THE TIDEWATER TALES

"Barth has never been more engaging, nor more engaged in his narrative complications."

The New York Times Book Review

"Those disheartened by the prophesied demise of literature may find solace in Barth's launching of another water-message. It signals that an old-fashioned, if decidedly post-modern storyteller, remains afloat somewhere off Maryland's Eastern Shore."

Philadelphia Inquirer

"If you crave to be lapped in the English language by one of its masters, fed and overfed with fiction, wooed and entranced and storied to your limits, Barth still does it better than anyone else."

San Francisco Chronicle

"Barth overwhelms us with his resourcefulness and invention."

Newsday

"*The Tidewater Tales* is probably the only piece of experimental fiction that can double as summer beach reading."

Library Journal

THE TIDEWATER TALES

A NOVEL

THE TIDEWATER TALES

A NOVEL

JOHN BARTH

Fawcett Columbine • New York

A Fawcett Columbine Book
Published by Ballantine Books
Copyright © 1987 by John Barth

All rights reserved under International and Pan-American
Copyright Conventions. This book, or parts thereof, may not
be reproduced in any form without permission. Published in
the United States by Ballantine Books, a division of Random
House, Inc., New York, and simultaneously in Canada by
Random House of Canada Limited, Toronto.

Library of Congress Catalog Card Number: 87-91351

ISBN: 0-449-90293-5

This edition published by arrangement with G.P. Putnam's
Sons.

Cover design by Richard Aquan
Cover Painting: Abby Aldrich Rockefeller Folk Art Center,
Williamsburg, Virginia

Manufactured in the United States of America

First Ballantine Books Edition: June 1988
10 9 8 7 6 5 4 3 2 1

FOR SHELLY

CONTENTS

OUR STORY

Security Agency's Espionage City at Fort George G. Meade.
And Not Far North of Us Are the Army's Edgewood Arsenal
for Chemical and Biological Weapons Development and the
Aberdeen Ordnance Proving Ground. And Just Northeast of Us
Is Dover Air Force Base with Its Heavy Hardware. And Not
Far Southeast of Us Is the Wallops Island Rocket Research and
Test Firing Center. And Not Far South of Us Are the
Bloodsworth Island Naval Bombing Target, the Norfolk Navy
Yard, Langley Air Force Base, and the Army's Forts Eustis and
Story. And Not Far South-Southwest of Us Are the Army's
Camp Peary and the CIA's ISOLATION Training Camp and the
Patuxent Naval Air Test Center and the Naval Electronics
Testing Facility. And Just Southwest of Us Are the Naval
Research Laboratory Firing Range and the Naval Surface
Weapons Center and the A. P. Hill Army Reservation and the
Blossom Point Proving Ground. And Not Far West-Southwest
of Us Are the Indian Head Naval Ordnance Station and the
Quantico Marine Reservation. And Just West of Us Are
Andrews Air Force Base and the Army's Fort Belvoir. And Not
Far West-Northwest of Us Are the Headquarters of the CIA,
the DIA, and the NRO, Not to Mention the Army, Navy, Air
Force, and Marine Corps—All More or Less Laws unto
Themselves, Very Imperfectly Answerable Even to the Imperial
Presidency Just Across the River or Down the Street, to Say
Nothing of the U.S. Congress Ditto, Which Presidency However
Has the Power and Authority to Mobilize the Fourscore
Pentagon Facilities on Chesapeake Bay Alone and All Related
Forces and with Those Forces Destroy All Human Together
with Most Nonhuman Life on Earth. Nevertheless, Bucolic
Tidewater Maryland Holds Its Breath on This Placid Presummer
June Late Afternoon As If the Year Were 1880 or 1780 or 1680
Instead of 1980. We Do Not Believe That What We See
Around Us Will Be Here in Any Agreeably Habitable State for
the Children of the Children We Are About to Bring into This
World. We Do Not Believe That the World We Value Will
Much Survive Us. For That Matter, We Have No Tremendous
Confidence That Our Children Will. Yet Nevertheless,
Nevertheless the Fair Tred Avon Pauses in the Hazy Sunshine;
Nothing Stirs; *Story* Slides Seaward Sidewise Now at Less than
Half a Knot on the Glassy Tide; and Peter Sagamore, Who Has
Not Told a Proper Tale for Longer Than We Like to Remember,
Clears His Throat and Begins for His Wife's Entertainment and His
Possible Own Salvation "The Ordinary Point Delivery Story"

The Ordinary Point Delivery Story

OUR STORIES:
THE NEW CLOTHES HAVE NO EMPEROR

DAY 0: NOPOINT POINT TO DUN COVE

DAY 1: DUN COVE TO DUN COVE

DAY 5: LAY DAY, ANNAPOLIS

DAY 6: SEVERN RIVER TO CHESTER RIVER

DAY 7: CHESTER RIVER TO WYE ISLAND

OUR STORIES: THE CLOTHES' NEW EMPEROR

DAY 8: WYE I.

DAY 9: WYE I.

DAY 10: WYE I.

DAYS 11 & 12: WYE TO SASSAFRAS

DAY 13: WHY TO SASSAFRAS?

DAY 14: ORDINARY POINT

THE ENDING

OUR STORY

KATHERINE SHERRITT SAGAMORE, 39 YEARS OLD
AND 8½ MONTHS PREGNANT,
BECALMED IN OUR ENGINELESS SMALL SAILBOAT
AT THE END OF A STICKY JUNE CHESAPEAKE AFTERNOON
AMID EVERY SIGN OF THUNDERSTORMS APPROACHING
FROM ACROSS THE BAY,
AND SPEAKING AS SHE SOMETIMES DOES IN VERSE,
SETS HER HUSBAND A TASK.

Tell me a story of women and men
Like us: like us in love for ten
Years, lovers for seven, spouses
Two, or two point five. *Their House's*
Increase is the tale I wish you'd tell.

Why did that perfectly happy pair,
Like us, decide this late to bear
A child? Why toil so to conceive
One (or more), when they both believe
The world's aboard a handbasket bound for Hell?
Well?

Sentimentality, was it? A yen
Like ours to be one person, blend
Their flesh forever, so to speak—
Although the world could end next week
And that dear incarnation be H-bomb-fried?

Maybe they thought that by joining their
(Like our) so different genes—her

Blue-blooded, his blue-collared—they'd make
A blue-eyed Wunderkind who'd take
The end of civilization in his/her stride?
What pride!

Or maybe they weren't thinking at all,
But (unlike us) obeyed the call
Of blind instinct and half-blind custom:
"Reproduce your kind, and trust them
To fortune's winds and tides, life's warmth and frost!"

Perhaps they considered all the above
(Like us, exactly)—instinct, love,
The world's decline from bad to worse
In more respects than the reverse—
And decided to pay, but not to count, the cost.
Fingers crossed.

Well:
Tell me their story as if it weren't ours,
But *like* ours enough so that the Powers
That drive and steer good stories might
Fetch them beyond *our* present plight

and navigate the tale itself to an ending more rich and strange than everyday
realism ordinarily permits; a bottom line that will make art if not sense
out of the predicament your sperm and my egg, with a lot of help from
their producers, have got us into; in short, yet another rhyme as it were
for *cost* to end this poem with, even if we have to abandon verse for prose
or prose for verse to reach it: a rhyme less discouraging, more pregnant
so to speak with hope, than *lost*.
    Okay?

PETER SAGAMORE, 39 YEARS AND 8½ MONTHS OLD,
AN AUTHOR WITH CERTAIN DIFFICULTIES
THOUGH CERTAINLY NOT A DIFFICULT AUTHOR,
AT THE TILLER OF OUR LITTLE SLOOP *STORY*,
RESPONDS IN PROSE.

Blam. Blooey.
Katherine Sherritt begs his pardon?

BLAM! BLOOEY!

Twin thunderstorms struck Chesapeake Bay at about the same hour two weeks apart in the last spring and summer of the eighth decade of the twentieth century of the Christian era and bracketed our story like artillery zeroing in.

The first storm—*Blam!*—was born to a sultry low-pressure cell that squatted over Maryland all Sunday, June 15, 1980, last weekend before the solstice. At afternoon's end she let go a squall below Baltimore that spun across the Bay like an uncorked genie and blammed the middle Eastern Shore of Maryland, in particular the lower Miles and upper Tred Avon rivers. Wondrous, thunderous, frightening lightning! Hail and mini-twisters: trees downed, roofs unroofed, doors unhinged, windows blown . . . and our story begun.

The second storm—*Blooey!*—offsprang from a Canadian high that swept pregnant across the upper Mississippi and the Great Lakes on Sunday, June 29, 1980, first weekend after the solstice. Astraddle the Appalachian ridge she delivered a passel of young roughnecks, the roughest of whom tore into Druid Hill Park and the Baltimore Zoo at happy hour EDST, knocked down with a ninety-knot punch a big traveling crane at the Dundalk Marine Terminal, lost steam drowning two hubristic sportfishermen in small boats out on the Bay, and blooeyed the upper Shore at seventy knots plus before cooling off in the cornfields of Kent County. Near the old fishing village of Rock Hall, a big cruising sailboat in dry storage named *Buy, Baby,* owned by a Philadelphia investment counselor, was blown right out of its cradle. Farther up the peninsula, behind Ordinary Point on the Sassafras, some yachts dragged anchor, some others didn't . . . and our story came 'round on itself.

Here's how.

SET ME A TASK!

As Kathy Sherritt will tell it next fall, when we're home in Baltimore and she's back at work as Director of Folklore and Oral History at the Enoch Pratt Free Library, *The Tidewater Tales: A Novel* saw daylight at about six P.M. during Blooey! along with the other things she gave birth to that remarkable evening aboard *Story,* at anchor with the weekend fleet aswarm behind Ordinary Point, up near the cervix of Chesapeake Bay. But it was conceived just prior to Blam! two weeks before at Nopoint

Point, the Sherritt spread on Goldsborough Creek, off the Tred Avon, off the Choptank, off that same Chesapeake, farther down that Eastern Shore, when pent-up Peter Sagamore, that Kathy's best friend, best lover, best husband, moderately celebrated author of short and shorter stories, and father of the whole kaboodle in her womb, cried For pity's sake, Kathy, set me a task!—thereby setting *her* one.

NOPOINT POINT

A lover's task is what Peter meant: something he could do to demonstrate to Katherine Sherritt that he loves her like life and language themselves despite mosquitoes, heat, humidity, her parents' trying unsuccessfully not to be a bother, precious little sex since Kath's on the cusp, no tennis but brutal with macho male Sherritts all save Andy the youngest of whom blow him off the family court in straight sets, every day less swimming in Sherritt Cove, less windsurfing and waterskiing out in Goldsborough Creek, because on each new tide the sea nettles move a bit farther in like a billion old condoms with their miserable sting and beautiful name, *Chrysaora quinquecirrha,* which means five-filamented gold-edge but ought to mean God's five-month curse upon the Talbot County Gold Coast, no respite from Kathy's old prep-school and college chums, family friends, and fellow ASPS (American Society for the Preservation of Storytelling), swarming like sheepflies on Nopoint Point, including her onetime (one time) lesbian lover, a black-belt balladeer and sometime pain in our marital tush, though Kathy won't hear May Jump spoken ill of except by Peter in extremis. And more.

Now, P welcomes these diversions for good K's sake, but so much company gets to a chap who, while no solitary, is a duetary unabashedly and for sure: Give him him and Kathy Sherritt; the rest of the world is just . . . material. And on the bottom line—by reason of these manifold irritations and distractions and the low-grade, high-level suspense of when for pity's sake will she unload, and what and how many . . . Well.

To be sure, it's been no picnic for Katherine Shorter Sherritt, these two weeks on Nopoint Point; P.S. knows that. She loves the man as does he her and is as grateful for his uncomplaint as is he hers, but *she's* the one with the fabulous bellyful, Estimated Date of Confinement two weeks hence by our best reckoning: 29 June '80, 266 nights since a certain blessed one last fall—though inasmuch as all such EDCs are ± two weeks, she might just unload here in mid-sentence and set him a task indeed. She's the one hors de combat, on maternity leave from the great Pratt's Word of Mouth Department; from supervising oral history projects through the neighborhood branches, collecting urban folklore and recording immigrant folktales out of Baltimore's ethnic smorgasbord; from telling apprentice-level tales under May Jump's ongoing tutelage to the very young and very old and the blind and the unlettered, working toward her brown belt in recitation; from conducting seminars in otolaryngeal narrative and taking them in narration; from assuming the wheel herself sometimes of the Inner City Talemobile in winter or one of the Storycycles in summer to carry forth the word from Cathedral Street as well as bring it back; and in general from looking after the library's Office of Oral Input as May (once upon a time) looked after its Out-. She misses that. A writer may be his own best company: Desert Island or Manhattan Island, for Peter Sagamore it's scratch and scribble, scribble and scratch. But a mouth needs an ear, an ear a mouth; Kath's as gregarious as Pete's egregious; it's mainly the human flow through Nopoint Point, with its freight of anecdote and inquiry, that has eased the tedium of this fortnight in the First Guest Cottage. Bored out of her skull is Katie, by enforced inactivity and unresponsibility; as gratefully surfeited as Peter with her parents' benevolent overkill; weary as he of making more shift than love, and on top of all straining her lumbars to haul who knew how many of who could say what, given that equivocal ultrasound scan, from poolside to courtside to dockside to dinnertableside to husbandside at last in bed.

P. Sagamore has been since early May on summer leave from professing the Art of Everdiminishing Fiction, and will be till September. Now's when he normally does the most of his raw inventing for the year, which then through the academic season he'll fret and tinker at, buff and burnish, trim and tighten and tighten and trim as he preaches to beginners and coaches his advanced apprentices at the state university's main campus down in College Park, until by spring each item glows with the Sagamore shine that's made his name. Eight or six tiny items, apparently artless but hard and luminous, as if the idlest objects on your desk or outside your window, the homeliest gestures of ordinary people, were composed, compressed, and caused to shine each with its own refulgence, a mysterious, sharp limpidity. Though nowise obscure or difficult, Peter's art is without pizzazz, and ever terser. The cognoscenti cheer; the larger public, regrettably, ignores him, and, regretfully, he them.

The month of May normally gets our man into high gear and happy fits of abbreviation: His teaching's done, but Kathy's still at work; our Baltimore apartment he has all to himself from half past eight to half past five. Four hours of making long notes for short paragraphs; an hour of lunch and mail; two of sweet mindless physicality in some nearby school's gymnasium or on its tennis court; another two of chores, odd jobs, and errands about beflowered Baltimore; two or three more of building and eating dinner with Katherine Shorter Sherritt, comparing days, conferring upon the wider world—our favorite time, which we do not rush: wine and candles every blessed weekday, Telemann on tape, good food and quiet talk till cleanup's done at eight or nine; the balance of the evening reading, walking, letter-writing, very occasional movie- or theatergoing, perhaps with friends. Some okay restaurant weekly, some better one monthly, a semesterly party of some sort. To this routine add typically those two weeks in June of sailing on the Bay; now and then a quick winter ski trip or Caribbean beach-out when the cash flow flows. The occasional off-campus lecture junket for Peter or, for Katherine, library scientists' convention. Twice in our decade together short visits to Europe, whither in our earlier decades apart Kathy Sherritt had gone often, briefly, and Peter Sagamore once for a corner-turning year.

Thus our life, reader, which we love. Thus, normally, our May. Come June, we'd normally close our Stony Run flat, spend a long weekend with the Sherritts at Nopoint Point commissioning and provisioning old *Story* and baffling Henry Sherritt once again with our preference for an engine-less, unamenitied little sloop over *Katydid IV,* his fifty-foot ketch with three staterooms, two hot showers, full electronics, and a mighty diesel, which we're welcome to use with or without the paid hand. After a happy fortnight's sailing and drifting, back to steamy Baltimore and to work, returning most weekends to Nopoint Point, where there's never not room aplenty.

A regular life and a tranquil; a privileged life and an easy. Yet a busy life, a productive—and a too too swiftly running. Normally.

This May, no; this June, no. Jack Bass, the family obstetrician-gyne-cologist, who delivered Katherine early in his practice, has half retired to a spread of his own across Goldsborough Creek, but is still sought after by Gold Coasties in the family way and supervises the pregnancies of those he once delivered. Kath's is a case Doctor Jack has followed with more than routine interest: He delivered her first husband, Porter "Poonie" Baldwin, Jr., and shrugged his shoulders at that marriage, which all four parents cheered; he tisked his tongue at its early breakup and aborted young Mrs. Baldwin's pregnancy back when abortion was not much done in Talbot County; he consoled Henry Sherritt on the golf course and pre-scribed Valium for Irma; he approved K's subsequent pairing with Captain Fritz Sagamore's son from across the broad Choptank, despite that family's much lower social rank; he applauded our decision eight years later to get married and pregnant if P's old vasectomy could be surgically reversed, and steered him to a Boston urologist whose specialty is iffy reanastomosis; he rejoiced with us at evidence of motile sperm, danced at our wedding, and coached our late-procreative efforts when success did not at once crown them; he toasted our eventual pregnancy and monitored its regrettable miscarriage; he counseled Kathy—who by then was thirty-eight and getting no younger—on our final long-shot strategy and cheered its clear payoff in early winter; he informed us in March that he heard two heartbeats in there, in April two at least, and ordered an ultrasound scan to clarify matters wombwise; then he put an arm about Peter Sagamore's shoulders, took Kathy Sherritt's hand in his, regarded with us in equal awe the won-drous video display of what looked like a sibling-incestuous, polymorphous-perverse prenatal orgy of Siamese septuplets, such was the tangle of shad-owy arms and legs and umbilici flickering before us, and could or would not say further than that the delivery was definitely going to be multiple and that a week or two might be subtracted from our EDC. He recommended that Kath begin her maternity leave on the first of June instead of its ides and move to Nopoint Point for the entire summer, where he'd be five minutes away from the First Guest Cottage by Boston Whaler and no more than fifteen by Jaguar from either Chez Sherritt or Easton Memorial Hospital. Inasmuch as he knows us Sherritt-Sagamores to be great lookers-up and checkers-out of information, he felt constrained to forewarn us that morbidity and mortality rates increase for second-born twins, second- and third-born triplets, second-, third-, and fourth-born quadruplets, to say no further. Delivery by cesarean section was more than a possibility, despite our hopes to go the natural route.

WELL!

We remind ourselves now that we reminded ourselves then that going on and then off the Pill plus hitting the fertilizer improves the odds not only for conception (that was our half-year long shot), but for multiple conception. Given Kathy's age, we told ourselves, and the seventy-percent lowered fertility rate of men with vasovasectomies, it is unlikely we'll give pregnancy another go. Something to be said, in short, for putting all one's eggs in this one basket, if one wants more than one.

But who wants? Though we both affirm that a child sans siblings is the poorer for that lack, we ourselves have each in fact one close to her/his heart, one not; it seems a toss-up. And even with Help, each privately sees—at the prospect of *two* (-plus) infants, *two* (-plus) preschoolers—our duetary peace and quiet, already but a dear memory since 1 June, receding that much farther into the future. Not till 1998, by Peter's gloomy private reckoning, two years before the millennium, when he'll be pushing sixty, will the kids be off to college and the apartment tranquil enough again for him to write—should world and colleges, himself and writing, survive so long. Broods Kathy to her glummest self Hah: quintuplets in a high-crime city low-rise? We're in the *housing* market, Peter *mio:* the *big* housing market. With eleven-percent mortgages a bargain already and thirteen-percenters soon to be nostalgia, but real estate prices booming in the Baltimore–Washington corridor, you and I are going to have to buy a multibedroomed, play-basemented, fancy-kitchened, laundry-roomed, central-AC'd, automatic garage–doored, quiet low-crime side-streeted play-yarded azaleaed dogwooded magnoliaed suburban for Christ's sake *house!*

As Hank and Irma Sherritt's only daughter, Princess Kate growing up on Nopoint Point had two of everything including brothers, trikes, bikes, cars, mailing addresses, coming-out parties, *r*s and *t*s in her family name, and, in time, colleges, degrees, husbands, and uncompleted pregnancies. One day she'll have the best of that again, compounded: her share of the old, abundant Sherritt pile. She's glad of that, because she honors her parents and because there are at least three causes she looks forward to philanthropizing massively: her husband, who has paid his workaday dues and should be freed to give his remaining prime time, all of it, to his ever-terser art; her ASPS, of which she and May Jump are founding members; and her HOSCA (Hands Off South and Central America), an organization devoted to the frustration of U.S. meddling in the governments of its southern neighbors. But in the middle while between rich and rich—if only, she grants, like a person stepping coatless into the cold from a warm room to which she'll presently return—she's pleased to do with little in the ownership way, K, a good deal less than our twin salaries could afford: our light and airy but spare apartment; a modest wardrobe from Loehmann's discountery and L. L. Bean's mail-order outdoorsery, her chief indulgence. No car of her own; no television; art mostly from the Baltimore Museum's rental gallery; tapes, records, and books on loan from the Pratt. It is marshy Hoopers Island Peter, public-high-school state-university Peter, who bought and treasures our secondhand BMW and thirdhand sailboat of his late father's manufacture, the threadbare Herizes, Tabrizes, and Bokharas on our floors, the Japanese brush drawings and stereo, Scandinavian furniture and French food processor and German coffeemaker and cabinetful of okay Bordeaux. But until we can afford to commission some architect friend to design us a simple, high-tech, energy-efficient, unostentatious, unobtrusive little gem tucked into the trees on some high point of land on the Chester or the Sassafras, say, where we can swim naked in the natural element instead of suited up in the Sherritts' filtered and chlorinated tank, he wants a house no more than she.

A house! And then, no doubt, pet animals; he sure loved his in boyhood days: the world of Kitty Litter, Hartz flea collars, fish tanks, gerbil cages. Are there Boy and Girl Scouts still? Merit badges? Peter Sagamore was born into a moderately poor family made poorer by the Great Depression in historically poor lower Dorchester County, Maryland; he grew up without benefit of baby-sitters, nursery schools, summer camps, special-education fast tracks, and pressure from his parents to excel, both of whom had gone to work at sixteen and were delighted to see their children finish South Dorchester High. Katherine Sherritt was born into a moderately rich family made richer by every declared war in U.S. history in historically rich Talbot County, Maryland; she too grew up without baby-sitters (the Sherritts had live-in nannies and governesses), without summer camps (the Sherritts spent their Augusts in Maine or Spain), without special-ed fast tracks (a Sherritt's ed is special from prekindergarten on), without pressure from her parents to excel (the Sherritts have taken excellence in one form or another for granted since the eighteenth century). Having so much inexperience in common, we understandably share some apprehension about dealing with Pampers and PTAs, especially in triplicate or quadruplicate.

But we made up our minds two years ago, not impulsively, to join genes, and we're not displeased with our success, only dismayed by its extent; Peter Sagamore especially. One child, small, was what *he* had in mind, by whose lights a windy sentence is one with more than two clauses or three commas; whose longest short story in recent years runs maybe six pages, his recenter ones three or two, his recentest—you'll see. The world has things enough in it already; more than enough; too many. One ought ever to add to their number with reluctance. Pete's Cartesian, Kath Rabelaisian. Sentences, paragraphs like these must be hers, under whose good breasts are lungs like a marathoner's, a Met soprano's. This green-belt raconteuse can recite Homer's Catalogue of Ships or Gargantua's of bumswipes at the clip of a Gilbert and Sullivan patter song and make you call not only Bravo but Encore. She can enjoy the Ocean City public beach and boardwalk on a July Fourth afternoon with a third of a million fellow humans schooled like smelts, or the common fitting room at Loehmann's just before High Holidays, for which no simile will serve. If Less Is More is Pete, More Is More is Kath. Pete's pet poet is Emily Dickinson: *zero at the bone*. Katherine Sherritt's is Walt Whitman: *I contain multitudes*.

In sum, a well-coupled couple, and not only Jack Sprat–wise. At abundant Kathy's core, her friend discovered years ago, like hurricane's eye or black hole in a plenum, is a small but central bubble not of nothing but of Nothingness: an empty point where some Big Bang must have banged, since from it her universe busies out in all directions, particularly his. Peter Sagamore's life has been by contrast all but void of scenes, events, things, relations, distractions; son of monotonous marshes stretching sky to sky, he thrives upon silence, sparseness. But as in fact those wetlands teem and nurse the elsewise lifeless oceans, so at Peter's center, his friend discovered years ago, is not only a wistful, detached affection for the variety and busyness of the world, but a certain hard tireless dedicated energy, like a quasar blazing X rays in the universe's crawlspace. From that core his lean art radiates, as do by the way his attraction to and patience with the busy life of Nopoint Point, in measured doses, and his measureless delight in Katherine Sherritt.

DO THE WOMAN.

That won't be easy from our coupled point of view—P's promptings, K's cadenzas—but she'll draw a great breath; we'll try. Here's the woman of us, in her man's opinion: Katherine Shorter Sherritt at thirty-nine is a rangy, long-limbed looker looking thirty-three tops and topped with beach-colored hair (both the dry beach and the wet), streaked straight past fine strong shoulders when she lets it down. She has Hank Sherritt's Episcopalian bright gray eyes, Irma Shorter's twenty-four-carat skin and cultured-pearl dentition. She'll dress to the nines when occasion calls and sophisticate in three languages, Kate, but she's easy in the preppie drag she wears to work: tweed skirts, cable-knit crewnecks over oxford-cloth buttondowns; easier yet in soft jeans and hiking boots and flannels, swapping stories with her ASPS across an Ozark campfire; easiest of all in the all-but-altogether with Peter Sagamore, spanking along in *Story* through a summer afternoon or splashing naked by moonlight with the noctilucae. When Katherine takes her clothes off later in this prologue and stands in the First Guest Cottage wearing only earrings, wedding band, and fine gold chain necklace, you'll see those aforesung breasts engorged by pregnancy beyond their normal trim, their russet aureoles stretched cookie-size: athletical buttocks fairly firm even this far gone; smoothmuscled, fineskinned calves and thighs, flawless; and what was till the turn of the year a hard flat belly with God's thumbprint for a navel. All this, mind, in her husband's opinion (and May Jump's). She's an Outward Bound type, Kath: backpacker, white-water canoeist, distance swimmer. She's a green-belt karatiste as well as raconteuse, don't mess with K.S.S., though that belly's thrown her balance off. Under all that skin she is intuitive but clearheaded, even hardheaded when necessary. She is memorious, practical, capable, Kathy, but more dependent than she wishes upon Peter's stability and good humor to level out her swings from up to down to up. Life having been generous to her, she is in his opinion generous with hers: Much of that Pratt work is hardcore inner-city, and she is forever volunteering for good-citizenly chores over and above: Operation Head Start, the League of Women Voters, the Museum board, the Better Baltimore Committee, her prep school's board of trustees, her college's alumnae association, the local chapter of Amnesty International, and of course her ASPS and HOSCA. She has enjoyed vigorously, Katherine, every stage of her privileged life—her childhood, girlhood, adolescence, young womanhood, mature adulthood—except the period of her marriage to Poonie Baldwin. Strong-charactered and principled, she learned from that experience to prize good character above all else in others. She dislikes pettiness, foolishness, weakness, coquetry, moral laziness, snobbishness, cowardice, dissembling, bad faith; also drunkenness, narcosis, philandering, and sexual sadism. She is not, is Katherine Sherritt, modish, intellectual, high-style, cute, very worldly, "sexy," very political, submissive, very dependent, carping, devious, vain, contentious, affected, very fastidious, "passionate," fearful, reckless, jealous. She is neither genius nor virtuoso, though she's a whiz at collecting stories and getting better all the time at telling them. What she is, in her husband's view, is knowledgeable, sensible, well-organized, ardent, reasonable, energetic, sexual, loyal, dependable, moodier than she approves of being, quick-minded and intelligent, well-educated, physically and morally courageous, articulate, resourceful, prevailingly cheerful, self-reliant but not entirely, damned good-looking, we said that already, and, she adds, much drawn to genuine talent and virtuosity.

Kathy Sherritt knows who she is. She does? She does. With the strength of a certain WASP cultural tradition behind her, of which she largely but not uncritically approves, she relates easily to others who know who *they* are, however foreign: an asset in her ethnic-oral-history work. She would hit it off with a Masai chieftain or the Baal Shem Tov. Homosexual men are not uncomfortable in Kathy's company; straight women like her; lesbians are powerfully drawn herward, Q.E.D., as are heterosexual men of various classes, races, ages.

Katherine, Kathy, Katie-Kath-Kate! *He*'s drawn to you, too, who just now helped draw you! Lucky the man whose woman is Katherine Sherritt.

NOW DO THE MAN.

With pleasure: Lucky Katherine, in her and this narrative's opinion, to have for the man of us good Peter Sagamore. That surname is Algonquian for "minor chieftain"—we remember Teddy Roosevelt's Sagamore Hill, up in Oyster Bay—but "Captain" Fritz Sagamore was a German immigrant carpenter's son. The word is not given in our German–English dictionary: *Sage mehr* ("Say more"), we wonder, metamorphosed by some immigration clerk like many another new American's name? *Zage mir?* Nobody knows. Capn Fritz felt more or less German, but was never taught the tongue; the Sagamores presume themselves a line of sturdy Kraut carpenters going back forever and take no interest in family history. Transplanted to Hoopers Island, on the Chesapeake side of lower Dorchester, Fritz's father enlarged his trade to include boat carpentry, in which the son specialized; Fritz established himself in time as a regionally famous builder of Chesapeake Bay workboats—especially those long, narrow oyster-tong boats with inverted, "duck's-ass" transoms—and, toward the end of his career, small wooden cruising sailboats built "by rack of eye," without full-scale laid-out plans. Our Peter and Jacob, his older brother, even their mother and Sue-Ann, their younger sister, all worked about the yard and became adept with the boatwright's tools—joinery and brightwork were adolescent Peter's special skills—but only Jake took up the trade. Some voice spoke to Peter Sagamore early on, who knows whose in those trackless wetlands, saying Honor thy father and thy mother and thy place of birth, but put kilometrage as soon as possible 'twixt thee and them.

Pete's parenting was benign but inattentive. Lapsed Lutherans, Fritz and Nora always smiled, never quarreled, but were too busy and indifferent to do more than work, eat, sleep. P felt affection for but not much kinship with his mother: A good-natured, rawboned farm woman used to self-sacrifice and hard work without complaint, she's in a down-county nursing home now, senile early, cheerful, deaf, incontinent. All day long she drinks coffee and smokes cigarettes (it is not a strict nursing home), turns the television up too loud but doesn't look at it, and makes pencil drawings that her attendants can't decipher but her children recognize at a glance to be of the wooden parts of her late husband's boats: knees, stemheads, keelsons, bitts. P respected and felt kinship with but not much closeness to his father: a sound craftsman; an honest businessman with little head for business; an energetic and incorruptible citizen who served term after term as county commissioner in addition to running the Sagamore boat-yard; a shrug-shouldered father like his father, who never disciplined and almost never rebuked his children because there was almost never need to, but who did not talk or do much with them, either. Peter sees Fritz Sagamore now as having been a principled, benevolent, hardworking, un-adventurous, good-humored, civic-minded, rather shy and selfish fellow who made the best of his limitations without complaint and mildly left his children to their own devices. Pete misses him, honors his memory, wishes they two had been able to converse and do more of the usual father-son things, wonders whether Capn Fritz felt the same about *his* father, and finally shrugs. He worries that for want of better models, experience, and genes he'll be no closer to our children, despite his resolve to be, than his father was to him. Don't worry, says his wife, but sometimes she does too.

So how does a lower-middle-class, unaffluent, semirural, semiredneck, semicivilized, semieducated boy make his way out of the salt marsh into the corridors of literature? He bloody doesn't, as a rule: not into literature's or any other profession's corridors. If he does, it will likely be by accident and indirection. What your Sherritts take for granted, he'll pay for with his youth. Though he may outstrip, he'll never catch up. Though he scale in his lifeswork the high, dry summit of Parnassus, he'll go to his grave almost as wet behind the ears as if he'd never crawled out of the marsh. He will? He will. He had better therefore make a virtue of this limitation, become a hedgehog as he'll never be a fox. He will stumble into some university on scholarship, nearly drown there but not quite, and learn to float if never swim in the academic enterprise. Coming from no very defined cultural tradition, he will have not only all civilizations to discover, but Civilization. Having unlike Kathy no very defined self, he will grope his way into art with the one advantage of being unable, ipso facto, to practice it as self-expression; he will be free therefore either to invent himself in and for his stories or—what in his opinion comes to the same thing—to efface himself in his invention. Because he has everything to learn, he'll approach the medium without preconceptions, and this innocence may not be altogether a liability. Because he does not quite know who he is, he may never quite learn what he cannot do, and this ignorance, if it does not ruin him, may be his strength. This sounds more like the man of us talking than the woman; let her have her say.

Okay: On the cusp of forty, Peter Sagamore is a handsome U.S. six-footer, lean and healthy, even athletic, with curly hair the color of his woman's and skin to match its darker locks; some south European input into that lost line of carpenters gave all the Sagamores mahogany eyes and permanent suntans. He wears no mustache, beard, or eyeglasses. When he takes his clothes off later in Day Zero and stands in *Story*'s cockpit wearing only wedding band, wristwatch, and brown bead necklace, you'll see long flat swimmer's muscles under more of that permanent tan, body hair barley-gold and fine but for the tobacco-brown bush of underarms and pubes, the latter fleecier than Kathy's tight-curled nap but identical in color. Exercise and a lucky metabolism have kept P. Sagamore almost as trim as a healthy thirty-year-old. The skin that girdles his butt and gut is less tan than the rest; Katherine Shorter Sherritt's pleasure is to kiss right 'round those borders when on warm weekends we're sailing stripped and out of ready view: more particularly if, as happens, her friend is steering momentarily with the tiller-tip squeezed between his buns while trimming *Story*'s mainsheet or making entries in the log. His genital equipment—there it hangs, mildly curious reader—is circumcised, normal in magnitude, reliable in function. Inasmuch as husband and wife, neither either green or jaded, are satisfied quite with each other as sexual partners, an aspect of our life together that we enjoy as much as any other, there'll be little more to say in our story upon this head, though there may be some.

When our chap wears clothes, they'll generally be in the khaki-slacks/navy-blazer/madras-shirt category on teaching days, the jeans-and-rugby-shirt on others, cutoff denims and deck moccasins in summer. Except in town and on special occasions, he wears neither shirt nor socks from Flag Day to Labor Day. We dislike air-conditioning and are fond of skin; we are neither exhibitionists nor voyeurs, but nudity comes as easily to us in humid tidewaterland as to north Europeans on a south European beach.

All right. Some things Peter Sagamore is not, in his wife's opinion, are colorful, eccentric, high-energetic, very outgoing, Romantic, religious, politically enthusiastic, vain, gregarious, affected, promiscuous, devious, personally subtle, and ideological, though he sure does have opinions. Some things he is are personable, introspective, vigorous, unassuming, mild-mannered, stoical, prevailingly serene and good-humored, moderate in his habits, well organized, firmly principled, rational, virile (though forty is not twenty), patient with himself and others, a touch absentminded and forgetful, a touch passive in his dealings with the world and therefore dependent in many ways upon Kathy—and immune to doubts about his vocation, though not about his accomplishment. His personal culture is less broad than Kath's, though she finds it deeper. He reads not widely, massively, or systematically, but what he reads becomes a working part of him; he has a gift for language, none for languages; neither a scholar on the one hand nor a primitive on the other, he is an okay instructor in the art of literature from its manufacturers' point of view and a first-rate coach and critic of apprentice writers. Fairly said. As a writer himself . . .

That is another story, ever shorter. Enough here to establish that while our woman, who is without invention, can recount spellbindingly anything except her husband's stories, which must come silently from the page through the eye and mind into the soul, our man can recount nothing to good effect; can't even tell a joke. He merely and strictly invents, sets down. And that for this inventing and setting down, the fellow *trains,* like a spiritual and physical athlete. *Mens sana in corpore sano:* All that swimming, running, stretching exercise and the rest are not just for his physical well-being, any more than his memory-, breathing-, concentration-, and relaxation-exercises are merely for his psychological well-being. They are to bring him to the mark—the last mark he put upon yesterday's white page—in both Olympic and Olympian condition.

Henry and Irma Sherritt, it goes without saying, had early trouble with this connection of Princess Kate's and even now are less than perfectly easy with it. But they are chastened by their former advocacy of Poonie Baldwin, Jr., and they cannot but like Pete personally and approve his character. They respect the chap's integrity, and so far from perceiving him as a threat to their conservative values, with Kathy's help they see him as a moderating influence upon their daughter: His politics, for example, are more skeptical and middle-of-the-road than hers. If he were more famous, they'd be less uneasy; if he were less so, they'd be more. Not only *The New York Times,* after all, but even *The Wall Street Journal* has assured them that their laconic son-in-law is something different: a writer's writer's writer?

The writer Peter Sagamore: That sums him up. As another, asked what he is, might say, "I'm a black militant poet," "I'm a fifty-year-old divorced chamber musician with grown-up Hasidic twin daughters," or "I'm a Chilean Marxist on the staff of Orlando Letelier, Salvador Allende's ambassador to the U.S."; as Henry Sherritt would say, "I'm a Republican businessman Episcopalian Sherritt," and Irma, "I'm Mrs. Henry Sherritt," and Katherine, "I'm Kath"; so Peter Sagamore would answer I'm a writer. And it is because this writer, honed to this edge, had been these several seasons ever more distracted by seven several circumstances from writing, and especially this fortnight pent on Nopoint Point like a Preakness thoroughbred stuck in the gates at Pimlico, that in the sultry mid-afternoon of 15 June '80 Peter Sagamore cried out to Katherine Sherritt in the First Guest Cottage For pity's sake, Kathy, set me a task!

Thereby setting *her* one.

TAKE US SAILING.

Katherine Sherritt Sagamore considers. We are sitting on the newly carpeted floor of the second bedroom of the First Guest Cottage, a complete small house done tastefully in the Gloucester clapboard style Kath

calls Seafood-Chain Traditional and Peter calls Neo–*Captains Courageous,*
designed to contrast with the Maxfield Parrish Georgian of the main spread.
Irma redid in May the whole bedroom and its adjacent bath into a much
more elaborate nursery than her first grand-offspring will have at home:
Kate Greenaway–figured wallpaper, Laura Ashley curtains and drapes; a
pair of eighteenth-century cribs cunningly modernized for comfort and
convenience without disturbing their original design, and a matching rocker
for nursing; a state-of-the-art double bassinet, double perambulator, and
built-in baby bath; closed-circuit television for monitoring cribs and bassinet from all the principal rooms of the cottage, including the nursemaid's
room (which now adjoins the nursery on the side opposite the main bedroom), as well as from selected locations about the Main House and grounds;
and a related, very high-tech audio intercommunication system out of which
the bugs have not all been got.

Here's how that Sunday'd gone. A light rainshower woke us early; sa-
voring the sound of it, we embraced a bit while the next generation played
tag between us. Then we slipped into cotton nightclothes to greet the day.
Fresh strawberries, croissants, iced coffee. For a while we exercised together, Pete his daily dozens and Kath her pelvic workouts to the roll call
(hers) of Santa's eight tiny reindeer, the twenty-three several counties of
the Old Line State, the itemized list of my true love's gifts to me on the
twelfth day of Christmas. Next Peter ran laps around the rainsweet grounds
of Nopoint Point while Katherine did her Kegels and her antivaricose
elevations. We took the kiddies—Hop, Skip, and Jump—for a quick dip
in the pool, no one else about yet, and at nine Peter went to his worktable
in the nursemaid's room: Since March he's been putting in an hour or two
even on weekend mornings, to maintain pressure on his muse. Kath hauled
into a maternity sunsuit, fixed herself another iced decaf, and took up
station in an Appalachian rocker on the cottage porch to do work of her
own and to shortstop visitors.

The day was forecast hot and muggy, but its A.M. was still fresh. Red-
winged blackbirds rasped in the reeds. Blue herons squawked in for gawky
landings on Shorter Point, across Sherritt Cove, from which rose wraiths
of mist. Resting her feet on a footstool and a clipboard on her belly, Kath
gave the next half-hour to another sort of exercise: First-Level Improvisation from a drill book prepared for her by May Jump. The woman of us
has no wish to be a writer of stories; but that her best talent should be for
their mere collection, her second best (under May's close and ardent tutelage) for their mere recitation, reminds Katherine Shorter Sherritt disagreeably of the homunculus theory of reproduction, which held the female
role in that familiar drama to be no more than the reception, nurture, and
delivery of the life thrust into her by the male, rather than the creation of
one of the two actors as well as the theater of their Aeschylean play.
Having warmed up with Dancer and Prancer, pear-treed partridges, Dorchester Talbot and Kent et cet, she now First-Levels into last lines for May's
three-quartered quatrains and limericks four-fifths limned:

> *A wise old owl sat in an oak.*
> *The more he saw, the less he spoke.*
> *The less he spoke, the more he heard.*
> ⌣ ⸍ ⌣ ⸍ ⌣ ⸍ ⸍ ⌣ ⸍ .
> _____

Which sort of reminded her of Peter. And

> *A certain gay black-belt balladist,*
> *Not content to be merely tribadist,*
> *Making love in the tub,*
> *Told her friend, "There's the rub:*
> ⌣ ⸍ ⸍ ⌣ ⸍ ⸍ ⌣ ⸍ ⸍ .„
> _____

She attempts next, for a quarter-hour only, a much higher degree of improvisation: reading her husband's latest story: "B♭."

B♭ OVERTURE

Once upon a time there was a storyteller who hit the ground running in his twenties with a fine fat novel of the sort blurb writers describe as "sprawling with life," "teeming with characters," "overflowing with narrative abundance," as if the book were a sloppily topped-up petri dish. Never mind what it was about: It happened to be set mostly in Katherine Sherritt's home waters, but she read it while jobbing in New York City in midst of divorcing Poonie Baldwin, and she was so taken by it that when she heard its author was visiting that town, she sought him out at a public reading at the 92nd Street Poetry Center, introduced herself, and began a conversation which to the surprise of both parties went on till morning, though the verbal part of it was largely done by midnight. Indeed, Peter Sagamore's re-creation in that novel of the place where she'd grown up, and which she rather felt she'd put behind her though she still revisited it often, so engaged Katherine Sherritt's imagination that instead of pursuing her advanced degree in library science at Radcliffe as she'd planned, she moved back to Maryland and raised her parents' eyebrows by matriculating at the state university: the first Sherritt in history ever to attend a public educational institution.

Peter himself, writer-in-residencing about New England at the time, did not return south until five years later, by when Kate had taken her master's, moved to Baltimore, and established herself at the Pratt. Nor did we meet or otherwise communicate in that interval, except that she read faithfully every word he published, as well as every word she could find *about* every word he published, passed along to her by her fellow library scientists.

She was thus aware—as her own professional and romantic careers expanded to include that aforeshadowed militant poet, that middle-aged chamber musician, that Chileno foreign service chap, also May Jump, the ASPS, HOSCA, oral history, and urban folklore—that the career of her favorite living American writer and lover-of-one-night had begun the strange contraction aforementioned. The fine fat novel she'd been floored by had been succeeded by a lean, which she found fine too but disappointing in its leanness: She craved more teem, more sprawl, more overflow. Came then twin slim novellas; after them a landmark story entitled "Part of a Shorter Work"; and after that (author and reader had remet now and commenced the story of our life together) those briefer and briefer fictions of the last decade. As Peter Sagamore himself never gave interviews, issued position papers, or answered public questions about his art, his critics freely theorized and conjectured: the Death of the Novel, the Death of the Novella, the Death of the Short Story, the Moribundity of the Printed Word in the Age of Electronics, the Personal Petering Out of Sagamore. It was speculated that the author was in despair; that he had written himself into a corner from which only silence could now meaningfully issue. Until the plots of our lives intertwined, Katherine Sherritt herself now and then wondered whether some such dreary symptomatical fate had befallen the fellow—but her own life was too full and various for her to think of him often.

The fact was (she discovered ten years ago when she began sharing our life and times), Peter Sagamore was at least as busy and, in the best sense, as productive as he'd ever been. Neither his vision nor his invention had faltered; between early breakfast and late lunch he made as many sentences as in the days of that teem and sprawl and overflow that had brought Katherine Sherritt to his downtown bed. But the demon Less Is More had so got hold of him, with its lieutenant demons Cut and Squeeze, that ten pages of notes now made one of first draft, ten of first draft one of second— and those celebrated minifictions were not infrequently refined through ten or a dozen drafts: diamonds sieved from very mountains of verbal ore.

All very well, up to a point: Preferrers of the free and easy carped, but those diamonds sparkled indisputably. Anon, however (Kathy herself puts the point of diminishing returns at Pete's reanastomosis, followed by our unsuccessful and then successful efforts at impregnation, followed by our unsuccessful and now all-but-successful efforts to bring pregnancy to term; but she knows there were other things, other things too), even the most ardent Sagamorians came to raise their eyebrows, tisk their tongues, and finally shrug their shoulders as P's prolific minimalism attained a purity beyond intelligibility. The saying *Brevity is the soul of wit* he found five-sixths too garrulous. His favorite moments in literature became those like that near the end of the *Agamemnon,* when, with the single name "Orestes," Aeschylus evokes the whole bloody sequel to the play at hand. He only wishes, does Peter Sagamore, that one didn't need the play to make the word make sense.

And in the two years past in particular, especially their last 8½ months, her friend has more and more written only to remove such Orestean kernels from their Agamemnonic husks, at whatever cost of readership and, finally, even of publication. In the same month when we felt our offspring quicken in Katie's womb, Peter Sagamore wrote his first unpublishable story since early-apprentice days. Based on an old tidewater duck-hunters' folk recipe for preparing the inedible old squaw duck (Stuff that duck with a single olive wrapped in bacon; stuff a large chicken with that duck; stuff a large turkey with that chicken. Roast that turkey twelve hours over low heat. Then discard that turkey; discard that chicken; discard that duck; discard that bacon. Eat that olive.), the story began as a Turgenev- or Maupassantlike hunting sketch with the humorous recipe as its center, reflecting a more general wastefulness in the lives of the hunting party: an advertising account executive from Philadelphia and a prosecuting attorney from Wilmington, on holiday with their wives at a private wildfowl preserve on Chesapeake Bay. In later drafts, this frame situation had been progressively whittled down and finally dispensed with, except by implication in an expanded version of the recipe itself, in which the turkey has come to stand for the Wilmingtonian, the chicken for the Philadelphian, and the olive for the latter's new young wife, whom the former covets but who in the end gives herself to the local bird-hunting guide. In still later drafts, the recipe itself was abbreviated, then eliminated. The finished story, entitled "The Olive," consisted of nothing but that title. No literary magazine would have it, even as a curiosity, and Peter Sagamore could no more blame them than he could bring himself to restore what his demon had bid him cut.

$$\text{B}^\flat$$

A regression, really, this one, back toward such works as "The Olive" (which Peter had come to call merely "Olive"): In recent months, the author's work had grown so pure that he himself could not say what narrative scaffolding, if any, had been removed. For such items as "Cellar-door," "Summer Afternoon," and "Theophany," one had to imagine, *invent* the settings. Not so "B$^\flat$," which two days ago had been "The Magnificent B$^\flat$" and two days before that "The Discriminating Critic and the Magnificent B$^\flat$." Once upon a time, went the old musicians' anecdote that Peter Sagamore had reorchestrated in early versions of this story, there was a music critic of such experience and discrimination that, out of all the music in the world, he could enjoy by age forty only certain composers of the Baroque period; of those, by age forty-five, only the orchestral portions of certain oratorios by J. S. Bach and G. F. Handel; of those, by age fifty, little more than the obbligato for twin recorders in close harmony played over the soprano aria "Schafe können sicher weiden" from Bach's

Jagdkantate of 1716, BWV208—in particular, by age fifty-five (when it seemed to him that both his judgment and his ear were at their most perfectly discriminating), the lead *Blockflöte*'s repeated B♭ which opens that obbligato. "What a loss!" his friends and colleagues would exclaim: "Out of all of music, to be able to enjoy but a single note in a single composition!" "No doubt," the discriminating critic would agree: "But what a magnificent B-flat! Especially in the Telefunken recording S-A-W-T Nine Four Two Seven B, with Wingerden of the Amsterdamer Kammerorchester on the descant *Blockflöte*. In the other recordings it is rather less affecting; even in the Telefunken, Wingerden's attack is not all that one could wish. But these are quibbles."

Katherine Shorter Sherritt Sagamore believed she saw not only the point of her husband's story thus far, but, not without alarm, what today's revision of it was likely to produce. She closed her eyes; she exhaled her worry. Placing her left forefingertip over Peter's new story, she silently invoked the muse of Very Invention, and under "B♭" she wrote the number 39.

Then, though still distressed, she set about her real work of the morning: making clipboard note of a few ideas she wants to try out upon the local alumnae of The Deniston School for Girls—her mother's prep-school alma mater as well as her own—whom Irma will be entertaining this afternoon. She means to develop these notes, does K, into a presentation at the next Deniston trustees' meeting, in September: Strategies for Coping with the Foreseeable Economic Problems of the Few Remaining Private Boarding Schools for Girls in the American 1980s, Given the Ongoing Trend to Coeducation, the Present Decline of the U.S. Economy, and the Possibility of Continuing High Inflation and Interest Rates, Whoever Wins the November Presidential Election.

The Deniston School for Girls sits on a handsome waterfront estate on the upper Shore, adjoining two other handsome waterfront estates now owned by the Soviet embassy as a vacation compound for its Washington staff. Kath's specific proposal is to sell to the Soviets, who want more privacy and who pay top dollar, cash on the line, a third to a half of Deniston's ample acreage, which the school uses mainly for bridle paths and horse pasture. She would put the money into crackerjack faculty and scholarships for gifted students, in neither of which the school presently abounds, to the end of making the name Deniston synonymous with excellence in academics and the arts, as well as with social quality. That synonymy attained, the school could hike tuition charges as needed and still operate at capacity.

But her reflections are several times interrupted. First comes a call from a colleague at the Pratt Library, who can't get the Talemobile started for its Sunday rounds: The key won't turn in the ignition lock. Kate reminds her of the trick: Repeat three times the formula *Once upon a time* while jiggling the steering wheel to free up its locking linkage with the starter switch.

Next comes Irma, dressed for church, a Bloody Mary for herself in one hand, a Bloody Shame for Katherine in the other, and a small package under her arm. The women kiss good morning and enjoy each other's company for a quarter-hour. Irma Shorter Sherritt—though she feels with Henry that, in marrying Peter, Kate was to some extent reacting against them, in particular against their having touted Porter Baldwin, Jr.—enjoys her new son-in-law and recognizes the marriage to be as sound as hers. That's saying much. All the same, she can't help feeling, and from time to time declaring, that her daughter is living out her life on too small a stage. She wishes Kath weren't spending her thirties in a library office in a provincial city with only the odd short trip to beach or mountains; that she would at least go shopping and theatering with her mother more often in New York, not to mention Paris, London, Rome (the senior Sherritts are active travelers). It's all Irma can do to get the girl up twice a year to the factory clothing outlets in Pennsylvania.

Katherine kisses her, and that conversation goes no further.

Regarding dear Deniston, Irma has her own ideas, which she sets forth upon hearing Kate's. Selling off the acreage contiguous to the Russkies will not only displease the rich hard-line conservatives who supply Deniston with their daughters; it will curtail the school's riding program as well, and in Irma's opinion where you don't have boys you'd better have horses. She is all for expanding the arts programs, especially theater and dance, which have more social appeal than painting, sculpture, and instrumental music, not to mention writing. Never mind a better academic faculty, says Irma, at least as a high priority: The three Ds—dance, drama, and dressage— are more important to the school's survival than the three Rs, in which honest adequacy will do. So far from selling out to the Commies, Irma would rub their ambassadorial noses in the sweets of capitalism. In warm September and late May, let the pretty Denistonians windsurf past the compound in their bikinis; in the cooler months, parade them past in their jodhpurs and riding finery. She bets we'd collect the better class of Soviet defectors like windfall apples in October, and she has reason to believe that our government would express its gratitude in appropriate form.

Says incredulous Katherine You have reason to believe *what?*

I have reason to believe what I have reason to believe, Irma pleasantly affirms, and don't ask me why I have reason to believe it, 'cause I won't tell.

You won't tell because I won't ask, K teases, disturbed all the same— for reasons that *we* have yet to tell—by this surely idle remark of her mother's. That is the single weirdest idea I've heard all morning.

Says Irma Wait till I play my ace, and then plays it with cool offhand-edness, as it were into what remains of her daughter's lap: I'm proposing we change the school's name to Saint Deniston.

K whoops, then covers her mouth, hoping she hasn't disturbed P's mus-ings. Saint Deniston!

Your father agrees it sounds very diocesan.

Who's Saint Deniston? Kath wants to know. John James Deniston was a small-time robber baron!

Irm stirs her drink with its celery stalk; sips; shrugs. We'll canonize him. Her. I see Saint Deniston as a teenage English virgin on a big bay gelding. Joan of Arc, but nicer.

You can't invent a saint!

I just did. Isn't Deniston a pretty first name for a girl, by the way?

Too boarding-schooly.

Maybe. But The Saint Deniston School for Girls is a winner.

Kath is equally admiring and appalled. You're serious.

Perfectly. Upgrade the performing arts building and staff, especially the building. Upgrade the horse barns and the waterfront. Give special privileges for a while to the upscale types we really want, like boarding their horses for free, and promote John Deniston from robber baron to virgin Protestant martyr. In four or five years you'll be able to afford your academic excellence and your scholarships, especially after Reagan wins in November and the rich get richer. This came for you yesterday.

The mailing bag is stamped BOOK RATE. Kathy sees it's from May Jump in Annapolis and sets it aside. A lettered van drives behind the cottage, en route to the Main House. Irma says That's Buck Travers for the intercom, and gets up.

Mom.

I know what you're going to say. He won't bother you and Peter; the problem's at our end. Buck can fix it now, and Peter can test it for me later.

Says Kath That's not my objection.

I know it's not, but humor me. And don't give birth till we're home from church. I'm going to go have a talk with Buck Travers now.

They kiss. Kath compliments her mother on her dress and instructs her to say a safe-delivery prayer to St. Deniston. Irma replies that without sainthood and riding stables, Deniston hasn't *got* a prayer. She will consult her daughter further at lunch about tea party arrangements.

Now Katherine opens the mailing bag and sees that her friend, sometime mentor, and erstwhile colleague has sent her a new dictionary of homosexual slang *in token of our common interest in folkspeech.* . . . Those suspension points are May's; the inscription ends *Always, all ways, M.* While she's sampling the entries, her father stops by, also dressed for church, to wish her good morning and deliver the Sunday *Times.* He'll need the financial section back when we've read it. His other mission is to recruit Peter as a standby for tennis after lunch: doubles with Jack Bass and a former U.S. interior secretary, now retired to nearby Wye Island, with whom Henry Sherritt has formed a business partnership as a retirement hobby. They have persuaded Doctor Jack to join the venture, which Hank sees as both profitable and patriotic—and, for the Sherritts, nostalgic as well. Roughly twenty-five percent of the fertile feed-corn acreage of Kent County, on the upper Shore, has been purchased in the past few years by foreign interests, mainly Dutch and German conglomerates who may or may not be laundering Arab oil money. They know, says Henry Sherritt, that after oil, the next great world resource shortage is going to be food. What he and his associates aim to do is buy up as much as possible of that grainland before the "Europeans" own it all; then either resell it at a proper profit to American agribusiness interests or hold it against the formation of the next OPEC, led by the USA, in which the *P* will stand for *protein* instead of *petroleum*.

DO OLD HANK THERE.

Sure. At sixty-six he's trim and tan, he's long and leathery, Henry Sherritt, but the leather is bookbinder's calf, not cobbler's rawhide. Hank's hair and mustache are the color of the U.S. quarter before Lyndon Johnson diddled its alloy and the old coin disappeared. They're handsome; so's the man. Behold those eyes, as straight as good teeth; those teeth, as white as the clean whites of his eyes. Behold strong fingernails, which we can no more imagine Henry Sherritt ever biting than we can imagine him spitting, farting, chewing gum. He's cool and easy in his light seersucker, white short-sleeved shirt, clocked socks, soft bow tie, and boutonniere of early black-eyed Susan. Dry cool too is Henry's accent, an Eastern Shore brogue filtered through Groton and Princeton without quite filtering out. Though she disagrees with his politics almost from the bottom up, Kathy thinks her father not only good-looking but in nearly every way exemplary, and much loves him. Howevermuch she treasures Peter Sagamore and our union, she doubts it can be as textbook a case of happy marriage as has been her parents': We are too different under our harmony, our tempers too volatile under their ease, our dispositions too skeptical and self-skeptical, to manage Hank and Irma's unclouded bliss, each of whom thinks simply wonderful everything the other is and does. Nor have we the assets of their uncomplicated High Church faith and their virtual freedom from self-doubt, which permit them to be both unassuming and tolerant of difference, up to a point. Henry Sherritt may joke about the tidewater version of Old Boy society, Irma sigh at the seasonal round of coming-out parties, yacht-and-country-club galas, dinners, teas: They not only would not dream of changing that order, that round; they profoundly approve of and enjoy it.

Father and daughter kiss hello. He smells of suntan lotion and light cologne. He sits. They chat. Pete's working? As usual; but she'll deliver the tennis message. No obligation, Henry makes clear: It's likely Katherine's elder brother and sister-in-law will stop by for lunch after church, and Willy may want to make the fourth himself when he sees John Trippe and Jack Bass on the court. But Peter is welcome in any case.

Kath has as always been enjoying the sight, sound, and smell of her father; his invocation of Willy Sherritt darkens her expression. Powerful, porcine, sleek, unprincipled, her elder brother seems to her the incarnation of nearly everything deplorable about the world and worldview of which she finds her father the embodiment of nearly everything admirable. I know very well, she says now, why Willy's sucking around John Trippe.

She sees her father register that vulgarism with a tiny eye-twitch. Don't judge your brother out of hand, he reproves her. Kath says spiritedly she doesn't need the man in hand to judge him, this late in the day. Willy Sherritt is organizing a Reelect Baldwin Bull Roast in Poonie's new district in the Maryland mountains and needs to recruit a few unimpeachable conservative *famosos* to put his impeachable *infamoso* in a redemptive light.

Kate. Henry Sherritt frowns. Peebie's trying to pick up the pieces again. He made himself a new life and a new constituency once before; now he's got an even harder job ahead. Show some mercy.

Katherine Sherritt will be damned if she will. Ex-Congressman Porter Baldwin, Jr., undeniably shifted his chief theater of political operations to southern Maryland after their divorce: no easy matter for an aspiring politician. He remarried—another innocent Denistonian, God help the poor woman, who has so far stood by him through the later scandal and his subsequent second base-change, from southern to far western Maryland. Until that scandal hit the fan two years ago, he moved in the odor of conservative sanctity, a darling of the Moral Majority. But in Kate's opinion he learned nothing from the occasion and experience of their divorce except to be an even more careful hypocrite in the indulgence of his portfolio of vices, which we now know to have diversified from mere alcoholism and heterosexual sadism to include pederasty as well. He is the same double-dealing, opportunistic, unprincipled sonofabitch he has always been, declares Katherine, and Willy Sherritt is another: birds of a feather except in bed. Her brother's motives in maintaining that old friendship (and certain business connections) despite Poonie's crimes against her, and in organizing the bastard's reelection campaign despite that later scandal, have nothing to do with the morality of redemption through penance; not even with the morality of friendship. All Willy wants is a crony in Congress—right- or left-wing, gay, straight, or crooked—and he'd sell his own sister to have one, were she for sale.

Really now, Katydid. Henry Sherritt is visibly impressed by the depth of his daughter's fury, so long after its chief occasion. You'll bother Peter.

Kath apologizes for having raised her voice, but makes clear to her father that Poonie Baldwin himself had better never set foot on Nopoint Point while she's here, or she'll go public at whatever cost to herself with the full story of their marital breakup and blow him and Willy both away: a story of which even her father knows only the gross outlines.

Those outlines, Henry Sherritt says with a grimace, are gross enough. Touching her arm, he assures his daughter that, reformed or unreformed, her ex-husband remains non grata forever in his and Irma's household.

Henry too deplores Willy's continuing association with the man, and his playing footsie with organized, self-appointed legislators of virtue, especially given Willy's own moral shortcomings. But if Henry will not allow Porter Baldwin, Jr., on Nopoint Point, he will certainly not close the door on his own son, any more than he would on the unfortunate Porter Baldwin Seniors, for forgiving what he and Irma can never. Katherine might as well know that her brother is bidding to buy into Breadbasket Incorporated, and that he, Henry, at least, is not opposed to the idea. As for Peebie's double life, Henry is confident that the revelation of all that (which cost Baldwin the '78 election) will oblige him at least to run for reelection less hypocritically: either genuinely repentant and reformed, or else openly as the first declared bisexual candidate for the U.S. Congress. Time for church now.

Kate's unconvinced: If old Poon really comes out of the closet, she believes, it will be because his managers decide he can draw more national attention and support by so doing. More likely they'll advise him to go the repentant-sinner route, as he did after '63, when the only thing he repented was causing himself so much political inconvenience. It sure paid off then.

Her father says with dignity That memory hurts my soul, Katydid, and Kathy sees it does. But she cannot help adding, as they kiss good-bye, It's a pain in my ass, too.

Henry says he'll have another talk with Willy, but the man is his own man. Will Katherine and Peter join the clan for lunch?

K doubts it: She truly cannot abide her older brother. She even wishes that her younger, whom she adores, didn't have to be around him. Maybe she'll have Chip to lunch with us here.

That would hurt your mother's feelings, Henry says. As for Peebie, you know, Kate, the pity of it is, he really loved you. Probably does still. He was a desperate and pathetic and sick young man.

Says Kathy He still is, only middle-aged. Also despicable.

Henry Sherritt sighs. Also despicable. He hugs her carefully. See you after church. Take care.

THE NEXT HOUR OR SO

A great virtue of the Christian faith, in our recent opinion, is the tranquility it brings to Nopoint Point between half past ten and half past twelve on Sunday mornings, when the senior Sherritts and most of their friends and help are in church in the village of Easton, a few miles away. Peter pops out at one point with a refilled coffee cup and stands a few moments beside Kath's rocker, stretching his arms and legs, contemplating the cove, registering the steamy forenoon with his skin. K wonders what's what with old "B♭," but keeps her worry to herself. The earlier mention of Porter

"Poonie" Baldwin, Jr., inclines her to embrace her husband's left leg lightly and lean her head against his hip. We do not speak of the work in progress or the version of it Katherine has just read. She mentions the tennis. Peter hopes Willy will stand in for him. Hank's crowd takes the game too seriously for his liking; he'll be glad when his favorite partner is back in action.

We think we hear the sound of Buck Travers testing the intercom: an amplified drawl in the stately distance. Kathy sighs: Mom wants you to check it out after lunch, or later if you play tennis. She made the man promise not to bother us this morning.

It amuses Peter but annoys Katherine that all Sherritts assume all Sagamores to be "good with their hands." But he is in fact handy, and unashamed of the blue-collar background that makes replacing a rotted dock-plank or troubleshooting a balky outboard no less agreeable an hour's sport than playing tennis. He'll get Chip to help.

Back to the nursery, he says now. A dry sigh in his tone tells Kath that little has happened in there so far. She thinks the associations counterproductive, under the circumstances, but those circumstances are themselves so mattersome that she chooses not to bring up the associations. For the next three-quarters of an hour she rocks, musing, her Episcopal peace undisturbed but for that passel of thrashers under her tum. Beach swallows make low-level passes across the lawn and around the pedestaled bronze all-purpose-allegorical pair—naked neoclassic gent and lady, he frowning forward at Main House and Goldsborough Creek, she smiling serenely over-shoulder at First Guest Cottage and Sherritt Cove—whom Henry calls Business and Pleasure and Irma calls Eb and Flo and Chip calls Cathode and Anode and Kathy calls Vamos y Quedemos and Peter calls More and Less. Mockingbirds move from tree to tree, eloquently discussing territorial boundaries. Like interceptors buzzing bombers, purple martins harass crows that would raid their nests. There's a snapping turtle at periscope depth out in Sherritt Cove. Near the red day-beacon where cove makes into creek, K's knowledgeable eye espies in a waterswirl the wingtips of a feeding skate, like the warped dorsals of twin sharks.

A FEW PAGES BACK, VIS-À-VIS HENRY SHERRITT'S GRAIN-LAND SPECULATIONS UP IN KENT COUNTY, WE USED THE ADJECTIVE *NOSTALGIC*.

Right. Here's why. If you sail the upper Chesapeake, you know "Ornery Point," a handsome spit of sand and locust trees jutting more than halfway across the Sassafras from that river's north shore: It is where this story ends and another begins. Though it can in fact be a stubborn obstruction for a sailor to fetch in a headwind, the point takes its name not from that circumstance but from a tavern, or "ordinary," where pre-Revolutionary Hermanns, De Courseys, and Sherritts sipped rum or cider while waiting for the ferry that used to cross there between Kent and Cecil counties. Nothing remains of the ordinary: As of this telling, the point is pleasingly undeveloped and uninhabited by humans except for the odd picnicker or stroller of its beaches. Downstream from Ordinary Point, the Sassafras is an imposing estuary, a mile and more wide, between almost unbroken eighty-foot banks; upstream, it's a secluded river winding peacefully mile after mile around lesser points, between lower tree-lined shores, up to the village of Georgetown and beyond.

NOSTALGIA

Captain John Smith of Virginia was the first cruising sailor to poke into the Sassafras, in 1608. To his English ears, the name of the resident Indians sounded like "Tockwogh." Rear Admiral Sir George Cockburn wound a small British task force up the channel in May of 1813 to harass the locals. From the point of Ordinary Point, you have a fair view eastward, upriver, and a fine one westward: those tall cliffs stepping out of sight into the open Chesapeake, where the weather comes from. No land visible on the far horizon, though the rest of the United States is over there somewhere. Oceangoing freighters and container ships slide by to and from the Chesapeake & Delaware Canal like targets in a shooting gallery. Georgetown, at the highway bridge some miles upriver, is a yachting center: Wall-to-wall marinas up there harbor thousands of pleasure boats owned mostly by Delawarians and Pennsylvanians, for whom the Sassafras is the first convenient access to Chesapeake Bay. It is an altogether lovely freshwater river with, however, few good overnight anchorages along its shores except the commodious lee of Ordinary Point. For that reason, on any summer weekend evening you can count a couple hundred cruising sailboats and motorboats anchored there, individually and in rafts of two to twelve. Their owners, crew, and guests will be swimming, partying, barbecuing beefsteaks off their taffrails; the youngsters will zip sailboards through the fleet, hop from boat to boat to make or visit friends, play guitars and radios on foredecks, fly kites off transoms, parachute up and out on untacked spinnakers to drop twenty feet into the water; they'll dinghy ashore to stroll the beach of Ordinary Point, picnic, skinny-dip off the far side, chug beer, make out, and wonder how it came to pass that a certain young locust there, six to eight inches thick at the trunk and ten to twelve feet through its spread of branches, is neatly collared at its base by an old Atlas automobile tire, intact.

NOSTALGIA

This *is* nostalgia, or will be, soon enough. On such weekends, the anchorage at Ordinary Point is short on privacy and serenity. But it is secure in most weathers, while open enough for a welcome breeze on muggy nights. The air there is normally bugless; the holding ground is good sand; all that high-spirited activity can be enjoyable, occasionally, as a change of pace from the secluded coves farther down the Shore.

Our *Story* is no stranger to the Sassafras. We sail up there ordinarily, Peter and Katherine, once a summer, usually in August, a little second vacation to escape the sea nettles of Sherritt Cove and environs. In any breeze at all, three days of leisurely sailing, two of pushing, or one of standing watches will carry us the seventy-five nautical miles from Nopoint to Ordinary Point. With our centerboard raised we draw two feet of water, and thus have access to certain fine creeks off the Sassafras that the yachtsfolk from Wilmington and Philadelphia can't negotiate in their bigger boats. We'll spend a few lazy, steamy dog days there, shaded by *Story*'s cockpit awning or the canopy of maples atop a certain high-banked islet. We'll swim and read and write and bask, sip and cook and eat, tell stories and make love in ninety-degree air, eighty-degree water. We'll go naked from the Tuesday through the Friday, the place is that private, while a quarter-mile off so much pleasure-traffic plies the river that its channel looks like a nautical expressway.

Then on the Saturday we'll slip into swimsuits and sail down to join the action at Ordinary Point. However crowded the anchorage, with our shallow draft we'll find ample swinging room, mooring almost on the beach if necessary. As we thread under sail through the anchored fleet or poke about later in the dinghy, we'll inevitably find or be found by friends of Hank's and Irma's, enjoying in their fifty-footers what we're enjoying in our twenty-five; or friends of Kathy's from her college days who've since become doctors or MBAs from the Wharton School of Business, or who've married them: They live out on Philadelphia's Main Line now but come down weekends to sail their gleaming thirty-eight-footers and talk about the market (*The Wall Street Journal* is delivered daily in season to Georgetown marinas). Less often we'll run into a couple or two we've come to know through Katherine's job or Peter's: fellow academics, library scientists or museum people, whose two-salary households can budget a second-hand thirty-two-footer until it's time to pay the kids' college expenses, or now they're paid. Sometimes we'll even meet an old high school chum of Pete's from lower Dorchester, who has scraped together from his wetlands realty business enough for a twenty-seven-footer and is taking his annual low-budget vacation thereupon with wife and two kids and another couple, all speaking the pristine down-county twang and all somehow sleeping, eating, sweating, and defecating in those tight quarters, their shrouds and lifelines festooned stem to stern with laundry. We'll board or be boarded by various of these for drinks and talk; later, all hands might row ashore to join the youngsters dancing on the strand of Ordinary Point to disco music broadcast from across the Bay. We'll end the evening by piling overboard from *Story*'s gunwales or some other's for a midnight swim in the tepid, harmless water, by ourselves or with our friends, trying not to remember that we swim in a floating village of two hundred families with no sewage treatment facilities. It is healthy U.S. poo; no one takes sick. If any air moves through *Story*'s cabin from the windscoop rigged to the forward hatch, we'll make late drowsy love upon the "double" settee berth, where there's just room, before Peter crawls into the quarterberth aft and Kath into the V-berth forward, where there isn't. We'll fall asleep to the cry of night owls real and figurative, whippoorwills, and the clink of halyards left unsecured by the inexperienced or oblivious to slap against extruded aluminum masts.

WHY ARE WE TELLING US ALL THIS?

Because before such demons as Less Is More possessed him, P. Sagamore prided himself upon the knowledgeable rendition of the natural and human history against which his characters played out their moral-psychological dramas. A Sagamore story from that period might have been about a loving, middle-class, early-middle-aged couple's coming to terms with childlessness, for example; Peter agrees with Aristotle that the subject of literature is the passions of the human heart, the happiness and misery of human life, not geographical places and historical events. But if that make-believe couple happened to be represented as Marylanders of such-and-such diverse background, and the action took place aboard a small cruising sailboat on the Sassafras River, say, he'd want to get it said that that boat is a hard-chined, wide-beamed, tiller-steered, engineless wooden centerboard sloop of traditional local design; that those eighty-foot sedimentary cliffs below Ordinary Point, like the whole Eastern Shore of Maryland, were dumped there as a giant shoal by the Susquehanna River when the glaciers melted at the end of the last ice age, just ten thousand years ago—the same river whose Pennsylvania waters now erode those cliffs and keep the general salinity of the Sassafras above Ordinary Point too low—under five parts per thousand—for *Chrysaora quinquecirrha*. That, finally (here's Hank's nostalgia, to fetch which we've tacked through these other nostalgias as toward an upwind mark), when an earlier Henry Sherritt came up from Talbot County in the late 1770s and sipped cider in the ordinary at Ordinary Point, he was laying the foundations of the family fortune by wartime speculation in wheat and corn from the upper Eastern Shore, "the Breadbasket of the Revolution": His leased vessels moved his brokered grain to feed General Washington's troops, at such profit to himself in both money and favor with our future first president that he rose above his Loyalist inclinations and accepted a colonel's commission in the Maryland Line in the last months of the war. Of the three granaries on the Sassafras still preserved from that time, two were once leased to Colonel Henry Sherritt; the third has been converted into a restaurant more popular than excellent, serving the marina crowd. The present Henry is dickering with the Kent and Cecil county commissioners, and others, to buy one of the two, a historical monument now, and restore it as a working mill and granary, the centerpiece of his nostalgic and potentially very profitable feed-grain enterprise, Breadbasket Incorporated.

In Peter Sagamore's previous opinion, even in his present opinion, such contextual circumstances as these—or as that those clouds that will build west of Baltimore late Sunday afternoon, 29 June '80, are cumulonimbi packing both thermal- and pressure-gradient winds that will blow the be-jesus out of parts of that city and then tear across the Bay to blooey the upper Shore at cocktail time and drag half the anchors behind Ordinary Point, *Story*'s not included, almost within sight of that same granary, while Katherine Shorter Sherritt commences giving birth—such contextual circumstances are as crucial to the flavor of re-created experience as the fact that K has never borne a child before, though she's had one induced and one spontaneous abortion. Peter Sagamore used to wish that he could know and render them *all,* despite his understanding that if he did, no story would get told. Leaving them incompletely said still feels to him like describing a fine champagne as merely alcohol, water, and carbonic acid in solution. Better sip in silence than thus falsify! Not to mention . . .

And so—increasingly, unhappily, but determined to work this and other demons honestly through—has he done.

DONE?

Done.

TIME FOR LUNCH.

Skip lunch.

LUNCH MAYBE; LUNCHTIME NO.

Willy and Molly Sherritt's ice-blue Mercedes glides up the drive at lunchtime behind Hank and Irma's saddle-brown Cadillac, and Kathy loses her
appetite. Not to be rude to Irma, we go up and say hello, but, hanging a
bum rap on the kids—morning sickness this late in the day, this late in
our term?—do not stay for the meal. Peter is excused from tennis; he'll
check out the video intercom instead. Chip Sherritt is excused from ball-
boying to assist him. Willy's Molly asks us can she have a look at Irm's
redoings in the First Guest Cottage. Kate can't say no, but such is her
antipathy for her elder sibling and her exasperated sympathy for his wife,
she will permit no further reference in this narrative to the Main House
luncheon: only a sketch of Molly and a summary of her visit.

Molly B. Sherritt was Molly Barnes of Chestertown, Circuit Court Judge
and Mrs. Barnes's only, when she graduated from The Deniston School
for Girls a year before our Kate. In those days she was a bright-eyed,
apple-cheeked, high-humored girl, ruddy, befreckled, and wholesome; sturdy,
even a touch thick in body and mind, but of so cheery, energetic, innocent,
and kindly a disposition that everyone loved her in what she sees now to
have been the happiest years of her life, when she was a three-letter varsity
athlete, president of her form, and busy member of a half-dozen extra-
curricular clubs. From Deniston she went down with a clutch of classmates
to a small southern women's college regarded more for social propriety
than for academic seriousness; she left it after two years to marry her
girlhood sweetheart, William Sherritt, in a handsome ceremony at the
Deniston chapel on a sparkling June blue day, reception after at the Chester
River Yacht and Country Club. At that latter rose-and-peony-girt affair,
both the bridegroom and his best man—Porter "Poonie" Baldwin, Jr.—
got sozzled on the champagne: Poon to the point of stumbling off the club
dock en route to take a summer-tuxedo'd swim, Willy less so, but enough
to mortify his parents, make the straiter-laced Barneses wonder, and reduce
his virgin bride to tears when, having heavily deflowered her some hours
later in a honeymoon suite of Philadelphia's Warwick Hotel, he rolled from
her flush, still-expectant body into boozy sleep.

The day proved prophetic. Though their first years together were not
wretched, Molly Barnes Sherritt found her husband to be a boorish fellow,
an inconsiderate and soon indifferent lover, and a frequent drunk. How
had she not seen him so before? Because he was her Willy! cries hapless
Moll. His principal interests were and remain the buying and developing
of waterfront real estate (through Sherbald Enterprises, his long-standing
business partnership with Poonie Baldwin), for which he has a savvy knack;
the Frankly Controversial Experimenting with agricultural applications of
activated sludge (through a newly acquired firm called Natural Recycling

Research, whereof we know little at this stage of our story), in which he professes a Sort of Scientific Interest; playing tennis and golf with his Annapolis business cronies, for which he has aptitude and skill; drinking rye whiskey with branch water; and—particularly in the years since Molly discovered herself infertile—philandering. As Molly once did, many women find Big Will Sherritt attractive. Despite the alcohol intake, which, combined with his fondness for cigars, ripe cheeses, and oversalted food, would one day have felled him with a massive coronary on his backyard tennis court had not this narrative a different fate in store for him, Kath's elder brother at forty-five is physically powerful, well dressed and groomed, invincibly self-confident. He picks up young women law clerks and dental hygienists in the brass-and-fern bars of Annapolis and Baltimore and spends weekends with them on his Owens sedan cruiser—though he is not above humping in the front passenger seat of that ice-blue Mercedes in one of his Sherbald Enterprises waterfront building lots in broad daylight, his overwhelmed partner's left heel resting upon the simulated walnut dashboard, her right foot thrust through the open window while he half kneels on the floor before her, slacks and boxer shorts at his ankles, spreads her yet farther, lubricates her with his spittle, and, grunting around his Schimmelpenninck cigar, takes her more carnivorously than his affable barroom manner had led her to expect.

All this we know because word thereof gets back to Molly from women who know these women—Will neither denies nor vaunts his promiscuity, but he makes no particular effort to be discreet—and because Molly inclines for consolation to her old schoolmate, who however has for fifteen years consistently advised divorce. Molly Barnes Sherritt's problem is that she loathes the behavior but, despite all, loves the man. Save for the project of "sticking by Willy through thick and thin," her comfortable life is empty of significance. She wishes too late that they'd adopted children; that she'd learned a profession. She knows herself to be empty-headed, useless, by comparison to her mother-in-law, say, who sympathetically enlists Molly into her own club and committee work. That wifely life-project, while it requires of Mrs. Willy Sherritt little more than self-abnegation and some obtuseness, seems to have drained her once-abundant capacity for other activities: She plays no sports; she organizes nothing beyond her household; she reads Harlequin romances two-thirds through and watches daytime television. Yet, curiously—since Willy abuses her every way except physically—the fidelity at which we shake our heads has in fact given luckless Molly a degree of moral depth that many a happier woman lacks. She does not reason, but she understands. Certain lines of scripture, for example, in a polite Episcopalian Sunday sermon, burn to her heart like a flaming sword; they seem to her to justify her life and affirm her sorority with millions of her predecessors. She needs then tentatively to register this understanding with someone whom, however sympathetically scornful, she can trust: Katherine Shorter Sherritt Sagamore.

In fact, Molly Barnes Sherritt is still apple-cheeked and befreckled. She is sturdier than ever. Her ruddiness is gone the way of her energy; her eyes are clear and grave now, rather than bright; her high-humoredness is tempered into stoical placidity. She has not been made love to in twelve years and does not expect to be ever again. K likes and pities her and hates having her around; the unfortunate woman can't look at her sister-in-law's belly or those double bassinets without tears.

Not long after this story's close, Molly Barnes Sherritt will undertake (perhaps even welcome, but that is not for us to say) the even more demanding project of dying for two full years of cancer, originally cervical, without recrimination or even complaint. In the final weeks of her agony, she will sustain herself with two or three psalms, repeated silently and continuously like mantras, and the pages of The Deniston School Yearbook for 1956.

Her visit with us on this occasion stretches to half an hour, in the course whereof we learn that Willy is being treated for the social disease of our American times, herpes simplex, contracted presumably from one of his brass-and-fern pickups. Less dangerous than syphilis (or than AIDS, which in 1980 has not yet hit the historical fan), less disgusting than gonorrhea or crab lice, it is nonetheless uncomfortable indeed, rampant, and, as of this warm June Sunday, quite incurable. At its most severe, it can make sexual inter-course unendurably painful; obviously, one is supposed to warn potential part-ners that one has it. Unvindictive Molly reports that she has urged her husband to do so, but Willy knows that if he were to, that would be that. Therefore, like many another herpes simplexer, he simply doesn't. *He* wasn't warned, he complains, and bids his wife mind her own fucking business.

Kath's outraged. Peter, perusing the intercom service manual, is be-mused, the malady strikes him as so heavily appropriate to our place and time. But his own, nonmedical problem so preoccupies him that he can scarcely concentrate upon the manual, much less be properly appalled at Willy's callousness.

I know I should leave him, Molly sighs, and, affirmed, prepares now to leave us. But it happens that both Katherine and Irma Sherritt regard her as the very windvane of opinion among rank-and-file Deniston alumnae; Kate doesn't let her go before trying out on her those Strategies for the Eighties, in particular the matter of selling campus acreage to the Soviets. She is not surprised to learn that her mother has already done likewise with her counterproposals.

We *are* surprised, however, to hear that both Molly and Willy not only had been aware of the Soviets' proposal before Irma mentioned it, but have been arguing about it some while between themselves; that Molly in fact thinks Kate's idea a good one, *despite Willy's opposition to it*. Why does Willy care one way or the other, Katherine wants to know: His only interest in Deniston is that we supply victims for the likes of himself and Poonie Baldwin.

If it's real estate, says Molly, Willy's interested, commission or no commission. But it's really Peebie and the politics thing: some anti-Russian group. I'm sorry, Kate.

Of those who grew up in Katherine's circle and generation, Molly Barnes Sherritt is the only one who calls Porter Baldwin, Jr., by his politer nickname. What anti-Russian group? Peter asks with a certain curiosity, still however reviewing the intercom service manual. We learn that among the cold-warrior organizations willing to support Poonie's reelection despite his fall from straight sexual grace is an association of Soviet and Eastern European defectors to the United States, who claim anyhow that the congressman was entrapped if not framed by the KGB. Kath begins to hum. Peter turns the pages of the manual.

I shouldn't talk about these things in front of you-all, Molly acknowledges. But I think you're right, Kate: We don't need all those woods and horse barns. I was sorry to hear about your friend Doug Townshend, by the way. Irma said you went to some kind of memorial service?

We have not yet even mentioned to the reader our newly late old friend Douglas Townshend, or Friday's memorial cocktail service for him in Georgetown (the Washington Georgetown, where Poonie's gay bars are, not the yachty village on the Sassafras), and their bearing upon this Sunday and this book. What is more, despite Molly's cue we shall not speak for quite a while yet of dear dead Doug. Forget she mentioned him, reader of this sentence: Ignore this sign. Molly Barnes Sherritt guesses she'll run along now and does, back to poolside with her knitting bag to add a square to our baby-afghan-gift-in-the-works while waiting for Willy to finish his doubles match.

**IN ADVANCED AS IN EARLY PREGNANCY,
A WOMAN'S APPETITE MAY BE CAPRICIOUS.
BUT WHY DID PETER SAGAMORE EAT NO LUNCH,
EITHER IN THE MAIN HOUSE OR IN THE FIRST GUEST COTTAGE?**

. . .

AH SO. EVEN THE B♭, THEN, AS WE HAD FEARED . . .

CHECK THE INTERCOM. CHECK THE INTERCOM.

In a subdued, sober dismay, which we have put off registering though Katherine has been perfectly aware of it, Peter Sagamore turns now with relief to the simple physical-mechanical task set him by his mother-in-law: checking out Buck Travers's adjustments to the new audio-video installation. The Sunday is stoking up. From across the grounds of Nopoint Point come the pock of hard-hit tennis balls and mature male exclamations of satisfaction or chagrin. How does Willy hack it, P wonders aloud, with a jockful of herpes blisters? Hisses K The swine.

Peter has dispatched his lieutenant, twelve-year-old Andrew Christopher "Chip" Sherritt, from station to station to transmit and receive while he himself monitors, tinkers with settings, consults the manual, gives instructions from the nursery, and pays attention to his young brother-in-law's advice. But their program runs afoul of Katherine Sherritt, who, while she appreciates to the marrow, to the heart, to the womb, the delicacy of the hour, not only opposes the whole installation, as has been seen, but has been thinking about our situation in general.

Her husband has agreed all along that it is an expensive bit of near uselessness, this intercom; but he has shrugged his shoulders, as is his sometimes exasperating wont, and gone along with it for Irma's sake. Katherine, on the other hand, has declared it from the first and declares it now again an invasion in principle and in fact of both our and the future nanny's privacy: a fucking spy-in-the-sky. What's more, while thumbing idly through May Jump's gift dictionary of gay slang, she has been thinking, about our situation in general. Now in mid-test she rather suddenly takes up a position between the twin cribs, in full view of the ceiling camera, and begins removing her clothes, at the same time reciting spiritedly from the work in hand.

In most cases, she announces, peeling out of the blouse of her maternity sunsuit, a new young convict's penis—his *johnson, jock, shovel,* or *swipe*—isn't given a second look by his fellow inmates. It's his virgin ass that turns 'em on.

Embarrassed Andrew wonders from the poolside station Hey, Kath? We're testing the system, okay?

So am I, his sister replies. With a level glance at wondering Peter, she drops her blouse into the starboard crib and, switching the book from hand to hand as necessary, removes the nursing bra she's been trying on for fit. In prison parlance, the asshole *faute de mieux* is generally *goosehole, Hawaiian eye, ring,* or *roundeye.* If the lad is still a virgin—anally—he is called a *kewpie doll,* his anus being his *bullhead, cherry,* or *prune.* E.g.: Use a lot of spit, man: this guy's still got his prune!

Make her stop, Pete, Chip complains. I'm not supposed to hear stuff like that.

I agree, Peter Sagamore agrees, interested all the same in the information, the show, and the odd resolve in his friend's expression. But your
sister is her own woman. How's the video from there?

How'm I supposed to tell? For pity's sake turn *around,* Kath, so I can
look.

Says Kathy sweetly Look all you like, Kewpie Doll; that's what the
telly's for. She steps out of her sunsuit shorts. We hear Molly, at Andrew's
end, giggle and say Kathy Sherritt!

After he has been *opened up,* the new prisoner's ass is referred to as
gash, nooky, or *pussy. Spread* once . . . and he is a *marked woman* or
punk for the rest of his *semester.*

Irma Shorter Sherritt now speaks firmly from the glass-enclosed orangery
of the Main House: This really is not amusing, Katherine. You're embarrassing your brother and me too. And people are coming. I've always liked
that gold chain of yours, by the way.

You're getting the idea, folks. K whisks her underpants down and kicks
them away. Anybody wants to keep his prune had better over and out.
Now she turns quarter turns, striking model's poses as best she can. The
first to gain anal entrance, she declaims, a highly prized honor, is called
the *welcome wagon.* The second in line is *sloppy seconds,* while the
third . . . fucker . . . is *bloody thirds.*

Andrew Sherritt says You're weird, Kath, and clicks off.

No other slang terms are used after thirds, probably because the prize
is such a mess by then. Anybody still there? *Wedding bells* are composed
of the victim's comments mixed with the squeak of the mattress.

Mildly but sternly then, when Irma does not reply, Peter says That was
a touch much, no? All we have to do is turn the thing off at this end. He
turns it off.

It shouldn't've been put in. Glum now, but still thinking, Kathy sits on
the rug, fingers one earring, and flips the pages of that lexicon. What do
you guess *draw the blinds* means in gay talk?

I don't care what *draw the blinds* means in gay talk. Peter closes the
intercom manual and sits beside her. Irma meant well.

Mom always means well. Kath fingers the leg of his corduroy shorts.
That was dumb of me. I must be getting my period.

Me too. Pete busses the belly that rises between us. Metaphor, Meto-
nymy, & Co. kick back. Things come quietly to a head. Steadfastly we
have resisted this clear association, reminding ourselves that Less Is More
antedates our pregnancy and that there is at least one other factor (some
say there are five others) in the calculus of our man's silence. Steadfastly
we have protested to ourselves that P's impasse is a compression, really.
Prolific superminimalism, really. And steadfastly at the same time, and
tacitly, we have assumed that it and our pregnancy will at worst reach term
together. We have been being good-humored and humorous for months
about it, years really, but a pressure has been building all the same, and
a double fear: for Peter Sagamore's career and actual sanity, should things

go and stay where they've clearly been heading; and for the unthinkable burden it will place upon our parenthood if, to our dismay, his art turns out to have been sacrificed partly upon that altar.

Unlikely! Unprecedented? And yet.

And yet this state of affairs is truly not the legendary, the celebrated, the unspeakably tiresome Writer's Block. It isn't? It isn't: Otherwise, why would we write about it? P. Sagamore's muse may be dead or pregnant, but she is not blocked.

His sigh is like a surfaced whale's. He flips that manual into the other crib and stands over his distended friend.

For pity's sake, Kathy, set me a task!

KATHERINE SHERRITT SAGAMORE CONSIDERS DEEPLY FOR SOME MOMENTS, THEN SPEAKS TO THAT SAME DISTENSION.

Take us sailing.

PETER SAGAMORE CONSIDERS, TOO,

in particular an odd, unKathylike dejection in the tone of the voice of this thoroughbred female animal his wife and friend, who now winces up at him, holds out her hand, says Please. Okay?

You want to go *sailing?*

Sailing. Us. Not a word to anybody.

We'd have to be careful. . . .

She grunts to her knees. I *am* careful. I'm thirty-nine and careful. I am full up to here with care.

Alumnae tea. Saint Deniston. Strategies for the Eighties.

Kate looks at him levelly. Fuck 'em.

Mm hm. We'll just tell Chip, then, and he can tell Irma.

He'll want to go.

Chip's always welcome, yes?

Forget it.

Kath? But Peter reads the message of her presently brimming eyes: Just the two of us, please. Indeed, there is as much more to that wordless text as to a Sagamore minifiction. It may be argued that the language of the human eyeball is limited to dilation and contraction of the pupil, more or less irrigation by the tear ducts, and movement of the ball itself—a minimal vocabulary enhanced somewhat by muscular contractions of the lids, brows, and related features—and that the famous eloquence of eyes is largely a literary convention. Peter Sagamore is quick to question such conventions. But the ensemble of his wife's expression, whose principal speaker is those Minervan eyes, delivers in less time than it takes to write "B♭" the following considerable communiqué: *The protracted holding of the U.S. hostages in Iran by the new and erratic revolutionary government which deposed the hated Shah, together with the usual Arab–Israeli tensions, reminds us how precarious is the "free world's" principal energy supply and the economies dependent thereupon. The flood of Cuban refugees and deportees into Florida, the intermittent violence in South Africa, the diaspora of "boat people" from Southeast Asia, the recent staggering genocide in Cambodia, the juntas and dictatorships and totalitarianisms of right and left which oppress three-quarters of the world's runaway population—all remind us how rare and fragile is any measure of freedom, justice, and decency, not to to mention happiness, upon our planet. The recent nuclear accident at Three Mile Island, by no means yet resolved, on the river that feeds our Chesapeake, reminds us how almost unimaginably dangerous is the world even of the lucky unoppressed twenty-five or so percent. And the recent explosion of Mount Saint Helens reminds us that even should we ourselves not further ruin or destroy our Earth in the short run, which every disinterested expert tells us we're doing apace, indifferent nature's program is to do it in the long. Now, on top of all these contingencies, it has come to pass that what has been the center of your existence finds itself at odds with, finally even thwarted by, what must necessarily at least for some time be the center of mine, or at least be at that center: an alarming, almost unmentionable circumstance in itself, not to mention the other unmentionable factor or factors in your growing and now full-grown literary silence. This is the world, this the situation, into which you and I have elected and then labored to bring a child—children— knowing that he/she/they will almost certainly at very least have a life at very best less materially prosperous and qualitatively fine than ours, and discovering too late that the price of their creation may be much higher than we had dreamed. The clock is running, darling friend—your clock, mine, theirs, the world's—running! Before Circumstance takes us further by the collar or History harder by the throat, I want an hour or two of sweet doing-almost-nothing upon these mesmerizing waters with sweet yourself and no one else (except the gang in uterine parentheses), as in sweet seasons past. There is a thing I have to say to you, I think, that can better be said in Story than on Nopoint Point. You have set me the task of setting you a task. The task I now set you—actually the first of what will prove to be a brace of tasks— is to take us sailing without qualm or quibble, while there is still time.*

Peter Sagamore kisses Katherine Sherritt's hands. Let's go sailing. Helps her up and back into her underpants and sunsuit, never mind the bra, which she inserts into May's lexicon as a bookmark. She smiles now, lotions his back against the sun, finds herself horny. He lotions her legs, which she has some trouble reaching lately, and ditto. She says My prune is yours, you know. Jack Bass won't mind. Want to dig my ditch?

P pauses before replying I'm too scattered to dig your ditch.

I'll draw your blind.

I have no blind. Let's go sailing.

Past Business and Pleasure, through roses, boxwoods, and wisteria, down colonnades of yew and arborvitae, under oaks old as our republic and pines taller than those oaks, we make it from First Guest Cottage to dock without interception. Plump bald brown Jack Bass waves to us with his left-hand fingers from the court, where he's playing net while Henry serves. We note without surprise that Willy Sherritt has got himself partnered with silver-maned ex-Secretary Trippe; he waggles his big Prince racquet like a fiddler crab its claw. All four men wear tennis shirts despite the damp heat. The play proceeds. Irma has joined Molly Barnes Sherritt at poolside to sip Perrier, scan the Sunday *Times,* and chat with Joan Bass and Maryann Trippe, who have come over with their husbands from lunch at the Basses'.

Out on the dock, however, is Andrew, idly netting early blue crabs off the piles, inspecting them for certain signs, and dumping them back into Sherritt Cove.

LET'S SEE ANDREW CHRISTOPHER "CHIP" SHERRITT.

Shy for a Sherritt, Andrew is his sister's love and hobby. The nickname comes not from his being off the old block; it is short for *microchip* and derives from his remarkable store of information, his formidable memory, and his quickness at mathematics and nearly everything else. An accident of his parents' middle age (Irm had thought herself done with ovulation), Chip has been raised languidly, by family standards, though not spoiled: Mother and father had expended their parental energies years since, on Willy and Kate, and at Andrew's birth had not yet geared up for the busy grandparenthood they now look forward to. Chip's discipline, what little he needs, and chief attention and direction, which he thrives upon, come from his sister and his brother-in-law; we are in fact older enough to have been his parents, while Irma and Henry seem to him a benevolent great-aunt and -uncle with whom he happens to reside.

At twelve, Chip is a delicate-appearing boy, though like all Sherritts he's nimble and good at sports. His hair is dark brown and almost shoulder-length, but his skin is fair and freckled, won't tan properly. He's skinny and bright-eyed as a fledgling heron, self-conscious about but interested in his body. This summer, displeased with his pale and narrow chest beside brown-muscled Peter's, he won't go topless; above his boxer swimtrunks he's wearing a beige Izod shirt given him by Katherine. Nor will he go barefoot, but wears athletic socks and untied Nike running shoes except in the water, in church, and in bed. His top front teeth are still too large for the rest of him; that will change next year or the year after, when he shoots into puberty. Except for them, his face is a pretty young girl's face, their best feature his unSherrittlike great green eyes. Tribadistic May can't keep her hands off Andy Sherritt when she's about; soon enough it will be straight women who cannot. Chip sometimes fears that despite the good examples of his parents, he'll wind up making a bad marriage like his sister's first, or being a bad husband like his brother, for whom he strives in vain not to share Kath's distaste. He is therefore lately resolved never to marry, and in fact will not until he's Kathy's present age. But should the world not end before this century does, Andrew Sherritt in the year 2000 will be, at age two-and-thirty, not the computer software tycoon his dad half expects him to become, but a celebrated actor, director, and scriptwriter in several media, a serious intellectual, and a notably successful, nonpredatory lover whose ex-lovers, unlike Willy's, will speak warmly of him. Just now, however, he lets his sister know with a quick cut of the eyes that he remains offended by her misbehavior, and goes back to wielding the crab net with one hand as adroitly as a lacrosse stick.

Kath hugs him from behind. I apologize, Kewpie Doll.

He stiffens, but permits his hair to be kissed. You probably hurt Mom's feelings with that stuff.

I'll apologize; I'll apologize. She shmoozles his head between her breasts; rubs her chin in his hair. Where's the nearest intercom? I'll apologize right now. Didn't you put one on the dock?

Use *K-Four*'s CB, the boy suggests at once; Olive's always got her scanner on. His references are to the citizens-band radio aboard his father's blue and white ketch, *Katydid IV,* looming beside us—also equipped with all-channel VHF and single-sideband transceivers, radar, LORAN, and SATNAV receiver duly interfaced with autopilot, all which gadgetry Chip understands inside out and we do not—and to the Sherritts' West Indian cook, whom it pleases to monitor the highway police, the watermen's traffic, and her husband while she works. Now he realizes that his sister is teasing him. He uses the excuse to disengage himself, but his left arm remains loosely about her waist, where she holds his hand against her hip, and she is allowed to massage the back of his neck between her right thumb and forefinger. Chip wears a brown bead necklace like Peter's: another of her gifts, and the boy's single concession to nonpreppie costume.

ON WITH THE STORY.

Peter Sagamore in this interval has been conning with skipperly eye the sky, Sherritt Cove, Nopoint and Shorter Points at its mouth, and the wider waters of Goldsborough Creek beyond, to guess what might be what out on the river. Tide's low and slack; sky's hazy-sunny; air's mid-eightyish and humid. Since lunchtime, the breeze has veered from south-southeast to west-southwest and picked up from six to what looks and feels like ten or twelve knots out there: good air for a sail, but, together with those other signs, suggestive of scattered thundershowers later on. He considers.

He considers. Though not a true blue-water sailor like Henry Sherritt in his younger years, who used regularly to place the earlier *Katydid*s in the Annapolis-to-Newport and Newport-to-Bermuda races, Peter Sagamore grew up in small boats and knows the Bay's humors well. Even Hank respects his "local knowledge" and his ability to put our little sloop exactly where we want it without an engine's aid. In present circumstances, he is above all careful for Kate's physical safety—though no more so than she, who did not lightly set this task; who has a further thing to say; who has been thinking, about our situation generally. He steps aboard *Story,* tucked in under *Katydid*'s windowed transom like a yawl boat. Tied up astern is the Basses' runabout.

Asks hopeful Andrew Going sailing?

Got to give old *Story* a spot of exercise, says Peter. We'll finish the intercom another time. He glances at Katherine.

She squeezes her brother. I've asked Peter to take me for a little sail: just him and me and your nieces and nephews here. We need to be alone for a little while, okay?

The boy's disappointment is clear, but he gamely says I'll help you cast off. He is instructed to report our project to the Main House, to announce that Katherine will be late at best to the Deniston tea, and to raise either the Come Home or the Call In pennant on the port arm of the Sherritts' flagpole (from whose top stream the Stars and Stripes; from whose starboard arm flies the motley banner of Maryland) if we need to be gotten in touch with, for we do not intend to leave our radio on.

Kathy eases herself aboard. Chip and Peter open hatches, remove and stow fenders and sail covers, fetch up cockpit cushions, raise the mainsail, and bend on a midsize genoa jib. Andrew then steps ashore and uncleats our docklines. We are blanketed by the bulk of *Katydid IV,* but a good push-off with our sculling oar sets us out into Sherritt Cove enough to catch the first of the breeze and reach languidly into the creek, whence we can beat through the clearer air out past the day beacons and into the Tred Avon River. We wave good-bye, but do not sound the conch we keep aboard to signal *Story*'s settings-out. Chip replies with a little left-handed wave from the hip and wanders back toward the tennis court and the Main House.

HAVING MILDLY DISTRESSED HER FATHER, WHOM SHE LOVES,
WITH THE DEPTH OF HER CONTINUING AVERSION
TO HIS FIRSTBORN;

**HAVING THRICE IN SMALL WAYS OFFENDED HER MOTHER,
WHOM TOO SHE LOVES—
BY NOT JOINING IN THE FAMILY LUNCHEON,
BY MISBEHAVING ON THE VIDEO INTERCOM
AND OBSTRUCTING ITS CHECKING OUT,
AND NOW BY VIRTUALLY PROMISING A NO-SHOW
AT IRMA'S DENISTON ALUMNAE TEA—
AND HAVING FIRST EMBARRASSED AND THEN DISAPPOINTED
HER BELOVED YOUNGER BROTHER,
KATHERINE SHERRITT SAGAMORE SETTLES DOWN TO ENJOY
OUR PRIVATE LITTLE DAYSAIL.**

Well, we make me sound awful when we put it like that, says Kathy—settling herself heavily on the portside cockpit seat, her back against the cabin bulkhead, and idly twirling a wet-sand-colored lock of her hair between two fingers while watching stately Nopoint Point slide astern as *Story* gathers way—but we all know we love one another, all but Willy, may herpes simplex rot his pecker and make a monk out of him, and the main thing is we had to get away from there for a little while, because much as I love my family, I love you more, and we need to have a little talk. How's the breeze?

Better in the river. We won't go far.

I wish we were starting out on our June cruise.

P.S. almost says Me too, but his heart catches as, checking our sail trim against the masthead tacking vane, he realizes for the first time, really, that there'll be no more June cruises on this boat until the babies are old enough to be left for a week or so in their nursemaid's care at the First Guest Cottage—two Junes from now? three?—though we might of course borrow *Katydid IV* and take nursemaid and babies and paid hand Bobby Henry along too. Hoo, boy.

I'm afraid of this little talk, he says.

Says Kathy So am I. Let's sail for a few minutes before we start it.

A mile-long bend in the Tred Avon, from Goldsborough Creek to Town Point and the village of Oxford, runs east-west, affording the breeze a good fetch and *Story* a fair beat into it on the port tack. At Oxford the river widens and turns south for two miles to join the Great Choptank, itself about four miles wide there. Peter's plan, wind and weather permitting, is a brisk close reach down toward the Choptank River Light, at the Tred Avon's mouth; a steady beam reach back up past Oxford; a gentle run home. Seven or eight nautical miles in all, counting Goldsborough Creek; ninety minutes or so of sailing, tidily divided among the three main points; home before the likeliest thunderstorm period begins and in time for Kath to freshen up and check in with the Denistonians, if she wants to, before they disperse. It is a route we have daysailed countless times, in every sort of weather, and seldom failed to enjoy: from secluded to open and back to secluded waters; from the all but boatless creek, through the thronging fleet off Oxford, into the endlessly commodious Choptank, and back to Sherritt Cove.

The upwind leg is fine: *Story* pushes along at four and a half knots and ten degrees of heel in twelve knots of apparent breeze. We could carry our big #1 genoa, but with the woman of us about as pregnant as a female animal can get, it is well not to heel us over any farther. Moreover, the #2 is cut high at the foot and will give us better visibility reaching through the fleet on the second and third legs. But as we fetch Town Point, the wind begins to fade; by the time we hang our left, we're making barely three knots and slowing down. We give this state of affairs a skipperly ten minutes to establish itself as a tendency rather than a lull; then Kathy takes the tiller and aims us south while Peter changes up to the #1: a big, lightweight, deck-sweeping thing, twice the size of our mainsail. Just when it's raised, sheeted in, its predecessor bagged and stowed below, and the man of us back in *Story*'s cockpit, the west-southwesterly sighs a last sigh and expires.

Feces, growls Peter Sagamore. His wife agrees: Bowel movement. Should we check with NOAA?

While we give it once again the old ten minutes, Peter tunes in the National Oceanic and Atmospheric Administration's weather station in Baltimore, whose recordings still prophesy widely scattered thundershowers late this afternoon and evening—the standard Chesapeake summer forecast—while reporting eight- to fifteen-knot westerlies and southwesterlies here and there about the Bay. Ours must be a local lull. Sails limp, we drift down slowly on the tide with half a hundred other hopefuls large and small, sans even steerageway. The still air is oppressive; Kathy takes her top off and lotions up her front while Peter does her back. Take a dip, she recommends. I'll stand sea-nettle watch.

But the previous tide has really fetched that nuisance in, earlier than usual in the season. They're everywhere we look: mostly babies, but enough junior-high-schoolers with three- and four-inch quinquecirrhas to discourage swimming.

If we were up in the Chester or the Sassafras, says Kate, we could swim. Maybe even in the Miles or the Wye. I can still get up and down that boarding ladder. Says Peter Another year. Let me have your considered opinion of that sky.

He means to windward, westward, Bayward, where the blue-white haze has darkened down through several shades. In these latitudes in this season, end-of-the-day thundersqualls are at once so common, so local, and so widely scattered that while any given lawn may go for weeks without a drop of rain, almost every afternoon somebody or other will get lambasted. You may be bracketed by nature's artillery on three horizons and never have to put away your knitting or gather up your Sunday *Times;* or you may be sunk and drowned, electrocuted, or squashed by a falling tree while folks on the next river up continue their tennis match without a pause.

Wise tidewater tennis players, therefore, knitters of baby-afghans, and poolside readers of the *Times,* go on with what they're doing even when the wind veers northwest, the air suddenly cools, and the first fat raindrops drop. Only when the next point of land to westward disappears behind the lumbering wall of the storm will they say Well, I guess this one's for real, and head for the house. Wise tidewater sailors, however—especially those eight point five months pregnant in engineless small sailboats—make different assumptions.

Sighs Katherine I guess it's for real. The far horizon grumbles as if foiled. We decide not to drop sail just yet, but Peter unships the sculling oar, raises rudder and centerboard nearly full up, and with easy, gondolierlike sweeps begins moving us back toward Town Point. Behind it is a marina-girt creek into which we can duck if push comes to shove; once upstream of it we'll hug the riverbank all the way home and—if things get nasty, as they probably won't—either anchor in the lee of something or simply beach the boat. We do not feel threatened, only warned. It is coming on to four.

Half an hour later, as we'd have predicted, the west is hazy-bright again. Now it's the northern sky that's gray and far-off rumbly: no threat at all. But the river is slick calm; the flag over the Tred Avon Yacht Club hangs unmoved. We see some skippers pack it in, furl sail, and chug back toward Town Creek or out to the Choptank and whatever their day's destination. Most sit hopeful of new breeze, knowing that their auxiliary diesels can fetch them to shelter in minutes if things blow up.

The sculling is sweaty exercise. Two sheepflies join our crew without invitation and sensibly go for Katherine's breasts and thighs and calves, as would I if I were two sheepflies, Peter Sagamore remarks. Two or three sweat-bees fly out from town to bop around his sticky hair. I would fly out from town and bop around your sticky hair, says Katherine Sherritt, if I were two or three sweat-bees. Want a bucket of water on your head?

Too heavy; you'll bust a kid. He ships the oar briefly to fetch from a cockpit locker the collapsible canvas bucket with line attached that we use to dip seawater for scrubbing down, washing up, cooling off; flips it adroitly rim-edgewise overside; fetches up three-quarters of a bucketful of Tred Avon River, the most that can be swung handily up over the lifelines without springing a vertebra. He dumps it like a welcome Niagara over his head, then at K's request does the same for her, where she sits, soaking her hair, her maternity shorts, the cockpit and its vinyl cushions. Another, please, she bids him, and is redoused. P gets his stomach and the pouch of his swimtrunks kissed; bends to kiss his friend's wet head, then over her head to kiss upside down the smooth brown space between her shoulderblades; goes back to sculling upriver.

The storm alert seems to have passed. On the other hand, Peter Sagamore sees in Katherine Sherritt's face—as she stands up dripping now from the cockpit seat to have a skipperly look around, steadying herself with one hand on the lifeline and the other on his head—that our little talk is about to commence. *Story* sweeps slowly on toward the Goldsborough Creek day beacon; it is at least a nautical mile away, but another half-mile beyond it we can see off Nopoint Point the red white and blue sail of Andrew Sherritt's Sunfish, stationary in mid-creek but aimed our way, while on the point itself—

Says Kathy Jesus. Hand me the binocs, hon, would you?

He does, from their holder just inside the companionway, and she verifies not only that the Main House is lined with the automobiles of ex-Denistonians, but that from the flagpole's port arm—starboard from our perspective—hangs the Day-Glo green pennant that in the flag code of Nopoint Point says to any waterborne Sherritt within view Not Urgent, But Please Check In At Your Convenience.

Fecal *matter!* Kate complains, but hauls herself dutifully down the companionway ladder all the same, to the radio. As has been seen, it is our pleasure to keep *Story* simple: The sternsweep is our auxiliary power, the centerboard our depth sounder; waves, trees, and flags are our anemometer, the look of our wake and the sound of our dinghy under tow our knotmeter. The only instruments we normally carry, besides wristwatch and binoculars, are a good compass and a portable radio with the government's weather band for NOAA broadcasts and the FM band for music. But for Hank's and Irma's sakes—and Peter's—Kathy has permitted us to accept her parents' gift, a month ago, of VHF and CB radio transceivers, just in case, with accompanying twelve-volt deep-cycle battery, and Chip has duly familiarized us with their operation. Now, in our first nondemonstrational use of either, K raises Olive Treadway on the citizens band, asks what's what with the green flag, and is told in mellifluous Bajan accents that Ms. Irma is not very happy about her daughter's skipping out on the tea party, from which however Ms. Kathy's condition excuses her. Also, that we have unannounced company standing by.

Kiss? A different female voice—dry, gruff, Yankee, familiar—speaks from the CB loudspeaker Kath's schoolgirl nickname, made from her initials when she was Katherine Shorter Sherritt. Peter groans.

Maze? Happy Katherine shushes him with a wave. How come you're here? Over?

I hear a husband groaning, May Jump replies. It carries. Don't come in for my sake, Kiss; we're on our way home from Ocean City and stopped by to see your children. Olive tells me they've grown. Over.

They're huge! cries Kate. There's seventeen of them, and they're never coming out. Over?

That's what you get.

Who's your friend, Maze? Who's we?

You don't know her. Did you get my book, Kiss? Over.

Yeah, we did. Kath smiles through the companionway at eye-rolling Peter. We thought all that rectal stuff was fairly disgusting. The Hershey Highway, for God's sake. Over.

Explains May Jump That's the way they are. Women tend to leave each other's prunes alone.

P says from the sweep I remind you and your friend that the Federal Communications Commission has rules about obscene language on the airwaves.

Kathy says Peter says the FCC says we mustn't talk dirty on the citizens band. Over.

Who the fuck's talking dirty? May wants to know. 'Scuse me, Olive. Okay, Kisses: Us lemmings got to get back from marching to the sea. Have a fun delivery.

I'm not going to deliver, Kath declares. I'm going to pop like a puffball, over.

You'll deliver, May Jump assures her. You always did.

May!

Okay: You never did. I wish I could be there. Love to you, Kisses. In a raised but still friendly voice she adds To you too, Machissimo, and over and out. Wait: Black Olive has something else to lay on you. Bye, Kiss. Over.

Bye, Maisie. Olive?

In hibiscus-and-bougainvillea accents reproduced here at risk of racism, Olive says You daddy diss wonda you comin' in now; dey talkin' stawns all cross de Bay. Ova?

We're coming in, says Katherine wearily. Dad knows we keep an eye on the weather, for God's sake.

I diss tellin' you, Olive says firmly. Ova.

Thanks, Oll. Over and out, now.

To hear this conversation, Peter has rested his oar. He goes back to sculling as irked Kath hauls up beside him. The flies resume their attentions. She bursts out I wish it *would* blow up!

Honey?

I don't want to Please Check In At Our Convenience. I wish a breeze would blow us right up the Bay and out of everybody's reach until the end of this story. I wish we could go with the wind and swim and play by ourselves, just the two and nine-ninths of us, till I finally unload. She swats at a sheepfly near her navel. Sheepflies, however, have evolved to un-swattability: This one takes insultingly minimal evasive action and settles promptly two handswidths away, on her wet shorts.

Peter frowns. Don't abuse our children. And watch what you say about the wind.

Fornicate the wind! Kathy swats again, again in vain—and again, as if it really does give her some satisfaction to spank the babies. I'm sick of everything.

The sky has darkened once more northwestward. We are without su-perstition, virtually, but it is a rare sailor whom such oaths as Katherine Sherritt's will not make uneasy. The woman truly feels about to burst, not only uterinely. Tears build behind her eyes. The man wants to go forward and drop sail, but decides he'd better stay by her just now. Anyhow, he hopes for a bit of air yet to help us home before the weather comes. With a sweep of the oar, he says I'm sorry, Kath.

Brimming Katherine cries What *for?* She draws a large breath to lay hold of her distresses.

Her husband explains I set you the task of setting me a task, and you did, and I blew it.

Says K The wind blew it. I wish the damn wind would blow us right out of here.

The far sky rumbles back at her, as it did some pages past. A touch genuinely nervous at his wife's recklessness, Peter Sagamore sizes up a little cove to starboard in case we have to duck in there. Four feet mean low water, if he remembers correctly: plenty for us. Set me another, he bids her, sculling. I'll try to do better.

TELL ME A STORY.

To Peter Sagamore's surprise, Kathy Sherritt puts a hand on each side of his rowing hand, stopping the action. Kisses the hand she has thus framed. Says, as if she'd been waiting to be asked, Tell me a story.
  What?
  Story.
  Can't.

A STORY,

she insists to her friend's brown hand. Tell me a story of women and men like us: in love for ten years, the way we've been; married for two, two and a half. What I want to hear about in particular is their house's increase.
  Their what?
  House's increase. Kathy pushes hair back off her forehead. House's increase. Like there they've been: healthy, happy, more or less successful, well enough off, in love and faithfully loved. The favored of the fucking earth, like us. And yet in early middle age, with perfect freedom of choice and the world going to hell in a handbasket all around them—I mean stuff like nuclear proliferation, the U.S. economy rusting out, the natural environment clogging up, the national infrastructure crumbling away and no money to rebuild it, that sort of thing—in the midst of this they break

their behinds and disrupt their lives to bring an innocent kid onstage, maybe just in time to see the curtain fall. Two or three innocent kids! What are they, sentimental? Hubristic? Oblivious? Nuts?

She rests her chin upon her frowning husband's hand and speaks now to his belly. I mean don't they *care* that their kids could be atomized, or caught up in the worst convulsions this country has ever experienced? Do they finally not *believe* what everybody says is almost certain to happen, since nobody's doing much to prevent it and probably couldn't do much even if they wanted to? Or do they think their genes are such hot stuff that any kid of theirs will ride the apocalypse like a hobby horse?

Says wondering Peter, who has seldom heard his friend at once so calmly and so impassionedly eloquent, Tell me more.

No, says Katherine to his chest now: You tell me. Did they consider all these things, just as we did, and go ahead anyhow, figuring they'll pay the bill but not count the cost?

Pay the bill but not count the cost, Peter marvels. That's very well put, Kath.

So use it in the story. Tell me all about it. Tell me their story as if it weren't our story, but enough *like* our story so that the gods of storytelling will take the helm and man the sheets and blow us and it to a harbor we never could have predicted.

Boyoboy. Peter's look is pained indeed. Don't I wish I could.

Kath assures his neck and chin You can. Start at the very beginning, if you want to: ab ovo. The sperms and eggs that got us into this mess, or the ones that hatched the Sherritts and Sagamores that hatched the ones that hatched us. You can start with the thawing of the last ice age, for all I care, when the Set Designer came up with Chesapeake Bay and the Eastern Shore of Maryland. What's ten-K years, between friends? Go clear back to the Big Bang.

Peter Sagamore straightens the smooth brown back that Katherine Sherritt likes to move her left palm around on. Can't do it, Kate.

Unfazed K says Start near the end, then, like Homer. Instead of the ninth year of the war or the wandering, start in the ninth month of their pregnancy, and tell their story the way the tide comes in at Ocean City.

How does the tide come in at Ocean City?

The tide comes in at Ocean City by chasing the moon of inspiration and washing a little farther up the beach of Where We're Going with each wave and then rolling back to pick up Where We've Been. At the tale's high-water mark, the past overtakes the present and sweeps us to a finale rich and strange. Sweeps them.

Oh, dear Katherine: How I wish.

Directly to his eyes she says Wish harder. This is a real task, not a play one. I'll help you every way I can.

Like how?

Like maybe here's a better idea, since it's the present and recent past that have strung us out: Start at the ending, or near it, and take it from there. The story of every pregnancy, she declares, sitting back now and folding her arms across Eenie, Meenie, and their siblings, begins with death and ends with birth.

Amazed Peter Sagamore wants to know what in the world Katherine Sherritt means by Pregnancy begins with death. I wasn't sure myself when I said it, K says: That's what I mean by stories chasing the moon and telling themselves. It just popped out and sounded right. But now that you ask, I see that I meant not only our miscarriage the first time up, but the death of your sperm and my egg and you and me as what we were before, which leads to the birth of what we're going to give birth to and become.

Aha.

Just like the wind has died now from the Choptank maybe all the way up to the Sassafras, Kathy goes on, still eyes to eyes, but actually it's just taking a deep breath, the way I'm going to. You take one too, and tell me this story. Inspire.

But Pete protests Tell ourselves a story we know already by heart? I don't get it. Even if I weren't et cetera.

Kath interrupts him one beat late to declare These children haven't heard it. That part's for them, old Stamen and Pistil. Tell them where they're coming from and what they're getting into. Tell them to be brave and patient and not to rush and get here too early or on the other hand hang on longer than they should. Also to take turns and love each other and quiet down in there. But what *none* of us knows is the ending: the thing that's going to happen any day now and be news to both of us, sound scan or not, and change our lives and start a different story altogether. Let's start with that.

Through the latter part of this apostrophe, Peter Sagamore has been stroking with his free left hand the back of Katherine Sherritt's head. He believes he understands now what she's asking him to try and why. She sees that he understands. Fish make circlets in the glass-calm water all about us, gray now in the woozy air: gray as but less bright than the level eyes of Katherine Shorter Sherritt Sagamore. Our foreheads touch.

Mutters Peter Can't. Seven dwarves, et cet.

The whole dark north mutters back at him as does his wife, to mind what he says. The tide sets us gently astern, downstream. Peter rests his forehead now upon his oar-hand, where Kathy's chin had rested for a paragraph. He says You aren't the only one in this boat about to burst. That asinine "B-Flat."

Lies K It was an okay B-flat.

It was an asinine B-flat. Now it's not even that.

It is *her* hand moving in *his* hair now. She considers. Thirty-nine.

Hm?

Katherine Sherritt Sagamore repeats "Thirty-nine." It's a story I made up this morning after I read your next-to-last version of "B-Flat." The title's in numerals, but I have to say it in words:

39.

Asks Peter Sagamore What do you mean thirty-nine? What's thirty-nine?

Kath settles back in the cockpit. Did I ask you what "B-Flat" meant? Or "Olive"?

You knew already, from earlier drafts.

"Cellardoor" didn't have any earlier drafts. Neither did "Summer Afternoon" or "Theophany."

They're just words I happen to like a lot. Give me *Anna Karenina*.

Give me early Peter Sagamore. But here we are. What does "Thirty-nine" say to you?

He sees she's sort of serious and ventures Our age, for a few months yet.

Nope.

My jacket size.

That's thirty-nine long. This is just Thirty-nine.

The year our parents conceived us.

Good try, but you're not even warm. Try harder.

A new way to make love.

I don't get it.

Try harder.

Katherine does. As in *soixante-neuf?*

That wouldn't make sense. A Sherritt-Sagamore story makes sense, even when it seems not to.

Now we're talking. What's the new way to make love?

Beats me. But if there is one, it's number thirty-nine. The *Kama Sutra* gives thirty-eight.

Kathy sits up, we're both enjoying ourselves now, kisses Peter's forearms, and says You're on the track, actually. But "Thirty-nine" is a story. None of the above is a story.

Peter bets our conceptions in 1939 are a story. The first atom split; Franco winning the Spanish Civil War and Hitler and Mussolini starting World War II; Hank and Irma and Fritz and Nora wondering what kind of world they were bringing children into.

Katherine asks seriously does he think they thought a lot about that. Peter answers does she think they didn't. The sky grumbles, maybe not directly at us this time. We feel on the trail of something. Says Kathy Did you know that May Jump can recite the thirty-eight positions in Sanskrit and accompany herself on left-handed guitar? She learned them because *Kama Sutra* and I have the same initials.

Peter says May Jump can probably *do* the thirty-eight positions with her guitar, in her bathtub. But May's another story.

You're getting warm! Kath cheers. It was May that told me the story that "Thirty-nine" is based on. It's an old prison joke—I mean a joke about people in a prison, not a joke that actual prisoners tell, though for all I know they might. It's an old joke about prisoners telling one another old jokes. That's the only clue you get.

Disappointed Peter says Everybody knows that joke.

So let's hear it; it'll warm you up for your task.

No it won't.

Eyes to eyes she says You'll try because you love me.

The man considers, nods, breathes. Chip Sherritt has paddled his Sunfish home with its daggerboard and furled the sail. There is definitely weather to north and northwest of us, but it seems not headed our way. Prison's no joke, Peter Sagamore declares to our three hands on the sculling oar, but prison jokes can be good jokes.

Yes?

Uh, once upon a time there was this bunch of convicts who'd done so much time together in the same cell block that without even trying they'd memorized all of one another's jokes, okay? So to save time . . . Why would anybody who's *serving* time want to *save* time? Anyhow, to save time they gave each joke a number: Instead of saying Have you heard the one about the rabbi and the priest who both survived the same airplane crash et cetera, somebody would just say Seventeen, or Three Forty-five, and the others would know which joke he meant.

P falters. Swallows. Kathy Sherritt rests her cheek on his hand. Uh so one day a new guard is assigned to this cell block, yes? And he hears one inmate say Fifty-eight, and the other inmates laugh a little. Another one says Seventy-four, and they laugh harder. Yet another one says Four Twenty-two, and everybody chuckles. The new guard thinks maybe they're talking in code so that the guards won't understand. He asks an old trusty what's going on, and the old trusty explains all that stuff I said before, and then the old trusty says You don't believe it, just watch: I'll tell them the one about the rabbi and the priest who both et cetera. So he goes Eighty-seven, and the cons all yuk it up. So the new guard decides he'll give it a try, so he asks the old trusty Do you know the one about the cons who've done so much time on the same cell block that they've all learned one another's jokes et cetera, and the old trusty says Sure, everybody knows that one, it's number Thirty-nine, give it a try. So the new guard hollers Hey guys: Thirty-nine! but nobody laughs. So the new guard wants to know how come, and the old trusty shrugs and says Some people just can't tell a joke.

The northwest horizon clears its throat. Peter Sagamore grins uncertainly. Katherine Sherritt politely smiles. P sighs See? Some people just can't.

Kath soothes You tried. Making Joke Thirty-nine be the joke about Joke Thirty-nine was very Peter Sagamore.

P.S. complains I'm not a teller; I'm a writer. Once upon a time I was.

Anyhow, says Kate, I like the other version better.

What other version, your husband duly inquires.

Row row row our boat, says K, and while you're working out the story I've set you the task of telling, I'll tell you

ANOTHER VERSION OF THE OLD PRISON JOKE.

Once upon a time, a new prison guard named Fred was assigned to guard a cell block of long-term convicts near Bellefonte, Pennsylvania. The first day on the job, he noticed that the convicts often spoke in numbers. Twenty-three, one of them said, and the others nodded knowingly. Somebody down the line said That reminds me of Forty-nine, and they shrugged. A third one asked with a kind of chuckle How about Seven Nineteen? but nobody cracked a smile.

Well, Fred got suspicious, so he asked an old trusty What's going on? We're just telling jokes to pass the time, the old trusty explained; but we've been together so long that we all know one another's stories by heart. So a long time ago we gave each joke a number, the way musicians in a dance band number their tunes. I mean their numbers. Instead of saying In this set let's do "Smoke Gets in Your Eyes" and then "Stardust" and then "One O'Clock Jump," all your bandleader has to say is Set up Forty-two, Ninety-seven, and One Oh Eight. In the same way, if I want to tell for example the joke about the rabbi and the priest who both survived the same airplane crash, all I have to do is say Two Sixty-one, and everybody in this block knows which joke I'm telling. Saves time.

The new guard Fred wondered why people doing time would want to save time, but he says Show me once. The old trusty hollers Two Sixty-one, and sure enough, all the cons on the block smile and nod their heads.

How come nobody ever laughs? the new guard wants to know. The old trusty shrugs and says We've heard 'em all before.

Peter chuckles. That's good, Kath. You tell a good story.

Complains Kathy Jesus, Peter. I haven't *finished* it yet. I'm just coming to the punch line.

Sorry. I thought that *was* the punch line.

Says K, who picks up expressions here and there, *Oy gevalt*. The punch line is when the new guard decides to give it a try, so he hollers Thirty-nine, and everybody in the cell block breaks up, including the old trusty. Now, this new guard Fred happens to know he's no good at telling stories, see, so he asks the old trusty how come his number was such a winner? When the old trusty can get his breath from laughing and wipe his eyes, he says We never heard that one before.

PETER SAGAMORE LAUGHS A LOT
FOR THE FIRST TIME IN MONTHS, REALLY.

Oh ha. Oh ho ho. Oh tishy whum fa ha ho ho margy fum tee whoop hoo haw. Hum! Hum.

Katherine Sherritt wants to know what's so funny. Laughs Peter Sagamore I never hee heard that one before. You made it up yourself?

Sighs Kath I wish. May Jump made it up and sang it to me, but in her version the number was Ten Oh One. I changed it to Thirty-nine because it seemed funnier to have the number be low in the series instead of a higher one than any they'd mentioned.

Oh ha. Peter Sagamore says he sees the point of K's "39" story, all right: why she told it in response to his "B♭." And he appreciates of course that you're not supposed to know what Joke 39 was, in the joke. All the same, he can't help wondering: the ontological paradox, et cet. Hoo! Hoo.

Kath kisses his fingers. Maybe it was another version of the old prison joke.

Says Peter: K. S. Sherritt, I love you, and I am more than a tad frightened by what has come to pass in our house. What all this prologue, so to speak, has barely hinted at.

I too you, his wife replies, and I too. Now, I think you'd better set about the task I set you. The sky has stopped giving us dirty looks. Why don't we just ride on the tide for a while and wait for a breeze, and you tell me that story I asked you for back in Chapter One.

WELL, WE DO,
DESPITE THE FACT THAT NOT FAR NORTHWEST OF WHERE WE FLOAT
ARE THE U.S. NAVAL ACADEMY AND THE NAVAL SHIP RESEARCH AND
DEVELOPMENT CENTER AND THE NATIONAL SECURITY AGENCY'S
ESPIONAGE CITY AT FORT GEORGE G. MEADE. AND NOT FAR NORTH OF
US ARE THE ARMY'S EDGEWOOD ARSENAL FOR CHEMICAL AND
BIOLOGICAL WEAPONS DEVELOPMENT AND THE ABERDEEN ORDNANCE

PROVING GROUND. AND JUST NORTHEAST OF US IS DOVER AIR FORCE
BASE WITH ITS HEAVY HARDWARE. AND NOT FAR SOUTHEAST OF US IS
THE WALLOPS ISLAND ROCKET RESEARCH AND TEST FIRING CENTER.
AND NOT FAR SOUTH OF US ARE THE BLOODSWORTH ISLAND NAVAL
BOMBING TARGET, THE NORFOLK NAVY YARD, LANGLEY AIR FORCE BASE,
AND THE ARMY'S FORTS EUSTIS AND STORY. AND NOT FAR SOUTH-
SOUTHWEST OF US ARE THE ARMY'S CAMP PEARY AND THE CIA'S
Isolation TRAINING CAMP AND THE PATUXENT NAVAL AIR TEST
CENTER AND THE NAVAL ELECTRONICS TESTING FACILITY. AND JUST
SOUTHWEST OF US ARE THE NAVAL RESEARCH LABORATORY FIRING
RANGE AND THE NAVAL SURFACE WEAPONS CENTER AND THE A. P. HILL
ARMY RESERVATION AND THE BLOSSOM POINT PROVING GROUND. AND
NOT FAR WEST-SOUTHWEST OF US ARE THE INDIAN HEAD NAVAL
ORDNANCE STATION AND THE QUANTICO MARINE RESERVATION. AND
JUST WEST OF US ARE ANDREWS AIR FORCE BASE AND THE ARMY'S
FORT BELVOIR. AND NOT FAR WEST-NORTHWEST OF US ARE THE
HEADQUARTERS OF THE CIA, THE DIA, AND THE NRO, NOT TO MENTION
THE ARMY, NAVY, AIR FORCE, AND MARINE CORPS—ALL MORE OR LESS
LAWS UNTO THEMSELVES, VERY IMPERFECTLY ANSWERABLE EVEN TO
THE IMPERIAL PRESIDENCY JUST ACROSS THE RIVER OR DOWN THE
STREET, TO SAY NOTHING OF THE U.S. CONGRESS DITTO, WHICH
PRESIDENCY HOWEVER HAS THE POWER AND AUTHORITY TO MOBILIZE
THE FOURSCORE PENTAGON FACILITIES ON CHESAPEAKE BAY ALONE
AND ALL RELATED FORCES AND WITH THOSE FORCES DESTROY ALL
HUMAN TOGETHER WITH MOST NONHUMAN LIFE ON EARTH.
NEVERTHELESS, BUCOLIC TIDEWATER MARYLAND HOLDS ITS BREATH ON
THIS PLACID PRESUMMER JUNE LATE AFTERNOON AS IF THE YEAR WERE
1880 OR 1780 OR 1680 INSTEAD OF 1980. WE DO NOT BELIEVE THAT
WHAT WE SEE AROUND US WILL BE HERE IN ANY AGREEABLY HABITABLE
STATE FOR THE CHILDREN OF THE CHILDREN WE ARE ABOUT TO BRING
INTO THIS WORLD. WE DO NOT BELIEVE THAT THE WORLD WE VALUE
WILL MUCH SURVIVE US. FOR THAT MATTER, WE HAVE NO TREMENDOUS
CONFIDENCE THAT OUR CHILDREN WILL. YET NEVERTHELESS,
NEVERTHELESS THE FAIR TRED AVON PAUSES IN THE HAZY SUNSHINE;
NOTHING STIRS; *STORY* SLIDES SEAWARD SIDEWISE NOW AT LESS
THAN HALF A KNOT ON THE GLASSY TIDE; AND PETER SAGAMORE, WHO
HAS NOT TOLD A PROPER TALE FOR LONGER THAN WE LIKE TO
REMEMBER, CLEARS HIS THROAT AND BEGINS FOR HIS WIFE'S
ENTERTAINMENT AND HIS POSSIBLE OWN SALVATION
"THE ORDINARY POINT DELIVERY STORY."

Ahem.

THE ORDINARY POINT DELIVERY STORY

Once upon ahem. There was this couple. More or less like us? That, um.
K kisses the crow's-foot at the outboard corner of her husband's starboard eye. On with the story.

Hum. Well, Him. Redneck bluecollar, right? Marshes, tides. Blue crabs.
Oysters.

You have a way with words.

Declares P.S., warming to his work, Brother sister parents? Yeah. Scholarship get out write, okay? Stay loose sterilize write! No wife lovers travel *write*. He beams: Then teach-write-Less-Is-More-write-write-pfff. How's that.

Pfff?

Him to a T.

Maybe. Her?

Her. P considers. Her: blueblood private smart beautiful et cet, two of everything terrific wow? Then Poonie blah lead Her own life meet Him kapow!

I'm on the edge of my thwart. More.

P. Sagamore closes his eyes, grips the idle sweep, draws breath. Her him futz around, other lovers? Remeet College Park Dun Cove zowie! Enoch Pratt, U of M, Doomsday Factor—

Uh-oh.

Right. Big decision fix plumbing tie knot make baby no go; Jack Bass finally bingo then whoops.

Hold on. Whoops is their miscarriage?

I'm going fast so I can get to the end, Kath, where you told me to start.

Katherine Shorter Sherritt says she appreciates his intentions, but still. She having aborted Porter "Poonie" Baldwin Jr.'s spawn and so wanted to deliver Peter Sagamore's, our Doomsday Factor miscarriage of 1978 was an important disappointment in our life. She thinks it merits fuller treatment in this so-called story, Less Is More be damned. What'd that couple there whoop, exactly, when they whoopsed? What did Whatsername misdeliver?

Says pained Peter What a question. Show me the way, Kath.

K. S. Sherritt takes a breath of her own and, not to replay touchy history, to her own surprise *invents:* The first thing our heroine will've miscarried is . . . Less Is More.

P guesses he's as relieved as *she* must've been. Tell him more?

Less is more. It's your story.

Theirs. But Pete's got the idea: Less Is More, he declares, misculminated in a certain magnificent B-flat, which relieved a *lot* of uncomfortable pressure and facilitated Whatsername's passage of some further miscarried items, including but not restricted to . . . your turn.

Katherine frowns but comes up with Oh, the names of certain long-lost acquaintances and the recipes for several dishes that the couple used to enjoy making but had lately sort of forgotten about—Hey! Shirley Ovenshine!

Peter wants to know who's Shirley Ovenshine.

The Ovenshines were our summer neighbors in Maine when I was six, and Shirley Ovenshine and I were best friends that whole August, but Willy teased her about her name in some dumb double-entendre way that didn't even make sense, like Shirley, let me see your oven shine. I loved Shirley Ovenshine and Shirley Ovenshine loved me and I haven't thought about Shirley Ovenshine since Nineteen Aught Sixty or thereabouts. Shirley Ovenshine. I think I like this story.

Peter says Barbecued chutney bananas in aluminum foil. Kathy says we haven't made barbecued chutney bananas for a hundred years and she wishes she had a barbecued chutney banana in aluminum foil in her pregnant mouth right now while Peter Sagamore goes on with it.

On with the story? Or on with the catalogue of miscarriages?

The story, the story, says K.S.S.: I'll wind up the miscarriages, and then you get on with the story. Whatsername there next miscarried, let's see . . . two Doomsday Factors, one nice one not, and a turnaround story called "Part of a Shorter Work"; also a green Crayola crayon, don't ask, and assorted burnt chestnuts and unfired pistols. Then she came out with the God on Wires to tidy things up, and that was it for her and that's it for me. Boyoboy, the lady said when she'd finally misdelivered the God on Wires: Do I ever feel better! On with the story.

Pete's impressed: May Jump's exercise books, he bets. He shakes head. But draws breath, says Jack Bass try again long-shot pill, Less-Is-More short few; then bingo shorter fewer, belly bigger shortest fewest; out of gas, Nopoint Point, frustration, set me task; take us sailing, out of wind, frustration, set me task; tell me story out of breath here we are.

Katherine Shorter Sherritt Sagamore hugs her winded husband, turning sidewise at the bottom to avoid *Story*'s tiller and to get her belly out of the way so that she can press her breasts against him. We both say That's terrific; what *she* means is that here we are and now we can go on with the story. She has recklessly cursed the wind, acknowledges Kathy, meaning also the woman Whatsername in our story. She has recklessly declared I wish the fornicating wind would blow us right out of the Tred Avon and on up the Chesapeake, where we could be alone together, just you and me plus Bed and Breakfast down there, no timetable no itinerary just sail whither the wind listeth until my time cometh. Go on.

Peter says The wind don't cotton to being cursed, especially by sailors in engineless small boats. Who asketh trouble generally getteth.

Blam! cries Kath. A storm at sea. At bay.

Says Peter Blam Blooey! *Two* storms. At once.

Katherine asks him what he means blam blooey two storms at once; she doesn't get it. Neither does he, says Peter: He just upped and said it. The moon of inspiration, he supposes. Says K That's a good sign, very good sign: story telling itself. Grants P maybe so, but he's buggered if he knows how two storms can strike at once or what their doing so means in and to the story, and he's a writer likes to know what he's about. All he had in mind, when Katherine spoke of a voyage without itinerary timetable or destination, was that after two weeks, say, of sailing whither the wind listeth and having certain small or large adventures and maybe telling each other stories as they went along, some they've never told before and some they know by heart but need or want to hear again or tell the kiddies; some real stories from their life together and their lives apart; some made-up stories; some found stories and some lost stories—after a fortnight or so of this, this couple find themselves up at the head of the Bay, say, in the Sassafras River, say, loafing and swimming in the fresh water there and thinking about the stories they've told and heard and the people they've met and wondering how in the *world* she can have carried whatever she's carrying past the solstice, out of spring and into summer, and they figure they probably have been being mighty reckless, provoking the wind in her condition, and the gods were considerate enough after all not to blow them out of the water but just give them what they wished for, no wires attached, and now they've had their little cruise and their private time together, and they really had better pack it in and get on back to Nopoint Point; maybe even put in upriver at Georgetown right now and ask the woman's parents please to send up a car for her while Whatsisname singlehands their boat back home. . . .

The sky to westward, reader, has perceptibly darkened again and now rumbles over Peter's suspension points, but the brightness in his face brightens Kathy's; she knows Invention's look and has for long not seen it in her friend, who says now Sure. Back at Day Zero she said Fornicate the wind and set her husband this task in verse. But before he could reply or begin, or as he was replying or beginning, a storm blammed out of the west and did what she said, blew them away willy-nilly, and they said Well, let's *go* with it, blah blah, and now on Day Fourteen or so there they are, up on the Sassafras, happy to've had what they needed and lucky to've gotten away with it and ready to come home now and deliver the goods. They're anchored in Turner Creek, say, off from the old granary and the county park, and they dinghy ashore after lunch and call her parents. Is there a pay phone in that park?

Katherine remembers Up from the granary wharf. At the old restored farmhouse where the public toilets are.

So they call and arrange to meet her parents for dinner in Georgetown, after which Buck McHenry—that's the paid hand on her father's yacht, who'll come up with them in the car—Capn Buck, let's call him, will bring their boat *Whatsitsname* back down to Goldsborough Creek, 'cause it's a three-day sail, and if her husband does it she's likely to let go before he gets there. So it's all arranged, and they up their anchor and go over to Ordinary Point for a final swim. About four P.M. they start for Georgetown, figuring they'll run up on the little southwesterly that's been blowing all day, and wouldn't you know it: No sooner do they get the hook up and the mud swabbed off the foredeck than the woman's water breaks blooey all over the cockpit sole, and her contractions start immediately—

And the wind dies, Kate says soberly, looking off to westward. The woozy sky over there agrees with her.

Says Peter The wind dies; that's how the gods get their own back. This situation's no joke. The guy sets to with the sculling oar (as does Peter Sagamore now), but the sails hang limp, the tide's against them, and it's four or five miles to Georgetown. What's more, those contractions are coming very strongly already and awfully close together, considering that her labor's just started. So they decide to radio ship-to-ship for a tow from some passing powerboat and an ambulance to meet them at the Georgetown bridge.

Ambulance from where? Kathy worries. It's a tiny town.

All those tiny towns have volunteer fire companies with good ambulance service.

K suggests having him call one of the Georgetown marinas to set things up. Rumble rumble.

Rumble rumble, agrees Peter Sagamore. It's the gods laughing up their sleeves, 'cause while the man's deciding he'd better get on the horn all right, the woman says something like Omigod and hauls herself downstairs onto the foldout double.

Really only a comfortable single.

At best. What the gods don't know—well, I guess they know it all right and have decided to put the screws to him on this point—is that back in undergraduate apprentice writer days, Whatsisname here took paramedical training and rode for a summer with the ambulance crew of the Hoopers Island Volunteer Fire Company. It is true that while he has administered CPR and the Heimlich maneuver, pried smashed teenagers out of wrecked Chevrolets, and grapneled drowned crabbers and tourists, he has never actually delivered a baby. Moreover, his training is chapters behind him now. All the same, he's not as helpless as another in his deck moccasins might be. So he ships the oar and drops the Danforth right where they are, not far from the fleet behind Ordinary Point. And he scrubs up and gets out a clean sheet and towel—

One of each is all they'll have after two weeks of cruising, Kathy frets. If that.

Says Peter What they have will have to do, 'cause things are really popping, and on top of all, the sky's piling up out over the Bay. Boyoboy do they ever feel childish for not coming in earlier, but what they've done is what they've done. He gives her a kiss—

She needs it.

So does he and tries to raise a fire company on the CB to raise a doctor to talk him through the delivery while they find another doctor or at least a real paramedic to come out by boat to help him. But the CB's out of action, wouldn't you know, so he VHFs one of those big marinas like you said to telephone a fire company et cetera and relay their instructions. He also puts out a general call to the boats anchored all around them, figuring at least a few of the big ones must belong to rich doctors from Wilmington or Philadelphia. For all he knows, Doctor Spock himself might have sailed his big ketch up from the Virgin Islands or the Bahamas is it and be parked for the night behind Ordinary Point, en route up the Intracoastal to Martha's Vineyard.

Good move, agrees Katherine Sherritt. There may be as much medical expertise at anchor behind Ordinary Point on an ordinary summer weekend as you'll find in professional practice on the whole upper Shore, plus Walter Cronkite aboard *his* big ketch to narrate the action. I feel a ton better.

So do these guys in our story, but while word's going out, that action comes thick and fast, and they're both too busy to be scared. If they thought that what they *mis*carried back in Seventy-eight was something!

Says Kathy Let her deliver up front whatever you need for this story, but when the decks are clear she's to have healthy normal kids. And I want her doctor to be there.

Such matters, her husband insists, are in the hands of the gods. What's in *his* hands, delivered intact as a sort of trial run and with only minimal discomfort to the deliverer, are first of all not a baby daughter or son but a bottle with a message in it. And a key.

Surprise.

The message . . . turns out to be a joke about a rabbi and a priest who et cetera. The key's purpose they have no opportunity to investigate, because before our man can read our woman the joke, she delivers assorted bumper stickers and printed T-shirts.

Read her just one of those bumper stickers.

He unrolls one for her amusement. HEDONISTS HAVE MORE FUN.

We'll see. One T-shirt?

More cryptic: WHAT YOU'VE DONE IS WHAT YOU'LL DO. Followed by a lovers' quarrel, task, and knot—

Intertwined.

No doctor yet to untwine them. She gives a uterine squeeze, our woman, and comes out with the storyteller's double. We nod but don't speak.

K sighs: That's my husband.

Hers too.

They're still in labor?

Are they ever. But like a storm at sea, once the thing's upon them they're too busy coping to be afraid. The author's double is scarcely delivered when the lady brings to light . . . your turn.

Kath considers, remembers, smiles: A clutch of bookmarks as unlikely as a nursing bra, plus a mysterious library book to mark with those unlikely bookmarks.

A Brandy rose, says P: her favorite kind. Aaand . . . Odysseus asleep on the beach at Ithaca.

The woman gives birth to sleeping Odysseus?

Plus the beach, plus Penelope's unfinished web, which depicts this birth scene all but the end. After those come a container and a thing contained, a wise old owl, tales within a tale, a whole new ball game, and a cry for help.

Says Katherine No wonder. Where are all the obstetricians in that anchorage?

A few boats move in closer and stand by to assist, but their crews are computer software people and corporation lawyers. The men wear socks and Sperry Topsiders or Nike running shoes and Izod shirts and shorts and visor caps and digital watches with many functions, though the air temperature's ninety F and the humidity's eighty percent. The women either are dressed likewise, except for the socks, or else wear long-sleeved linen beach tops by Pierre Cardin over their swimsuits. Since our man is as usual wearing only swimtrunks, and our woman just now nothing, he asks them please to stand by and keep radioing for medical assistance, but does not invite them aboard. His wife's cry for help, however—I mean the one she gives birth to—is fortunately answered by her very next contraction, which produces a middle-aged, semiassimilated Italian-American midwife named Ma Nontroppo, who pins back her hair, washes her hands, and says *Lento, lento;* I'll take-a charge-a from here on.

Thank heaven.

And just in time, 'cause in rapid succession now our woman gives birth to the facts of life, to an adjustable latch for keeping options open, to a python with three Plymouth Rock hens perched upon its scaly back, to half a peck of Chincoteague oysters, some with cabalistical engravings on their long narrow shells, and to a Crisfield oyster knife. Also to the emperor's new clothes and a series of seafarers as unlooked-for on Chesapeake Bay as old Odysseus there: a series limited to but not necessarily including the Flying Dutchman, Arthur Gordon Pym, Huckleberry Finn, Sindbad and his friend Scheherazade, the Old Man of the Sea, Francis Scott Key, Queequeg, and assorted Vietnamese and Haitian boat people. All these are no sooner delivered along with their craft than they disperse through the astonished anchorage in pursuit of their several destinations, while cameras click and Walter Cronkite, though retired, radios his old network for a helicopter minicam crew. Mother and midwife rest from their labors for a welcome minute.

But even resting, presses Katherine, she delivers the punch line of that joke about that rabbi and that priest who both survive that airplane crash. Also two locked caskets, one barnacled, the other bejeweled, and a brace of fortune cookies. Would you open one for me?

One of the cookies. It says uh. It says um. It says *To finish this poem I'm too modest.*

Peter!

Your exercise book was lying open in the portside crib.

Stay out of it. What was the other one?

The other cookie. Uh, the other cookie goes unopened on the starboard settee, because just then Ma Nontroppo exclaims in amazed Neapolitan and displays four bases to be touched . . . and seven several dwarves.

Seven several sounds familiar to Katherine Sherritt. Their names, please?

Names. Uh Vug.

Vug?

Vug for short. Uh Vug and Crump? Crump, yeah. Fougasse and Dingle. Words I like to say. Coomb. Cubby? Coign.

Says Kate These seven several came not from nowhere. You'd better tell us more about these dwarves.

These seven several dwarves came from the inexhaustibly fertile womb of the woman of this couple of ours, engendered there by the union of her plenteous ova and her fellow's copious sperm, and delivered at just the right pace by the vastly experienced gentle Eyetalian hands of Ma Nontroppo. I don't know what they are yet; just who.

Who's Vug?

Uh Vug: No neck. Speaks in grunts? Squat, powerful, hirsute, surly. But dependable all the same, right? You may not *like* Vug, but you can count on him.

Crump.

Crump's ah bark is worse than his bite. Crump's . . . bite exceeds his chew. Crump's chew . . . surpasses his swallow. But *what Crump swallows, Crump digests*. Try Fougasse?

Warns Kath A slippery trickster. Watch out for that Fougasse.

Ably done. Do Dingle.

Dear dark dopey Dingle's done. Who's left?

The inseparable trio Coomb Cubby and Coign. Coomb I see as a quiet one: deep, circuitous, phlegmatic, unpredictable. Cubby of course is cute and cuddlesome; you want to hug Cubby, and you may.

I might. Coign?

The leader who goes last, says Peter Sagamore, directing his six companions from three paces behind. Except when he rides upon Vug's shoulders, shading his eyes with his left hand and pointing the way with his right. More about these guys later, we bet.

Katherine Sherritt points with her left, worried again about that sky over there.

Acknowledges P We should have kept sculling, but we didn't. Chances are et cetera, and anyhow et cetera. The same case obtains at Ordinary Point at cocktail time two weeks from now, where after Ma Nontroppo takes charge our man ups anchor and sculls into snugger shelter in the lee of the point, almost on the beach, all the while keeping a weather eye upon his wife. I forgot to say that Whatsername is in no pain throughout this remarkable episode, which entertains and astonishes her as much as it does him and even Ma Nontroppo, who in her long experience of midwifery has never presided over so abundant and various a delivery. The other eye he keeps upon the weather, which has piled up to west-southwest of them as dark as that mess off to west-northwest there. At this point—

Uh-oh, Peter: There's lightning.

Saw it. Followed by the first sharp thunder: fanfare for our woman's delivering a complete inventory of both the items she miscarried two years ago and the items presently delivered, including the inventory itself. A fortunate circumstance, that, without which we could never have logged this catalogue later, inasmuch as not a few items in both categories were forgotten, mislaid, resorbed, or pilfered, and others lit out for the Territory like those boat people before we'd even counted heads. The woman of our couple says I have a feeling we're getting to the end: Check over that list, would you, honey, and see whether anything's left to come besides the main thing. Ma Nontroppo wipes her brow with a red-and-white-checkered tablecloth and says I can tell you before you look that that list won't have the main thing on it. They never do.

Kath says That's as it should be. I don't want to know in advance.

Anyhow, says Peter Sagamore, no bad news on here that I can see. Or that *he* can see, either, the father of all this stuff. But he does notice that after the inventory item that reads *Complete Inventory of Items Delivered by Whatsername Aboard Sloop* Whatsitsname *Behind Ordinary Point, Sassafras River, Maryland, Six Twenty-nine Eighty,* there's one final entry, which his friend gives birth to even as he reads it: a book.

A book! What book?

This book is what the inventory says, in italics: T-H-I-S B-double-okay. But what actually proceeds from the mother of us all is a letter addressed *To the Mother of This Book*. Ma Nontroppo delivers it; the addressee reads the message inside, which says Pick one oyster from that half-peck of Chincoteagues. Any oyster.

Says Kath She picks one of the ones that have cabalistical inscriptions.

Open it, the letter says, Peter says. She shucks it open expertly with the Crisfield oyster knife and finds it to contain neither oyster nor pearl nor grain of sand, but—

A little clam! cries Katherine. Like those Japanese trick ones I got when I was a girl! A real baby clam that you drop into a glass of water and it sinks to the bottom and you watch it and watch it till it opens.

Says Peter Sagamore They watch it and watch it, the way we're watching and watching it with our mind's eye now, at the same time watching that black stuff getting closer over yonder while they're watching *their* black stuff getting closer and flashing and rumbling, just as her uterus gets its breath again and starts rumbling a bit too as if clearing its throat for the finale.

I'm scared, hon. Hurry.

This is *Story*'s only speed.

At last the clamshell opens. . . .

At last the clamshell opens, and there unfolds from inside it a miniature paper castle with a little American flag flying from its battlements, and above the flag—

Even as the first cool cat's-paws of the approaching storm dart from the northwest shore—

Both here and there, and both couples swallow hard and cross their fingers, as in your poem—

Fingers crossed.

Fingers crossed, they see unfurl above the little flag a poem in tetrameter couplets aabbc ddeec et cet beginning Tell me a story of women and men like us like us in love for ten et cet and asking how come they decided this late in the afternoon to have a child when the world's about done with. . . .

Boyoboy, says Kath, it *looks* about done with, over there. It's not going to miss us, Peter.

Nope. But we can handle it; hold tight while I get the sails down. We understand now what I meant before by two storms striking at once, two weeks apart, one up at Ordinary Point on the Twenty-ninth and one right here right now, just as the poem's last stanza unfolds to read Tell me their story as if it weren't ours but *like* ours enough so that the powers that drive and steer good stories might fetch them beyond our present plight and—

Blam!

Go the twin storms exactly then, their force doubled by their combination. They slam together into the Eastern Shore of Maryland just as above the clamshell castle with its flag and its poem (with the last line still unglossed) there unfolds—

Blooey!

This book:

THE TIDEWATER TALES,

OR,

WHITHER THE WIND LISTETH,

OR,

OUR HOUSE'S INCREASE:

A NOVEL

OUR STORIES:
THE NEW CLOTHES
HAVE NO EMPEROR.

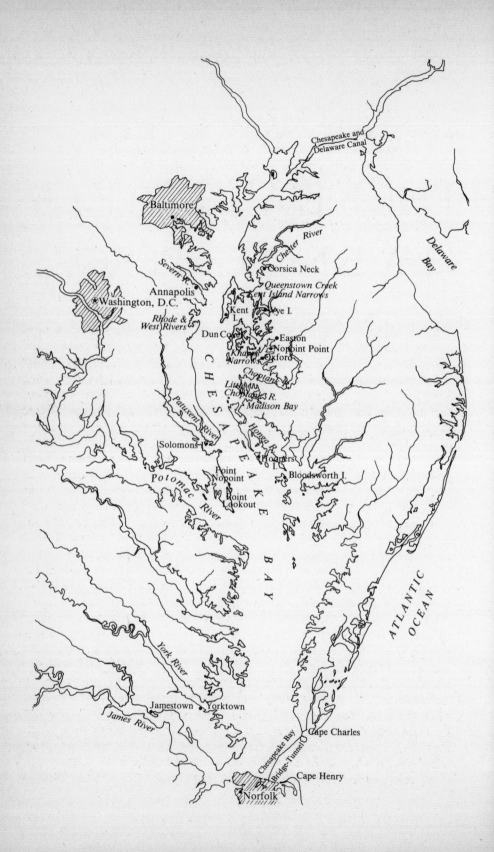

DAY O:
NOPOINT POINT TO
DUN COVE

The wind's fists pound down from north instead of northwest, slick calm to twenty knots in a double knockdown, laying *Story*'s lee rail under while the water's no more than ruffling up, almost pitching Katherine Sherritt and family across the cockpit. But our woman's center of gravity is low; her nautical reflexes are quick: She cries Hey! but grabs a lifeline stanchion and the tiller, braces her feet against the seat opposite, and stays put. Peter Sagamore, on the low side, springs with a great grunt to the high, dropping our oar into the cockpit as he springs, and scrambles on forward to shorten sail as our combined weight rights the boat. Herself a seasoned sailor, Kath quickly bears us off downwind for stability and so that the mainsail will blanket the jib and make it easier to hand in. By when Peter achieves the mast and uncleats the jib halyard, we are roaring downriver, planing and surfing over brand-new gray-green waves. The breeze settles in—fifteen, eighteen, puffs of twenty-plus—but the wave-fetch here is not long. What's more, the sky to westward, which we seem about to take off and fly into, is bluer by the moment: The heavy action is to the north, on the next river-system up, the Miles and the Wye, which are in fact being briefly blasted flat.

Peter wrestles down the headsail but does not try to bag it, merely lashes it fast, then lowers the centerboard and moves carefully around the mast to reef the main, keeping a low profile and a secure grip. Already we've passed Town Point and are coming up on Oxford. There's another thunderclap, but it's north-northeast; the sky's lighter and lighter where it matters. All the same, P's feeling mighty reckless, mighty unskipperly, in fact damn foolish, to have brought us out in K's condition, task or no task, when there was any chance at all of weather. But as he goes to jiffy-reef the main before we come about and beat homeward, Kath cries No! Looking back, he sees her jubilant. A sunburst lights her up, the boat, the scene; it has been a while since he has seen his friend exhilarated.

We tear past Oxford. Calls Katherine Let's *go* with it! She has lowered the rudder to reduce *Story*'s roll in the quartering seas; she is turning the corner where the river widens, where we ran out of air in our prologue; she is aiming us south, toward the open Choptank. We are a pair of adults, mindful of each other's needs, respectful of each other's judgment: If he insists we go back, she'll yield; if she insists we go on, he'll go. Call home first, she orders, and then let's set a smaller jib. This is just what we need.

He regards the sky, the waves, her face, our course and speed; goes below and turns on both CB and weather radio.

Henry Sherritt is calling already, as we'd have guessed; the paid hand, Bobby Henry, is coming in the family runabout to tow us home. Peter reports politely that we need no rescuing; that having run downwind to shorten sail, we are off Oxford and will sail ourselves home presently. The squall line has passed, he points out as NOAA reports that news to him. More thundershowers are predicted, but not until later in the evening. Hold on, Hank: Kath wants to talk to you.

Indeed, she has been signaling from the tiller for the mike. Now she sweetly apologizes to her father for our not having radioed in at the first sign of weather and for her missing the Deniston tea. But we are out here, she tells him firmly, at her insistence; she needs to get away for a bit. Henry Sherritt sounds mollified, but relays to us the truly remarkable storm-damage reports coming in on local radio from the upper Tred Avon and the Miles as well as from Baltimore. He knows we're good and responsible sailors, but still. Katherine then, to Peter's surprise, announces that we're going to spend the night aboard, probably in Dun Cove, off Harris Creek, some ten miles down the Choptank from the mouth of the Tred Avon. We are? We are. We have no ice aboard, but we keep *Story*'s water tank topped up, a small supply of canned food and drinks in the lockers, a duffel of fresh towels and bed linens. We'll radio when we're anchored in the cove, only forty minutes away by runabout. And we'll be home tomorrow, maybe the day after.

We hear Henry assimilate. It does look like the heavy stuff's gone by, he admits. And it's a good reaching breeze to Dun Cove, if it holds. Irma will want to send Bobby Henry in the chase boat with something better than canned beans and franks for us to make for dinner.

Insists Kathy We don't need it. But then she sees Peter's Don't Be Stubborn look and yields. Tell Mom to send whatever she feels like sending. Ice. Caviar. Barbecued chutney bananas in aluminum foil. Nothing. Anything.

That's my Katydid, her father says. He will send Bobby Henry as soon as he knows we're in Dun Cove. Sooner, if the wind drops. We are to watch the weather and enjoy our sail.

Over and out. The wind promptly drops, but for minutes only, as the storm fades; then it sets southwesterly, warm and damp at ten and twelve knots: our prevailing Chesapeake summer breeze. Peter raises the midsize jib; Katherine lays a starboard tack for the Choptank River Light, from where a port tack should fetch us directly to Dun Cove.

Says her husband, beside her now in the cockpit, So we're going sailing. One leg at a time, says happy K. S. Sagamore. On with the story.

Peter complains I *finished* the story. Once upon a time, he means, the storm of the past overtook the storm of the present, or the storm of the present the storm of the future: blam blooey. And Whatsisname and Whatsername and their offspring abode in all pleasaunce and solace of life and its manifold delights, for that indeed Allah the Most High had changed their annoy into joy; and on this wise they continued till there took them the Destroyer of Delights and the Severer of Societies, the Desolator of Dwelling-Places and Garnerer of Graveyards, and they were translated to the ruth of Almighty Allah, and their houses fell waste et cetera. He beams. Over?

Katherine duly declares, in hormone-rich contralto, Then there reigned after them a wise ruler who loved tales and legends, and he found in the treasury the marvelous stories contained in the thirty volumes called *The Stories of the Thousand Nights and a Night.* So he read in them a first book and a second and a third and so on to the last of them, and each book astounded and delighted him more than that which preceded it. My friend Chip tells me, by the way, that a thousand and one nights divided by thirty volumes comes to thirty-three and a third nights per volume: a very long-playing record. We sure are moving on this tack.

Peter Sagamore agrees. Then asks Chip said that? Then says Boyoboy, that boy doesn't miss a trick. Then asks further whether she happens to know why there happen to be exactly 1001 nights in *The Thousand Nights and a Night,* rather than 5047 or 39. Katherine does not, other than the pretty symmetry of the number. Peter doesn't either, but he bets there's a story in it somewhere. We are indeed moving on this tack, down and out of the Tred Avon, feeling more lifted with every water- and airborne kilometer. Kath's hunch has proved as usual sound: that this is what we needed, even if, as would be doubtless prudent, we sail back to Nopoint Point tomorrow. Would she meanwhile, from her boundless memory, recite more of the ending of our favorite book in the world? That is a base it's time we touched, in Peter's delicate condition.

Croons Kath With goodly gree. That book we love and base you feel a need to touch ends with the word FINIS, and there is a very great deal more one could say about it, including why there aren't say thirty-nine nights or sixteen hundred thirty-four nights. That FINIS is only the beginning. On with our story?

Says Peter, sighting sidewise westward over our compass, Time to tack, Scheherazade.

We tack, just past the girdered, rock-girt frame of Choptank River Light. The wind over this expanse of water is stronger; the waves are steep and short and cresting. But our new course is a comfortable close-to-medium reach; *Story* lifts and slides almost parallel to the seas instead of punching into them, a fast and lively hour's ride out to Harris Creek. No land on the far horizon; no other boats in sight. As always in such circumstances, we wonder whether everybody else knows something that we don't and should.

What are we doing out here?

Says Katherine at the helm We're taking us sailing and telling a story to these postmodern children of ours: Show and Kiss and Tell.

Our children, frowns Peter at the sheets, are going to be postmod?

Ineluctably. Blooey and Blam, she explains, have blown us willingly, though a touch riskily, out of our comfortable, even luxurious, but nevertheless antsy-making routines. A cruise through the Ocean of Story, since you ask, is what we're up to out here.

Says Peter Hum. Anyhow a one-nighter, up the fictive creek with nothing but a paddle. What day's today? Replies K Day Zero, and tomorrow's the first of the rest of your narrative life. We've touched one base already: On with our stories.

Peter Sagamore isn't sure there *are* any more, for him, though he grants there is allegedly many a story in everything and everyone: a thousand and one stories in the naked Bay, so to speak. He so speaks as we leave to starboard the mouth of Broad Creek—thus called though it's bigger than our Tred Avon River. Puns musing Katherine "The Naked Bey" sounds like a story right there itself: a Tunisian romance. Ease the jib a bit; it's stalling. Or like The Emperor's New Clothes.

Peter does, and says suddenly Our story's vice versa.

Tell it. The Clothes's New Emperor? Tell it.

Not quite. The man squints, checks windvane and telltales, eases the main too till its luff just starts to flutter, trims it in a touch till the flutter quits, says

THE NEW CLOTHES HAVE NO EMPEROR.

Over.

What do you mean *Over?* You haven't started!

But Peter Sagamore insists he's done. For just as, in that folktale, the vain king advertises for new regalia from the finest tailors in his kingdom, and is gulled by sharpsters who scissor and stitch thin air, declaring their cloth so fine as to be invisible to cuckolds, and thereby con both ruler and ruled into praising their work while each man privately gnashes teeth at the revelation of his cuckoldry, until a stripling lad too green for sex and a fortiori et cetera cries out Hey, the emperor's bare-ass naked! and the barefaced shame is shown. So we, in P.S.'s opinion, just contrariwise, have laid out upon Imagination's bed a true new suit of Story: shirt socks and shoes of Situation, pants of Plot, drawers of Dramaturgy, Viewpoint's vest and Method's mufti, even cravat cuff links cummerbund and crown of Character—but those new clothes have no emperor. All that, however, he says, goes without saying.

No!

Less *is* More, Pete says seriously, but adds Look how we're tearing along. Five and a half knots? Six?

Five anyhow. But in his wife's opinion, what goes without saying in *his* opinion would fill a book—maybe the book that grew out of the poem that grew out of the castle that grew out of the clam inside the oyster that Whatsername gave birth to at the end of the prologue of our story. And the emperor waiting imperiously to don those nifty duds . . . is the emperor Do It.

WE REACH HARRIS CREEK IN NO TIME,

but before we do Peter kisses Katherine's cheek, where strands of dry-beach hair hang breeze-loosened from their bun, and helps her into her sunsuit top because the air's cooling down, and puts on a short-sleeved sweatshirt himself, and grimly observes, but does not remark, that back yonder to starboard on Ferry Neck is the estate with the big brick house lately listed for sale by the U.S. Central Intelligence Agency, who for years used it as a safe house for e.g. interrogating Soviet defectors and debriefing the former U-2 pilot Francis Gary Powers after his release by that government in exchange for the convicted Soviet spy Colonel Rudolf Abel. The place is no longer needed by the Agency, P does not remark, since their purchase of Sagamore Flats, his name for the old white clapboard house on Middle Hoopers Island where he and his siblings were born and raised: a house built by his grandfather, enlarged by his father, and extensively remodeled by its present owners; a much remoter and more secluded place for their sundry activities than Ferry Neck in thriving Talbot County.

Remarks Kath with a shiver Ferry Neck: Get me out of here. Poor Doug Townshend.

A curse, grim Peter says, upon all spooks and Doomsday Factors. Off with their stories.

On with ours, says Katherine. Do it.

We reach Harris Creek in no time—another Choptank estuary long and broad as a river itself, the last before the Bay proper—and hang a right for the short run up to Dun Cove. P takes the helm. K radios home, chats with Olive and with Irm. Olive complains she's having trouble with her CB; Chip promised to fix it, but has done strange things to it instead; now it picks up stuff she can't make head nor tail of. Will Mister Peter have a look at it when we get home? No, says Katherine: He's not a repairman. Yes, calls Peter. Says Olive Here your mother.

Mom, says Kath, we've only got this one battery on board and no alternator to keep it charged. Can't we write letters? I'm sorry I misbehaved on the telly and stood you up on the tea party. I'm ashamed of myself. Hi.

Hi. It was not your finest hour, Katherine. If you want, we'll send Bobby Henry back in the chase boat with a spare battery. Do you know Russian when you hear it?

Da.

Well, you won't be hearing it at Saint Deniston's. The price of Kate's dodging the alumnae tea, reports Irma cheerily, turns out to have been having her, Irma's, Deniston proposals warmly received by nearly all present and no case made for Katherine's except, surprisingly, by Molly Barnes Sherritt, whom Irma worries something must be wrong with, pleased as she is to see the poor woman take a stand for a change. Anyhow, she says, you and the Commies and academic excellence lose this round.

That's show biz, Mom. I'll sock it to 'em at the trustees' meeting. Kath declares that we do not need the chase boat, but will not refuse it. Irm says that's considerate of us, since it's on its way already: Andrew and your father did some time-speed-distance calculations and sent Bobby Henry, let's see, twenty minutes ago with a few little things, so you won't have to wait around for hors d'oeuvres and dinner once you get parked. We'll send him again with a battery.

No, Mother. But the women chat and chuckle all the way up Harris Creek. She *did* mention Katherine's proposals to the group before presenting her own, Irma now reports among other things, but left their exposition to their author for a later meeting, should it take Kate's fancy to attend one. Molly Barnes Sherritt had weakly seconded the idea of selling out to the Russkies—but then Molly always followed Kath's lead when not following her husband's orders. I wish she'd follow my advice instead, says K, and leave Willy. Irma says I know you do, dear, but Molly's problem is she loves the wretched man. If only Willy were *completely* hateful. However, he's a Shorter-hyphen-Sherritt. For a Shorter-hyphen-Sherritt, says Kath, Big Will comes very close to completely hateful. What'd you serve with tea? Sighs Irma Champagne. Plus everything. Bobby Henry's bringing you the leftovers. Daddy says you're being reckless, but you've put a bee in his bonnet all the same: Now he wants to take *me* sailing. If you go, says K, for heaven's sake take Chip; we felt creepy going off without him. Irma says firmly You needed to. Everybody understands. I love you, Mom, says Katherine Shorter Sherritt Sagamore: Dad too. Irma says We know that, Kay; likewise, I'm sure.

To Peter Sagamore, such conversations as this by ship-to-shore radio-telephone between a thirty-nine-year-old woman and her sixty-four-year-old mother—who had had already two considerable tête-à-têtes that day—are an ongoing remarkability; he never to the best of his recollection had a sustained, relaxed, quarter-hour general-interest chat with either of his own parents in his adult life. As an erstwhile storyteller who pays some notice to the souls and skins of others, he acknowledges notionally that the difference between Sagamores and Sherritts in this particular is less a matter of class than of individual family tones: that many a privileged Gold

Coast clan are numb and dumb with one another; that many a marsh-country waterman's house is aglow with mindful and articulated love. All the same, every time we sail down the Great Choptank, with low-lying Dorchester on our left and high-banked Talbot on our right, his heart tells him that while much authenticity lies aport there, where his roots draw salty nourishment yet from the mosquito-rich, seafood-infested marshes of his youth, nearly everything civilized lies astarboard—where also are all the best natural anchorages on the river. Almost always, when we turn, we turn north.

We reach Harris Creek in no time and turn north; in no time we are two miles up it, approaching Dun Cove. Ten years ago, when we remet, we first retrysted in this cove and began our continuing voyage together. Then, too, we made a turn: for Katherine Sherritt, an ongoing though qualified return to home waters; for Peter Sagamore, a qualified putting of home waters behind him at last for keeps. Ten years it took Odysseus to sail home from Troy; it took P. Sagamore thirty to cross the Choptank from Dorchester to Talbot County, from Hoopers Island to Dun Cove and beyond.

Kate kisses his tiller-arm as we enter the capacious cove. Does her husband want to tell our children how their folks got it on here in 1970?

He does, but doesn't just then, because even as we hang a right inside the bifurcate, tree- and farm-lined cove to anchor in its empty upper tine (there being two large rafted cabin cruisers already in its lower), we hear and see a familiar small motorboat astern: the forty-horsepower outboard which serves as tender for *Katydid IV* when that vessel goes to sea, slung in davits over its transom, and as an all-purpose runabout when the big ketch is in port. Before our anchor's down and set, Bobby Henry and Andy Sherritt are circling us, Chip waving from the wheel. Elbow on the coaming and cheek in hand, Katherine smiles at them. As soon as Peter cleats our anchor rode and moves to furl our sails, Andrew flips out a pair of white rubber fenders and brings the runabout expertly alongside. Hi Kath; hi Pete.

Well hello there, Kewpie Doll. Good evening, Bobby Henry.

Stocky Bob—yellowbearded, redfaced, crow's-footed, no-necked, thick-armed, T-shirted, bluejeaned, and early-swagbellied like many a commercial waterman—touches the green bill of his yellow Dekalb feed-cap and makes the runabout's painter fast to *Story*'s midship cleat. Howdy.

We're not staying, Chip quickly assures us. Mom sent stuff. He smiles. They're going sailing, too. He holds the runabout alongside with one hand on our gunwale, near his sister's elbow. She lightly covers that hand with hers.

Right smart of goodies here for you, Bobby Henry allows. Like Peter, he is from lower Dorchester County and used to work in Fritz Sagamore's boatyard. As always when the two cross paths for the first time in a day, they shake hands, and Bobby Henry winks. Peter Sagamore thinks Bobby Henry thinks the bond between them to be not alone their common marshy origin, but that they both now live high and easy off the Talbot rich. There is no cynicism in Bobby Henry on this score—Hank Sherritt would detect it and cashier him promptly if there were—only such pleasure in his good fortune that he does half again what his job requires in the way of maintaining the Nopoint Point flotilla and waterfront in show condition (*Story* not included; Peter is fussy on that score) and still finds time over and above, except when *Katydid* sets out for Maine or Florida, to run a crabline from his own bateau in summer and tong oysters in winter, for extra money and to keep his hand in. Peter Sagamore thinks Bobby Henry thinks that he, Peter, writes and teaches in that same spirit: just to keep his hand in.

We load our cargo: a bottle of Chandon brut, another of Beaujolais, a six-pack of Molson's ale and another of Perrier. Three several dips with crudités and English table-water croquelins for dipping. Two gorgeous artichokes vinaigrette for appetizer. For entrée, four magnificent loin lamb chops to barbecue off our taffrail, and a Tupperware container of cucumber-and-onion salad with Olive's special Barbadian herb dressing. A baguette. A wedge of peppercorned brie. Fresh pears and apples. And for tomorrow's breakfast, almond croissants and local strawberries. Also two twelve-pound blocks of ice and a seabag packed with our windbreakers, cotton pajamas and cotton nightgown, a change of underwear for each of us, Peter's wallet just in case, and our traveling toilet kit. Finally, a bouquet of assorted tea roses from Irma's garden: one Peace, one Sonia, two velvety damask reds. Andrew hands these to Katherine last. Bobby Henry stands hands on hips and grins. Think that'll hold you?

Peter frowns. Nothing to read? But Bobby Henry is not long on irony. Tell the Sherritts we're wowed, as usual.

We have to go now, Chip says to his sister. And to Peter, Dad says the weather's not finished yet.

Bobby Henry says Your daddy's about right, too. Yall have fun now.

Thanks again. We sit among our provender, tisking tongues; then Peter stows it. The vase of roses fits nicely into a winch-handle holder in the cockpit. Katherine radios to thank her parents—but is told by Olive that they have indeed gone for a sail in their big boat. Olive is amused. You put ideas in they head.

Katherine hopes they have enough to eat.

SOLIPSISME À DEUX

Rigging the swim-ladder and the barbecue grill, Peter Sagamore observes that while a few black flies wander over from a nearby dairy farm to check us out from time to time, some tidal fluke has left Dun Cove clear of sea nettles. He strips his swimsuit off and gingerly tries the water. Near eighty degrees, clean and green and buoyant. Get your tush in here, he commands his expectant friend.

Is he sure? He's positive.

K does as bidden, but before letting herself very carefully down the transom ladder, puts a water-ski belt between breasts and belly to take the effort out of floating. Her husband paddles over to the bottom rung and receives her into his lap. For a while we hang there, steeping in the solitude, exhilarated still by our little truancy and our rousing sail, but fast relaxing in the circumambient deliciousness, the rightness of Katherine's judgment, the happy prospect of dinner and a night aboard. *Solipsisme à deux.* As usual at the bottom of *Story*'s boarding ladder in the north fork of Dun Cove with Katherine Sherritt in his lap, Peter Sagamore erects. Says K For heaven's sake Do it. I don't know, says P; but *she* knows, and does it for him. Again she's right. In antiphonal murmurs we recite our memorized litany from *The Merck Manual:*

P: Oh, my. Normal activities and customary exercise may be continued throughout pregnancy.

K: Swimming and mildly strenuous sports are permissible comma and . . . there is no reason a pregnant woman cannot ride horseback or engage . . . in similar vigorous activity if she is accomplished at it and is cautious.

P: You're accomplished; I'm cautious. Many women find . . . that their sexual desire is changed . . . parenthesis increased or decreased close parenthesis . . . during pregnancy.

K: Not mine. Sexual intercourse . . . is permissible . . . throughout pregnancy.

P: But should be prohibited if there is any vaginal bleeding, pain, or leakage of amniotic fluid. . . .

K: There's none! There's none. Several . . . maternal deaths have been reported from blowing air into the vagina during cunnilingus Amen.

Says Peter Amen and holds us in place like pintle and gudgeon so that Katherine with her free hand can now leisurely assist herself to orgasm's edge. Her dear sound crossing it—and our recollection of P's pleased surprise at her similar self-ministration ten years ago in this same place—does him as well. Still connected, now we float, he holding her breasts raised by the ski belt as by an eighteenth-century bodice and soothing their erected nipples.

Tell Gudgeon and Pintle about it, their mother murmurs. Their father vows he shall, one day. It will be called

DAY ZERO IN DUN COVE,

and that story, reader, subject to later trimming and tidying, will go something like this: Hot young writer having met warm young reader in 1964 after cool young fiction reading up at the 92nd Street Poetry Center, and they having spent steamy young New York night together down at the old Gramercy Park Hotel—

God, remembers Katherine: We were twenty-four, and you were already there, and I wasn't anywhere. A fucking failure.

Only your marriage was, protests Peter.

We didn't fail that night, for sure. To our children, K explains He was the first man I'd ever slept with, guys, except my unmentionable first husband aforementioned. Your mom was wowed.

Writer and reader (P.S. would say if we went on telling this tale in this fashion) agreed that that Gramercy Park June night was a success indeed. But so used were both of us to successes hard and easy, considerable and inconsiderable, that, alas, nothing therefore followed from this one. *She* finished shucking old Poonie Baldwin, Jr., and went back to Maryland and to graduate school; *he* went writer-in-residencing about the U.S. of A. We did not remeet until an early-autumn evening six years later, at a party in College Park, Maryland, given in honor of Ms. Katherine Anne Porter.

In which interval, would say Katherine Sherritt Sagamore, a *lot* of water went under the Chesapeake Bay Bridge.

In which interval, agrees Peter, our brackish Chesapeake, like a Rive Gauche tart, douched herself with four thousand tides from the great bidet of the North Atlantic. But we can't go on telling this story like this.

Katherine arches at least one eyebrow. The father of her children has known Rive Gauche tarts?

One, once. That tart, however, happened to remark We French wash only one thing, monsieur, but we wash it constantly. Such a remark is hard to forget. Tidy Thérèse. But look here: You tell your water under the bridge, I'll tell mine, if we're really going to do this. It should be a team effort, like pregnancy.

Says Kath We *are* really going to do it. We're going to crank your motor till it catches and goes. *Her* water, she declares to Dun Cove, bore off her Black Panther poet, her Hasid violist, and her Chileno foreign service officer, good men all, plus lesser flotsam whom she may have neglected to mention, just as Peter neglected to mention Tidy Thérèse. Such things happen. Having mastered the science of libraries at the U. of M.—where by the way she'd come to know Ms. Katherine Anne Porter on the strength not only of writer-reader bonding but of some relation between the Porters of O. Henry/Sidney Porter fame, cousins of K.A.P., and the Shorters of Irma Shorter fame, mother of K.S.S.—she was in place, as they say, at the Pratt. But she came down from Baltimore for that party that night with her new roommate, also a great fan of Ms. Porter.

People don't talk like this, Kath.

Do it.

Well. Her new roommate, children . . .

You had your well-washed Left Bank tart; I had my Brandeis balladeuse, at that time only a green-belter, under whose spell I had certainly fallen and to some extent respectfully remain, but into whose bed I had ventured, though pleasurefully enough, one night only, not long before this party we're making our separate ways to. Partly in the spirit of the High Sixties, kids, which we'll get to another time. But not entirely. In any case, that's water under the bridge—in Nineteen Seventy still a single span rather than a twin. Over?

Water under the nation's bridge. Peter Sagamore was at that party more out of respect and protocol than out of literary enthusiasm, though the respect was real enough. K.A.P. was the U. of M.'s senior literary ornament; young Sagamore was their tenured new associate professor of Where It Allegedly Is At. A bold appointment, in the department's view, since where it's at is famously subject to argument and change, but tenure is forever. And no small step on P.S.'s part, in his view, since his early vows to the muse enjoined him from, among other things, marriage and tenured academic appointments. But like K. S. Sherritt, he was at a fork in his road.

The difference, in Kath's opinion, is that P thought he'd just *made* a major sexual-emotional-personal career decision, whereas K thought she had one imminently to make: May Jump was stepping up the pressure. We were both partly right and partly wrong.

Right.

To Tweedles Dum and Dee, Katherine declares It wasn't just New England your father put behind him when he swapped the Charles for the Chesapeake.

It was not. After Portugal, he'd winged it for some while along the cerebral cortex of our republic, the River Chuck, with one of those Briggs–Copeland lectureships at Harvard and similar plums for promising young transients. What had fetched him there—as to Portugal, Paris, and Portland, Oregon—was his deep wish not to become a marshy Mark Twain, a Faulkner of the Free State fenlands.

But what *kept* him there, longer than in those other places . . .

Pete Sagamore sips his Chandon brut; Kate her Perrier. We have disconnected, climbed *Story*'s transom ladder, slipped into our dry swimsuits: we are taking now our narrative ease before firing up the barbecue. How much of this do we literally say, in this articulated wise? When old intimates rehearse what between them goes without saying, they do it with cues as brief as recent-Peter Sagamore fiction. The old Gramercy Park, Room One Seven Six. That Katherine Anne Porter party. But we know what has us by the larynx; we do our best to do it. Whatever our actual words, we rehearse as if to our unborn this chapter of our actual story: the *first* Day Zero in Dun Cove.

What kept P there in lively Beantown was as serious a connection as he'd enjoyed in his three decades on our planet, with an able ex-Swarthmorean who at twenty-nine was already an assistant producer at WGBH-TV and clearly going places in her medium. Their relation, of some two years' standing, had taken a curious turn: Though he had no interest in parenthood, Peter Sagamore was prepared to marry the lively, the befreckled Marcie Blitzstein, had she been inclined to marry. Ms. Blitz (her professional self-abbreviation), on the other hand, had no interest in matrimony, but awfully wanted children once her career position was secure, if ever: so much so that she was prepared to have shiva sat upon her by her steadfastly pious family, whom she loved and honored, for having a child out of wedlock by her goyishe lover, who didn't want one, had he wanted one. A sad impasse, since they cared about each other, and it was at first complicated but ultimately resolved by another problem, one of temperamental chemistries, which both parties were experienced enough to recognize: Much as they admired, respected, enjoyed each other, each was finally more in love with his/her calling than with their life together. Such things happen.

At the same time, even in his recent "Portuguese" and "Boston" stories, even in his more recent and shorter and less realistical ones, there kept appearing the marshes, tides, and webfoot passions of our author's youth. His fancy fed still upon Chesapeake seafood. The question posed itself whether, recognizing this circumstance, he were better off musewise to shrug his shoulders and stay put, or go back down there and live on location for some years at least, as the state university had in fact invited him to do, and either sink for real into the bog of literary regionalism or work through to more transcendent terms with those staples of his imagination.

Not a heart-stopping problem, *niños,* on the scale of human problems, but for an artist—for *this* artist—a fundamental problem nonetheless, and given resonance by his and Marcie Blitzstein's troubled love.

On a certain fine May weekend at this juncture, they happened to cruise from Scituate Harbor down Massachusetts Bay and through the Cape Cod Canal with another couple, aboard that other couple's fancy sailboat, and to pick up a mooring at lunchtime on the second day in Marion Harbor, off Buzzards Bay, where, to his happy surprise, Peter Sagamore saw riding at another mooring nearby a small wooden sloop unmistakably of his father's manufacture: Broad-beamed, hard-chined, bowspritted, barn-door-ruddered like a miniature oyster-dredging skipjack, it looked as mislocated in New England waters as a Chinese junk. What's more, life had imitated art to the point of naming that sailboat *Story,* after a similarly named vessel in Peter Sagamore's fat first novel.

Well! The foursome chuckled and clucked tongues over the coincidence. Dinghying ashore for a lunch of lobster rolls, they circled that Sagamore 25 and saw it to have been handsomely maintained. A hunch warned Pete to let the coincidence lie; it was the tireless, the enterprising Marcie Blitz who insisted they make a little project of tracking down *Story*'s owner before returning to the city. Their first inquiry revealed the boat to be in brokerage: Its owner had unexpectedly died; the widow hoped to sell while the boat was in its freshly recommissioned state.

Incomprehensibly to Marcie Blitz, her friend shrugged his shoulders. Back in Boston on the Monday, she took it upon herself to telephone the widow, represented herself as a prospective buyer, and along with more pertinent matters, inquired into the craft's odd name. She then reported to her lover that *Story*'s late owner, while no fan of Peter Sagamore's newer fiction, had been an ardent admirer of his earlier—just the reverse of Marcie's own, high-tech sentiments. John Basel had bought the boat secondhand in sorry shape on Chesapeake Bay because he recognized it to be one of Fritz Sagamore's; he had restored it and named it *Story* out of admiration for his favorite contemporary author. So much had Mrs. Basel and her late husband enjoyed sailing it together, she could not bear the thought of sailing it without him; moreover, while still physically able, she was too old to manage without an engine, and to hang an outboard on *Story*'s virgin transom would offend her purist husband's memory. The vessel was for sale otherwise "fully found," in excellent condition, reasonably priced and ready to go.

Said Peter Sagamore in effect Mm hm and went back to work. He could not much longer stall both College Park and Boston U., which had also offered him a residency. As is sometimes his way with a difficult decision, he pretended to turn his back upon it and lose himself in his fiction, while actually monitoring that fiction with a certain third eye for clues to where his heart of hearts inclined. Like his apparent indifference to the *Story* coincidence, it was a habit that drove forthright Marcie up the wall.

The piece under his hand happened to be that pivotal one long since aforementioned, which had begun as an average-size short story entitled "The Point" and then had mushroomed, to its author's disconcerted surprise, into four or five drafts of an attempted novel, but which would wind up published as a very short story indeed, entitled

PART OF A SHORTER WORK.

Once upon a time, across Sherritt Cove from Nopoint Point, there was a handsome, low, wooded headland, "unimproved" but for a collapsing gooseblind on its Goldsborough Creek side and a path to that blind from the county road through becreepered stands of oak, ash, and pine. Three generations of Sherritts coveted that headland, called Shorter Point, to complete their ownership of all the property bordering Sherritt Cove and thus to forestall the construction of any houses thereupon besides their own. But the Talbot County Shorters, while less rich, are as old a clan as the Talbot County Sherritts, and as confirmed in the place's pleasures: Successive senior Sherritts made their bids to buy—handsome bids in the dollars of their day—and were refused by successive senior Shorters, farm folk mainly, each of whom declared his intent to use Shorter Point for goose hunting only, but to use it for goose hunting forever. Nor were they lured by Sherritt proposals with explicit goose-hunting easements: Shorter goose rights guaranteed in perpetuity. They vowed they had no particular mind to build there, but it was their pleasure to walk through Shorter woods on Shorter Point to reach the Shorter blind.

Thus endured an uneasy peace punctuated by small and large alarms, for the view of Shorter Point is the very centerpiece of the Sherritt Cove flank of Nopoint Point, from every principal window of both Main House and First Guest Cottage. Merely to *see* a Shorter over there at any time other than goose season, or in that season doing anything but gunning geese, called forth binoculars and consternation across the cove. Who was that other man walking the shore with old John Shorter? Why did he point at that loblolly pine, that stand of cordgrass, if not to suggest what might be cleared to make way for a fine house, two fine houses, maybe two not-so-fine houses, maybe even a grain dryer, a chicken ranch, a whole residential subdivision with attached marina?

Henry Sherritt's grandfather, who had himself caused much of Nopoint Point to be selectively cleared for additions to the Main House and construction of the First Guest Cottage (then called the Guest Cottage), was therefore in his elder age as fearful for the health of his Shorter counterpart as for his own, lest that patriarch's heirs be moved to build, or to sell Shorter Point to any save himself. He did not trust John Shorter, Jr.—his own son's age—precisely because the two younger men were fast friends since boyhood and equal enjoyers of the life of Sherritt Cove. Surely John Junior would buy out his siblings' interest in Shorter Point when the time came; he would fell trees, raise a modest clapboard house, run out a dock, keep one of those gasoline yachts that everybody nowadays was buying—and there would go the eastward view from Nopoint Point. But those Shorters who left the county or otherwise evinced little interest in Shorter Point were no less dangerous, should John Junior die or in some other wise be unable to buy them out: Surely they would sell to the highest bidder without regard for the future of the property, and even the Sherritts might not be able, merely to protect one of their views, to outbid a syndicate of real estate developers with plans for a Shorter Point Estates, a Shorter Village.

Both gentlemen went to their rewards, the reigning Sherritt a touch before the reigning Shorter. Despite the Great Depression or because of it, John Shorter, Jr., was in fact able to buy out his siblings' interest in Shorter Point, and for a day in 1932 it seemed to Henry Sherritt's father, Samuel—whose inherited and growing concern for the fate of his eastern view had gradually distanced him from his old friend—that the worst had happened. Workmen appeared across the way; a piledriver was towed into Sherritt Cove! It seemed incredible to Sam Sherritt that he had not the right to forbid entry upon that water which bore his name; but even a Sherritt owns, even of Nopoint Point, only down to the mean high-water line.

Two hours passed, *a pile was driven,* before he could set down with shaking hand his father's old Zeiss binoculars, which rested always ready in their mahogany holder on the seat of a central bay window in the library of the Main House—and row across the cove in the tender of his new gasoline yacht to verify his ex-friend's perfidy. Even as he rowed, he expected at every stroke to hear behind his back, between the guillotinelike slams of the piledriver, the crash of falling trees.

It turned out that John Shorter, Jr., was merely building a better goose-blind to replace the collapsed one, with access by a short pier instead of by skiff. Not a tree was topped, much less felled; the new blind was an aesthetic improvement upon the old; the two men gunned geese in it together, their friendship restored. Even their wives took up the sport.

Some goose seasons later, however, John Junior succumbed in middle age to a coronary, leaving his wife and their only child, a daughter. On Nopoint Point, the familiar alarm resounded, especially when the widow Shorter remarried: Her new husband was a rich Philadelphian! Goose-hunting enthusiast! And, though only late-fiftyish, *retired!*

His name was Parker Pink, and within a season of his taking Marge Shorter to wife, the direst Sherritt fears were realized. As Mr. and Mrs. Sam Sherritt watched and listened helplessly from across the cove—he clutching the Zeiss binoculars, she weeping on his arm—crews of men and machines assaulted Shorter Point. Saws, axes, bulldozers, backhoes, stump grinders, a piledriver with a whole bargeload of piles. Two weeks later, half the trees were gone, the underbrush was cleared, the footpath widened to a road and ditched; piles were driven for a hundred-foot lighted dock with two slips and a cross-T; excavation was completed for what was clearly to be a substantial house; and a natural prospect that had altered little in the last ten thousand years was gone. Even before a check of building permits in the Talbot County Courthouse confirmed the fact, young Henry Sherritt reported to his father that young Irma Shorter had reported to *him* that her mother, of whom she was fond, and her stepfather, of whom she was not, were selling the old Shorter farm and farmhouse and building a major seat on Shorter Point.

Alas, Marge Shorter loved her Parker Pink, and Parker Pink, alas, loved the color of his surname. The major seat proved to be no tasteful red-brick Georgian or beige half-timbered Tudor, but an ostentatious pink and white stucco pile in the very worst of taste: a marriage of Andalusia and early Florida presided over by Cecil B. De Mille. Tiles, turrets, Moorish arches! Fountains and terraces stepping down to the illuminated dock—at which there steamed in one day to its new home berth, to complete the rape of Sherritt Cove, neither a natty sailing yacht nor a gleaming cabin cruiser, but—how to utter it?—a huge *houseboat,* done in the colors of the castle and named . . . *Pink Lady II* . . . complete with tender named . . . *Pinkie Too* . . .

On the scale of human misfortunes, the loss of a view from one's mansion's eastern windows cannot be ranked high, even when that view had been undisturbed since the last ice age. But in the emotional economy of a happy family, it may loom larger than the death of certain loved ones. Samuel Sherritt lost a brother in Belgium in World War I and both parents to Talbot County natural causes; another son would die at Iwo Jima in World War II. Such losses are irreparable; the death of those young men, in particular, caused deep mourning on Nopoint Point and for years subdued the pleasures of the family. But they were understood to be and accepted as casualties of major history, as the death of elder parents is accepted as natural loss. The atrocity on Shorter Point was of a different order, actually much harder to accept: an awful caprice, a galling fluke, a permanent affront. The Sherritts could neither bear to look across Sherritt Cove nor avoid doing so. They could not come and go in their cars and boats, or work or play on their estate, without having their noses rubbed in the works and pleasures of Parker Pink. The man was gregarious; the man was loud. He entertained copiously in his castle, on his grounds, aboard his houseboat—which was equipped with horns, a siren, even an amplified electrical calliope. Two likewise loud and grown and rufous sons he had by his first marriage, who raced powerful speedboats in and out of Sherritt Cove, and gave high-decibel parties of their own, and stood to inherit, with their new half-sister, Shorter Point.

The Sherritts took to traveling; but even in the Cotswolds and Provence, young Henry's mother would fall despite herself to stifled sobs, his father to snuffled Episcopalian curses, at recollection of what had befallen their eastward view. Dorothy Sherritt came to seriously begging Samuel to sell the place: an idea as unbearable to him as living across from Parker Pink. Their excellent marriage suffered; on their return from Europe, Dorothy took to bed. Too late Sam saw that he should have mortgaged every Sherritt asset, if need be, to make John Shorter Jr.'s widow an irresistible purchase offer upon her first husband's death (he had in fact made a generous one, but, not wanting to intrude upon her bereavement, had accepted her plea for time to think it over, and had neither raised nor pressed his offer). Too late now; too late forever. And terrible Parker Pink climaxed his vulgarity by more than once advertising his awful spread for sale, at inflated prices, as if to taunt his neighbor—half a million, when such properties went for a quarter-million; a million, when they went for half—for he was one of those people who, whether they love what they have or not, need always to know what they could get for it in the market, and who if their inflated asking price were met, their half-bluff called, might in fact sell without regret, but would more likely back off without compunction and next time raise the price.

There was moreover in the distress of the Samuel Sherritts yet another factor, which may literally have turned the loss of their eastern view into the death of both of them. When Marge Pink had been Marge Shorter and John Shorter, Jr., was still alive, both families smiled with favor upon the childhood friendship, early romance, and not-unlikely eventual marriage of Henry Sherritt and Irma Shorter, as uniting two so-long-cordial neighbor clans. For Samuel Sherritt, in particular—Irma being his friend's only child and thus the likely sole inheritor of still-pristine Shorter Point—the match bid to consummate a family dream. But with the advent of

Parker Pink, the Pink Palace, *Pink Lady II,* and that brace of strapping, high-volume, hydroplaning Pinksters, Henry's and Irma's affiancement became a bone in the Sherritt throat. No matter that they loved Irma like a daughter and that the young woman herself quite deplored the Pinking of Shorter Point: She honored her mother and was therefore a polite stepdaughter and half-sister in her new house. It followed that Henry, as a gentleman, would be obliged to be a polite stepson-in-law and half-brother-in-law; that there would be not only a marriage but a wedding, and no doubt a showy wedding reception on Shorter Point, with attendant and ongoing social obligations between the two houses: the iron fist of propriety gloved in pink velvet. No Sherritt would have it otherwise, but for Henry's parents the prospect was literally unendurable. Shortly after the engagement was announced, Dorothy Sherritt was absolved by a paralyzing stroke; a second killed her before the wedding. Broken Samuel did his duty, but withdrew thereafter to the west wing of the Main House, closed every window blind and drapery on the Sherritt Cove side, and forbade his maid to open them while he lived. The newlyweds set up housekeeping in the town of Easton and visited their families with a discretion amounting almost to surreptitiousness, especially in the outdoor season.

A few years later, in 1942, Samuel Sherritt took perhaps the sole unfastidious action of his life: He committed suicide with his favorite goose gun, a twelve-gauge Remington, long unused. Nopoint Point passed equally to Henry and his older brother, who together maintained the property but closed the house and went off to war. Thus Samuel did not live to see one of Parker Pink's sons and one of his own killed in military combat, the other Pink son move to California, and Henry and Irma and their two children to Nopoint Point. Parker Pink succumbed to a galloping melanoma; and his widow, who had loved the man but not his works, decided to put Shorter Point up for sale, but, discovering a lymphatic cancer of her own, gave the property to her daughter and her son-in-law instead.

Relieved of the burden of buying Shorter Point, Hank and Irma Sherritt were enabled to spend a small fortune restoring it to pre-Pinkhood. Though two-thirds of their affluent friends, nine-tenths of ordinary Eastern Shore folk, and their own son Willy thought them deranged, at huge expense they razed the Pink Palace; removed the dock, fountains, terraces, walls, landscaping, even the heavy stone rip-rap along the shore; filled the excavation and regraded the land to its original contours. Working from old photographs and advised by botanists from College Park, they reforested the cleared land, not with saplings, but with large-caliber trees of the same varieties felled by Parker Pink—and not fine nursery-grown specimens, such as one would ordinarily choose who could afford the tremendous cost of transplanting and reestablishing mature trees, but lean and scruffy oaks, pines, and ashes dug from actual woodlands and replanted in their natural crowded state. It was an operation unprecedented in the experience of Eastern Shore landscapers, even those used to catering to the whims of rich "Come-Heres" (the locals' term for nonlocals who "come here" to retire). The state university's botany people took such an interest in the project—especially when the Sherritts insisted that even the scrubgrowth be "landscaped" in, down to briars and creepers—that three doctoral candidates did their dissertation fieldwork there.

Last of all, the access road was de-paved, de-ditched, replanted, and narrowed to a weedy footpath leading to a modest gooseblind: Parker Pink had long since replaced John Shorter Jr.'s sturdy blind with a huge heated and plumbed affair, which the Sherritts razed along with his other improvements. Irma first proposed buying or building a ruined blind for the old site, but upon reflection she agreed with ten-year-old Katherine that that idea was a touch tacky. In John Shorter Jr.'s honor, then, they replicated his, and used it every hunting season.

Not surprisingly, given the scale and nature of the enterprise, a number of those trees died. But they do that in nature, too, and nature quickly took over where art, science, and money left off, building osprey nests in those dead trees, modulating the ecosystem in a hundred small ways from expert artifice and cunning approximation into the real thing. By 1955, only a sharp-eyed botanist could have guessed that Shorter Point had once been Pinked; by 1965, only an archaeologist. And if earlier Sherritts had enjoyed their eastern view across Sherritt Cove, their enjoyment was as nothing beside Hank's and Irma's, who many and many a time still in 1980, as we tell this story, catch themselves gazing bemused at Shorter Point. They smile; they touch hands or lips or wineglasses with unspeakable satisfaction.

Now: Just as Shorter Point Restored was to their happy Sherritt eyes a different bit of geography indeed from the all but pristine Shorter Point that Parker Pink "improved," so the story P. Sagamore was to publish in 1970 as "Part of a Shorter Work" was very different from the story "The Point," which had ballooned into the novel *Shoal Point,* which was then ablated down to "Part of a Shorter Work."

THE POINT

had had nothing to do with Shorters and Sherritts and Parker Pink, for though at the time of its composition our man had met Katherine Shorter Sherritt that evening in New York City and spent the night with her, and had in fact enjoyed from her, in course of that night, that story, told apropos of something or other in the tumid darkness of Room 176 in the Gramercy Park Hotel, and had even remembered it long after, "The Point" was a realistic midsize conventional tale inspired by Jacob Sagamore's sale of Sagamore Flats on Middle Hoopers Island to the United States Central Intelligence Agency.

The family property—which, with the two other siblings' agreement, had been bought by their older brother upon Fritz Sagamore's death and Nora Sagamore's decline—did in fact include, though it was not built upon, a point, called Shoal Point. A reedy, sandy, and finally muddy spit, Shoal Point projected maybe ten feet into the Chesapeake at high water, when most of the point became Shoal Point Shoal; as much as two hundred feet at low water, when most of that shoal became Shoal Point—this though the tidal range at Hoopers Island, as throughout the Bay, seldom exceeds two feet.

This property of the Sagamore property was not the point of "The Point," though it was to become part of the point of "Part of a Shorter Work." What Peter Sagamore's original story concerned itself with was Elder Brother's indifference, quite like Jacob Sagamore's, to the possibility guessed early on by Younger Brother: that the federal agency outbidding a retired New Jersey dentist for Sagamore Flats under Department of the Interior cover was in fact the CIA. The Come-Here dentist, Peter Sagamore had argued by telephone from Boston, would likely restore and improve the house and grounds, which were in some disrepair, and use them for the unobjectionable purpose of retirement residency. The CIA would not only use the property for who knows what unsavory business (only their counterintelligence and clandestine-services people would have any use for it at all), but might to that end disfigure it with e.g. chain-link fencing, a helipad, big radio antennae—might perhaps even raze it and replace it with some nonresidential structure more to their purposes.

Jacob Sagamore—who with his sister, Sue-Ann, was still sorting out their late father's affairs, settling their mother into a nursing home, and reorganizing the Sagamore Boatyard—replied from Hoopersville that his brother was once again talking more like an Outside Agitator than like a good American; that a government operation on Sagamore Flats might benefit lower Dorchester's chronically depressed economy; finally, that if Peter wasn't happy with his management of Sagamore Flats, the Sagamore Boatyard, and their Sagamore mother, Jacob would be happy to turn over their management to him and go off on extended holiday in his brand-new Winnebago RV, as he planned to do anyhow before long. The truth was, Jake declared when the discussion heated up, he had spent his whole life down in dear damp Dorchester and paid his dues in spades while Younger Brother gallivanted around Europe and Yankeeland writing stories about webfoot rednecks on the good ol' Eastern Shore. It was Jacob's intention to convert the Sagamore yard away from workboats and sailboats, away from wooden boats entirely, to build for a few years a line of flashy-looking cheapo plastic runabout hulls under subcontract to a Pennsylvania firm, and then to sell the whole shebang, take the money, and run to Florida. If Peter didn't like it, he could lump it.

Peter lumped it. Sagamore Flats was sold to that "government operation," and in the story, as in fact, paradox ensued. The disappointed New Jersey dentist bought a similar property just upshore, on Taylors Island, which included farm and woodland acreage. Soon after, in partnership with two fellow retired Come-Heres, he caused the farmhouse to be razed, the woods cleared, roads run in, and the acreage developed into one more low-budget residential subdivision, Bayside Estates—which however failed to attract the anticipated out-of-town buyers and was soon rezoned into a mobile home park. That park was then promptly singled out for wreckage by a small spring twister, as such places are, and only partially rebuilt by the developers, all of whom had moved on to Florida. The CIA, on the other hand, while they gutted the Sagamore Flats house to a clapboard shell and redesigned the inside entirely for its new functions (in Peter's story, the "heavy interrogation" of Soviet defectors suspected of being KGB double agents, and the electronic reception of transmissions from certain of our "spy in the sky" satellites—though most of that latter activity is the business of the Defense Intelligence Agency and the National Reconnaissance Office), carefully preserved the exterior and grounds as an innocuous, perfectly unremarkable waterfront farm, indistinguishable from its appearance in Fritz Sagamore's best days. Elder Brother gloats off to Fort Myers in his Winnebago; Younger Brother is morally perplexed up there in Transcendentalist country. "The Point" closes with Y.B.'s being politely but unequivocally warned away by a very nonlocal fellow when, on an impulse, he drives south, charters in Annapolis a sailboat of his late father's manufacture, crosses the Bay, and sails up to the old family dock beside Shoal Point.

Or so it was meant to close. But as its narrative tide ran, "The Point" enlarged and lengthened into a bulky, unSagamorian saga whose working title was

SHOAL POINT.

Every successful writer, early on in his/her experience, develops a more or less characteristic matter, manner, and method, which thereafter he departs from at his risk and persists in equally at his risk. The latter risk is staleness, self-parody: a dead marriage between the artist and his art. The former is regression to novicehood, as when a woman long and faithfully wed loses her spouse to death or divorce, begins after due mourning to "date" again, and feels and acts at forty-five as awkward as the green teenager she once was. Between these poles, among artists as between spouses, is mature development; but its course is neither always clear nor, when clear, always followable nor, when followable, always smooth. Peter Sagamore once tried for half a September afternoon in *Story* to fetch through the bridge at Knapps Narrows on Tilghman Island, playing a fluky fair wind against a steady foul tide in his engineless boat, by turns as amused and exasperated as was the bridge-tender. That worthy quite understood the situation and several times halted traffic and obligingly opened the draw as *Story* broad-reached to within fifty feet of it or less, only to be blanketed by the bridge piers or the bascule span itself and carried back by the tide despite P's sculling. Rather than tie up at a pier for three hours till tide-turn (by when the daylight and probably the breeze as well would fade), he reversed course and sailed the long way around, under the island, from the Bay into Choptank River: ran out of light and air anyhow, miles from any proper anchorage; was then "caught out" by a rare Chesapeake fog as a cool front glided in over the still-warm water; missed one mark after another that he would have sworn he could find even without a compass; and wound up sculling blindly till past midnight to find what he had to hope in his then entire disorientation was safe anchorage till morning. Whew.

Dissatisfied with the point of "The Point," Peter watched uneasily as it grew toward novel size, and not his kind of novel at all: talky, loose, expansive, humorless—even politically and socially concerned! But some imp of the perverse bade him scull on: The antipathy between the brothers was elaborated far beyond the mostly cordial distance between himself and Jacob. The moral paradoxes were extended back into U.S. history: The CIA's often illegal activities were shown to have a provenance back to Thomas Jefferson, even to George Washington, and to pale before the rape of the land and the near or total obliteration of species (not excluding whole nations of Indians), at the hands less often of Come-Heres than of established settlers and their local descendants down to the present, who incline to resist any curbing of their exploitation, who market whatever resource is marketable as nearly out of existence as they are able and then move on to some other marketable resource or shrug their shoulders in the manner of mining or utility companies and move away.

Shoal Point's epigraph Peter took from the nineteenth-century Maryland writer George Alfred Townsend:

> *And the county clerk will prove it by the records on his shelves:*
> *That the fathers of the province were no better than ourselves.*

The protagonist-narrator, a local himself, born into a family of Hoopers Island watermen, grows up with their values in the first four chapters: He is more or less contemptuous of the Come-Heres, whose money however is never refused; of conservationists and other experts from across the Bay; even of recreational sailors, who use wind and water for mere sport. In Chapters Five through Eight he becomes the first of his family to leave the county and attend a university; his perspective enlarges to the point of distancing him from his family, not alone on matters environmental: These are the years of the black civil rights movement, of which Cambridge, in Dorchester County, becomes one stormy focus. A tumultuous scene (Peter wrote it in Portugal, in a *pousada* in Sagres, near Cape St. Vincent) finds the narrator there on Race Street, fresh from a year's European excursion, in the midst of an incendiary riot, confronting his redneck brother across a police barricade. . . .

The civil rights act is passed by Chapter Nine, and in the next three chapters the racial violence subsides. The new environmentalists come to the fore, their ranks swelled by the Come-Heres retired to the area on the fruits of their own exploitation of other resources elsewhere. In the Bay there are lean years and relatively bountiful ones of what harvestable species remain, but except for Canada geese and whitetail deer, who thrive near cultivated cornlands, the curve is unambiguously, inexorably down.

The curve of moral complexity, on the other hand, goes up with the narrator's understanding, perhaps in Chapter Twelve, that as an outsider he is working for causes whose consequences he himself does not have to live closely with. He makes uneasy peace with his family. An opportunity presents itself in Chapter Thirteen for him to return to live in the area he cares most about in the world: His father dies, the family business must be renovated or sold; a government agency, probably the CIA, expresses discreet interest in purchasing "Shoal Point Flats." Literally to reconnoiter his native waters, the narrator decides to charter a sailboat out of Annapolis and spend a few days reviewing the area incognito, as a Come-Here. He finds and rents a sloop of his own father's manufacture, a "Shoal Point 25"; he singlehands it across and down the Bay to Hoopers Island. Though he knows those waters as one knows one's bedroom in the dark, he misgauges the tide in his own front yard, so to speak, and ignominiously runs hard aground on Shoal Point itself.

No problem: The boat is a shallow-draft centerboarder. All he need do is winch up the board and drift free, or, if it has been driven up into its trunk and the hull aground on its shallow keel, get out and push. As he sets about the former, he sees a pair of crabbers pause at the end of their nearby trotline and chug over to see whether he needs assistance. He expects the familiar twangy sarcasm, teasing but not necessarily unfriendly. He smiles and waves them off—though the centerboard, he discovers, is indeed clear up in its trunk. He secures its slack pennant, kicks off his deck shoes, and prepares to go over the side and push, leaving his blue jeans rolled down against sea nettles.

But the chaps come over anyhow and offer him a tow. The narrator observes that while their vessel has the lines of a typical local workboat— long waterline for stability, narrow beam for easy access to both sides, low freeboard for working trotlines or lifting crab pots and oyster tongs over the gunwales, a small wheelhouse for foul weather—it is improbably clean for this time of the season, as if it has just been launched and commissioned. So are the crabbers, their work clothes unsoiled, their hands and faces smooth. Moreover, their accent is neutral Network American, not local; their faces, their eyes, their manners are white-collar professional; and their offer to help, while cordial, is a touch insistent. Though the narrator knows little about the ways of undercover agents at that point in his and his author's life, it occurs to him to wonder whether the crab trotline is a cover for the CIA's scouting "Shoal Point Flats" over an extended period, perhaps assessing the degree of its privacy and penetrability from the water. . . .

Here, however, the novel itself had run aground, even as its narrator declines the proffered towline, steps into the chill, hip-deep water, and manhandles the sloop stern-first off Shoal Point. It was a story that Peter Sagamore by sheer persistence could eventually get told, he realized; but it was not a Peter Sagamore story. As a grounded mariner without a centerboard may, in extremis, lighten ship by jettisoning everything expendable, so in the weeks just prior to this Boston weekend of which we speak, our author had thrown out of *Shoal Point* the entire CIA business— what did he know, really, of such matters?—the environmentalist theme, the whole civil rights imbroglio, and every sticky parallel between the narrator and the author in the "grown-up" sections of the story. Now on this present Monday he reviewed what he had amputated and with a bold coup de main struck out all the growing-up chapters as well, so evocative of a thousand other up-from-the-boondocks novels. By lunchtime he had reoutlined the project in what would be its finally published form: a quite short story whose realistic aspect was based on the one part of the action he had utterly invented. The narrator-protagonist by chance comes across a sailboat of his late father's manufacture; he charters and sails it back to his home waters, even to his home, after long absence; and he runs aground in his own front yard upon the piece of marine geography he has known most intimately since birth.

This same narrator, Peter decided over lunch and after talking by phone with exasperated Marcie Blitz, would himself be a disaffected young CIA officer at work upon a book-length exposé of his fellow ex-officers' sale of their expertise to sundry nefarious or at least questionable interests. (It would be seen in retrospect that with remarkable intuition—since Peter Sagamore had in fact at the time no special knowledge of such matters— "Part of a Shorter Work" anticipated in some detail the Watergate break-ins and such enormous, sinister international operations as those of the rogue agents Edwin Wilson and Frank Terpil.) But the sailor-author's manuscript, merely summarized in the story "Part of a Shorter Work," is fated never to reach completion—hence the story's title—for the reason that, even as he raises the centerboard of his rented sailboat and waves away the crabbers chugging over from a nearby trotline, apparently to assist him off Shoal Point—

So when Ms. Blitzstein came home from work that evening (Peter Sagamore in effect now tells his unborn children in Dun Cove), and I told her I'd scrapped the whole *Shoal Point* novel except for the running-aground business, which I hadn't mentioned to her before, and she learned about the similarity between what had just happened to us in Marion Harbor and what happens to that narrator of mine in Annapolis, she said For pity's sake buy the damn boat and take that Maryland job and let's sail that boat from up here to down there, and then we'll just see what's what with us. We'd had a fine two years, she said, that she'd never forget; it was probably time we each went on to our next thing. And she was right, as Marcie usually was about such matters. In fact, she was telling me what I'd already decided to do, and making the decision easier by promising to take off that summer and sail *Story* down to Chesapeake Bay with me.

So I bought this boat—and immediately hung a secondhand six-horse outboard on the transom, for convenience as well as for emergencies. I said no to Boston and yes to Maryland; I took a few weekend shakedown cruises to check out the systems and get the feel of her; I packed my Boston stuff to be picked up later (Marcie didn't pack hers) and then bought charts and provisions for our long coastwise cruise. Nearly five hundred miles: two to four weeks, depending on the weather and how much poking around we did along the way. I placed "Part of a Shorter Work" and began doing even shorter pieces: Less became More.

But as sailing time approached, Marcie Blitzstein changed her tune. There was a new assistant producer at GBH who would jump at the chance to replace her while she was away, even if she were off filming a documentary for the station. In fact, her rival aside, she didn't see how she could justify to the production crew or to herself so long an absence—unless Peter was maybe willing to let her *do* the trip as a documentary: maybe as a pilot for some kind of Writer in America series for PBS? Now *that* idea struck her as not half bad, what with the boat's name and P's going back to his roots, et cet! In two weeks she could work out a format and get a crew together to follow *Story* with a chopper and a chase boat; Peter could do excerpts voice-over from his fiction and talk about Regionalism versus Internationalism, or the Sense of Place in American Lit, blah blah blah, while they sail on camera from Melville and Hawthorne country down past Whitman's Long Island and right by Manhattan, work in a little Thomas Wolfe You Can't Go Home Again, Hart Crane and the Brooklyn Bridge et cet, then down through Whitmanville again, Camden and Philly—Do we sail through Philly, or is that just the train?—on down to Baltimore, Poe Mencken Scott Fitzgerald Francis Scott Key, and end up in the nation's capital. Dynamite! That is the way dear Marcie talked, sort of, and that is how her busy mind worked.

P told her her heart wasn't in that project. She said she *knew* that, but her heart wasn't in their splitting either, any more than in their staying together, and neither was his. Right, as usual. He told her he didn't dig using their connection as grist for the mill: If she wouldn't dishonor it by televising it, he wouldn't dishonor it by writing about it, okay? Now just hold on there, said Ms. Blitz, and then made a truly eloquent pitch, right from the ventricles, the burden of which was that they were artists, for Christ sake, both of them; that their love affair and every other thing good bad or indifferent that they'd ever experienced or imagined separately or together *was* grist for the mill; and that to grind that grist in that particular mill was to honor it, not dishonor it—as long as they ground it honorably.

Says Katherine Sherritt Sagamore You miss that Marcie Blitzstein. You wish I was an artist. Were.

Peter Sagamore assures her he does not.

Wish or miss?

I'll always miss old Marcie now and then: a spirit swift and free and brave. But that machts nicht.

Says K glumly I'm a nothing. A little librarian, potentially rich.

A big librarian and plenty besides. Queen of my heart. Light of my soul. Mother of our posterity. More.

Not queen of your *whole* heart, though, the way you're king of my whole heart. Do I go around missing Poonie Baldwin now and then, or Saul Fish or Jaime Aiquina? Maybe Jaime a little. So on with your story: Do it.

Our story, soon. He sailed down here alone, little ones (Peter Sagamore would say if he were literally putting all this into words): a terrific experience, here and there hairy. Sagamore Twenty-fives weren't designed for ocean work, but Capn Fritz knew what he was doing, and old Charlie Bunting knew even more: the yard's chief carpenter, who'd really designed the Twenty-five. *Story* sailed down from Buzzards Bay through Narragansett Bay and Long Island Sound, through Hell Gate and down the East River to Sandy Hook, then down the Jersey coast and inland waterway and through the Cape May Canal, up Delaware Bay and River, through the C and D Canal, and into our Chesapeake, and those three weeks brought its skipper to complex terms indeed with his departed father and, by extension, with his origins. P. Sagamore is not a romantic: neither about origins nor about wooden sailboats nor about writing fiction. *Story* leaked a little on the way down and had a few spots of dry rot in unimportant places; once he'd moved his stuff down from Boston and settled in Annapolis, Pete laid on the epoxy and the fiberglass without a qualm, and modernized the rig a little here and there for more speed and easier handling. Charlie Bunting and John Basel would have been offended—but it wasn't their boat any longer.

On the other hand, he couldn't bring himself to use that engine—not even at Hell Gate, where the current is a bona fide bitch, or in the Jersey waterway, where the channels are too tight for tacking. He practiced patience and waited for the right wind and tide, sometimes for days, damned if he knew why. One is not allowed to transit those two canals under sail alone: In the Cape May he turned the engine on for the first time, but left it in neutral and ran the three miles through on a slack tide and a following breeze. In the Chesapeake and Delaware the traffic is monitored by TV, and the rules are enforced; he did the same trick for fifteen miles. If there'd been a moment's danger to anyone else or any real threat to himself or the boat, he'd have said Screw this and shifted into gear; but it much gratified him that there wasn't.

For a while, once he'd berthed *Story* in Annapolis and himself in College Park, he kept the O.B. in a cockpit locker. The very day before the evening of that Katherine Anne Porter party, he sold it to a chap down the line at his marina on Whitehall Creek. Then he went home, looked over some student papers, made notes toward a certain new story even shorter than "Part of a Shorter Work." He shaved, he dressed, and he went to do his duty by K. A. Porter. There. Over?

Says Katherine Sherritt, almost literally, Not quite over. The name of that story, kiddies—the one shorter than *Shoal Point,* shorter than "The Point," shorter even than "Part of a Shorter Work," was, in your daddy's own fewer and fewer words . . . Over.

SHORTER POINT

Grist, grist, grist for the mill: Marcie Blitz was right about that. As long as one grinds it honorably. Who's to say who jumped whom that night at the 92nd Street Poetry Center? But after it developed that these children's da was billeted in the Gramercy Park, and that their ma's overpriced closet of a flat was not a whole lot farther down in the Village, on West Eleventh, and we shared a cab to carry on the conversation we'd started over autographs, it became fairly clear by say Fifty-ninth and Fifth that we two Eastern Shore folk had a *lot* to say to each other besides bookchat and good night. Old Poon was out of Katie Sherritt's twenty-four-year-old picture, and Yussuf al-Din wasn't quite in it yet, though he was rapping darkly at her sexual door. Marcie Blitzstein was but a befreckled freshman Swarthmorean, four years yet into Pete's libidinal future, and while there were several items of note in his libidinal past, there was none quite in his present. All this we gathered from each other not in any detail but by tactful general inference as the Checker cab banged south—the year was after all Nineteen Sixty-four, when U.S. sexual promiscuity had not yet really got into overdrive, and well-raised types like us still thought of sex as something special. How on earth do you suppose it will be, Peter, Katherine says now, when *these* innocents are twenty-four? In, let's see. . . . Oh, Jesus: Two Thousand and Four?

P.S. says soberly that he has little confidence of anything's being anything in Twenty Aught Four; but that's another story. The Checker banged south.

The Checker banged south—

Stavros Petrakis at the wheel! I just flashed on the license by the meter with his picture and his name on it: Stavros Petrakis. Mustachios and all.

Living with your father, says K. Sherritt to our children, is mighty spooky sometimes. And to Peter What am I wearing, that you'll soon take off me?

Hum. One-piece pullover light knit jersey sleeveless dress. Scoop neck scoop back blue and white fine horizontal stripe bra no stockings some kind of sandals. Shell necklace gold loop earrings some kind of pin some kind of hair-clasp barrette whatever. No rings no bracelets Omega sport wristwatch I forget what color underpants small navy ditty-bag purse containing wallet keys Kleenex aspirin and diaphragm. And some unobtrusive scent . . .

Children! Your father has forgotten your mother's perfume!

No he hasn't: Le De, *par* Givenchy. And you took your own clothes off.

But there in the cab, pleased K continues, Stavros Petrakis's south-banging Checker . . .

We touched fingers to forearms (our story goes on) and traded Did-you-knows about growing up separately together down on the Shore. It is clear that we find each other's young persons mighty attractive there in that cab in that big town. Somewhere in the high Twenties we drop the Checker, it's such a fine night to walk. We stroll on down Fifth and pop in someplace for a drink, but it's better outside, where every time we come to a Did-you-happen-to-know-Whatsisname, we can take the other's arm. On a bench in Union Square, halfway between your place and mine, we decide but do not say that we will not be saying good night this night. Feeling very bold and liberated, K.S.S. stands up and takes the writer's writing-hand and says Let's have our nightcap at your hotel.

First time P's ever been directly propositioned, except by professionals. He springs up, kisses her, and grabs a left-handful of her perfect buns, which along with the rest of her he's been admiring all the way down from Ninety-second, but which he has scarcely hoped to lay actual hands upon— K happening to be, by a factor of several, the classiest young woman in his moderate experience. Fancy his delight, children, when your mother responds by putting *her* left hand on *his* tush, and her right over his left on hers, and pressing us together from knees to bellies while running her tongue around his. Hoo boy.

It had been a while, Katherine Sherritt would have our listeners know; it had been a while. And what it had been, when last it was, was Poonie Baldwin, Junior, and to keep her head clear she'd kept her legs together right through the divorce. She had even half thought she might be done with men altogether after what Poon did, but the fact is that our children's father is this handsome hunk, wait till you see, kids, and all through his fiction reading at the Poetry Center she'd been thinking Why not? and deciding to introduce herself and thinking maybe she's ready to get back into dating, quote unquote, but not really expecting him to say Come on, let's tell some more tidewater tales, I'm at the Gramercy Park, where are you? And the whole time, banging south in that Checker, she's wetting her pants—

Robin's-egg blue!

—her robin's-egg undies and thinking If he doesn't, she will.

While *he's* been thinking Do you suppose? Probably she's just being *friendly,* for Christ sake, a smashing high-class bird like this: don't get your hopes up, Webfoot. Remember the immortal words of Jasper Johns: that we artists are the elite of the servant class.

Reverse snobbery. But kiss we do, there in the Square, and go for the old buns, whereupon comes a groan from a nearby bench, and there's some freako with his shlong out, watching us and whacking away. Good old New York.

We run to the hotel, so amused and excited that we forget about the nightcap till we're in the elevator, by when we're too busy getting it on to bother with room service till ninety minutes later. When in fact we *do* order up a bottle of Taittinger brut with which to toast a number of things. Some obvious ones, of course: your perfectly splendid face and body . . .

Yours. Cheers.

A bout of lovemaking more gentle than athletic, when we got down to it: careful and caring, even, given that we're newly met and hot as two pistols. A surprising long sweet sweaty *after*play that can only be called affectionate, seeming as it seemed to be directed less at rearousing us for Chapter Two, though anon it did, than at stretching out our pleasure in Chapter One. A pleasure, at that, not alone in a happy roll in the hay with a nifty new number, but in finding and bedding a *paisano* to whom one doesn't want to say good night.

Whom in fact, little ones—and this is how it happens you're hearing this tale—whom in fact we enjoy swapping stories with as much as swapping kisses from head to foot and around the world by both the equatorial and the transpolar routes.

Sex and stories, stories and sex. Teller and listener changing positions and coming together till they're unanimous. About three A.M. you lifted your head from my lap to ask me Had I ever happened to anchor behind Shorter Point on Goldsborough Creek off the Tred Avon River, across Sherritt Cove from Nopoint Point? And to tell me how your mom and dad rebuilt Nature by undoing the mighty works of Parker Pink—and I wanted that story as much as I wanted you not to pause to tell it.

Stories, stories. In the dark, with sirens in the background as New York's other night-business went on. Now, what Katherine Sherritt would like to know is how in the world two people who found so much pleasure in each other all that night and next morning—as much pleasure in taking as in relinquishing both the narrative and the sexual initiative, so to speak—

I like that.

Could then say good-bye after a *very* long brunch—room service again, as the G.P.H. doesn't open its dining room for breakfast—and not see each other thereafter for six long busy years? I mean six years of our mortal life, children, that he and she could have spent together and didn't! Six yearsworth of doing everything together before the Doomsday Factor gets us all! It's not as if the world'll end any later because we held off. I hate our being apart for twenty-four hours, and we lost six whole mothering years that we needn't have! How did that happen?

Shrugs Peter Sagamore Don't ask them. We weren't ready, obviously, and that would've been a pity even if we *had* somehow put doomsday on hold by kissing good-bye on the corner of Twentieth and Irving Place and me going up to New England and you going down to West Eleventh and then down to College Park and then up to Baltimore. What a consoling idea, Kath: that by staying apart we maybe kept the world together. Who knows but what?

We know.

We know. And therefore we console ourselves and our offspring with twin other considerations: that those six years gave us a many another tale to tell each other when our paths recrossed; and that thanks to a perfectly unlikely chain of perfectly fortunate coincidences, culminating in the co-incidence of Kate's admiration for and Pete's obligation to the elderly author of *Ship of Fools* and other opera, P.S. put down his trusty Parker pen on a certain early evening in early fall Nineteen Seventy, after an hour's trimming of a certain story-in-the-works, and ambled across campus to pay his respects, thinking all the way about Parker Pink and Parker's ink and Shorter Point and Katherine Anne Porter and Katherine Shorter Sherritt of the egg-blue knickers and peach-pink knockers, whom and which he had not forgotten over those six years, no indeedy—a windfall like that is rare in the luckiest man's life—though he'd not followed up on it, either, except in his imagination, where that Gramercy night lived its narrative half-life aglow like pitchblende in the dark. While at the same time K.S.S. and her roomie are hauling down the BW Parkway to pay *their* respects ditto. P's distance is shorter, but he gets there later because he's woolgathering about Shorter and Nopoint Points and Less Is More. He even gets to wondering specifically whatever happened to classy Kate Sherritt: probably found herself a sharp young international banker years ago and divides her time between London and the Upper East Side with him and their gorgeous preppie kids, Pounds Shillings and Pence. They *would* be gorgeous, for sure, and no snobbery in them if their dad's genes matched their mom's. I imagined, says Peter, you would have remembered our little adventure with a smile now and then when you saw me being patted on the head by the *Times* or trashed by *The New York Review of Books*—

Loyal Katherine pats his head. On with it, says Peter.

Maze and I get there and pay our respects and swap a few Shorter–Porter stories with old K.A.P., who is in fine fettle, and I learn from our hosts that the university's new writer-in-residence will be stopping by. Says Katherine Anne He wrote a fine first novel a few years back about the tidewater country, and I haven't finished anything he's written since. But don't tell him I said that, she told us with a wink, 'cause he's sexy and single. Her very adjectives. When she was our age, she declared to me and May, she'd have run off to Mexico with him. Young fellow named Peter Sagamore. When you were my age, May said to Katherine Anne, I'd have run off to Mexico with *you*.

She got Porter going then, May Jump did, on Mexican revolutionaries and the Weimar Republic, and Katherine Sherritt was glad of that, because while she'd read somewhere that Peter Sagamore had moved to College

Park, it somehow hadn't occurred to her that of course he might be at this party. Ms. Porter's remark brought that night in New York back to her so strongly that she felt like a character in a romantic flick: as if Yussuf al-Din and Saul Fish and Jaime Aiquina had been digressions in the plot, and now we were getting back to the main story-line. She got trembly in the gut, and when she saw P.S. come in, smiling and salty-looking from his summer, she went to get a drink so he wouldn't see her right away. Not that he'd recognize her six years later in a roomful of strangers—he hadn't been seeing *her* in the *Times* and on book jackets and bookchat shows and in David Levine caricatures, getting leaner and handsomer and intenser-looking all the time, in K's opinion, with his Less Is More. For all she knew, he'd had hot-assed little sophomores and Sagamore groupies jumping into bed with him every other night for the past six years, a thousand and one one-nighters, and didn't even remember Union Square and the Gramercy Park. She watched him shake hands with the host and hostess and kiss Katherine Anne's powdered cheek hello and be introduced to May Jump—who as a matter of fact knew we'd gotten it on once years ago because Kath had mentioned it to her in passing in the library while praising some new piece of Peter's she'd just read. But the subject had never come up again, and K wasn't even sure May'd made the connection when Porter said what she said. I sort of hoped she hadn't, Kath declares: It surprised me to be feeling so *nervous* about such a thing at age thirty. I actually decided I'd go find a bathroom, because I figured you'd be heading for a drink at the bar about now, and anyhow my bowels were acting up. But just then I see May point me out to you across the room— across *two* rooms—and that's where I freeze the frame.

Says Peter Sagamore I owe May one forever. To our unborn offspring he goes on In the world whereinto your mom and I have seen fit to bring you people, women and men are engendered by the physical coupling of one with the other and in no other way, normally. Got that? But their coupling is not confined to that purpose; it is done recreationally and in other spirits as well, most often across but not seldom within the genders. And when, as happens, man couples with man or woman woman, engenderment is precluded but not pleasure, so one hears. You will now understand, your Auntie May being in love with your ma, that it was either a calculated risk or a considerable altruism for her to tell me that she believed I might remember her apartment-mate and fellow library scientist, a major fan of mine whom I'd met once in New York City some years before. That's her in the spiffy Anne Klein fall colors, over by the bar. Kathy Sherritt?

Says K.S.S. Up with the music: Your father's smile across those rooms, kids, would have lit the suburbs from College Park to Alexandria. Without even an Excuse me to May Jump and Katherine Anne Porter, he swarmed through that party like a seal through kelp. People turned to see what was happening; I didn't know myself quite what to expect. . . .

But, says Peter Sagamore, she smiled! With a roomslength still between us, your ma gave her head a small toss and raised her chin a bit and laid one forefinger along her cheek and smiled—and oh, I tell you that if biology were romantic, you'd be going on ten right now, 'cause then and there you'd have been conceived, in a roomful of people, before your parents even touched.

Katherine Sherritt must have wondered was the man literally going to sweep her off her feet? Not his style nor hers! A Hollywood clinch, then, to the party's mild amusement? Not impossible: sort of nifty. And then run hand in hand, grinning and lushing our undies both of us, from College Park clear back to Gramercy Park?

We wish. But the prosaic fact was, P. Sagamore lost his nerve—if that's fair to say when he couldn't have been said to have any plan of action to abandon, beyond crossing that room and bringing those smiles together. It was the smashing *coincidence* that had propelled him, and the unexpected sight of that woman—still six years later the finest he'd ever shared a bed with, and her beauty more seasoned and womanly at thirty than it had been at twenty-four. When we were close enough to touch, Katherine Sherritt set down her drink, not knowing just what would happen next, and leaned back against the edge of the bar-table. And at that moment Peter Sagamore ran out of spontaneity, though not of heart-feeling, and of all things stuck out his right hand toward her as if to shake hands. But Ms. Sherritt put out her left instead, fingers up and slightly spread, a surprising gesture, as if half reaching out and half holding off, and without glancing from her smile he found his fingertips touching hers, point for point—a light mild innocent friendly moment's business, not lingered over as in a B movie. Except that *then, bambini,* one or the other of us spread those fingers the rest of the way, wide open, for a long second as we both looked down at them before dropping our hands and raising our eyes and saying something like Well hi! and laughing lightly and beginning our Boyoboy-talk-about-*coincidence* conversation. And ten years later we both agree that few moments in our two lives have been more sexual than that one there: that opening, that spreading of our fingers.

However, that was pretty much that, for then. Neither wanted to presume upon the past, though it was clear from across two rooms that we both remembered it with unembarrassed pleasure; and neither of us knew yet what the other's present circumstances were, or his/her own desires. So our conversation quickly turned to general pleasantries and catching-ups, though with a special voltage on it, a curiosity beyond the just polite. May Jump joined us as Peter Sagamore was getting to the *really* odd coincidence of his having made notes that very afternoon on the Parker Pink/Shorter Point story Katherine had told him apropos of something or other while sixty-nining back in Sixty-four. All the signals were that this friend of hers was "butch," as we still said back then, or at very least bi-, and that she took a proprietary interest in our Kath. May was on her guard already, a touch too breezy, with an edge, and that made the man of us wonder what was what—especially when he registered now that the pair of them shared a flat. At the same time, he was pleased to understand that K wasn't presently living with another man (he had checked already those spread left fingers for a wedding band, and she, shortly after, his cocktail-holding ditto ditto).

He tells them both the Funny Coincidence, looking for signs that lovely Kate remembers being disrobed and arsey-turvy when she told him the exemplary saga of Shorter Point. No sign: Either she doesn't remember, or she is one cool cookie indeed.

Not so cool, guys, as she looked: Fact is, her guts were churning, her ears were burning, her nipples tingling, her vulva jingling with the memory of those narrative circumstances, which she's sure are being advertised to the room. *May* sure felt the amperage in our air.

May Jump's radar is even finelier tuned than that of your average library scientist. In any case, all hands concurred that that coincidence was some funny coincidence, all right, and then we chatted some more, and then May steered you off to meet Whatserface the Computer Folklorist, and I spent some hors-d'oeuvres time with my new academic colleagues and the guest of honor. But I knew exactly where you were in whichever room at any given minute of that three-hour party.

I you too.

And I'd made up my mind to follow up on our remeet.

As had I. We found it exciting then (goes on our story) to keep the party between us for those couple of hours, feeling the pull across a houseful of people and knowing that the point of the evening now was our coming back together for bye-byes at its close. It was Katherine Sherritt, it turns out, who, when that happened, volunteered that she and May were in fact driving over to Sherritt country for the weekend, to introduce May Jump to Hank and Irma. If there was anything further Peter Sagamore needed to know about Parker Pink and Shorter Point, she would be happy to check it out and phone in a report, if he'd give her a number.

Well, would he ever, now. Address too; just happened to have Parker and paper right on him, he being a writer. But look here; talk about coincidence: *He's* hopping over to the Shore tomorrow too, for the long Columbus Day weekend! But driving's such a drag: the last Ocean City traffic of the season. . . . He's sailing over from Annapolis, no particular destination in mind, whither the wind listeth et cet, maybe touch base at his parents' old place on Hoopers Island, maybe not. He might just check out Shorter Point himself, an easy day's sail with any breeze at all. If you girls happen to see a beamy little twenty-five footer—named *Story,* he's embarrassed to confess—becalmed off the Sherritt doorstep . . .

Amused K wants to hear again: Your boat's named *Story,* like the one in your novel? That's a touch much, no? Says blushing P That's another story and yet another coincidence: I'll lay it on you next time. The woman smiles: Next time? Says our fellow thinking fast Eight A.M. tomorrow, which is when the tide turns at Slip Thirty-three in Beasley's Boatyard on

Whitehall Creek at the foot of Whitehall Road off U.S. Fifty, just before the Bay Bridge. Your instructions are to pack lunch for three and an extra sweater apiece and meet me there at eight sharp, and we'll ride that tide to Shorter Point. The three of us.

May quickly says Thanks but no thanks: *She* mal-de-mers at mere mention of Winslow Homer. Besides, they'll want the car through the weekend and to get back home, right? But Katherine Shorter Sherritt takes a lock of beachy hair in her hand and remarks to it that there's always a car to spare on Nopoint Point, and she hasn't gone sailing in approximately one hundred years. The gentleman asks whether May Jump has tried Bonine? Keeps your muffins down but doesn't toddle you off. There is Bonine aboard. At eight A.M. on a Saturday, says May, I *want* to be toddled off. Also at nine. We'll honk from the bridge. May doesn't need Bonine, Kathy scoffs: She's a hotshot white-water canoeist. Says Peter Sagamore Well, then.

Anyhow, you're welcome at Nopoint Point, Ms. Sherritt declares. Seriously. We'll look for you. Up the Tred Avon, she goes on, possibly embarrassed at having let May Jump decide for the both of them, and hang a right at Oxford. Goldsborough's your next real creek to starboard after Town Creek, and Sherritt Cove is your first serious cove to starboard in Goldsborough. You'll see a humongous blue-and-white center-cockpit ketch in there named *Katydid Four,* unless Dad's out sailing.

Says the man of us *Katydid,* is it. He has lost this round to Miss May, he sees, but scores a point yet by divining that that nickname was doubtless Daddy's for our woman when she was a tot and remains her pet-name yet—maybe her love-name? Tit for tat for twitting him with *Story.* He's pleased to see her color a bit behind her merry eyes. Says May Off to Baltimore, Kiss. But Katydid Sherritt asks Peter Sagamore Do you live here in College Park?

He does, temporarily, though he's scouting to rent something on the water. Tonight, however, he'll be sleeping aboard in Whitehall Creek, to get a jump on the tide. He smiles. Slip Thirty-three, Beasley's Marina, foot of Whitehall Road, eight A.M. Little Sagamore Twenty-five named you know what. Says May Don't hold your breath, skipper.

I didn't. Bade good night to all, walked back to my flat, changed into sailing clothes, popped a few things into the cooler, and drove out to Whitehall Creek, full of handsome Katherine Sherritt. Katydid. *Kiss!* It was exciting as well as flattering to've been told that that old novel of mine had not only brought the woman up to Ninety-second Street one famous evening, but had fetched her back to Maryland not long after for her graduate degree. In a way, you'd let me know at the party, I was responsible for your being there; and I'd replied of course that in a way you were responsible for *my* being there: the Shorter Point tale you'd told me . . . once upon a time . . . which had become, in a way too complicated to go into at a party, the story of my literary working life. So, you'd said: We are responsible for each other. May moved in on us then, and that was that. But the future parents of these children of the future exchanged over that remark a smile of understanding that we were being responsible *to* each other as well, by curbing our curiosity and going easy on the innuendo. The man of us sat a fair while right here in *Story*'s dew-damp cockpit, regarding the stars and—having paid his dues to responsible restraint— thinking horny thoughts. Missing good Marcie Blitz for sure, since leaving whom he'd not in fact been laid, but hugely lusting for Katydid Shorter Sherritt. Went below to sleep. Couldn't. Masturbated. Slept.

The woman of us rode back to Baltimore, comparably though not iden- tically preoccupied, to May Jump's clear chagrin. Her thoughts were less pornographic; anyhow softer porn: voice hair eyes and smile instead of knickers and knockers and sixty-nining in Room One Seven Six of the G.P.H., Two Lexington Ave. But warm they were, her thoughts, and while she didn't blame May for trying to turn her arousal to advantage, she wasn't up, thank you, for going down. A touch too gaily, excuse me, she said Why *not* sail over and drive back? You know you won't get sick. Replied May I'm sick already, but I'll survive. Go take your boatride with Mister Straight; I'll sleep in and maybe drive over later. Maybe not.

A thing we appreciate about May Jump is that when she says a thing like that, she means it. When May's bruised, she lets you know; but cynical as she is in some particulars, she does *not* believe all's fair in either love or war. Even if she and K had been a couple, May'd have honored what she took to be the limits of anyone's proprietary rights. But they weren't a couple; what had passed between them, May knew to have been mainly experimental on Katherine's part, at a time when she'd ended her Chileno affair and was approaching thirty feeling somewhat jaded and not greatly pleased with her emotional biography. In truth, when Kath reviewed them, as she did that night, not one of her four major affairs, her marriage certainly included, had been deeply satisfying, though all but the marriage had been much more agreeable than not. Only that remarkable one-night stand with the writer Peter Sagamore remained an unalloyed satisfaction in her memory, perhaps because its nature guaranteed inconsequentiality. Nothing had been at stake for either of us, but our talk, as well as our sex, had been serious under its high spirits. In retrospect she felt she'd felt— in the Gramercy Park then, in College Park again tonight—that center of energy beneath P's laid-back manner, the dark small nothinghood beneath her animation. And that center of his had filled and swelled that center of hers; hers had actively received, accommodated, enfolded his. . . .

She set her bedside alarm for six-thirty, deciding she'd see how the idea looked when that hour came. At six she waked and thought she wouldn't go; the invitation had been just party talk, inspired by those crazy coin- cidences. The dawn was gray; the bed comfortable. But the man *had* remembered not only our night's adventure but her story, and he had come back to it six years later. At a quarter past she aborted the alarm, not to wake May in the other bedroom; tossed into her ASPS backpack the few things she had decided during the night she'd need if, as was unlikely. . . . She wondered briefly about lunch and settled upon three apples, two granola bars, and two cans of Tab, understanding he'd never *count* on her appearing. Wrote out a note for May which she'd composed in her mind already, with driving directions, appeals to her patience and understanding, urgers to rendezvous at Nopoint Point about cocktail time to carry on with their weekend plans; even a request that May telephone the Sherritts later in the morning to explain what was what.

So *bon voyage,* May had grumbled into the kitchen then. He's a lucky stud. She would *not* be driving over, May had decided, frankly because her feelings were hurt: It was to have been *their* weekend. Not to worry, though; these things happened; they'd do their weekend another weekend. Better for K to leave this one open for improvisation, should one tack lead to another; better for May's pride not to divvy up with Mister Straight. Complained Kath You talk as if I'm sleeping with the guy! We're just going sailing. Said May Yes, well; kiss me good-bye, Kiss. And dress in layers; it'll be warm this afternoon.

Me (P. Sagamore tells our listening children), I was asleep in *Story*'s quarterberth, or awake but not up yet at half past seven, warm in my sleeping bag in shorts and T-shirt and enjoying the damp air coming cool down the companionway onto my head. I watched the sky clear and listened for a breeze and looked forward to the day's sailing and not for a minute really expected the ladies to show, even when I heard tires on the gravel near Beasley's docks and a car door open and close. Half the marina would load up and head out by mid-morning; by noon there'd be a thousand and one sailboats between Annapolis and the Eastern Shore. But then I heard your mother call from the finger-pier Ahoy there, *Story:* Anybody home? And my adrenaline whooshed, even before I said Welcome aboard, girls, just give me a minute here, and popped my head out and saw that we were but one salty-looking lady, soft tight faded jeans and white marl sweater, her hair tucked up under a ragg-wool watchcap against the early chill. My my my. No May? No May. We didn't pursue it. Said our Katydid, all business, tossing Peter Sagamore her pack, Get your pants on, skipper; I'll single up the lines.

Breakfast?

Oh eight hundred is oh eight hundred, our Kath called back from the bow. Let's get under way and then talk breakfast. *No nonsense* is what her tone told him: I have taken a certain initiative in showing up here alone, as I did once before in seeking you out at the Ninety-second Street Poetry Center. The situation between us is reasonably clear and should not be forced. Let things take their course; do not presume by dallying over breakfast with me in your drawers when I have offended my friend by coming here and have pushed a bit to arrive on time.

My tone said all that?

And more, and properly. I hopped to it; didn't so much as pee or brush my teeth till I'd gotten my clothes on, compass and binocs out, mainsail uncovered and up, and *Story* threading through the aisles of boat slips and out into the creek. My guest had expertly cast off and coiled our leeward lines; when I dispatched her aft to tend tiller and mainsheet while I cast off the last of our windward lines and warped us out of the slip by hand, she asked with pleasure We're going to sail her out? No choice, I was able to give her one moment's pause by replying: no engine.

All *right!* When he got the jib up and came aft, she volunteered to go below now and fix his breakfast while he sailed us out; she'd had her morning muffin, but wouldn't mind a second coffee. Said he You sail; I'll fix.

That, K. Sherritt tells the audience, was a good move. No quicker way to get the feel of a boat or a situation than to be put in charge of it. She was too happy remembering how to sail, and too busy sailing, to feel further uneasiness about May Jump and what she herself was doing there; and of course it pleased her that P had dropped the What's-our-hurry stuff and put her right at the helm. The guy took his leisurely time down there—in the head, at the washbasin, in the galley—leaving her in charge as long as possible while he heated water, stripped to the waist and washed and shaved, tidied up the quarterberth, and served out juice and croissants and coffee for two, all the while chatting and smiling up through the companionway and calling out from memory what marks to steer for and what courses to steer. We had six or seven knots of northwest breeze, as Kath remembers: an easy downhill glide out of Whitehall Creek, wing and wing under main and #1 genoa while the sun came through and dried the dew off us. Just right for getting reacquainted with winches and cleats and buoys and day beacons, and the bare brown arms and shoulders of the controversial minimalist author Peter Sagamore, at which she sneaked a look while he was shaving, and which she well remembered around her in New York.

P swears he wasn't showing off, except by remembering all those buoys and compass courses in order: If he'd thought she was coming, he'd have been shaved and dressed and ready. But he did his surreptitious share of sizing up too, from down below, while making black coffee and light conversation: sized up the woman, the wind and windfall, the situation. That she was here, alone and admittedly at cost of miffing her good friend, argued that she remembered with pleasure our story's first chapter and was prepared not only to see where the next might lead, but to steer it along a bit, help compose it. Pieces of vanilla-caramel hair curled out from under her watchcap, especially at her neck-nape when she turned to look aft. Such one-night adventures as Gramercy Park are no common feature of P.S.'s biography: He recalled very clearly the look of what was under that oiled wool sweater and those faded Levi's—all of it under, around, atop him, kissed and kissing; the caramel hair let down and tenting our two faces half a dozen years past.

Was he, then, merely moistening his shorts with hope and expectation of a waterborne replay of that scene? Is that what our story comes to?

Not even mainly, much less merely—though moisten his shorts he did, Peter Sagamore, even at sight of her smooth fingers light upon the tiller-tip (shucks, so did she, when he came gleaming up into the cockpit at last with mugs of hot coffee in gimbaled holders and a paper-plateful of day-old croissants, just as we cleared Hackett Point, entered the Chesapeake, and laid a course for Bloody Point Light and Poplar Island, fourteen miles magnetic south, our lunchtime destination). With no May now to constrain us, and all those preliminary What-are-we-up-tos evaporated with the dew and washed down with the coffee, we got truly under way: relaxed in the warming air, the easy downwind sail. The man did a few small go-fasts to our sail trim, which the woman took an interest in. Then he relieved her at the helm; she swung her long legs up onto the cushion opposite and sat comfortably facing aft with the cabin bulkhead for a backrest and bright October for a backdrop, and we talked southward down Chesapeake Bay.

Twenty-nine June Sixty-four, declared Peter Sagamore candidly now for openers, remained a red-letter night in the calendar of his life. He'd wanted to tell her that, last evening.

You did, said happy Kate: more than once, and I told you the same. I think we told the whole party.

You're not remarried.

Nope.

Involved, though?

Well . . . A great smile. You?

Not really. Shall we do love-lives first, or get right to art and politics? Jobs I think we pretty well covered at the party.

Oh, love-lives, K supposed. She'd gathered from various review articles that her shipmate was neither married nor celibate. She recalled his remarking in the course of 29 June '64 that the nature of his medium (the profitless short story: full-time vocation, no-time profession), together with his reluctance to commit himself to regular teaching, made him a poor bet as a breadwinner. Since in addition he had no particular wish to reproduce himself or to devote a large measure of his energy and attention to raising children, he regarded himself as inferior husband material—though he was not by temperament promiscuous and much enjoyed sharing his life with a woman.

He said all that in the Gramercy Park Hotel?

One way or another. And K.S.S. told *him* that after Porter "Poonie" Baldwin, Jr., she felt much the same way. Though she had the luxury of trust-fund income past and present and some inherited wealth in the future, she was resolved upon financial independence and a useful working life; even her high-rolling brother Willy was far from *just* a playboy. On the other hand, unlike Peter Sagamore she took eventual remarriage and parenthood for granted. She had too much enjoyed her own growing up, and her parents their parenting (of her and young Andy, at least), not to look forward to wife-and-motherhood herself in the coming decade. But she was in no great hurry. No doubt, she supposed in conclusion, the parental urge was stronger in ordinary civilians like herself than among artists, who famously sublimate it into their work.

Well, now, P.S. wasn't sure how famously. Seemed to him his writer/painter/musician friends had kids at about the normal clip. Their divorce rate, he'd heard, is higher, but he wouldn't swear to it. As for excellent parenting, that seemed to him a gift of temperament and couple-chemistry, about as rare as any other real talent and quite uncorrelated therewith. Many nonartists of his acquaintance were wretched parents; some artists he knew were also first-rate moms and dads. He himself would be on the low side of average, he predicted, but better than wretched. She?

Laughed Katherine Sherritt she'd be terrific! How'd they get on this subject?

So we dropped it, somewhere abeam of the Thomas Point Light, coming onto ten hundred hours and the morning warming toward sixty. Peter rigged a little sheet-to-tiller self-steerer; folks going upwind were still bundled and watchcapped, but we offwind sailors peeled out of our heavies, down to turtleneck jerseys the both of us, sleeves pushed up, and made a second breakfast of Kate's apples and Pete's canned iced tea. For the next hour we did Major Involvements, more or less circumspectly and yet in some detail. The sailing kept us just busy enough to move moment by moment toward or away from intimacy: One paused and looked up to check the windvane, trim a sheet; or one consulted the other's eyes with whole attention. Peter learned, in no detail, about Yussuf al-Din, Saul Fish, Jaime Aiquina. He'd heard tell of that poet and that musician; was impressed; said as much. Said K You got me going on artists, I suppose. Al-Din had been the most difficult and demanding: the cross-racial and cross-class hangups on both sides. Fish had been the sweetest, most dependable, and most talented; Aiquina the most important both emotionally and intellectually. He had awakened her politically, just as Peter Sagamore—but she hadn't mentioned this, had she? She laughed and truly blushed. That night in New York, sir, you awakened me sexually, just like in the storybooks, after Poonie Baldwin had closed me up. I didn't particularly know I'd been asleep! Maybe Peter'd thought she was an old hand at all that stuff we did—she'd tried to make it seem so—but she'd never voluntarily done half those things before, and certainly never enjoyed them so. You turned me on. And I stayed turned on.

Exciting news that was for Peter Sagamore, the same remarked—and he knew pretty surely now that before very long, maybe even that day aboard *Story*, he and this woman would strip off their remaining layers and move their conversation out of language.

Jaime Aiquina's influence, K said now, had led her and May Jump, whom she'd met by then, to help establish HOSCA, the anti-interventionist group which could by 1970 boast chapters on fifty major U.S. campuses and serious infiltration by both the FBI and the CIA. The acronym was English—Hands Off South and Central America—but the word was Spanish. Did Peter know Spanish?

A little and badly, he answered in Spanish. But he remembered from somewhere that a *hosca* is a female mulatto, no? K colored again: As an adjective, it means dark or sullen; Jaime worried that what he'd taught her about U.S. politics south of the border was costing her her sense of humor. But it was a racial tease, too: He'd heard about Yussuf's hard time with her parents, and he himself was not quite white—some royal Inca blood in there. Any daughter of ours, he used to say, would be a *hosca* for sure. But HOSCA was their only *hosca*.

Said Peter Sagamore So. And where was Jaime Aiquina now, even as we spoke these words on the placid Chesapeake? He was in Santiago de Chile, Katherine replied, trying unsuccessfully to keep our government's hands off his hero and leader, Salvador Allende. It was Jaime's prediction that the combined forces of ITT, Anaconda Copper, the Chilean right wing, and the CIA would never permit a Marxist administration in Chile even if legally elected, and that the coup when it came would be a bloodbath in which Chilean democracy would drown like Argentina's, for the rest of the century at least.

She smiled thinly across the cockpit. I don't think we're *that* awful. Do you? Jaime Aiquina, she continued, was Marxist, Catholic, married, and separated. He'd wanted her to live with him in Santiago, and she'd said no. This might sound queer in 1970, but the fact was, she was patriotic. She despised what we were doing in Vietnam and South America; she deplored about half of what we'd done in our history. But she did not admire any other major country more, and she liked being American Kathy Sherritt and living right here on Chesapeake Bay. You taught me that, too, she said, as a matter of fact. Your early books.

Peter wanted to know what, exactly, those fictions had taught her in that line. K replied at once To be plenty skeptical, but to steer clear of easy cynicism as much as chauvinism.

Well.

Mainly, they taught me not to lose sight of the tragic view. Didn't I mention that in New York? It's not an easy lesson for a natural optimist, but I learned it. Later on, when you start carrying the Less Is More business so far and talking about the tragic view of the tragic view, you lose me.

Serious Peter Sagamore declared he sometimes lost himself as well in those ill-charted waters, which he was nonetheless determined to navigate, for more reasons than he could readily set forth or was even confident he understood.

Let me wrap up Jaime Aiquina, Katherine said, and then it's your turn. Jaime Aiquina believes that the generals are going to overthrow Allende and turn Chile into one more strong-arm state, with a lot of help from Uncle Sam. He believes that thousands of people like himself will get *desaparecido*'d: tortured and shot. Jaime Aiquina hates injustice, but he's skeptical of revolutions and has no confidence in the ultimate victory of good over evil. Nevertheless, he went home to do what he could, and he honored me enough to want me to come with him, whatever the consequences to myself. It would have been so easy for him to do the other thing!

She looks our children straight in the eye. She'd said no, she said, partly out of fear. Her ex-husband had once drunkenly raped and tortured her, and she'd been terrified right through it, even though he wasn't a professional thug or a certified sex maniac, just old Poonie Baldwin, Jr., whom she'd wanted to kill and should have. But with Jaime Aiquina it hadn't been just or even mainly fear: She'd said no to Jaime Aiquina because she'd wanted to live here, as happily as she was in fact doing. She was political, all right, but she wasn't *passionately* political, the way Jaime had been. Was still. She brightened: There. So who've *you* been going to bed with? Everybody?

Said pensive Peter Sagamore You think your awakener never sleeps, but in fact he is a middling performer except when inspired by the likes of yourself. The truth was, he went on, that by contrast with those distinguished affairs of hers—in particular with Señor Aiquina's high seriousness and the startling revelation of her former husband's brutality (of which P.S. trusted he would hear more another time; she must pardon his writerly lust for detail), his own sexual-romantic life made mild telling indeed: two extended liaisons, several shorter ones, the odd weekender or one-nighter. All more than agreeable; none truly soul-stirring. Couple of real heart-wrenchings, but no heartbreaks. He had said simple truth when he declared our New York night to have been a high point in his erotic career. In his adult life he had seldom lived alone for long, but he guessed he was no great shakes as a sexual activist, much less a sexual imperialist. A busy scribbler, not particularly gregarious, who spent three-fourths of every working day talking to himself, so to speak, and in the other fourth enjoyed athletics, reading, and the company of a friend or two, with one of whom he was usually in love. The most serious since '64 had been energetic Marcie Blitzstein: To square his narrative debt he now briefly summarized that affair and its denouement. Nothing there to make a story from, much less to ennoble with the tragic view: Marcie Blitz would have found another man before he and *Story* reached Chesapeake Bay—and that man would be a good man, and a lucky.

Katherine Sherritt regarded Peter Sagamore across our cockpit in 1970 and does likewise now, a decade later. It looked to her, she declared back then with furrowed brow, as though we two really had little in common. He's a solitary; she likes people. She's an organizer (hasn't even told him yet about ASPS, which she and May founded in '69); he won't even join the Authors Guild or the American Association of University Professors. She's a citizen, a true participating democrat; he seldom even votes. He's fairly indifferent to and distant from his family; she loves hers busily, all save shitful Will. She's been given the best of everything since before she was born; as far as she can gather, he never had the best of anything until as an adult he achieved it for himself. What were we doing on that boat together?

Well, what are we? Peter asks her. Apples and Oranges hold their breath.

Kath's gray eyes flash. Just taking the long way home, she says as she said then, and reached and reaches out her left hand. Grave Peter does/ did with it what she did with his at the Katherine Anne Porter party: palm to palm, fingers up, tips kissing and then slowly spread—and then slips his between hers and squeezes. Just now she is too offspring-fraught to do more than smile; but at that shipboard squeeze in October '70 she was off her seat with a bound and upon him.

At this point our twin narratives had fetched us wing and wing through the warming forenoon, past Bloody Point aport and across the mouth of Eastern Bay; we were bearing directly for Poplar Island: a wooded, all but uninhabited little archipelago off the Eastern Shore. Anchor this boat or beach it, K. Sherritt ordered, thrusting our clasped hands deep into her lap; I'm going off in my Levi's. Growled Peter Me too: We'll run under the lee of Poplar there. Fifteen minutes. Too long, groaned K, working *his* lap now. Can't we drop the fucking anchor right here?

That is the one we dropped, in the lee of nothing, right there on the eight-foot shoal just north of Poplar Island. Bit of wave action, but good holding ground. Dropped anchor, sails, inhibitions. As Peter set the hook, Kath scrambled below; she was shoes off and out of her jeans by the time he came down the companionway. Got himself proper jumped, he did: She was at his belt, his fly. But *he* couldn't wait, either: dropped to his knees on the cabin sole, whisked her undies down—nope, canary yellow— grabbed both cool buttocks and buried his face in fleece. Kath clutched handfuls of his curls, she loves them, held his head there while she stepped out of those step-ins and pulled us both to the port settee. Bit of a flurry then: Each wanted *all* the other's duds off to see it again, inspect, savor; but who could hold still for that? He managed to kick free his Topsiders and ankle-down his jeans and drawers, and that was it: Our woman's knees were up, thighs open (socks on); with one hand she seized his jersey-front, his penis with the other; she pulled him on, and even as she lifted to take the thrust, we felt him fire at our first deep stroke.

Which was therefore also our last, for the time being. Unexpectedly shot, the man went limp at once and dropped laughing atop her. She was chuckling too, at our hurry, but hooked her legs behind his back, reached down under to hold him literally by the balls, and kept in place his wet little slip there while we kissed, nibbled ears, murmured Less Is More, and rubbed Katherine Shorter Sherritt to climax. Which, after all (Peter Sagamore could not avoid reflecting with some small chagrin), her friend May Jump could have fetched her to about as well.

However, we were unburdened then of urgency. Leisurely now, though it was not summertime in *Story*'s cabin, we finished undressing, each for the other's delectation, and fixed ourselves a lunch of tea and tuna, admiring each other's bodies at their ease in our slightly pitching craft. Much touching the while: her shoulderblade, his butt and cleft; light buss of collarbone, underside of breast. Few words. In mid-salad, Kate felt and announced a great gush from her of Peter's semen; not to stain the settee cushion, she tidily tucked her lunch napkin into the fold of her vulva and retired to the head compartment to clean up. Those several movements—tucking that napkin; sliding out from behind the dinette table, her hair down to her breasts; moving sideways between him and the table leaf to get through the narrow cabin to the head—restirred P.S. past leaving her alone. Nuzzled those buns as they passed before him (she'd expected he might); followed her in there, mighty close quarters; stood before her while she did her business—he wants to watch her do everything always, naked and clothed, he finds her ordinary movements that appealing. She was not displeased. Since there he hung, she cleaned him with a tissue for the pleasure of handling his equipment and then sipped him back to size.

No fans of the sexually explicit, our children ask whether that tuna salad ever got eaten. Sure it did, dearies, every bite, and our tea drunk dry, dishes washed, bodies more or less reclothed, sails reraised, anchor weighed and voyage voyaged, all in time's fullness. But there was no hurry; rarely has been since, from that hot first stroke to this present point of your parents' pen. We paused an age off Poplar Island, making second love; the Bay's geology was in greater haste than we. No slight meant to lesbian pleasures, but good May Jump cannot do *this,* or have *that* done, unless with artifice with which our Kate will have no truck. Less became More, More Most, in no hurry, and this time stayed that way a proper while. When presently we sailed again, though our vessel was the same, we were a different crew, upon a different voyage.

Where to? It scarcely mattered. On the original Columbus Day, light left the Chesapeake about six-thirty Algonquin time. Given daylight saving, not quite spent, and a two-o'clock second start, we had yet five hours plus to fetch wherever. Fifteen miles to Nopoint Point at, say, four knots in the easy air, less something for the tide (now turned), gives home by dark if we had an engine to push us through Knapps Narrows into the Choptank. Said happy Kate Who cares? We were beside ourselves in *Story*'s cockpit with satisfaction. The forecast was clear; the wind iffy. We could have taken the long way around, under Tilghman Island, and sailed the last leg after dark, wind permitting; but Peter was loath to risk a repeat of last month's fog. What's more, if May'd done us her favor, wouldn't the Sherritts have the Coast Guard out in force by dusk?

Well, yes. Unable to worry, but resolved not to worry others, we decided to heave to off the Narrows and hitch a ride through behind the first boat willing to tow us, dropping off just before the bridge to pay-phone Hank and Irm. If we could then scrounge a second tow out into the river, we'd aim for Nopoint Point as long as the breeze held, or scull to the nearest shelter should it fail. If we could not (scrounge a second tow), we'd either ride the tide back into the Bay and anchor for the night in empty Poplar Island Harbor or leave *Story* tied up where she is, near this hypothetical pay-phone, and sleep aboard.

Alternatively, of course, we could have asked the Sherritts to send a car for Kate or both of us; it's not a long drive, and Peter could have gone his way next morning. But we knew we weren't going to do that: We'd too much yet to say to each other, even in word language, before we rejoined the world. We had scarcely broached e.g. the weighty subjects of library science and literary art: how we had got ourselves involved therein and what we hoped to accomplish. Hadn't touched What next? with which our hearts were full. Oh, we scrounged those tows, both the first and the second—first behind an obliging oysterman coming home from work, who likely had no use for pleasure sailors but thought we needed help; second behind an elegant Canadian yawl en leisurely route from Toronto down the Intracoastal to winter in Florida—and Kath made her call (no May at Nopoint Point, but she had faithfully phoned the Sherritts, and so K was glad *she* did: told Mom and Dad she'd get there when she got there, not to worry, and she loved them; tried to call May as well: line busy). But as we rode out then behind *Moonraker, Dawn Treader,* Whatever (the oysterman had been *Rosie B. Giles*), we were arms around each other and grinning, not at hokey yacht names. There was indeed just enough breeze yet to sail. When *Sundance* dropped our line at Peter's signal and puttered off eastward into the wide Choptank, Kate hung a left and aimed us north, toward Harris Creek.

Where to? our man called back from the mast. She'd been enjoying the sight of him working there, barefoot and shirtless now in Indian-summer late afternoon: raising sails, coiling with easy motion halyards and towline. She was thinking things, too—making comparisons, in fact—and didn't answer him right off. He admired the way she handled herself there in the cockpit, steering with one brown leg while she hauled in jib and mainsheets. She's barefoot too, jeans rolled to the knee, denim shirttail out and knotted in front, sleeves rolled, top three or four buttons open. Good Marcie B. had been strictly a fair-weather sailor; this one he could imagine weathering storms. He was pleased to stay put awhile and watch her trim our sails; push her hair back and check windvane, shoreline, compass, chart. She saw him watching her. Smiled. Said Dun Cove?

THAT'S THE END OF OUR STORY?

ask To and Fro, disappointed: the story of Day Zero in Dun Cove?

Nope: That's its beginning. At this point in Nineteen Eighty, our paired narratives have fetched us through dinner and cleanup; we're back in the cockpit at half after eight, enjoying the warm last light and considering yet another family swim. It goes without saying that between Peter Sagamore and Katherine Sherritt, the long story we've just told goes without telling: We have reminisced, in fact but nowise in full, about our meet and our remeet, our first Chesapeake night together, here aboard *Story* here in Dun Cove, which led to a weekend which led to much more and which is not done yet, though its culmination may be said to be yourselves. But in October Seventy it was just four-thirty when we ghosted out of Harris Creek into this cove, turned right, sculled up into the fork, and dropped anchor for the night in approximately this very spot. Couple of hours of daylight left, but we wanted our attention free of sailing. A few other yachts rode at anchor; a few more might yet come in; but that time of year there's privacy aplenty. Then as now it was warm enough to swim, though the autumn air would cool fast as the sun set. The sea nettles, however, were at fleet strength. The water was theirs; even the canvas bucketfuls we would haul up for foredeck showers must be inspected for medusae before we dumped them on each other's goosebumped skin.

That is what soon we did, *pour le sport* and because a warm day's sail is well washed off. But at first, distracted now by neither boat-tending nor imperious desire, we shared a short self-conscious spell, a different sort of What next. Anchor down, sails furled, Dun Cove examined and agreed to be mighty handsome but alas unswimmable, we sat about wondering, until, without realizing what she was doing, Sherritt set Sagamore a test. So what do you think? she found herself asking when our eyes next met across this famous cockpit. She could scarcely herself have said about what, much less have understood that About what? would have been the wrong reply— until her new lover smiled, held out both hands, and said I think so!

He was right. Unease dispersed; we resumed the dialogue that continues yet. God bless a sailboat! We chattered away now, as busy being new friends as lovers. In time, of course, our very animation would rearouse us: There was that pouch in Peter's pants, the peep of Kate's free breasts from her knotted workshirt, the rest of America to be discovered. We would soak, soap, and rinse each other's skin with buckets of Dun Cove; go off again like fireworks in the cabin—but you've had enough of that for this chapter. Eventually we'd settle down, congratulate ourselves with wine upon our good fortune, make late dinner, even sleep (not well) in each other's arms in *Story*'s largest too-small berth. Would we go together then tomorrow to Nopoint Point? Introduce Pete to Hank and Irm and Chip, and spend the holiday weekend there, pretty obviously lovers? Would we in fact leave *Story* moored in Sherritt Cove, borrow a spare car to get back across the Bay, and do our voyage in reverse the following weekend? Would we, however, in that four-day interval, crave each other's company to the point of long nightly phone calls and a Thursday dinner date? Would we, on the homeward sail, weather our first foul weather of both sorts (rain, plus a thoughtless crack of Peter's re May that fired into anger K's self-reproach at having just quarreled with her over the obvious subject), so satisfactorily that we understood by weekend's end that we wanted to be together much much more? Were we, on the strength of one week's reacquaintance, ready to begin a life together?

I think so!

UH-OH.

Off to bed now, Mother Kate says to our brood; but just as they begin to settle down in her hold, Peter goes Uh-oh. He's looking south, down-fork, from where a warm light air is just beginning to stir and swing us. Katherine looks too, and lets go a Lithuanian obscenity—she picks these things up in her line of work—that sounds something like "roopoogee" and means something like "pigdogdamn" at sight of a familiar big blue-and-white center-cockpit double-headsail ketch gliding into Dun Cove in the waning light. That will be Irma there at the wheel, though we can barely make her out; Andrew on the bowsprit (transferred from the chase boat by Bobby Henry en route home) unlashing the anchor; Henry Sherritt manning the seven-by-fifties. Presumably he espies us; *Katydid IV* swings up our way. Demonstrative Kath hollers Double damn! and springs to our foredeck, alarming the household; does the TV trick again, peeling out of maternity shorts and halter and exposing herself to broad view, feet apart and arms akimbo. She calls back to Peter to come do likewise; help; they've probably got Jack Bass aboard too, in case she delivers in Dun Cove. But Pete won't return overzealous generosity with offense. Thinking of shrug-shouldered Fritz and Nora, he shakes his head, fetches out our own bin-oculars, watches amused to see who wins.

It is a standoff. *Katydid* steams close enough for Hank to see what his daughter's not wearing; sharp-eyed Irm and bright-eyed Andy, forewarned by the afternoon preview, have guessed already. Signals are given; the ketch slows in reverse. Henry Sherritt raises the binocs again, quickly puts them down, picks up the cockpit mike, realizes we're not going to be tuned in, maybe considers the hailer (there's a loudspeaker at his mainmast spreaders for hailing purposes and giving foredeck instructions in noisy weather), says something in exasperated Episcopalian. Not for the first time, Peter wonders why they do not stand their ground, come right along-side if they want to: It's just their naked, pregnant, thirty-nine-year-old willful daughter, and Chip is beyond reembarrassing in this particular; he's grinning and waving at us. Let the naughty girl beaver their bowsprit, if that's her pleasure; Hank ought to cluck tongue and proceed with the evening. But Kate knows her dad: *K IV* withdraws a discreet way down-cove and anchors, still within view but at soft-focus range, from where one can tell at seven magnifications that a person's naked, but can't really *see* anything.

I swear! K cries moving aft, annoyed nearly to tears. P gives her a hand

and says Look *now.* Sure enough, a sleek Ericson sloop, Jack and Joan Bass's *Off Call,* is sliding in to raft up with *K IV.* Relax, Peter advises, and she really tries to, but one can't do that, *try* to relax. Wails Katherine Why don't they leave us *alone?* Her husband, still thinking of his indifferent parenting, reminds her We know why.

So she does in fact manage to calm down by the time Andrew Sherritt reaches us on his Windsurfer (that southerly has settled in now, balmy, steady). Her brother rounds up two yards astern, not to bang us; calls Hi; and in a display of sailboardsmanship even manages to lower mast, boom, and sail into the water without losing his balance. He's wearing a ski belt and a T-shirt with the legend HEDONISTS HAVE MORE FUN; we've heard that before. Hi yourself, his sister says, slumped glum in her seat: Come aboard if you want; I'll put clothes on. Sure enough, now-worldly Andy says not for *his* sake; if he was his dad, he'd've thrown a moon right back at her. Says Peter Good man; says Katherine If you *were* Dad: subjunctive mood. Couldn't they park in some other creek? You're too hard on them, Chip chides, still balancing his skinny body on the drifting board; why not come over and be nice? Peter Sagamore smiles at his wife. She's smiling too now, but says No, and they're not to waste time radioing, either; Andrew may report that she's sorry again for misbehaving again, but she'll do it again if they crowd us again, even if she has to be sorry again again. It's privacy or privates.

The boy shrugs, almost goes over. He and the board are drifting up-fork. Want to windsurf, Pete? There's no nettles. The man does indeed. Reading his muscles, Kath says Do it; it's a perfect evening; my time will come. She pulls a towel over her lap for Andy's benefit when the men change places, but doesn't bother covering her breasts. The light's going; anyhow, anytime now there'll be a suckling suckling each. Chip drips aboard, squeezes out and hangs up his T-shirt—a present from May Jump from Ocean City, he announces—dries off, digs a Coke from the icebox, lounges on Peter's seat, and, shivering under a towel, asks Kath questions about James Joyce's early short story "Araby," which he has read several times that afternoon at our recent suggestion. He understands that times were different then; even so, *that* twelve- or thirteen-year-old boy was a real dork.

You've never felt shy with girls yourself? his sister queries. In over your head? Or worked up in a way that you realize you're not experienced enough yet to handle? She doesn't mean just sex; she means what the lad in the story *feels* for his friend's older sister but can't effectively follow up on. You know: first love.

Yeah, Andy knows all that: He's felt stuff like that, and he guesses Joyce portrays it pretty well. Katherine smiles at that "portrays." Andrew thinks he caught most of the symbolism, too (Kate's still smiling—but it turns out that in fact he did. Under her and Peter's tutelage, Chip Sherritt is a closer reader than any English teacher he'll likely have till his second year of college). What strikes him as dorky about Joyce's *protagonist* is that when he discussed the story with his father just now on the way to Dun Cove—

You talked about James Joyce's "Araby" with Dad? Sure I did. Dad and I discuss stuff. Dad's no dork, Kate. Well of course he's no dork; but early-modernist lit is hardly Daddy's long suit. Says bridge-learning Andrew A good player knows how to play his short suits as well as his long ones. Katherine squeezes her brother's hand—they're holding hands across the cockpit—and says How old did you say you are? But back to Daddy and dorks.

Math-minded Henry Sherritt, she learns now, had been less interested in the "Araby" boy's preadolescent agonies than in the story's financial transactions, and had set his son the following arithmetical problem: The orphan lad's uncle in Joyce's story gives the boy a florin to go to the Dublin bazaar called Araby in pursuit of a love token for the girl with whose image the boy is infatuated. He takes a train across town, reaches the bazaar just before closing time, pays his admission, comes to realize the futility of his errand, and, as "the two pennies fall against the sixpence in his pocket," experiences an epiphany of humiliation. *Now,* had asked Henry Sherritt: Given the pre-decimal currency of the time, in which a florin (two shillings) equalled twenty-four pence, and assuming that the boy had no money of his own, and further that his return train-fare would be the same unspecified amount as his fare to Araby: (1) How much was round-trip fare from Dublin's North Richmond Street to the bazaar and back in 1894, the year of the action? And (2) how much would the boy have had to spend on a gift for "Mangan's sister" if he hadn't been unmanned by his excursion into the adult world?

Holy mother of God, breathes Kate, wishing Peter were here to hear. But Peter has of course windsurfed down to *Katydid IV* and *Off Call* to be nice, inasmuch as he *is* nice, and enjoys his parents-in-law and the Basses. I could never even figure a London restaurant tip till the Brits went decimal. Fifteen percent of four pounds three shillings tuppence! So?

Says Chip The kid has to pay a shilling to get in, because the sixpenny entrance is closed. That's a symbol right there, right? The sixpenny entrance must have been the kids' entrance, and he has to pay the grown-ups' price of admission. Anyhow, there goes twelvepence: half his florin. Since he has two pennies and a sixpence left in his pocket, the train fare out must have been fourpence, and if the train fare home is another four, he's only got fourpence to buy his gift for Mangan's sister.

Corrects wowed Kath Not *only got* fourpence, Chipper: *got only* fourpence.

That's what struck bright-green-eyed Andrew Sherritt as dorky: Even allowing for inflation, what did the kid think he was going to find for fourpence, or even for ten if he hadn't had to pay the extra admission? Dad said maybe the kid thought his uncle was going to give him more than one florin; but we agreed that a florin's about right for the time and the occasion and the social class. Anyhow the kid didn't seem disappointed to get it, and once he had it he should've done his arithmetic down the road. Plus we wondered how come the dork didn't have a penny to his name for such a big-deal errand. We'd just been going over my finances.

Says smiling K So you and Daddy didn't think much of the story. I'm not crazy about it myself, but it's one of Peter's favorites.

Says Andrew I'll appreciate it better when I'm older. Like that first-person narrator remembering an experience that still burns his buns maybe twenty years later, when he's a grown man. I agree with Pete that the narrative viewpoint is the bottom line of that story.

You do.

They speak of other things and not at all, soaking the evening in. P presently glides back in the dark and splashes down with a laugh, less gracefully than his brother-in-law. Your options, he calls to Andy from the water, are to sleep here tonight or sail this thing back now so your folks can quit worrying that you'll drown in the dark. Sighs Kate You can stay; but Chip digs night windsurfing. He dons his wet T-shirt, joins Peter overside, belts up, scrambles onto the board, hauls mast and sail out of the water, calls good night, grabs the wishbone, and sets off upwind. Katherine keeps his sail in sight with our largest flashlight as he tacks easily back and forth toward *Off Call* and *Katydid IV,* lit up for him to steer to. Such a fine moon rises as he draws near that an hour later no lights would have been needed: Even without the binoculars, we can see the two rafted boats in silhouette a quarter-mile off.

By then—so delicious is the air, the night—K has joined her friend for yet another swim: Only afloat is she free of the weight of her great belly. Hank says that if you're going to show it to everybody, you should rent the space for advertising, Peter reports, like the Goodyear blimp. The south wind soughs at eight and ten knots through the woods onshore; the water is perfectly comfortable, silky on our skin. There are noctilucae: microscopic algae that phosphoresce with our every motion, sparkling our bodies and the water round about us. There are luminescing jellyfish— untentacled, harmless, magical—glowing like incandescent lemons in our wake as we tickle by. No human life has many such evenings; most, we suppose, have none. Peter marvels duly at the "Araby" dork story. But that moon!

Proposes Kath We could just sneak out. We're back aboard now, splitting unequally a split of champagne by way of nightcap (that sip of alcohol won't hurt you, kids) and listening to one barn owl and two whippoorwills. Sail all night. Give 'em the slip. Replies her husband Irresponsible. It's going to be *brunch,* then, you know, Kate reminds him. Or they'll board us with chafing dishes. Crepes, melon balls. I can't stand it.

Grins he It is a hardship.

Well, it is, in its tiny way. Why *can't* we just sail for a while like that couple in our story, whither the wind listeth, till further notice from down-stairs? Our last duetude until apostrophe Ninety-eight?

Muses Peter Hm. But sighs: Irresponsible.

We could radio home twice a day, to keep them from worrying. *Three* times a day. At the teeniest sign of anything, we get on the horn and head for the nearest marina. Rough weather, we scoot for shelter or don't start out.

She's serious. It's not as if we're in mid-Atlantic, she points out. Chesapeake *Bay,* for Christ's sake: a Mickey Mouse crack in the coastline.

Hm.

DAY 1:
DUN COVE TO DUN COVE

PYTHON AND CHICKENS.

In the reptile house of the Berliner Zoologischer Garten, in a glass cage the size of a small room, lived a large python. As Peter Sagamore and Katherine Sherritt watched, a carrot-haired, milky-skinned zoo attendant put into that cage three white leghorn chickens, who flapped and fluttered and fussed for a minute and then clucked and pecked contentedly about the cage floor, separately and together. Flaked down and torpid in a corner, the python paid his guests no apparent heed for a very considerable while. The life of the reptile house went on round about the cage, the life of the zoo and its attendants round about the reptile house, the life of Berlin round about the zoo.

We watched.

In time the python leisurely uncoiled and glided forth. The chickens clucked, moved slightly away, and went on with their business, until with surprising swiftness and economy of motion the python seized one of their number. White feathers flew; the cage rang with hen screams: those of the victim, held fast and dying now in the python's jaws, and those also of its companions, thrashing terrified about the cage. Then only the companions squawked, for the python, with a movement almost too quick to follow, shifted its bite, unhinged its lower jaw, and began the unhurried process of swallowing its prey alive, headfirst. For a full half-minute the other chickens flailed from corner to corner, beating their wings against the glass walls, alarming themselves further with their own attempts to flee. But before their hapless fellow, feet still twitching, had entirely disappeared from view, they were back to their scratch and peck, their strut and cluck.

One of them perched sometimes upon the very back of the python, torpid again now with the great labor of digestion.

At 0630, Monday, 16 June 1980, a brief thundershower wakes Peter Sagamore: Yesterday's weather front is still slowly passing through Maryland. *Story* rocks and rustles but slightly in the associated wind; we're in the lee of trees on the fork's west bank. The rain is cozy upon our deck and cabin-top; we closed the forward hatch and companionway slide at bedtime against this forecast possibility, and not enough rain blows back through the companionway proper to require further buttoning up. Snug in the quarterberth, P enjoys light drizzle in his face while the thunder moves off, and reflects upon his vivid, unsettling dream.

Were you ever in the Berlin Zoo? he asks quietly through the cabin, not to wake Katherine if she happens to be still asleep. Peter himself has never visited that city; is only assuming that it has, in fact, a zoo. His friend replies from the forward V-berth Sure. She's been awake for a while, listening to the little storm, thinking sober thoughts and wishing Up and At 'Em wouldn't start their morning soccer practice before sunup. It's right by the Tiergarten, off one end of the Kurfürstendamm. Once when the folks and I were touring West Berlin it was just this time of year, but the weather was so cold we had to take shelter in the crocodile house. The only heated room we could find.

We have lived together too long for her to ask Why do you ask? Over breakfast we share dreams; this morning K can't quite remember hers, though she remembers having had some. P's, we agree, was inspired by that item in that ad-lib catalogue of what Whatsername gave birth to in our prologue—where, however, those hens were Plymouth Rocks instead of white leghorns, weren't they. Anyhow, says K, you dreamed a real dream. That's a good sign, no?

We are pleased to take it so to be. Perhaps because he is or has been a professional waking dreamer, so to speak, Peter Sagamore's night dreams are normally dull stuff indeed. Much of the time they're scarcely even visual, much less exciting: spelled-out words and punctuation, scanning by as on a trans-lux, or a neutral voice speaking like a proofreader in his skull: *Anyhow comma says K comma* et cetera. But at anchor aboard *Story*, particularly on the early nights of a cruise, we both tend to dream more lively and narratively coherent dreams, and to recollect them better, as it is said one does if one decides to record and report them. More anon.

Gray day, the forecast unpromising: intermittent rain, a raw stiffening northwesterly, chance of further thundershowers. We nibble strawberries, chew croissants, swallow coffee, speak little. Yesterday's lark seems now to each of us just that; yet the stakes remain as high as they are vague and still incompletely exposed. We don't know.

Through white mist rising from Dun Cove, we see *Off Call* unraft and motor out, doubtless homeward bound. *Katydid IV* stays put. We do not talk about it, but after breakfast, while Peter on the can reads *faute de mieux* the *U.S. Coast Pilot 3: Atlantic Coast: Sandy Hook to Cape Henry,* he hears Katherine say affably to her parents by VHF that she doesn't care, we're heading out anyhow for a few days, no destination, whither the wind listeth et cetera over. Says Henry Sherritt Whither the wind listeth today is right back home, Katie. Anyhow upriver, not out to open water.

Replies Kath Yes, well. But I guess we'll give it a try, Dad. No trip should begin by going backward.

Hank requests a word with Peter. K half teases, half bristles: The old man-to-man thing? Her father says Yup. And then to Peter, who has emerged from the head, What exactly are you-all up to? Instead of quite answering, Peter says I guess we'll try the Narrows, Hank, while the wind's light and the tide's with us. If we can't get through or the weather blows up, we'll run back and regroup. Otherwise we'll tuck in behind Poplar Island and call you from there about mid-morning.

We are a touch surprised at our firmness of purpose, considering. Irma, we suppose, is unhappy, but Henry Sherritt is impressed enough to say merely that he trusts we won't object to *K IV*'s standing by at this end till we've either shat or got off the pot, excuse him. Says Katherine I object. Says Peter Overruled. Overruled, Hank and Irma agree. Andrew Sherritt comes to *Katydid*'s microphone and says Hi, Kath; hi, Pete; overruled. Democracy, sighs Katherine; I swear.

The clear purpose of Knapps Narrows in the universe is to put the screws to our principles and projects; to test whether we're still serious. How many times already in our narrative have we tried to get through that mile-long cut, here to there or there to here, and failed, or nearly, for want of engine? Okay, Knapps Narrows, here we come again, despite last evening's prudent weather-amendment: About nine, we suit up in foul-weather gear, secure everything below and on deck, weigh anchor, raise sail under the sodden overcast, and ride out of Dun Cove on a light northwesterly that seems less light already once we're into the broader waters of Harris Creek. *Katydid IV* powers out in our wake, Irma and Katherine chatting by radio as busily downstream as they had chatted up. Henry means literally to stand by at the green day-beacons off the east end of the narrows. You'd think we're setting out for Portugal, Kate complains. Eleven months pregnant, Irma retorts, you shouldn't set out farther than our swimming pool.

As Peter has reckoned, we'll have to short-tack back and forth up the first half-mile of the narrows, to the bridge. Once we're through it, a single starboard tack should fetch us the remaining half-mile out into the Chesapeake. On any weekend in the boating season, traffic in the channel would make tacking through it unfeasible; on a drizzly Monday there'll be few or no pleasure craft abroad, and the working watermen will have cleared the narrows hours since. We bet we can do it, bridge-tender willing; then, we promise ourselves, we'll reconsider what we're up to.

But that wind is piping up. At the last minute before committing us to the passage, Peter tucks a reef in the mainsail; Kate calls the bridge-tender as we approach. It is the one we have come to know, the patient one,

Howard: He recognizes *Story* and reminds us, as has become his habit, that he knew Peter's dad, yes indeedy, Capn Fritz, God bless him, over. We promise to make only one pass this time. No sweat, says Howard as he raises the draw, and nothing coming our way from bayside. He'll keep the lift open till he's sure we've got a purchase on the wind—Happy phrase, thinks P—and won't be blown back through. But he warns us that it is right rough out there this morning.

With the tide's help, we coast easily through the draw. Peter tucks a second reef in the main, and we strap life jackets clumsily over our slickers. Rain resumes, light but pelting in the wind that whistles now through shrouds and stays as we clear the west end of Knapps Narrows.

Howard was right: The lee of the land has been uncommonly deceptive. To leave secluded for open water when that water has a bit of a chop on it is always gut-tightening; pleasurably so, as a rule. But today those brown-and-pewter seas—steep, short, breaking—roll under the dirty sky straight at us, rank on rank as far as we can see, which is not far. Loudly into the wind, Kate says Gulp. Pete agrees.

Our problem is that we must negotiate that narrow channel through shoals on both sides for another half-mile of exposed water before we can turn either up- or downwind: no joke at all in those two- and three-foot seas, with no engine to help us and not another boat in sight.

We have been foolish.

This comes clear in five rough minutes of slamming into those waves, each one stalling our forward motion, knocking us to leeward, drenching us with cold salt spray. Katherine says nothing, but is truly frightened, not least by the tight concern in Peter's face. The kids huddle and cling like a passel of possums or steerage immigrants in a storm. In the first of those minutes, Peter understands that we must retreat; it takes him the other four, of supremely watchful seamanship, to gauge the right moment for coming about in a situation that will permit us no second try. Coming about, he calls hopefully when that moment arrives: A puff gives us just enough drive at the crest of one sea to bring *Story*'s bow through the eye of the wind, so that the next sea slams us the rest of the way around. Steering with his knees, P quickly eases the sheets for our run back into Knapps Narrows. A deft, even masterly bit of skippership, this whole maneuver, in which, however, our skipper takes small satisfaction, so wretched does he feel for having thus exposed us at all. Would he ever have, he wonders, if life in the First Guest Cottage had not so relieved us lately of responsibility for ourselves? He asks Kate to take the tiller now as we swoosh back into the sheltered narrows, our dinghy surfing left and right behind us down the following seas; he radios first Howard and then Hank Sherritt that we've packed it in, are heading them-ward. Not to worry, Irm. Do have that draw up, Howard, so's not to oblige us to kill our headway as we once more balance wind against tide.

A DELICATE MOMENT IN ANY VENTURE

Irma won't, for the present. Howard does. There is the now-familiar moment in the lee of the drawbridge when the tide offers to carry us astern before *Story* regains a purchase on the wind. Who cares? The spirit's gone out of our adventure like the fizz from stale champagne. Here wind and water are easy again; the rain stops to congratulate us for coming to our senses, however belatedly. Peter peels out of his life vest and foul-weather top and takes the helm so that Kate can do likewise. Out yonder where Knapps Narrows and Harris Creek conflue into the huge Choptank, *Katydid IV* rides serenely at anchor. We feel chastened, childish, low.

Here is a delicate moment in any venture. Mighty tempting now to pack it in altogether, as surely Hank and Irma expect we shall, and go tails between legs back to the First Guest Cottage: to comfort, safety, and unresponsibility except to the imminent offspring. Back to work.

And there, reader, is the rub. Our man is no boy; would he ever imaginably have put his wife and our all-but-delivered family at risk; would Katherine ever imaginably have let herself and them be so put, not to mention initiating the adventure that so put them; would we be spinning out a book of some size thereabout, called *The Tidewater Tales: A Novel*—if this were merely one instance more of restless richies amusing themselves until the doctor comes? *The storymaker Peter Sagamore is stuck:* For seven several reasons, if not nine, the man literally does not know where he will go next, what do; and that state of affairs terrifies him, when he looks it in the eye. It frightens the bejesus out of K. S. Sherritt, too. What you're reading, reader, is P's and K's *story*. But what husband and wife are living, and trying rather desperately just now without success to read ahead in, is not their story. It's their life.

MORE ON THIS SUBJECT, BUT NOT FROM THE SAME SOURCE

A wave of remarkable despond breaks over us as we exit the narrows and head for the anchored ketch. We profoundly do not want to follow it back to Nopoint Point and the First Guest Cottage. Neither do we now want to proceed with our whimsical, yes, but nonetheless fairly desperate expedition. No need to speak further just here of the reasons; we don't want to do anything that we can think of to do next. More than halfway to *K IV,* Peter Sagamore, who has been standing expressionless at the tiller, lets go of it with a grunt, sits down heavily on the cockpit seat, puts his head in his hands. *Story* rounds up by itself into the wind and luffs quietly. Alarmed by this extraordinary irresolution—unknown among Sherritts and by no means characteristic of Sagamores—Katherine nevertheless understands that for her to take the helm herself at this volatile moment (as she had done at a less volatile one ten years before, near this very spot) would be an entire error. But does going whither the wind listeth include drifting into a day beacon, or down upon *Katydid IV,* or right aground?

Here is a moment when, in stories, something happens because it must: Mere narrative pressure, dramaturgical suction—manifest in such expressions as *Just then,* or *Suddenly,* or *Even as she looked desperately about her for some sign*—calls The Next Thing into existence, and the narrative proceeds for good or ill. That is our art's great lie (one of them), for in fact we and our little craft really can simply wash ashore or be ignominiously taken in tow by an uncomprehending Hank and Irma, who will come to realize with dismay that, under our apparently irresponsible larkishness, their able son-in-law was desperate almost to the point of literal catatonia; their never-before-nonplussed daughter so anxious on his, on our, account that she simply can do nothing about the situation and its maybe seven several causes.

As a child in the pre-television 1940s, on the family's twice-a-month expeditions from Hoopers Island up to Cambridge, when he and his brother and sister were sometimes treated to a movie at Schine's Arcade Theater, Peter Sagamore intuited that the hero of no matter how perilous a wartime shoot-'em-up was by the nature of fiction rendered *perfectly safe,* from death if not from injury, right up to the climax of the story at least: as safe as Styx-dipped Achilles in the first nine years of the Trojan War. Whereas in fact gray rainy nature can not only kill us, as she will eventually in any case, but kill us quite stupidly, meaninglessly, interrupting our story between any two of its words to smash us into hamburger with a jackknifed trailer-truck, or eat us leisurely alive with cancer apropos of nothing, or in any of her million ways derail our lives without foreshadow or significance. Perhaps this fact of life goes without saying; perhaps not. At age seven and eight, Peter Sagamore tried explaining it and its corollaries to his parents: how John Wayne, at the beginning of some film they had just seen together, might imaginably have flung himself parachuteless from a B-17 at 15,000 feet or under the wheels of an express train without fear of dying, since if he died there could have been no movie, and there *was* a movie. Said Fritz I spect you're right. Nora felt the boy's brow for fever. Twenty years later P mentioned it amused to Katherine Sherritt, who understood immediately what he meant but confessed to its never having occurred to her. Our conversation then was apropos a "story" in Peter's notebook called "Apocalypse," never submitted for publication and here printed for the first time, in its entirety:

APOCALYPSE

One drizzly Baltimore November forenoon, as from an upstairs work-room window of our little house I mused over the neighbors' lawns—some raked clean, some still leaf-littered—and considered whether

For that, Peter had explained, is how—in the first-person narrative view-point from which each of us leads life—the world can end, whether at that *whether* "I" am felled by a coronary or thermonuclearly incinerated by an ICBM meant for Washington, D.C., but slightly diverted by a minuscule error in its inertial guidance system. The twin facts are (first) that we are on the one hand so lulled by ubiquitous narrative convention that we may indeed forget, reading a realistic story, that in it even the meaningless is meaningful, it having been put there by the author just to remind us that real life comprises much meaninglessness. When, in a story, nothing happens next, that is the thing that happens next: The nothing becomes a thing, which, we may be sure, the author will quickly cause to be followed by the *next* thing, a more conventionally dramatic thing, and on goes the story. Whereas (second) in fact, nothing is no thing, and our story does not at all necessarily go on, for the reason that our lives are not stories.

THE STORY OF OUR LIFE IS NOT OUR LIFE. IT IS OUR STORY.

And in our story, Katherine Shorter Sherritt Sagamore looks about us now in the most desperation she can recall having entertained since the day (much worse than this one, to be sure) Porter "Poonie" Baldwin, Jr., held a cocked and loaded pistol to the nape of her neck and, among other terrorizings, forced her rectum. The expression on her face so startles her mother, watching our non-progress through *K IV*'s binoculars, that Irma drops those dandy Fujinon precision opticals—fortunately they are sheathed in rubber, and the lanyard is around her neck—and grips the teak cockpit coaming, her own face drained. And, crazily, there bobs by *Story*'s drifting bow just then ... *a container*—a Day-Glo orange canister, actually— which in fact, taking it maybe for a crab-pot buoy, Kate scarcely registers in her distress.

But look again: The thing's free-floating, and it's the shape and color of a popular brand of marine signal canister. Crab-pot buoys aren't that. Look, she says to Peter, and dumbly points. Distress-flare canister. Wonder what's in it.

He looks; looks dumbly back. USCG-approved Alert-and-Locate-signal canister, so what, we have one already. The house is on fire; the ship's going down; who needs a distress-flare canister?

But the thing has done its narrative job, which was to be The Next Thing. Our low trance is broken. Says Kathy dully, but with resolve, Let's go back up to Dun Cove and regroup, okay?

BACK TO DUN COVE, OKAY?

Back to Dun Cove, okay?

On her second saying, Peter Sagamore gives his head a vigorous shake. Yeah, sure: Dun Cove, regroup. On with the story.

By the way, says K, that canister there might really have something in it besides search-and-locate signals. Make a pass by and let's see; then I'll call Mom and Dad.

We do, the man of us still dazed by his unexpected sudden view over the edge of the known world. Be it understood, friends, that what has shaken and appalled him is *not* his having his nose rubbed in the unpredictability of his personal future: the reminder that while what *he* doubtless had in mind for himself, when he thought about it at all, was a fairly uninterrupted flow of professional inspirations large and small—fairly smoothly turned into paragraphs and public pages, fairly regularly enlarging his readership and repute into a fairly successful and honored elder age enriched by long and happy marriage—what fate might have in store for him is early poop-out, ever-dwindling reputation, perhaps untimely demise, perhaps disease, failed marriage, wretched parenthood, death of spouse or child, psychological ruin, derelict old age, not to mention explosion of world. Who knew? Such dark night thoughts by day are *not* what had P momentarily there by the Adam's apple; anyhow not purely and simply. It was rather the reminder of what so goes without saying that we are ever forgetful of it: that Nature is not naturally narrative; that whatever the nature of natural cause and effect, it is not except by accident dramatically meaningful. K. S. Sherritt might yet miscarry as before or give birth to monsters, or she might healthily deliver a brace or two of dear and robust babies: Dancer and Prancer, Cause and Effect, Pure and Simple. Peter Sagamore's biography might turn out to follow any of the paths aforementioned—and all will be equally "meaningless," inasmuch as in fact, so far as we can tell, we are not characters in a story.

Thanks be then for our story, in which we are! In which now we fish that Day-Glo canister out of Harris Creek with a crabnet; try to unscrew its top to see whether the thing's full of old flares or seawater or what; find out we can't. (It's Kath who's trying it; Pete's still unfocused. She hands it to him; he wrenches the top loose in one motion and hands it back to her. Perpend this detail.) Now she finishes unscrewing the top, looks in, says Wow, and fishes forth a worn-out black beret—the emperor's old clothes?—which she promptly pops onto her head, right dashing she looks in it, too, and . . . what has she here? A rubber-banded roll of ruled, three-ring loose-leaf binder paper sealed up in a transparent plastic food-storage bag, secured with a twist-tie? Hey, wow, she says: a real live message in a bottle, and tries to read through the Baggie what looks to her to be a pen-scrawled title page. *EXEDUC,* is it? *EX-EDUCATION,* is it? Some joker is polluting our birth-waters with cranky pedagogical tracts?

She puts the whole business aside (P's still reviving; light rain resumes) and calls *K IV* to tell the folks we're heading back to Dun Cove to regroup, recoup, reconsider. Canister or no canister, message or no message, that irresolute, open-ended, vertiginous minute is still what's mainly upon our minds. Irm's on the binocs while Hank's on the radio: What's going on? What was in that thing you fetched up? Did Katherine check that hat for lice before she put it on?

Peter now believes he understands, by the way, his early-morning dream; in any case, shaking his head hard again, he sees a sense to it, even a parable.

THE PARABLE OF THE PYTHON AND THE CHICKENS

It is true, we agree, that legend on Chip Sherritt's T-shirt: Hedonists doubtless have more fun. What's more, those chickens in that python cage in that reptile house of that Berlin Zoo in that dream of Peter Sagamore's did well to go on chickening till their turn came, inasmuch as no amount of valor, organization, or ingenuity on their part could alter their particular fate. Pete in the busy whole cast of his mind, Kate in that still inner sanctum of her heart, agree with Robert Louis Stevenson that except for the ephemeral pleasures of sex and a few other satisfactions, the human facts of life and death and history are so dismaying that only some reflexive numbness or self-mesmerism keeps even the most favored of us from going screaming mad. A good morning's work, a fine afternoon's sailing, half an hour of love, a good dinner and a balmy evening's anchorage divert us, and we may be grateful for such diversion, inasmuch as the python does not go away. It is the sea we sail upon, the warp and woof of ongoing history, the very ground beneath our feet. The wonder then is not that courage, magnanimity, altruism, mercy, and the rest are rare; it is that here in the reptile house they occur at all.

So we reflect, beating steadily up-creek while K chats with *K IV*. She acknowledges, without detail, that it was hairy out there, all right, and announces our intention to wait out the weather in snug Dun Cove, reading relaxing eating reconsidering. You're sure you're all right, asks anxious

Irma, who will not soon forget what she saw in those binoculars. Says Katherine We're all right. Maybe not all *there,* but all right. Tell Chip we found a gen-you-wine message in a bottle, but we haven't read it yet.

Irma hopes it's not more naughtiness; Andrew has heard enough naughtiness for a while. Well, they guess they'll head on home; she hopes we'll follow soon. Wait: Daddy wants to talk to Peter. Katherine sighs and declares she enjoyed the sport of sailing a whole lot more back when *Story* had no two-way radio. Henry Sherritt's unamused voice says crisply Pete?

The age of word-processor technology is upon us, about to make *writing,* as Peter Sagamore and the author of our bottled manuscript have known it—the muscular cursive of pen on paper, connecting drawn letters into a literal flow of language—as quaint a handicraft as fletching or scrimshaw. Yet it still bemuses P.S. in 1980 to chat by wireless with a man he cannot see, in a bridge-tender's station around the bend or aboard a boat growing smaller astern, not to mention on the moon. He takes the microphone: Here, Hank. Over.

But Henry Sherritt can't think now just what it was he wanted to say. Katie's all right?

We raise eyebrows, but have no heart for irony. Instead of saying I'll ask her, P gently repeats our intention to make ourselves cozy till the weather improves and then do whatever seems appropriate to the situation, always keeping the homefolks posted. Just now we're going to make late lunch and read a good book. He goes further—calculatedly, Katherine sees in his expression as his eyes check hers: *Katydid* is welcome to raft up with us for the afternoon. . . .

No, well, they guess they'll head on home. We-all take care, now; over and out. Hold on: Chip wants to know did you read that message yet?

Katherine says It's a longie. In a Baggie, which she's looking at as she talks. Tell Chip there's a genie inside in the shape of a longhand manuscript called *SEX EDUCATION* colon *Play.* And tell Mom that the colon is the punctuation mark, not the large intestine. Over and out, now, Dad; we've got stuff to do.

Asks everybody aboard both vessels It's called what?

SEX EDUCATION: Play,

Katherine Sherritt Sagamore repeats, holding the bagged roll sideways in the gray light of the cabin. She has given it a turn to urge that title page into better view. Stage play? Foreplay? Recreation play? Don't ask her. Over and out and let's open this Baggie.

But extraordinary as they are, the contents of that canister are not our first concern. Kath keeps the beret on, but sets aside the roll of papers. Before we turn into Dun Cove we see *Katydid IV* make sail and stand upriver toward the Tred Avon; then here we are again, anchoring this time for variety's sake where the two forks join, the cove to ourselves on a rainy cool Monday. A few short tacks put us where we want to be; while Katherine dries off below, Peter luffs up, goes forward, drops and sets the anchor, lowers and furls the dripping sails, and rigs a boom tent to help keep rain out of the cabin. Kate's fixed lunch. We've food enough left to make shift for dinner, she announces; breakfast will be bread and coffee. After that, it's retreat or reprovision.

Lightly but seriously we kiss across the dinette table upon which our Baggied water-message sits as centerpiece, flanked by paper plates of Portuguese sardines, sliced purple onion, halved cherry tomatoes, wedges of Gouda, celery sticks, stoned-wheat crackers, paper cups of apple juice. Peter adds his foul-weather gear to hers in *Story*'s wet-locker, washes his hands, sits on the opposite settee. His wife looks good in that beat-up old beret.

Well. Another T-shirt motto, maybe? THIS IS THE FIRST SENTENCE OF THE REST OF OUR STORY? Proposes Katherine Let's don't talk about it.

All right. Though it's not our general way, at times there's much to be said for saying nothing. It *is* cozy in the little rain, no? The cabin's cool enough for jeans and sweatshirts. Peter's plenty worried, but you can't just go on being plenty worried. We munch lunch.

Aren't we going to open it?

Says Peter I've read enough manuscripts this semester, but he picks the thing up, reads its title through the plastic, undoes the twist-tie, plops the roll onto the table. Who can't wonder what *SEX EDUCATION: Play* might be and what it's doing with an old beret in an orange jug at the confluence of Harris Creek and Knapps Narrows?

What *I* wonder, says Katherine Sherritt—remembering how her husband had shortly before managed, with mere more muscle, the thousand-and-first thing in our history she's tried to do herself and couldn't, though she is no weakling—is not why God made men stronger than women in the first place, but why He goes on doing it when it's no longer useful for survival of the species, if it ever was. That proves He's male. Why couldn't I get that canister open? Hey, don't hog that water-message. Says Peter, dabbing at the sheaf of papers with his paper napkin, I'm not hogging; I'm blotting. That canister left a wet spot on the table. Kate complains You're reading, too. It's a playscript, P reports, adding that there is no God and that furthermore He didn't do what K says He did, make men stronger than women; what He did was distribute physical strength between the genders on a scale best represented by staggered brackets, thus (he puts the manuscript back down in the wet to make staggered brackets with his thumbs and forefingers, thus—[]—and Katherine snatches the moment to snatch the top page; snatches two or three by mistake; hands back all but the first, which she presumes he has perused to his satisfaction; all it says is *SEX EDUCATION: Play*). You're up near the top of that right-hand bracket. So you agree with Plato, Kate charges—echoing May Jump, who hates this particular passage in Book Five of the *Republic* because she fears it's true—that while a great many women are superior to a great many men in a great many respects, on the whole men are superior to women. Says Peter That proposition is a minefield of equivocations into which only a fool would blunder. Hey: This really is some kind of a playscript. Read it first, if you want to; I'm in no hurry.

Read, read, bids Katherine. But don't hog. And so for the next while, over lunch and after, as the universe continues its explosion and Earth spins upon its blood-greased axis through Monday, 16 June 1980, we read *SEX EDUCATION: Play.*

ACT I: THE CONFLUENCE

Scene 1: Shooting the Tube

K wants to know Since when do scenes in a play have titles? How would the audience see "The Confluence" and "Shooting the Tube"?

Bemused Peter, who's on page 2 already, says Read. Evidently this was meant to be a TV play. *Tube* could be the telly screen, no? But you'll see what else it is.

Katherine thinks it sounds like what we just did: shoot through Knapps Narrows into that confluence where we found this canister. And many's the time she's felt like shooting the Idiot Box at Nopoint Point. Let's not ever have one in our house, okay?

Says Peter Read; you'll dig it. It's about white-water rafting.

We read:

(Total darkness. Continuous sound of rushing water. JUNE'S *voice-over: a young woman's voice, excited but mainly businesslike, as if the speaker is dictating into a tape recorder or making radio transmission while attending to other business. Titles and credits appear on the dark screen during* JUNE'S *soliloquy, which is punctuated by the sounds and, gradually, the sight of her busy navigational maneuvers, like those of a self-contained white-water rafter.)*

Wonders Katherine *Self-contained?* But she does dig white-water stuff.

JUNE *(Voice-over)*: The end of this Tube can't be far off. The Branch current has slackened half a knot; there's a very dim light downstream at one five five degrees. *(We see the light: a faint spot in the center of the screen.)* Whoops . . . I'm spinning counterclockwise a bit . . . *(The spot of light moves accordingly.)* "Hard right and right along!" That does it. Full ahead now. *(She does something momentarily strenuous, then sings unmusically.)* Drifting and drea-ming . . . *(We hear a rush of water.)* That was a tricky one! *(She sings again.)* On-ward and down-ward . . .

Onward and downward, echoes Kate: That's us this morning.
Read, says Peter.

(The spot of light is now an area of light, holding fairly steady.)
JUNE: Definitely less current along here. Less spin, too. Easier to steer
now. Whoa . . . Ah. *(More officially)* Right Ovarium, Right Ovarium: This
is June Graduate Eighty, June Graduate Eighty, forty-eight hours out and
floating. Do you read me, Right Ovarium? Over.

Whoops Kathy: Right *Ovarium*?

JUNE *(Pauses, hand to ear. There is no reply.)*: Damn! *(Louder)* Ms. R?
Can you hear me? Your prize pupil J. G. Eighty says Damn it to hell!
Over? *(She pauses again, hand to ear, amused at her own impudence, and
sighs. Sounds of business.)* Now hear this, girls . . . *(Business)* This is your
class valedictorian and pride of our dear Right O., making her post-com-
mencement report from somewhere *way* down the Right Branch—*oof!* It
is mighty dark and lonesome down here, friends, just as Ms. R warned us
it would be. . . .

Says Katherine I get it: It's the Saint Deniston senior class play.

*(As JUNE speaks on, she begins to become dimly visible: a young woman
whose bare arms, legs, and head protrude from a light, flexible inflated
envelope, egg-white, diaphanous but tough, through which the rest of her
body will be discerned as the light improves. In this envelope she "floats"
as in a rubber raft, busily steering with movements of her legs and right arm
while speaking into her cupped left hand as if it held a microphone. JUNE
is fresh and somewhat delicate-appearing, but entirely competent, energetic,
even athletic.)*

Yay! says K: The Deniston Girl.

*(Indeed, one sees now that the terse, preoccupied tone of her soliloquy is
owing to her navigational activity: In addition to steering and speaking, JUNE
seems to be taking sights through her hands as through binoculars, closing
one eye to line up ranges or take bearings with her raised forefingers, logging
navigational data as if her finger were a pencil and her flotation-envelope a
writing surface. Foam or wavelets may now be seen on the surface around
her, moving downstream past rubbery boulders and soft stalagmites. They
and the smooth walls of the Tube reflect ripples of light, as does JUNE's
envelope. The effect is of a soft and resilient undergound watercourse.)*

K's never heard of navigating while you shoot rapids; you're too busy
staying right side up. And what's this *envelope*? P says if she doesn't stop
interrupting, we'll have to write her lines into the script.

JUNE: And it's mighty strange making these reports without knowing
whether anybody reads me or not. Speed three point five. Heading one
five zero. Now I know how Jan and April felt, calling home from clear

down at the Confluence and never knowing whether we could hear their good-byes.

KATHERINE: Jan? April? June?

JUNE *(Pauses, hand to ear):* Definitely some light ahead, at one five five magnetic. Can't estimate distance. *(She caroms expertly off a stalagmite.)* Wo-*ho!* Shooting the Tube is some terrific ride! Take those white-water seminars seriously, girls, and don't neglect night practice. Are you there, Ms. R? I'll hang a right at the Confluence, ma'am, like you taught us . . . *(She sweeps adroitly around a boulder.)* I mean *as* you taught us. *(She declaims.)* "Hang *tight* all *night,* then hard *right,* at first *light,* and you'll *sight* Mister—" Ouch! *(She bumps over a rock; grabs her backside.)* Well, sisters: I'll keep making these reports till Mister Right swims along or I'm Down and Out, whichever happens first. But I could use a word from home before I hit the Mainstream. *(Lightly and a touch waveringly, she sings.)* Some day my prince will come. . . . *(More strongly)* Some da-a-ay . . . *(Peering downstream, she breaks off to report urgently.)* Right Ovarium, Right Ovarium! This is Jay-Gee Eighty, June Graduate Eighty, Juliette Golf Eight Zero! I've got *Tube's End,* do you read me? I have definitely got Tube's End, dead ahead at one five zero! Plenty of light now. No hazards in sight; no sign of any Swimmers, either. *(She looks directly at the viewer.)* Now I can see past the Tube to the Confluence: loud echoing noise where the Right and Left Branches come together. *(We begin to hear the sound she describes.)* Current's picking up now, but it's easy to manage; I'm going to shoot it. Three point two knots. Three point five. There's the Confluence! *(The rushing sound crescendoes.)* Three point seven; four knots . . . Here comes your dream girl, Mister Right! Onward and Downward and awa-a-ay we go!

(She shoots down and out of sight in a spray of white water toward a large area of light as if at the end of a long tunnel—from where, blending with the sound of cascading water, comes now an almost choral reverberation.)

KATHERINE SHERRITT: Is this damn thing what I think it is?

PETER SAGAMORE: I think it's what you think it is. But for pity's sake read on. Here comes Scene Two.

Scene 2: At the Confluence

(Holding wearily and warily onto a spongy boulder in a calm eddy between swift currents streaming toward us from great tunnels on her left and right is MAY, *breathing hard.)*

KATHERINE: May! Did you write this, Peter Sagamore?

PETER *(Shakes his head):* Cross my heart and hope to die.

(May's envelope is of greenish paisley, tougher-appearing than JUNE's *but considerably the worse for wear. In the faint light we see that* MAY *herself is*

an attractive young woman, but, like her envelope, battered and disheveled: a survivor. From the Right Branch, over the sound of rushing water, JUNE *speaks the last words of Scene 1.)*

JUNE: Here comes your dream girl, Mister Right! Onward and Downward and awa-a-ay we go!

(At the words "Mister Right," MAY *scowls and draws closer to her boulder. Her expression is nervous and hostile. She holds fast with her right hand. Her left—she is left-handed—is open and ready to deliver a karate blow.)*

K: I don't believe it! But May Jump hates green.

P: Mess not with the distinction between life and art; things are tough enough already. Are you up to the Swimmer/Floater business yet?

*(KATHERINE *is too busy reading to answer.)*

(Now JUNE *shoots out of the Right Branch, trying hard to steer to starboard.)*

JUNE: "Hard *right* and right along . . ."

(But the current sweeps her into MAY, *who loses her grip on the boulder. Cries of consternation from both women; they spring in opposite directions, but are at once swept together again by the opposing currents. For a few seconds they mix it up vigorously in the eddy; both are able in the arts of self-defense.)*

KATHERINE: Yeah, well. But May Jump's a brown belt, not a green. A brown belt can throw a green belt nine times out of ten.

PETER *(From some other page):* What?

(Then each recognizes that her adversary is of the same general sort as herself.)

JUNE: Hey, you're one of Us. . . . ⎫
MAY: You're not one of Them. . . . ⎭

(They laugh and embrace. In the eddy behind the boulder they bob and circle gently. Each finds it difficult to realize the other's presence; both are breathless from the wrestling. MAY *coughs from having swallowed water.)*

JUNE: I thought you were a Swimmer!

MAY: I thought *you* were, Sister! *(Coughs)* You can thank Mother Moon I didn't sink you before I realized . . . *(Coughs)* . . . you're a Floater.

JUNE *(Laughs and raises her eyes as she pounds* MAY's *back to ease her coughing):* Thank you, Mother Moon, for not letting her sink me before she realized I'm a Floater.

MAY *(Still coughing):* Don't think I couldn't do it.

KATHERINE *(To herself):* She could. *(To* PETER) What's this Mother Moon, and all these women named after months?

(Without looking up from his page, PETER *points to hers, by way of saying Read on.)*

MAY *(Sarcastically, now that she has her breath):* Okay. Float along down to your Mister Right now, Dreamgirl.

JUNE *(Lets go of her, embarrassed):* I was being *ironic* when I said that! *(MAY reaches out quickly and holds onto her through a spell of coughing.)* Are you all right, Sis? *(MAY nods.)* What in the world are you doing here? I don't even know you!

MAY: *Right*'s a dirty word where I come from: I'm all *left. (She displays the rips and tears in her envelope.)* And this is all that's *left* of me!

JUNE: No kidding! You're a Lefty?

MAY *(Nods):* I'm a left-*over,* too, believe it or not.

JUNE: I've never met a Floater from the Left Branch before!

KATHERINE: Left Branch?

MAY *(Dryly):* The pleasure is mutual. *(She looks* JUNE *over appraisingly.)* How did a Right-O manage to stay afloat this far?

JUNE: I managed.

MAY *(Scornfully, but holding onto* JUNE'*s knee):* Without even getting her hair wet! Shooting the Right Branch must be a breeze.

JUNE *(Unfazed):* Must be. *(She removes* MAY'*s hand from her knee and pushes off into the current.) Auf Wiedersehen,* Lefty; pleased to've bumped into you.

MAY *(Splashes after her):* Hold on a minute!

JUNE: Onward and Downward! *(She shoots expertly the first short stretch of the Mainstream, where the current is noticeably less strong and the boulders and other hazards are less numerous than in the Branch.* MAY *comes tumbling pell-mell after. At the next eddy, in the lee of a large boulder,* JUNE *pauses and plucks* MAY *nimbly from the current. Dripping wet,* MAY *hangs exhausted onto her rescuer.)*

MAY *(Out of breath):* Okay, Right-O: You're not bad.

JUNE: For a spoiled little Floater from the Right Ovarium?

MAY: You're not bad, period. But you haven't been *floating* for a full month, either. You haven't been *down* yet, much less down and back.

JUNE *(Impressed):* You really have been?

MAY *(Nods):* I told you I was a left-over.

JUNE: That's amazing! What's your name?

MAY: Mike Alpha Yankee Eight Zero: May Graduate Eighty. *(She holds out her hand.)* May.

JUNE: May! *(She takes her hand.)* How can you still be here? I'm *June!*

KATHERINE: I get it. Boyoboy.

MAY *(Shrugs):* I've done two or three things that I was told no Floater can do. Swimming upstream, for example.

JUNE *(Smiles and shakes her head):* Only Swimmers can move upstream. Floaters can steer and navigate, but only downstream.

MAY: Watch. But be ready to catch me: I'm too far gone to go far.

(By dint of much thrashing, MAY *actually manages to "backstroke" a few yards upstream, toward the Confluence, before spinning exhausted back to*

JUNE, *who, laughing, once again plucks her safely into the eddy.* MAY's *grateful grip this time begins to resemble an embrace.)*

PETER: This will never do for Saint Deniston's.

JUNE: I'm astonished! *(She moves* MAY's *hand from the neighborhood of her breast.)* Where'd you learn to do that?
MAY: Swim? You can bet I didn't learn it from my Floating coach, Right-O.
JUNE *(Moves free):* I've got to try it. What's the trick?
MAY: Draw yourself in as narrow as you can, to reduce drag, and then kick like crazy.
JUNE *(Merrily):* I'll pretend I'm one of Them, heading for one of Us!
MAY: Oh boy.
JUNE *(In false baritone):* Onward! Upward!
(As MAY *watches skeptically, arms akimbo,* JUNE *manages to hold her own against the current by merely kicking; when a wave accidentally turns her belly-down, she cries out but improvises at once a sort of crawl stroke, much more effective than* MAY's *awkward backstroke.* MAY *is impressed.)*

KATHERINE: So am I, sort of. Who in the world wrote this, Peter?
PETER *(Shrugs):* Are you up to the lesbian part yet, and the Lunations?

JUNE: Look out, girls! Here comes Mister Right! *(Another wave tumbles her over; she floats expertly back to the eddy, laughing and clearing her wet hair from her face.)*
MAY: I've got you! Don't worry! *(She seizes* JUNE *in another embrace, from which, exhilarated,* JUNE *firmly extricates herself.)*
JUNE: I don't need *getting.* What fun!
MAY: Didn't I tell you? We aren't really built for it; we've got all this drag . . . *(She spreads her envelope wide with both hands.)* where the Swimmers have nothing but a streamlined head and a long tail.

KATHERINE: Uh-oh.

JUNE: But we can *do* it! That's amazing!
MAY: We can do it. Whereas if *they* tried to float downstream the way we do, they'd sink in a minute.
JUNE: We can actually swim! Why weren't we told that?
MAY: *They* have to keep thrashing upstream just to stay afloat.
JUNE *(Muses):* Maybe that's all they want to do! Maybe they actually don't want Us at all! *(She laughs at the heretical idea and lifts her arms to fix her hair.* MAY *watches with dour appreciation.)* Maybe they're just trying not to go under!
MAY: Like you and me? I doubt it.
JUNE: Not like me. *(Pensively)* I may not be sure what I want, Lefty, but it's more than just not going under.
MAY: That's what I thought, this time last month.

JUNE *(Looks at* MAY *with new interest and sympathy and offers her hand, which* MAY *takes readily):* You've really hung on here since the last Lunation? That's incredible!

KATHERINE: I don't believe it: a menstrual comedy, yet.

PETER: A lesbian menstrual-show. I think it's a first.

MAY *(Nods):* I agree. No floater in history ever did it before, as far as I know.

JUNE: And you made your way back to the Confluence from clear downstream!

MAY *(Modestly):* Not from *all* the way downstream. But from a lot farther down than this. It took me three weeks to swim back up to the Confluence, and I've been resting here for nearly a week.

JUNE: How'd you ever do it?

MAY *(Shrugs):* I'd swim a little and then hang on a lot. There are caves and coves and things, where I was able to hide out, and low banks and ledges where I could climb out of the water and rest.

JUNE: Climb out of the water!

MAY: Watch. *(She heaves herself laboriously up to sit on a small projection of the boulder.)*

JUNE: I can't believe my eyes!

MAY *(Nods and smiles grimly):* Not only do we not die on dry land; we don't even get stiff, if we splash a little water on our envelopes now and then. Those rest periods saved my life.

JUNE: Move over, Lefty; if you can do it, I can too. *(She scrambles up, more agilely than* MAY, *and perches beside her, laughing.)* They didn't say a word about this in the Right Ovarium!

MAY: Nor in the Left. Much less that we can actually swim against the current.

JUNE *(Indignantly):* Excuse me, Sister. I've got a bone to pick with a certain teacher of mine. *(She speaks to her cupped left hand.)* Right Ovarium, Right Ovarium: This is Jay-Gee Eighty, just below the Confluence. Do you read me, Right Ovarium? Over. *(No reply.* MAY *watches, amused, lightly fingering* JUNE's *envelope.)* Ms. R? This is Jay-Gee here, high and dry and mad as a wet hen! Come in, please: I've got some things to ask you and some more to tell you. Over! *(No reply.* JUNE *smacks her hand against the boulder;* MAY *takes her other hand.)*

MAY: What could she say, Right-O? She's been lying to you and your sisters for a hundred Lunations.

KATHERINE: This is too spooky. May Jump used to talk just like this May here.

PETER: Read on: It's a lesbian feminist undergraduate menstrual television comedy.

JUNE: Ms. R never lied to us!

MAY: My teachers sure did.

JUNE: I *loved* Ms. R!

MAY: I loved my teachers too, doll. *(Wryly)* And they loved me. But they were *wrong*.

JUNE *(Hopefully):* Maybe our teachers didn't know any better, even in the Right Ovarium. *(MAY grimaces.)* Or the Left. Ms. R never claimed she'd been downstream herself.

MAY: Neither did Coach Lefkowith. She'd been around plenty in other respects—

JUNE *(Merrily):* We had a coach like that, too!

KATHERINE: So did we, at dear old Deniston.

PETER: What's that?

K: A butch riding coach.

P: Never mind your butch riding coach; I'm up to Mister Right and his fellow rapists.

JUNE *(Swims again, experimentally and to keep her distance from* MAY; *she backstrokes and sidestrokes lightly against the current as they talk):* I can't believe this!

MAY: I hate to think what your Ms. R told you about the Swimmers.

JUNE: She told us the truth. With full-color illustrations.

MAY *(Baiting her, but watching with admiration):* Handsome Mister Right, chugging up the Tube with his gold medal for the long-distance backstroke.

JUNE: *That's* just a way of speaking, too, Lefty. *(She tries her crawl stroke.) I* never seriously believed there was just one right Swimmer in the Sea for every floater. Some of us did, but I didn't. *(An afterthought, as she floats back)* You did call them Swimmers, didn't you?

MAY: *Rapists* is what we called them. Hey, you make swimming look easy! *(She joins her, to get closer.)*

JUNE: It *is* easy. You called *all* of them rapists?

MAY: How many does it take?

KATHERINE: It only takes one, honey. And he can be the Mister Wrong you're married to.

PETER *(Knows what she's reading):* How come Hank didn't put out a contract on old Poon?

(Through the following, MAY *lightly pursues* JUNE, *and* JUNE *lightly evades her: around, beside, and over the boulder, in and out of the eddy.)*

JUNE: All of you called all of them rapists?

MAY: Not all of us. I personally call them cantino macho pigs.

JUNE: That's disgusting, Lefty!

MAY: *They're* disgusting. Wait till you see them. Millions of them, thrashing and slavering . . .

JUNE: I refuse to believe that they're *all* like that.

MAY: You've never seen them. I have.

JUNE: Maybe you saw the wrong ones. *(She climbs up onto the boulder to wring out her hair and envelope.)* A couple of my girlfriends back home were pretty disgusting, as far as that goes. Real slobs. And from what we were told about the *Left* Ovarium. . . .

KATHERINE: I don't know about this June here.
PETER: Keep reading. I like her.

MAY *(Splashes* JUNE *from below):* I'm sure you think *I'm* a slob.
JUNE: Not necessarily.
MAY *(Climbs up beside her): We* were told that the Right Ovarium turns out spoiled little pansies with no guts, no brains, and no ambitions except to find Mister Right and settle down with him.

KATHERINE *(To herself):* Well. There's more to Saint Deniston's than that.

MAY: My teachers used to say, "Better slobs than snobs."

KATHERINE: May is May; no question about it. Does that make me June?

JUNE *(Unprovoked, fixes her hair):* So you think I'm a gutless, brainless snob.
MAY: Not necessarily. *(She touches her.)* In fact, you're okay.
JUNE: You too. *(She moves off, climbing around the boulder.)* So let's don't believe everything we were taught, all right?
MAY: I've learned not to. *(She follows her.)* But get this: We were taught that Mother Moon is greater than Father Sun, because the Moon gives us light at night, when we need it, whereas the Sun gives us light in the daytime, when there's plenty of light already. Not bad, huh?

PETER: There's a line here about the Moon's being greater than the Sun that's not half bad.

JUNE *(Laughs, shakes her head; returns to the water):* The fact is, we were taught to look for a good, dependable Swimmer with the right background—
MAY: I knew it!
JUNE: Not too much of an egghead, you know, but not one of your macho whipcrackers, either—and then . . . settle down, as you said, after we shoot the Tube together, and . . . *(She glances at* MAY.) Merge.
MAY *(Frowns):* Merge! Merge?
JUNE *(Embarrassed):* You know. *(She presses her finger-ends together several times, uncertainly.)* Merge.
MAY *(Understands):* Oh, that. We called it Fusing. So: They told you all to go Merge with Mister Right and make a Baby. *(She touches* JUNE's *leg.)*
JUNE *(Merrily takes* MAY's *hand):* We didn't even know what a Baby *was!*
MAY: I still don't. But I know I want none of it. *(She touches* JUNE's *knee with her free hand.)*

KATHERINE: I've heard that Sun-Moon joke before. It's Number Thirty-nine.

JUNE *(Catches that hand too):* I don't think *they* knew, either. The same with Merging. They said we'd understand when the time came. Maybe we will, if it's not too late already.

MAY: My time isn't coming, if I can help it. *Merging!*

JUNE: It doesn't sound so terrible to me: Floaters and Swimmers putting their Identities together. I'm going to keep an open mind.

MAY *(Pulls free and pats* JUNE's *behind):* It's not your mind they're after, Right-O.

JUNE *(Moves away):* Who knows what they're after? What are *we* after? I must say our other option never impressed me.

MAY *(Shakes her head): We* called it the Big Wash-Out; but we were supposed to choose it over Fusing with Them. Coach Lefkowith said that to Fuse our Identity is to *lose* our Identity. I used to ask her what good our Identity was, after the Wash-Out. There we'd float, all by our lonesome on the Flat Sea, still clutching tight to our precious Identities. . . .

JUNE *(Coming in closer, now that* MAY *isn't pressing):* You asked your coach that?

MAY: I was a troublemaker. I used to pester Coach Lefkowith to tell me why there were just shes and hes. Why not three sexes, or five?

JUNE *(Joins her, genuinely puzzled):* What would the spare one do?

MAY: I'll demonstrate. *(*JUNE *stops her quickly, but not rudely.* MAY *does not insist.)* The Coach demonstrated. Then I asked her seriously: Why couldn't there be just Us? Who needs Them? She said she'd spent her life wondering the same thing.

KATHERINE: All Floaters and no Swimmers? That would be boring.

JUNE: But that would be boring! It would be just like the Ovarium, right?

MAY *(Points):* Left. And that's exactly where I'm headed.

JUNE: You can't! Once you're launched, there's no going back. Is there?

MAY *(Gestures at herself,* JUNE, *their surroundings):* There's no precedent for *this,* either, Right-O, but here I am. Seems to me all I have to do is bear left at the Confluence and keep on upstream.

JUNE *(Points):* You mean bear *right.*

MAY *(Considers):* Right. It was left at the Confluence coming *down.*

JUNE: It was *right* at the Confluence coming down. . . . *(She understands.)* No, you're right. We both are.

MAY: So to get back left I have to keep right. Who'd have believed it?

JUNE: Do you actually *want* to go back, Lefty, if you can? *(She smiles and corrects herself.)* I mean May?

MAY: No, you mean *can. (She sees her misunderstanding; is pleased.)* Oh: You mean *me.* May.

*(*JUNE *nods and smiles.)*

PETER *(Frowns and shakes his head):* A lesbian feminist undergraduate *grammarian* menstrual television comedy.

MAY *(Seriously):* Well, sure. Why not? I'll be the first coach in history who's ever really been down here and knows what she's talking about. Maybe I *should* bear left and drop in on your old Ms. R: I could fix her head about Merging and straighten out your little sisters. *(She does not say this disagreeably.)* They'd have to believe me, because I've *been* there! I've dealt with Them! *(She has been looking thoughtfully downstream. Now she turns to* JUNE.*)* Wouldn't *you* rather be back in the Ovarium than here?

JUNE *(She has listened attentively. She considers, looks around, shakes her head.):* No. It was fine, May; I loved it. But it was School. School's over now. I guess I'm going to float on down.

MAY: No! *(Urgently)* It's terrible down there, June. And lonesome! You don't realize. You're not out of danger just because you've reached the Confluence. Those Swimmers will scramble you!

JUNE: I'm no Baby. *(They look at each other in sudden wonder, both apparently realizing for the first time what that word might mean.* JUNE *smiles;* MAY *frowns.)*

JUNE
MAY } *(More or less simultaneously):* { You're really going back?
You really want to go down?

(They embrace affectionately, both nodding yes.)

JUNE *(Climbs down into the eddy):* It's a very strong current up there in the Branches, May. They say that even most Swimmers can't manage it.

MAY *(Following her):* What's down there is worse than current.

JUNE: Well. So. *(She smiles.)* Good-bye, Lefty; you've taught me a lot. *(She eases herself gingerly into the Mainstream, holding her position with a light backstroke, at which she is now adept.)* Say hello to Coach Lefkowith from all us little snobs in the Right Ovarium.

MAY *(With some emotion):* Sure. *(She enters the Mainstream too, almost crossly, and begins to kick her way upstream with her earlier vigorous backstroke. She calls back to* JUNE.*)* Tell Mister Right he doesn't deserve you!

*(*JUNE *smiles, waves, steers off downstream out of sight behind yet another large boulder, less craggy than its predecessors.* MAY *watches her go, sniffs, turns furiously over into the crawl position invented earlier by* JUNE, *and thrashes off upstream, grunting "Onward! Upward!" at each stroke. Her voice fades into the sound of flowing water as she moves out of sight.)*

PETER: There's still a third scene. Shall we take a break and talk about this thing?

KATHERINE: No! I'm only up to the swimming-back-home business; don't interrupt me.

P: This June here sure does remind me of present company in some ways.

K: She doesn't remind *me* of present company. Read on ahead; I'll catch up.

Scene 3: Onward and Downward

(The same eddy, a few moments later. MAY's *voice-off still grunts faintly "Onward! Upward!"* JUNE *reappears from downstream, sidestroking easily and pensively; she has evidently circled the boulder, either to watch* MAY's *departure or to reconsider her own next move. Drawing into the eddy, she listens bemused as* MAY's *voice and splashing vanish in the general sound of flowing water.* JUNE *turns her eyes uncertainly downstream and splashes idly, humming "Some Day My Prince Will Come." She recognizes the tune and breaks off, smiling and shaking her head. Now she turns sharply back upstream, from where come sounds of* MAY *in distress. At first concerned,* JUNE *smiles as* MAY *is swept back onto the scene, spent.* JUNE *catches her as before and pulls her into the eddy.* MAY *resists groggily for a moment.)*

JUNE: It's me, May. Don't worry: It's not Mister Right.

MAY *(Out of breath):* It's *I* . . . Predicate nominative.

JUNE: What happened? *(Teasing)* Wouldn't the Coach let you back in?

MAY *(Recovering, wipes water from her eyes and rolls them at* JUNE's *remark):* I came back because you're going to need help fending off the Swimmers.

JUNE: *Me* need help! Did I call for help?

MAY: In that current I'd never have heard you. How come you're still here?

JUNE: I'm in no hurry. Ms. R said "Enjoy each stage before you move on."

KATHERINE: Ms. R is right.

MAY: You *had* moved on, and you came back. Admit it: You're a little chicken.

PETER: *Oy gevalt* and *sacré bleu.*

JUNE: I am not! And no wonder if I am, after listening to you. I wasn't before.

MAY: Hmp.

JUNE *(Her feelings still hurt):* If you can manage by yourself now, I'll float on down.

MAY: Wait, June! *(Determinedly)* You're not going without me.

JUNE: I'm not?

MAY: Okay: *Please* don't go without me.

JUNE: You're scared, too.

MAY: I'm scared for your sake. . . .

JUNE *(Moves away):* Bye-bye, May.

MAY: For both our sakes! Both, both. *(*JUNE *pauses, mollified.)* Look, Right-O . . . June . . .

JUNE *(Accents the first syllable):* Call me *Jay*-Gee.

MAY: I like you. You're a good Floater. *(She grins.)* Always sunny side up.

JUNE *(Accepts the compliment with a quick nod):* You too, May: I like you, too. Bye.

MAY *(Grabs* JUNE's *foot):* I've *been down there,* Jay-Gee! Part of the way, anyhow. Why shouldn't you have a guide?

JUNE: No, thanks. *(She frees her foot and pushes out into the Mainstream as before, but holds her position against the boulder.)* I don't want a guide. *(She smiles and extends her hand.)* But I've no objection to a friend.

(As MAY *laughs and splashes over to her, a sudden new distant sound comes from downstream: faint, echoing male shouts, curses, splashes, whistles. The two* FLOATERS *hold each other in alarm.)*

KATHERINE: Here it comes.

MAY: What *is* it?

PETER: We know what it is.

JUNE *(Equally alarmed, but surprised at* MAY's *question):* I guess it's . . . Them. They? The Swimmers.

(MAY closes her eyes, bites her lips, beats her free hand against her knee, almost weeps with anger and fright. The sound fades.)

JUNE: How did I know right away it was them, and you didn't, when I've never seen them and you've already dealt with them once?

PETER: My very question.

MAY *(Miserable):* Oh, Jay-Gee . . . there *weren't* any Swimmers before!

JUNE *(Astonished):* You had a Dry Lunation! *(MAY nods, shamefaced.)* You lied to me!

KATHERINE and PETER *(Separately, as each reaches this line):* A Dry Lunation.

MAY *(Defensively now.* JUNE *still holds her place in the stream;* MAY *has retreated to the eddy, still clutching* JUNE's *hand tightly.):* Dry Lunation or not, I damn near drowned down there!

JUNE: And *you* want to teach my sisters how to escape the Swimmers, which they're not even supposed to do!

MAY *(A bit desperately):* There's plenty to deal with besides Swimmers, Jay-Gee. Whirlpools! Cataracts!

PETER: Diaphragms and dildos.

KATHERINE *(Minutes later):* Forest-green Crayola crayons.

JUNE *(Unimpressed, pulls her hand free):* Good-bye, May.

MAY: Look, damn it: I *survived!* I'm the only Floater in history who ever came back to tell the tale, and I know the next leg of the stream. I can help you!

JUNE *(Less annoyed;* MAY's *accomplishment is undeniable.):* You're the one who needs help: "Cantino macho pigs," and you've never even seen one!

MAY: Okay: We can help each other. I'll help you navigate the tricky stretches, and you can help me keep an open mind about rapists.

KATHERINE: Now she's talking.

JUNE: Now you're talking. *(She begins an old Ovarium song.)* "Sis-ters to-ge-ther . . ." (MAY *waves off the song, but gratefully takes her hand.)*
JUNE *(Teases):* We'll double date with Mister Right and Mister Left!
MAY: Yech.
JUNE: Ready?
MAY: Sure.
JUNE: A one. And a two . . .
(Another sound from THEM. MAY *and* JUNE *clutch each other again, until the sound fades.)*
JUNE *(Dryly):* You can let go now, May.
MAY *(Sighs and releases her, but holds onto her hand. Seriously):* I don't *want* them, Jay-Gee.
JUNE: I noticed.
MAY: I hate them!
JUNE: You're afraid of them.
MAY: I hate them and I'm afraid of them too!
JUNE: Sight unseen.
MAY: But not sound unheard. I don't want to Wash Out alone, though, either. *(Pauses)* I think I want *you*, Jay-Gee.
JUNE *(Admonishingly):* Lef-ty . . .
MAY: I really like you.
JUNE *(Draws away):* Bye-bye, Lefty.
MAY: I'm coming with you!
JUNE: Come on, then.
MAY: What's your rush? "Enjoy each stage . . ."
*(*JUNE *smiles lightly.* MAY *makes a desperate pass, which* JUNE *easily parries.)*
JUNE: That's enough of that.
MAY *(Not very derisively):* Saving it for Mister Right?
JUNE: We'll see. Come on, if you're coming.
(But a third wave of cries comes up from THEM, *distinctly closer.)*
MAY *(Makes an obscene gesture downstream):* You want *Them?*
JUNE *(More brightly):* Certainly not all of them. Let's look them over: Maybe they're as different from one another as we are. Maybe some of them are *nice! (She positively disengages herself from* MAY *and sets off slowly downstream.)*
MAY: Jay-Gee!
JUNE *(As she passes down behind the boulder):* I think I like this part! Come on, May!
MAY *(Dives in from the eddy):* I'm coming, damn it! Hold on!
JUNE *(Out of sight now, sings excitedly):* "On-ward and Down-ward!" Whoo! Come on, May!

MAY: I'm coming! I'm coming!
(The scene dissolves quickly in the persistent rush of water and the rising sound of THEM.*)*

Groans Katherine I'm barely past the Dry Lunation, and you're finished already! How can it end so fast, when the plot's just begun to thicken? Don't tell me. Replies Peter I hate to be the one to break the news, but all we have is Act One.

No!

You like it that much?

Katherine declares it to be the queerest mix of sophomoric and serious she's seen in a while, but her main questions about it aren't literary. Leave her alone now, till she's done. Peter goes upstairs for a walk, but circumambulating *Story*'s deck takes about one minute. He stows the empty orange canister beside *Story*'s full one, never used, and considers dinghying around Dun Cove for the exercise. Decides to wait for Kate. Those responses of hers we've included in the script are only samples; in fact she reacts aloud to nearly every line she reads. Wash Out! Cantino macho! Forest-green Crayola.

Professional Peter ponders the subject of Improbable Coincidence, which Aristotle allows may begin a story but must not be rung in to end one. The problem is not only, Q.E.D., that life is not a story, but that even if it were, we characters in it wouldn't normally know at any particular moment where in its plot we are. Will the birth of our children end a drama, begin one, or close some act and open another? In literal fact, none of the above; in fiction, any or all. And the coincidence of our finding, in the pregnant month of June, at a sort of confluence, the floating script of a play about "Floaters," one named June and the other May and gay, about to encounter at another sort of confluence what clearly will be a school of spermatozoa. . . .

Katherine claps her hat and wails Where's my Act Two? Who do we know that knows about me and May and writes Woody Allen comedies and floats them off in canisters with their old clothes? She hauls upstairs and covers her husband's face with kisses. Jesus, I'm glad we're straight and I've got you.

Well, likewise, for sure. It is Peter Sagamore's fear that there is not only an Act Two, but an Act Three as well: if not in this world, then in the heaven of dramaturgical obviosities.

The what?

Says Peter We could write the rest ourselves: All the clues are right there in Act One. It's you know what.

What?

Old hat. Want to take a dinghy ride? Stretch muscles?

We do, taking turns on the oars, round about both arms of Dun Cove, which now remind us of fallopian tubes. Few or no nettles, but the afternoon's too raw to make the water inviting. Though she does not herself invent stories, black-bereted Katherine has told enough of them to agree with Peter, once she thinks about it, that in Act Two those two young females—Floaters, ova, whatever they are—must encounter the "Swimmers," no doubt including the heavily foreshadowed "Mister Right," and be menaced by them, if not by him, or at least perceive themselves so to be.

Says Kath He'll look like you. I wish we were in bed with you right now.

Says Peter Yup. Then the screws will have to be put to May's and June's separate preconceptions, excuse the expression. That's why that Right and Left business was established. Each of them will find that her education was a half truth. June is openminded, but May won't come off her opinions easily. How does he know? Because that's what second acts are for. Maybe Mister Right will have a few things to learn, too—such as that fertilization normally takes place *above* the Confluence, not below it. But that's show biz.

Katherine bets May will be jealous, the way May Jump was.

You bet she will. Do human ova ever survive menstruation, by the way?

Not that Katherine ever heard of: Superfetation works the other way. But she guesses anything is possible; anyhow, it seems okay as a working premise. And remember, we're only assuming they're human ova. Maybe they're sea urchins? In any case, Peter declares, Act Two must end with Mister Right and May's rivalry exacerbated, June's sentiments painfully divided, and the threat to all hands sharply escalated by some new turn of events. . . .

Pleads Kate Stop! You'll spoil the story. How do you know all that?

Freshman Dramaturgy, in Pete's opinion. So's the script, doesn't she think?

Is he sure he didn't write it?

Says P Please. He is by nature a narrator, not a dramatizer. He cannot deny that should he ever presume to playwrighthood, his efforts might not be superior to *SEX EDUCATION: Play;* but he denies the presumption. That denial brings us back both to our sloop and to the main question: All extraordinary coincidences aside, what kind of oddball would put a playscript, finished or unfinished, into a plastic canister along with a worn-out hat and float it off on the tide? If he hopes some agent or producer will come across it, he's casting his seed upon the wrong waters; he'd be better off on Long Island Sound than on Chesapeake Bay.

Kate declares she sure never thought of her eggs as being little women, much less self-contained white-water rafters with individual personalities. The idea gives her the heeb-jeebs. What she mainly remembers about her first menstruation was feeling like an unsuccessful chicken: It would've been more satisfying to *lay* the thing and cluck over it than to bleed it out and not even see it. Wait: She now also recalls searching for it, in vain, in those early Kotexes. Her mother had been amused, her first-form girl-friends disgusted, but she hadn't cared: The thing was after all hers, and she was simply curious.

And unabashed, says proud Pete, and unsqueamish: That's our Katydid. Anyhow, I enjoyed the whole business.

Of course you did.

Growing tits and fur and connecting with the moon and the tides—terrific. Brother Willy, she reports, and his bosom buddy Porter Baldwin, Jr., had been first-class pains in her behind, snooping and teasing. Yech.

Enjoy each stage, quotes smiling Peter. We are back aboard. In fact she *had* a sort of Ms. R, Katherine reminds him: one of those wonderful high school English teacher ladies who are forty when they're twenty and no more than forty-five when they reach sixty: a woman of unusual skill, wisdom, firmness, patience, and industry, without children or living spouse, whom generations of Deniston girls stood in classroom awe of and affectionately mocked among themselves as an old maid, while she did more for their minds and characters than most of their parents and subsequent college faculties combined, with an individual concern for her charges that would put to shame any doctor, lawyer, or psychiatrist Kate has ever known, in a profession without the rewards of rank, riches, fame, or community prestige: a profession that one enters as a high school English teacher and retires from, forty years later, a high school English teacher. Irma Shorter and Katherine Sherritt and many another had loved Mrs. Florence Halsey as one would adore a personal god, with a love that deepened as the decades taught them how much they'd learned from her—and that love was Florence Halsey's chief reward. Near eighty now and confined to an Easton nursing home—her health had failed promptly upon her retirement from the Deniston School for Girls—Florence Halsey has, for attending family, the half-dozen ex-students of various ages who both revere her and reside in the area; for posterity, hundreds of others scattered about the world; for immortality, neither more nor less than any first-class teacher ever has: the words (spoken by her former students to their own students, spouses, children, friends) "Mrs. Halsey used to tell us . . ."

What Mrs. Halsey used to tell us was a lot less dippy than Enjoy each stage, Katherine Sherritt declares. Mrs. Halsey used to tell us stuff like Always give your adversary credit for at least as much common sense as you yourself have. And Remember, girls, that the opposite of reason is not emotion; it is unreason. And the opposite of emotion is not reason; it is frigidity on the one hand and sentimentality on the other. Florence Halsey's sayings were not old hat.

Peter's glowing, both because he finds Mrs. Halsey's obiter dicta congenial and wise and because we're making love again down in *Story*'s cabin, Kate wearing only her beret *trouvé*. Whatever its shortcomings as dramatic literature, Act I of *SEX EDUCATION: Play* has managed after all to rouse us. The languor of our passion—it is that kind of afternoon; we are in that kind of humor—seems to calm the children, Body and Soul, as if Pete's slow motions were fatherly caresses. When at last he ejaculates, K sighs I hope there's no Mister Right in that batch, now that school's closed for the season.

Over dinner we ask So are we going sailing tomorrow, or home? That partial comedy remains much in our minds: the work of some not-untalented amateur, we have decided, who either whimsically thus abandoned it with a symbol of his self-criticism or made a copy and whimsically thus launched the original as a waterborne offering to the muse: a simulacrum of its principals, those Floaters. We are duly awed by the odds against any sperm's connecting with any egg; the grossly improbable coincidence of life itself—which nevertheless contrived to come to pass in the case of each of us, and which we have contrived to perpetrate at least for another chapter. Toward dusk there is a final small thundershower, with distant lightning bolts such as may have catalyzed the first living cells in the primordial molecular soup. Even as its thunder rumbles oceanward, the sky clears: new crescent moon, bright stars; the promise of a calm night and a breezy fine morning as the high moves into Maryland.

Maybe it's the weather change, or our lazy lovemaking followed by the weather change. Or maybe it's the story of our lives thus far with its slowly building impasse, culminating in today's crisis, broken by the whopping coincidence of a manuscript-in-a-bottle, revealed to be a more whopping coincidence yet and followed by a certain amount of reflection, by satisfying though awkward sex, by a good dinner, and by the weather change. In any case, it seems to us just now that though the apocalypse might possibly arrive before the end of this sentence, we have just now no problems that we can do anything about. If fate still has us in its jaws, it is not at the moment swallowing us headfirst. It makes sense, just now, to us, right here, to enjoy the evening and think not of the morrow until it come. Kate radios those tidings to Nopoint Point. We have a nightcap ale—just a sip for her—and go to bed early.

Tell Pride and Prejudice a bedtime story, their mother insists from forward to aft. You have to do that every night now until they're born. New rule.

ONCE UPON A TIME THERE WERE TWO LOCKED CASKETS,

Peter replies instantly from the quarterberth—one of those occasions that astonish Katherine and sometimes him too, as if the muse, surprised, speaks before she knows what she's saying. Not burial caskets; treasure caskets. Uh. Each of which contained . . . the key to the other.

DAY 2:
DUN COVE TO
MADISON BAY

Even when we're sailing, it's K.S.S. who usually dreams our better dreams. Early this morning she has a jim-dandy:

THE CONTAINER AND THE THING CONTAINED.

After our bread-and-coffee breakfast (decaf for Kate), we ran out of Dun Cove and down Harris Creek on the promised high, north-northwest by north at twenty plus, a blue Canadian air that cleared our souls and, once we were under way, so recommitted us to our undestinationed voyage that it went without saying, when we reached the place of yesterday's impasse, that we would not even enter Knapps Narrows to reprovision, but run on whither the wind might list, out of the Great Choptank, into Chesapeake Bay—there had to be a can of *something* aboard for lunch, and who needed ice on so brisk a morning?—down to wherever, where supplies were bound to be.

Wherever turned out to be Madison Bay, in the *Little* Choptank: twenty miles of splendid southing back toward *Story*'s launching place. We considered running on through the afternoon, down to Hoopers Island, Shoal Point, Sagamore Flats, to say hello to Peter's boyhood if not to the U.S. Central Intelligence Agency; but feeling the wind weaken after tide-turn, we decided instead upon the Little Choptank, next river system below our own, which however we had somehow never gotten around to sailing together. P recalled there being a little Coast Guard Search-and-Rescue station there on shallow Madison Bay, on that river's south shore, and a working watermen's wharf, and some sort of crab-and-oyster restaurant, perhaps with an ice machine, maybe a small grocery store as well. Who knew?

Those are Dorchester County waters. The land lies low; soybean farms and pine woods begin giving way to salt marsh. Houses are few, frame, plain: Millionaires are scarce down here. The anchorages, though innumerable and snug enough, are for the most part shallow, full of unmarked shoals, and often loud with mosquitoes from Easter to Thanksgiving. Cruising yachts are not abundant.

We did well to heed that flagging breeze. The first ten miles of the day we sailed in two hours; the second ten took nearly four. At half past two, in mid–Little Choptank, our breeze failed entirely, and we crept with the sculling oar into Madison Bay: a wide creek, really, walled by loblolly pines; maybe a mile long, half that across; seven feet mean low water at its deepest, most of it two to four. There were the low white workboats; the USCG S&R; the restaurant-crabhouse, bigger than Peter had remembered; a small working marina that he had forgotten, with fuel dock and haul-out lift. Ice machines. Freshwater hoses, hooray. And, anchored off to one side about halfway in, away from the wharves and the channel traffic, the oddest-looking vessel we had ever seen in Chesapeake waters.

That is saying much. Halfway along the intracoastal thoroughfare from Massachusetts to Florida, our Bay floats every sort of traffic except the deepest-draft supertankers. In a few hours' daysail, you may pass a nuclear submarine, a four-masted square-rigger, a Windsurfer, a Texas Tower under tow, a Chinese junk converted for cruising, a syndicated million-dollar "maxi" racing machine, a kid in a kayak, a Monrovian freighter bound for Sri Lanka, an oyster-dredging skipjack built in 1889 and still working, a round-the-world cruiser manned by one young woman, a drug-running superspeedboat, a hydraulic clammer, a U.S. Navy rowing shell, a fishing charter boat packed with half a hundred black gentlemen anglers, a ten-Brownie war canoe, a Russian Caribbean cruise ship, an air boat, a flying boat, a hydrofoil, a Hovercraft, a missile frigate, a water-skier, a paraglider, and a man bent upon walking from Annapolis to St. Michaels in Styrofoam pontoon-shoes of his own design. All those we've seen, and more, over the summers, from *Story*'s cockpit, but we had never before seen . . .

A weathered black hull with a bank of rowing ports, its transverse bow thrust forward at the waterline as if for ramming, its high stern curved and curling like an outsized Venetian gondola's, with no visible rudder. A single short mast amidships with squaresail or settee-sail brailed to its yard. No name board, no registration numbers. No flag or burgee. No tender. No sign of anyone aboard.

Well, now, said we to ourselves: We Americans are a stunt-happy, replica-crazy folk, and we are not alone. Following the likes of Thor Heyerdahl, men and women in recent decades have sailed from just about everywhere to just about anywhere in faithful replicas of just about everything, from balsa rafts and bulrush dhows to Baltimore clippers and carracks of St. Brendan's bullhide. More often than not, they have gotten where they were going. So why *not* a Homerical swart ship in Madison Bay, in the Little Choptank, in Katherine Sherritt's predawn dream?

That dream, inspired by our play-in-a-canister, was in fact about sperms and eggs. It imaged the ovum as a sort of Penelope, beset by spermatozoic suitors until rescued by her Odysseus, who has, so to speak, the key to her casket. As in Homer's poem, that key is neither a figurative phallus, such as a literal key, nor a figurative key, such as her husband's literal phallus. It is the answer to an intimate marital question rich in sexual suggestion: the secret construction of the couple's immovable marriage-bed, its stout chief post a living olive-trunk. The dream-scene then changed to Chesapeake Bay: Penelope/Katherine was one of those white-water Floaters in that "television play," about to be carried under by the horde of suitors clinging to her envelope like shipwrecked sailors. When Peter/Odysseus turns his key in her lock, she sheds that envelope like a buster crab its shell, leaving them to drown, and floats off in her true husband's embrace, at once (so spoke the voice-off narrator in her dream) the Container and the Thing Contained.

Now, in Madison Bay, we understand that we have done righter than we knew to undertake this aimless, unlikely voyage at this delicate juncture in our lives. What we actually do this Tuesday is much as was just recounted as if dreamed, except that over breakfast, while our heirs do their A.M. aquabatics, we listen to the morning news. Some of the truth begins to emerge about the Soviet invasion of Afghanistan, theretofore characterized as a revolution in that country, and we hear of the U.S. Supreme Court's ruling that novel life-forms created by the gene splicers may be patented.

That latter item reminds bereted Katherine of her dream. For our entertainment she recounts it, objecting however that it makes her and her eggs into passive little patsies—Sleeping Beauties waiting for Prince Charming's wake-up call—whereas in biological/historical fact both ova and ovulator are assertive, even aggressive actors in our life's story.

Says Peter Dreams are dumb and tells us now his less fantastic one, inspired in part like hers by that *SEX EDUCATION* script and his twin-casket bedtime story, but mainly by the fact that one early morning at age twelve or thirteen he set out alone in his crabbing skiff on the Honga River, behind Middle Hoopers Island, with what he took to be basic survival gear, resolved not to touch his oars but to drift like Huckleberry Finn whithersoever the tide might fetch him.

Is each of these dreams, we mildly wonder, a casket containing the other's key? We decide we'll see. As aforenarrated, we set out, our souls cleared in Harris Creek by the fresh blue breeze. Off Knapps Narrows we understand that we shall neither turn Nopoint Pointward nor pause to reprovision, but carry on simply south. Pete radios that tiding home. We pour second coffee from the breakfast Thermos and feel the breeze falter. Provisionless, we skip lunch, turn into the Little Choptank at four knots, sail up it at three, at two, at one. Finally we scull into tree-flanked Madison

Bay, named for the author of *The Federalist* and fourth president of our republic. And we espy that black . . . Phaeacian 35?

Indeed, mighty curious, we scull marveling right around it. Half the size, maybe, of those in Homer's catalogue? We are not classicists; cannot even say for sure that the lines are ancient Greek: They seem so, but we may be being cued by Kathy's dream. In any case, the vessel is as above described. On closer inspection, all but one of those pairs of rowing ports turn out to be cabin ports. The spars are varnished wood; the standing rigging is tarred rope, not stainless cable. Deadeyes instead of turnbuckles; belaying pins instead of cleats; no winches in sight. Even the blocks have varnished wooden cheeks—but sharp-eyed Peter notes that their sheaves are molded nylon, and that the running rigging is not laid hemp but braided Dacron, like ours. There's even a VHF antenna on the stubby mast.

We halloo; get no reply. Well, now.

With no breeze to sail by, and the waters down here already too nettled for swimming, we've time on our hands. Let's see what's to be found and learned ashore. We scull in, tie up at the bulkhead near the restaurant, take on water, ice, and what simple provision K can charm the restaurant kitchen lady into selling us: enough for one day's makeshift meals. We'll anchor in Madison Bay this afternoon and dinghy in for dinner this evening at the restaurant, where the fare will be homely but the seafood strictly fresh. The few folks about are clearly local: three red-eyed, grizzled watermen of various ages, drinking Budweiser at the bar; a gaunt, fiftyish barmaid like a surviving Andrews Sister with wrinkled neck, high-piled bleached hair, rhinestoned pointy eyeglasses, twang-voweled speech. We perch on bar stools, split unevenly a National Premium beer, and ask about the odd craft anchored yonder.

Demands one of our barmates, a younger fellow with shoulder-length hair and a John Deere cap, She's a pisser now, ain't she? Must of sailed in last night; she was parked there at five this morning when he went out. Never saw neither person aboard of her.

His companion, a burly older chap who will not look Katherine in the eye or belly, figures it's likely one of Capn Jim Richardson's jobs. This is a plausible hypothesis: The man referred to is a Dorchester boatbuilder of wider renown than Fritz Sagamore, whose yard turned out the full-size working replica of the seventeenth-century pinnace *Dove* now moored at St. Marys City off the Potomac, where Lord Baltimore's Maryland colonists first settled. The younger waterman is of the opinion that this one here's most likely a Viking ship: He remembers Kirk Douglas aboard of one like her on the television. The Vikings, he has heard tell, got here way before Columbus. Like as not, some boat museum like that one up to Saint Michaels hired Capn Jim to build them a Viking ship.

His third assertion is reasonable, his second true, his first mistaken, but we let the error go, except that Katherine wonders good-humoredly how sailors as expert as the Vikings intend to reach St. Michaels (on the Miles River) from Jim Richardson's boatyard (on the Choptank) by sailing south to the Little Choptank and Madison Bay. Why honey, says the older man at once—loudly, so we'll know he's teasing, but looking at the Andrews Sister instead of at Kate—they'll go right round the world and come down on her from the C and D Canal! That's how they come here in the first place, ain't it, Shirl?

Shirl reckons so. The young waterman laughs. The third neither speaks nor smiles. Katherine Sherritt chuckles, as entirely at ease with these people as she is with everybody. Not so Peter: He hopes he is neither elitist nor populist; he has outgrown his undergraduate prejudice against redneckery, but he will not sentimentalize the homefolk. The burly waterman's riposte he finds fairly witty of its kind; more familiar and less engaging is the ragging, bluff, loud, endless and meaningless sarcasm that prevails and passes in parts like these for wit. In those red-rimmed eyes he sees the bullies of his childhood and the Negro-lynchers of generations past, as well as the hardworking, generous, self-reliant people he grew up among. He feels as much a part of them, and as uneasy in their midst, as a wrasse among groupers.

Anyhow, he wants to get back to *Story,* get out and get anchored, for a particular reason, which he lays on his companion as soon as he can pry her politely away from her newfound friends. These dreams we have been dreaming, these stories we've been telling each other and the children over the past two days, some of them spontaneously and to our own surprise . . . It has occurred to Peter Sagamore, he allows as we push off from the marina bulkhead, to write at least some of them down, as the basis for, you know, whatever.

Almost too joyed to speak, Kate is not quite. She declares from her perch on the cabin top I have a different suggestion: Let's do a Doctor Jack.

I.e., she explains, tucking some hair under her beret, just as when, unable to reconceive, on Jack Bass's advice we took oral contraceptives for half a year and then fertility drugs and wham, here we are, so she proposes Peter *not* write down these tales and dreams and anecdotes. Not yet. Why not let's dream and tell, tell and dream, narrate and navigate whither listeth wind and tide until we are delivered of our posterity, or about to be, and *then*—by when you'll be as about to burst as I am now—deliver yourself of our several stories, duly arted up.

Says Peter Sagamore immediately Yes.

YES!

He puts by the sculling sweep for a moment; goes forward to kiss her neck. But I'm afraid I'll forget them.

His wife advises So keep a list. Keep a log. Keep an inventory, like

What Whatsername Gave Birth To. Then when your time comes, use that list as your table of contents.

Another kiss! But suppose we come to forget what those titles are titles of? "Thirty-nine," for example, or "The Container and the Thing Contained"? Replies Kate No matter: You'll dream up new tales to fit those titles.

Normally we anchor well away from neighbors: the Second Principle, after security, of Overnight Anchoring. But so eager now is Peter to get going on that tabulation—already he despairs of recollecting *all* we've told since leaving Nopoint Point—and so curious do we remain about that "Phaeacian 35," as Peter has dubbed it, we wind up parking just astern of it instead of elsewhere in Madison Bay. The spot is at once convenient to the docks and yet out of their earshot and comfortably away from the watermen's traffic in and out of the creek; anyhow, our neighbors are evidently not aboard. Our anchor down, K puts the Sun Shower out to heat up for later, does her preggers exercises, then makes herself comfortable in the awning-shade to write May Jump a letter about Act I of *SEX EDUCATION: Play.* P wishes he had the faithful little loose-leaf notebook in which for twenty years he has recorded story ideas and other potentially usable matter, from the look sound smell taste feel of things to overheard dialogue and general propositions about human life, its happiness and its misery. On second thought he's glad he doesn't have it, since what he's about to do he's never done before. It seems apter to fish out *Story*'s log, which needs updating anyhow, and in it reconstruct as best he can the succession of our seaborne dreams and tales (by title only), interpolated with the usual sailing data.

The late still afternoon stokes up. Did "Another Version of the Old Prison Joke" come before or after "The Ordinary Point Delivery Story"? The day before yesterday he calls Day Zero, because we didn't then know yet quite what we were doing. Under it he enters "The New Clothes Have No Emperor" and "The Points: Shoal & Shorter." Under yesterday, Day One, go "Berlin Zoo," "Sex Ed Act I," and "Parable of 2 Locked Caskets." Weren't there others? Under "Day 2: T 6/17/80: Choptank R (Dun Cove) to Little Choptank R (Madison Bay)," he registers first his own early-morning's dream, which, by the time we get around to re-creating it in written sentences, will have been reinforced and clarified by the dream he'll have tonight and be called

HUCK FINN ON THE HONGA, PART ONE.

Peter Sagamore drifts away from home, thirteen let's say, alone, just as on a mid-June early morning he once did—not running away, because there is in his Hoopersville childhood nothing fearsome or hateful enough to flee; not yet running toward, because he scarcely knows yet what he craves instead—but drifting in his ageless, hard-used, well-kept wooden skiff on the running tide just as he had done in fact, except that in the dream he leaves behind his oars. Down the wide, shallow Honga River he floats in the warming calm, hour after hour, through a featureless blue-green seascape whose every non-feature he knows by heart. He has chosen this day carefully—a windless forecast with high tide about dawn—and has notified his imperturbable parents that he's going crabbing, though he isn't. The still air steams and hums; so slick is the Honga's surface that a swimming crab leaves a black and silver wake visible at a hundred yards. Our lad lies now in the skiff's warm odorous bottom, rough with dried fish-scales and crabfat, the scorings of bait knives over who knows how many years, and coat upon coat of flaking paint. Stretched out under the midships seat, he watches gulls and cumulus clouds. He imagines Portugal, the coast of Africa. As always, he is stirred by the knowledge that his homely Honga joins the Bay, the Bay the Atlantic, that ocean the others, and that therefore a message floated out from Hoopersville in a bottle, say, might just wash ashore in Morocco or Zanzibar. The young real Peter Sagamore more than once dispatched such messages and never failed, espying a washed-up bottle in the marsh, to check it for reply, but never found one. Peter Sagamore in last night's dream had dozed off in the bilge of the skiff and been startled from his sleep-within-a-sleep by a rap on the deadrise. Crabfloat, no doubt, or lump of driftwood, but at second knock he pulls himself up and is glad he did. Awash at the skiff's hard chine is a small wooden box, like a miniature sea chest, strapped in rusting iron, grown with barnacles and algae, barely afloat. Because Katherine yesterday fished out that Alert-and-Locate canister with a crabnet, there is a crabnet now in the dream-skiff: Young Peter uses it to draw the box alongside for hefting aboard. It is not lightweight: for one thing, it is both waterlogged and at least partially water-filled, as he hears when he shakes it. It is also locked, and the lock mechanism is no doubt corroded and seized, though the sturdy escutcheon and keyhole are of brass or bronze and only tarnished to green. When he tips the front side down, water drains sluggishly from the keyhole for a long while. Now the casket is lighter; instead of a slosh, there is a satisfying muffled rattle of contents when he shakes it.

Awake, he would be hungry and thirsty by now; in the dream, he is free to set undistracted about the task of opening his treasure. His only tool is his pocketknife. He probes the keyhole with its auger bit; he slips its smaller blade under the lid and feels a fairly hefty bolt, but is afraid to damage either his knife or the wonderful box by further force. He will wait until he can have at the lock with more suitable tools. Meanwhile, he contents himself with carefully scraping off algae and barnacles—he leaves a few of the latter on the iron straps, for effect—and with wondering what might be inside.

He loses track of time. A small north breeze rises, welcome in the muggy forenoon. When the sea chest is as clean as can be managed in the circumstances, the boy looks around to check his bearings and finds that wind and tide together have carried him farther than he had supposed: out of the Honga, into the confluence of Hooper Strait and Chesapeake Bay. To eastward is the open water of Tangier Sound: no land visible on that horizon, because while the distance is not great—seven or eight miles— the land is scarcely higher than the water. To westward are the even more open waters of the Bay, toward which he is being carried: no land visible that way either, because while the shoreline over there is more substantial, it is a dozen and more miles distant at its nearest. Just south, he recognizes marshy, uninhabited Bloodsworth Island, a restricted area used as a bombing target by planes from the Patuxent River Naval Air Station. To the south-southwest, where he's drifting, are the hundred-plus miles of the lower Chesapeake between Hoopers Island and the Virginia capes, where bay becomes ocean.

In waking fact, in 1953 when Peter Sagamore roused from a dream-fraught doze and found himself being carried into the Bay, he had entertained a moment's thrill of fear and then, child of these waters, had sensibly broken his resolve not to touch the oars and had used one to steer toward Bloodsworth Island, knowing the folly of braving either the Bay or Tangier Sound in an open skiff with neither sail nor engine. He was after all *not* running away from home (had he been, he would have set about the thing very differently); he was conducting a simple experiment, for which he had knowledgeably prepared: to test whether, setting out exactly at tide-turn on a windless dawn and never touching the oars, he would be carried downstream for six hours twenty-five minutes (he had estimated from the tide tables and current charts that his position at 2:40 P.M., when the tide next turned, would be just about here, at the confluence of the Honga, Hooper Strait, and the Bay) and then carried back up—here was the point of the experiment—to regain his approximate starting place at 9:05 P.M. Or, failing that—since no messaged bottle cast from the family dock had ever been seen again—back to wherever those bottles went, where he would recover every water-message he had ever sent to the world, and perhaps among them find the world's reply.

But the unpredicted wind had spoiled the experiment: There remained two hours yet to tide-turn, by when he would be at sea indeed. What was more, even the present gentle breeze would cancel out the returning tide; he would have to row the six miles home. Fair enough: He was wiry as a muskrat and tireless at the oars. But he also knew that should that wind increase more than a few knots he'd have to seek shore and wait it out, and his parents would be justly concerned.

In fact he steered to the reedy shore of Bloodsworth, where few adults and no children ventured: strictly off limits, even between the well-monitored bombing exercises, because of the danger of unexploded munitions. So shallow are those waters, the skiff grounded in six inches a hundred feet offshore; he had to drag it gingerly through the mud, keeping an eye out for the larger sea nettles and hoping not to step upon an unexploded bomb. In his dream, on the other hand, oarless, he finds himself fetched by a slow curve of current not onto Bloodsworth but around it, into the open Bay—where, to make matters worse, he now sees unpredicted thunderheads building in the west. It is clear to him, in the dream, that he must either wake up or go over the side and swim the skiff half a mile to shore: no great feat except for the sea nettles. He is about to try to wake himself when he finds himself awake in *Story*'s quarterberth, rocking gently in Dun Cove, wondering what that chest contained.

Not yet having dreamed Part Two, Peter logs the above as "Drifting Down the Honga," and under that title, for further expanding, enters merely "Round-trip Huck Finn, to Bloodsworth without oars. Floating box, locked."

He is in course of noting Katherine's dream—"The Container and the Thing Contained"—when its dreamer, who has gone forward to check whether the Sun Shower is warm enough to use, calls back quietly Pee-ter, in a tone that says You're not going to believe this until you see it. Bring the binoc-u-lars, she croons, and waves politely back at the couple who have waved politely herward from the fiddleheaded stern next door.

The man is curly, burly, tan and gray, grizzled of hair and beard that once were auburn; middle-aged, robust, rather handsome, at once weathered and subtle-appearing—and dressed in a short white tunic loosely belted at the waist: a chiton! His companion, similarly robed, is a slender younger woman: A gold fillet circles her light-olive brow and smooth black hair; her eyes are large and dark—set off strikingly by mascara, Katherine notes, who herself never uses makeup when we're sailing. From this distance, at least, she looks a beauty. The pair lean languidly on the starboard quarter-rail, having evidently just come up from below—where they've spent the whole hot afternoon?

By when Peter gets there with the glasses, it would be rude to use them. He waves hello; the gentleman waves back. His arm about Katherine's waist, Peter is emboldened to call across the windless water Unusual boat you've got there. The chap replies pleasantly Not so unusual where it came from. His accent sounds to us Oxbridge: more accurately, Oxbridge-as-second-language. His companion smiles. Is yours a local design? she inquires, politely. Interesting lines. Her voice is as elegant as her smile, and free of identifiable accent.

Responds Peter Very local design. *Intensely* local. You're welcome aboard, if you'd like to look us over.

The sturdy gentleman says After a bit, perhaps, thank you. But he does not at once return the invitation, which we'd have jumped at. They remain at their quarter-rail, taking their ease but not pursuing the conversation. As they were there first, we withdraw from *Story*'s bow, not to intrude upon their privacy, and, full of curiosity, take our showers swimsuited in the cockpit. Katherine wonders sotto voce What *are* they? Peter replies

It's Odysseus running off with Princess Nausicaa. Isn't she smashing? In Kath's opinion they're *both* smashing: a pair of Greek movie stars doing *Odysseus Among the Muskrat-Eaters*. Where's the film crew?

We slip into clean go-ashore clothes and mosquito repellent and at about seven climb into the dinghy to row in for dinner, first rigging the anchor light on our headstay to guide us home after dark. No sign of Nausicaa— Down there doing her face, P bets, and K says Her face doesn't *need* doing; her face is done—but blocky Odysseus calls mildly from amidships Ahoy there, *Story:* Would you care for an aperitif?

Kathy says for both of us as we check each other's eyes Why not? Peter has the dinghy swung their way already. Their boat's gleaming black free-board is high, but the gentleman rigs an ample midships boarding ladder as we pull alongside. With his aid from above and her husband's from below, K manages the climb easily in the calm water. Peter secures the dinghy and follows.

There is no proper cockpit. Four folding deck chairs are arranged around a low table amidships on the teak deck, just aft of the mast, where we suppose rowing-benches must have been fitted in the prototype. The un-cluttered decks, sturdy bulwarks, and high sheer give the craft a serious, seaworthy look, but Peter can't figure out for the life of him how the thing sails.

Theodoros Dmitrikakis, Odysseus declares, shaking our hands. We are to call him Ted. Peter Sagamore. Katherine. We are seated, pleased that our host neither jokes about nor hastens to explain his unusual vessel and costume. Diana, he calls quietly down a companionway leading aft under the raised quarterdeck: Our neighbors are here. The vowels are European: Deeahnah replies she'll be right up; he should ask us what we'd like to drink. Ted is afraid that they keep no hard liquor aboard: There is light white wine; there is retsina. Katherine says happily A drop of retsina— and a glass of water, she adds, pointing to her tum. Retsina, Peter affirms. Retsina, Ted says down the companionway, adding something in presumable Greek. Diana presently emerges with a serving tray which, when we move our eyes from her to it, we will find holds an unlabeled clear glass bottle of retsina, four small faceted wine goblets and a water tumbler, and a plate of Calamata olives and feta. She is gorgeous.

You are gorgeous, Katherine says as Ted pours. And don't we envy your waistline!

The woman replies easily Yours too is enviable. She seats herself beside Ted, puts a hand lightly on his bare brown knee, smiles him a wistful quick smile of such beauty that Peter Sagamore's heart goes buzz. She crosses two perfect brown legs and lifts her wineglass in salute. *Moment,* bids her friend, this time in French; goes to the rail; gravely empties his glass overside. Returning, he says pleasantly: To Poseidon. He repours; says to Diana, Peter Sagamore and Katherine . . .

Sherritt, Peter says from habit. K says Sagamore, actually: Katherine Sherritt Sagamore. Kathy.

We are pleased to meet one another. Here's to us.

Well. They are smiling, amiable. Their cheese and olives are delicious. Though Peter is no fan of retsina, this is ice-cold and only slightly resinous and certainly appropriate. Now: We don't want to pry, but who's going to get to the point?

I see neither wheel nor tiller, Peter observes, smiling. Do you really use a steering oar? Diana looks at her senior companion with light amusement; he replies offhandedly and not very informatively that an autopilot does most of their actual steering. He does not know whether we know well *The Odyssey,* one of the great epic poems of the ancient Greeks. . . .

We know it well, Peter assures him. Adds Katherine Practically by heart, in English alas. My husband is a writer and I'm a storyteller, she goes on straightforwardly—I mean I'm a library-science person who's learning oral narrative. Peter makes 'em up and I tell 'em, and your *Odyssey* is practically our favorite story in the entire world.

Her American candor wins Diana, who (when Ted has done reminding us that the dream-swift ships of the Phaeacians, that godly race of sailors in Homer's poem who finally deliver Odysseus back to Ithaca, had no mechanical means of steering at all, for they could sense where their skippers wished to go and aim unerringly in that direction) identifies her companion as a former classicist and undersea archaeologist, herself as his former protégée and associate, now his wife. To your good health, long life, and lasting happiness, Peter proposes, lifting his glass. Fair winds, snug harbors, et cet. The Dmitrikakises wish us likewise. Says Kath cheerily As soon as we sailed in here we said Phaeacian Thirty-five, and when you guys came on deck in your chitons we said It's Odysseus and Nausicaa.

Responds Ted smoothly You do us honor. But he does not go on to explain the chitons; instead he says, with clear interest, Storytellers, are you. Are you quite famous for it? Dee and I are out of touch.

He's famous, says Katherine, among people who know. He's the best. I'm only an apprentice. Says Peter Some apprentice: You should hear her do the Catalogue of Ships. You can sing the Catalogue of Ships? Ted asks her, impressed. With enough retsina, K acknowledges—but in English, remember. And in prose.

Our hosts exchange a glance. Will you have dinner with us? Diana asks. Lamb kabobs: We've enough for four. Katherine says unhesitatingly We'd love to; I'll help; and we sip more retsina. The watermen in the restaurant over there this afternoon, reports Peter, thought your boat was a Viking replica on its way to a museum somewhere.

Amused Dee cries Viking! Serious Ted says We rarely go ashore. All right, thinks Katherine: If we have to pry, we'll pry; you wouldn't invite us to dinner and expect us not to ask questions. Underwater archaeology must be exciting, she declares to Ted straight: Is this about what you'd guess from *The Odyssey* that the Greek ships looked like?

Not from *The Odyssey,* says Ted. He reminds us that the paradoxical scarcity, in that great sea-story, of knowledgeable nautical detail (compared to the authoritative ship-lore in *The Iliad*) is one of the characteristics which, with others, has led some readers to infer, erroneously, that its author was a woman—indeed, that it was "Nausicaa" herself.

Ted's self-assurance, in our opinion, borders upon the arrogant, but somehow does not cross the border; we let that "erroneously" go. The vessel, we are now told, is indeed "a sort of replica, more accurate than anyone could likely imagine." But it is not bound for any museum, nor do he and Diana sail it for reasons of nostalgia—we have noted, surely, that some of the rigging is of materials unknown in classical times. Declares Ted We prefer it because it is faster and more seaworthy than any other vessel its size. Not that we're interested in racing.

Her voice rich in disbelief, Katherine asks Really? It goes to windward? Diana replies, amiably if not quite to the point, that certain of their archaeological discoveries in the Mediterranean proved profitable enough for them to retire from their profession, build the boat to their specifications, and cross the Atlantic in record time. Now they migrate like wild waterfowl up and down the flyway from Nova Scotia to the Caribbean.

We Sherritt-Sagamores find it hard to believe—impossible, actually—that so primitive a design, with its single, yardarmed sail, could perform well even against our little *Story,* not to mention a modern ocean racer, especially to windward. If we are not experts in naval architecture and ancient history, neither are we ignorant of them: Odysseus's crew did more rowing than sailing, except offwind. Peter ventures this observation, by no means contentiously. To our surprise, Diana appears to take some offense; she excuses herself to get dinner going. Ted frowns too, but explains that the boatyard was in Diana's hometown, a certain Greek island. The designers and builders were her relatives. And—our understandable skepticism notwithstanding—the boat sails much better than we suppose.

Katherine assures him we were merely questioning, not challenging—Peter's father was a boatbuilder, too!—and excuses herself to go straighten out Diana and help with the meal. Her directness and goodwill carry the day, as Peter has seen them carry many a yesterday: In five minutes the little tension is dispersed; the four of us fall to building a splendid dinner of lamb-onion-and-tomato kabobs, grilled over a brazier on deck and accompanied by a good unlabeled red table wine which Ted decants and serves mixed with mineral water, again pouring the first glass overside.

Our conversation keeps to the less touchy ground of our common enthusiasm for classical Greek literature, especially Homer's *Odyssey.* Though we are not scholars, P knows as well as loves the poem, and K is wise in the ways of the bardic tradition.

Over the meal, as the red sun sets into battleship-gray haze, Ted asks us what our favorite moment is in that story. Without hesitation Peter Sagamore replies that his is the scene in Book Thirteen, halfway through the poem, where after ten years of war and nine of wandering, Odysseus wakes at last on the beach of his homeland, having been fetched there by the Phaeacians in their dream-dark ships and put ashore in his sleep. The man doesn't know he's in Ithaca, says Peter; he laments that the Phaea-cians, who seemed so obliging, have tricked him after all and put him ashore in one more alien country, and that still more wandering lies ahead. He walks up and down the beach in despair—*dragging his feet along the shore,* Homer says.

We all know the passage, and so listen with pleasure to P's paraphrase. Athene appears in the guise of a young shepherd, tells Odysseus he's in Ithaca, and asks him teasingly who he is. Out of a nature deeper than his fatigue, Odysseus conceals his elation at being home and spins out one more false identity, one more elaborate fiction, all the while kneeling on the beach in supplication before the stranger. With a smile, Athene casts off her disguise and stands before him: tall, beautiful, and wise. Even as he yarns on with his umpteenth cover-story, she reaches out and caresses him. In a voice full of love, she chides him for his cunning—*so like her own,* she says—and for not recognizing the goddess who has watched over him right through his odyssey.

Peter shakes his head: What a moment.

Our hosts are clearly pleased and affected by his choice—which he has also done an okay job of rehearsing, K thinks, given that *telling* stories is famously not her friend's long suit. Theodoros is actually moved to breathe in deeply and drain his wineglass. Diana touches his arm. What I think about that scene is this, declares Peter Sagamore: To recognize that his nature is the earthly counterpart of Athene's, and to realize that he's home at last—they're the same thing, right? He won't need to disguise his identity any further.

Ted nods and gruffly says Just so! Of course, puts in quick Katherine, five minutes later Athene disguises him as an old peasant, and off he goes to live incognito with Eumaeus the pig-man. But that's another story, I suppose. Ted repeats Just so: The story of his wandering is done, and the story of his homecoming is begun.

Exclaims beautiful Diana You two really do know our poem! And to Katherine What's *your* favorite moment?

Kate has seen her turn coming—the Dmitrikakises, we think, play this game with all their dinner guests—and has considered. I'm glad you asked, she declares, though we are not certain our hosts understand American irony. The fact is, I had a dream only last night about my favorite passage in *The Odyssey*. Murmurs Peter *Quelle coincidence.* I guess it's in Book Twenty-three, the reunion scene, goes on unperturbed Katie. The big bow has been drawn, the suitors have been massacred, the collaborationist maids have been forced to clean up the mess and then hanged, the place has been fumigated, and Penelope's out of danger. In fact, she slept through the whole thing, the way Odysseus slept through the boat ride home. Nineteen years of stalling for time and hoping against hope are over with; the old nurse wakes her up and tells her that her husband's home at last—and the poor woman can't quite believe it. Not only that: She can't set aside two decades of waiting and worrying in five minutes. She comes downstairs, but she doesn't know how to handle the situation. Should she run up and kiss the guy? Should she stand back and question him awhile, look him over and make sure? But she can't even think what to ask him. She sits by the fire, opposite him, and finds she can't say a word; she just looks and looks at him. Their son scolds her. She admits she's in shock, that she can't even look the man in the face—although she's been busy doing just that. But if it really is Odysseus, she says, they'll work it out, 'cause they have secrets between them that no one else has heard of.

Old Odysseus likes that; he also sees that the woman needs time and mustn't be rushed. So he and grown-up Telemachus work out a trick for dealing with the dead suitors' families—it's a typical Odysseus-trick, and he explains it in Penelope's hearing as a sort of preliminary proof. Then he goes and gets himself cleaned up and dressed to the nines, and only *then* comes back to the hall where Penelope's still waiting and wondering. He scolds her, in an affectionate way, for her obstinacy: Homer's people are forever scolding one another, like a big happy Mediterranean family. What other wife could keep herself out of her husband's arms after twenty years? As if the question shouldn't be What other wife would still be waiting patiently and faithfully after twenty years! And Homer has Penelope say this wonderful, womanly thing: *You're* strange, too, she tells Odysseus. I'm not being haughty or indifferent, she says; I'm not even unduly surprised. *But I have such a clear picture in my mind of the way you looked twenty years ago, when you sailed off to Troy in your long-oared ship. . . .*

Then she plays the bed trick, telling old Eurycleia to move Odysseus's big bed out into the hall for the night, when she knows that the real Odysseus knows that it can't be moved: The secret of the marriage bed is that it's there for keeps. Seems to me she's testing not only whether this handsome middle-aged stranger is really Odysseus—that fact must be pretty clear to her by now—but whether he's *her* Odysseus: the one she remembers so clearly. If he has forgotten the secrets of their marriage bed, then no matter what his name is, he's not her husband.

Bravo, Diana says. Hear hear, agrees proud Peter. Theodoros nods. Continues Kath He takes the bait, no faking now, and explains in a great swivet that the bed can't be moved, 'cause he built it around a live olive tree, blah blah blah. So that proves he's Odysseus. What he *doesn't* know, he says very pointedly then, is whether their bedpost-tree still stands, or whether someone has cut it down in his absence. That does the trick: Penelope melts, and it occurs to me now that there's a similarity between this scene and the one Peter told. First we see that Athene loves Odysseus because he's so much like herself: She shows herself to him for the first time undisguised, and that means he's home. Now we see that Odysseus and Penelope are perfect for each other because she's just as cagey and resourceful as he is. She demonstrates that, and then they put by all such game-playing—and that means he's *really* home, and the story's over.

Bravo again! cheers Peter. Kate's heart tingles. Our hosts have grown mighty pensive. Ted nods at his wineglass; Diana regards first him and then the gray-and-salmon sky to westward. Says Peter Sagamore So: I'd say that that's another one of those bits that led people like Samuel Butler and Robert Graves to imagine that *The Odyssey* was composed by a woman. The Homer's Daughter business.

Ted sits up, pours out another round of red and water, which we're learning to like though Kath's is nine-tenths water. The author of *The Odyssey* was not a woman, he firmly informs us. You might say that it was a man who had learned to pay attention to women as well as paying attentions to them.

Says Kate Sherritt *Okay*—once again because while the man's self-assurance is potentially insufferable, what he said was so nicely and unarrogantly put that we can't take offense. Peter now asks Diana directly what *their* favorite moment is (something tells us they do not have separate ones). She and Ted at once exchange so loving and wistful a smile that we excuse them any amount of over-self-confidence. And we have guessed correctly: Their joint favorite episode in all of literature, Diana tells us, is another beach scene: the story in *Odyssey* Book Six of young Princess Nausicaa of the Flashing Arms doing laundry with her maids at the river shore and then playing ball with them on the beach, while unknown to them poor ship-wrecked Odysseus—naked, sea-grimed, exhausted from swimming, and alone—sleeps dead to the world in a clump of wild olive bushes nearby.

Yeah! cries athletic Kath, delighted at the memory. Playing ball! Old Nausicaa there with her major-league arms. I love it!

Goes on smoothly smiling Diana She never misses a catch. But one of the maids does, and the ball goes into the river, which is deep just there and has a fast current too, and they all make a shriek, the way girls do. The noise wakes Odysseus. He groans and wonders where he is—for all he knows, the people might be cannibals, like the Cyclopes—but he has to ask for food and shelter or die, so he steps out grizzled and naked except for an olive branch to cover up his privates. Diana smiles and smiles. *Like a mountain lion,* Homer says, she says, *forced by hunger to besiege the very walls of the homestead and attack the pens.* The girls catch sight of him; they scream; they scatter—

All except Nausicaa, Ted puts in, turning his wineglass by the stem as if examining a thornless rose.

Says K Good old flashy-armed Nausicaa: She's all sand. Ted smiles at her questioningly. Guts, Kath explains. *Cojones.* Balls. Did she ever get her ball back, by the way?

Kay-tee, Peter warns. Kate says Excuse me, Dee; I'll shut up. But this scene knocks *me* down, too.

Says Diana Dear Homer draws such a picture of both of them. Odysseus on his knees says just the right things to flatter her and calm her fears and state his case all at the same time. Then, once he washes himself up and puts on the clothes they give him, and Athene makes him particularly handsome, Nausicaa flirts with him shamelessly! She tells her maids that he's just the kind of man she hopes to marry, and then she tells Odysseus himself that she's afraid the gossips in town will think she's bringing this handsome stranger home to be her husband, since she has spurned all the local princes who would like to marry her. Diana grins. She's shameless!

I love her, says Kate, grinning too. Peter wonders: Dear Homer?

Says Ted Every scene between them is beautiful, including the last one, two books later. King Alcinous has offered Odysseus Nausicaa to be his wife, even though they don't know who he is yet; but Odysseus has declared he must get home—without directly mentioning that he has a wife waiting for him there. Nausicaa was brave down on the beach, but she is even braver when she hears this news and accepts it. She stands in her father's hall beside one of the great pillars—*in all her heaven-sent beauty,* Homer says—and greets him. Good luck, my friend, she says. Isn't that splendid? Not Noble Sir or Distinguished Stranger, but *my friend.*

Quotes beautiful Diana, looking at him serenely, warmly, *I hope that when you are in your own country you will remember me at times, since it is to me before all others that you owe your life.*

Princess Nausicaa, Ted seriously says back, *I do indeed pray Zeus the Thunderer and Lord of Hera to let me reach my home. If he does, then even there I will never fail to worship you all the rest of my days. For it was you, lady, who gave me back my life.*

They reach out and touch each other's fingertips. We are thrilled. We reach out and touch *our* each other's fingertips, too. Says Peter Beautiful. Good choices and well told. It is not difficult to see why the Dmitrikakises like that story: its obvious parallels to their own May–September connection. We bet it's a relatively new marriage, and not Ted's first.

Dinner is done, the sun is down, but no one feels like setting about the cleanup yet. Ted fetches a citronella candle from below; passes around some bug repellent with a pleasant pine scent and Greek letters on the phial. Diana brings up baklava and offers coffee, but our consensus is to retrieve the cold retsina for postprandial sipping. Katherine (mineral water for her, thanks) says she's sure they know all those sequels to *The Odyssey* in which for one reason or another—Penelope's infidelity or death, Odysseus's restlessness, whatever—the old sailor makes a final voyage to meet that "easy death from the sea" that Circe foretold for him. Dante has him leave the Mediterranean and sail for five months down into the Southern Ocean, to sink at last in sight of Mount Purgatory: the classical era overwhelmed by the Christian era. But late-classical writers have him going back to Calypso in search of the agelessness she once offered him. K believes there's even a version in which he goes back to Nausicaa, who's still carrying the torch for him in those flashing arms of hers.

Diana wonders: Carrying the torch? Kate explains the old slang expression, to their amusement.

Laughs Diana Yes, I suppose she was . . . carrying the torch. We've heard all those stories. And some naughty ones, too.

Ted fingers his red-and-gray beard. My friends: Diana and I do not see people often, and we have enjoyed this evening with you, Katherine, and you, Peter. You seem to us to be wise about both sailing and poetry, and to be in love with each other as well. The three great things, yes?

Applauds Kathy Hear hear, and we drink to those things. We Sherritt-Sagamores, some of us anyhow, are beginning to feel our wine.

And you are about to have a child, adds Diana. A fourth great thing.

Says Peter Or fifth or sixth. There's twins at least in there, named Iliad and Odyssey. He raises his glass. May you be likewise blessed, if that's a blessing you seek. May you be oppositely blessed, if it isn't. We drink. Declares Kate *We've* enjoyed this evening, too. We think that Theodoros is handsome and Diana is beautiful, and that this here now Phaeacian Thirty-five is the fleetest, swartest ship that ever clove the wine-dark, fish-infested sea, is what we think.

We drink. Ted says good-humoredly You make a little joke about the boat, but we don't mind. On the contrary: Dee and I will tell you two stories to add to your story collection, if you wish to have them. Two of those *follow-up stories* you speak of. But these you have never heard before. What do you say?

Kate says she's all ears and so's Pete, and says it so they'll know she means it. Peter adds that we began this little cruise with more cause than purpose, if they know what he means—sailing *from* more than sailing *to*—but the thing seems to be becoming a sort of narrative scavenger hunt. By all means tell on; we're honored and delighted.

Satisfied Ted declares that the second of these twin stories is the *true* story of Odysseus's so-called last voyage. The first has to do with that famous web of Penelope's, the last corner of which she wove by day and unraveled by night for more than three years to stall the suitors, having promised them she would choose a new husband from their number when it was done. The story has to do with what she wove into that last corner: what the web was about.

On with that story, urges Peter Sagamore.

Says Ted I shall tell one and Diana the other. Which is your pleasure, my dear?

The second, of course. In fact—Diana rises, smooths out her white tunic; Peter's hormones exclaim By Aphrodite, she is a magnificent specimen!—I'll clean up dinner while you tell the first.

She won't permit us to help. But all four of us need to pee before further narration, and so at last we Sagamores get a real glimpse belowdecks. A showboat, a gold-plater: gorgeous woods, meticulous joinery—inlays, even, and intricate hand-carving everywhere. The galley fixtures and the plumbing in the head compartment are modern, but our not-inexperienced glance espies no electronics, no navigation station—just as there were abovedecks no engine controls or instrumentation that we could see. To be sure, they could all be concealed for effect behind that handsome woodwork.

Bladders relieved and legs stretched, three-fourths of us return to the main deck and at Diana's request move our chairs close enough to the aft companionway for her to overhear the story. Katherine Sherritt props her legs up comfortably on the quarterdeck rise. Peter Sagamore pours out three dollops of retsina, one of mineral, and hands a glass down to gleaming Dee. Theodoros Dmitrikakis takes a sip and a breath, and with an assurance in this case pleasing, begins by glass-candle-light

THE UNFINISHED STORY OF PENELOPE'S UNFINISHED WEB.

After Odysseus had drawn the great bow and slain the suitors and caused the wanton maidservants to be strung up all on the same rope like hapless sparrows in a fowler's snare, and after Penelope, as Katherine says, had overcome her doubts by means of the marriage-bed secret, husband and wife so long separated retired at last to that very bed. As you recall, Athene made that first night of their reunion long, holding back the dawn to give them time both to make love and to hear out each other's stories.

But although Homer doesn't mention it, their *second* night together was even longer, for in its course, after making love, they raised and answered a question much upon their minds. It was Penelope who voiced it, as they lay now lightly separated in the great bed Odysseus had fashioned for them, their hands touching in the dark. Granted that each of them had been essentially faithful over all those years: Whatever his trials, temptations, perhaps even lapses, Odysseus had come home to her; nor had he ever doubted her to be his destination. And whatever hers, Penelope on her part had never really ceased to believe that he would return, and had not committed herself to any other; and here they were, back in each other's arms. Yet it could scarcely be imagined that both had remained strictly celibate for twenty prime and mortal years! Leaving aside as unworthy of mention any fleeting, inconsequential alliances—a slave girl or temple prostitute here, perhaps an itinerant princeling there—what, if any, had been their major side-engagements of the heart? Whom else had each of them *loved*—though never so much, Q.E.D., as they loved each other? Between two so fit to each other's souls as they, such stories might be told.

Odysseus spoke first, and, though all guile with others, to Penelope as to Athene he spoke straight truth. As his canny wife supposed, there had indeed been one such "side-engagement of his heart": not with any mortal woman—what mortal woman could hold a candle to his Penelope?—but with a goddess, as dangerous as she was beautiful. Tell the story, Penelope directed, and tell it whole and plainly. I fear nothing, now that we are together.

So Odysseus told her the story of his liaison with Circe the enchantress on the island of Aeaea, to which he came with his one surviving ship and crew after those ruinous adventures with the Cicones, the Lotus Eaters, Polyphemus the Cyclops, Aeolus on his floating island, and the cannibal giant Laestrygonians. Everybody has heard that it was this Circe's pleasure to turn men into beasts, and that she turned Odysseus's scouting party into swine. The common story is that she did this by means of a certain charmed potion slipped into their wine, against which the herb Moly alone was proof. But the truth is that that potion was Circe's unusually keen intelligence and formidable learning, in the presence of which—combined as they were with her striking beauty and her excellent and plentiful wine—men turned themselves into whatever beasts lurked inside them: some into lions, some into wolves, others foxes, others dogs. In the case of that particular party, swine.

Touché! cheers Katherine Sherritt, and asks if that's what Circe's potion was, what was the Moly?

Says Ted That was Penelope's very question, to which Odysseus answered The Moly was my experience of you, who alone besides Athene have always seen through my every pretense and pretension. As I see through this one, Penelope replied. Don't flatter me: There was more to that Moly than myself. Responded Odysseus I speak the truth, but so do you: There was indeed more to the Moly. Its deep root, I say again, was my experience of you, which taught me how to love unpatronizingly a woman my equal in authority and intelligence. The difference is that Circe was not my equal but my superior, with whom I had always to be at my very best, once I had disarmed her with that Moly and she had taken me to her high bed. Not for a moment, in the year I spent with her—

A year! Penelope cried out, and let go her husband's hand and sat up in the dark bed. You stayed with this enchantress a whole year?

This night, Odysseus reminded her, we're honor-bound to tell the truth. Not for a moment in that whole year did I dare relax my guard and simply be myself with Circe, or I'd have joined the other swine in her pen.

A whole year! Penelope lamented. She lay down again beside her husband, but did not take his hand as before.

He could not have managed longer, he told her, so unremittingly upon his mettle did the enchantress keep him. What was more, he needed not only to preserve himself from being turned into ham and bacon, so to speak, but somehow to rescue and restore his crew from that condition, and moreover to extract from Circe the sailing directions to Ithaca from Aeaea, which is off the charts: *A place where East and West mean nothing,* Homer says. It is a route that carries one straight through Hades, past the fateful Sirens and the Wandering Rocks, and then—at cost of ship and shipmates—between Scylla and Charybdis to Ogygia, the enchanted island of Calypso.

Penelope could only whisper once again A whole year!

The most demanding year of my life, declared her husband: so exhausting that I lost track of time altogether, and had to be reminded by my men what season it was. In the end I got everything I wanted from her; but I swear to you that beside that year with Circe, my ten years of fighting before the walls of Troy were child's play, and my seven years with the nymph Calypso were a vacation.

Says grinning Peter Sagamore Uh-oh.

Your seven with the nymph Calypso! cried Penelope, sitting upright. Tell me you mean seven hours! Seven days!

Ssh, Odysseus bade her: You'll waken old Eurycleia. Will you hear the truth, or hear nothing? Oh, the truth, Penelope wept; we shall have the whole truth. With this *other* other woman, then, it was seven whole years!

Odysseus implored her to calm herself, declaring that he expected equal candor from her in her turn, when her turn came. Penelope told him to proceed, but her head was dizzy, and she would not lie down beside him while he continued. Seven years!

I understand your distress, Odysseus assured her, Ted said. What *you* must understand is that whereas with Circe I was free to leave as soon as my men were restored to me and I had my sailing directions, with Calypso I was in effect a prisoner, though a splendidly treated one. I had no men, no ship, no choice but to put myself at the nymph's disposal and to do her bidding in her perfumed cave.

Penelope steeled herself and asked what had been this Calypso's bidding, exactly. Just what I needed after Circe, replied Odysseus, next to being here in this unmoving bed with you. Where are you going? Penelope answered from across the room that she would hear the rest of his story from the chair at the foot of their bed. And hear the story she would; but he must understand that such news required some assimilating. On with it.

Odysseus himself sat up now and said frankly through the darkness between them that after the extraordinary challenge of his year with Circe, and the heartbreaking loss of every ship and crewman he'd set out from home with, it was an unspeakable relief that the immortal and beautiful nymph Calypso expected of him nothing but that he be a ready fellow. Theirs was a relation without responsibility, except amorous performance.

Katherine Sherritt bets *that* news cheered Penelope right up.

Don't forget the woman's strength of character, bids Theodoros. Stricken as she was, she *did* understand the situation as her husband described it. Did you give her children? she wanted to know then, or she you, as I gave you Telemachus? He had not, Odysseus replied, for Calypso had wanted none. It is said that the embrace of a god is never fruitless, but goddesses have their ways; they get children by mortal men only when they choose to. And fortunate it was for him she was disinclined, for a man who sires children upon a goddess is typically a wreck thereafter: Look at old Peleus, Achilles' father by the nymph Thetis; look at old Anchises, Aeneas's father by Aphrodite. As for where his heart lay, Odysseus went on, Calypso herself would testify that though at her bidding he went to her high bed for two thousand five hundred nights and there did his manly office without stint or respite, every morning he returned to the seashore, there to bewail his idyllic isolation and rack his brains for a way to get home to his mortal wife.

Eight years with other women! Penelope repeated like a refrain, but more quietly than before. A year with Circe, seven with Calypso! You were out there actually sailing for only one year of the nine!

Odysseus firmly begged her to remember in her distress that, unforgettable as those two women and those twin interludes were, they *were* but interludes. Moreover, with Circe he had been in danger and in need, and with Calypso, though not at risk, he had been powerless to leave without her consent and assistance. Bear in mind also, he appealed to her, that both affairs, being as they were with goddesses, did Penelope a kind of honor, as did the fact that while both Circe and Calypso had admittedly engaged her husband's heart, neither had captured it. But now, he said, it is your turn to be the teller and mine to be the told. Will you not rejoin me in our bed?

You made our bed, Penelope said quietly, and now you must lie in it, alone, till I've told my tale. And tell it I will, though at less length. For one thing, there is less to tell. For another, I am still short of breath before the fact that you and I have spent fewer nights together in this bed than you spent in the high bed of Calypso.

Yet you have, after all, a tale to tell? Odysseus asked uneasily.

I have, his wife affirmed. No god, she declared, came down from Olympus to interrupt her loom-work with irresistible importunings, nor did any wandering Aeneas make her his Dido-of-a-season. She did not, like Spartan Helen, run off with some royal houseguest, nor like Clytemnestra install a noncombatant noble in her warring husband's bed—though among her one hundred eight late suitors had been numbered many a handsome lord. What's more, they had pled their several suits not adulterously, like Aegisthus, but on the honorable and reasonable presumption of Odysseus's death—for they had been as ignorant as she that he was neither dead in Troy nor sunk and drowned, but sleeping one year with Circe, seven with Calypso. Yet to none of them had she lent her heart, nor had she gone to any's bed even for an hour, much less admit him to this moveless bed of theirs.

Thoughtful Odysseus said Mm hm. No god or demigod, you say; no wandering hero or well-born suitor . . .

Dear husband, Penelope said: Word has perhaps reached you of the device by which for above three years I forestalled my suitors' pressure to choose a husband from among them. I mean the loom trick.

Odysseus acknowledged that news had come to the hut of Eumaeus the swineherd, who subsequently passed it to him, that the impatient suitors at one point had agreed to let her finish weaving a shroud for Odysseus's old father before she chose a second husband, and that for three years she had unwoven every night what she wove by day, until the ruse was discovered and she was obliged to finish the piece. But everybody knows that a tale recounted is likely to be a tale improved. Tell on.

What he heard was essentially correct, Penelope told him, but it was not the whole story. She had indeed begun a shroud for old Laertes at one point to delay the suitors, and had been obliged to finish it when they discovered how slowly she was proceeding. But that was a trifle: a work of her left hand, so to speak. Her major web-work for the past nineteen years, and the source of the unweaving-device, was quite another matter; it is that one which both tells and is her story. She began it soon after Odysseus sailed for Troy, to keep her mind and hands busy in his absence. It was to be a sampler of sorts, into which she meant to work little reminiscences of their too-brief time together. She had fully expected him to return victorious before it was complete. As the years passed, however, it grew into a mighty tapestry, in three panels.

The first panel, on which she worked no less than seven years (Penelope's voice failed her for a moment when she spoke that number), depicts the story of their life together from their courtship in Sparta through Odysseus's departure on that ill-starred military expedition to Troy: a period three years shorter than the time it took to weave it. There is bandy-legged, thigh-scarred young Odysseus, a suitor himself then, winning her hand in the Spartan footrace. There are the bride and groom leaving her homeland in their honeymoon chariot, Penelope modestly veiling her face to indicate that her first loyalty is now to her husband. Even the intricate lacework of the veil is duplicated in the tapestry—weaving about weaving, so to speak, of which the then-novice weaver was particularly proud. There is Odysseus building their palace and fashioning the newlyweds' marriage bed. There is Penelope giving birth to Telemachus in that same bed the very next year; and, but one year thereafter—woven in darker thread— there is Odysseus feigning madness in order to dodge the fateful draft. He yokes together an ox and an ass to plow his Ithacan fields; he sows the furrows with salt. But Agamemnon and Menelaus, the recruitment team, neither believe him mad nor recognize the sane prophecy in his behavior: that it is they who are mad, for mounting a war which will leave their fields and wives barren. There is the counterprophet Palamedes proving Odysseus's sanity by snatching infant Telemachus from Penelope's breast and setting him in the tenth furrow, which the father will not plow lest he kill his son. There is that other draft-dodger, Achilles, hiding among the women until Odysseus, now recruited, tricks out his sex. There is the fleet's false first start from Aulis; and there—in the panel's last, lower right-hand corner—the second: In red thread is stitched the blood of sacrificed Iphigenia; the whole catalogue of Argive ships sails Troyward into the background, while in the foreground of the final square inches, in lieu of artist's signature, the tiny figure of Penelope, her son in her arms, her back to the viewer, stands alone on an Ithacan headland, staring out to sea.

Why, that sounds epical! Odysseus ventured. I much look forward to seeing this tapestry of yours.

Penelope did not reply. The second panel, she declared presently, turned out to be another seven years in the loom. Seven years! And it would never have been embarked upon, had she not believed from year to year of those seven that, despite certain prophesies to the contrary, her husband's triumphal homecoming would interrupt it. There are tales, my friends, that one begins in hopes of never having to reach the end.

In two views, this panel recounts the ten years of the Trojan War. The first view (occupying only the upper left-hand corner) shows their house, steadfast and unchanged. Her father-in-law Laertes, the old nurse Eurycleia, the dog Argos, the swineherd Eumaeus, the goatherd Melanthius, the herald Medon, the bard Phemius (who of course was too young then to be a bona fide bard yet)—all go about their domestic business. . . .

Phemius, Odysseus mused. That will be the young fellow who begged for his life when I was killing your suitors the day before yesterday. I was about to dispatch him with the others when Telemachus confirmed the fellow's story that he had never sung for the suitors of his own free will. I spared him and sent him packing.

From across the room he could hear Penelope's breathing. When you sailed, she said presently, this Phemius was a boy, one of the goatherd's helpers. But early on he showed such a way with the lyre and with his voice, amusing the servants so with his clever songs, that Eurycleia set him the task of keeping up my spirits with his music as I wove.

Then it's well I spared him, said Odysseus. For that work he deserves my thanks. What else is in this second panel?

That same upper left-hand corner of it, Penelope declared, shows Telemachus going through his boyhood and herself at her loom, weeping at her husband's absence and weaving Panel One. A more accomplished artisan by then, she was able even to suggest, in the finest stitches, the contents of that first panel in its miniature replication here—a trick she could never have brought off seven years before. As for the body of Panel Two, it shows the war in Troy, first as she and the rest of the household imagined it, and then, when the fighting was over and the other heroes began to make their way home, from their reports—which young Phemius, like every other bard in the known world, turned into song.

As he sang, said Penelope, she sewed; as she sewed, he sang. His words became her images, her images his words. There is Achilles sulking in his tent; there shameless Helen promenading the Trojan battlements, et cetera. But the focus of this panel, as of the first, is Odysseus and his several celebrated exploits. Here is shown his revenge upon Palamedes for exposing his madman act; here his capture of Rhesus's horses, his quarrel with Ajax, his retrieval of Philoctetes's magic bow, his theft of the sacred Palladium, and many another heroic feat—culminating, of course, in his grandest stratagem: the wooden horse.

Said Odysseus This second panel must be a formidable piece of work, for that was a complicated and a bloody decade. The Trojans lost their city, but so many on both sides perished that to this day I can't decide who lost the war. I say let's put it behind us and get to the third panel of your collaboration with this young bard, this Phemius.

People called it the Book of Homecomings, Penelope reported, for it shows the principal Greek veterans returning from the war, each to his fate as news of it reached Ithaca and Phemius turned the story into song. Six years now in the making, the panel remained still unfinished, and thus the story of it was conflated with that of Laertes' shroud. To old Nestor, alone of all the Greeks, is granted a safe, direct, and happy return: There is Agamemnon, caught in Clytemnestra's net and butchered in his bath; there is this one wrecked, that cuckolded, these betrayed in other wise. But there are Menelaus and Helen, the origin of all this woe, after many vicissitudes sitting as comfortably together at their Lacedaemonian fireside as if nothing at all had happened. They are shown receiving young Telemachus, in search of news of his father; wanton Helen even *knits,* and so skillful a weaver was Penelope by this time, she was able to show that the whole disaster of the war and its aftermath has not cost the hussy one dropped stitch.

And down toward the lower right-hand corner, Penelope concluded, is pictured this high hall, infested with my suitors. They reasonably believe you dead and beleaguer me to choose a new husband from among them, meanwhile devouring your substance daily. Aided by Phemius's ingenuity, I delay them with every possible pretext. We do the shroud trick not once but twice: once in fact and again in the stitches of this panel. We send Telemachus off to Pylos and Sparta, hoping that Nestor or Menelaus will have word of you. . . .

We send Telemachus away? Odysseus echoed.

Myself and good Phemius, declared Penelope, without whose resourcefulness I would long since have been obliged to surrender myself to the suitors. It was Phemius's idea to send our son off traveling, so that I could swear not to remarry until his return. It was Phemius's idea to weave your father's shroud, a warp here, a woof there. And when I was constrained to press on and finish it, it was Phemius's inspiration that I should plead to finish my tapestry as well before making my choice. Such a small area remained to be done, the suitors reckoned it the work of a month at most; they settled in to gorge and guzzle and make free with our womenservants till I had completed that lower right-hand corner. And it was Phemius's device to unravel each night what I had woven by day.

I begin to see, said Odysseus: perhaps more than I wish to. The part not yet woven is my homecoming. The suitors slain. Ourselves here in this bedroom, telling these stories.

Not at all, Penelope replied. For even had I known as I wept and wove through the years, fearing you dead, that you were enjoying yourself for a year in Circe's bed, seven in Calypso's—even then I would have woven the great climax which I wove in fact: my husband home at last; the suitors slain; order restored to Ithaca. You'll see in the morning this very scene, stitched clearly in stitches not put there yesterday but firmly in place and never loosened. For upon that scene depended our liberation from the suitors. You were our only hope.

Our, repeated Odysseus.

Telemachus's and mine, Penelope said. And Eurycleia's and Eumaeus's, and the thirty-eight maidservants who like myself held out against the suitors' advances.

Also Phemius, Odysseus declared.

Also Phemius. No warrior he, Penelope went on to say, her young friend could scarcely have picked up Odysseus's great bow, as Telemachus used longingly to do, much less have drawn it. So far from presuming to slay the suitors, he dared not so much as provoke their irritation. Every night, at their demand, he had sung for their entertainment, hoping to distract them from their lust. But his songs had been double-edged, as she knew by listening from her loom. Pretending to flatter them, he had exposed their grossness and presumption. Pretending to sing of her heart's hardness, between the lines he had praised its constancy. Pretending to scoff at the possibility of Odysseus's return, he had in fact kept that possibility always before them, to temper the suitors' outrageousness and to give courage to the rest of the household. Then at evening's end, when the unwelcome guests were besotted with Odysseus's wine and off to bed with the maidservants, Phemius would slip upstairs, go to the great loom, and unweave all or most of what his mistress had that day woven.

So, Odysseus said: It was not your hand that did the undoing. . . .

Mine, said Penelope, was too weary from having woven to unweave. Once or twice an artist may unmake and remake what she has made. Ten times, a dozen—but not ten times ten times. In particular when it is not the art that she is displeased with, or not she whom the art displeases.

I see more and more, Odysseus declared. And yet he believed his wife had mentioned that this undone corner was *not* the scene of yesterday, and today, and tonight? Replied Penelope It is not. In my tapestry you are home; Phemius has withdrawn; the guilty are punished; you and I have exchanged our stories. We are there as we are here—and here we are, you and I, just as Phemius foresang and I forewove. What was yet to weave, she continued, was tomorrow and the days thereafter. Many a version she had stitched in, and though the web-work every time was above reproach, if Phemius had not unstitched them she would have done so herself, for none would do.

The fact is, declared grim Odysseus, this minstrel Phemius has been your lover for twenty years.

Twenty years! Penelope cried, and Odysseus heard her laugh for the first time since his return. Never twenty years! Twenty years ago, she reminded him, Phemius had been an ignorant stripling boy, frisking with Melanthius's goats while she labored over Panel One. Through the seven years of Panel Two, he had reached young manhood and minstrelsy, moved into the palace, practiced and refined the art he'd learned in the rocky highlands with none but the goats for audience. It was only in the six years past, the years of Panel Three, as the suitors had pressed and her hope and courage had waned, that Phemius became first her most loyal supporter (after Eurycleia and Telemachus, to be sure; but those two had ever been as much Odysseus's guardians of her morals as Penelope's confidants and friends); then her fellow tactician, her fellow artist, her closest friend . . . and, yes, finally her lover.

Odysseus groaned.

Though never once was he in this bed, Penelope concluded firmly, herself still sitting in that chair in the dark. The vow she had made upon her husband's departure, she said, neither to admit another man into their marriage bed nor herself to go to the bed of another man, she had kept—though at last in its letter only. In her weaving room, beside her loom, was a couch piled deep with the yarns of her art. There Phemius had sat and sung as she wove, often putting by his lyre to hold between his out-stretched hands the skeins she wound into untangled balls. There too they made the love that tangled them. After which, as she lay slaked and drowsy among the yarns, he would rise and gently undo what she'd done. Whether that day's scene showed the two of them running off together to live in love and art and upland poverty, or dead at Odysseus's hand together with the maids and suitors, or (the most frequent denouement) wife and husband reconciled and Phemius gone off to woo some other woman or his mere music—whatever the day's version of their end, she would feel the thread of it unwarped, unwoofed. The ravelings would fall lightly upon her breasts and thighs and belly, to be refigured next day; then presently she'd hear her friend go off to his pallet belowstairs, whereupon she'd rouse herself, shake off those undoings, and come to this cold high bed to sleep alone.

There ends my story, Penelope declared; my tapestry remains unended. When Eurycleia recognized your scar and told me you were returned, I pretended disbelief, but bade Phemius good-bye and begone, both for his own protection (though it is quite like him to have lingered on and had to beg for his life) and because my loyalty remains to you, even now that I've learned of your year with Circe and your seven with Calypso.

Your loyalty may be mine, observed Odysseus, but your heart belongs to this young singer, this Phemius.

Penelope replied that her heart was divided and would doubtless remain so, for a while or forever. About her erstwhile lover she had no illusions: He was neither a hero nor a husband, but a singer of tales. He was not hard nor strong nor brave nor rich nor nobly born—though neither was he soft, weak, cowardly, destitute, or ignoble. He was handsome but not rugged, insightful but not shrewd, sensitive but not wise. If she had enjoyed him as a lover, she had most valued him as a friend, and most admired him as an artist. She had no wish to be his wife, nor any man's save Odysseus's—who might now do with her what he would.

Heartsore Odysseus went to where she wept, kissed her forehead, and brought her back to their bed, where presently, despite her tears, he heard her breathe the breath of sleep. But he himself lay sleepless through what remained of that night, turning over in his mind the story of her tapestry and the problematical task ahead. Next morning, as Athene had directed, he dressed once again in humble clothing, to evade the wrath of the slain suitors' families; he put a well-cut oar upon his shoulder, bade good-bye to his newly regained household, and set out upon his wearisome inland task—not only to appease Poseidon, but to assimilate his wife's story and to give her time to assimilate his.

As luck would have it, on the third night out, up in the craggy highlands behind his palace, he came upon a goatherd singing lightheartedly beside a small campfire with only his goats for audience; drawing nearer, he recognized the very fellow whose life he had spared before Penelope told her story. His heart full, he saluted the singer out of the darkness and, disguising his voice as he had disguised his appearance, asked to share that campfire for the night. The young man welcomed him, passed the wineskin, and asked who he was and why he was strolling the mountains by night with an oar upon his shoulder. Pleisthenes, a servant of Antinous, Odysseus replied at once, laying down the oar and seating himself far enough from the firelight to assist his disguise. *Former* servant, I should say, since my former master, the leader of those suitors for the hand of Odysseus's wife, was the first of those gentlemen to die when that ruffian showed up two days ago and butchered the whole crew. I myself barely escaped with my life; I must now make my way back to Boeotia, my home country, with no other reward for my years of service than this oar, which I made free with as a souvenir. But I daresay it will fetch a good price in Boeotia once Odysseus's story becomes better known, for it is the only oar in Greece from a genuine Phaeacian dark ship. And who are you, young fellow? You look to be a ready enough cocksman: What are you doing up here singing songs to the goats instead of to the ladies down below?

Phemius laughed—and Odysseus, who had scarcely looked twice at him during their confrontation in the banquet hall, observed that he was a wiry, clean-limbed, canny-looking fellow, handsome enough in his way but mainly quick-eyed and supple-featured. He too, he said, was a fugitive from Odysseus's halls, but for a different reason, which he could better sing than say. Do it, do it, bade disguised Odysseus. Taking up his lyre, the bard struck a few chords, retuned a string or two, and then launched into a ribald ballad about a young goatherd, Phemius by name, who learned from his billy goats how to sing to please the nannies, and from a certain noble lady how to hump like a billy goat. Then, oh then (he sang), while Odysseus plowed the wine-dark sea and Penelope's suitors plowed their way through Odysseus's wine, randy Phemius plowed Penelope herself. *And oh he kissed the freckles on her hey-nonny-no, the pretty freckles on her hey-nonny-no!*

Now Odysseus, in telling Penelope of his year with Circe and seven with Calypso, had avoided any intimate detail; and Penelope had done likewise but for the business of those unravelings upon her postcoital skin: an inadvertence that had burned into Odysseus's imagination like a cattle brand. Such was his rage therefore at hearing Phemius now boast so flippantly of cuckolding him, and advertise so lewdly that detail of his wife's complexion (which he himself had recollected fondly through their twenty-year separation and kissed lovingly at last just a few nights since), he sprang across the campfire, struck the lyre from the startled bard's hands, seized him by the throat, and set about to do what he ought to have done back in the banquet hall.

The instrument fell with a clang; the goats bleated, leaped, and scattered; terrified Phemius found himself once again begging for his life. He had made the whole thing up! he cried. He was but a lying songster, whom Odysseus's faithful wife had never been more than friend to! Those freckles he had borrowed from the backside of a serving-maid, who had boasted to him of that resemblance to her mistress!

Odysseus held the fellow by the gullet. Till now, Phemius, he declared, you had committed two offenses, the second graver than the first. You made love to Odysseus's wife: a trespass which, howevermuch it stings, I was prepared to forgive you, under the circumstances, as I have forgiven her. But then you put your private offense into public art, multiplying the felony. Don't claim to me that you mean this song for your goats' ears only: I know a thing or two about minstrels. For this second offense I ought to kill you, to preserve not only my own honor but my wife's: Whatever her feelings for you, she cannot be imagined to enjoy the prospect of your publishing those intimacies to the world. And now, having dishonored me by bedding my wife and dishonored her by trumpeting your conquest to strangers, you dishonor yourself by denying that your trumpetings are true.

Desperate Phemius then swore, with what breath he could draw, that if Odysseus would once again spare him, he would devote the rest of his career to singing his savior's exploits and Penelope's steadfast virtue. Odysseus scoffed: He could imagine, he said, how far such a promise might be trusted; he chose to leave the matter of his fame to bards with no vested interest in singing it. For Penelope's sake, he decided then, and because he was weary of killing, he would for the second time let Phemius live. But should he ever hear of his singing again of that affair, he would search him out and cut his throat.

Hardly able to believe his good fortune, the grateful bard swore never again to speak of the matter, much less sing of it; not even to the goats.

To ensure that you do not, Odysseus said, I'll take a measure painful enough for you but nonetheless preferable to death: a measure inspired by the example of a bard far greater than yourself, who in Phaeacia sang of the moon and the stars and of the great deeds done in Troy.

That would be Demodocus, frightened Phemius said: a master singer indeed, who unfortunately—

He spoke no further, because grim Odysseus clapped one hand over his mouth and with the other blinded him in both eyes, in order that when he sang in future, however far from Ithaca, he would never be able to know but what watchful Odysseus was among his hearers.

This cruel measure taken, Odysseus left the bard wailing in the wilderness and, with somewhat calmer heart, went about his arduous work. The oar upon his shoulder, he trekked from city to inland city until he reached a village so landlubberly that its folk mistook that oar for a winnowing fan, and there he completed his long penance to Poseidon. Then he returned to his own high hall, making livestock raids along the way to replenish his herds, depleted by the hungry suitors. With the help of his old father, his grown son, and gray-eyed Athene, he made civil peace with the families of those suitors. Penelope received him, and not indifferently: In this second separation they had each come to terms with the other's story, and now between them as well was made civil peace. Never mind who had outwronged whom; they wisely resolved to put the passions of the past behind them, and settled down to enjoy a tranquil middle age.

Here Theodoros Dmitrikakis falls silent; smiles; sips his retsina.

Asks Peter Sagamore with a disbelieving chuckle That's it? Says Katherine Sherritt I like that tapestry business, but everything's unfinished!

Beautiful Diana has long since joined us; instead of taking her deck chair, she sits upon the deck itself, leans back against Ted's knees, and with the fingers of her left hand touches the fingers of his, upon her shoulder. That is just about it, says Ted.

But not quite. After a few months, and even more so after a year or two, Odysseus found himself restless: On this, nearly all the late-classical sequels agree. He would return often to the seashore below his high hall, to the spot where the Phaeacians had put him at last ashore, and would stare out at the distant islands and the open sea beyond them. His conversation came to be of nothing but Troy and his adventurous voyage home. Without mentioning his encounter with Phemius, he hired a vagrant bard at fair salary to stay on in Ithaca and sing that story, using Penelope's great tapestry as his cue card. For Odysseus had been shown that formidable work, and so far from being jealous of it, had been ravished at first sight. This bard, however, had no talent; his singing bored them all, and Odysseus soon sent him packing.

The tapestry then became his chief bond with Penelope. In order to admire it the more, he had it moved from her weaving room to their dining hall, where he could lose himself in it every mealtime. In particular he loved its second and third panels, especially that third. At his direction, Penelope willingly rewove the course of his voyage, of which in the first instance she had had no firm details: Now there were the drugged-out Lotus Eaters, the blinded Cyclops, the man-eating Laestrygonians. To be sure, Circe and Calypso were not depicted in their own persons, any more than young Phemius was shown in the loom room. But there was the Aeaean isle, the men turned into swine; there was perfumed Ogygia, with a fern-lined cave-mouth in the middle distance, and in the foreground Odysseus constructing his raft. And there was the Phaeacian shore, where an inland river meets the sea: Nausicaa of the flashing arms was now in place, playing ball with her maids and girlfriends. . . .

The lower right-hand corner, however, Penelope had never really finished, though for display purposes she had filled the empty area; it was all background and no foreground. Given her skill, Odysseus thought, she might easily in the space available have stitched in his hike with that oar, a bit of a highland odyssey itself; perhaps even some foreshadow of his death, as Tiresias had foretold it in Hades: an easy death from the sea in his comfortable old age.

Ted sips. In Dante's *Commedia,* as Katherine mentioned, that death comes in the Southern Ocean. And so perhaps it will. But what has happened so far is this: After two years of that featureless tranquility in Ithaca, marked only by Odysseus's absorption in that tapestry, Penelope—who seemed scarcely to have aged at all during their twenty-year separation—found that time had made up for lost time: She aged two decades in two years. Except for the distraction of reworking the tapestry and the diversion of overseeing Telemachus's wedding (but the bride's family did most of that), nothing much interested her any longer. She came almost to miss missing her husband. The importunings of her suitors, unwelcome as they had been, had kept her on her mettle, as had the original weaving of the tapestry.

Most sharply, of course, she missed her friend Phemius, and wondered why she'd had no word from him whatever, not even word of his marrying and having children. By contrast with his lively youthfulness, her husband (who, if never delicate, had been similarly young and lively when he sailed for Troy) seemed now like a heavy, scarred old olive trunk. She no longer resented those long trysts of his with Circe and Calypso, which it had so wounded her at first to hear of. In his absence she had come to endow him with her lover's better qualities as well as his own; now she found herself endowing Phemius, in *his* absence, with Odysseus's better qualities, remembering the bard as stronger, braver, shrewder than he had ever been. She missed him; and while she scarcely craved him back as a lover (she could see in the glass how she'd aged; anyhow, she no longer felt up to a lover), she did not welcome her husband's embraces and never herself took the sexual initiative with him, as she had learned to enjoy doing with Phemius.

Nor did Odysseus, for his part, often press those embraces upon her. He truly felt that he had forgiven her her interlude with Phemius; why in the world should he not? But her revelations and Phemius's had left their mark. Would he have been more or less bothered, he wondered, if her lover had been an Agamemnon, an Achilles? But it was your noncombatants, he decided with chagrin—it was your Parises, your Aegisthuses, your Phemiuses, in a word your doves—who laid their eggs in the eagles' nest. In any case, while he could never dislike a woman so fitted to his soul as his Penelope, there was no longer much between them besides that tapestry, before which more and more they found themselves entranced, thinking their separate thoughts.

Now for Penelope, who knew every stitch of that work by heart, its most attractive moments were those views in Panels Two and Three of the weaving room, herself at the loom weaving Panels One and Two respectively, their own scenes replicated in exquisite miniature. And of those, her special favorite was that tiny square in Panel Three which showed her weaving Panel Two. Even the casual viewer noticed and properly admired the little panel-within-a-panel, but there was a further detail known only to the maker and one other. In an area no larger than her fingernail (in a tapestry itself wall-size), she had managed to suggest in the tiniest stitches of the very finest thread the scenes from Panel One, being woven in Panel Two, being woven in Panel Three. That idea she had gotten from Phemius, who, as he sang of Troy, once improvised an interlude wherein an old minstrel entertains disguised Odysseus with a song of the war itself, in course of which is described the shield forged for Achilles by the gods, on which in turn is figured the story of the war thus far. Penelope herself had judged the device a touch too visible, though charming, and therefore had so buried that most artful bit in her own tapestry that no one noticed it unless she pointed it out. This she had done one mild summer night to her lover alone, who had been so delighted that he kissed her from head to foot, front and back, and improvised on the spot a naughty little song in goatherd's Greek about some freckles on a certain part of her body, which she herself had never seen. That bit of stitchery had become the secret symbol of their connection, as the bedpost-tree had been of hers and Odysseus's.

As for Odysseus, it was Aeaea his eyes returned to: the hall with the swine before it and sleek Circe invisible within. The expression on her face when, so far from succumbing to her potion, he had stood erect before her and unsheathed his sword! The timbre of the voice with which she then had invited him to her bed! And even longer than upon Aeaea— seven times longer—his eyes rested upon that dusky yet dainty cave-mouth on Ogygia's flowered shore, into which he had gone nightly for seven years and emerged fragrant with hibiscus, bougainvillea. Not just immortality had Calypso promised him, but perpetual youth, and he had—incredibly!— declined. He too could read the mirror's message: While he credited himself with aging ruggedly, aging he certainly was; Calypso would not likely make him that offer now.

Yet, almost to his own surprise, where his imagination lingered longest was before neither of those two beaches but a third, where a frisky young princess played at catch with her friends while a naked, weary, salt-grimed castaway watched captivated from his hiding place among the sea grapes and wild olive, wondering how to approach without frightening her away.

When, as eventually came to pass, Odysseus announced one evening to Penelope his intention to take a bit of a sailing cruise, he politely invited her to come along. Laertes and Eurycleia were dead; Telemachus was established as manager of their estate and was bursting with new ideas he was eager to try out; Odysseus and Penelope were retired folks, really, with little responsibility. Wouldn't she enjoy seeing something of the world beyond Ithaca? Second honeymoon, et cetera?

As he had expected, she declined. Their new grandson, and the second grandchild on the way, meant more to her than any second honeymoon;

she couldn't bear the thought of leaving their care entirely to their mother. Anyhow, she knew without trying it that sea-voyaging would make her ill. The fact was, she had been thinking seriously of going back in earnest to her loom-work, as more than a hobby. Maybe she would open a little crafts shop. Who knew: Perhaps she would finish at last that final corner of her old tapestry. Shall we stretch our legs before Diana tells the rest of the story?

Well, okay. The hour is late, but the night's too muggy to make going below an inviting prospect, and we have told so many stories ourselves since Nopoint Point that it is agreeable to be told one, even at epical length. Peter checks with Katherine; she's all right and ready for more. And we want to see and hear Diana Dmitrikakis in action. The two couples take a turn about the decks. No more liquids for Kate; Peter has had enough retsina. Ted finds cold beer below: Alpha, brewed in Athens. We reapply insect repellent against the formidable salt-marsh mosquitoes and gather again around the citronella candle aft of the mast, in the ship's waist. Diana brushes back her hair with a copper-braceleted wrist; she frowns handsomely, like a pianist about to strike the first notes of a recital piece; she begins

THE LONG TRUE STORY OF ODYSSEUS'S SHORT LAST VOYAGE.

So, she says, Odysseus and Penelope bade good-bye to each other again, and with a small picked crew of veteran sailors, he set out to westward. His official mission was to express his gratitude to the Phaeacians for having carried him home; perhaps to lay a wreath upon the rock into which, he had heard, Poseidon changed their black ship upon its return, in full view of home port. But his actual hope was to see bare-armed Nausicaa again—and beyond that he had yet another objective in mind, which he scarcely acknowledged even to himself.

The voyage from Phaeacia to Ithaca had taken no time, for it had been accomplished as Odysseus slept, in a boat very much like this one. The voyage from Ithaca back to Phaeacia, all hands wide awake in an ordinary sailing-and-rowing vessel, was another matter, whose hazards and—I have forgotten the English for *longueurs* . . .

The English for *longueurs,* says Peter Sagamore, is "longueurs."

Thank you. Whose hazards and longueurs I shall pass over. Somewhere in the course of it, Odysseus and his weary crew, laboring to windward, actually caught sight of one of those dream-dark Phaeacian boats streaking in the opposite direction, skimming the waves like a flying fish with scarcely any effort at all on the part of the crew. How they envied it!

But after what seemed to them an age of hard wind right on the bow, alternating with slick calms, the island came into view, just as Odysseus remembered it except for a ship-shaped rock in the harbor-mouth and, behind the town, a ring of mountains that had not been there before. They landed—Odysseus as always in disguise—and made themselves known as Ithacan sailors on a trading voyage, who unfortunately had had to jettison their cargo in a storm and now sought only to rest and reprovision their vessel before moving on. Old Queen Arete received them, coolly but civilly, and accepted their captain's gifts, including the memorial wreath and a ball of pure silver. These he declared were from their king, Odysseus, who had commissioned him to deliver them to King Alcinous and his family should their journey fetch them near Phaeacia. The wreath was to mourn those seafarers he had heard were petrified on their return voyage; the ball was for the princess Nausicaa, to replace one she'd lost in the river years ago.

To his surprise, the queen covered her face with her black shawl like any peasant woman in mourning. For some moments she rocked back and forth in her seat—the throne of Phaeacia. Then she mustered her royal composure, uncovered her face, and told the stranger that the Phaeacians' hospitality had indeed cost them dearly on that occasion. Not only had the flagship of the royal navy, with the finest officers and crew on the island, been turned to stone in full view of the harbor and the city been ringed on three sides with impassable mountains—Poseidon's punishment for their ferry service on Odysseus's behalf—but she had subsequently lost her husband and their daughter as well, and stood perhaps to lose her three unmarried sons, all on that same Odysseus's account. The man had intended them no harm, but from the bottom of her heart she wished he had never set foot in Phaeacia.

Nausicaa dead! cried shocked Odysseus. And great Alcinous too! He begged Arete to tell him the story before she withdrew, so that he could relay it to King Odysseus, who would be heartbroken to hear how the gods had repaid the Phaeacians' generosity. I should hope so, said Arete, and later that afternoon obliged him with the unhappy details. Princess Nausicaa was not in fact known to be dead, she said; however, she might well be worse than dead. Always previously a model daughter, though a strong-willed one as befit her mother's child, she had not been the same after Odysseus's departure. Day after day she paced the shingle down where the river meets the sea. She would have nothing to do with the eligible young gentlemen of Phaeacia, whose attentions, whatever she might say to the contrary, had pleased her enough before. Incessantly with her maids she did the royal laundry, as if by that magic she could once again conjure briny Odysseus from the olive bushes. To their shame, Arete and Alcinous had indulged this folly, even encouraged it, without really meaning to do so. For to them as well, after Odysseus's departure, the local young men seemed second-rate; they found themselves wishing for another like him—younger perhaps, unmarried certainly—to be their son-in-law. But Poseidon's revenge had sharply reduced their interisland commerce; few strangers called on the court of Phaeacia these days.

As Nausicaa's lovesickness had grown, she had hounded blind Demodocus to leave off singing of Ares and Aphrodite and the moon and stars
and sing only the Trojan War, specifically the episodes starring her hero.
Indeed, she had pestered the old bard to make up an entirely new song
based upon the grand tale Odysseus had told them of his long voyage
homeward, which had fetched him to Phaeacia. Arete even feared that the
girl had driven the poor fellow into early retirement, for he was too gone
in years to attempt another epical composition. She was possessed, Nausicaa was, and no amount of reminding her of Odysseus's age and marital
status could unpossess her.

Both to appease their daughter and in hopes of weaning her from her
passion, when Demodocus had hung up his lyre not long since, the king
and queen had replaced him with a younger bard who had lately become
the rage of the Mediterranean, chiefly on the strength of his Odyssean
songs. The stipulations of their contract with this Homer—that was the
young virtuoso's name—were that he would sing of the wandering Ithacan
as often as the princess demanded, but that always the song must end with
the joyful reunion of devoted husband and faithful wife. The bard had
readily agreed: That general topic was his specialty already, and inasmuch
as his version was at particular pains to emphasize Penelope's fidelity,
Odysseus's steadfast longing to return to her, and their triumphant reunion,
the stipulations were no burden.

But by no fault of Homer's, Arete explained, the stratagem had back-
fired. Happy ending or not, the song so enflamed Nausicaa's craving for
that man old enough to be her father, she would have young Homer repeat
and repeat the beach scene, wherein the salt-stenched castaway flings himself at her white knees. Then she would flee the room before the bard
began the second half of his work, which, depending on his and his audience's mood, took him from two to twelve more evenings to get through,
and which to tell the truth was less interesting to the Phaeacians than the
first half—especially Books Six through Twelve, with their local setting.

Not many months ago, said grim-faced Arete, a night came when Nausicaa fled at that familiar moment not only from this room but from the
palace and evidently from the island, presumably in search of the hero of
her fancy, since none of us has seen or heard from her since. When it
became apparent that she was nowhere in the city or the surrounding
countryside, her three unmarried brothers put to sea for Ithaca in search
of her. But my husband so feared that she had fallen into the hands of
pirates, and so blamed himself for having offered her hand to Odysseus
in the first place, he suffered a stroke soon after her disappearance, and
a few days later died. I carry on in his stead as best I can, managing our
simple affairs of state, receiving the rare visitors to our island. You and
your shipmates shall enjoy our customary courtesy, short of ferry service.
You are to make yourselves comfortable and remain in Phaeacia for as
long as necessary to repair and reprovision your ship. However, you must
excuse me from the evening's entertainment. I have no quarrel with good

Homer's art; indeed, I hope against hope that his Odysseus-song may somehow sing my daughter home again. But I cannot abide hearing of its hero.

. You can imagine with what emotion Odysseus heard all this. But he kept his own counsel and maintained his incognito, declaring to Queen Arete only that King Odysseus would be grief-stricken to learn that his innocent and helpless stay in Phaeacia had had such lamentable consequences. He then paid formal tribute to the stone ship, sacrificing to Poseidon down at the harbor; the wreath he laid on the grave of Alcinous. He even made a courtesy call on old blind Demodocus, who echoed in more professional terms Arete's praise of his successor. All artists, the bard declared to his visitor, have their tricks and specialties. Among this young Homer's was a gift of singing so artfully of women that Demodocus had been moved to ask him whether, like the prophet Tiresias, he had not once been a woman himself. Homer's answer had been that he was not nor had he ever been a woman; he was only a man who had learned to listen to women, and who, when he had had eyes to see with, knew how to look at them as well, and to understand and remember what he saw.

I see, said Odysseus: Like yourself, then, this Homer is blind?

Quite blind, Demodocus replied. And to me alone he has entrusted the story of how he became so. As you may know, my friend, there are tales that we bards sing to the public at large, and other tales that we sing only to one another.

Had Demodocus himself been sighted, he would have seen Odysseus's eyes narrow then as he said Though I am no bard myself, sir, I pray you tell me that story. I shall pay you any fee you name. Replied Demodocus I will not do it for any price; not even for my life.

Tell me then, Odysseus said to Demodocus: Do you or this Homer chap know anything of Princess Nausicaa's whereabouts? Queen Arete has been so courteous to me despite her grief that I am determined to discover her daughter's fate. Or is that perhaps another of those tales sung only by one bard to another? If it is, Demodocus answered, then my gifted young colleague has not seen fit to sing it to me. There is yet a third category of songs, he added: those a bard sings only to himself. But I suspect that Homer knows no more than you and I of Nausicaa's whereabouts. How beautifully he sings of her!

Odysseus declared that rather than wait for the evening's performance, he would speak privately with this Homer at once. Where did he live? Alone, said Demodocus, high up in the new mountains behind the city, like a solitary goatherd. He, Demodocus, did not know the way there, nor had any of Homer's numerous admirers been able to follow him home at night after one of his performances; for though blind, he was nimble as a mountain goat.

By now Odysseus had strong suspicions of this Homer's identity; that same evening they were confirmed. So long had it been since a trading ship had called on Phaeacia, despite her mourning Queen Arete treated her visitors to the first of what turned out to be a week-long series of state dinners. After the entrée, as a dessert of sweet butter cookies called *kou-lourakia* was being served, she excused herself from table but bade the company remain to hear the fastest-rising star in the firmament of minstrelsy, the famous Homer.

Two serving-boys led him in, one guiding him by the elbow, the other carrying his lyre. Odysseus's shipmates, who had scarcely known the bard Phemius in Ithaca, did not see through the prematurely white hair, the gaunt and weathered face with its closed blind eyes; but Odysseus recognized at once the man he had assaulted in the Ithacan hills for singing lewdly of his wife. Despite Arete's testimonials, he put his hand upon his sword-hilt and prepared to strike, should "Homer's" song so much as hint at Penelope's affair with her minstrel.

Diana smiles. Ted and I believe that a genius is not a person dramatically different from ordinary people. He is a man or woman much like others, but more finely honed, to the point where his difference in degree becomes almost a difference in kind. Homer took up his lyre like any other bard; he sipped red wine unmixed with water; and he sang the dignified and touching first four books of *The Odyssey:* Athene's visit to encourage Telemachus; that young man's debate with his mother's suitors; his embassy to Nestor in sandy Pylos, in quest of news of his father; his calling on Menelaus and Helen in Sparta upon the same errand. Familiar topics, every one—but sung with a discernment, an economy, a pungency of detail, and an artfulness of arrangement that made them seem as if seen and sung for the first time and forever. That is what genius is, in Ted's and my opinion.

Moved to the marrow, Odysseus applauded more loudly than anyone in the hall. When Phemius then bowed, drained his wine cup, and left the room without assistance, he hurried after to question him privately about Nausicaa. But at the sound of pursuing footsteps, the bard broke into a nimble run, darting like a rabbit this way and that once he was clear of the palace and outside in the forecourt. Though Odysseus snatched up a lantern from a drowsy guard to keep him in sight, he soon lost his sightless quarry in the dark.

The same thing happened on the second night, after Homer had sung the beautiful story of Calypso; of Odysseus's near-drowning and his beach encounter with Nausicaa of the flashing arms; of his reception by Arete and Alcinous in that very hall; of the Phaeacian games; and of the bard Demodocus's singing first of jealous Hephaestus's snare for the lovers Ares and Aphrodite, then of Odysseus's great stratagem of the wooden horse. What a bard this Phemius had become! Hearing him sing how Demodocus's song had moved disguised Odysseus to helpless tears, disguised Odysseus was very nearly moved to helpless tears.

Says Peter Sagamore Bravo, Dee. And Bravo says cool Diana cried the Phaeacians, who had crowded the hall to hear themselves so sung. Now: Enraptured though he was, Odysseus believed that in Homer's description of Calypso's beauty he detected some details of Penelope as she had been rendered in Phemius's sex-song to the goats of Ithaca. But so well-imaged were they, and so forgivable, he could not take offense: Homer had after all never seen Calypso, and the nymph thus described was sleeping with Odysseus, not with the bard. In Homer's rendition of Nausicaa, on the other hand (except for yet another repetition of the freckle motif), there was a clearly firsthand accuracy and authority: so much that Odysseus found it difficult to believe that the bard had never seen the princess with his own eyes, and had been in her presence for only the short period from his arrival upon the island until her disappearance. Once again he pressed after the singer to question him, but in the crowd Homer eluded him even more easily than he had done the night before.

So it went also on the third night, after Homer sang Books Nine through Twelve, Odysseus's rehearsal of his story thus far; and again on the fourth night, and the fifth, the sixth, the seventh. As the audience thinned out, Odysseus was able to pursue his quarry a bit farther each evening: out of the forecourt, through the town and the dark suburbs, up into the steepening hills. But invariably, blind Homer slipped away in the black high mountains behind the city. Moreover, he arrived at and left the palace by a different path each evening, so that even when Odysseus stationed crewmen along his first six routes, his seventh turned out to be different from all its forerunners. Yet Odysseus dared not collar the fellow in mid-performance or for that matter in the hall itself, for fear of offending good Arete, revealing himself prematurely—and cutting off the marvelous story.

He approached the eighth and final evening with trepidation. In the ongoing story, Odysseus had landed in Ithaca and moved in with Eumaeus the swineherd; Telemachus had returned from Pylos and Sparta and been reunited with his father; disguised Odysseus had entered his own house as a beggar, had been insulted even by the other beggars, had gone unrecognized by his wife but not by his old nurse Eurycleia, and had suffered with his son the taunts of Penelope's suitors while he reconnoitered the situation and made his murderous plans. Tonight must bring the climactic massacre and the delicate business of his reunion with Penelope. Once again Odysseus stationed his men along Homer's seven previous escape routes; once again the bard appeared as if from nowhere after the quince compote, and Queen Arete excused herself, announcing somewhat pointedly by the way that after this final state dinner, her guests were free to entertain themselves as they pleased. And once again Odysseus sat hand on buckler through the bard's performance.

What a performance it was! Though the audience after the first four nights had steadily dwindled, the hall was packed for Homer's conclusion of his *Odyssey*. Unable to curb their enthusiasm till the end, the crowd applauded separately Odysseus's drawing of the great bow, his slaughter of the suitors, his sparing of the bard Phemius (which Homer made a comic scene of, so mimicking the frightened bard's plea that Arete's hall resounded with laughter). Then he sang the meeting of husband and wife:

Penelope's confusion, Telemachus's chiding her, Odysseus's admiring patience, the riddle of the marriage bed—all with such discretion and insight that despite himself Odysseus wept aloud, just as he had done years before at that same table when Demodocus sang of Troy.

The blind minstrel paused in his conclusion of the story. As before, the Phaeacians asked their guest of honor why he was so overcome—particularly since, as an Ithacan himself and loyal to Odysseus, he ought to be gratified by the story's happy ending. It was the first time he had been thus publicly singled out; the bard quickly made to leave the hall. Odysseus bolted from his chair and called across the room: Phemius, wait! It is Odysseus himself who has pursued you these seven nights, but I intend you no harm! I wish only to praise your art—and to ask a few questions about Princess Nausicaa!

Everyone was astonished. But unmasked Homer did not wait to hear his art praised; in his usual zigzag fashion he dashed from the hall, out of the palace, and through the forecourt, easily eluding the men positioned to intercept him. He headed for the hills by an utterly different way, more difficult and dark than any of the others. Odysseus had after him like hound after hare—at first despairingly, not only because he had never yet been able to follow very far, but also because this time he was himself blinded, by his own tears, and in his haste he had left behind the lantern he used to follow the slippery bard's trail.

Before long, however, he came to realize that these handicaps were an asset. Unable to see, he was obliged to listen, and in order to hear he had to move quietly as well as quickly. He no longer called after his quarry, thereby announcing his own whereabouts. Once out of the town and up in the craggy hills, he no longer raced, but stalked. As the incline steepened, he sprang from rock to rock; even leaped crevasses in the dark. When he heard Phemius pause to listen, he paused too, and moved only when Phemius moved—until, after more than an hour, the bard, no doubt believing himself once again free of his pursuer, carried on more leisurely and less cautiously. Indeed, once he'd gotten his breath back he began to sing, and the work of following him up the high black trails became easier yet.

His song, which Odysseus could hear plainly, was about how wrathful Odysseus had gouged out the bard Phemius's eyes for his having sung the beauty of his mistress, Odysseus's own Penelope—in particular the freckles on her hey-nonny-no, pretty freckles on her hey-nonny-no. Odysseus drew his sword. But the song was neither a taunt nor a lament: In its next verses the bard thanked his assailant, who in thus blinding him had done him unwittingly a triple service. Sighted (he sang in the following stanza), he would have seen fair Penelope grow old and lose her beauty; he would have seen younger, fairer women and would have sung their beauty instead of hers. But as it was, Penelope's former beauty remained the last his eyes would ever know; she was ageless in his imagination; he would sing forever the freckles on her hey-nonny-no, dainty freckles on her hey-nonny-no.

Furthermore (the next stanza declared in a sober Phrygian minor mode), his blindness, like Demodocus's, had enabled him to see the world more clearly. Despite Odysseus's threats, it had made him Homer the epic bard instead of Phemius the ribald minstrel, that mere singer of freckles on hey-nonny-nos, sweet freckles on hey-nonny-nos. No sighted Phemius could have composed blind Homer's *Odyssey,* which would make both its hero and its composer immortal. Nevertheless—and here the song grew gay again—in the singer's inmost self, behind Homer's blind eyes, horny Phemius still pranced and capered: Odysseus's third favor was to have made him into a Homer so admired that Princess Nausicaa herself had run away from home to become his mistress! What was more, as fate and poetry would have it, she was the very image of youthful Penelope, right down to the freckles on her hey-nonny-no—hi ho! Twenty freckles on her hey-nonny-no!

That was a song, however, his song concluded in a flippant coda, to be sung only to the singer by himself.

By turns moved, chagrined, outraged, dismayed, and astonished, Odysseus at the song's end found himself really mainly curious. He put away his sword as Homer rounded a final rocky corner and hove into sight of a small lamplit cabin in a level clearing. That light, in a blind man's cabin, made Odysseus's skin tingle. Sure enough: Forth came a white-armed young woman with a cup of wine to greet the returning bard. From the concealing darkness, Odysseus marveled: She was the same tall, trim-limbed beauty he remembered from the beach, only a few years older, more womanly than girlish now, and if anything lovelier than he remembered. Her black hair was let down; it spilled about her face and shoulders as she handed rough Homer the wine cup. Shocking, to see the former goatherd's helper so familiar with a princess! Homer guzzled the wine, then drew her face to his for a kiss. It did not escape Odysseus's eye—he seemed to see things this evening more sharply than ever before—that Nausicaa turned her cheek to take the kiss. But when Homer then good-humoredly smacked her behind and led her into the cabin, she put her arm about his waist and made no protest.

Having heard what he had heard and then seen what he had seen, Odysseus was after all inclined to leave the couple in peace. Clearly the princess was there of her own choosing; the affair was not finally his business. But having come so far, he could not resist drawing nearer, to use his eyes and ears together. Through a shuttered window he saw Homer seated on a low chair, drinking more wine. Nausicaa, sitting cross-legged on a clean black goatskin on the floor with a goosefeather in her hand and some sort of parchment on her lap, asked him whether he had been pursued from the palace yet again that night. He had, replied Homer, wiping his mouth with the back of his hand, and now that he knew by whom, he would be obliged to stay up in the hills for a while. In fact, popular as he was in Phaeacia, he and she must consider moving to some other city. I'm ready, Nausicaa said at once. But who is it pursues you?

Her voice, breaks in Theodoros Dmitrikakis: Don't forget to tell what the sound of her voice does to Odysseus.

Diana touches her companion's muscled leg. Katherine Sherritt bets she can guess what the sound of Diana Dmitrikakis's voice is doing to Peter Sagamore; it's even doing it to her. She touches *his* leg; her husband squeezes her forearm reassuringly.

Odysseus is in love with the sound of Nausicaa's voice, Diana says simply. Never mind, said Homer: It's only a hostile critic from the old country; every bard has his share of them. He had no fear of the fellow, he declared to her, especially now that she had copied out his *Odyssey* in her writing. Even if his pursuer should catch and kill him, he would live on in those written verses. It was for Nausicaa's sake that he had given the fellow the slip night after night, not to betray her hiding place. For that, Nausicaa said, stroking the goathair indifferently with her feather, she thanked him, she supposed. Homer stood, drained his wine cup, and supposed she could thank him in their bed just as well as from where she sat. Later, maybe, the princess replied, and Odysseus's heart stirred: No doubt Homer was tired from his evening's performance and his flight from his pursuer; he should turn in and sleep. But she was restless from having done nothing the day long but copy out his endless *Odyssey,* the final book of which she had still to review for errors of transcription. She guessed she would sit up and copy-read until she grew sleepy.

You may sit up and read copy all night, said Homer cheerfully, just as you please. He knew very well what copy she'd be reading, he declared: not Book Twenty-four, but old Book Six, wherein bare-arsed Odysseus breaks up her ball game. But first she must come soothe her singer to sleep with the freckles on her hey-nonny-no, et cetera. You are one-third poet and two-thirds goat, Nausicaa chided him: you and your hey-nonny-nos. But she dutifully put down her vellum and rose to join him in his low bed—whereupon Odysseus, unable either to withdraw or to stand quietly by, burst into the cabin, calling her name.

Startled Homer sprang upright in the bed, his tunic open, his phallus fast descending. Nausicaa of the flashing arms had already dropped *her* tunic to the rug, atop her manuscript; now with a squeal she snatched it up to cover herself, sending papers flying—but not before Odysseus with his newly sharpened senses had observed that her buttocks were as unfreckled as her famous arms. Don't be alarmed, he wanted to tell her: It is your friend Odysseus. But he could only repeat her name.

Nausicaa looked, looked again, covered her face with a corner of the tunic, and collapsed into the nearby chair, upon several manuscript pages that had fallen there. She looked yet again, closed her eyes, and let her head fall back. It really is you, she said. What in the world are you doing here?

He has come all the way from Ithaca to butcher me, Homer answered, quite in control of himself now. He believes that I have broken a certain vow I made to him years ago, when he poked my eyes out in the Ithacan hills. In this belief he is mistaken—not that that fact ever stayed the hand of an epic hero. But Homer does not beg for his life, Odysseus, the way twice-craven Phemius did. He asks only that you preserve the tale that this young woman has copied out, who gives herself to me for no other reason than her adoration of you. My *Odyssey* does you the honor you have heard already; it is, in fact, your scribbled immortality.

The bard's self-possession returned his own to Odysseus. Great Homer, he said, placing his hands upon the fellow's shoulders to show him that his sword was sheathed: Be assured that I will injure neither it nor her nor you. I have heard the songs you sing to the world, the songs you sing to Demodocus, and the songs you sing only to yourself. The first I honor; the second I forgive; the third I will not betray. For having blinded you in my blindness, I ask your pardon.

Forgiven, forgiven, Homer said. That little business made my day no brighter, but in making my night it made my life. He perched on the bed edge, crossed his legs, and asked How are things in Ithaca? Odysseus replied that Penelope was well and thought often of her old friend Phemius, lamenting that she had heard nothing from him. That her great tapestry was done at last, but that, himself being no poet, he would not presume to describe its finishing touch, the lower right-hand corner of the Homecoming panel. Homer must return to that high hall himself one day, to her weaving room, where he would always be welcome; he must hear from Penelope's own mouth, feel with his own skillful fingers, what ending she has brought that story to. As for the lady herself, Odysseus swore gallantly that she remained in every particular exactly as Homer remembered her from the days when he was her friend and comforter Phemius.

Mm hm, said Homer. As for himself, Odysseus went on, he remained that excellent woman's great admirer, her steadfast friend, and her lifelong provider; but they were no longer truly husband and wife. At this news, Nausicaa—who had been dabbing at her eyes with her tunic sleeve and listening amazed—grew still and redoubled her attention. He had installed his son Telemachus, his daughter-in-law, and their children in his high hall, Odysseus declared, speaking now directly to her. Their life was Penelope's life, unless and until she should see fit to take another husband or another friend—and that lucky fellow had Odysseus's blessing in advance.

Nausicaa found something of her voice and asked What about you? Smiling Odysseus sat down on the goatskin rug between her chair and the bed. Nausicaa tucked up her legs and drew the tunic more carefully around herself. He had thought at first to retrace the route of his odyssey in reverse, Odysseus said: beginning in Phaeacia, then calling upon Calypso and Circe, perhaps even sailing back to Troy, to see how their postwar reconstruction was proceeding; thence home again to Ithaca by the route he first sailed therefrom. Now, however, he understood that rocky Ithaca was home to him no longer; his black ship was, and the wine-dark breast of the sea. Not impossibly he might one day revisit there, to see how his grandchildren grew; but it would be simply one more port of call. His destination was undecided—though he had a certain plan in mind. But now, Princess, he said, it is your turn to answer questions. Are you here altogether of your free will, as it appears to me?

Nausicaa nodded, cleared her throat, and said I am.

And is that because you love this noble bard, Odysseus pressed, beyond any pain you might cause your family? The young woman's eyes lowered. Homer himself supplied her answer: Of course not. Nausicaa turned to face him sharply and spoke his name. From the first, said Homer, it had been perfectly clear to him that it was not "noble Homer" she loved, but his songs and stories, and in those not the art, but the images of herself and Odysseus, fixed forever there like figures on a terra-cotta vase. And this despite the likelihood that, never having seen her with his naked eyes, so to speak, he hadn't got her quite right.

You have me exactly right, Nausicaa assured him, flashing Odysseus a certain look. You have me down to the last detail. To Odysseus she declared then her great regret for having caused her parents pain—though for that, as they themselves acknowledged, they shared some responsibility. She regretted that her brothers were out scouting the Mediterranean for her in vain, though a journey beyond their little island would do them a world of good, as it would do her. When they learned in Ithaca, as they doubtless had done already, that Odysseus and Penelope had separated, they would be more convinced than ever that he and their sister had arranged a rendezvous. They would then hurry home to see whether the lovers had sailed away somewhere together—to the land of the Lotus Eaters, for example, which she understood to be especially pleasant this time of year—or whether Odysseus had taken advantage of their absence to relieve their noble but weary mother of the burdens of state and to reign over Phaeacia with their sister as his queen.

Homer rolled his eyes and began humming a tune to himself.

I have no such ambitions, Odysseus told Nausicaa. I am done myself with the trials of both administration and herohood—though I do have one last epical cruise in mind. But back to our subject: Is it your wish to remain here, in the service of this great bard?

Of course it isn't, Homer answered for her again. Do you think I don't see that the girl is bored to death up here with me? She has stayed on this long because she's ashamed to go home and has nowhere else to go—and because here she can at least reread Book Six of my *Odyssey* to her heart's content.

Dear Homer, Nausicaa protested, firmly now: You do yourself discredit. I have preferred you to all the young men in Phaeacia, an island rich in attractive young men. Don't dishonor Homer the man by imagining that I've cared only for Homer the singer of tales.

Nicely said, said Odysseus. Even Homer agreed.

But I cannot deny, Nausicaa went on, that the latter was the former's glory, or that in loving your *Odyssey* I was loving my memory of its hero.

Pleased Odysseus then declared to Homer that in the same way, perhaps, in making love to Nausicaa, the poet had been loving the memory of a certain former mistress, whom some details of his image of Nausicaa fit more fairly than they fit the flashing-armed princess herself. In my condition, Homer replied dryly, it could scarcely be otherwise. Then back to the matter of your intentions, Odysseus said to Nausicaa. . . .

What can I say? the young woman cried. That girl on the beach in Homer's poem is I and not I. She'll go on just so, my immortal self, however misrendered, while I get older like my mother. Her maids will miss that catch forever and ever, and shipwrecked Odysseus will come forth naked except for that wild-olive branch in his left hand, to approach her but never really reach her. . . .

χρειὼ γὰρ ἵκανεν, Homer murmured: σμερδαλέος δ' αὐτῆσι φάνη κεκακωμένος ἅλμῃ, τρέσσαν δ' ἄλλυδις ἄλλη ἐπ' ἠιόνας προυχούσας.

But Nausicaa stands fast, said proud Odysseus: frightened but resolute, her royal mother's daughter.

And there she'll stand forever, Nausicaa sighed: neither losing her friend nor having him. She swallowed; took a breath. I wish you'd carried me off, in your ship or one of ours, and that we had loved each other even for a little while, like Dionysus and Ariadne! Even if you had abandoned me then as he did her, to grow old with my memories, at least I'd have had something to remember besides dumb Eleni's missing that catch!

So you would have, Odysseus said tenderly. I share that wish of yours— all but the part about abandonment. He wondered aloud what she would think of the voyage he now proposed to undertake: a voyage so unlikely of accomplishment that he dared not even bring along his faithful crew. It was not for Ogygia or Aeaea he meant to steer, but for somewhere no one he knew had ever sailed, if the place truly existed at all.

Aha, said Homer, and fetched up his lyre and struck a major chord. On his odyssey, Odysseus continued, he had managed to sail right off the charts, to where East and West mean nothing, nor North nor South; to where sleek Circe rules and the spirits of the dead abide. . . .

I can't imagine wanting to go there, Nausicaa said. Nor I wanting to return there, Odysseus assured her.

Homer struck another chord. This time, said Odysseus—but then corrected himself, declaring that *time* was the wrong word. Where he proposed to sail for was a place that Circe herself had spoken of during their final night together: a place where East may be East and West West, but where Past and Future disappear. As he had sailed before out of charted space, he aimed now to sail right out of measured time, to a place called The Place Where Time Stands Still.

That's a song I've heard before, said Homer, improvising a light cadenza. Did sleek Circe give you sailing directions to that famous place?

Unruffled Odysseus replied that the course was neither a secret nor a problem: One steered a touch more to the north or south, depending on the season, but always to westward, directly for the setting sun. If that's all there is to it, Nausicaa said, why doesn't every mariner go there and spare himself the pains of old age, which I gather is what this journey is all about? If it's so easy to sail out of time, why are there any ancient mariners?

Homer nodded approval and struck a chord. The fact that the bearing is simple, Odysseus responded, doesn't mean that it's generally known: Many a great puzzle has been found to have a simple key—once that key has been found. In this case, however, he added, the heading was not the problem. Homer sounded another chord. The problem was time. Three chords more. As Circe had explained it to him, and Calypso had subsequently confirmed, The Place Where Time Stands Still does not stand still; it recedes to westward at exactly the speed of the sun itself, a speed no ordinary vessel could hope to approach. And if by some bewitchment one could match that speed—flying through the pillars of Hercules and across the River Ocean so swiftly that the sun hung fixed upon the far horizon— even then one would draw no nearer; one's distance off would merely not increase. To reach The Place Where Time Stands Still, one was obliged to sail so fast that the sun would appear to reverse its course and rise in the west. Evening would then become afternoon, afternoon morning; the sailor himself would actually grow somewhat younger!—until he overtook that fleeing, flowering shore. Which, once attained, would carry him and his vessel along, with no further effort on his part. Neither ship nor sailor would thenceforth age; he might cruise those flower-girt waterways forever, never tiring of them, for what stales our pleasures is time, and there he will be out of time.

Well, now, said disappointed Nausicaa, who had hoped to hear a more practical romantic proposal: That is a fancy worthy of our friend here. But it seems to me that your ship, fast and seaworthy as it doubtless is, is after all just another boat, which by your own acknowledgment took a great while merely crossing from Ithaca to here. How do you expect to overtake the sun in it?

Such a feat, Odysseus admitted, was out of the question. Nor in fact did he have any idea at all how to get where he wanted to go, determined as he was to get there. But the experience of his original odyssey had taught him that the solutions to such problems are seldom to be found by sitting on the beach; that was why he had come to Phaeacia rather than racking his brains in Ithaca. He had pondered the matter there as thoroughly as he could and had made what preparations he could imagine for the voyage (given its nature, those preparations were more spiritual than physical). Then he had set out, trusting to fortune and his own wits to show him as he went along what could not be seen from shore.

If I may say so, Homer put in from the bed edge at this point, I approve of your method, which I have more than once employed myself—though it can be recommended only to the most knowledgeable practitioners of any art. He ran a deft arpeggio. Tell us, then: What trick have fortune and your wits disclosed, to drive a mere sailing vessel faster than the setting sun?

As to his means, Odysseus replied, fortune and his wits remained as mute as ever they'd been in Ithaca, except to confirm by his recent journey that his boat and crew were of no further use to him in the project. He might perhaps sail on with them to Aeaea and seek further advice from Circe; after that his men would return with the boat to Ithaca. As to his end, however: Only that very night, there in that room, speaking with the Princess Nausicaa, hearing her story while admiring her beauty and then telling of his private plan, had he seen what he ought to have seen before: how lonely that timeless place would be for the singlehanded sailor who found some way to reach it.

The princess brightened and shifted in her seat. To sail alone is one thing, Odysseus said: Sailing through solitude has its pleasures. But to sail *to* solitude is another matter. What good is eternal youth, alone? What I therefore propose, Nausicaa—

I accept with pleasure, the princess interrupted, holding out her white right arm to him while pressing her tunic to her chest with her left. Odysseus protested that she hadn't yet heard his proposal. Living with this poet, Nausicaa replied, has taught me narrative navigation. From a story's heading and position, I can reckon where it's bound.

And from its pace, Homer added with a sigh, its Estimated Time of Arrival.

What you propose, Nausicaa went on, is that I return home, make peace with my noble and sorrowing mother, and ease her burdens while you and your crew sail off to Circe for advice. You propose that if you survive that voyage, and if Circe knows in fact how this magic country can be reached, and if you can persuade her to tell you that secret (which she wouldn't likely do if I were with you), and if she then permits you to sail back here with that information, and if you survive the return voyage as well, which you only barely did before; and if, having managed all that, you still feel as you feel tonight—why, *then* you'll propose that I risk that crazy westward journey, in hopes of sharing with you its improbable reward. And if I feel then as I feel now—and if indeed I myself, on that who-knows-how-distant day, am still alive and well, rather than wrecked by disease or accident or war or mere despair—then, my friend, with all due respect to good Homer here, I shall accept your proposal with great joy.

Very well spoken, Homer applauded. You have the makings of an ironist.

Odysseus declared himself duly chastened by her words. But how else was he to proceed? It was quite true, as the princess had implied, that shrewd Circe would not likely proffer advice without recompense. One knew further to what sort of recompense she inclined, which she would not likely demand or he tender if Nausicaa were with him; powerful and dangerous the woman was, but neither wicked nor perverted. He regretted as keenly as Nausicaa the length and perils of a round-trip voyage from Phaeacia to Aeaea, when what he most wished was that the two of them could step directly from Homer's cabin into The Place Where Time Stands

Still. But a boat is but a boat; otherwise they could set sail for that place this very night.

Your wits, man, Homer muttered, tinkering with a melody on his lyre. Use your famous Odyssean wits.

Unless, Odysseus said, putting a forefinger to his brow, as it now occurs to me might be possible, my Aeaean voyage could be shortened by a faster boat, like the one that once carried me from here to Ithaca as if across the street. . . .

I thought he'd never get around to it, Homer confided to his chord progression.

Now at last Odysseus took Nausicaa's hand. Persuade your mother to lend me a boat like the one your brothers are racing around in, he said to her, and I'll be back in two days instead of two years.

If Circe lets you go, Nausicaa reminded him, regarding their clasped hands. And if you don't come to prefer her to me as your sailing-partner, once you're back in bed with her.

Homer strummed. Odysseus assured the princess that it was she alone he hoped to sail out of time with: not a goddess already timeless like Circe or Calypso, but a mortal woman, as he was a mortal man. He hoped further that she wouldn't begrudge his going back to sleek Circe to learn the secret of super-high-speed sailing; that was the ticket price for their voyage together.

So it seems, Nausicaa said. And not the only price, either. There's another, which I've already paid.

To Homer's accompaniment, in the Dorian mode now, Odysseus supposed she meant by "another price" the leaving her mother and brothers and her native island: a price he too had already paid, in Ithaca. Your payment, Nausicaa observed, was in a somewhat different coin. Well put, said Homer. Anyhow, the princess went on, that was not the price she had in mind. Obviously, she declared now to Odysseus, she was his. Out of love for him she had spurned her worthy Phaeacian suitors, fled the palace, broken her parents' hearts, led her brothers on a wild-goose chase, and given her virginity to a wandering minstrel, whose song of Odysseus had been her only recompense for such misbehavior. She had done all that, moreover, not because she was weary of her family, as Odysseus had become of his, but solely because she had loved him beyond reason, like one possessed.

I see what you mean by the price already paid, said flattered Odysseus. But Nausicaa now declared that even that was not the prepaid price she meant. She removed her smooth hand from his scarred, and looked down at her fingernails. If you had said to me, she said over Homer's new and wistful strain, Nausicaa, I love you; let's forget about Circe and The Place Where Time Stands Still. Now that I've found my way back to you, let's grow old right here together, looking after your mother, advising your brothers on the government of the island, maybe raising sons and daughters of our own: little Odysseuses and Nausicaas. You might have said to me that living out together what time we have left seems to you a sweeter fate than staking our lives upon such a far-fetched escapade as sailing out of time. Oh, my friend: If you had said *that* to me, I'd have felt more loved than any woman in love's history. But you didn't. What's more, if I were to propose such a course to you, you would make diplomatic apologies and tactful expressions of regret and then sail off to Aeaea and from there to The Place Where Time Stands Still, either with Circe or with some other companion or alone after all, your heart is so set upon that voyage. *That's* my admission price, Odysseus: the knowledge that what you want is not Nausicaa herself, but Nausicaa as your shipmate on this voyage, and the further knowledge that your interest in herohood and kingship, even in fatherhood and grandfatherhood, is behind you. That is the cost of my ticket to this perpetual retirement cruise.

Said uncomfortable Odysseus You make it sting. What can I say?

Nausicaa smiled and brushed her hair back with one hand. Nothing. It is a price I prepaid willingly, though not joyously, before you ever returned here.

Peter Sagamore takes his wife's hand and paraphrases one of her verses: She decided to pay, but not to count, the cost. His reward is a brilliant pleased flash of Diana's eyes.

Nausicaa then briskly got down to business. To borrow a Phaeacian ship for the voyage to Circe was out of the question: It was to punish her countrymen for just that sort of generosity that Poseidon had taken such hard measures against them already. Even though Odysseus had presumably settled his own debts in that quarter, the Phaeacians would never dare risk the sea god's wrath again.

Well, then, Odysseus lamented, the game is up. He had taken for granted, before, the hazards and hardships of the expedition to Circe. But having seen Nausicaa and learned what he'd learned this night; having now imagined the possibility of a fast Aeaean weekend, after which he and Nausicaa could set out upon their great race together—*now* the prospect of an arduous, perilous two-year separation so discouraged him that he was indeed tempted, almost, to put the whole enterprise by, send his ship and shipmates back to rock-rich Ithaca, and settle down on Nausicaa's island in the capacity she had described. Perhaps he could get interested in farming again; he hadn't stood behind a plow since the day a quarter-century ago when Palamedes had set baby Telemachus in that tenth furrow.

Homer's chords turned appropriately nostalgic, and young Nausicaa began to appreciate how old her longed-for lover really was; how much was behind him; how more important to him than to her was this adventure out of time. She was not unmoved to hear him consider abandoning it, even though belatedly and in despair. I have an idea, she said then, which just might spare us your trip to Aeaea and the price of Circe's information, if indeed she has any, and get us going very soon on this cruise of ours.

Odysseus, Homer declared, you have found yourself a proper new partner. This young lady is as ready with inventions and expedients as you used to be yourself, back in Trojan days.

What Poseidon had chastized the Phaeacians for, Nausicaa explained, was their former unfailing generosity to castaways on their island; their ferrying them home gratis like a magic water-taxi service, while they slept. He would not punish her brothers, for example, for flying from port to Mediterranean port in search of her; nor would he likely punish a Phaeacian couple for embarking together upon a voyage of exploration. Their rights in such matters seemed clear enough. Now: Her brother's boat was a new design embodying the very state of the art of Phaeacian naval architecture, a field in which her people were unrivaled. It was as much swifter than all previous Phaeacian designs as those were swifter than anyone else's. Furthermore, while her brothers were justly regarded as the winningest racing skippers in Phaeacia and therefore in the known world, the truth was that when she and they had been children, racing their sailing prams about the harbor, she used to beat them two times out of three. And even though the customs of the country judged it unsuitable for well-born young women to go to sea, more than once at her urging they had smuggled her aboard with them, dressed as a man, to advise them in a particularly important race; and her tactical skill never failed to fetch whatever boat they were sailing across the finish line first.

You astonish me, said happy Odysseus.

Yet what neither I nor my brothers have, Nausicaa went on, we being strictly racing sailors, is exactly what *you* have aplenty: experience in navigating through such cruising hazards as Lotus Eaters and cannibals, and survival skills like raft-building and jury-rigging. In short, she concluded, if he were to renounce his Ithacan citizenship and become one of them, and were he and she to ask her brothers, upon their return, for the loan of their marvelous vessel, and were they to put it at her disposal, and were she and he to set out to westward in it with no other crew than themselves and the lightest possible cargo, to minimize displacement—*then,* by Zeus, she believed that while they might fail nevertheless to attain that magical escape-velocity, they would have the best chance of attaining it that any mortals ever had, and they should at least approach that timeless shore more closely than mortals ever did.

She lowered her eyes. But maybe you're not prepared to become one of us.

Odysseus rose to one stiffening knee before her and would have taken both her hands this time had she not needed one to hold her tunic over her breasts. In the presence of this great bard, he declared, I here renounce all past citizenships, loyalties, and identities. I declare my wish to become one of you and to pursue exactly the course you have just proposed. You've given up so much for me, Nausicaa, that being Ithacan is the least I can give up for you. I do it freely and readily.

Homer's accompaniment grew restless. *One of you,* the man says, he told his lyre, and *that's the least he can give up for her.* If I had eyes, I'd look just now to Nausicaa's and would see there something less than joy. But look here, Odysseus: Why should Nausicaa's brothers put their pride and joy at your disposal, the fastest boat in the fastest navy in the world? They wouldn't be just lending it, you know, the way a friend or relative might lend his dearest possession. If your stunt works, they'll see neither their sister nor their boat again. What you're asking for is another outright gift, like Nausicaa's love, and one almost as extraordinary.

Odysseus had to admit that the bard was right. Even his poor sluggish Ithacan boat, in which he'd made only one voyage and that an uncomfortable one, it would pain him to part company with. The loss of its predecessor, which had carried him faithfully from Ithaca to Troy and as far homeward as Scylla and Charybdis before it went down into the whirlpool with all hands but himself, had broken his heart almost as much as the loss of his comrades. He had no right to expect Arete's sons to donate their prize possession to a virtual stranger.

He sat again on the goatskin rug, altogether dejected. Nausicaa tapped her fingers on her cheekbone. Your wits, man, Homer urged, and then sang again, with different emphasis: *I wish to become one of you; that is the least I can give up for you.* Hey nonny nonny and aiyiyi . . .

Odysseus clapped his brow. Good Homer! *Great* Homer! Again I owe you! He rerose to one knee and clasped both of Nausicaa's, which were bare and pressed together. Splendid woman, he said to her: more patient and forbearing than almost anyone I know: My wits are so dulled by age and fatigue that if we do not soon find a way to turn time back, I'll be too addle-headed to navigate at all. How could I have spoken of giving up the least for you instead of the most, or of becoming one *of* you instead of one *with* you? Forgive me all that: Let's marry our fates and fortunes, you and I, and find out not how much we can give up for each other but how much we can have together!

Homer struck a more satisfied chord and set down his instrument. That took a while, he said. Now then, pretty Nausicaa: You came to me freely, as did another noble lady once before, without seductive designs or blandishments on my part, and you made me the most satisfied of men for the second time in my life. For that, my thanks. My only regret is that this time around I never saw the details of my good fortune, except in my mind's eye, and it's in the details that reality abides. *Caress the details,* old Demodocus used to sing to his apprentices, and he's right. Even so, in what I've heard tonight there is the stuff of a second *Odyssey,* or maybe a *Nausicaad,* which I'm so eager to begin working out that you must not only consider yourself released from all obligation to me—you never had any, really—but also excuse me now, the pair of you, from your company.

Good Homer, Nausicaa murmured, not taking her eyes from Odysseus's face. It seemed to her that already he was looking younger, more like the man she had fallen in love with when he had washed the salt off himself that morning on the beach and her maids had decked him out in one of her brothers' robes.

Great Homer, Odysseus echoed. If it was the bard's pleasure, he declared, his men would give him free passage back to Ithaca, where he could reinstall himself in the palace and sing his new song as well as the old one and any others in his repertory. For just as there are those who quickly tire of anything familiar and forever hunger for novelty, so there are others who believe the old songs to be the best.

I believe I understand your invitation, Homer replied, and I promise to consider it seriously.

In return, declared Odysseus, I hope you'll let Nausicaa and me be your guests here till tomorrow morning. Then we shall go down to Queen Arete and tell her a tale that will do honor to both yourself and this young woman. After that, when her brothers come home, she and I will marry. They'll give us their boat as a wedding gift to get me out of their way, and we'll set out for the setting sun.

The tale you'll tell Arete is a tale I'd like to hear, said Homer, but not tonight. Very well, my house is yours: not in return for your Ithacan invitation, which I may after all end up declining with thanks, but in return for Nausicaa's past favors, which I am not likely ever to forget. And now, friends, I'll say good night—as soon as I've heard Nausicaa accept, after the fact, the proposal she accepted in advance.

Nausicaa declared she did, and Odysseus kissed her for the first time at last, somewhat clumsily on account of their positions, the bard's presence, and her continuing modesty with respect to her tunic. Homer withdrew with his lyre to the farthest corner of the little cabin, where for some while he sang and played to himself to give the couple what privacy was possible in the circumstances. Impatient to get on with it, Odysseus nevertheless restrained himself at the princess's bidding until presently, as Nausicaa had reason to expect he might, the bard fell asleep over his composing. Even good Homer, she declared, sometimes sleeps. Finally then she took her friend's hands in both of hers, stood up as straight and brave as she had stood once upon the beach, let the tunic fall, and herself initiated what she had dreamed about awake and asleep ever since her friend Eleni had missed that momentous catch.

There was one awkward moment only: When at Odysseus's delighted bidding she turned so that he could admire at leisure what he'd only glimpsed on first entering the cabin, she was mortified to hear suppressed laughter, and shocked to see that the man was in fact grinning, not merely with ravishment! Her eyes stung; she spun about, snatched up her tunic from the floor. Her own opinion, confirmed by Eleni and her other girlfriends and more recently by Homer himself, was that her backside was as perfectly perfect as the rest of her. It is, it is! Odysseus hastened to assure her: A flawless marvel! A pearl! A peach! But so long had she sat upon those manuscript pages in that chair while this story unfolded to its present moment, those splendid buttocks were now befreckled with the ink of Homer's *Odyssey*. Life had imitated art: The poet's description of her charms was no longer poetic license. But those freckles, declared Odysseus, darling as they are, belong elsewhere than on white-limbed, blemishless Nausicaa. Forgive me my amusement, dear friend, and permit me to remove them.

He made to do so, with a corner of her tunic. But bold Nausicaa, her composure regained, let that garment fall again, and, leading him to the bed, ordered him, as penance for having embarrassed her, to remove those literary blemishes with kisses. And so he rapturously did, until of inky freckles on the royal hey-nonny-no there remained not one iota.

Now great Athene in her wisdom, as if to compensate for having made epically long Odysseus's first night home with Penelope, made this first night with young Nausicaa lyrically short. Her protégé was after all a decade older than Homer; his staying power was no longer something to sing about. All the same, when presently the lovers fell asleep in each other's arms—Odysseus much sooner than Nausicaa—both were content. He had made love to a number of women in his half-century, but never to one so fresh, lovely, and eager, despite her inexperience, as the clean-limbed princess of Phaeacia, at once dainty, athletic, and without inhibition once that matter of the freckles had been clarified. As for Nausicaa, in bed with the second man of her life: If she had been in the mood for objective comparison, she would have found young Homer the more imaginative and longer-winded performer. But she was in no such mood. In the dark with Homer, she had been more blind than he, every night pretending it was Odysseus who embraced her and turned her this way and that. Now it so excited her that her long love-dream had come literally true, she insisted the lamp be left lit so that she could see Odysseus seeing her body and taking his pleasure in it. Well after he had satisfied himself for the present and fallen sound asleep, she continued to touch him, feasting her eyes upon his hard-used, muscled flesh, the famous scar along his inner thigh, and those parts which, on the beach, he had kept covered by that olive branch.

In the morning, Odysseus made breakfast for the three of them. When the princess and the poet were awake enough to pay attention, he briskly set forth the general outline of the story he proposed to tell Arete, and with their help—especially Homer's, whom not surprisingly they found to be a gold mine of invention—worked out its details. So impressed were the couple with the bard's contributions, they prevailed upon him to carry the tale himself to Arete and try its effect before they presented themselves and apprised her of their plans. Truth to tell, Homer was not displeased to oblige them, for while he was in his turn impressed by Odysseus's inventiveness—so ready and fertile that the poet began to wonder how many of those adventures recounted to the Phaeacians in Books Nine through Twelve of the *Odyssey* had actually occurred—as a professional, he found the man's delivery somewhat wanting.

The lovers then disguised themselves as goatherds and followed the bard down the mountain with a few of the flock Homer kept about the cabin in honor of his former occupation. While still in the Phaeacian suburbs, they heard that the palace was in an uproar: Nausicaa's brothers had returned during the night from their fruitless search. At once Homer suggested a detour to the cottage of his senior colleague, Demodocus, who always heard every rumor first and had the best nose on the island for sniffing out fact from fiction.

Arriving at the old man's house, they heard him singing of, of all people, Telemachus. From the doorway, Homer struck a single chord; Demodocus at once put down his own lyre and welcomed him by name, as respectfully as if Homer were the emeritus minstrel and himself the newcomer. Between you and me, Homer said after greeting him, let never a false note be struck. The couple with me are Captain Odysseus, formerly of Ithaca, and his lover, formerly mine, the Princess Nausicaa. We three have made peace among ourselves; we mean to do likewise with Queen Arete and her sons. But we've come to you first, both to pay our respects and to hear from you what's what down in the palace before we go there.

The surprised old minstrel bade the lovers come closer and speak certain dialogue lines from Book Six of Homer's Odysseus-poem, so that he could verify their identity. He had suspected, he declared, that his Ithacan caller might be Odysseus come back for Nausicaa, but had dismissed that suspicion as too dramatically interesting to be true: an occupational hazard of bards, he said, to whom reality's unrestrained melodramatizing is a continual embarrassment. Though he regretted Alcinous's death, he found it highly amusing that all the while Nausicaa's brothers were turning the known world upside down in search of her, she was in bed with worthy Homer up in the hills. He could not imagine a finer literary prize, he declared, or a more deserving winner; for once, "poetic justice" had turned out to mean justice for a poet. And he was prepared to sing them the palace news, if Homer in turn would sing him Odysseus's alibi for Nausicaa and himself.

With pleasure, Homer said, glad of the chance to try out their story on a world-class colleague before performing it in court. You first: You were doing Telemachus, I believe, when we interrupted you.

Following Homer's example, Odysseus and Nausicaa sat on the floor at Demodocus's feet, exchanging warm glances and touches while the old man retuned his lyre and sang that Nausicaa's brothers and their crew of handpicked oarsmen had expected to sail their new vessel to Ithaca as one might step from one room into the next, but that in fact, to their disappointment and mystification, the voyage had taken above a week: nowhere near so long as an ordinary ship would require, but far longer than their design specifications predicted. Be that as may, they had been hospitably received by Odysseus's wife and son and daughter-in-law, the master of the house being not at home. Taking Prince Telemachus aside to spare

Queen Penelope's feelings, the young men had told him all about their sister's infatuation with his father, which had so possessed her that she had disappeared altogether from the city, presumably to seek him out. In return for the Phaeacians' having once returned Odysseus to Ithaca at very considerable cost to themselves, the brothers begged Telemachus to beg his parents not to take offense at Nausicaa's unrequited and embarrassing passion. should she somehow make her way to that high hall, but to pity it for the madness it was and see to it that the princess was safely returned to her family.

I feel just awful, Nausicaa said. Odysseus squeezed her hand.

Prince Telemachus readily agreed, sang Demodocus, but then much alarmed the three brothers by reporting to them that his estimable parents were alas no longer together: They had seen fit to go their separate ways, his mother back to her loom, his father back to seafaring. That Odysseus had in fact set out some time ago for the brothers' home port, ostensibly to pay tribute to the Phaeacians' ill-rewarded hospitality to him. It might be, Telemachus speculated, that Princess Nausicaa's regrettable passion was not unrequited after all.

This news, Demodocus sang on, had aroused mixed emotions indeed in the brothers, who were additionally chagrined that to get back home in their defective new boat would take another full week. In fact, however, they and their crew retraced their course in a mere eyeblink of time, and realized that their outbound problem had been not in their autopilot, but in themselves. The older Phaeacian vessels had been able to intuit where their skippers wished to go and to steer them unerringly there; their new, state-of-the-art design did likewise, but so much more sensitively that in certain circumstances it could be at odds with itself. The brothers' direction had been, in effect, *Take us to Ithaca, to where our sister and Odysseus are;* the autopilot knew where Ithaca was, but must also have sensed that neither Nausicaa nor Odysseus was there. It had subtracted the second directive from the first, at great cost of headway.

This vindication of their yacht-designing skills, however, was a pleasure much muted by their discovery, only last night, that Odysseus had indeed arrived in Phaeacia just after they had left it; that he had been their mother's guest, incognito, throughout their absence; and that having heard from Arete the story of Nausicaa's disappearance and from Homer the story of the *Odyssey,* he had himself disappeared earlier that same evening—for some reason chasing after the famous bard, who for some reason strenuously eluded him. The sibling princes were now reorganizing and arming their crew as a posse to go up into the mountains in search of Homer's cabin, though they could have little hope of stumbling upon what no one else had ever found, and like all Phaeacians they were terrified of any altitude above sea level. And that, Demodocus concluded, is the morning's news.

He's right about our fear of heights, Nausicaa told Odysseus, although *masthead height* would be more accurate than *sea level*. It took more nerve for me to follow Homer up that path than it did to stand and face you in Book Six. We Phaeacians call it acrophobia.

We poets, Demodocus rejoined, call it poetic license when we say "sea level" instead of "masthead height."

And the gods, wry Homer said, call it poetic justice, I suppose, to punish a race of sailors with a ring of mountains. It was the local acrophobia I counted on to keep my fans from following me home and learning who my roommate was. Only another Ithacan like myself could be equally at ease on the wine-dark sea and in the goat-delighting hills. Last night, exactly such a one came along (here Homer took up his lyre, struck a chord, shrugged), and my honeymoon was over. Now it's back to my nimble-shanked goats and my hexameters, which I hope may be as nimble. Tell me what you think of this bit of theater, Demodocus.

At Homer's bidding then, Nausicaa pretended to be her own mother; Demodocus took the role of her brother Laodamas, the late Alcinous's favorite son, who always sat at his father's side; and Odysseus played her other two bachelor brothers, the princes Halius and Clytoneus. Where have you been? Nausicaa demanded sternly of the poet, in a voice so like Arete's that both Homer and Demodocus gave a start. What was it between you and Lord Odysseus these past few nights, and what connection does it have, if any, to my headstrong daughter's whereabouts?

Don't be alarmed, Homer said with a strum—

Don't be alarmed? Odysseus cried, feigning the angry young men. We were about to drag you and that lying Ithacan down from your mountains to the level seashore, where a man can see what's what! He and Nausicaa smiled at each other. You had better sing your piece, Demodocus warned Homer gravely, and it had better be a good one.

Homer thereupon invoked the muse Erato—not his customary muse, he noted—to sing Princess Nausicaa of the peerless arms, unharmed and safely en route home, thanks to noble Odysseus—who, like her, was guilty of no worse crime than love. Quickly he synopsized the story thus far, omitting only his own affair with Penelope, Odysseus's revenge upon hapless Phemius, and the liaison between himself and Nausicaa. He reminded the court of Alcinous and Arete's early offer of their daughter's hand to Odysseus, and their later plan to cure her lovesickness with songs of that man's fidelity; how those songs had only fed the girl's infatuation to the point where she fled the palace—not, as everyone supposed, for Ithaca, but for Homer's own goat-girt cabin in the dizzy-making hills, that she might hear nothing the day long but songs of Odysseus, Odysseus, Odysseus.

Nausicaa blushed; so does Diana of the snow-white teeth. Ted squeezes her shoulder, as did Odysseus the princess's. I took her in, gave her food and shelter, and respected her royal maidenhead, sang straight-faced Homer—but then toned the line down to *her royal maidenhood*. When she threatened to run off to Ithaca or over the nearest cliff, as she did every second afternoon and some mornings, I dissuaded her with songs of unrequited lovers who found new and greater happiness elsewhere. Most of these I was obliged to invent: Our myths are not rich in happy endings, especially of that sort. When the Ithacan sailed in a while back, I guessed early on he was Odysseus; I dodged him night after night because he had not yet made his intentions clear, and I wanted to spare Nausicaa's feelings if they were not honorably directed at her. But who can get the best of that cunning fellow? The gods led him across the storm-rich seas and up the goat-fraught cliffs to his beloved. For so she is, my friends, as is he hers. His intentions are every bit as honorable as were mine. He has put Ithaca and all things Ithacan behind him; neither does he covet the throne of Phaeacia: only Nausicaa's white hand in marriage—plus a certain wedding gift to speed them upon what bids to be the longest honeymoon in marital history. But I shall let the lovers sing that song themselves.

Well done! the audience applauded, both then in the old bard's cottage and a few hours later in Arete's palace. At Demodocus's suggestion (he was no Homer for invention and performance, but his long professional experience had made him wiser in the ways of audiences), he himself went first to the disarrayed and angry court, from which the princes' posse was nervously making ready to set out, and declared that great Homer was safe and sound and came bearing good news of Nausicaa, which would spare them their mountain-climbing expedition. When they had assimilated this report and settled down, Homer entered and sang them an already more polished version of the trio's story.

Well sung! old Demodocus cheered, to cue the royal family's reaction, and from the rear of the discombobulated hall Odysseus and Nausicaa echoed his applause. The crowd made way for them; they shed their goatherd wraps and came forward as their proper selves to kneel before Arete and the frowning princes. Nausicaa's arms, her mother noticed at once, were white no longer, but sunburnt as any peasant woman's; her hair, however, was clean and neatly brushed, her tunic spotless, her expression radiant. She was no longer virginal, Arete understood at once, but she had not been forced. In a clear voice, the princess declared that great Homer had sung the truth from first to last. She would regret forever the sorrow she had caused her father and mother in the name of love, as well as the trouble she had put her good brothers to—though she was pleased to hear, she added with a smile, that their new hull design had lived up to or exceeded its predicted performance values. She prayed their forgiveness, Arete's consent to her marriage, and their blessing. Likewise, said Odysseus, and discreetly said nothing further just then about wedding gifts.

Arete regarded for some moments this man halfway between her daughter's age and her own, and so marked and weathered by experience that his face and hands alone were a living logbook of his odyssey. Frankly, she told Nausicaa, I had hoped you'd marry someone more your age, whose children by you would be his first and only heirs. As it is, every chorus you sing with this man, new to you, will be a repeat for him, only in a different key. But so be it: You've made your choice, and it may well be that an impetuous young woman like you will be happier with a seasoned, older husband than with a young one as headstrong as yourself.

She then embraced her daughter, saluted Odysseus, gave her consent and blessing to their match, and welcomed him to serve her and the princes as their chief state counsellor, whether officially or without portfolio.

Odysseus saw Laodamas and his brothers exchange uneasy glances. He thanked Arete for her offer and her blessing, the three brothers for their fraternal concern for Nausicaa; he also congratulated them enviously, as one sailor to another, upon the reported success of their new design. But he disclaimed any interest in Phaeacian state offices. He had seen enough of Arete's statecraft and general wisdom, he said, to know that the young princes could have no better advisor in the administrative arts than their mother, against the day one or more of them succeeded to the reins of government. As for himself and his bride-to-be—he looked to Nausicaa, who nodded—they had in mind by way of honeymoon a long voyage of exploration: a voyage in one respect brief, in another perhaps endless. But it had better be proposed and discussed among the royal family only—plus Homer, whom they should regard as court historian and keep no secrets from.

The queen agreed; the posse, to its great relief, was demobilized; an engagement luncheon was ordered for the immediate family and the two bards, in the course of which Odysseus set forth his plan. He described the land Circe had told him of and the peculiar difficulty of reaching it, without mentioning that whoever overcame that difficulty would age no further, but could never return. It was his ambition, he said, to end his long nautical career with a honeymoon cruise to that country in the brothers' new boat, the only vessel remotely capable of getting there. Should he and Nausicaa make a successful landfall, the fame of the Phaeacians—their hospitality and their nautical prowess—would be sung forever in the new principality he hoped to establish there. And who could say what rich commerce would then ensue between the two nations, which no competitor would have the technological know-how to share in? If, on the other hand, his attempt should fail—well, those were the fortunes of the sea, which his fiancée had declared her readiness to hazard at his side.

Nausicaa affirmed that readiness and implored her brothers to lend them their boat as a wedding present, even though the loan might turn out to be a gift. Otherwise, she supposed, she and Odysseus would have no choice but to accept the appointment Arete had offered him, as her prime minister.

The household then divided to confer and consider. Arete withdrew to question her daughter a bit more on the period of her disappearance and on Odysseus's obligations to his first wife and his son, as well as to elaborate on the pros and cons of the difference in their ages and to review with her some intimate facts of married life. Nausicaa, who much loved her mother, answered her questions as fully as she could without saying more than she wanted to say and made it plain that she meant to go with the man from that day forward wherever he went.

I can see that you do, Arete said, not displeased. I hope profoundly that your friend feels likewise about you.

As for Odysseus, he questioned Nausicaa's brothers in technical detail about their boat, in order to gain their confidence, flatter their abilities, and forestall their questioning him more closely about his intended destination. Then the lovers changed places: Odysseus did his best to reassure Arete that he loved her daughter wholeheartedly, that he had provided generously for his former household, and that in marrying the princess he would not be committing bigamy, since Ithacan law did not apply in Phaeacia, much less where he meant to go. Nausicaa for her part found her brothers' regret at the prospect of losing her more than offset by their relief that Odysseus would not be staying on in the palace. Sorry as they were to give up a vessel they'd barely tested, she soon had them discussing excitedly the possibility of an even better version: a Phaeacian Thirty-five Mark Two, based on their sea trials of the prototype. When she promised not to sail until they'd completed their testing of the Mark One and drawn their plans for its successor, they agreed to lend her the boat for as long as she and their prospective brother-in-law should need it.

So it came to pass, not long afterward, that Odysseus and Nausicaa were married in a splendid three-day celebration, at which the bride excelled all her bridesmaids and most of the ushers in the ball-throwing events, and Odysseus left behind all the local skippers except the three princes, against whom he refused to compete, in the around-the-buoys sailing events. Demodocus and Homer went one-on-one at a series of banquets for the newlyweds, and while the younger bard won hands down, Demodocus seemed to have gotten a new lease on life from the inspiration of the projected honeymoon voyage, which everyone agreed he turned into his best song since the one about Ares and Aphrodite snared in the golden throes of love by jealous Hephaestus. Stripped of its music, betrayed into workaday English prose, and much summarized, his new song—which turned out to be accurate prophecy—went something like this:

Ted rises to his feet and takes over Diana's narrative as if launching into Demodocus's song: The nuptials done, bride and groom retired joyfully to their honeymoon bed and embarked upon a different sort of exploratory voyage, about which they were in no hurry whatsoever. . . .

Next morning, responds smiling, blushing Diana, thanks to the wisdom of Queen Arete, the bride's maids were able to honor an ancient custom of squid-rich Phaeacia: that of displaying to the assembled court their mistress's wedding-night bedsheet, so copiously blazoned with Nausicaa's hymeneal blood that, as the great bard Homer himself observed, it looked like the legendary field of battle between the Cocks and the Cuttlefish. All summer then they stayed on in the palace, giving joy to Arete and working daily with the young princes on the fine tuning and inmost secrets of their craft.

Says Ted: Odysseus was perfectly delighted with his young bride. He could not have said himself where his energy came from, but there it was, when he needed it, as if he had already achieved Circe's promised land. And at the naval cunning embodied in the princes' ship, he was simply astonished: Its outward resemblance to the vessels of the time was a virtual camouflage, concealing technologies so unfamiliar as to amount to magic. But with brown-limbed Nausicaa's help and patient Laodamas's (who was already thinking yet farther ahead to his Mark Two version), he got the hang of sailing it.

As for Nausicaa, chimes in Diana, it turned out that her romantic fantasizing had been as accurate as it was obsessive: A girl who had always loved her father, she was exactly as pleased with her middle-aged bridegroom as she had expected to be, in exactly the ways she had imagined. It excited her that he had had a former life; that what was fresh to her was refreshment to him. It excited her that rousing him sometimes required a bit of doing on her part; she enjoyed the doing. Finally, it excited her that her youth and inexperience, combined with her imagination and uninhibition, excited him: Did Calypso ever do *this*? she would ask him, and then do something she had never heard or thought of before, but which it had just occurred to her might be possible. If what she did turned out to be news to Odysseus too, that was exciting; if on the other hand he said Circe herself used to do that, except she'd put her left leg *here*—that could be more exciting still.

What with so much and various excitement, says lucky Ted, it is not surprising that at summer's end, when all was ready for their setting out, they both gladdened and broke Queen Arete's heart by announcing that her first grandchild, whom in all likelihood she would never see, was definitely in the making: about as far along in his or her development as the brothers' *new* new boat. At Homer's suggestion they even chose a nickname for their first child, should it be a son: *Mark I.*

We watch and listen raptly as our practiced hosts wind up their tale. On the cloudless equinoctial day, declares Diana, their farewell banquets done and tearful farewells made, at exactly mid-afternoon Nausicaa cast off their boat's bow line, Odysseus the stern. Homer and Demodocus struck twin chords, and the newlyweds glided from the cheering harbor, past their petrified predecessor, and away from mountain-ringed Phaeacia. Once clear of the island, they secured their safety harnesses and set a winged course straight for the declining sun.

For the next several hours, Ted goes on, they accelerated from fast to faster to faster yet, employing every device known to canny racing skippers plus the radical new ones built into their craft. It is perfectly safe to say that never since the world began had a manmade vessel moved so swiftly through the water: well beyond anything they had managed in their practice runs. The sun continued on its downward path, but ever more slowly as their speed increased—until, just as they had planned and hoped . . . He gestures smiling to his wife, who takes his hand and holds it.

As they'd planned and hoped, she echoes, at the moment the sun's golden lower limb just touched the far horizon and Nausicaa called *Mark!,* Odysseus made the last go-fast adjustment Laodamas had taught him—a tiny final flattening-reef in the mainsail, it was—and mirabile dictu, as the Romans say, they reached what Circe had called Holding Velocity. For what seemed an eternity, the sun hung poised exactly there, neither setting further nor retreating higher.

Says Ted, exchanging with Diana an actor's expression of nervous dismay, Their exultation turned into nervous dismay. Another half-knot, a *tenth* of a knot, would do the trick; a breath more of wind; they had done everything they'd planned to do; they had far exceeded even the sound of their own speed—and yet they were not going fast enough; the sun hung still. The terrible thought crossed Odysseus's mind: *We aren't going to make it.*

Then, Diana quietly declares, in the spectral silence of Holding Velocity— a silence that must be experienced before it can be imagined, surrounded as it is by the visible rush of unbelievable speed—Nausicaa took her husband's hand and spoke to him in a voice no louder than mine now. When I was a young girl racing against my brothers, she said, and all else failed, I used to win sometimes by whistling into the sails. In Phaeacia we call it *whistling up a breeze.*

We had better try it, Ted responds. And so they did, Odysseus whistling in the normal fashion, as if to make music, and Nausicaa letting go a shrill blast between two fingers in her mouth.

Yay for Nausicaa, says Kathy Sherritt: I admire a girl who can whistle like that.

Was it wishful thinking, asks Diana, or did they see the sun actually rise a millimeter above the horizon? They scarcely dared look, for fear of injuring their eyes. Again Nausicaa whistled. No doubt about it this time: The sun perceptibly lifted—but sank again at once to horizon level. Well, she couldn't whistle continuously; she was hyperventilated already. Honey, she said, I'm out of ideas.

But your idea gave *me* one, Ted says Odysseus said then. He had heard Demodocus remark of Homer (using another Phaeacian idiom): That young fellow certainly can sing up a storm. Being a prose-minded Ithacan, he had asked Homer whether that tribute was literally correct and, if so, whether Homer could teach him the knack, to use as a last resort when becalmed. The bard had replied that it was trick to be used only as a last resort indeed; that said, however, there was nothing very tricky about it: The secret was to find the right song for the singer and the occasion, and then (in Homer's own words) to let 'er rip.

For Odysseus, says Diana, Homer recommended the song he himself was in midst of composing (don't forget that all this is in *Demodocus's* song, being sung at the wedding feast): It began with the story of the unfinished corner of Penelope's web, and it would end with Odysseus and Nausicaa's sailing off into the rising sunset—but he hadn't worked out the ending yet. All you have to do, Demodocus sang that Odysseus said that Homer told him, is get the first line right, and the second; the rest will follow as does the night the day.

Nausicaa raised her lovely eyebrows at that, says Ted, among other reasons because neither of them could carry a tune, even when they knew what the tune was. Could Homer be settling some score with them? Odysseus thought not, inasmuch as the bard had taken the trouble to teach him the first two lines of that new song. In any case, they had no other expedient: As best he could—for it was a case of the blind leading the blind—he rehearsed with Nausicaa what Homer had rehearsed with him. Then he took a deep breath and sang loudly into the sail: *Once upon a time . . .*

In heartfelt harmony then, Diana says, Nausicaa joined him in Line Two, which they sang together like this:

There was a story that began, the handsome couple sing together, in very approximate unison, and Diana continues It worked, in a way they hadn't anticipated. Not only did the boat surge forward and the sun climb visibly a few degrees above the horizon, but when it did, instead of facing the problem of Line Three (which neither of them knew), they found themselves back at Line One: *Once upon a time.* And when they followed it with Line Two—*There was a story that began*—there they were, back at Line One again, and the sun another few degrees higher.

Eureka, exclaims laughing Peter Sagamore.

Indeed, says Theodoros, they had found it. How long they went on repeating those lines it is strictly impossible to tell, for while their boat flashed forward under the climbing sun, time seemed to flash back.

Before his wife's eyes, says Diana, Odysseus lost ten years. He looked fortyish again, and handsomer than ever. Nausicaa hoped he wouldn't get any younger than that. . . .

As for her, Ted says now in a grave voice, and Diana looks away: She lost fewer years, for she had fewer to lose. But alas, in losing fewer she did not lose less. She became the radiant, white-limbed young beauty she had been before Odysseus stepped out of the olive-scrub onto the foreshore of her life. In that regress, the little swelling in her belly flattened out—

Katherine Sherritt makes a pained small sound; Fear and Trembling clutch each other, wide-eyed.

—and the grandchild Arete never would have seen, says quiet Ted, its parents have also yet to see. Sperm and egg returned to their launching places; father and mother became groom and virgin bride once more.

For all their sadness, goes on brave Dee, they regarded each other with delight. It particularly gratified Nausicaa that she was virginal again, so that she could give her experienced friend the pleasure of her first experience.

A pleasure he would have taken then and there, Ted declares, upon the whistling afterdeck, except that just then a bird streaked by, the first they'd seen since leaving port. And a few moments later, land hove into sight:

white beaches, royal palms, an air more perfumed than the air of Calypso's isle. The ship slowed to normal sailing speed, but the sun stayed fixed at the point to which they'd raised it: midway between its zenith and the western shore. They ran up easily onto the surfless beach; they stepped ashore near a clear and sparkling natural fountain in a grove of navel oranges. Her throat quite parched from singing those two Homeric lines for who knows how long, thirsty Nausicaa wondered—

Do you think the water's safe to drink? recites Diana.

Ted responds Let's take a chance, handing her wine goblet and raising his own in salute. They drink. They drank. And at the first swallow, Dee declares, they understood that they had arrived at their destination.

With an air of finishment, our hosts take their seats. God knows how late the hour must be; we have lost track of time and don't want to regain it. Dew-damp Katherine says Whew: What happened after that? Replies Diana, brushing something invisible off the front of her chiton, Nothing. They lived happily ever after.

Ever after? musing Peter presses. For all practical purposes, Ted affirms. The sun resumed its normal course, but once having drunk from that spring, Odysseus and Nausicaa virtually ceased to age. Nature does not go in for absolutes: The technical fact is that from that time on, they have aged at the rate of about three months per century, or about ten years in three thousand, and their boat along with them. Its name is *Mark One,* by the way, as their child's had been going to be; but even though they call it that, they've never had the heart to paint that dear name on the garboards or the stern. Another technical peculiarity of their situation rules out east-west travel of any length: They can neither recross the Atlantic nor go much farther west than the Eastern Time Zone. Nor for that matter below the Equator, for some reason that's not altogether clear. No punishment involved, you understand: That sort of thing went out with the Olympians. They just can't do it; their boat won't go there.

Within those limits, however, they're free to move north and south at their pleasure, and that is what they've done ever since. Early on, they fell into the natural pattern of cruising north through the spring and summer toward Maine and the Canadian maritimes, then south through the fall and winter back to Florida, where they first landed, and on to the Bahamas or the Caribbean. Mostly they stay in the open ocean, like stormy petrels, and are seldom seen; they enjoy each other's company more than other people's. But since the Intracoastal Waterway was opened, for variety's sake they sometimes take the inside passage instead. Once a century, on the average, they'll manage to revisit any given anchorage among the thousands along their route, to see how it has changed since their last visit.

For the first two and a half millennia, says Diana, there was scarcely any change at all, and *never* another sailboat. Talk about privacy! Nowadays, of course, it's a different story.

In which, says smiling Ted, once in a while a fellow sailor will anchor for the night in Nova Scotia or Tobago or Chesapeake Bay and discover himself moored next door to an honest-to-God Phaeacian Thirty-five, Mark One. My friends, your health!

We applaud. We toast *their* health, too, which clearly needs no toasting. We drink to Poseidon and Aeolus, to Ithaca, Phaeacia, and the Eastern Shore of Maryland. Then Peter Sagamore declares that it seems to him the story's not quite done: Whether or not Homer returned to Ithaca, we still don't know what Penelope wove into that last corner of her web.

Theodoros Dmitrikakis nods and says, not quite to Peter's point, You have been first-rate listeners, both of you. . . .

All of us, murmurs Katherine, patting her belly—and wondering too late whether she's being tactless.

But it is late, goes on Ted, even for people who have all the time in the world. Tomorrow evening, if you like, we'll tell you

THE END OF THAT STORY.

Or the next time we find ourselves in the same anchorage.

Agreed. And you must let us return the favor. Eye for an eye. Tit for a tat. Tale for a tale.

What a brace of smiles! *Quel* cool couple!

Agreed.

DAY 3:
MADISON BAY TO
RHODE RIVER

Wrecked in the head from retsina, groggy still at eight next morning from so late a bedtime, Peter Sagamore awakes feeling anyhow like making love to Katherine Sherritt and so, well hung as well as well hung-over, navigates through *Story*'s cabin to her snug berth. Planting his face between her sleepy breasts, he advises Don't breathe my breath. One whiff will embalm those children and their mother too.

Says stirring Katherine You've been dreaming about Dee-ah-nah Dmitrikakis.

No.

You're allowed. Kate yawns and stretches as best she can. Tell those children last night's bedtime story while you're there.

No.

She holds his head: A story a night. She fingers his hair. Odysseus and Nausicaa got you off the hook, but a rule's a rule.

Rules shmules, Peter mumbles: Jesus says the Sabbath was made for man, not man for the Sabbath.

Replies K Today's Wednesday, and yawns again. That Dee is *gorgeous*! Mm.

Presently Katherine wants to know So are they or aren't they what we think they are but know they can't be? Peter thinks we should discuss that question fully at breakfast and not at all now, but Kath's wide awake and racing her motor. Still holding his head she says That Ted's a sexy thing, too. *I* sure dreamed: dreams dreams dreams, this whole cruise. Do it. Do you wish we were supercool like them instead of plain old us? Ah. Ah.

Presently in turn Peter says It's me that's plain old us. *You're* supercool.

Bids kinky Kate Now set me a task. It used to bother May Jump that it excited Katherine Sherritt to be given sexual work-orders by her lovers.

That has got to be a sign of hang-up, May would say, but had to acknowledge that when it came to carnal pleasures, Kiss was about as un-hung-up as a body can be.

Enough sex: Let's check the world. It is a hazy calm morning in Madison Bay, still cool—and we have the anchorage to ourselves.

They did it. Over tired doughnuts from that restaurant and coffee, we agree we half thought they might: slip out quietly at dawn; leave the big questions as unresolved as that final corner of Penelope's web. We know very well we'll never see "Ted" and "Diana" again; that the end of that story really was

THE END OF THAT STORY.

We're not even going to think about it, Peter declares, aware that for some while we shall of course be able to think of little else, and that from time to time for the rest of our lives we'll be asking ourselves whether the obviously preposterous circumstance might just possibly be the case and, since it can't be, it being so obviously preposterous, what then *is* the truth about that handsome, supercool couple and their spooky boat, *Mark I*? Us, we like a story with a proper ending to it: no loose ends, no red herrings, no fade-outs; all mysteries resolved, virtue rewarded, wickedness brought low, true lovers at the altar and presently pregnant.

Katherine Sherritt suddenly says Mark Twain. Says unsurprised Peter Yup.

You know what I mean? Sure he knows what she means: That was going to be *his* story if, as we might have known wouldn't be the case, *Mark I* had still been there this morning and we and the Dmitrikakises had gotten together again and old flashy-limbed Nausicaa there and her bandy-legged, thigh-scarred friend had told us the end of that story of Penelope's web and our turn had come to tell *them* one. Kate's not the only one aboard this vessel that all they do is dream dream dream. And has she noticed—pret-ty far out for us no-nonsense types—how what we're dreaming and what we're sailing into on this cruise of ours so play off each other lately that a body can't sort out cause from effect? Take that *SEX EDUCATION: Play* play, for example, Act I of which floated in just when we needed it and caused or colored the dreams, both his and hers, that led to Odysseus and Nausicaa and Penelope's unfinished web and N's three brothers' first boat and their second, also unfinished like Peter's dream of two nights back, which he now sees retrospectively to have been entitled *Huck Finn on the Honga, Part One,* inasmuch as he wound it up last night with

HUCK FINN ON THE HONGA, PART TWO, OR, THE *MARK TWAIN*.

Pay attention to your father now, Mason and Dixon, their mother orders: This is your last-night's bedtime story. Me, I remember now I dreamed I was in bed again with Poonie Baldwin, Junior. Yech! Yech!

Asks Pete Did Ted and Diana mention or show us the jeweled box that Arete gave Odysseus and Nausicaa as a wedding-plus-going-away present, or did I dream that?

Katherine opines from the cockpit, where in white underpants and gray sweatshirt she's curled up now around her decaf, You dreamed that. Unless we dreamed the whole shebang. Hey, yeah, she muses: Maybe we're not really *on* this boat here in Madison Bay, okay? Maybe we're back in the First Guest Cottage at Nopoint Point, you checking out Mom's intercom and me kvetching about invasion of privacy. Peter muses with her: I asked you to set me a task, and you were just about to do it when one of us dozed off and dreamed all this. Katherine declares We're back in the Gramercy Park Hotel in Nineteen Sixty-four, still making love and falling asleep and waking up and making love, and one of us has upped and dreamed a flashforward about how we split after that and then got back together again at the Katherine Anne Porter party in College Park and got married and pregnant and antsy and here we are. Want to wake up or go with it?

Go with it, says Peter Sagamore, and maybe he's still thirteen years old and never left old Dorchester County. Maybe he's still stuck on Bloodsworth Island there, waiting for the tide to turn and fetch him home in the *Mark Twain,* aha.

In the?

You'll notice, the man of us tells our children, once you're born, that your working Chesapeake watermen do not characteristically name their workboats *Windsong,* for example, or *Sundance* or *Moonraker* or *Dawn Treader,* not to mention *Tiltin' Hilton, Yom Clipper, Ahoy Veh, Daddy's Playtoy,* or *Buy, Baby.* Your working Chesapeake watermen call their boats *Captain Earl P. Batchelder* or *Rosie M. Conway,* and sometimes *Edna Mae.* Your father's right, says Katherine: Bobby Henry calls his john-boat *Ruth Marie Ann,* which is his wife and daughters. Further, announces Peter, if your working Chesapeake waterman's workboat is accompanied by a dinghy, skiff, or tender—as it will not normally be except in the case of the motorized yawl-boats used to push oyster-dredging skipjacks in windless weather—then that dinghy, skiff, or tender will decidely *not* bear an amusing name played off the name of the mother ship: *Night Watch* followed by *Watch Out; Allegro* followed by *Allegretto; Sloop du Jour* followed by *Crouton; Shapely Lady* followed by *Tender Behind,* et cetera. Your working waterman's dinghy, skiff, or tender will have no name at all, unless perhaps *A F Four Four Six Five M D.*

Now, then: We boatwright Sagamores down on Shoal Point, Hoopers Island, were not working Chesapeake watermen and waterwomen, but we worked with working waterfolk, we lived like working waterfolk, and we named our boats like working waterfolk. The elderly skiff, therefore, in which on an airless June A.M. in Nineteen Fifty-three your sire set out to discover whether the tide would fetch him six hours twenty-two minutes-worth down the Honga River and then six hours twenty-two minutesworth back to his home dock, with no assistance or interference from himself—that skiff had no name when I set out, neither in fact nor in my dream of night before last. And it was still anonymous, that skiff was, when in both cases a northerly breeze sprang up that promised to carry your pa out into the Bay if he didn't go ashore on Bloodsworth Island, which he did. Not by swimming the skiff in through sea nettles, as I was about to do two nights ago when I woke up from dreaming this, but by steering myself aground and then walking the skiff up through the muck, hoping I wouldn't step on an unexploded souvenir from the Patuxent Naval Air Test Center. I did not and therefore survived to grow up and leave Dorchester County and become a strange sort of story writer and meet, make love to, lose, remeet, and marry Katherine Shorter Sherritt and beget you guys upon her as they say and dream this dream and tell this story.

Unless, K reminds him, you're still asleep and dreaming down there on Bloodsworth Island.

Right. Now, Katie: Where do you suppose a person comes from?

A person comes, says Katherine promptly, from the felicitous encounter of sperm and egg in fallopian tube. I refer you to *SEX EDUCATION: Play,* Act One. She sees that Peter's serious, leaning on his arms on the companionway sill. She touches his hair. But that's not what you have in mind.

Nope. What he has in mind is this. A person from K. S. Sherritt's background would scarcely be able to imagine—if it weren't that her ethnic-folklore field work and her long affair with Peter Sagamore have led her many and many a time to see and shake her head at it—how homogeneous, how variety- and idea-poor, though no doubt rich in other ways, was life in an isolated fishing-and-farming village like Hoopersville, Maryland, especially before the advent of television. The biweekly expedition to Cambridge, with its occasional movie, was in the 1950s still a big event. Almost nobody read any books ever, except the Bible. All hands were Methodist or lapsed Lutheran except a few descendants of Lord Baltimore's original Catholic colonists. Everybody was of English or Scotch-Irish extraction but for the odd turn-of-the-century German immigrant. Everybody was white but for the blacks—proportionately far fewer in the salt-marsh communities, which had little use for slaves, than in the agricultural areas and the towns. Racial segregation was absolute. Visitors of any sort were few. The nearest bookstore was in Talbot County; it had as well been on the moon. A trip to Baltimore was an excursion to Babylon. Whatever positive might be said for such a growing-up place—in the way of physical independence and self-reliance among its people, the virtual absence of crime, a strong community spirit, and (except for the blacks) a classless society in which wealth was as rare as indigence—the fact is that until he left for college, Peter Sagamore had never met anyone who'd been to college, other than his schoolteachers and the family doctor. Nor had he ever met e.g. an Italian-American (not to mention an Italian Italian), an Asiatic, a Jew. In those Dixiecrat days he had scarcely known even a Republican, and had never to his knowledge encountered an atheist, a political radical either left- or right-wing, or anyone who could speak a tongue other than down-country English except his high school Spanish teacher and a couple of Holy Rollers. No doubt things are different now. More?

No. It is possible that when *she* was thirteen, Katherine Sherritt knew no one except the help whose parents weren't five-generation professional and business people. While Peter was dozing down the Honga in that nameless skiff, she was as at ease on the Paris *métro,* a London bus, a Cunard liner, or a Boeing 707 as she was on her three-speed bike or her father's ocean-racing *Katydid*s. She could distinguish Pombaline from Manueline in Portugal, plateresque from *pavo* in Spain, not to mention Romanesque from Gothic all over the rest of Europe, more from casually accumulated firsthand experience than from study. . . .

Enough. Phenomena like Katherine Shorter Sherritt, who remember which side their ancestors were on in the War of the Roses, do not wonder where a person comes from, until they come to know phenomena like Peter Sagamore. But we digress. Mark Twain? Dream?

If Hannibal, Missouri, had been in central Tennessee, Peter wonders, would there have been a Mark Twain? The river that carried Huck Finn away from Hannibal carried Sam Clemens into the world and around it. The Chattahoochee or Monongahela wouldn't have done, not to mention the Honga; the point is that *anything* in the USA could come down that Mississippi, so to speak. It only doesn't come back, any more than Mark Twain went back to being Sam Clemens of Hannibal. Okay? Whereas— P's tidewater fantasies notwithstanding—*nothing* he ever saw went down the Honga that didn't start there, and it all came back on the tide, no different but for a few barnacles. It's just us Hoopers Island waterfolk going out to work and coming home again, generation after generation. Except for the odd war veteran or nineteenth-century skipper in the Indies trade, the last brush Hoopers Island folk had with the wider world was the arrival of the British invasion fleet of 1813 and 1814, which foraged around there while burning Washington and attacking Baltimore. When Peter Sagamore was a boy, folks still talked about those raiding parties as if they had happened in their lifetimes. Them Redcoats, now, they were sumpn: Give 'em what they wanted, they'd pay you in pound sterling; didn't, they'd take and burn you to the ground.

It is a fact about islands, Katherine Sherritt agrees, that they tend to be insular.

Which is why Peter wonders how—when at age thirteen he heard the

much-revered local Methodist minister explain to his Hoopersville con-
gregation that when Jesus is called King of the Jews, the biblical Jews thus
referred to are not to be confused with the sharp-trading moneygrubbers
we all know today—he understood at once that the man was a bigot, though
he hadn't yet learned that word. The only Jews anyone on Hoopers Island
had met firsthand were two or three families of Cambridge shopkeepers
who everyone agreed were upstanding people; yet no one questioned the
stereotype, which Peter, who'd never met even those families, knew at
once to be unjust. What was more, at about the same moment he came
to understand the more complex injustice of the condition of the Negroes,
whom everyone *did* know more or less closely without that familiarity's
disturbing their stereotypes. It promptly appalled him that not only all his
friends but his family as well shared these attitudes, about which—he
discovered over midday dinner that same June Sunday—they were good-
humoredly impervious to argument.

After the chicken and the lima beans and the mashed potatoes, the boy
went soft-crabbing to be alone with these revelations, and as he stalked
the Shoal Point shallows, he decided among other things that all people
are created equal before God and ought to be equal before the law, but
aren't; that he didn't believe in God anyhow and therefore wouldn't join
church next Easter, as he was scheduled to; that though he liked his family,
he was not truly a member of it and was not destined to pass his life on
Hoopers Island; and that tomorrow, if the weather was right, he would
try the drifting experiment he had been planning for some time, not simply
to see whether it worked, but to clarify one final matter that the minister's
casual anti-Semitism had somehow brought into near-focus.

All this, mind, in a single Sunday in the life of a mild, cheerful, nowise
rebellious, and utterly unsophisticated boy. Hence Peter's question: Where
does a person come from? What on earth, for example, could that lad have
been reading down there in Hoopersville to put such liberal, outlandish
ideas into his head?

The less bloodthirsty portions of the Holy Bible? Katherine suggests.
The U.S. Declaration of Independence? *The Adventures of Huckleberry
Finn*? Listen: It impresses her that in the fancy circles she grew up in,
bigotry was regarded as a vulgar no-no, and all hands were expensively
schooled in critical thinking, cultural pluralism, and the rest, but when you
came right down to it the prevailing attitudes weren't a whole lot different
from those on Hoopers Island. Everybody in her set knew very well by
age thirteen that ethnic stereotypes are vicious, Jews obnoxious, and Negroes inferior. Such things went without saying. What Katherine Sherritt
believes is that it is enough for the heart's elect, even on a desert island,
to hear one chorus of e.g. the old Protestant Sunday-school song *Red or
yellow black or white, they are precious in His sight; Jesus loves the little
children of the world,* or see one UNICEF card with its holiday greeting
in half a dozen languages, to make that child a lifelong partisan of liberty
and justice for all; whereas the spiritual-imaginative hoi polloi, no matter

how privileged, never really question their assumptions, but wear their cultural blinders to the grave.

Heart's elect! marvels Peter. Spiritual-imaginative hoi polloi! What is this fount of eloquence I'm sharing an engineless small boat with? Who wants flashy-armed Nausicaa in all her heaven-sent beauty when he has Katherine Sherritt Sagamore?

Laments K God, she was gorgeous. On with your story.

In fact, Peter Sagamore at thirteen *had* begun reading *Huckleberry Finn*. He'd borrowed it from the Dorchester County Public Library in Cambridge *faute de mieux,* having used up the shelves of Tom Swifts and Tarzans that the librarian steered all boys to, and while he couldn't have said then what's clear to him now about the difference between Twain's homely-artful truth-telling and the voiceless innocuosity of Victor Appleton and Edgar Rice Burroughs, surely Huck had had a hand in this drifting project; very likely in that Sunday's insights as well. He pulled his anonymous skiff ashore on Bloodsworth Island, fiddled further with that locked sea-box— no, wait: The box was only in those dreams. All right, then: He can't remember *what* he did while waiting for the tide to turn and the breeze to die out or not, besides wish that the Honga ran one way like the Mississippi, out to the world. Presently he dozed off again—he'd had a wakeful night and a very early start that morning—and dreamed that Huckleberry Finn was with him there on Bloodsworth Island.

In those days, says Peter, I had a best friend whom without quite noticing it I'd come to be half afraid of: a redneck neighbor-boy my age, Howard Something-or-Other, with papery skin and straw hair and a pointy face full of bad teeth. Also sour breath and red-rimmed eyes. Howard Some-thing-or-Other smelled like stale crabfat and crushed saltines, and he picked his nose and ate his boogers and was a great gooser in the ass of his male friends and rapper of them smartly in the nuts, as we chaps called our testicles, besides having so large a craving to witness my little sister naked that he was forever offering me dollars filched from his mother's purse to set him up to spy upon Sue-Ann Sagamore in her bath, which I didn't. Howard Findley.

Holy Jesus on the Cross of Calvary, says Katherine Sherritt: This was your best friend?

Says Peter The available selection was not wide. In this dream of mine, old Howard Findley there gets conflated with Huck Finn: So much for the famous subtlety of dreams. He's all for smashing the lock on my floating lockbox and getting at whatever's inside, is Howard Findley. I realize I'll have to sleep curled up around it even though Howard Findley will goose me in the ass; otherwise he'll break into the thing before I can get it home and let it open by itself. Sorry to be so obvious.

Katherine decides it's okay. Your unconscious was only thirteen, and you were asleep.

Says Peter Well: But in *last* night's dream, there he was again, old Huckleberry Findley, age thirteen and forty at the same time—as Howard sort of was, in fact—and when I saw and smelled him, I understood a few truths that even Mark Twain wasn't telling. I don't know. Yes I do: stuff about hair lice and crab lice and circle-jerks and wino sodomy in empty boxcars. The fact is, I smelled Howard Findley's fate on him back then, and couldn't have said what I was smelling except that it was sad and squalid. Jail cells and drunk-vomit. Knife fights and phlegm and cracked black leather shoes. Baggy wool pants. Pecker tracks. You know? In the same way that I knew Huck Finn was realer than Tom Swift or Tarzan, I knew that even in my dream, Howard Findley was realer than Huck Finn. So in Nineteen Fifty-three I woke up and rowed home knowing that I didn't have to *reject,* as they say, Howard Findley and that Methodist minister and my family and Shoal Point and the Dorchester marshes. On the contrary. What I had to do was get myself out of there and write about them respectfully and truthfully from somewhere else, maybe Portugal, the way Mark Twain wrote about Hannibal from Hartford, Connecticut. Huck Finn lit out for the Territory, but Sam Clemens lit out for civilization. Peter Sagamore lit out for college as soon as he was able.

And that, children, says K.S.S., is how your father came to become a moderately celebrated writer of short and shorter fiction. We suspect he's left a couple of things out.

Responds Peter Leaving things out has been the name of the mothering game.

Whereas in last night's version of this dream, prompts Kate.

Last night I woke up from the Huck Finn dream of Nineteen Fifty-three and was relieved to find Howard Findley gone. In fact, he joined the U.S. Merchant Marine, I believe, and is possibly now a tattooed habitué of the greater world's waterfront bars, but just as likely he's a well-groomed and competent deck officer with high school–age children in Philadelphia. All I had to do was load my unrifled box back into my trusty skiff *Mark Twain,* row us all back home, and hide the box in the steamer trunk in my bedroom closet till it steamed open by itself. Sure enough: nothing inside but a rusty iron key.

Corrects Katherine Nope: a filigreed and jewel-bedizened key worth much more than its weight in gold because that's what it was made of: gold fetched from the New World to the Old by Christopher Columbus himself, like the gold in the custodial in Arfe's monstrance in the treasury of the Toledo cathedral. A key so precious that by comparison the box that held it was worthless.

Okay. But the box that held it is not the box it opens.

Of course not. The box it opens is the jewel-encrusted treasure chest given by Queen Arete to Nausicaa and Odysseus as a combination wedding and going-away present.

Which, says Peter Sagamore, when opened with that jewel-bedizened key worth many times its considerable weight in gold, will be revealed to contain the rusting iron key to the box of my Huck-Finn-on-the-Honga dreams, Parts One and Two.

Our children chorus You both have got it wrong. It is true that we lack experience of the world; on the other hand, we have an umbilical connection with transcendency, and it is our unanimous opinion that these keys together unlock the mystery of where a person comes from.

I swear, we proudly agree: Those kids of ours are chips off the old blocks.

ALL THIS WHILE WE'VE BEEN SAILING, SAILING,

through a sweet June early morning of warming air, clearing sky, and light and variable mainly westerly breezes, out of Madison Bay and the Little Choptank River, vaguely down past Taylors Island toward Hoopers, thinking maybe we'll touch base with P's mother at her nursing home, though she won't know who we are; say hello to Sue-Ann Sagamore Hooper and her husband, one of the originals; have a side-of-the-eye look at the old home place; take *Story* back to its Once Upon a Time, et cetera. But just about here, Peter having told with help from his friends the tale he'd have told Odysseus and Nausicaa in exchange for theirs, had they hung around to hear it, a fresher breeze moves in from the south. Ten knots and steady. Your choice, Skipper, says our happy woman, and our man says Let's get out of here, turns our transom respectfully on his home waters, and runs us for the next several hours north, out of there.

No more stories, he declares, about my youth. Let's have some music to run free by. Between Vivaldi and Telemann, the D.C. FM apprises us that at least fifteen and maybe three times that many black South Africans have been killed in a new outbreak of racial violence in Cape Town. No whites. Katherine groans And pretty soon they'll have the Bomb down there, and then Argentina and Pakistan will have it. God help us all. Peter Sagamore says nothing; but he reflects, to put it mildly, that the civilization that Huck Finn fled and that himself and Sam Clemens lit out for is what has him so by the throat—containing as it does not only domesticity and the bittersweet responsibilities of parenthood, but Doomsday and other Factors—that he is reduced to saying nothing.

A dignified elderly gentleman in a three-piece summer seersucker sails by, necktie and all, apparently singlehanding a big skipjack impeccably converted for cruising: the second sight in two days, that get-up, we've never seen before on our Chesapeake Bay. We wave; he waves. We pass the leaning Sharps Island Light, cross the mouth of the Great Choptank, wiggle our fingers in the direction of K's home waters, to which we're not returning either, yet. Behind Poplar Island—Welcome back to our story, Poplar Island, where we first made shipboard love!—we anchor for a light late lunch and swim before deciding where we'll go next. No nettles yet this far up, at least not on this tide, and so welcome is the silky water to our two skins, we resolve to stay above the slowly advancing nettle-line for the rest of this book or until Kate's labor day, whichever comes first.

Is this how Flaubert operated?

But look here, says Pete: We really must make a serious pit stop today. We're out of everything. By our constraints, says Kate, are we defined; but not *only* by our constraints. She makes a pacifying position-report to Nopoint Point—to young Andrew, as it happens—and then out of nearly nowhere observes to her husband that Tonio Kröger, in Thomas Mann's 1903 story of that title, is born in the uptight north, flees to the libertine south, and settles into artistic maturity in the middle latitudes. Munich, as Katherine remembers. Peter Sagamore did it the other way around—with different voltages on the compass points.

Yeah, well. Sort of.

Old Chip there says he's reading Mann's stories in the *Death in Venice* collection. Long-winded, Chip reports, but a groove.

For the second time in this book, Peter says Chekhov says What the aristocrats take for granted, we pay for with our youth. We ex-peasants, Chekhov means. What I like about your little brother is that he *doesn't* take his privileges for granted: All the great things wow him. I'll bet they did you, too.

Did and do. But K. S. Sherritt's delight in Life's Finer Things is like the pleasure of touring the family estate, whereas P. Sagamore's is the thrill of exploring country newly discovered, or newly won. Apropos of his question—Where does a person come from?—K is reminded by her chat with Chip that the newly fledged author Tonio Kröger, in Mann's story, returns incognito to his hometown, finds that the house he grew up in has been turned into a public library, locates one of his own books on the shelves in what used to be his bedroom, is questioned politely by the local police for suspicious behavior, and has no other validation of his identity (in those innocent pre-passport days) than some proof-sheets of his fiction. In more than the usual sense, in short, he has become an author. Our woman is being teleological: Her point is that a person may come from where he's going as well as go back to where he came from. As the sapling may be said to be the product as much of the oak tree it's programmed to become as of the acorn it used to be, bemused Kröger at that moment in his and Mann's story is the particular writer he is at least partly because of the wiser, mellower, greater writer that his life's experiences—including this revisit to his origins—destine him to become. Okay?

Marvels Peter My my my. Okay indeed.

His wife's not done (We're sailing, sailing, west now across the Bay from Poplar Island toward Rhode River, on the Maryland mainland, an attractive anchorage with nearby marinas to reprovision us. Our choice of this destination has been influenced, if not determined, by three factors: We don't want to go back yet to anywhere we've been already on this voyage; we hope to stay above sea-nettle territory so that we can swim; and we've done enough lazy downwind sailing for today and would rather beam-reach briskly now across the south-southwesterly. These add up to a course anywhere from west to northwest. Subtracting from the anchorages in that quarter—that eighth, really—those we deem insecure, aesthetically unappealing, inconvenient to supplies and obstetrical assistance if needed, or beyond the estimated radius of our remaining sailing time gives us Rhode River: specifically, the snug attractive lee of an uninhabited tiny island over there called Big Island because nearby there's one even tinier): It has occurred to her to imagine her husband in Tonio Kröger's position, changes changed. Moderately acclaimed spinner of ever-dwindling yarns and for better or worse the least political of storytellers, he sails back incognito to Hoopers Island, Hoopersville, Shoal Point, Sagamore Flats; he penetrates to the very bedroom where as a lad he read *Huckleberry Finn* and dreamed of drifting out on the tide and then back to his starting place—and he is detained for interrogation by the house's new owners.

Glum Peter thinks he sees her point: What proof-sheets could *he* show these days? Not even that "B♭." He would have only Katherine, Katherine, he declares to her: more than ever his best proof to himself of his existence and identity. We wish we had Ted and Dee's autopilot so that we could simultaneously make love and headway.

And one other thing, his stirred friend reminds him: *Story*'s new log, with its list of these tales we're telling. Did you add Huck Finn on the Honga, Part Two?

Peter did, and another after that, and though he can't know it just now, there'll be two more before Day 3 is done: that much-foreshadowed one about the culmination of Kath's troubled marriage to Porter "Poonie" Baldwin, Jr., and a less foreshadowed one called something like

THINGS WE NOT ONLY NEVER SAW BEFORE
IN OUR PEACEFUL CHESAPEAKE,
BUT HOPE NEVER TO SEE AGAIN EVER ANYWHERE.

This second gets told first, or would so get if not that between ourselves it wants no retelling, only a reminding of: a grim sort of "39." What's more, we're reluctant to apprise little Stars and Stripes so early of this aspect of the world they're about to enter. What's more yet, this one is a mixture not of fiction and truth, but of facts and lies. Finally, the thing has no more ending than Penelope's web, at least not yet that we know of, and on *our* boat an open-ended story is no story at all. But after Kate's conjuring of the CIA "safe house" that Pete's birthplace has become— her imagining his being interrogated by counterintelligence people in the very room in which he began his own interrogation of life and language and the world—it is enough now, as we sail innocently across the afternoon, for Peter to sigh to her The old DDF too, I suppose?

Kath nods: I know what you mean. Her tone is as sober as what those initials put us in mind of. Then she adds, surprisingly and cheerily, But the reader doesn't—as if it's understood between us that her favorite writer's next is going to be no narrative vanishing point, but something beyond that vanishing point: a regular story, a by-Godly *book,* maybe even a sizable one, of a sort very different from what he's been down to lately. He finds himself declaring with an edgy grin that he wishes we were home in Baltimore right now with our new babies, Rock and Hard Place, so that between diapers and feedings he could get to his writing table. Kath's eyes shine, but she firmly says Nope: We're going to stay on the narrative pill and sail and tell stories stories stories till you're ready to pop.

Repeats Pete Pop. We thrill; we sail to westward. Pop.

Well: Readers who haven't done time with us *don't* know what "DDF" has come to signify in our house; why it is that every time the Central Intelligence Agency floats through this narrative, we twinge separate but equal twinges. Unpolitical? Boyoboy, are we unpolitical: just your average, sappy, middle-class, high-minded liberals, Katherine and Peter, Pete especially: mildly patriotic but nowise chauvinistic, opposed to imperialist aggression all around. Get out of Southeast Asia; Hands Off South and Central America (Kate's fierce on this one). Equal opportunity, justice for all, save the environment, no nuclear first strikes, no nuclear second or third strikes either, beware the military-industrial complex, make our government obey the law like the rest of us—that sort of thing. Otherwise, political skeptics, if not quite agnostics. Why, Peter Sagamore doesn't even hate the National Security Agency, at least not in principle (Katherine Sherritt does); *he doesn't even despise the CIA* (Katherine Sherritt does), not in principle, how about that, though he believes both agencies to be somewhat crazy, ill-regulated, and therefore—because rich and powerful and sophisticated—dangerous. In principle, Peter Sagamore agrees (Kath doesn't) that because the U.S. government is not the only organization on earth somewhat crazy, ill-regulated, et cetera and dangerous, it is well for our leaders to have good information on our other-than-harmless adversaries, even in peacetime, when there's any real consensus on who those adversaries are. He's even willing to grant (not Kathy) that despite the overkill, ill regulation, self-serving, et cetera, our "intelligence community" actually provides our leaders from time to time with a certain amount of useful information and thus some justification for its expensive and otherwise unsavory existence. *Sic* Pete (not Kath).

What we're against, sentimental stock liberals that we are, is our government's collusion in—not to say its systematic, well-funded direction of—assassination, torture, clandestine warfare, the clandestine undermining of other people's elected governments, the clandestine harassment of and illegal general snooping upon our own citizens—things like that, you know, by anybody from our intelligence community down to our local cops. As also of course by other people's intelligence communities and cops, but they're outside our jurisdiction.

We also object, the sentimental pair of us, to the contamination of our beloved Chesapeake by e.g. industrial discharges and toxic wastes; by agricultural run-offs of fertilizer, pesticides, and silt; by acid rain, oil spills, and the decomposing bodies of CIA spooks who have met their end in circumstances so ambiguous that the only unworrisome explanation is the sad and mildly implausible one of suicide by reason of domestic personal unhappiness, whereas the *most* worrisome ones are about as worrisome as worrisome gets. We happen to have met, once, one of these last contaminants. The whole story would overflow this book like Goldsborough Creek its banks on a major spring tide and still not be finished, because people and institutions sit yet upon secret parts of it, and other parts were doubtless known but to the victim. Here's a short version of the long chapter involving us:

Whatever else we are, Katherine Sherritt and Peter Sagamore are principally the principal characters in a work of fiction entitled *The Tidewater Tales: A Novel*. But the Chesapeake Bay is real; so are all the federal government operations on and around it, such as that partial list in our prologue chapter-head beginning "Well, We Do, Despite" et cetera; so are all the active and retired military and civilian government employees, thousands upon thousands, who use these ever more contaminated waters for their recreation, as do we; so was the corpse our *Story* ran into several cruises back, on Sunday, 1 October 1978.

We were thirty-seven then, nine months married, three and a half pregnant for the first time in our coupled life. Andrew Sherritt, who was with us too, was then ten. Early fall's a golden season on our Bay: The maples and sumac dazzle the river shores, the geese honk in from Canada, the water's still warm (that's important to this story), and there's more breeze to sail by than there is in summer, though the air temp can be anything from tops-off to oiled-wool sweaters. We'd got a late start on a weekend cruise that we might even carry into Monday if the weather held: Back-to-school time had as usual preempted September's weekends. All three of us were up for sailing, and Chip had an enthusiastic plan that Katherine agreed was interesting enough and Peter had consented, with misgivings, to pursue, as he was pursuing some other things in those days.

On the previous Monday morning, September 25, a thirty-four-foot Columbia sloop named *Brillig* and registered in Wilmington, North Carolina, had been found aground between Point Lookout and Point Look-In, just above the mouth of the Potomac on the western shore of the Bay. Mainsail and #1 genoa were set and trimmed. When a search-and-rescue vessel from the Coast Guard station at St. Inigoes Creek on the St. Marys River, off the Potomac, came around Point Lookout to investigate, the crew found no one aboard. The Coast Guardsmen pulled the sloop off and towed it back to the St. Inigoes station, where it was found to belong to one John Arthur Paisley, fifty-five, of Bethesda, Maryland.

In the week that followed we learned from our morning newspaper, in addition to the above, that the missing Mr. Paisley was estranged from his wife of some twenty-five years, who lived with their two grown children across the Potomac in McLean, Virginia. That he was a former CIA officer who after thirty years with the Agency had upon his retirement in 1974 been deputy director of the Office of Strategic Research. That upon his retirement, which coincided approximately with his marital estrangement, he had been employed by the Washington office of a large accounting firm, Coopers & Lybrand, and maintained no connection with the Agency. That he had set out alone from *Brillig*'s mooring (above Solomons Island on the Patuxent, next river up from the Potomac) on the nearly airless mid-morning of Sunday, September 24; had chatted by radio with the owner of the mooring, a retired Air Force colonel named Norman Wilson (who subsequently returned *Brillig* to its mooring after officers of the Maryland State Police had routinely examined it at St. Inigoes), and with another friend sailing nearby: one Michael Yohn, of the Agency for International Development. That at about two in the afternoon this Mr. Yohn had radioed over to *Brillig,* still in sight, that for lack of a decent breeze he was packing it in to watch the afternoon football game on television: He thus became the last person known to have seen John Arthur Paisley alive. That Colonel Wilson, however, had had yet another radio chat with his friend later that afternoon—Some radio freaks, these guys, we remarked to each other—in the course of which Paisley reported that he was anchored off Hoopers Island Light, fifteen nautical miles across the Bay. He would be returning late that evening, he declared; Wilson wasn't to wait up. Next morning the sloop was found as aforedescribed, about twelve miles southwest of Hoopers Island Light and twice that far from Colonel Wilson's Patuxent River moorings.

Singlehanders, Katherine Sherritt observed over breakfast on the Tuesday, should always wear a safety harness on deck, even in a calm.

Said Peter Mm. After Kath left for work, he made a telephone call.

Nopoint Point on Goldsborough Creek is locally so called because there's no real point where the land humps into Sherritt Cove, just a shoal marked by a day beacon. You won't find the name on your chart of the Choptank and Tred Avon Rivers. You will, however, find a Point Nopoint on the *western* shore of the Bay, named for the same reason: It is the merest kink in the shoreline, not far above where *Brillig* went aground. Indeed, an old mnemonic rhyme for mariners sailing north from the Potomac was

> *Point Lookout and Point Look-In;*
> *Point Nopoint and point again—*

the last being Cedar Point at the mouth of the Patuxent. Chip Sherritt's float plan for our first fall cruise of the 1978 season was to sail from Nopoint Point to Point Nopoint, a round trip of maybe eighty nautical miles plus upwind tacks and detours to overnight anchorages.

Okay, said Kath by telephone from her library office, I'll be your straight man: What's the point of spending a whole weekend sailing from Nopoint Point to Point Nopoint and back to Nopoint Point? And Chip, who all that summer had been riding high on Lewis Carroll, replied You've got it. Plus we can look for that *Brillig* fellow.

Said his sister Don't be morbid. I'll talk to Peter.

The man whom Peter tried to telephone on that Tuesday—and again on the Wednesday, the Thursday, the Friday—was an elder friend of ours who, like the still-missing skipper of the sloop *Brillig,* lived in Bethesda and was not at home. P did not mention these uncompleted phone calls to his wife. It *is* the name of the game, K acknowledged, reporting Chip's proposal: Destinations are just excuses for sailing. Yes, well, allowed Peter, we haven't been down that way for a while. We might even slip over to Hoopersville and say hello.

We decided we'd see what was what, windwise, when the time came. So after work that Friday we hauled across the Bay Bridge and down Route 50 with a hundred thousand fellow Baltimoreans and Washingtonians headed for the ocean beaches. We checked in for the night at Nopoint Point, and on September's last morning made Hank and Irma wonder once again why the three of us would rather crowd into engineless little *Story* than luxuriate aboard *Katydid IV*—especially with Katydid Five (Chip's name for our then-baby-in-the-works) in the works. The forecast was fair, the breeze westerly and usable; once we'd beaten out of the Choptank in two or three extended tacks, it made the best recreational sense to spend the afternoon on a long beam-reach down and across the Bay to the Patuxent.

The least spoiled anchorages on that river are up past Solomons Island, in St. Leonards Creek. According to the Baltimore *Sun,* Colonel Wilson's mooring was "near Solomons Island"; according to the Wilmington, Delaware, *News-Journal,* to which the Sherritts subscribed, it was at Lusby, a little settlement on a cove off St. Leonards Creek. En route downBay, Chip Sherritt teased his sister by pretending to look for the missing Mr. Paisley; when she told him to for pity's sake knock it off before he gave K Five a conniption, he pretended *not* to keep an eye out for drowned bodies. But Lewis Carroll was often in his talk, and once he asked, apropos of nothing, why anybody except maybe a fisherman would drop anchor off Hoopers Island Light, exposed from all sides in the open Bay, as *Brillig*'s skipper had reportedly done. Now he voted we park for the night up by this Lusby place, which he had located on our chart of Patuxent River. Sort of check it out?

A singlehanded sailor, Peter Sagamore declared, in any waters less open than mid-ocean, does well to drop anchor if he needs to go below for more than two minutes. There's not enough sea-room out here for heaving to or sailing with nobody on watch.

I'll bet Paisley was a spy for the Borogoves, the boy said surprisingly, and the Slithy Toves got him.

Upset Katherine said That's enough of that, Chipperino. The military roar and clatter around Patuxent Naval Air Station made the two of us edgy, as always. She reminded her brother that the glamorization of espionage and counterespionage is not approved of on our boat. Like police work, she declared, national intelligence–servicing is ninety percent routine monitoring, cataloguing, and analysis, of a plodding, painstaking character; the other ten percent is more sordid than not. We deplore the mystique, the aura of names like Central Intelligence Agency, and we would have our young crew member learn to do likewise. The missing skipper of the sloop *Brillig* was one of hundreds—nay, thousands—of early-retired intelligence-service employees in the Washington area who take another job for a few years to augment their already comfortable pensions, amortize home mortgages and sailboat loans, make alimony payments, and build up their investment income for genuine retirement. He had no continuing connection with the CIA, we have been told by the CIA, where anyhow his job seems to have been of an administrative character. He was apparently between lives; he went sailing by himself, evidently not an unusual event; he parked for a while in the calm air off Hoopers Island Light at the afternoon's end, doubtless to make and eat his dinner; he radioed his friend not to worry; presently he weighed anchor and made sail for a lazy evening ride home, as we have many times done ourselves. Then he inadvisedly left the wheel and went forward sans safety harness or flotation vest to check or adjust something or have a look around behind the big genoa—Peter Sagamore confesses to having inadvisedly done the same himself more than once, while sailing alone—and against all odds he tripped or slipped and fell not only down but under the lifelines and overboard. Perhaps he struck his head along the way and drowned without ever knowing he was in the water; more likely he was less lucky and saw his boat glide away from him just a bit faster than he could swim. Unless *Brillig* had a permanently mounted boarding ladder on her transom, he might even have overtaken the boat—if it rounded up and luffed before bearing away again, as *Story* would do in that circumstance, in a series of retreating arcs like a deer checking its trail—and found to his dismay that there was nothing whatever on the hull for him to hold onto, and so good night. For that very reason, as Chip Sherritt doubtless had read, many singlehanders trail a light bouyed line astern, or at least tow a dinghy on a long painter when weather permits: one last chance. Accidental drowning is terrible in any circumstances, horrible in some. Let us not add to and cheapen its horror by melodramatic invocation of the magic letters *C-I-A*. Okay?

Said subdued Andrew Sherritt Okay. We anchored, as it happened, in the mouth of the fifth cove to starboard up St. Leonards Creek, the one that goes in toward the village of Lusby, because that's where we happened to be when anchoring time came; *not* to park there would have been a kind of negative attention to what we now wished to deemphasize. It is an ordinary, unremarkable little Chesapeake cove. By sundown, Pete had a headache: the red wine, we supposed, from dinner, on top of the afternoon's sea glare.

Next morning the westerly resumed: just right for reaching on down to Point Nopoint and then either running over to Hooper Strait and up the Honga to touch base with surviving Sagamores or, more likely, reaching back toward Nopoint Point and home. Our night's dreams had not been the best, but Chip Sherritt's mind, at least, seemed clear as the weather. He stood the first trick at the helm and amused himself, as was already at ten his wont, by doing time/speed/distance calculations in his head for every leg of our course, with corrections buoy by buoy and landmark by landmark, as if we were skirting a reef-girt coast instead of poking out of placid St. Leonards Creek. Now and then we grazed bottom with our centerboard because the helmsman was busier plotting our course than steering it, but no matter: Like his dad, Andy will grow up to be a first-class yacht navigator, among his other accomplishments. We were pleased to leave the sailing mainly to him; to stretch out on our "porch," as we call *Story*'s little foredeck, and enjoy being healthy, pregnant, thirty-seven-year-old Americans on a blue October Sunday morning, the sun warming us already through our jeans and sweaters as we ran wing and wing under the Solomons Island bridge and out of the Patuxent into the Bay.

Was there more helicopter and jet-trainer action than usual for a Sunday at PAX, the air station? Who knew? After so many years of Vietnam footage, the sight of even two military choppers in formation is enough to give us doves the heeb-jeebs. As we cleared Cedar Point and turned down the Bay, we could just make out low-lying Hoopers Island across the water, six miles eastward. Despite himself, Peter Sagamore began reflecting upon that Shoal Point story of his, which had wound up being called "Part of a Shorter Work" and had turned his literary career around a questionable corner. Because he happened to know that for many years the Central Intelligence Agency had operated a safe house on Solomons Island and another on Ferry Neck in the mouth of the Choptank, as well as their new one over there in Sagamore Flats, he was moved to the further reflection that our projected weekend cruise described a sort of Safe House Triangle: a reflection that made him feel no safer. Indeed, a CIA sailor (Peter knew of at least two such; no doubt there were hundreds) who sailed from Solomons to Hoopers Island might simply be going from office to office.

To himself he swore God damn it, the germ *is* contagious. Had he infected Chip, or Chip him? He was about to advise his kid-brother-in-law to ease the genoa a bit (its leeward telltale was stalling) when Katherine, sitting up to ward off a touch of morning sickness instead of lying down beside him, squeezed his right hand with her left and started out calmly to declare I see the biggest dead fish over yonder that I ever did see in thirty-seven tidewater years, but ended up saying Oh Jesus Peter look!

She was pointing off to starboard, shoreward, almost abeam. As Pete sat up, Chip saw the humpy white thing too and rounded *Story* up for a closer look. A beamy shoal-draft hull like ours does not shoot far into the wind, but the dead man was no more than three boatslengths off; Chip at the helm was so overwhelmed to realize what it was, instead of the former carp or drumfish he'd supposed it to be, that he simply let go the tiller and sheets. The sails luffed; we lost way quickly, but not quickly enough to avoid a soft collision. The corpse slid partway along our starboard waterline, then forward and away as *Story* stalled and gathered sternway. P got only a glimpse from his position, of a fat naked face-down dead white human body; he scrambled aft through flopping sheets and sails to take the helm. Andrew Sherritt saw further that his first dead person was a man neither young nor freshly deceased: Fish, crabs, warm water, and time had been at him. The boy went white-faced, dizzy; his gorge rose; he swallowed sourly and broke into a sweat. K's view was best of all, so to speak: The face-down rotting heavy bald white man was naked from the waist up, but wore blue jeans and, above the exposed elastic band of his jockey shorts, some kind of bulky belting that quietly bumped our bow and shuffled along our bootstripe before we drifted back. *Her* gorge, primed already by the morning sickness, rose past the swallowing point; she flattened herself belly-down under the swishing headsail and threw up blindly overside.

. That did for Andrew: He popped his head under the stern pulpit, over the transom, and followed suit. The only crew member in control of his breakfast, Peter gybed us around, summoned Katherine to come aft as soon as she was able, patted Chip's back, and eased *Story* corpseward. One doesn't just sail away. By when we luffed up just above it, Kath had got her stomach in hand as it were and returned to the cockpit to assist her ailing brother. In those days we had no radio: Peter instructed Chip to run our distress flag up to the mast spreader and help Katherine wave down the nearest motorboat or large sailboat while he kept the dead man in sight.

And that he did, with both the unaided and the aided eye. Unlike Andrew and for that matter Katherine, Peter Sagamore had seen drowned folks before, of various ages, sexes, and social classes and in various stages of disrepair, from both the general circumstance of his having grown up in an island community where boats far outnumbered cars and the particular circumstance of his having done rescue work with the Hoopers Island Volunteer Fire Company. He had helped drag river bottoms for and sometimes assisted in the vain effort to resuscitate drowned watermen, who seldom knew how to swim; drowned youngsters who swam out too far; drowned teenagers reckless with their beer and high-speed runabouts; drowned ladies and gentlemen fallen for one reason or another from passing yachts; pilots and their passengers dropped from the sky in malfunctioning private aircraft or military training jets; the odd merchant mariner inexplicably lost by night from a passing freighter; even an occasional casualty of plain old heavy-weather shipwreck. Now, in the twenty minutes or so until a large sedan cruiser called *Mama's Mink* noticed our commotion and chugged over to check it out (where were all those helicopters when we needed them?), he was able to observe through our 7 × 50s that the former person floating chest-down in the water near us was a middle-aged-looking bald white male, not fat but bloated from the gases of decomposition, worked over by the marine life of the Chesapeake—blue crabs especially, we suppose, whose size and appetite peak at summer's end. The fellow looked to have injured his head: Pete couldn't quite see, but there was some sort of ugliness behind the left ear. He wore only blue jeans and . . . a lead-weighted scuba-diving belt? Nope: *two* lead-weighted scuba-diving belts, which must surely have kept him on the Bay bottom until the bloating brought him up. In water still in the low to mid sixties, that would take . . . about a week?

Mama's Mink now saw what we were pointing at. Much high-spirited reaction from Mama and daughters, presumably, on the cruiser's foredeck, but the white-uniformed professional captain agreed to call the USCG and (against the red-faced owners' inclination, it seemed) to stand by at least until another radio-equipped and engine-powered vessel relieved him. It was clearly much easier for him than for us to maintain position; indeed, without wind in our sails and steerageway, we had no maneuverability at all and had to let *Story* drift well clear of *Mama's Mink*. Normally unsqueamish Katherine was not well; it was Chip now who patted *her* back. Nevertheless we felt obliged to stand nearby until *MM*'s captain notified us by hailer that the Coast Guard was on its way. Others, too, evidently monitored the transmission: We saw a sportfisherman and a motorsailer under power change course usward. Then there was a helicopter overhead, not Coast Guard white and orange but unmarked olive drab, the wash of its rotors bad news for us sailboats. Seeing no good reasons to hang around and several to go (here came two or three more pleasure boats; the VHF channels must have been buzzing), we put the helm over, let the sails fill, and headed north for home.

Chip was still pale; Katherine nauseated. Peter for his part was furious, and something more. For reasons shortly to be set forth, the old question resurfaced, in his mind just then more than in hers: Why bring a child into this world? Our crew of course gets around to wondering Was that that *Brillig* fellow there? Mister John Arthur Paisley? Maybe so, maybe not: some luckless boater, anyhow. Were those weighted belts Kath thought she saw around his waist? Well, yes. Diving accident, maybe? Nope, says Chip: no wet suit. Nobody dives in blue jeans. Yes, well.

Well?

Look here, reader: What finally appalls us, prospective-parentwise, is not that the world contains death and even disasters natural and manmade: holocaust, earthquake, plague, famine, fire, flood, war, the destruction of our natural environment. On the somewhat less than total scale, the world has ended many times: Where are Maryland's Indians these days, Europe's Jews, the citizens of Pompeii, Masada, Lidice, Gomorrah? When we look about us at beflowered Baltimore, thoroughbred Worthington Valley, the manicured waterfronts of Talbot County, we do not forget that we are chickens on the python's back. If our particular reptile happens to have slumbered since the Civil War, in his sleep growing fescue and flowers on his scales, perhaps that's because he's still digesting the East Coast Indians, long since swallowed whole. He will rouse and strike again, by and by. What finally appalls us (P in particular) is not that even good governments have secret forces, more or less laws unto themselves, who harass, sabotage, torture, and kill—in short, "make policy"—no matter what the law, the Congress, the president, and sometimes even their own directors and department chiefs authorize or prohibit. That is your civilized world as it has no doubt virtually always been, only higher-tech these days and more expensive. Our beautiful wisterias and rhododendrons are fertilized with blood, our hybrid tea roses mulched with crime; we do not approve of, but have made uneasy peace with that circumstance. We *don't* like the heat and therefore *do* stay out of the kitchen: grit our teeth; try both to protect Chip Sherritt (say) from these ugly realities and to strengthen him in them, as we shall our own offspring when the time comes. We accept all that, more or less. Though it is heart-heavying enough merely to fly in over our Chesapeake after heavy rain and see its failing tributaries brown and red and yellow with ruin, we can even still hope, swallowing hard, that our kids-in-the-works will have something left to enjoy down there, if . . .

But then our US Air flight (say) banks over the Potomac on its glide path into Baltimore–Washington International, and Peter sees not only those natural neighbors, Arlington National Cemetery and the Pentagon, and the grim H-shaped headquarters of the CIA over yonder in Langley, but (because he happens to know it's there even though its existence is as of the time of this novel still officially unacknowledged) the astonishing National Security Agency complex down there at Fort Meade, and one or two other things. Whereupon raises its ugly head the biggest python of them all, so different in degree from those familiar sleeping ones as to amount to a difference in species and make us think ourselves insane to be deliberately pregnant. We mean

THE DOOMSDAY FACTOR.

Though our CIA had officially denied that Mr. J. A. Paisley was anything more than a retired intelligence analyst with no current role in the Agency, Peter Sagamore had private reason to know otherwise; to associate Mr. Paisley and *Brillig* with

THE DOOMSDAY FACTOR,

which, whether or not the chap *Story* just bumped into was J.A.P., keeps floating to the surface of our life like deadly fact to the surface of our fiction or rotting corpses to the surface of our Bay.

THE DOOMSDAY FACTOR,
OR,
AT LAST: A FINAL REASON FOR PETER SAGAMORE'S LATE INCREASING
SILENCE

Our Bay.

When the Chilean generals arrest and kill three or was it ten thousand noncombatant civilians, the Argentine generals six or was it thirty thousand, the Khmer Rouge two or was it three million, the Nazis about ten million, the Soviet Stalinists twenty million; when unacknowledged official murder grows so enormous that one has to add "give or take a few million" to some particular estimate, why bother our heads about one middle-aged American dead body more or less? One American infant-in-the-works more or less? Oh, because not only is no man an island, but that was *our kid* inside that Kathy there; our *Story* here. This land is our land et cetera, and thus that CIA is our CIA, and what we bumped into that blue October Sunday morning was our dead body, though it was identified in next week's papers as J. A. Paisley's. That mark Peter Sagamore thought he'd seen behind its left ear was a nine-millimeter bullet hole; those weights, sure enough, were 38 or 39 or 40 pounds of scuba weights, depending on which account we read in which newspaper. Those blue jeans and jockey undershorts would turn out to be a bit of a problem for investigative reporters following up the story: Size 30 waist, they were, and the corpse itself weighed in at 144 pounds once the belts were off, whereas Paisley alive weighed 170 and wore size 34 to 36. Well, corpses lose weight, the Maryland State medical examiner would explain, especially perforated corpses: Intracranial and other body fluids run out. Even waterlogged corpses? And their clothes lose weight too, do they? Even the printed size-markings lose half a foot of waistline? Her own girth growing, Kath would say wistfully Some dandy diet, death.

Those are but two of several mysteries and discrepancies that the reporters would turn up in the months to come. The CIA, true to its nature, routinely lied as long as it could, even to the Senate Select Committe on Intelligence, to whom it is supposed to tell the truth. That is its second principal business, lying, and its problem. Having at first denied that Paisley had ever been a CIA man and then reluctantly acknowledged that he'd been a very high-ranking one indeed, the Agency continued to deny that he was still on the payroll at the time of his disappearance, until reporters reported that an attaché case full of CIA documents had been found aboard *Brillig* by CIA investigators who inspected the boat along with the Coast Guard, the Maryland State Police, and Mrs. Maryann Paisley—to whom we here apologize for dredging up this sore material, but goddamn it we were minding our own business out there when etc. The Agency denied that report, along with the report that the documents were marked *secret*, but now acknowledged that Mr. Paisley at the time of his death was in fact a $200-a-day consultant for the Military Economic Advisory Panel, established to assess for the CIA the Agency's own assessments of Soviet military expenditures and related matters. By the Wednesday after our Sunday bump, angry senators had obliged the Agency to admit that there were indeed Agency documents aboard *Brillig,* which were not classified top-secret only because they were draft reports by Paisley himself which had not yet been delivered to the Agency for classification. But they still denied taking an active role in the investigation of Paisley's death, and that his death had anything to do with his familiarity with our new spy-satellite system, the Keyhole 11 "Big Bird," which he had helped conceive to monitor Soviet compliance with the SALT I arms-control agreements, and which the KGB had managed to obtain secret information about from a young CIA double agent arrested earlier in the year.

By that same Wednesday, October 4, Mr. Paisley's fellow yachtsman, Michael Yohn, of the Agency for International Development, the last person known to have seen the chap alive, was reported to have left the country hurriedly for an extended visit, it was not known to where. Colonel Wilson, too, of the Lusby mooring, left soon after for Perth, Australia, for an indefinite time. It was reported that Mr. Paisley was despondent over the marital separation; also that he was in financial straits. But it was also reported that he was *not* in financial straits, and that so far from being despondent, he had a new lover, former friend of his wife's, whom he sometimes took sailing and to whom he'd loaned his car just prior to telephoning Maryann Paisley, on the Saturday before his last sail, for a cheerful chat. He remarked that he planned to go sailing tomorrow and invited Maryann to meet him for dinner should the weather keep him ashore.

"People whose business, position, or character involves secrets they will lie and lie and lie to protect," a certain friend of ours in Bethesda used to say, "are not especially to be believed on any particular point, even when they swear that *this* is the truth, whereas what they'd said before was a lie. It is well to have as little as possible to do with such people." Any nation's "intelligence community" is rich in such secrets: the hidden truths which its expensive business is to discover but only selectively to reveal. Its members therefore routinely lie as necessary to the public, to their colleagues and families (who, to be sure, learn not to ask questions), even—less routinely—to their superiors, as well as to their rivals and their enemies and ultimately to themselves. Peter Sagamore, at the time of this earlier cruise, had been lying in similar fashion for some while, mostly passively, like Agency officers, by withholding what he knew; in some instances, more seriously, by withholding *that* he knew. We hate this part of our story. On with it.

More exactly, by withholding from Katherine Sherritt what or that he had been told: He *knew* nothing, inasmuch as he had been told what he had been told over the several years past by the Agency officer whom he'd tried to telephone when we first read of *Brillig*'s discovery below Point Nopoint, and again after *Story* collided with that yacht's unfortunate skipper. On the Friday, October 6, he got through to him: our Bethesda friend quoted above.

Townshend here.

Peter Sagamore, Doug.

Peter. I expected you might call.

I've been calling.

I've been away, said Douglas Townshend. What have you and Katherine been up to.

Sailing and making babies. Peter breathed. We were out on the Bay last Sunday, Doug, just below Solomons Island.

Really.

Bit of a stir out there.

You saw it, did you.

Lunch tomorrow? I'll pick you up.

Doug Townshend paused. Let me drive up there Sunday evening after dinner. I've seen neither Katherine nor Baltimore in too long.

Make it for dinner, Doug. We'll go for a drive after.

Well. Dinner it is.

"Our telephones must be assumed to be tapped, our lodgings wired. Do not ever talk business with us on the telephone, or in our quarters or our automobiles. Always let *me* decide where and when to speak of business matters. Remember that I myself may be misinformed or disinformed, or I may be lying to you for one reason or another. Our kind may tell you six true things, as subsequently verified, in order to set you up for believing a seventh thing, which may be false. I speak of course of ordinary business circumstances, not of our special situation, in which I have no motive for anything less than total candor."

None that I know of, had said Peter when Doug Townshend first spoke words like those to him in 1974; and Douglas had replied, Townshend-fashion, inflecting his questions as declarative statements, Just so; then what will you believe. Countered Peter I didn't sign on to believe, only to listen.

That had been the correct response. Douglas Townshend in 1974 was a pink and portly sixty-year-old who looked like an aristocratic Eisenhower and was just becoming our CIA friend. In those days, his royalty income having dropped with his production, Peter sometimes conducted writing classes in the university's evening college for extra cash. In addition to the pleasant but usually unhelpable permanent amateurs—middle-aged housewives and schoolteachers, retired civil service clerks and lieutenant colonels, all hoping to hit the jackpot with novels about spies or flying saucers or their own lives—such classes attracted an occasional ringer, of interest whatever the degree of his or her talent. One such was an ex-warden of the Maryland State Penitentiary, whose novel was a plea for leniency for most first offenders, even murderers other than assassins and hired gun-

men, but Islamic punishment for all second commissions of the same offense: cutting off the hands of two-time thieves, surgically emasculating
two-time rapists, brutally beating two-time assaulters, et cetera; the novel
lacked form, language, character, invention, and plot, but not a certain
vision and rough justice in the theme. Another was a retired rear admiral
whose previous bibliography consisted of the Navy's sight-reduction tables
for navigation stars; a former combat officer, he contrived under Peter's
tutelage not only to write his war novel but actually to publish it, once P
had persuaded him to scrap the common sailor's point of view, of which
the admiral knew nothing, and concentrate on maneuvering those big boats
and bureaucracies from the bridge-deck level, about which he knew much.
A third was Douglas Townshend.

Witty, soft-spoken but firm-principled, urbane and thoroughbred like a
gentler, unathletic Henry Sherritt, in his beautiful three-piece pinstripes
and dark silk neckties Douglas looked to Peter Sagamore like a misplaced
Princeton trustee. His fiction, like its author more polished than anything
else in the room, nevertheless did not quite have it: light comedies of
manners among the old Maryland family aristocracy, under threat from
arrivistes like the Vanderbilts; blustering eccentric gentlemen, daft or scrappy
elder ladies, well-mannered but troublemaking youngsters; no sex; no violence beyond the odd wrecked roadster or spoiled lawn party—it was
P. G. Wodehouse country-place humor displaced to Greenspring Valley
and attenuated in transit. The author himself was diffident; one got the
idea early on that his literary interest was in proving to himself that he
could *not* after all write fiction, rather than that he could. He admired
exquisitely the certain quasi-fanaticism or roughness of spirit he saw in
great writers, not only in the Lawrences and Hemingways (and the Peter
Sagamores, he insisted) but in the Henry Jameses and Marcel Prousts as
well. It was absent from himself.

After a few months, Doug Townshend quietly dropped the course, but
not its instructor. A Maryland aristocrat of sorts himself, whose grandfather
had been a Princeton trustee, Douglas Townshend had studied literature
before following the family path through law school into government service. In all but quite contemporary letters, the breadth of his reading was
superior to Peter's. Doug knew very well and much admired P's own early
fiction, up to the turning point represented by "Part of a Shorter Work";
and while he could not warm up to the subsequent increasing minimalism,
he could appreciate and discuss it more sympathetically than many professional critics. Moreover, he knew the Sherritt family well at second hand
and slightly at first, from sundry horse-shows back in Katherine's riding
days and similar casual path-crossings.

He therefore had us to dinner in honor of his withdrawal, over Peter's
polite protests, from the field of literary creation, and the evening was a
success. Doug Townshend's house was a Federal-period Georgetown gem
which by reason of his late divorce (first we'd heard of it) he was exchanging
for a no-maintenance condominium in Bethesda. His companion for the

evening was the widow of a noted diplomat and a functionary of the Kennedy Center; though bejeweled to the nines, she had an Alice Roosevelt Longworth caustic wit and was friendly besides. There were two other couples: a once-celebrated hardboiled-detective novelist, now old and stoical about his fallen fame, and his wife, a plain country lady with nothing to say; and an attractive young assistant professor of American literature—a Baltimore girl now teaching on the Eastern Shore and living in Annapolis with her rather older husband, a husky, gray-bearded, athletic-looking colleague of Douglas's.

Colleague at what?

Assorted as we were, Doug had seen to it we would discover connections among ourselves as the evening proceeded. The diplomat's widow had attended The Deniston School with Irma Shorter; had once even dated Henry Sherritt! The erstwhile-famous hardboiled-detective novelist claimed to Peter that it was himself, not Gaudier-Brzeska or Walter Gropius, who first said Less is more. What's more, he cautioned, Least may be most: but Nothing is nothing. The assistant professor had begun her doctoral work in College Park just as Kath was finishing her master's in library science there; she and her new husband, moreover—second marriage for him as ours would be for Kate—shared our love for sailing the Chesapeake. Even the plain country lady turned out to be a refugee from the Maryland marshes, whom the once-celebrated hardboiled-detective novelist—an old alumnus of Washington College in Chestertown, it developed, where young Professor Leah Talbott now taught—had met in their Depression youth when he was briefly a high school principal over there. She remembered Capn Fritz Sagamore, all right, and was moved to ask Katherine whether, when she cooked muskrat for *her* family, she served the beast with the head on or off. Peter can't look at them, Kath declared; me, I crack their little skulls with a nutcracker and spoon out their brains: delicious. Said the lady Me too, honey, and patted K's hand.

Colleagues at what? Peter asked politely of Franklin Talbott, the professor–young lady's rather older husband, who not only knew and liked Peter's pre–Less-Is-More fiction but wanted to talk about it, whereas Peter wanted to talk about sailing. He had in fact no idea what Doug Townshend did for a living; had inferred from some remark or other that he was "with the government," a safe enough inference in that neighborhood. They're spies, rasped the Alice Roosevelt Longworth lady before Frank Talbott could reply. The nice kind, she added: all cloak and no dagger. Kate Sherritt believes she remembers Lee Talbott's missing a beat here in their conversation and Douglas Townshend's not missing a beat in his. Her own blood went momentarily cold: HOSCA, the Chilean coup, her disappeared ex-lover. Franklin Talbott frowned perceptibly enough to let the A.R.L. woman know that he did not find her brashness charming in this instance and then said pleasantly to Peter No cloak either, I'm afraid. Doug's an analyst; I'm an editor. We're supposed to make the difference between Information, which there's always too much of, and Intelligence, which there's never enough of. Said the Alice Roosevelt Longworth lady Less is more. Unless it suits their purposes, our leaders ignore what the CIA tells them anyhow.

I can never remember, Frank Talbott said smoothly, whether it was Mies van der Rohe or Giacometti who said Less is more. Declared his wife It was Edgar Poe's raven after hearing one stanza of that dippy poem.

The ex-famous hardboiled-detective novelist drank off his wine. His wife smiled broadly and patted Katherine's hand again. Leah Allan Silver Talbott, Douglas Townshend told us, is a putative descendant of Mister Poe. An imputation she denies, said Ms. Talbott, but enjoys. And Franklin Key Talbott, Doug went on, is directly and inarguably descended from the author of our national anthem. Said the Alice Roosevelt Longworth lady Long may it waver.

Thus was the subject changed. But we remarked the little voltage introduced into the room by those charged initials. Indignant Katherine restrained her urge to make a speech against the Agency's role in destroying Chilean democracy. To Townshend and Talbott together, friendly Peter said Maybe you gentlemen can tell me whether the outfit that bought my parents' place on Hoopers Island really is the CIA; we're convinced it is. Doug Townshend replied easily We're not in the real estate department and asked his colleague whether he knew Peter's story "Part of a Shorter Work," involving an Agency safe house on Hoopers Island and the narrator's approach thereto. To our surprise, both Talbotts did; what's more, though their own boat was a thirty-three-foot blue-water cutter, they knew and admired the Sagamore 25. The ex–hardboiled-detective novelist knew neither the boat nor the story nor the distinguished quarterly it had been published in. American fiction had long since gotten too fancy for his taste, he allowed; he wondered whether that had to do with the fact that our writers all drank table wine nowadays, like damn Frenchies. Wine wine wine, even for cocktails. Could we imagine Dashiell Hammett ordering a chablis spritzer? Douglas Townshend refilled the man's glass; the plain country lady put her hand over hers.

Later that year, Doug told Peter in Peter's old BMW Some genuine writer needs to know what's going on, not just the pop novelists and the exposeurs. My stories, Peter warned him, will never even be topical, much less political. And I've become a taker-outer instead of a putter-inner. Less *is* more, more and more. They had been driving around the Baltimore Beltway for ninety minutes; now they were parked in front of our Stony Run apartment. Said Doug It will show up somewhere. Don't count on it, Douglas; you've picked the wrong priest to confess to. Doug Townshend smiled: If I had Herman Melville or Mark Twain for a friend. But I've got Jim Michener, Jim Cain, Herm Wouk, and you. Fine writers every one— but I'll take you.

His enrolling in Peter's evening-college class turned out to have been a cover for meeting and sounding out its teacher, though his love of literature and his mild interest in writing were real enough. He kept abreast even of the literary quarterlies—more so than Peter himself. Thus he had tisked his tongue twice, so to speak, over "Part of a Shorter Work" and its terse successors: once at the radical minimalism, an aesthetic value he questioned in Peter's case; once at the coincidence of the CIA material. For a special reason, he had been curious to meet the author and to learn what the author *knew;* in particular he wanted to find out whether there was any connection between the United States Central Intelligence Agency and the writer's turn toward taciturnity.

P could scarcely believe the man was serious. Did Doug really mean intimidation, KGB-style? He'd been writing long; he wanted to try short— or short wanted to try him. Who knows why we do what we do? The connection question had come up two or three social evenings later, by when we and Douglas Townshend were by way of becoming friends. When he had satisfied himself that no connection existed, that we were aware of, between his longtime employer and Peter Sagamore's recent literary corner-turn; that the Sagamore-Sherritt household knew nothing about the CIA beyond what any attentive reader of *The Washington Post, The New York Times,* and *The New Republic* could infer, and cared only as any stock-liberal Americans busy with their nonpolitical lives and careers might care—when, in short, he had come to know his man and his man's woman— Douglas Townshend put into operation an odd idea he'd been entertaining for a quarter of a century.

Male Townshends go to the Gilman School in Baltimore; thence to Princeton University; thence to law school, preferably Virginia; thence back to Baltimore or Washington, to divide their careers between legal practice and government service. The family is as old as white America. Townshends are always well-enough to do, but seldom really rich and never ostentatious. They take moderately high place for granted, but shun highest place as too conspicuous. Townshends are conservative, but high-principled and so profoundly fair-minded—a sort of intellectual Henry Sherritt, Katherine came to say of Doug—that not infrequently they find themselves siding with the radical position on matters of civil rights and social justice. A Townshend despises jingoism, flagwaving, and bullying of any sort but is so deeply patriotic that he characteristically makes trouble not only for his department, to which he is finally less loyal than to the government as a whole, but also for the government as a whole, to which he is finally less loyal than to his ideal of it derived from knowledgeable allegiance to the Constitution, especially its Bill of Rights. In government work, this is the very recipe for trouble. Townshends believe in an aristocracy of neither blood nor wealth nor talent—though they would err on the side of talent— but of character, which they suspect some families and some schools may help transmit. What noblesse oblige obliges a Townshend to is nobility of thought and action, whatever the consequences. Oh, the very recipe for trouble.

Douglas Townshend took his baccalaureate in English literature at Princeton in 1942 and, through family and university connections, got himself assigned to "Wild Bill" Donovan's wartime Office of Strategic Services, first as an intelligence analyst under the supervision of Herbert Marcuse and young Arthur Schlesinger, Jr., later as a behind-the-lines liaison agent among resistance troops in occupied France, finally as a counterintelligence officer in the OSS's X-2 division in the Balkans, where the Other Side was already the Communists rather than the Nazis. After the war he dutifully took his law degree, but fresh upon receipt of it he rejoined his comrades in Allen Dulles's new CIA. Under the "open cover" of being once again a mid-level information analyst, he grew more and more involved in liaison work between the covert gatherers of information and its overt interpreters; thence he moved into a darker liaison between counterintelligence and covert operations, or Clandestine Services. He found himself at odds with certain of his colleagues and superiors, while being defended, protected, and promoted by others. When his adversaries were in the ascendancy, he would be eased from Covert to Overt; when the weather changed, he would—while still overtly Overt and on the outs— be covertly welcomed back.

His problem (Doug told us early on, in our apartment) was that while helping the Agency learn what it wanted to know about the nation's presumable or potential adversaries, he had learned one appalling thing after another about the Agency itself, and therefore about the nation. Even in wartime, Douglas Townshend had had reservations about the OSS's paramilitary adventures, as opposed to its intelligence-gathering escapades. But war is war; he had set his reservations aside. Quite another matter, in Doug's opinion, to conduct such operations in peacetime. The NKVD and later the KGB, his colleagues naturally pointed out, were doing the same thing, all over the world: Whole secret shooting-wars were mounted, like Frank Wisner's Ukrainian and Baltic campaigns against the Russians during Harry Truman's second term.

If we're going to fight a war, Douglas Townshend believed, Congress ought to declare one. His closest colleague, Frederick Talbott (older brother of the chap we'd met at Doug's, who had preceded his younger sibling into the Agency and risen like a rocket in Clandestine Services), would reply There'll never be another declared war, Doug, except among small-timers.

If we're against the CP in Turkey and Greece and France and Italy, Douglas Townshend truly believed, we should help their opponents openly. Even the French government doesn't know everything we're doing in France! Frederick Talbott would reply with a smile that to do those things openly would be to meddle in the domestic affairs of a sovereign state: unAmerican and inefficient.

If we're going to shelter hundreds of Nazi war criminals in the United States, Douglas Townshend truly believed, our president should tell us so and explain why and take the consequences. Our president doesn't know half of what we're up to, Frederick Mansfield Talbott would reply, and he wished he didn't know half the half he knows. Plausible deniability, et cet. Presidents come and go; the Company gets it work done.

If we're going to deceive and therefore corrupt our official friends both foreign and domestic, Douglas Townshend truly believed, and secretly harass, subvert, and even arrange the killing of unofficial enemies foreign and domestic, and traffic with the vilest people we perceive to be possibly useful, and lie as necessary to the people whose interests we're supposed to be defending, what on earth *are* we defending, and why? How are we better than the other side? Who says we're better than the other side? Rick Talbott would ask. What we mainly are is on the other side from the other side. In my opinion, Doug, you lack the Tragic View. In *my* opinion, Rick, you lack any moral view whatever. Spoken like a scoutmaster, Douglas, which you aren't. Spoken like the Prince of Darkness, Rick, which *you* aren't.

Though that is what we called him, Douglas Townshend told Peter Sagamore, zipping around and around the Beltway, and still do, and they soon got to calling me Mister Clean, though my hands were soiled enough.

Now, it goes without saying, reader, that Frederick Talbott and Douglas Townshend never said exactly those things to each other in exactly that way. Professionals don't talk like that. Nevertheless, those things got said. Same goes for these exchanges between Douglas Townshend and Peter Sagamore. What Doug wanted Pete to understand was that though his in-house criticism of the Agency's skullduggery had been at first unrelenting, and though there were lines he was not invited to cross because it was understood he would not cross them, no knowledgeable colleague doubted him to be the most trustworthy of critics. On more occasions than he enjoyed remembering, he had participated in operations he disapproved of, in order to remain as much as possible *in the know*. To this end, once he had made clear his general position he came to leave off asserting it, lest he cut himself off from learning as much as he could of what we were doing, and how and why we were doing it.

The Faust of the CIA? Peter Sagamore wondered. That's my first question, Doug: your motive. My second—

Said Douglas It's obvious what your second is; don't ask it yet. As to your first: This Rick Talbott fellow is your Faust of the CIA. His middle name's Mansfield, but if I were a novelist I'd make it Manfred, after Lord Byron's Prince of Darkness. Quite a different chap from his brother Frank! Douglas Townshend's interest in knowing the worst we're up to, he declared, was never knowledge for its own sake, much less (like Frederick Mansfield Talbott's) the secret making of history for *its* own sake. It was— at first simply and then less simply—to do what he could to temper or stop what he judged to be a betrayal of what he valued about his country. When he found, early, that his in-house criticisms were acted upon only when they addressed the relative effectiveness of particular agents and techniques, not the general morality of means and ends, he kept his own counsel and did his share of the devil's work with the intention of writing a thoroughgoing exposé of what we had become by deluding ourselves that fire must be fought with fire. As the first such exposés began to appear, however, he had realized that their publication virtually ends the author's critical effectiveness. Franklin Key Talbott, Doug happened to know, was at work upon such a book, as were others. Once the author resigned from the Agency to complete it, he would have nothing more to expose except what little he might learn at second hand from his former colleagues. Moreover, while such exposés are necessary and valuable to a democracy, their effectiveness, too, is limited. Aroused public opinion might temporarily encourage and enable a congressional watchdog committee; might even lead a president to appoint a strong and scrupulous Agency director. But the likes of Frederick Mansfield Talbott would be constrained thereby merely to work that much more carefully and covertly, not to terminate their work.

Doug Townshend had therefore come to and acted upon a different resolve, not an easy one for a person of his fastidious character. The Agency had crews of "mole hunters," whose job it was to uncover and neutralize double agents among its officers. He himself had had a hand in such investigations, where the leaks were plausibly damaging the nation's security. In fact, however, the most deeply penetrative mole he knew of was himself.

At this stage of their acquaintance, Peter Sagamore did not know Douglas Townshend well and had not yet had his Obvious Second Question answered. He felt his skin thrill unpleasantly at the above declaration, made perhaps in their second private conversation. Not a mole for the KGB, Doug assured him. They're a nastier outfit than us, from a nastier government. Believe it or not, I became a mole for the USA. And not even in the elevated cause of general morality, mind; simply in the cause of legality. Plus one other cause.

In this self-appointed capacity, he gave Peter uncomfortably to know, he had become in recent years the chief anonymous source of inside information on the Agency's illegalities and excesses: the "Deep Throat" of the CIA, he would call himself after Watergate. Under exquisitely careful cover, he had provided to certain members of the Senate Select Committee on Intelligence, to certain newspaper reporters, and to certain Agency ex-officers writing responsible exposés of their former employer, all the information on such illegalities and excesses that he could reveal without revealing himself and getting his colleagues killed. His disclosures had been to some good effect, he judged, though less so than he had hoped; he expected them to be more effective in the current, no doubt temporary public reaction against the Agency in the wake of our Vietnam war. He hoped to be of particular assistance to Senator Frank Church's investigative committee and to Franklin Key Talbott's book *KUBARK* (the Agency's cryptonym for itself), though neither man would ever know for certain his informant's identity.

At this point Peter Sagamore had said Look here, Doug: It's time we got to my Obvious Second Question. Also to your One Other Cause of a while back.

Agreed Douglas Townshend with a gentle pink sigh It is. The One Other Cause for which I am a mole—rather, *against* which I am a mole—is

THE DOOMSDAY FACTOR.

He meant the word *factor* (Doug explained as the pair lapped the Washington Beltway this time) in the older English sense: a trading agent. Just as Moose Factory, Ontario, is not an establishment for the making or processing of moose, but a place where Indians in the James Bay moose country formerly traded furs for goods of British manufacture; and just as the sot-weed factor in colonial Maryland was not an element in a situation, but a wholesale buyer of cured tobacco in similar exchange; so the rogue or double agent whom prudent citizens must most fear is your dealer in potential apocalypses: your Doomsday Factor.

Rogue agent, Peter more or less inquired. I hate spy talk.

No more than I. A rogue agent is not quite the same as a double or a triple. A double agent is either a spy for some other agency who has penetrated your own, or a spy of your own who has penetrated another agency, or a spy of your own who has been penetrated by another agency. A triple is an agent of your own who pretends to be doubling for someone else while pretending to work for you, while actually working for you. Either of these becomes a Doomsday Factor if and when he traffics in thermonuclear-weapons information or material in such a way as to make the use of such weapons more rather than less likely, in whatever circumstances or cause. Do you follow me.

Far from eagerly.

Not all Doomsday Factors are intelligence people. Not all doubles, triples, and rogues are Doomsday Factors. The Venn diagram, however, shows a small but awfully dangerous overlap.

Rogue agents, Doug.

Rogue agents are agents or ex-agents out of Agency control in a way different from doubles. There are at least three kinds of rogue agents, I'm sorry to report. By far the most numerous is your ex-officer who uses his Agency skills and connections to go into nefarious business for himself. This sort runs from the lowest level, like Nixon's hired burglars, up through mercenary terrorists and trainers of terrorists, to multimillionaire dealers in illegal narcotics and weapons, to Doomsday Factors, who for a sum of money will put whole populations at risk. All but the last of these have reached near-epidemic numbers.

Let Doug explain as he and Peter circle the nation's capital, counterclockwise: When, out of concern for its security, a household buys a pistol, it may in fact increase its security to some degree. It also increases, to a much larger degree, the likelihood that someone in the household will be pistol-shot, whether because an armed intruder meets fire with fire, or because an out-of-hand family quarrel now has an escalated last resort, or merely because an accident happens that couldn't have happened before the pistol joined the household. This was George Washington's objection to large standing armies, Dwight Eisenhower's to the military-industrial complex, and, so Katherine tells me, the Sherritt-Sagamores' to firearms in your house. Of those objections, only yours has so far been heeded.

Go on.

In the same way, when you conscript a great many ghetto black men and train them to be able killers of Vietnamese and then return them from the dope-soaked natural jungle to the dope-soaked asphalt one, you have provided the means, the motive, and the opportunity for a good deal more urban violence than you had before. And when you hire lots and lots and *lots* of clandestine-service and counterintelligence people in the manifold divisions of your national intelligence community—particularly when you do so in a low-ideology, high-profit-minded republic like the USA—and you give them skills and information and accesses worth a great many dollars to someone who knows how to take advantage of greed, grudges, boredom, jealousy, rivalry, lust, fear, and other human failings, you have got a loaded pistol in your nightstand drawer indeed.

Said Peter Sagamore No question. But Doug.

Patient friend, said Douglas Townshend, we are getting there, counterclockwise. A second and much smaller category of rogue agent is represented by the likes of Frederick Mansfield Talbott: knowledgeable and competent, respected and influential—and at once so independent-minded in word and deed and so utterly devoted to the Agency that almost nobody in the Agency completely trusts him these days. Rick's chief responsibility at one time was the sniffing out of moles, even of the Deep Mole we perennially suspect to have penetrated nearly to the top of our outfit. Because this particular sniffing-out proved inconclusive despite Rick's expertise, some people inevitably came to suspect that the Deep Mole was either Rick himself or the deputy director to whom he submitted his report, and who shortly thereafter transferred him back out into the field. There he became your true Prince of Darkness: first in the Middle East, lately in Latin America.

Now then, Peter: In Joseph Conrad's day, your rogue agent was more of a nuisance and embarrassment to his original patron than an outright menace to civilization. Even today, he *may* be no more than a megalomaniacal private-empire builder or a high-tech crook: an updated Lord Jim or Mister Kurtz. His rogueries may be as petty, however reprehensible, as G. Gordon Liddy's and E. Howard Hunt's, or as multifarious and profitable as Edwin Wilson's and Frank Terpil's.

In that last season of his innocence, Peter Sagamore was able to ask Who are those people? I hate all this. Said twinkling Douglas Townshend You shall come to know who they are, if you want to know, and to hate all this as much as I do. Your present-day rogue agent, on the other hand, may be a Doomsday Factor.

Is that Frederick Talbott fellow a Doomsday Factor?

Rick could be a Doomsday Factor. But if so, he's not out to make dollars; he's out to make policy. If a Frederick Mansfield Talbott decides that Israel must have weapons-grade plutonium to go nuclear, as they say, for the sake of its national survival, then weapons-grade plutonium will manage to disappear unaccountably from a nuclear installation in Pennsylvania and appear in the keeping of Mossad, the Israeli CIA. This is only by way of a hypothetical example. If I then say Look here, Rick: Now that the Israelis have the bomb, the Syrians are going to buy into the club from the French, he'll reply That's a bridge we'll blow up when we come to it. There is your second category of rogue agent.

What is the third, Douglas, Peter asked, inflecting his question Townshend-style. What is the third.

Said Douglas Townshend I'm the third, and the neutralization of Doomsday Factors is my One Other Cause. I double for the Constitution against the CIA, and I rogue for the human race against Doomsday Factors. There we are, and here we are.

A losing race, that one, it seemed to Peter Sagamore. Seemed to him that the class of Doomsday Factors includes all who advance their careers, line their pockets, or gratify their ideologies by commissioning, designing, manufacturing, testing, selling, deploying, or manning the likes of thermonuclear weapons, as well as those who traffic in their legal or illegal proliferation. No? Also those who domesticate Doomsday by scaling such weapons down or seriously considering their deployment for any purpose except deterrence of their use; who speak of limiting or winning a nuclear war, et cetera. Yes? Seemed to Peter Sagamore that the Doomsday Factors have the antifactors outnumbered by about a hundred thousand to one.

Quite so, acknowledged Douglas Townshend. But one can effectively weed only one's own backyard. I can't stop the Pentagon from making and deploying the neutron bomb or the cruise missile. But I may be able to stop a rogue agent from peddling plutonium in Libya or Argentina. And I do my best to stop a rogue agency from subverting the law of the land and its own charter in the name of national security.

Even if to do so, Peter prompted . . .

Quite so, unruffled Douglas Townshend said. That is the Tragic View, to which, despite Rick Talbott's taunt, I am a long-term subscriber.

He was telling this, Peter Sagamore once again reminded our friend, to the least political of fictioneers. In private life, a halfhearted liberal with the usual contradictions: his mind a socialist, his heart an anarchist, his belly a shameless capitalist. And his girlfriend a rich, halfhearted radical. At the worktable it was another story. Doug Townshend's allegiance was to the U.S. Constitution, long may it wave; Peter Sagamore's was to the muse. He had no notion what her politics were; job enough to find out her aesthetics.

Nevertheless, Doug pointed out, the Agency appeared in "Part of a Shorter Work."

If he were writing that story today, P replied, it would be shorter yet. He would take the Agency right out of it; the wrong-looking watermen who came over ostensibly to aid the grounded narrator would remain an unresolved mystery, as would the true identity of the buyer of Sagamore Flats. At the time, he had allowed the Agency to appear in the story because it seemed to have appeared in his life: an apprentice error.

It has appeared again, Doug Townshend observed, pointing to himself.

But not to the same writer.

What exactly changed him.

What exactly changed the world? America moved from the sixties into the seventies; Peter Sagamore moved from his twenties into his thirties. His bones, he forgot to mention before, are nihilist. No wife, Doug, no children; just habits of decency and concentration. In four point five billion years, by Peter's reckoning, the sun will exhaust its hydrogen fuel and expand to apocalypse us anyhow, if a rogue comet doesn't knock us off earlier. In the long-winded novel of the universe, the history of life on Earth from beginning to end is one tiny episode, and the evolution of human civilization and art is one single moment in that episode, shorter than the shortest Peter Sagamore story. The rest of God's novel is about something else. That single moment, like a certain magnificent B-flat, happened to be the only moment that much interested P.S.—but his interest was not especially in prolonging it.

Surely, on the other hand, it is not in seeing it shortened even further.

Not especially. But you should know with whom you're dealing, Doug. Pete tapped his sternum. Bit of a Black Hole under there.

Douglas Townshend nodded. Melville would have said the same: *No!* in thunder.

Said Peter It's time we heard why you're dealing with me: my Obvious Other Question.

YES.

He too, our friend reminded Peter Sagamore somewhere back then, was single and childless; no more of a philosopher than P; certainly no ideologue, either moral or political. Nevertheless, he subscribed with calm passion to certain values whose ultimate justification he had long since lost interest in questioning. One's thirties, he observed by the way, in the case of scrupulous and concentrated spirits like Peter's, are a decade in which one may discover within one's nihilist bones a moral marrow—but never mind that. On the plane of personal aesthetic practice, at least, his young friend had exchanged freewheeling exuberance for parsimonious rigor, and had accomplished admirable work in both spiritual modes, so to speak. Though he, Douglas, preferred the products of the former, he found the exchange more than sympathetic, perhaps exemplary. In any case it was almost certainly a *stage,* which, if the writer and the world endured, might well lead to something more disciplined than Stage One, yet richer than Stage Two: in short, to work at once masterful and human.

Or to silence, terse Pete reminded him.

Or to silence. With the merest side-glance at the analogy between these twin prospects and the civilized world's, Doug next remarked that one serviceable bridge from those first and second stages to that noblest third was the Tragic View: the view he personally held of the U.S. intelligence community, of his own covert efforts to keep it honest, and of many another thing as well, not excluding the alliance he was about to propose to Peter Sagamore.

Mused P It's not easy to be original this late in the day, Doug, but you may have a first there. What in God's name is the Tragic View of the Central Intelligence Agency, and why am I being let in on it?

Replied in effect smooth Doug The Tragic View of the Central Intelligence Agency is this: Covert government security operations, like organized criminal operations, are cancers in the body democratic. They have in common that they corrupt and falsify individuals and institutions. They widen the gap between what things represent themselves to be and what they are. They debase the very language. The famous links between the Mafia and the CIA—involving Cuba, for example, during the Kennedy and Johnson administrations—they're quite natural. The stock-in-trade of both are hit men, cut-outs, dummy companies, fronts, plants, puppets, and extortions. Also coercions, briberies, lies, cover-ups, entrapments, conspiracies, and collusions. A crooked cop and a double agent are cells of the same cancer.

This is the Tragic View?

Not yet. The Tragic View follows upon the recognition that covert operations are sometimes justifiable, perhaps even necessary, for the protection of a good society, but like other aspects of security they are inevitably abused. In good faith as well as bad, definitions vary of defense, security, justice, and our other best interests. Protection shades off into coercion, aggression, self-serving. The best cop on the force will Make Policy from time to time when he's got a big fish right on the hook and knows the fellow's going to slip through the cracks of the system. He becomes a small-scale Frederick Talbott. The Tragic View involves the realization that judgment, discernment, determination, vigilance, courage, goodwill, and the rest can only help keep in check what can't be eliminated. We control and suppress the cancer as much as possible for as long as possible, though we can never cure it and may very well succumb to it ourselves.

Said Peter Sagamore I see and agree. Now you'll tell me why you're telling me.

I've told you nothing, Doug Townshend declared. I've only expounded, for several straight chapters. What I propose to do, with your consent, is tell you plenty: as much as I know of exactly what we've done and are doing in this line, and how we do it, and what I'm doing in the other direction, and what I have to do in *their* direction to cover my tracks. I propose to start small and work up, with your go or no-go at each level. I know what I'm about, Peter.

I can't say *I* know what you're about. Think who it is you're talking to, Doug! Surely I'm the wrong repository.

No. You're my literary repository; I have others. But the others have to decide whether to believe me and whether to act on what I tell them. All you have to decide is whether to listen.

Even for your literary repository, you should have an American Solzhenitsyn. My stories aren't *about* those things.

About! Douglas Townshend's pink face briefly reddened on the northeast quadrant of I-495: the nearest Peter Sagamore would ever see him approach the emotion of anger. Let them not be, he said then, calmly. There are different ways to be *not about*. Your stories are not about the Holocaust, either, for example; if you were a Jewish writer who'd survived the camps, your stories might still be not about the Holocaust—but they'd be not about it in a different way. What we're dealing with here is no holocaust yet, but it's a cancer in our own body. If your stories come to be not about that in a different way, I'll have accomplished all I hope to accomplish on the literary front. I should add that you needn't withhold from Katherine what I tell you on this first level, though obviously discretion will be called for.

He consulted his wristwatch and smiled his twinkly-pink Townshend smile. It's Nineteen Seventy-four already. Yes or no?

Peter Sagamore consulted his. Considered. Shrugged.

YEAH.

Story is anchored at sunset behind Big Island on the Rhode, after our longest but not our best day of sailing in these pages. No babies yet. Hours of light and variable southerlies have ghosted us up and across the Bay to our first real pit stop of the voyage: Galesville, in the marina-fraught West River, next door. Thence—properly iced, watered, and provisioned now for several days' cruising, should K's uterus permit—we sculled two miles through the dying air to our anchorage, under a sunset like a baroque Ascension. What did we speak about through this weighty exposition? Not about Douglas Townshend, John Arthur Paisley, the Doomsday Factor, the CIA—but not about them in a different way from the way we didn't talk about them in more innocent seasons past.

Douglas Townshend became a special friend, our only one his age. That model of courtliness could, like Katherine, enjoy himself in many sorts of company while remaining quite himself. In those days we sometimes smoked dope with our younger friends—colleagues and graduate students of Peter's; apprentice library scientists from the Pratt—sitting in a ring on the floor of our Stony Run apartment, firing up "zilches" made from knotted plastic trashbags hung over a tub of water. The young men wore beards and beads, bell-bottoms, shoulder-length hair; the young women wore miniskirts or jeans or Mother Hubbards, granny glasses, headbands, long straight ironing-boarded hair. Close-barbered, shinily shaved Douglas would lounge above us on a chair arm in English suit and club tie, sip a perfectly iced julep for which he had brought fresh mint and special tumblers with him, and benignly oversee the general narcosis. He was equally at home with the Sherritts and the Basses at Nopoint Point, and made us welcome in his Georgetown–Bethesda circle. The Alice Roosevelt Longworth lady was often with him, as often not. He had other close women friends, but there was an air of celibacy about him. Except for occasional marijuana, we younger folk were all putting cigarettes behind us, with more or less difficulty; not so Douglas. His match-hand, we noticed, sometimes shook. We would have enjoyed crossing paths again with Franklin and Leah Talbott, but that did not happen; Doug seemed to prefer it so. His friends were literate doctors, architects, lawyers, theater people, career civil servants from State, Justice, Interior. Or so they represented themselves.

Over the next two years—in Peter's car around and around those beltways, in our apartment after dinner on evenings when Katherine's manifold commitments required her presence elsewhere, over lunches in College Park or downtown Baltimore, aboard *Story* on occasional Kathless daysails, and in odd moments of privacy here and there about Nopoint Point—Douglas Townshend carried out the first level of his program.

Doug says we *were* responsible for doing Patrice Lumumba in, Peter would report to Katherine, though it wasn't literally the Agency's finger on the trigger. And he would give her details of what went on in Katanga in 1960 and early '61. Doug says the Agency really *did* help Mafia hitmen try to nail Castro; the mob wants back into Havana. He won't tell me yet whether John Kennedy's assassination was arranged by Castro and the KGB or by Lyndon Johnson or by Cuban exiles pissed about the Bay of Pigs. Doug says this guy Rick Talbott that they call the Prince of Darkness went down to Chile in Seventy-three under Mafia cover to help ITT and the U.S. Navy help Pinochet's people knock off Allende. Doug says they lie to our ambassador about things like that so that the ambassador can deny them with genuine indignation. Doug says we have a poison for assassination purposes made from the natural toxins of a certain subarctic shellfish; it leaves no chemical trace whatever. Doug says people like Kennedy and Johnson and Nixon and Kissinger don't ordinarily order assassinations just like that: All they have to do is let it be known that the absence of that sonofabitch So-and-So would be good news. Even Joe Stalin didn't always have to name names: It was enough to frown and suck on his pipe when a certain name was mentioned, and the guy was dead. Doug says even Frank Church's committee won't believe it at first when they hear about plots to make Castro's beard fall off and to blow him away with an exploding cigar and to use a submarine sound-and-light show to fool the Cubans into thinking that the Second Coming has come, but it's true. Doug says we're using these humongous herbicides and defoliants in Vietnam to kill the rice crop and the VC's jungle cover without telling our own men how toxic the stuff is to handle. Thousands of our soldiers are going to have long-term disorders and disabilities without knowing it's Dioxin poisoning from Agent Orange. Doug says the Pentagon did the same thing with radiation exposure in the Nevada and Bikini bomb tests, even with long-term casualty estimates in hand. Some of it's pure callousness, Doug says; some of it's machismo on the command level. Doug says good old Dwight Eisenhower knew about the dangers of atomic-test fallout to the U.S. population and authorized the AEC to lie about it. Doug says that torture medicine is becoming as distinct a specialty as sports medicine. We've trained whole squads of counterrevolutionaries right next door on the York River, Doug says, without their ever knowing for sure they're in the States. We also train goon squads and interrogation teams for various friendly dictators. Our Chesapeake Bay is a fucking moral cesspool, Kath.

Even liberal Katherine got defensive: The Russians do all that too!

Sure, said Peter; but they're them. I'd kind of thought we were us. Doug says we've already sprayed San Francisco and New York City with test strains of respiratory bacilli in limited dosages and counted the results: how many extra old folks die of respiratory dysfunction; how many extra healthy people check in with upper-respiratory complaints. Doug says we're testing all kinds of nasty things on our own war veterans in VA hospitals. Not even the doctors always know about it, much less the patients. Doug says we're running a program called Color Hearing to see whether certain combinations of hypnotism and LSD and stuff can improve the perception of analysts interpreting spy-satellite photographs. They're mostly volunteers. But Doug says we're running another program called MK Ultra to test the effects of mind-altering drugs on thousands of people who don't know they're being doped. Our own people. A couple of the subjects have committed suicide already, and some others have blown their circuits altogether, and their families don't know why. The idea is that an enemy who's freaking out can't fight. Interrogation Medicine is interested too, of course; they run their own drug-testing programs.

Cried Kath Our whole freaking *government* is freaking out!

Here and there, for sure. Doug says his Prince of Darkness pal can kill a man in public by standing behind him in a London bus-queue and touching his leg with the tip of a bumbershoot; the chap'll never know what hit him unless he's up on our R and D. Ricin, the stuff is called. Doug says the KGB's ahead of us on nontraceable cardiac arrest, but we'll catch up and go them two or three better. Doug says the Rumanian Wet Affairs people have a fountain-pen delivery system for their heart-attack juice, but our fellows find it awkward to empty a fountain pen inconspicuously into the other guy's martini, especially since nobody but me uses a fountain pen these days. Doug says Wet Affairs means liquidation; I forget whether the joke is ours or the KGB's. Termination With Extreme Prejudice is ours, Doug says.

Shrieked Katherine, by then a patriot despite herself, I don't *believe* all this shit Doug says!

However, we came to know, it was true.

Then Kath didn't want to hear it. Neither after a while for God's sake did Peter. But he could not *not* listen, any more than she; he could not ask not to hear more of what he didn't want to hear as item after item, in considerable part owing to Douglas Townshend's covert tips and leaks, was revealed—by the *Post* and the *Times,* by Senate investigators, by disaffected ex–Agency officers promptly denounced by their former employer—to be true, true, true. To be, even, understatement.

Peter Sagamore's stories got shorter. Also less frequent. They were not about our successful efforts to overthrow the legally elected Marxist government of Salvador Allende in Chile and establish the bloody generals in his place. We don't even enjoy Sherlock Holmes in our house, reader, much less James Bond. Peter's stories were not about Douglas Townshend's very heavy interrogation, with the help of Frederick Mansfield Talbott and John Arthur Paisley, of the eminent KGB defector Yuri Nosenko, whom James Jesus Angleton, our counterintelligence chief, believed to be a Soviet plant. Doug said we never quite trust such defectors, because the consequences of being mistaken are so great. Nosenko told us that the KGB did *not* train Lee Harvey Oswald in Wet Affairs during Oswald's stay in Russia, and Townshend, Talbott, and Paisley believed him, but Angleton remained convinced that the KGB had planted Nosenko to give us exactly that disinformation. We grilled Nosenko for years in isolation in our Wilmington, North Carolina, safe house before giving him a new identity and a house in the D.C. suburbs and a thirty-eight-thousand-dollar salary as low-level analyst for the Agency. Doug said he himself sailed down to that safe house one summer with the Talbott brothers on Franklin Key Talbott's cutter *Reprise* and sailed back on Paisley's sloop *Brillig,* but Peter Sagamore's stories were not about that. Neither were they about Operation KITTY HAWK, the CIA's Master Mole hunt conducted from 1972 to 1974 by the same quartet—Douglas Townshend, Frederick Mansfield Talbott, John Arthur Paisley, and James Jesus Angleton—each of whom was himself necessarily a suspect. Another high-ranking Soviet defector and sailing friend of Paisley's, Doug said, the naval officer Nicolas Shadrin, was a double agent with the dangerous assignment of feeding the KGB disinformation provided him by one of the aforenamed quartet; but another member of that quartet was persuaded that the Master Mole was in fact supercoding that disinformation into genuine information, thereby reestablishing a communication link that National Security Agency decoders had broken not long before. Even the clever and knowledgeable spy novels

of John le Carré are not enjoyed in our house, reader, and so Peter Sagamore's ever-briefer literary utterances were programmatically not about
that same ex-Captain Shadrin's vanishing in 1975, Doug said, from a public
square in Vienna in broad daylight and full view of our CIA station there,
presumably disappeared by the Komitĕt Gosudarstvĕnnoi Bezopasnost'i.

Operation KITTY HAWK was completed, but did it fly? Doug said that
upon its completion in 1974, his colleague John Arthur Paisley was promoted to the post of deputy director of the Agency's Office of Strategic
Research; but it was the liberal (by Agency standards) William Colby,
successor to the old-guardsman Richard Helms, who received the mole-
hunter's report, and later that same year Paisley retired, expressing his
disillusionment at the revelations of Senator Church's investigating committee. Colby awarded him a going-away medal, for distinguished service,
and Douglas Townshend told Peter Sagamore that Paisley and a number
of other officers were overtly retiring with such grumbles of disaffection
in order to go on the covert consultant payroll, or to set themselves up for
doubling or tripling, or—like Wilson and Terpil—to go into the lucrative
roguing business for themselves. About the time Captain Shadrin disappeared in Vienna, Doug said, the Paisleys separated after more than twenty
years of marriage; marital breakdowns, Doug said, like psychological
breakdowns, occur with such heightened frequency among counterintelligence and clandestine-service officers as to be regarded as an occupational
hazard. His own marriage had been at least in some measure another such
casualty; the Paisleys' would have borne the double burden of Maryann's
also having worked for the Agency (she had been, for example, a book-
keeper for the Nosenko interrogation team). Peter Sagamore's stories were
not about all that—but so possessed by these matters was his reluctant
imagination, very little was left for his stories to be about.

Porter Baldwin, Jr., amid groans and yechs from Katherine Shorter
Sherritt, was elected to the U.S. House of Representatives from his southern Maryland district in 1974 on a flaming conservative platform that included the restoration of Christian prayer in the public schools, equal time
in the curriculum for creation science as against Darwinian evolution, the
reestablishment of antiabortion laws, an end to busing as a means to racial
integration of our public schools, a hawkish defense of our wound-down
war in Vietnam, and a denunciation of Senate critics of the CIA. Among
his chief financial backers were Willy Sherritt and the Moral Majority. In
1976, though Jimmy Carter defeated Gerald Ford, Rep. Baldwin was swept
back into office despite his past connections with Spiro Agnew and Richard
Nixon, on a platform that now included all the previous planks plus repeal
of the Freedom of Information Act and "unhobbling" the CIA's dirty-tricks
department. By Seventy-eight, said Katherine Sherritt, the hypocritical
sumbitch will be nuking the gays. Baldwin's backers, Douglas Townshend
mildly reported to Peter Sagamore, had come to include a highly unofficial political action committee among the old guard in the Agency itself.

Asked startled Peter Sagamore, who had become a hard man to startle,

Money? The CIA is buying our own politicians? Doug couldn't say. Big government agencies, like other big interests, maintain their public relations officers and unofficial lobbyists; they are certainly aware of their congressional friends and enemies, and no doubt rejoice in the victory of the former and the defeat of the latter. Human enough. Election "targeting," after the manner of official Political Action Committees, would of course be impermissible on the part of the U.S. Navy or the Federal Reserve Board, for example. But using laundered money for smear campaigns, rigged elections, and associated dirty tricks abroad is the Agency's daily business: An officer placed as Douglas Townshend had once been placed, with a group of like-minded colleagues, could budget and execute similar operations domestically, at least on the occasional congressional level, without their division chief's knowing it, much less the director of the Agency. Just as the CIA's budget itself is concealed in other government appropriations, many a covert enterprise can be hidden in that budget. One must hold onto the tragic view, the tragic view, Doug said, if one can find it.

Doug says he's resigning from the Agency, Peter Sagamore told Katherine Sherritt in 1976. Said Kate Thank God; no more Doug sayses. We had read together Victor Marchetti and John D. Marks's 1974 exposé *The CIA and the Cult of Intelligence,* Doug supplying us with approximations of the passages deleted by the Agency; also Philip Agee's 1975 exposé *Inside the Company: CIA Diary,* which inspired Katherine to redouble efforts on behalf of her HOSCA organization. Is he really resigning, she wanted to know, or just going underground? Doug says it's to celebrate the Bicentennial, Peter reported. He'll get consulting fees like everybody else, and the Company's paying him to write his memoirs for the archives, like everybody else. Doug says that that Franklin Key Talbott fellow has the job of editing all those memoirs, which nobody ever reads, while he's secretly working on his own exposé. Doug says the Agency likes to maintain some connection even with its rogues, like that Edwin Wilson fellow, to keep tabs on them; but Doug says the rogues use that connection as part of their cover. The tragic view. Hey, Kate? I hate all this.

She does too. It was better when you were just a writer.

Yeah.

I really like Doug Townshend, Peter. I wish we'd never met him.

Yeah.

Maybe now that he's resigning, you can stop being his literary archive.

Yeah.

But the truth was that Doug Townshend had told Peter Sagamore that their confidences had reached the point where Peter's curiosity and sense of plot must be weighed against the absolute candor of his relation with Katherine Sherritt. The matters of which he wanted to speak next came closer to home in two respects: They were transpiring partly in the Sagamore Flats safe house on Hoopers Island, and Doug's report of them must not this time be shared with Katherine.

Said Peter with relief That's that, then, Doug. No deal. Hooray.

Quite all right. It's the choice every Agency officer has to make.

Anyhow, said Peter, all this central intelligence has done nothing for my writing except constipate it.

So far, said Douglas Townshend. And not quite so, either: That special not-aboutness is beginning to be there. Your last piece reminds me of Thomas Mann's novella *A Man and His Dog,* which he published in Nineteen Eighteen and which is loudly *not about* the world war. The sound of two hands not clapping.

My story, said P, is approximately one hundred twenty-seven times shorter.

What I propose to tell you next gets us back to the Doomsday Factor.

Nope.

Quite all right.

But Peter found himself not mentioning this conversation to Katherine, and so the infection touched us anyhow. We maintained our friendship with amiable Douglas Townshend, but it was clearly now a bit constrained. Early that summer, Doug had a mild heart attack; we visited him in Walter Reed Hospital, and Peter much wanted to ask him whether the Agency, maybe his legendary colleague the Prince of Darkness, could possibly have etc. But it seemed not cricket to ask, P having declined to listen, and so our bedside conversation was not about that.

In the fall, Peter made his seasonal visit to Hoopersville—alone, as it happened, Katherine being off at an annual ASPS get-together in the Great Smokies—to pay his respects to the family. He took his mother out for their ritual drive around the place she'd spent her life in: the bridge to the mainland; the wildlife refuge, where tens of thousands of Canada geese were arriving for the winter; her daughter's house; her other son's house; the Sagamore Boat Yard, next door to the former family house. He wanted to see whether the dock was still there from which he had set himself adrift on the tide a quarter-century before. The new owners had replaced it with one more substantial, with a light at the cross-T and two improbably clean white wooden workboats moored alongside. As he returned along the chain-link fencing to his car, where his mother smiled absently and smoked her Winston cigarettes, another automobile left the newly re-sided house, drove down the new blacktop driveway that had once been paved with oystershells, and paused while the driver, a neatly dressed black woman, stepped out to unlock the gate. When she paused again on the outside to relock it, Peter saw that the nearside backseat passenger was Douglas Townshend, lighting a cigarette with unsteady hand. They were not ten feet from each other. Through the closed car window, Peter saw that Doug saw that Peter saw him; they looked into each other's faces for some seconds while the driver returned to her place, but Doug's studied impassivity was enough to check Peter's reflex of greeting. Cigarette lit, Doug turned back to his companion, a weathered-looking fellow with gray billy-goat chin-whiskers but no mustache; the car drove off. There was no other sign of activity in Sagamore Flats, to which a large new garagelike structure and a helipad with windsock had been added since Peter's last visit. The venetian blinds were closed at a number of downstairs windows. Nora Sagamore said Your colored people have certainly come up in this world, and that's a fact.

Troubled by the degree of his complicity and equally of his curiosity, Peter told upset Katherine of the proposal he'd kept secret from her: to keep secrets from her. We talked; we talked more. In the period of that small bad faith, P's literary production had quite ceased. Even our love-making had become less frequent. Whatever the psychodynamics might be between Less Is More at the writing desk and more more more in his tête-à-têtes with Townshend, the relation was undeniable. Both, Peter had come to feel, must be worked through to some Other Side.

Katherine Sherritt, for her part, believed there to be an important distinction between secret information that she's not to know the nature of but does know the fact of, and the secret that her friend even has such secret information. That latter sort of secrecy, she believed, would likely be corrosive; Peter's experience of the past few months was demonstration enough. Need the former sort be? Let him get on with it. She would know it was going on, but wouldn't ask questions. Said Peter Seems risky. You don't have to tell me that, said Kate. But you're hooked on this Doomsday Factor business, and we're hooked on each other. Just don't get recruited, okay?

As happens after some mild estrangements, we felt more solid than before for that clearing of the air; we even decided in the new year to get Peter reanastomosed and us married and Kate pregnant, if we could, in that order. P re-presented himself to both Douglas Townshend and the muse: The former gravely regreeted him; even the latter seemed to loosen up a bit. In a mere three months, he wrote a six-page story which was received not only as something of a literary event but as a considerable literary object; it subsequently took honors in both major American collections of the year's prize stories and has been much anthologized since. We read KUBARK by Franklin Key Talbott (sent down to us by Peter's New York literary agent, who turned out to be Talbott's too) and *Decent Interval: An Insider's Account of Saigon's Indecent End, Told by the CIA's Chief Strategy Analyst in Vietnam* by Frank Snepp, whose royalties were denied him by a court ruling when the Agency sued in order to intimidate future authors of such exposés. *KUBARK*, which dealt mainly with our covert operations in South America's Cono Sur, we found much the better written; it provoked less reaction from the Agency because its author's most damning revelations had already been made public by Senator Church's investigating committee by the time the book appeared. In keeping with our new understanding, however, we did not discuss these books together as we had discussed their predecessors.

Speaking with scarcely a movement of his lips as was his habit in these sessions, Doug said What I'll be telling you now is mostly secondhand, Peter, and might possibly be disinformation, though I think not. I'm resigning because they're nudging me out to pasture anyhow because they're pretty sure I've been leaking to Congress and the *Post,* but they can't prove it because I know how to diddle the polygraphs.

Before we hit the Beltway, Doug: Did the Agency do your heart attack?

Douglas Townshend smiled. No way to tell; that's the beauty of it. Rick Talbott says some people can be warned off with a glance, while some need a nine-millimeter bullet in the cerebellum to get their attention. In between, I suppose, is the perfectly ambiguous cardiac episode.

They were driving out Massachusetts Avenue in P's old BMW, which Kath had come to call the Expository Vehicle. The man you saw me with on Hoopers Island lives up there these days, Doug said, nodding at a nondescript apartment building. His neighbors are KGBers from the Soviet embassy, one of them in Wet Affairs. John is fluent, and his specialty is Soviet strategic weapons strength. Now that Bill's out and George is in, John's as busy as he ever was. He told me last week that he has less time for sailing these days than he did before he retired.

Oh? Bill was Colby. George was Bush. John was Paisley, whose present assignments had to do with Doomsday Factors. Having written nothing since that six-pager, Peter went up to Boston late in the summer for bilateral reanastomosis of his vas deferens. Marcie Blitzstein, now a freelance feminist filmmaker, dropped by Mass. General to inspect his operation scars for old times' sake, but he wouldn't show them to her. That much he told Katherine, who said You're allowed, you're allowed, for Christ sake; just don't put the thing in her. But he didn't tell Kath about Bill and George and John.

John Arthur Paisley, reader, was born in 1923. At age seventeen he joined the U.S. Merchant Marine and was trained as a radio operator. During the war he made several Lend-Lease runs to Murmansk, learned the Russian language, and became established in three of what were to be his four lifelong loves: things nautical, things electronic, and things Russian. The fourth came toward the war's end, when, still in his very early twenties, he was apparently recruited to do OSS work under Merchant Marine cover. In 1948 he went to Palestine with Ralph Bunche's United Nations mission, which laid the groundwork for establishing the new state of Israel. According to Douglas Townshend, Paisley was already working for the equally new CIA, and under UN cover helped set up a radio intercept system for monitoring traffic both among the Arab governments and between those governments and the Soviet Union, at a time when it was feared the Soviets might make a power play in the Middle East.

The conversation in our house was about waiting for Peter's sperm to come down their new pipeline; it was not about John Arthur Paisley's marrying Maryann, fathering children, and receiving advanced CIA training under State Department cover at the Defense Nuclear Agency and in the Air Force staff course in ballistic missiles. It was not about his working with the Color Hearing and MK Ultra programs afore-exposed, or his helping to develop OCTOPUS, the Agency's computerized data-bank on all matters Soviet, or his association with our airborne espionage program via the U-2 and SR71 "Blackbird" aircraft and SAMOS, our early spy-in-the-sky satellite.

We crossed our fingers and waited. Come on, spermies, Kath encouraged. They're shy, Peter worried; they've been underground too long. Following the Nosenko interrogations, he didn't tell her, Paisley was assigned to the U.S. embassy in London under light cover to attend the Imperial War College and do Soviet-surveillance work out of our nuclear weapons depot and SR71 base at Newbury Air Station. A very senior spook by '72, he took part in the Strategic Arms Limitation Treaty negotiations—SALT I—in Vienna and Helsinki, as an expert on satellite surveillance of Soviet compliance with the agreements. Here (so said Doug Townshend, who was doing the same dangerous thing) he made contact with one or more potential Soviet defectors and/or double agents, of the status of Yuri Nosenko—and we approach the Doomsday Factor.

P. Sagamore's stories through that fall, had he written any, would have been not about the fact that in the period just prior to and after John Arthur Paisley's deputy directorship of the Agency's Office of Strategic Research, the CIA's estimates of Soviet military capability (the preparation of which was that office's principal responsibility) were regarded by the hawkish, especially in the national defense establishment, as consistently too low. Inasmuch as high estimates, whether correct or exaggerated, would lead to an increased American armaments buildup, it was clearly in the interest of the USSR that those estimates be low. Doug himself believed them to be very close to correct and the complaints against them to be inspired by Pentagon paranoia and the greed of the Doomsday Factors in our weapons industry. Others, however, believed the Office of Strategic Research to have been misled by the likes of Yuri Nosenko into underestimations clearly to the Soviets' advantage in the SALT negotiations. In 1976 the Agency was prevailed upon to compare the estimates of its in-house experts—the "A Team"—with those of an ad hoc committee of independent authorities on such matters: the "B Team." To do its work, the B Team needed access to all the classified data from which the A Team made its calculations; someone knowledgeable in the field but not currently an active Agency officer was required to coordinate the experiment, supply the B Team with its materials, act as liaison between the two groups, and draft a report on the comparative findings. Director George Bush, Doug said, called Paisley out of "retirement" for this work.

The following year, the year of our reanastomosis and our crossed-fingered vigil, the Doomsday Factors moved again, Doug said, and Paisley was given an even more consequential assignment. The SALT II negotiations were approaching: Great powers being what they are, it was assumed by each side that the other would demand more arms cuts from its adversary than it expected that adversary to agree to, offer less than it expected its adversary to demand, fall back in both areas toward more acceptable positions, and, if agreement should be reached, cheat as much on that agreement as it could get away with. It was therefore of the first importance to each side to know in advance what the other's "fall-back" position was, how the other intended to cheat on that position should it be agreed upon (so that appropriate surveillance technology could be developed to detect that cheating), and what anti-cheating surveillance technology the other intended to deploy (so that appropriate cheating technology could be developed to get around it). In Douglas Townshend's opinion, faithfully unreported in our family conversation and unreflected in Peter Sagamore's unwritten stories of 1977, John Arthur Paisley had been approached in Helsinki during SALT I by his KGB counterparts and "pitched" to double. He had reported the approach to J. J. Angleton and been advised like unlucky Captain Shadrin to "take the pitch" and—this was Operation KITTY HAWK—had fed the Soviets certain data on our fall-back position: Whether information, disinformation, or supercoded disinformation, Doug did not know.

Either stung or encouraged by that experience, the KGB then scored one enormous success and was strongly suspected of having scored yet another. Between 1975 and 1977, two genuine young Doomsday Factors (from the U.S. point of view), Christopher Boyce and Andrew Lee, sold thousands of pages of technical data on our spy-in-the-sky satellites to the Soviets, with the help of which, it was feared, they were cheating on SALT I with impunity. As we looked for sperm, the pair was arrested, tried, and jailed—and John Arthur Paisley, Doug declared, was given the job of assessing our loss and the USSR's gain. Specifically, in addition to his rare "all-building" pass to CIA headquarters and safe houses, Paisley was issued portable high-technology equipment to detect and monitor Soviet interception of U.S. spy-satellite transmissions—and now we come to Sagamore Flats, the end of the year, and the fulfillment of one of Mr. Paisley's lifelong wishes.

Sperm! Sperm! Sperm! cried in order Dr. Jack Bass, Peter Sagamore, and Katherine Sherritt, examining in turn, like spies in the sky, a glop of Peter's ejaculate under the doctor's microscope at Thanksgiving. To the delight of all hands, we wed, in a much smaller December ceremony at Nopoint Point than Irma Sherritt had had in mind: the family, some neighbors and friends, including May Jump and Doug Townshend—fewer than a hundred guests in all. We honeymooned on a chartered sailboat in the British Virgin Islands, endeavoring to make a baby and to write something not about Doomsday Factors, while back in cloak-and-daggerland the KGB prepared a stunning follow-up coup.

The principal U.S. espionage satellites by this time, replacing our older SAMOS designs, were the Keyhole series: KH11 and KH12, nicknamed "Big Bird" after a popular character on an American television show for children. They are almost unbelievably perceptive instruments: The best LANDSAT photograph of Chesapeake Bay—a false-color image taken from 570 miles up, on which we can clearly see not only Nopoint and Shorter Points but *Katydid IV* lying at its dock and every shoal we've ever run *Story* aground on—was made from "inferiorized" Keyhole technology, to prevent the Soviets from knowing exactly how good the real thing is. Big Bird, Doug told Peter, could distinguish between lamb chops and T-bone steaks on *Katydid*'s taffrail grill. It was Keyhole technology that the Soviets were principally after in their dealings with Boyce and Lee; there could be no realistic SALT II agreement until the loss of all that data was assessed and somehow repaired. Early in the spring, Doug said, under the cover of his job at the accounting firm of Coopers & Lybrand, John Arthur Paisley worked with an intelligence think-tank called Mitre Corporation, who determined that the Soviets would require even more information on Big Bird's workings in order to make best use of what they already had. If they were successfully intercepting the Bird's transmissions, then they had somehow got that additional information; if they were not, then getting it must be among their highest intelligence priorities.

Katherine Sherritt Sagamore menstruated. We retried and reretried; she remenstruated, reremenstruated. Likewise the muse. George Bush was followed at the CIA by a retired Navy man, Admiral Stansfield Turner, to whom, Doug told Peter, John Paisley proposed a project combining for the first time all of his several enthusiasms, and by whom (Doug said) he was given permission and additional equipment to carry it out. While still preparing his draft report on the A-Team/B-Team experiment, he outfitted *Brillig* with yet more exotic electronic gear lent him by the Agency, so that while sailing he could "sweep" the Chesapeake area between the Sagamore Flats safe house on Hoopers Island, the National Security Agency complex at Fort Meade, and the Soviet embassy's vacation compound on Corsica Neck, next door to The Deniston School at the confluence of the Corsica and Chester Rivers, where (said Doug) the KGB maintained its principal electronic installation within the United States. If KH11's transmissions to Forts Meade and Belvoir were being intercepted on Corsica Neck or, worse, relayed there by a deep mole at Sagamore Flats, *Brillig* would intercept those interceptions, confirm and assess the damage to Big Bird's usefulness, and perhaps uncover the mole as well.

John's riding higher than the Prince of Darkness, Doug said. He reports directly to Stan Turner, and he's a great friend of Comrade Nosenko these days, who is back in the Agency's graces and may even be involved in the project.

To heat matters up yet further, Doug said—shades of the Nosenko affair—we had as of April a first-class new defector: Arkady Schevchenko, the Russians' UN ambassador and one of their disarmament experts. Schevchenko, according to Douglas Townshend, was now telling his interrogators just what Paisley wanted to hear and the hawks didn't: that the A Team's low estimates had been accurate, and the B Team's were substantial exaggerations of Soviet military strength. Not surprisingly, the B Team suspected Schevchenko of being another high-level KGB plant and Paisley of "delivering" him to discredit their report, if not for more sinister reasons. The interrogation was continuing.

Doug's own current consultancy was not unrelated to the Big Bird business, though his equivocal standing in the Agency kept him more removed from the main action than Paisley, not to mention the Prince of Darkness. The Iranian revolution would surely cost the CIA its listening outpost and SR71 base near Tabriz, partly for the sake of which we had supported the shah, helped train his infamous secret police, and thereby indirectly fueled the revolution. Diplomatic negotiations with mainland China had led us to shut down our surveillance station at Lien Ko in Taiwan, from which we monitored China's missile and nuclear weapons testing facility at Lop Nor. Part of Doug Townshend's new job was liaison work among the Agency, the NSA, and the governments with whom we must arrange new installations to make good those losses. His real interest in the assignment stemmed from the fact that the "take" from both of those listening outposts was sometimes funneled into the KH11 for transmission to Fort Belvoir, and he suspected that other Doomsday Factors were to be found around the Big Bird's nests. Perth, Australia, he told Peter, where our National Aeronautics and Space Administration already maintained a satellite and spacecraft tracking center, was one feasible fall-back from our abandoned listening-post at Lien Ko. He expected to have business in Perth.

The KGB's next blow fell, however, not in Perth or Ankara or Helsinki but in middest America: in Hammond, Indiana, where in August—owing partly to Rick Talbott's undercover work—the FBI arrested a young Agency watch officer named William Kampiles on charges of having sold to Soviet agents in Greece the most intimate technical manuals for KH11, including one signed out to former director George Bush himself. Indiana! Doug had groaned in July, just before the arrest. Who could have guessed that SALT II would be torpedoed in Indiana? The Big Bird was now so seriously penetrated, he believed, that hawkish senators opposed anyhow to arms-limitation treaties would use its compromising as a strong argument against our ratifying the new Carter–Brezhnev negotiations. As there was every prospect of an enormous conservative resurgence in the 1980 U.S. elections, Doug feared that the days of Soviet-American détente were numbered, and that the new decade would see us at best prodigiously escalating the arms race, at worst preparing to wage a "winnable" nuclear war.

Sore-souled Peter Sagamore did not tell his wife about the Doomsday Factor in Indiana—though the fuss was soon enough in the papers—or about the intensified new Deep Mole hunt subsequently initiated by Rick Talbott in almost as freelance a style as John Paisley's waterborne search for links between Sagamore Flats and Corsica Neck. The two enterprises Doug understood to have overlapped, to the point where Paisley and the Prince of Darkness were said each to have named separately the same man to Stansfield Turner in their short list of suspects—as well, it was rumored, as naming each other.

Who cared, reader? While the mushroom-clouded specter of the 1980s approached, and Peter Sagamore appealed to his muse in virtual vain for stories *not about* the end of civilization, one of his June swimmers turned out to have made its way after all through Katherine's plumbing and to have penetrated successfully her floater-of-the-month. In July she missed a menstrual period for the first time in fifteen years. We held our breath . . . and Peter his tongue on the subject of Doomsday Factors. In August, as young Mr. Kampiles joined the arrested ranks of Boyce and Lee, and Arkady Schevchenko's interrogation continued, and Frederick Mansfield Talbott spent more and more time at Sagamore Flats, and Congressman Porter Baldwin, Jr.—a newly appointed member of the House Intelligence Committee—stridently denounced, among other evils, the SALT II Sellout and the Carter Administration's Betrayal of Our Great Ally the Shah of Iran, and John Arthur Paisley tended *Brillig*'s sails and twiddled his dials, she missed another. After consultation with Jack Bass, we announced to the Sherritts that we were pregnant.

Clear tears in his gray eyes, joyous Henry at once established over Katherine's objections a mighty trust fund for his first grandchild. You did that back in Poonie's administration, Kath reminded him, and look what happened: I don't trust trusts. Irma counseled Let Daddy have his fun, and we did. Alfred North Whitehead, Peter said, said that worship is the natural human response to the perception of order in the universe; trust funds are the natural response of the affluent to pregnancy in the family. Chip Sherritt, among whose pastimes that summer was biological mathematics, named our fetus Katydid V and for our amusement calculated on his Apple computer the odds against any given human spermatozoan's accomplishing its mission. They were satisfactorily astronomical.

Speaking of Kate's former husband (Douglas Townshend told Peter Sagamore toward that happy summer's end), Rick Talbott sees a Doomsday Factor in the making there, and our differences on that question are coming to a curious head. Have I told you that among Congressman Baldwin's anonymous supporters these days is the KGB.

He had not; he now did. It was expected that reelection to his House seat in the fall would set Porter Baldwin, Jr., up to run in 1980 against Maryland's liberal Democratic senator, particularly if the Republican presidential candidate that year turned out to be a strong one. It had come to Frederick Talbott's knowledge that the KGB hoped to penetrate the Congressional intelligence-oversight committees—not by way of the doves, as might be expected, but via their most hawkish members. In Poonie's case, their tactic was to be homosexual entrapment followed by anonymous blackmail: Their prediction was that Baldwin would sell his soul to cover his ass; that having first helped elect and then crucially compromised him, they could at least pressure him to vote their way in committee, at best tap his access to U.S. intelligence, even groom him to be a high-level Doomsday Factor. Rick Talbott's intention was to thwart this penetration by arranging a scandalous exposure: not of the KGB connection, of which the congressman was ignorant, but of the gay connection, which ought to be enough to end Baldwin's political career despite the fact that an estimated one out of every ten male DCers is AC/DC.

About this counterstrategy, Doug Townshend's feelings were divided. For Baldwin the man and congressman he had only disdain; but if the United States was in for a binge of nuclear escalation in the 1980s, it might be better to have a muzzled hawk on the intelligence committee than an unmuzzled one, as Baldwin's presumable replacement would be. Rick Talbott, in his independent way, was for the Agency right or wrong; Doug's first concern had been for his country's welfare above the Agency's and in recent years for the world's above his country's, where the two conflicted. The likes of Boyce and Lee and Kampiles could be said to have been Doomsday Factors mainly from the American point of view, though their contribution to the undermining of SALT II Doug regarded as a general victory for the side of death. Poonie Baldwin unpenetrated was a Doomsday Factor (junior grade) from the world's point of view, for in Doug's opinion a belligerent new U.S. administration would be more of a threat to human civilization than the Soviet Union—outside its own borders— currently is. Poonie penetrated, on the other hand, would be a menace only from the U.S. point of view, while Poonie *defeated* might well be replaced by an even more dangerous hawk.

Don't of course tell Katherine any of this, Doug advised. Said worried Peter Don't worry: I can barely follow it myself.

And yet you must, Doug declared. This isn't fiction; it's the world we really live in.

As their conflicting views of Congressman Baldwin illustrated, Doug was coming more and more to see Rick Talbott himself as a potential Doomsday Factor to be undone, lest he undo the wrong people, or the right people at the wrong moment; and it was to be feared that Talbott had come to see Townshend likewise. Their colleague John Arthur Paisley, on the other hand, they agreed was now dangerously exposed, a prime candidate for Doomsday Factorhood from either point of view. His domestic situation was unstable; a chronic depressive, he had joined a therapy group called Lifespring; among his closest personal connections were those always-equivocal Soviet defectors and a circle of ex–Agency freelancers; his unusually large command of and access to our most sensitive intelligence, and his counterintelligence expertise, must be much coveted on Corsica Neck. From Frederick Talbott's perspective, Paisley could be or readily become a Doomsday Factor in any of at least three ways; by being himself the KGB's Deep Mole in the Agency; by quietly covering the Deep Mole at Sagamore Flats while making his elaborate seagoing sideshow of discovering him; and/or by misidentifying, innocently or otherwise, Rick Talbott as the Deep Mole, thereby neutralizing a chief neutralizer of Doomsday Factors—from Talbott's point of view. Whereas from Townshend's point of view . . .

Jesus, Doug! protested Peter, who once upon a time had found James Joyce complicated. More than once, in the course of this endless Beltway exposition, he had come to wonder whether our friend Doug Townshend

mightn't after all be not only disinformed but, in his dignified way, deranged. But then so was he, for hearing out such vertiginous madness, for
not sharing it with Katherine Sherritt, for coming back for more though
his muse was speechless with appall! Katydid V completed her first trimester, during which her father made reams of notes for stories *not about*
Deep Moles and Doomsday Factors, and composed scarcely a sentence of
them. For all he knew for certain, this Frederick Mansfield Talbott and
John Arthur Paisley did not even exist. Perhaps Doug Townshend was
practicing a mode of fiction other than the written?

Then, at 1100 hours on Monday, 24 September 1978, the sloop *Brillig*
was found aground below Point Nopoint, mainsail and #1 genoa set and
trimmed, steering wheel unbraked, VHF radio on, a life jacket lying about
in the cockpit along with a navigational chart, on which had been plotted
the leg home to the Patuxent from Hoopers Island Light. The dinette table
was pulled loose from its hinges; a sandwich was in the making on the
galley counter, where lay an open package of lunch meat and a mustard-
smeared knife. Nobody was aboard.

Mildly over Tuesday morning's paper, in which it was denied that the
missing skipper had any present or much past connection with the CIA,
Katherine wondered Do you know anything about this? Whoops: I didn't
ask that. Said Peter I don't know whether I do or not, and called Douglas
Townshend. For three days he got no answer, while the Agency was caught
out in lie after barefaced lie and congressional intelligence committee members—Porter Baldwin, Jr., excepted—grew more and more annoyed with
Admiral Stansfield Turner. On the Friday morning, a Jamaican housemaid
in Bethesda explained that Mr. Townshend was in Perth, Australia, until
next week. Chip Sherritt, deep into chess and *Through the Looking Glass,*
proposed a weekend sailing trip (the reader now appreciates in what grim
bad faith Peter Sagamore concurred with the general itinerary), and we
intersected the misfortunate corpse subsequently identified as John Arthur
Paisley's.

For the first time, and without telling Katherine, Peter sought out Douglas Townshend upon his return, and to our friend's undisguised satisfaction
pressed him for information instead of merely consenting to receive it.
They met on a mid-week mid-afternoon in Carla's Cavern, a bar-restaurant
selected by Doug in the Fells Point neighborhood of Baltimore. At that
hour they were the only patrons. A handsome, Latin-looking woman in a
striped caftan, whom Doug seemed to know well, was tending bar. The
two conferred closely for a while; then the woman brought Perrier with
lime for Doug, Molson's ale for Peter, and withdrew.

Carla B Silver, said smiling Douglas. No period after the middle initial,
don't ask me why, and one calls her by her full name. She owns this place.
Carla B Silver is Rick Talbott's housemate of many years, but never mind
that. She's also the mother by a former marriage of Rick's brother's wife,
the young professor you and Katherine met once at my house. But never

mind *that* complicated business, either. The point is that Carla's Cavern is a good place to talk. Rick was with me part of the time in Perth, as it happens, or rather I with him.

Said Peter Perth, remembering that Perth is where Paisley's friend Colonel Wilson was reported to have gone after returning *Brillig* to its mooring. Is that a coincidence, Doug?

Not nearly so remarkable a one as your colliding with my late colleague. I am a great respecter of coincidence; otherwise I'd wonder how you happened to be at that particular spot on the ample Chesapeake at that particular moment. What can I do for you, Peter.

What you've been doing, only more so. Tell me what's going on.

Doug squeezed his lime. Lit a cigarette. You don't mind not sharing what I say with Katherine.

Of course I mind. But that's my Bay out there with those Doomsday Factors floating around in it, and it's my kid in the works. What's going on?

How's the writing coming along, Doug wanted to know.

Said grim Peter I haven't written a bad line in months. Tell me Paisley stuff.

Cool Douglas replied I'll tell you Paisley stuff. Colonel Wilson says *Brillig*'s table was broken already. Paisley's girlfriend says it wasn't. The question is whether there was a struggle.

Paisley's girlfriend doesn't know boats, Peter opined. I've fixed our bulkhead table on *Story* half a dozen times, but any heavy bump could knock it loose again.

That's interesting to hear.

No it isn't. What else?

Doug considered. A good bit of it will come out in the papers eventually. The questions will be Was it really John's body you-all bumped into out there, and Did he do himself in or was he done in, and Why and how and by whom. My information is that nobody who knew John well identified the body. The state medical examiner invited Maryann Paisley to do it but suggested she not, on account of the decomposition, and she declined. She thought Colonel Wilson did, but he didn't, thinking *she'd* done it. The Coast Guard brought the body in to the Naval Ordnance Lab at Solomons Island after you left, and it was inspected by the deputy medical examiner for Calvert County and a local marina operator, who happened to be socializing on the deputy's boat when the state police call came through. Neither of them knew Paisley well enough to make a real identification, even though *Brillig* was serviced at that marina now and then, and neither of them noticed the bullet wound, although it was a nine-millimeter hole. What they did notice was a mark on the neck like a cut or a rope burn, but they didn't mention it to the authorities because word was out that the Agency wanted things kept quiet. The mark could have been skin slippage, after a week in the water. The state medical examiner didn't make the identification or mention the neck lesion; he measured the body, noted the bullet wound, and amputated the hands for the FBI to make dermal prints from—the only kind you can get at that stage of the game. But get this: The FBI, to everybody's surprise, couldn't find any fingerprint records fresher than thirty-eight years ago, when Paisley joined the Merchant Marine at age seventeen. This despite the fact that people like us are refingerprinted every time the weather changes. The body and the hands were then cremated in an Agency-approved funeral home; that takes care of future exhumation. The other basis of identification was a partial upper dental plate identified by Paisley's dentist in McLean, who serves a number of Agency people. It was an eyeball identification, which the dentist himself admits would fit a million other middle-aged men, but he couldn't do better because guess what: Paisley's dental records are also missing. The office had changed its filing system, the dentist said—evidently by throwing out all its files—and the partial lower plate that John also wore wasn't brought to him for identification, if indeed the fellow you bumped into had one. The four-inch-undersize jockey shorts and jeans and the twenty-five-pound-underweight corpse, you've already heard about—it was also four inches short, by the way—but you may not have heard that those thirty-eight-year-old fingerprint records were supplied to the FBI after several days' delay by the CIA itself, and that when a newspaper reporter turned up a better set of prints the other day in U.S. Merchant Marine files, the FBI refused to release its old set for comparison with the new one. How's that.

So was it Paisley we bumped into?

Doug sipped. Doug puffed. My understanding is that my nautical ex-colleague is indeed dead. As to the how, Peter. No blood or brains or spent cartridges in the cockpit. Bullet behind the left ear. Two scuba belts around his waist—nobody has questioned that they were his belts—but no mask or snorkel or flippers or air tanks aboard. One gathers he didn't take the weights along for diving purposes. The suicide scenario is that he loaned his car to his girlfriend to help her move her furniture with, telephoned his estranged wife to tell her cheerfully that he might be going sailing but might meet her for dinner if he didn't, and then went sailing by himself on a windless Sunday with a boatload of high-tech electronics, a suitcase full of special antennas, two scuba belts, a handgun, and a briefcase containing his draft report on the A-Team/B-Team experiment. Also a draft agreement for marital separation and a redline telephone book so sensitive that nobody is supposed to take it out of Agency headquarters ever. He motors over to Hoopers Island Light and drops anchor. He radios Colonel Wilson not to wait up. Maybe he works on his report; maybe he tunes in on Sagamore Flats or Corsica Neck or Meade or Belvoir or the Big Bird. Sometime later—it must have been next morning, since nobody has reported that *Brillig*'s running lights were on—he plots his course home, weighs anchor, raises sail, turns on the VHF, and breaks out the mustard and the lunch meat—all to make it look as though everything's normal. But instead of eating, he puts on the scuba weights, jumps or leans overboard, and shoots himself left-handed through the head. Decomposition then sheds twenty-five pounds of body weight, four inches of waist-line, and another four of height, as well as opening up some neck skin. Unless your bumping him did that. But contrary to John's plans, we presume, the gases also float the corpse a week later. Otherwise we'd all have presumed an accidental death, wouldn't we have. Can you credit that scenario.

Said Peter All but the thirty-waist pants. The work he was into was dangerous or cranky or both. His kids were grown; his marriage was kaput; the new girlfriend probably wasn't a major item, just a souvenir from his other life.

Doug nodded. John was in group therapy, or had been: not unusual for people in his domestic position, and almost par for the course in counter-intelligence. His mother is dying of cancer in a Midwest nursing home; Maryann had gone out there not long before to tape some reminiscences with her for the family archives, and John had the tapes.

That has to have been a downer, P agrees: playing those tapes at age fifty-five in his bachelor flat while he went on with his freelance life. So he thought more and more frequently of turning himself off. Being a professional in the tracks-covering way, when he decided to do it he took a few simple measures to make it look like an accident, either to spare his family the embarrassment or to get around some clause in his life insurance, or both. It's plausible, Doug.

It is. What about the left-handed pistol shot.

No problem: When it's one hand for yourself and one for the ship, either hand may take priority. Paisley happened to find himself hanging on with his right hand, so he went ahead and shot himself with his left. It's not as if he was trying to write a letter or hit a target fifty feet away.

Good. And the size thirties.

Peter paused. If our authority for that detail is either the state medical examiner or the Calvert County coroner, we have evidence that neither gentleman is incapable of oversight. And the clothing was cremated with the corpse, I presume, so that's that. Anyhow, things get mixed up in laundromats. Maybe the son left a pair of jockeys in his dad's apartment, and Paisley stuck them in his seabag by mistake. No big deal.

Okay. Did the fellow you bumped into have white chin-whiskers. That would seem to be a clincher.

Couldn't see. Did yours?

Mine, Doug Townshend smiled. I have no information on that point, nor do I happen to know whether the beard would still be there after a week's recycling. Seems to me it would be.

Declared expert Peter Usually yes and sometimes no; depends on who's been swimming through the neighborhood. No rings on those amputated hands, by the way? No wristwatch?

I have no information on that. Is it possible for you to imagine the corpse *wasn't* Paisley's.

Replied P.S. It's possible for me to imagine anything; getting it written is my problem these days. There is ample precedent in our fallen world for the substitution of corpses by people who want themselves or someone else thought dead. But if you were going to such elaborate trouble, plus weighting your proxy down with just enough lead to let the crabs mess up his face before he floats back up, wouldn't you put the right size pants on him plus your wallet and watch, to clinch the ID?

Said Doug approvingly I would. Unless I were unusually pressed or not very professional.

Speculated Peter If an Agency hit-boat from Sagamore Flats dropped off a size-thirty frogman near Hoopers Island Light to nail Paisley, either because he was the Deep Mole or because he'd uncovered the Deep Mole, and Paisley managed to nail the frogman instead and then said to himself Hey: Since I have this perfectly satisfactory dead frogman on my hands, why don't I change identities like my pal Nosenko and fake a suicide so that old Maryann can collect a bundle in honor of our years together, and at the same time I'll avoid the consequences of having nailed my ex-colleague here, who is already conveniently weighted down with lead. I'll do a Captain Shadrin, except I'll disappear myself to Pago Pago, where the sailing's nice, instead of to the Gulags, where it isn't. But shit, Doug, this is bad spy fiction. What's the truth?

The truth, Doug Townshend said with a little grimace at Peter's language, is upstairs in Carla's Cavern. But I haven't told you about the break-ins yet, and we haven't done the simpler murder scenarios, have we.

Weary Peter, hooked, said Paisley was killed because he was the mole. He was killed because he wasn't the mole but knew who was, or was about to find out with his fancy radios. He had a wet affair with the KGB types in his apartment building, for any of a dozen reasons. He was terminated with extreme prejudice by a consortium of the DIA, the NSA, the NRO, the NSC, the FBI, and the IRS; also Colonel Wilson and Mrs. Paisley. They broke into his apartment, stole his scuba belts, planted a few nine-millimeter bullets in his nightstand drawer, zipped over in an unmarked helicopter from McLean or Lusby to the Hoopers Island Light, where they knew he was parked, on account of his call to Wilson, and neutralized him. Since the medical examiner's ballistics tests matched the bullet in his head with the ones in his nightstand drawer, it was reasonably inferred that he'd shot himself with his own pistol.

Marveled Douglas How did you know about the bullets.

I didn't.

They were on the closet floor, not in the nightstand drawer. Paisley's apartment was a busy place while he was out on the Bay or in it. *Brillig* was found aground about eleven A.M.; the Coast Guard found the briefcase full of CIA stuff and promptly notified the Agency, who seem promptly to have notified the firm of Coopers and Lybrand; but Maryann Paisley wasn't notified till eleven that evening. She sent their son to check his dad's apartment, and the boy found papers scattered about, the family tapes and tape machine missing, and a number of nine-millimeter bullets

spilled on the bedroom closet floor. He assumed the place had been bur-
gled; in fact, people from both the Agency and Coopers and Lybrand had
dropped in. The Coopers and Lybrand visitors took a Rolodex with sensitive numbers in it—not the same as that redline phone book on the boat,
which the Agency confiscated along with the briefcase. The Agency visitor
found two cartons of classified material, including a note in John's hand-
writing that read *Now what about Schevchenko?*—but he didn't find Paisley's debriefing reports on Arkady Schevchenko, which matter a great deal
to the verification of the A-Team/B-Team business. Those reports are still
missing. So are the terminal-mother tapes and some others in which John's
girlfriend claims John talked about suicide. The girlfriend might well have
dropped in, too; she had a key to his apartment. But you didn't really
need one to join the party: Both Eddie Paisley and the chap from Coopers
and Lybrand simply asked the super to let them in, and people like Rick
Talbott and John's Russian neighbors ask for keys only when they're being
polite. I forgot to mention—

Said Peter Sagamore suddenly John Arthur Paisley was neutralized by
a neutralizer of Doomsday Factors.

Doug Townshend put down Perrier and cigarette. Patted his lips with a
paper napkin. Beamed. It's time we went upstairs.

Through Carla's Cavern—an agreeable, unremarkable bar and grill—
Peter followed him as he had followed him through these years of exposition, wondering no longer Whether but as always Why. An unremarkable
door toward the rear of the establishment was opened from behind at their
approach by a remarkable-appearing young woman who must have seen
them coming, P could not guess how. Thin to the point of gauntness, large-
eyed, wild-haired, mournful of expression but not unattractive, she wore
over braless tiny breasts a T-shirt with the legend I'M SO HAPPY I COULD
JUST SHIT. In a distracted voice she said Hi, Doug. Douglas Townshend
said gently Mim, and bussed her proffered cheekbone. The girl looked
shyly sidelong at Peter, but thereto infallibly courteous Doug made no
introductions. Rick and Ma are upstairs, she said.

Townshend nodded. Up the men went, the spare young woman remaining below, to a comfortable apartment above the bar. In the living
room, which smelled of fresh mint, the Latin- or maybe Gypsy-looking
Carla B Silver rose from a leather couch, smiling wonderfully around a
cigarillo, straightening her caftan, smoothing her glossy hair. A man beside
her, with whom she had been speaking closely, remained seated. Both
seemed to Peter to be sizing him up, Carla B Silver a good deal more
warmly than her companion.

He reminds me a little of Jon, she said huskily to Douglas Townshend,
while looking with sad goodwill at Peter. The hair and eyes? Doug touched
her shoulder. Everything reminds me of Jon, she admitted. I'll be downstairs.

To himself Peter wondered John Paisley? The man on the couch said
evenly, as if in reply, Jonathan's our left-wing son. He disappeared in Chile

last year. Peter Sagamore, Douglas Townshend said to the man, who shook hands without getting up. Frederick Talbott. Is that mint tea, Rick.

More reserved than diabolical-appearing—a beardless, leaner, more polished-looking, less ruddy and amiable version of that Franklin Key Talbott fellow we'd met at Townshend's early in this chapter—the Prince of Darkness smiled and poured two fresh glassfuls from a silver teapot, elongating the hot stream with dextrous panache like a Moroccan waiter. The Israeli cabinet did something the other day that Carla B Silver disapproves of, he said dryly. She's been A-rabbing ever since, to teach them a lesson. He advised Peter to try the couscous special downstairs, if he and Doug were staying for dinner. This tea needs half a cube of sugar.

Said Peter I'm sorry about your son. The three men stirred in small sugar cubes passed from a saucer by their host, raised their tea glasses in half salute, and sipped. Doug then sat by, clearly letting the newly-mets feel each other out.

Frederick Talbott ignored the condolence; shrugged. You've caught a famous habit. The main reason we have a Central Intelligence Agency is that Doug Townshend and Allen Dulles got bored after V-J Day. Peter said nothing. But it's a habit you can still kick, at your stage of it, Frederick Talbott said presently, checking his wristwatch. Writing a spy novel, are you?

A touch irked by that disingenuousness, Peter declared without explanation I'm not even writing a novel *not* about spies. I'm an innocent but curious bystander who grew up in Hoopersville and sails on the Bay. Things bump into me.

With plainly calculated unamiability Frederick Talbott asked What does it matter to you whether Jack Paisley killed himself or the Russians killed him or we killed him or somebody else killed somebody else? Why not stay home and write your stories?

You make the idea sound attractive.

I intend to. Why should you give a damn?

Aware that he was being tested, but not at all sure what was at stake, Pete considered. The Paisley business seems to give a damn about me, he said, not displeased with that formulation.

At once and shortly, Frederick Talbott replied No it doesn't. Peter felt an uncomfortable thrill at the professional interrogator's refusal to be nice. As if reading his thoughts, Frederick Talbott now said Look here, comrade: We're not nice. You're nice; my little brother's nice. You write stories; you teach college; you're used to nice people. You think Doug Townshend's nice 'cause he comes on nice. But he's not nice and I'm not nice and Jack Paisley wasn't nice.

P echoed neutrally Wasn't. He saw Talbott's eyes flicker toward Doug Townshend as if pleased. Doug sipped his cigarette and his tea.

You're one of Doug's hobbies, Frederick Talbott declared. I have my own. Your curiosity about Paisley doesn't interest me.

Holding onto his adrenaline, Peter said Your curiosity about me interests me. If you're such a big-deal baddie as Doug makes out, how come you're futzing around with a small-time storyteller?

The man now positively grinned his approval to Douglas Townshend, who was also smiling. In a more cordial tone he said Let's forget about motives and talk price. I know more than Doug knows about the Paisley affair; that's why you're here. I know more about the Paisley affair than anybody I know knows. What's it worth to you to know what I know about the Paisley affair?

Peter took it he didn't mean in dollars.

Of course not.

Well, it's worth my sitting here and being bullied. But just barely.

Said Frederick Talbott, more correctively than unkindly, Now *you're* the one who's futzing around. So far it's been worth it to you to keep some things you know from your wife, by mutual understanding. Apparently it's been worth it to you to set aside your writing career for a while. Not quite that simple, maybe, but that's about what it comes to, no?

Peter didn't argue.

That was a fork in the river, Frederick Talbott declared, and for one reason or another you made your choice, as we all do. Now you're at another fork in the river.

He looked to Douglas Townshend, who now with his customary courtesy reassured Peter that he was not as yet exposed to any real danger by knowing what he, Doug, had confided to him thus far. It was the confider, if anyone, who was at risk. The next level of confidences, however, involved a more active complicity on the part of the confidant; not only the nature of the information but the fact of it would for example have to be withheld from Katherine Sherritt Sagamore, for her own protection, and Peter would be at some risk—of the same sort though by no means to the same degree— as Douglas himself and Frederick Talbott—for knowing what he would know. Early on in their relation, Doug reminded him, Peter had invoked the image of Faust. The situation now did indeed have its Faustian aspect: The price of his knowing more about the Paisley case and related matters would include some further estrangement not only from his wife but from his innocence in general and his innocence about the United States of America in particular. The presumable reward would be an enlarged understanding of where and what the powers are that move our government and the world: no small reward for one whose vocation is registering in language the experience of life. An enlarged understanding especially of Doomsday Factors (Frederick Talbott lifted his mint-tea glass as if to toast that phrase; Doug Townshend soberly returned the toast), who might well terminate the whole shebang. Mister Sagamore's motive, Doug declared to his colleague—if you'll permit me, Peter—has been less idle and more estimable than he'd have us think. It is nothing less than driving his art through reticence and his spirit through innocence, both to some presumable farther shore.

Talbott grimaced. That's over my head.

Replied Townshend smoothly No it isn't. And then, to Peter, As your Virgil on this tour—or your Mephistopheles—it falls to me to remind you that that innocence of yours is really long since lost. You are a little bit pregnant. If saying yes now has its price, the price of saying no is artificial innocence, which is another name for arrested development.

Uncomfortable Peter Sagamore said to bored Frederick Talbott I don't think that was the price you had in mind.

Nope. Your wife and her mother are both trustees of The Deniston School, right?

Doug Townshend frowned and set down his tea glass; Peter's surprise was evidently shared. Maybe they'd like to do their school and their country a little service, Frederick Talbott said.

Tight-lipped Douglas stubbed his cigarette. Frederick Talbott ignored him for the length of an extended statement. The Soviet embassy wants more privacy on Corsica Neck. They've put out feelers about annexing land from Deniston, and pretty soon they're going to make a quiet offer to the board of trustees. We have it in mind to stir up a big redneck fuss on the Shore at that point, so that some unimpeachable Deniston friend of ours can come to the Russians' rescue and quiet the fuss and shepherd the deal through. Somebody respected and patriotic and blue-blooded, you know, but liberal in the Averell Harriman style. By then we'll have saturated the campus with our people and our gear; we've got some in place already. We'll also benefact the school anonymously. Is "benefact" a word? Our Deniston angel might get to know one or two embassy people or their wives, though we never count on that. The bottom line is that between the bugs and the angels we get a better idea what they've got in the attic over there.

Peter looked to Douglas Townshend, who said with a sigh This shouldn't be news to me, but it is. Business never stops, Peter. Feel free to say no.

Okay, said Peter: No.

Said smiling Frederick Talbott The angel needn't report to us. She needn't even know she's our angel. You've established yourself as a CIA-hater who's appalled but fascinated by messy goings-on in your own backyard. She shares your feelings, makes friends with her Russian neighbors, and tells you what she hears, and you tell us. The main things we find out for ourselves.

Feel free to say no, Doug Townshend repeated—a touch edgily, it seemed to Peter—and rubbed his forehead with three fingertips.

I said it already. Look, guys: I'm sorry if I led you-all to believe I was recruitable. My curiosity is cured.

He stood, but Douglas Townshend did not at once stand also. Frederick Talbott kept his eyes on Peter. Feel free to say no, he echoed disagreeably. You really *don't* know anything about us.

Said Peter I'll read a few spy novels. I'm ready to go, Doug.

Checking his watch again, Frederick Talbott said Maybe you *should* read a few spy novels. You're free to feel any damn thing you like, professor. What you're free to *do* could be another story.

Doug Townshend said Come on, Rick.

You're supposed to be coaching this boy, Doug, Frederick Talbott teased, and you tell him to feel free to say no? Tapping the saucer of sugar cubes, he said lightly to Peter I've sent all three of us a valentine: two-hour delay and clean as a whistle. Does he know what a valentine is, Doug?

Good Lord, Rick, Doug Townshend said. Peter's skin thrilled. Frederick Talbott rotated a bezel on his watch and said with satisfaction Seventy-five minutes to the end of the chapter, just like in a spy novel. Am I pulling your leg? From his sports-shirt pocket he removed a small yellow sealed envelope. Here's the antidote, also clean as a whistle. He tore it open and dumped its contents, three bright capsules, onto the sugar server, where several of those half-cubes remained. One capsule was red, another white, the third blue. Ignore the colors, Frederick Talbott instructed; they're all the same inside. My advice to you is to believe me and take one, even though *this* might be the valentine, or one of them might not be the antidote. That's what kind of nice fellows you're playing games with. He passed the saucer first to Douglas Townshend. What's *your* advice, Doug?

Douglas Townshend calmly said You're being outrageous, Rick. But without hesitation he picked up a capsule, the blue one, and washed it down with the last of his tea. Pleased Frederick Talbott took the red one, but did not at once put it in his mouth, and offered the saucer to Peter. You see how we have to trust one another in our business, even though we mustn't. He swallowed his capsule. Are you in? Feel free to say no.

Take it, Peter, Doug advised with another sigh. I'm terribly sorry.

Peter Sagamore perspired.

Is Doug your friend or my accomplice? Frederick Talbott teased. Swallow hard. Tea? Dizzy Peter swallowed the white capsule; it caught in his dry throat and had after all to be washed down with gulps of tea. I'm really sorry, Doug Townshend murmured. Frederick Talbott poured himself another glass but did not sugar it; the remaining cubes he shoveled into his pants pocket. Think it over, he said affably to Peter: the Deniston caper. You're free to say no.

Katherine Sherritt and Peter Sagamore suppose that in a spy novel, this long episode would climax in an explosion of physical action; an indignant lunge, an expert parry; at least a curse, a smashed tea glass, a regurgitation. But in this truth-seeking tidewater tale, a tisking Townshend, still apologizing, merely ushered a sweating Sagamore down and out of Carla's Cavern. No sign of friendly proprietress or crazy-haired girl in T-shirt; a lean and sullen West Indian tended the bar, at which early patrons were beginning to gather.

Patient reader: To have lost much innocence does not condemn one to losing all. To realize that one bears some guilt does not condemn one to becoming ever guiltier. Our late friend Douglas Townshend's conviction, if it *was* his conviction (we have chosen to believe it was)—that a gifted artist, purged of illusions, might come thereby through to some profounder art and perhaps even help save the world—may well itself have been an illusion. But even had Peter Sagamore been guaranteed such a payoff (he told Doug in their final conversation, by telephone a few days later), he'd have said No, no, no in thunder! And wished he had done earlier.

Then you *have* made your choice, said still-apologetic Doug—who long since had opined that both "valentine" and "antidote" were almost certainly "blanks," but just possibly were real. Your wife is more important to you than your writing is. Who can blame you?

Said still shocked Peter The choice isn't that clean. I haven't told her yet what happened in that bar, but I will. To hell with John Arthur Paisley! To hell with you all, Doug.

Quite so, said Douglas Townshend. This is what Rick wanted—to recruit you or turn you off—but I'm disappointed, of course. There's more to that fellow than the side you saw, by the way.

Doomsday Factors, for Christ's sake. I'm ashamed of myself.

Yes, well. Obviously I wish you and Katherine the best, and your literary projects too, though I'm not at all confident you've made the right choice. That unhappy hour in Carla's Cavern could have led you into things that no American writer of your gifts has ever been even close to. Rick was much taken with you, I should say.

Screw Rick.

Mm. Me too, I gather. Peter said nothing. So be it, Douglas Townshend sighed. Porter Baldwin, by the way, is going to lose next month's election. His defeat won't be unrelated to all this, and to the Doomsday Factor. Peter said nothing. For heaven's sake don't imagine that we do our serious business as elaborately as that mint-tea thing, Doug said. Well, we do, sometimes, but that was Rick's idea of a literary demonstration. More often he'll go for a simple kick in the crotch or an umbrella-point in the leg, if not a bullet behind the ear. Seriously, Peter: Setting aside the Deniston business, if you should change your mind . . .

Peter hung up the telephone. The U.S. Central Intelligence Agency, we read soon after in our newspapers, pressed the Maryland State Police to drop their murder investigation in the Paisley case and rule suicide. Maryann Paisley attempted to retrieve her late husband's car from his girlfriend, one Betty Myers, but Ms. Myers refused to return it until certain personal items of hers had been returned to *her* from Paisley's apartment—including, reporters speculated, those never-located tapes she spoke of in a *Look* magazine interview: the tapes in which her friend John had allegedly spoken of suicide. The Maryland State Police and the State Medical Examiner ruled that the corpse *Story* had bumped into was a probable suicide. The FBI concurred, but the Senate Select Committee on Intelligence, annoyed by Admiral Stansfield Turner's false denials of Paisley's status, opened their own investigation. A sister of Paisley's out in Oregon declared to reporters that if she ever wanted to kill somebody, she sure would do it in Maryland. Late in October, supporters of Congressman Porter Baldwin Jr. (R., Md.) were shocked by the revelation that he was a solicitor of homosexual favors from young male prostitutes in Georgetown gay bars; the damning evidence, together with witnesses prepared to testify, had dropped into FBI hands as if from nowhere, in connection with a routine police investigation of one of the gay hustlers. The congressman at first denied the charge, insinuating that his political rivals—who were of course jubilant—were behind the whole thing. Finally he more or less acknowledged the truth of the allegations, repented, apologized publicly to his family and constituents, but refused—rather spunkily, Peter thought—to withdraw from the congressional race, and lost the election. Two Soviet spies were convicted for trying to buy U.S. antisubmarine-warfare secrets from a Navy officer in Connecticut; they claimed entrapment, and though they were soon exchanged for five Russian dissidents, the newspapers speculated that John Arthur Paisley might also have been trying to entrap certain KGB officers, maybe his Massachusetts Avenue neighbors, and had been killed by them as a heavy signal to the CIA.

Katherine followed these stories with avid appall and wondered why her husband had apparently lost interest, particularly as she knew he knew more than the reporters knew about the case. Thanksgiving Day, which normally we divide between Nopoint Point and Hoopersville, we spent in our Baltimore apartment so that Peter could tell his wife everything we've now told here. Two weeks later, at the end of her second trimester, she spontaneously aborted our child.

We made certain New Year's resolutions.

Peter Sagamore's muse, however, did not change her tune. Take it out; less is more. We had, then, it seemed, lost both ways. Grim Kath conferred with Jack Bass; we went on the Pill. The Senate committee's investigation of the Paisley case bogged down and was given over to the Justice Department, who gave it over to the FBI, who submitted a twelve-page report reaffirming the Maryland State Police ruling of probable suicide. Maryann Paisley wrote a long letter to Admiral Stansfield Turner, demanding that the Agency vindicate her late husband by acknowledging the secret and dangerous work which had culminated his long career of service. In a brief reply, Admiral Turner (who had by no means necessarily been lying to that Senate commitee: Agency chiefs can report only what their aides tell them) expressed his regrets at the cloud still hanging over Mr. Paisley's death, but pointed out that the Agency had no jurisdiction in the matter and must properly defer to the Maryland State Police. The Agency put its Choptank River safe house, on Ferry Neck, back on the market. Said glum Katherine, reading the Baltimore *Sun* over breakfast, Let's both of us become spooks; we're spooks enough already since last Thanksgiving. Said glum Peter I'm free to say no.

More tea?

Then in late March 1979, Frederick Mansfield Talbott disappeared, Paisley-style, from his younger brother's cruising cutter, *Reprise,* on which he'd been taking an early solo sail from his parents' farm on Wye Island. The cutter was found lightly aground in Eastern Bay, not far from the mouth of the Wye, but the missing man's body was never located. As might be expected, the media gave much play to the similarity of the two cases; some even picked up on the cutter's portentous name. In April, the Senate intelligence committee declared its dissatisfaction with the FBI's report and reopened its Paisley investigation: a delicate business in view of President Carter's preparations-in-progress for the SALT II negotiations with the Soviet Union. We read that Frederick Mansfield Talbott had probably been despondent over the disappearance of his radical son Jonathan in Chile. In May, the insurance companies Mutual of New York and Mutual of Omaha both announced that they were withholding payment to Maryann Paisley of the death benefits in her husband's policies, citing their doubts about the identification of the body. The flamboyant lawyer Bernard Fensterwald, Jr., hired by Mrs. Paisley to investigate her husband's death or disappearance, declared to reporters that Paisley had been, among other things, the CIA's liaison with ex-President Nixon's Watergate "plumbers," one of whom Fensterwald had also represented.

Douglas Townshend telephoned us once, just wondering.

No, Peter said to Katherine. Katherine said to Douglas Townshend Peter says No. Quite so, said Doug: Only wondering. In June, Attorney Fensterwald arranged a press conference on Solomons Island, at which that deputy Calvert County coroner and that marina operator declared their shared conviction that Mr. Paisley had met with foul play. Said Eddie Paisley This removes any doubt that my father did not kill himself. Bernard Fensterwald, Jr., agreed, but the state medical examiner scoffed. Reporters speculated that Fensterwald had staged the conference for the benefit of the insurance companies, who did indeed subsequently pay off; but a spokesman for the Maryland State Police pointed out that cause of death was not an issue with the underwriters, as there were no suicide clauses in the policies. At Jack Bass's instruction, we now went off the Pill and onto a fertility drug; a few months later, Peter's sperm came through as his muse would not, and by the autumnal equinox Henry Sherritt reinstated that trust fund.

Maryann Paisley—$235,000 wealthier, minus attorney's and private investigator's fees—disclosed to reporters in November 1979 that CIA files on her late estranged husband, which she had acquired under the Freedom of Information Act, showed fifteen years of his Agency career blacked out. He had been, she was now convinced, while overtly Overt, covertly Covert, and at the time of his death was in all likelihood eavesdropping from *Brillig* upon a mole transmitting KH11 data from the Hoopers Island safe house up to the KGB installation on Corsica Neck. At the same time, now that the insurance companies had paid off, she reaffirmed her conviction that the body in the Bay was not her husband's. The state medical examiner, she revealed, had showed her photographs of the corpse. Its nose was not her possibly late estranged husband's nose.

In January 1980, ex-Congressman Porter Baldwin, Jr., formerly of St. Marys County in southern Maryland, announced his complete rehabilitation from both alcoholic and homosexual tendencies and his intention to run again for Congress from his new base in western Maryland. The Moral Majority withheld its support, likewise the Caucus for Gay Pride, but others cheered his announcement. Maryann Paisley reported that her home in McLean, Virginia, was broken into while she was out with friends, and that though apparently nothing was stolen, her possibly late estranged husband's effects had been strewn about in an obvious attempt to frighten her: His scuba gear, for example, had been hauled out of storage along with a marine radio and placed prominently upon a workbench, as if by its owner's ghost. Her attorney, Mr. Fensterwald, opined that the break-in was in all likelihood a scare tactic by the Central Intelligence Agency to dissuade her from pursuing her Freedom of Information suit to recover all documents pertaining to Mr. Paisley—a suit Fensterwald expressed little confidence of winning, the Agency being the Agency. Of Frederick Talbott, whose loss we could not bring ourselves to grieve, there remained no trace, no news; his son, too, remained *desaparecido,* swallowed up in the Southern Cone with the thousands of others. And from Peter's muse, as our new and apparently redoubled pregnancy approached its term, there was likewise no report.

We moved to Nopoint Point in June to await parenthood.

On Tuesday, June 10 last, the newsdealer in Easton happening to be sold out of the day's Wilmington paper, Henry Sherritt picked up along with his *Wall Street Journal* a copy of *The Washington Post,* though he himself does not at all care for that newspaper, and dropped it off at the First Guest Cottage for his daughter and his son-in-law, who he knows rather do. Among the obituaries was Douglas Townshend's: The retired CIA officer had died of a ruptured aneurysm aboard an airliner en route from Los Angeles to Sydney, Australia, whence he was bound for Canberra and Perth on business as a government consultant. Though we know no other members of his family, shocked Katherine set to work on the telephone, which is to her as is his flute to Jean-Pierre Rampal. By the time shocked Peter finished his distracted morning's toil upon a draft of "The Magnificent B$\flat$," she was able to report that both the Alice Roosevelt Longworth lady and the widow of that once-eminent author of hardboiled-detective novels (who had gone to his own denouement) were persuaded—on no particular evidence that Kath could coax from them—that the Central Intelligence Agency had done in our erstwhile elder friend. Indeed, inquiring of a sister of Doug's about memorial services, the Alice Roosevelt Longworth lady had met with a cynical hostility reminiscent of John Paisley's sister's, which she duly reported to Katherine: The Company killed him, Kate quoted the A.R.L. lady quoting Douglas's sister: Go to *their* memorial service.

There were, it turned out, at least three such services: a small funeral ceremony, restricted to the family of the deceased, when his body was returned from the Antipodes to the Townshend family graveplot in Baltimore County; a full-fledged in-house memorial service at CIA headquarters in Langley, arranged and attended by Doug's former colleagues; and a small informal memorial cocktail party in Georgetown for his non-Agency friends, hosted with dignity after all by the Alice Roosevelt Longworth lady on Friday, 13 June, and attended, our fingers crossed, by us. At the door, our hostess said to Katherine's belly Good Lord look at you, but that was that. She acknowledged that she was probably handing the Agency a bum rap; we agreed that its covert operations arm well deserved any raps and charley horses the likes of us could hand it, for so often turning paranoid speculation into understatement. Katherine took the two sips of memorial champagne permitted her by Jack Bass and then drank tonic water with lime. Peter endeavored to maintain the Tragic View of clandestine operations on the part of governments equipped to destroy the world many times over; indeed, of governments period. We had rather expected to see Franklin and Leah Talbott among the guests; would have been pleased to, within the limits of our strained attention, for we had admired Frank's *KUBARK* exposé and had enjoyed both husband and wife. They had gone off on a Caribbean sailing trip, we were told, in part to recover from the shock of Frederick Mansfield Talbott's presumable death and to escape the attendant publicity. That matter, too, was by some at the party attributed with knowing tisks and shrugs to the Agency; by others just as knowingly to the KGB. There had been a rift, some said, between the brothers upon publication of Franklin Key Talbott's book. There had been no rift, said others: The exposé was in secret fact orchestrated by the CIA itself, to throw the KGB off track in certain matters. Et cetera. A memorial cocktail party, we decided, is not a wonderful idea.

There fizzles out the chronicle of our only brush to date with Doomsday Factors. A proper novel, we agree, would know what *really* happened to John Arthur Paisley, to Frederick Mansfield Talbott the Prince of Darkness, to Douglas Townshend. But these are mere tidewater tales, wending whither listeth wind and water no matter how seasoned the tiller-hand, or almost no matter. The reader understands now what final strain was in the First Guest Cottage and upon our discourse on that Saturday and Sunday, 14 and 15 June 1980, when Peter Sagamore wrote his final version of "B♭" by deleting all that remained of it: its abbreviated title. That ultimate kenosis, so long in the works of his works, was thus completed as Katherine's filling was all but fulfilled. The latter vessel stood ready to be emptied, the former to be replenished, when pent Peter said Set me a task! and careful Katherine Take us sailing, and both vessels ventured out upon a third.

Between you and us now, also, reader, as between ourselves, there remain, despite certain mysteries, no further secrets. Bunk to bunk through *Story*'s cabin next morning, behind Big Island on Rhode River, Peter asks Katherine Shall we get on with it. His inflecting that question as a statement is his salute to the late Doug Townshend. I mean now that we have everything on board we need. Or shall we sensibly go home and have our babies.

Replies wakeful Katherine, as promptly and soberly as if waiting to be asked, Let's take us sailing.

DAY 4:
RHODE RIVER TO
SEVERN RIVER

But to sail wants wind; this mild June Thursday morning there is none where we are. New rioting in South Africa leaves forty-two more blacks dead. Decline of U.S. "smokestack" industries continues. People on engineless small sailboats had better be fair-weather friends as well as foul. To wait out the calm, after breakfast Kath baby-sits on *Story*'s front porch, reading Charles F. Chapman's *Piloting, Seamanship, and Small Boat Handling* while doing delivery exercises. She practices reciting, to herself and to Odds and Ends, the thirty-two points of the compass until she can do it at patter-song clip both clockwise and counterclockwise, but she cannot come up as could May Jump with a melody to fit. She tries unsuccessfully to dismiss from mind the memory of being forcibly sodomized, seventeen years since, by her former husband, former Congressman Porter Baldwin, Jr.; her Let's take us sailing was said soberly because for two nights in a row now she has redreamed that disagreeable episode. Down in the cabin, her incumbent spouse does isometrics and remarks to *Story*'s log that

THE FOREST-GREEN RECRAYONING OF MRS. PORTER BALDWIN, JR.,

was to have been told the reader yesterday but wasn't because Day 3 was overlong already by the time we got the hook down behind Big Island; he goes upstairs to entertain K with the story of his meeting himself forty years later in the middle of the Atlantic Ocean seventeen years since: the same year she got herself recrayoned.

Poonie Baldwin, Katherine Sherritt had told Peter Sagamore in Dun Cove sometime during our first nautical night together after the Katherine Anne Porter party in 1970, was no villain. Her new lover had known, since our busy stay in the Gramercy Park Hotel six years before that, that she had been married and to whom, but hadn't yet heard the tale of that match's end. She was telling him it now (ten years ago) because at her climax-time in our then latest shipboard coupling, which happened to wind up with her atop him, he had happened lightly to press a helpful fore-fingertip into his new woman's rectum. Instead of revving up her joy, the friendly move had caused her to cry out into his open mouth (we were kissing), snatch his hand away, and bound off him in mid-orgasm, bumping her head hard on the cabin headliner. She apologized at once, before *he* could—and only then he remembered a similar push-of-the-wrong-button that energetic night at 2 Lexington Avenue; a similar apology. Though his erection was entirely spooked, she insisted upon remounting him and upon his replacing his fingertip in that touchy socket. No go: He'd felt her tighten up all over. For pity's sake, he'd suggested; let's leave the poor thing alone. There's so much else. But she wanted him to have the works; demanded that he lead her gradually in our nights and years to come to enjoy even occasional anal copulation with him, not to mention the odd friendly goose— We'll see, said Peter—and told him the story of her forest-green recray-oning.

He was only a weakling, old Poonie, and, I understand in retrospect, a disoriented boy in matters sexual. His nickname you'll have guessed to be the affectionate diminutive for "poontang," a then-popular slang term for the main thing you men were alleged to want from us women. Said Peter I know what "poontang" means; I was there. Went on fascinated Kath It's a peculiar class of partitive, no? *Some* nooky; *a little* poontang. Not Let me see your nooky, or I'm going to stuff my putz into your poontang.

Affirmed Peter Sagamore Poontang is never the female genital qua gen-ital, but the female genital sexually delivered or claimed. You were saying.

Willy gave him that nickname when he and Poonie were first learning naughty language, and it stuck. A funny thing about naughty nicknames is that they're just as tenacious as clean ones even though they can never be used publicly. Poonie's parents probably still don't know that that's what nearly everybody who knows their celebrated son calls him among themselves. Most of the Upper Shore upper-crusties sent their kids to the same private lower schools and dancing and riding classes and one another's parties, and so even though the Baldwins lived two counties up from the Sherritts, Willy and Poonie were best friends from kindergarten on and spent lots of time at each other's houses. Poon was always hanging around me and my girlfriends, pestering and teasing us when Willy was with him and wheedling in on our games when he wasn't. I might mention that your public-school type of intersexual bullying was rare in our crowd, and that even back in the late forties and fifties, the cruder sorts of gender distinction were frowned upon, though plenty of less crude ones operated full force. Few of my little girlfriends played with dolls or did needlework, nor did the little boys go in for Cowboys and Indians or GIs and Japs. What we played was sports sports sports, and while the team sports were always segregated and never played outside school, things like tennis and riding and sailing and swimming we were encouraged to do together, as part of our general social training.

All that, said Peter Sagamore, is as foreign to what went on on Hoopers Island in my day as would be the court of Louis Quatorze to New Guinea bushmen.

Said naked Katherine as we gently perspired together in 1970 there on *Story*'s settee berth, she fiddling bemused with her new lover's now flaccid penis, I mention it in order to establish that even Willy kept a foreskin of public manners over the glans of his essential swinery, and that Poonie Baldwin was as charming when he wanted to be, which in fact was most of the time, as he was deceitful and weak and kinky whether he wanted to be or not. I happen to believe that there are unfortunately bad-charactered children who really take pleasure in doing bad things, and okay-charactered children who try out bad things but then feel properly ashamed even if they're not caught, and some really good-charactered children who can rarely be tempted even to experiment with bad things, because they truly dislike them. They think the bad things are bad.

Well, now, said Peter.

By bad, his new friend hastened to explain, she didn't especially mean stuff like You show me yours and I'll show you mine—although that particular category of naughtiness was in fact rare in her childhood circle. What she meant was, you know, lying, stealing, cheating (like maybe *not* showing you mine after we'd agreed and you'd shown me yours), and, let's see, gratuitous cruelty to our fellow animals and so forth. Said Peter I was your middle kind: okay-charactered et cet. Said Katherine So's my kid brother, Chip, whom I'll be glad when you meet: a normal first-rate kid who experiments carefully now and then with the limits and makes the right moral inferences from his experiments. But you're both firm-charactered fellows. Peebie Baldwin—his official nickname, made from his initials— was a weak-charactered middle kind turned into a baddie by his internal contradictions and the intuitive exploitation thereof by Willy Sherritt, himself a baddie at least from the hour of my birth. Yours truly (K was obliged to establish for the purposes of this narrative) was a ninety-nine-percent goodie. To overtease or take unfair advantage of another kid or lie about anything significant seemed as creepy to her as shoplifting or torturing a pet cat.

I did some of those things, Peter confessed. And felt properly creepy.

What I did, once, said Kate, was let Poonie and one of my second-grade girlfriends talk me into playing doctor with them.

God be praised, said gratified Peter: common ground at last between Talbot and Dorchester.

It was at my girlfriend's place on the Wye: a gorgeous spread next door to Wye Plantation, with a swell gazebo down by the river turned into a playhouse for the younger kids. The day before had been Heather Foulke-Stoughton's seventh birthday—

Marveled Peter Heather Foulke-Stoughton. *My* little nurse-patient down in Hoopersville was Sue-Ann Sagamore's gum-cracking girlfriend Ramona Mae Pinder. Heather Foulke-Stoughton! Excuse me.

If Willy had been in on it, K declared, or it'd been Poonie tout court, I'd never have agreed. But the Foulke-Stoughtons were very high-carat even by Gold Coast standards, and I had a crush that fall on red-haired Heather, which is why I'd been allowed to stay over till next day. I forget how come Poonie was there, but he was. The daughter of some doctor-friend-of-the-family had given Heather Foulke-Stoughton a play nurse kit for her birthday, which her mother confiscated right away: Our kind weren't supposed to aspire to the taking of temperatures and the changing of bedpans. Inappropriate items of that sort were passed on to the help, from whom Heather Foulke-Stoughton wheedled this particular item back, so that we could check it out in more detail. I doubt whether I'd've done the same; but Heather Foulke-Stoughton was a girl both willful and a touch intimidating. Green eyes and freckles. I allowed myself to believe with her that we had a right to know what exactly was so terrible about the thing she was being denied.

Uh-oh.

Yeah. So of course after half an hour of taking turns with the stethoscope and the bandages and candy pills, Doctor Baldwin is ready to move on to more interesting areas of internal medicine. So is spunky Heather Foulke-Stoughton, who is currently the patient: Having bound me and Poonie with the usual oaths of reciprocity, she peels out of her undies and presents herself for our examination. Poon's in second heaven; I'm reasonably tit-illated but ever more alarmed as Heather Foulke-Stoughton keeps upping the ante. When she insists that we both check her out all over with the stethoscope, it's *my* heart I hear. She makes a urine specimen for us while we watch, in an empty champagne glass that somebody left in the gazebo and the maids missed. When Poonie says Nurse Sherritt, we'd better have a look at this patient's hiney, Heather Foulke-Stoughton bends over the edge of the picnic table and spreads her own cheeks for us. Heather Foulke-Stoughton graduated from Wellesley summa cum laude and married an Alsatian beer-baron's son and divides her time these days between Strasbourg and Monte Carlo, but her little gray-pink seven-year-old A-hole is fixed forever in my mind's eye: the first I'd seen up close. Tidily puckered, I report, and clean as a whistle.

My turn next, and I was close to tears. I had a strong feeling that Heather Foulke-Stoughton went as far as she did 'cause she knew I'd have trouble doing the same, and that she and Poon were more interested in examining me than I'd been in examining her. But a promise is a promise: I dropped my drawers; I made my pee; I let them count my pulse between my legs. And when hiney-time came, I bent over that table and spread my nervous cheeks.

Stroking his new lover's handsome upper arm, Peter Sagamore said Kiddie porn is not a medium I relish. All the same, I wish it had been me instead of Poonie Baldwin there in Heather Foulke-Stoughton's redheaded gazebo.

Said Katherine Sherritt The point of this episode of this story is that in the interval between patients, Doctor Baldwin's imagination had been at work, with the result that whereas red-haired Heather Foulke-Stoughton's high-carat anus got no more than an intimate visual inspection, mine got its temperature forcibly taken. The manufacturers of kiddie doctor-and-nurse kits apparently know better than to include thermometers, but resourceful Poon had spotted a box of Crayola crayons in the gazebo and, without letting the patient know it, had evidently signaled his intentions to the nurse. When he said We'd better take Miss Sherritt's temperature, Heather Foulke-Stoughton held me chest-down on the table while Poonie pushed a forest-green crayon halfway in. It *hurt,* man, and I yelled loud enough to scare them twice: The main house wasn't all that far from the gazebo, and even Poonie at that age wouldn't have wanted to really hurt me, only to make me say Ouch. He was playing sadist the way he was playing doctor.

Remarked Peter Sagamore Forest green.

Perpend that detail, Katherine instructed. I pulled the crayon out myself, ashamed of my crying but very much afraid that the thing would break off in there and I'd have to be taken to a real doctor. When it was out I threw it away and piled into my panties and out of that gazebo, but not without registering that the color of that Crayola thermometer had been dark green. Nurse and doctor were full of apologies and fears that I'd tattle, which of course I didn't. Soon enough we all made up and went riding on our junior bikes, me somewhat gingerly.

So Poonie never had to deliver.

He'd have been more than happy to, I'm sure, since it was just us girls. What he *did* deliver, some days later, was a *P.B. LOVES K.S.* note written in forest-green crayon, which he teased me by claiming was the same he'd taken my temperature with. It would've been like Poonie to comb the Foulke-Stoughton's gazebo for that crayon. He carried it around with him for a while after; he would take it out when other kids were around and claim that forest-green Crayolas had a particular fragrance that he liked.

Old Poon, said Pete, has a definite down-county streak.

He also from that day forward declared to his parents and my parents and the other kids that he was going to marry me when we grew up. The years pass, and with them, we would have imagined, all recollection of that interlude in Heather Foulke-Stoughton's gazebo. My mortification at which, I forgot to say, was compounded by Poonie's telling Willy about it, who teased me in his usual oafish way for a week or two. Poonie's ongoing crush on me became a standing joke in Talbot and Kent Counties, more at his expense than at mine. Even Willy couldn't mock him out of it.

Observed Peter That bespeaks some character, no? But it's time for me to fade out of this narrative.

Okay. I never doubted that in his peculiar way the boy was attracted to me. And I'd better emphasize that he wasn't a creep: Poonie was lively and witty and bright and a good dancer, and after puberty he grew lean and sort of handsome. He knew how to charm the grown-ups with his manners, and it was flattering to be so adored year after year, even though when dating time came it was usually other boys I went out with. But sometimes I dated Poonie, and we always enjoyed ourselves. With me, at least, he was less aggressive about making out than some of the boys I liked better. He would make me say Stop, the way he made me yell Ouch in the gazebo; then he would not only stop but apologize and quit trying for that evening. It may be of mild sociological interest that, as a group, we Gold Coasties were not sexually precocious by the standards of U.S. public high schools in the Nineteen Fifties. With a few exceptions, the boys who scored scored with public-school girls. Going steady was discouraged both by our parents unanimously and by our separation after puberty into girls' and boys' schools, many of them boarding schools. On weekends and school vacations, we did a lot of dancing and a fair amount of petting in cars and boats and rec rooms and gazebos, but while blouses were unbuttoned and bras sometimes undone, nearly all of us kept our legs together. A lost world.

Up through lower and middle school, Poonie's nickname had been so little more than Willy's joke that we scarcely remembered what it referred to. However, when we all went off to our various upper schools, my brother became the aggressive whoremonger, drunk, and general scapegrace that he remains, and Poonie was his steadfast sidekick. How much poontang they actually *snagged*—that was the locker-room verb then in fashion— may be debatable; the stories Willy brought home from boarding school to Nopoint Point had more to do with the pursuit than with the score, or with Willy's making out in the backseat while Poon passed out in the front. He wrote to me regularly—Poonie, I mean—and I usually wrote back. We were in fact old friends. Despite his declarations of love, I regarded Poon as a wayward but basically decent older brother, less willful and less obnoxious than my real one. Mom and Dad, too, were inclined to sympathize with him and blame his lapses on Willy's influence, which they felt responsible for but couldn't do much about. My brother was impervious to discipline. To get closer to me, Poonie invited my criticism. I'd tell him to drink less and behave himself better, and he'd go through the motions of self-reform, but quickly lapse into his excesses—excessive apology included.

It was generally accepted among the parents that the boys were merely sowing more than the usual crop of wild oats. There was ample precedent in our set for piled-up sports cars and country-club punch-ups and nights in the drunk tank. More particularly, it got to be assumed that eventual marriage to me would straighten Poonie right out, and that Poonie's straightening out would have a good effect on Willy. None of this was put baldly, but it was so consistently in the air that I got the habit of thinking that way myself. Very few of us married till we were done with college, and the end of our college years seemed so far away that it was easy for me to put off thinking clearly about what we were more and more taking for granted.

Dear God, the innocent fifties! Why didn't it ring bells in my head that Poonie Baldwin was overdoing his contempt for queers, who were as unfamiliar to us as Martians in those days? And with all the traveling and reading I'd done by the time I went off to Radcliffe, how come I didn't laugh when he did the old number about being driven to booze and easy pick-ups because I held out on him? The answer is that I really cared about him because our families cared about him. We even cared about Willy Sherritt, whom we didn't like—and Porter Baldwin, Junior, with all his failings, was a likable fellow in those days, and very popular.

Also patient: He had been officially after my virginity for at least four years before I let him in, at the end of my second undergraduate year. I'd dated a number of boys who'd turned me on as Poonie never did, but somehow it worked out that not one of them wowed me enough for long enough for me to want to go to bed with him. This was still only Nineteen Fifty-nine; not many of us saved it for our wedding night, but as a rule we didn't fuck unless we thought we were in love. Poonie had just graduated from Penn and was on his way to law school; in a week we'd have both been back on the Shore for the summer, but he came all the way up to Cambridge to propose that we get engaged that weekend and marry when I finished college. Every year he got more sensitive-looking; that spring he was especially attractive, in a vulnerable-looking way, with his new dark mustache and his ash-blond hair, and that weekend in Boston he was charming. This could have waited a week, I told him; but he admitted he thought his chances were better away from where we'd grown up together. When I turned him down as gently as I could, he started crying, right there in Lockober's Restaurant, where he'd been putting away a lot of champagne to get up his nerve for the proposal. I took him back to my dorm on Linnaean Street—still against the rules in those days—and to cheer him up I promised to reconsider his proposal over the summer.

The boy went into a fit of gratitude: weeping all over me, kissing me up and down—and begging me to go to bed with him. By some odd reasoning it seemed to me that since I wasn't ever going to marry him, I ought to give him what he'd been after for so many years, and that's what I did: a sort of go-away present. Poon had trouble getting it up, he was so excited; then he came right away. My whole deflowering took less than a minute. Afterward he kept gravitating to my ass, begging me to let him kiss it even though he didn't deserve to, et cet.

Remember, it was my first time out: I had expected more attention to other areas—but then, I'd expected a number of things that hadn't happened. I let him go to it, till I found out that it wasn't my buns he was after, but my asshole, with his tongue. When I turned him off, he made his usual apologies and asked me whether I remembered what we'd done when we were kids in Heather Foulke-Stoughton's gazebo. I guess I hadn't, till he mentioned it; *he* not only remembered every detail, but managed to turn the story into a disarming explanation of his eagerness to get back there again. If you knew Poonie, you'd understand.

Well: A week later, back home for the summer, I found out from Jack Bass that what had been itching me like crazy for the past couple days was crab lice. You really *can* get them nonsexually, Doctor Jack told me, from a bedspread or a toilet seat or a laundry bag where your underwear gets mixed in with somebody else's. I told him not to bother; that I'd got mine in the usual way, and that he'd better check me out for clap and syphilis while he was down there. Then I called up Poonie Baldwin in a grand rage that got grander yet when he hemmed and hawed and finally confessed that he'd been scratching himself since the day *before* he came up to Cambridge, and had found out two days later that he and Willy and four other guys had all got the crabs from a fraternity-house whore in Philadelphia. He hadn't told me, he said, because he'd been busy praying that he hadn't passed them on to me, and he was afraid I'd have nothing to do with him if he told me to check with my doctor right away after I'd given him my virginity. His phrase.

You're right, I told him, and hung up. That should've been that. But it was summertime, my last summer at home, and all our old crowd would get together on the weekends at Nopoint Point or this yacht club or that for the sailing races, and Poonie was simply contrite about what had happened. No more sex, but we got to be friends again, and he tried hard to watch his drinking when I was around. By the time he went down to law school at Emory and I went back up to Radcliffe in September, I'd forgiven him, and he was pressing again for us to get engaged.

Why in the world did I say yes, Peter? I guess because after the crab-lice episode, the man seemed more grown-up than he'd seemed before. He'd behaved himself for a whole summer, while Willy raised more hell than ever. And because Jeanne and Porter Baldwin, Senior, were such dear friends of Hank's and Irma's and had always been so good to me. And because no *real* man had ever managed to touch my heart. I'd had such a happy and privileged life, and I loved my parents and our whole crowd so much . . . it's as if I was mesmerized, the way people get at the beach sometimes or out sailing on a perfect afternoon. But there has to have been something wrong with me, right? Some kind of vacuum at the center, that made me love the life around Nopoint Point more than I loved any particular man. It was as if by marrying Poonie Baldwin I'd be strengthening the team. I got engaged to Poonie pretending to myself that I would come to love him, when what I really felt was some kind of school spirit left over from Deniston.

As far as any of us knew, our engagement and Poonie's law studies really did straighten him out for the next year and a half. He and I didn't see much of each other except on school holidays; the next summer he was legal-interning in Baltimore, and I took a cataloguing job at one of Harvard's libraries to see whether I was interested in making a career of it. When we were together we had sex, as they say; it was never terrific, but I guessed it was normal enough. What did I know? Old Poon was a better cunnilinguist than a cocksman, but at least he left my rectum alone. Mainly we danced a lot and made plans for the wedding. He was a very happy and very nervous fiancé; I was pleased because our parents were so pleased. Only Jack Bass seemed less than delighted—the crab-louse business, I guessed, which he had put two and two together about—but he kept his reservations to himself.

At our wedding reception, the bridegroom overdid it with the champagne, as he did once or twice in Bermuda on our honeymoon, and the bride didn't get humped till the morning after. By the time we set up housekeeping in Centreville, where Porter Senior's law offices were, I was already having a few dark doubts. Whether we were making love or just horsing around in our new swimming pool, Poonie had a habit of hurting me—playfully, you know, but repeatedly—until it really did hurt and I made a noise or scolded him. Then he'd either sulk or go into his abject-apology routine. Soon enough his anal interest reared its head again, so to speak; he called me a prude for not letting him grease me up and go in there. I understood that anal intercourse was considered okay by some broad-minded couples, but so was group sex and wife swapping, which I didn't have any taste for either. It hurt enough when Poonie stuck his finger in there, which he did as often as he could. Asshole rights got to be such an issue between us that I checked with Jack Bass, who told me very firmly not to let the guy in there more than rarely: No matter what the permissive sexologists claim, anal copulation weakens the bowel action, quoth Doctor Jack, and conduces to rectal infibulation, hemorrhoids, and various kinds of infection. Poonie complained that I wouldn't do it even rarely, and I realized that I simply didn't love him enough to take pleasure in doing things with him that were uncomfortable and distasteful to me. I began to worry seriously then that our marriage was a dreadful mistake; but we were still newlyweds, and Mom and Dad and the Baldwins had given us such an elaborate wedding that I was too embarrassed to tell them my troubles. I had to hope we'd work things out.

Assholes. Since I wouldn't let him into mine, Poonie kept after me to finger-fuck him in his. In his way, he was as innocent as I was. He thought of himself as liberal-minded and me as frigid; he must have had a few homosexual connections already, but he didn't understand yet that he was basically gay, and I didn't realize that with a normal man I'd have shed my inhibitions with my underwear, the way I finally did in the Gramercy Park Hotel. When I said no to him, he got angry and drunk and did the old If You Won't Do It I Know Somebody Who Will routine. A couple of times he tried to force me, and I really blew up. A couple of other times he went off with Willy to the city for a weekend; he'd come back subdued and apologetic, or else resentful. After three or four months of marriage, we both knew we were in trouble: There was virtually no sex between us anymore; I was beginning to think maybe I *was* frigid. Poonie regarded himself as normal because Willy was a drunk and a bully too, but the differences between them must have been coming clear; in his heart of hearts he was *hoping* he was normal.

So we argued, and I worried, and he drank too much and got either abusive or weepy or comatose. Finally I told him he had to see a shrink about the alcohol, and we'd do marriage counseling together about our sexual problems. At first he refused: There *was* no problem, except my frigidity. Then he agreed—but to the sex counseling only, and only after we were pregnant. He'd got the idea that having a baby would solve our problems; he actually told me that motherhood would make me feel more like a woman, when the truth was that fatherhood would make him feel more like a man. He was also beginning to think about running for Congress, and he wanted the family image for his campaign.

I said Absolutely not, and laid down the law: six months on the wagon and joint sex therapy over at Johns Hopkins, where there was a counselor Jack Bass trusted. If we felt good about our marriage at the end of that time, we'd try for pregnancy. Poonie got so furious—and so drunk—that for the first time he raised his arm to hit me. I threatened to leave him if he did, and that night I refused to sleep in our bed with him: another first. He turned on the tears, and we made an appointment with the shrink for the following week.

Poon obviously sensed that he had deep problems. He felt so relieved at the step we'd taken that for one whole evening he was perfectly charming. He drank straight tonic water; he was witty at the dinner table, the way he'd always used to be. We put records on after dinner and danced on our patio, and for the first time in our married life we made love like a normal couple: affectionate foreplay followed by a solid fuck. I even had myself a little orgasm, which I pretended was a big one, and fell asleep afterward in his arms. *That* made him feel so good about himself that he slipped out of bed and downstairs to the bar and drank himself into a stupor.

When I found him down there toward morning, I told him that was it: We'd made a big mistake and had better unmake it and get on with our separate lives before things got worse. I would pack some stuff and get out while he was at the office; we'd work out the details later. Poonie begged me to forgive him once again; he'd been so excited at taking a step forward that he'd let himself slip two steps back. I told him I *did* forgive him, but didn't want to be his wife. I hoped he'd get help with his booze problem and find himself a partner more to his taste.

So he got ugly and called me things. Then he calmed down and agreed that I was right to leave, but hoped we could straighten ourselves out. Then he phoned from the office, all choked up, and begged me to stay; he said he was afraid of himself, what he might do or turn into. He'd never talked like that before. I quit mooning over our wedding gifts and started collecting my stuff in a hurry to get out of there and down to Nopoint Point.

But I didn't make it. Centreville is a tiny town, reader: The offices of Baldwin and Baldwin were five minutes from our house. I had hardly got my suitcases out of the attic when his car came up the driveway, and I heard Poonie come in the side door and start banging things around downstairs at the bar. Oh boy, I thought. I was up in our bedroom, still in my nightgown, with clothes and luggage spread all over the bed. I thought to call the police, but it's harder to bring yourself to do that in a small town than it is in the city, where you don't know all the cops by name. Anyhow, the chances were that the most I was in for was more tears and namecalling. My main concern was to get out of that nightgown and into street clothes.

I heard him start upstairs, grumbling to himself, so I pulled off the nightgown and popped into underpants and a skirt, and I couldn't find my damn bra so I grabbed a blouse and was just buttoning it up when Poonie came in like a refugee from a Eugene O'Neill play: necktie loose, hair messed up, a bottle of Jack Daniel's in one hand and an ugly little pistol in the other, that I didn't even know he owned. Good old America.

He asked me where I thought I was going. I turned my back on him and started tucking in my blouse. He actually fired a shot—through one of the suitcases and the bed, it turned out, and into the bedroom floor. The bang was so loud I jumped. Poonie stood between me and the telephone with a surprised grin on his face, looking at the pistol. There was actually gunsmoke in the room! I said That does it, Poonie, and ran around him to the phone. I think he was a little dazed; he didn't stop me at first— but I didn't know the police number, so I had to ring the operator. Before she answered, Poonie put down the bottle and snatched at the phone, and when I wouldn't let go he yanked out the jack and wrestled me down on the bed on top of all my spread-out clothes and put the pistol to my neck.

If a stranger had broken into the house and done that, I'd have been too scared to resist. But this was my old pal Poonie Baldwin, that I'd grown up with! Gun or no gun, I kicked and hollered and slammed him around the face with the telephone until he gave me a whack upside the head with the flat of his pistol. It shocked and hurt me so much that I rolled over onto my stomach and wailed. Maybe I thought he'd apologize then, the way he always did when he went too far. Instead, he tied my wrists behind me with the telephone cord and raped me.

Strictly speaking, what he did was force me against my will; in those days it was still legally impossible for a woman to be raped by her husband. Once he had my hands tied, he pulled my skirt and underpants off and turned me on my back and put the pistol to my neck again. I should've kicked and yelled like before; I didn't really think he'd shoot me. But the side of my face hurt so much where he'd hit me, and I was so stunned and upset by the whole situation, I just bawled. Damn me for that!

Poonie drank another slug or two from the bottle and took his time getting his own pants off. Then he opened my legs and wet me with spit and fucked me in the missionary position: very uncomfortable with your hands behind your back and a Princess telephone under your shoulder-blades. As a rule the guy came fast, as if he were nervous about being in there in the first place. But the combination of flat-out sadism and Jack Daniel's bourbon improved his staying power. He talked at me the whole time, and paused every now and then to take a left-handed swig from the bottle on the nightstand without withdrawing, while he held the gun to my throat or my forehead. He told me I was a frigid snob who needed loosening up. He told me he'd fucked a hundred women in his life and every one of them had been better in bed than I was. He accused me of accusing him of not being man enough for me, when the fact was I wasn't woman enough for him. In fact I'd never said any such thing; it was his own insecurity talking. He still had his shirt and tie on: a maroon club tie I'd bought him in Easton just before we were married, when I was persuading myself that I loved him. It dangled in my face while he was raping and haranguing me, like a taunt to my bad judgment.

When he finally came and climbed off me, he kept up his tirade from a chair beside the nightstand. I was too miserable to say anything. The left side of my face hurt so much that I wondered if he'd broken something, and on top of my other worries his ejaculation reminded me that I was ovulating. On the rare occasions when it was needed in those days, I used a diaphragm, but that morning I'd stowed it in my suitcase, not expecting to need it again for quite a while.

I asked him please to undo my hands; the phone cord hurt, and I wanted to go douche and put an ice pack on my face. He said You and your douches; you're always in a rush to wash me out of you. I told him this was no joke; he'd hurt me, and I was ovulating.

That was a mistake. Poonie started in about my refusing to have children with him: another example of my being too good for him, and he was damned fed up with that; I'd been lording it over him since we were kids, and from now on things were going to be different. If I didn't give him what he wanted, he'd take it, et cetera.

He made me stay put and drank some more whiskey. He'd loved me all his life, he said, and I'd never really loved him back, and that's why he drank too much and went to whores who'd give him what I wouldn't, blah blah blah. Drunken postcoital schmaltz. Did you know that human sperm can be retained alive in the cervix for two or three days until an ovum comes along? But if the egg's already in the pipe, they can do their job in five minutes. Poonie made me lie still for half an hour, holding the gun on me and saying things like maybe having his baby would make a better woman out of me.

After a while he started fiddling with himself, and I thought Uh-oh. While he was doing that, he had to put the pistol down on the nightstand every time he picked up the Jack Daniel's. If my hands had been free, I'd have made a go for the gun. Maybe I should've screamed bloody murder anyhow, but nobody would've heard me, and Poonie had enough liquor in him now to make me worry.

Hey: I forgot to mention that this was a beautiful late-winter morning: a little glaze of snow on the ground, and the trees glistening from a sleet storm the night before, and the bedroom full of sunshine. It broke my heart, what a huge mistake I'd made with my life. Poonie kept saying Princess Kate, too good for anybody; it was time he showed Miss Sherritt how to share it.

Well, I just lay there, sniffling and hurting and feeling sorry for myself, and when he ordered me down on my knees in front of his chair with my face in the blue shag wall-to-wall and my ass in the air, I guess I knew what was coming, but I got down there. He undid my wrists and made me spread my cheeks and greased me up with Vaseline from his nightstand drawer—I never knew he kept Vaseline in his nightstand drawer—and sure enough, he tried to bugger me, but his erection wasn't hard enough to force me open. The anal sphincter is a mighty muscle, and it can have a mind of its own. So he used his thumb, to the hilt, and when that didn't work I heard him scrabbling around in his nightstand drawer again. I was afraid he'd use the gun barrel, or the Jack Daniel's bottle; I told him I was *trying* to relax for him, but just couldn't do it.

He said We'll see about that and stuck something slender and hard and pointy in there that made me cry out. He pushed it in and pulled it out a few times and then scared the bejesus out of me by putting the tip end of the gun there after all and telling me to open up for him or else. As if my ass was a safe-deposit box! But that did it, thank God, and the man got what he was after at last. He drove clear in and stayed there a few seconds while he scraped something across my back. I let out a yell, as much fright as pain, and he drove in again and came with such a groan you'd have thought he was the one getting hurt, and collapsed on top of me. Right away then he started crying, rolling us over onto one side and shmooshing his face into my hair and begging me to forgive him, and in his drunken remorse he made the mistake of letting go of the pistol while he hugged my shoulders.

There it was, on the rug, right in front of my eyes. I grabbed it and jumped away from him and tore out of that bedroom and downstairs to the other phone. Poonie got himself up and came after me, sort of wailing. I'd never held a pistol in my hand before, much less fired one, and for all I knew the thing didn't have any more bullets in it; but I was in such a fury that when he followed me into the kitchen I shot at the floor in front of him and managed to nail him in the foot by mistake. It turns out that what actually happened was the bullet ricocheted off the quarry tile before it grazed the inside of his left heel; otherwise it would've done real damage. Poonie hollered and thrashed, and there was lots of blood, and I nearly fainted from shock.

But I didn't. That gunshot cleared my head the way the one upstairs had stunned me. I changed my mind about calling the sheriff and got out the first-aid kit instead. It was Poonie who fainted, from shock and alcohol, while I put a bandage on his heel to stop the bleeding and saw that despite the mess I hadn't much more than nicked him. By the time I had him bandaged up, he was breathing normally; he woke up enough to apologize all over himself again and then fell into a drunken sleep on the quarry tile. I put an afghan over him—our wedding gift from Molly Barnes—but I let him lie there bare-assed in his shirt and tie and blood while I telephoned Porter Baldwin, Senior, and my father and told them to come over, there was a sort of family emergency, and Dad to bring Jack Bass with him if he could, but not to say anything yet to Mom.

Mister Baldwin was there in ten minutes; it took nearly an hour for Dad to collect Doctor Jack and drive up from Easton. I turned up the thermostat to keep myself warm, but refused to put clothes on or set down the pistol till everybody was there. A mighty uncomfortable fifty minutes for Porter Senior. Did Peebie *attack* you, honey? Shouldn't we get you both to the hospital? He didn't want to stare at me, and he was plenty worried about the blood and the pistol and my beat-up face and Poonie's bandaged foot. I told him I'd been attacked, all right, and his son would explain it when he woke up from his nap, and maybe I should make us all some coffee.

A main concern of fathers and fathers-in-law in these circumstances is to get the young lady's clothes back on her and the firearms stashed away; but sorry as I felt for Mister Baldwin, I wouldn't be rushed. When everybody was there, I told them what had happened and showed them the bullet holes upstairs and the ripped-out Princess phone on the rug and the bottle of Jack Daniel's on the nightstand. Poonie was stirring by that time, so I let Doctor Jack wake him up and check out his foot, and I gave Daddy the pistol and told him and Mister Baldwin to ask Poon a few questions while Doctor Jack examined me: I wanted evidence for legal prosecution. We two went back up to the famous bedroom, and while Jack Bass poked around inside me, he told me he'd had his doubts about this marriage all right, even before the crab lice and my questions about anal intercourse, but he hadn't wanted to be a killjoy. He confirmed that there was semen in both my vagina and my rectum, as well as green markings on my buns and my back. I told him what I'd felt down on that rug, but I didn't put two and two together till we looked around on the floor and found a forest-green Crayola with blood and shit and Vaseline on it. I checked Poonie's nightstand drawer; there was the Vaseline jar, with the top still off, but no crayon box. All Poonie wanted was the forest green.

For the first time in all this ruckus I felt embarrassed then, and a little ashamed of myself and sorry for Poonie Baldwin. I didn't tell Jack Bass what had happened in Heather Foulke-Stoughton's gazebo a hundred years before, but I asked him to hang onto that forest-green Crayola as evidence for the prosecution, and I put a robe around me at last, and we went downstairs, and I let myself cry a little when Daddy hugged me and Mister Baldwin fixed me an ice pack for my face.

Well, old Poon there was a pretty sick boy by that time, and a pretty sorry one. He'd been throwing up and making excuses and blaming me for not doing my wifely duty and blaming Willy and his parents for turning him into what he was. But Porter Senior was an old trial lawyer, and Hank Sherritt was one very upset daddy, and the two of them got the truth out of him between upchucks. Jack Bass corroborated that I'd been sodomized and Crayola'd as well as beaten in the face and bound and raped—the men had seen those green marks on me already. But when I told them I was ready to talk to the police now, they clucked and hmmed and then explained to me that I could bring assault-and-battery charges if I was determined to, but not rape, since the attacker was my husband.

I was wild! Never mind that a jury might let Poonie off, though I couldn't imagine why—but not to be able even to file the charges! I hauled up my robe and made them look at the marks on my ass again and told Jack Bass to show them that crayon, and I said You mean he can get away with this too? They were three uncomfortable gentlemen, but they explained that that would come under aggravated assault. I swore I was going to tell every detail to every newspaper and TV reporter who'd listen, and get the wretched laws changed; never mind anybody's reputation, and Poonie could just forget about running for public office. They let me go on till I was ventilated, and they promised to stand by me whatever I decided and to testify if I wanted them to. But they hoped for everybody's sake that I'd consider a quick and quiet divorce with a generous settlement instead of a big public fuss that would make life sticky for all of them, not just for Poonie, small towns being what they are.

That must be what I wanted to be talked into—all but the settlement. Give the money to a rape crisis center, I told them; give it to some outfit for battered wives. I ended up not calling in the sheriff at all, much less pressing charges. I wouldn't even take half the value of our house and furniture when the time came; *I* hadn't paid for any of it, and the associations were all painful. Dad helped me finish packing my clothes, and I moved back home till I could get my bearings. I told Mom the story and let her scrub the crayon marks off me, so she wouldn't feel left out. But I didn't tell her or anybody else till you just now the real secret of the forest-green Crayola.

When the smoke cleared and the lawyers started talking, Poonie came to see me. He'd already apologized to Hank and Irma. He asked me what in the world he could do to get us back together again and straighten out his life before he went off the deep end for keeps. I told him I believed he really was sorry and really did love me in his way, but that our marriage had been a huge mistake all around, and nothing on earth would get us back together. I told him he was off the deep end already, in my opinion, though maybe not for keeps, and I advised him for his own and our families' sake to move away from the Eastern Shore, as I was going to do for different reasons, and to get on the wagon and stay there, and to come off his scornfulness about dykes and faggots, because he sure had hang-ups of his own, and to consider some heavy shrinkage for his impulse to hurt women, but not to expect any fantastic results, and not for pity's sake to run for public office till he got his private life in better shape. And if none of the above panned out, I advised him, he should seriously consider using that pistol of his on himself instead of on other people, for he was a miserable, worthless, dangerous sonofabitch as he was.

Well, he did try some of those things, as a matter of fact, but they didn't work. When we were safely split and things had quieted down, Poon found himself another nice dumb Deniston girl to marry, whom I should have warned but didn't, and they set up housekeeping over in Saint Marys County, and things seemed to go his way. He had himself a pair of children to be photographed with and became an archconservative, and he's rising fast in the state Republican organization these days and hopes to run for Congress in a couple of years, even though it's an open secret now that he's a lush if not a flat-out alky and a closet gay as well, who covers his ass by cozying up to the Moral Majority. I worry now and then about the physical integrity of his new wife's rectum, but that's her business, no? At least he's out of mine.

So I found out I was pregnant from aggravated assault, and Doctor Jack took care of that, and I went up to New York for a while for a change of scene and jumped you that night at the Ninety-second Street Poetry Center and got a taste of what I'd been missing. You must have wondered what you'd fallen into! And then down to D.C. and the U. of M. and those other boyfriends and then May Jump and now you again. Good old May was so indignant when I told her the Poonie Baldwin story that she made me learn karate so I can cripple the next sumbitch tries to lay a hand on me where I don't want one laid, but I haven't gotten that good yet, but I will.

So now you know why you found me a little skittish back there and also up in the Gramercy Park Hotel when it came to hineyholes, Katherine Shorter Sherritt told Peter Sagamore aboard *Story* in Poplar Island Harbor in 1970. The reader understands now too our woman's particular fascination with that lexicon of homosexual slang from which she gave her closed-circuit reading in the First Guest Cottage early in this book. Boy-oboy, she sighed (Poplar I., 1970): I bet your friend Marcie Blitz there took it up the tush and loved it.

Said Peter Sagamore Never mind my friend Marcie Blitz, and let's get tushes off our minds for a while. I'm gratified to hear the tale of your sorry first marriage and the subsequent seasoning and annealing of your heart. I do not tire of such confidences, unless boastful on the one hand or abject on the other, and they are safe with me.

Well, then, his fine new woman said, your turn, but her fine new man said Another time: I didn't promise to show you mine yet. It is a long way, he tells her now while we wait on Rhode River for a breeze, from the Doomsday Factor to the Forest-Green Crayola Factor. But the seamy undersides of power and the seamy backsides of the powerful are as one in the seamless web of our tidewater tales, which should likewise incorporate

THE STORY OF PETER SAGAMORE'S MEETING HIMSELF
FORTY YEARS LATER SEVENTEEN YEARS SINCE.

Back in Sixty-three, while Poonie B. was doing his number on you in Centreville, Maryland, I was over in Sagres, Portugal, getting myself dehicked and recovering from Jean Heartstone of blessed memory.

K murmurs Yeah: Jean Heartstone. She knows this part of the story, all right: Peter Sagamore's graduate-school romance, which had led to both his vow of bachelorhood and his precocious bilateral vasectomy. No need for him to retell it. Jean Heartstone was an apprentice poet from Portland, Oregon, who believed, among many another unusual thing, that proper names have the power of self-fulfilling prophecy and that language in general and writing in particular have such magical properties that the future is highly contingent upon what we read and write as well as what we are called. Jean Heartstone had been a little daft and a little scary but also gifted and in her rangy way beautiful when Peter Sagamore met her in Baltimore. Her surname was in fact a corruption of Hearthstone, and by inclination she was both passionate-hearted and domestically inclined, a great baker of fruit breads and maker of love and macramés back before the sixties became the Sixties; a keeper of injured birds in shoe boxes; an antivivisectionist and vegetarian whose zucchini frittatas could make a Bengal tiger forget about meat, briefly. But while the horny young men among her fellow graduate-student apprentice writers spoke yearningly of getting into Heartstone's jeans, the poet herself took her name as a genealogical instruction to harden herself against consequential emotional attachments (her parents were unamicably divorced) and to give herself altogether to the causes of radical politics and a politico-magical poetry wrought from left-wing charms and curses. In lines as spare as Emily Dickinson's, though less cool, Jean Heartstone assisted the overthrow of Fulgencio Batista by Fidel Castro's Oriente guerrillas and the election to U.S. president of John F. Kennedy—whom she would later inadvertently overcurse for permitting the Bay of Pigs invasion and unintentionally thereby cause to be assassinated. Her guilt in this matter, together with her abuse of lysergic acid and her admiration of the wrong role models among latter-day American poets, would lead before that volatile decade's end to her severe mental breakdown and ultimately to her suicide by unassisted headlong flight into a Pennsylvania granite quarry in the conviction that she was recycling her flinty heart.

Jean Heartstone's interest in Peter Sagamore had begun more with his first name than with his second. He had loved her so furiously from October through May of their one-year graduate program that he took for granted they'd do Europe together upon becoming certified masters of arts and set literature ablaze with their mutual talent and reciprocal passion. During the university's Easter break, however, he made the misstep of drafting a story about two talented apprentice writers, not unlike themselves, who marry and beget children. The man of the couple becomes an internationally successful poet but a failure as a father; he regards his books as his true offspring, and his merely human ones grow up to despise both him and literature. The woman turns into so excellent a mother that she neglects her fiction, regarding her children as her true creation, and never quite makes it as the novelist she had promisingly bid to become.

Merely hearing this plot summary of that story had caused Jean Heartstone to conceive Peter Sagamore's child on Good Friday afternoon despite diaphragm and spermicidal douche—she happened not to trust birth control pills, but they would have availed her nothing in any case against the power of language—and then to abort it "spontaneously" but deliberately two months later, on Commencement Day, having refused in the interim either to terminate the pregnancy or to marry the fetus's father despite his entreaties to that end and his protests that the story (which became his first published work) was pure fiction, as witness his reversal of the two writers' métiers. In a desperate effort not to lose her, he talked a progressive young urologist into vasectomizing him and offered to defect with Jean Heartstone to British Columbia in June, though U.S. involvement in Southeast Asia was still less than massive at that time. Impressed by the audacity of his gesture, but convinced that that story had irrevocably hexed her literary career, Jean Heartstone dismissed him and became the shrug-shouldered sexual property of perhaps the only overtly lesbian ex-con writer in Greater Baltimore at that time: a pretentious and ungrammatical poetastress with one-tenth Jean Heartstone's talent, who was not at all nice to her but had done time in both the Rosewood Training School for delinquent girls and the Patuxent Institution in Jessup and was never dopeless. In short order, this person pimped Jean Heartstone out to a number of her male drug connections, some one of whom impregnated her. This second fetus she carried with her on her short flight into that granite quarry.

But by then, heart-wounded Peter Sagamore had hitchhiked and backpacked from Le Havre down through France and Spain and over to Portugal, in defiance of Jean Heartstone's metered curses upon Messrs. Franco and Salazar and the tourist dollars that helped support their governments; he was wintering cheaply out on the Sagres end of the Algarve, in those days and in that season still richer in fisherfolk than in tourists. For months he watched the Atlantic roll in from the wrong direction and searched the rock-locked beaches in bemused vain for those water messages he had dispatched as a boy from Hoopers Island. He was neither lonely nor self-sorry, though when word reached him of Jean Heartstone's end, he spent a devastated week on the dizziest cliffs of the Sagres headland, where Prince Henry the Navigator's navigators' college was, imagining how it would be to smash himself like the surf upon those rocks a hundred meters below. He resorbed into his bloodstream nearly a billion of his spermatozoa and dedicated his more or less enforced celibacy to his late lover. He did not regret having had himself sterilized except for the metaphorical implications, to counter which—since his bereavement and isolation precluded ready sexual encounters despite his good looks and his ease with strangers—he engendered a very swarm of fiction, and in the process discovered his authorial voice and his essential subject matter. He completed his apprenticeship under no further masters save the mighty dead, and commenced his professional writing career. By the time he rearrived in the USA, he would find himself arriving in its literary magazines, have an agent and a contract for his first novel, and be busily drafting his second and planning his third. Meanwhile, having mourned Jean Heartstone in energetic celibacy on the Ponta da Piedade, through the rest of his European reconnaissance he exorcised her the other way, sowing his semen but not his seed in Portugal, Spain, Italy, Austria, Germany, Denmark, the Netherlands, Belgium, France, England, Scotland, and Wales. The more he traveled, the more his imagination fixed fruitfully upon the lower Dorchester marshes; once home, he took a writer-in-residency at Oregon State University, in honor of Jean Heartstone, but spent that fine rainy Northwest year telling midAtlantic-modernist tideflat tales. There followed similar appointments in New York and Boston, in which latter city began the next major chapter of his romantic-erotic life, starring Marcie Blitz *née* Blitzstein—and that is where the reader came in, but it is not the story P's telling K now to whistle up a breeze behind Big Island.

Back there on Ponta da Piedade, he declares, I could read Spanish okay and Portuguese poorly and neither well enough to enjoy books in the language. I was so thirsty for written English that I reread over and over the few books I'd brought with me: *The Odyssey,* the Modern Library abridgment of *The Arabian Nights, Don Quixote, Huckleberry Finn*—even my pocket dictionary and encyclopedia and my own manuscripts. It was partly to have something new to read that I wrote so much that year; I even transcribed my dreams every morning before breakfast, and here we go:

My undergraduate dreams at College Park were the dullest I ever heard of; I seriously used to wonder whether anybody whose unconscious was so tiresome could ever become the writer I'd made up my mind to try to be. In graduate school, they got even worse. Day after day from dawn till past midnight I wrestled with literature and language and lean Jean Heartstone, and night after night all I'd dream was my voice saying things like *In graduate school comma they got even worse new sentence.* By Thanksgiving, my dreams were like the hum of an electric typewriter between typings; by Christmastime, they were like the ongoing intergalactic echo from the Big Bang, detectable only by the most discerning sensors.

Jean Heartstone, who happened to be both an expert on dreams and an expert dreamer, told me that my trouble was I didn't take dreams seriously, which was true. It was part of Heartstone's Magic Language Theory that to dream more interesting dreams, I'd have to take more interest in them, and that the way to do that was to resolve—in writing—to keep a detailed written record of them, as she did.

For a while, it worked. As soon as I decided to write the damn things out every morning, a whole Dickensload of memorable characters swarmed onstage night after night. The scenes and situations were terrific; the action was lively; the plots weren't half bad even when I recollected them in the morning. I was particularly impressed that these dreams had nothing whatever to do with my waking concerns—not even symbolically, as far as I could see. Both asleep and awake, I related to those dreams the way a good reader relates to a good novel: with detached but total absorption.

As my dreams got better, my fiction got worse, so I gave up transcribing my dreams for Lent and wrote that fatal Easter-vacation story, but that's beside the point of this digression. The point of this digression is that since dreams belong in the category more of things that happen to us than of things we do, the Heartstone dream-improvement theory really was a self-fulfilling prophecy. And the bearing of that point upon the story of my meeting myself in mid-ocean is that almost the only thing I could find to read in English in my part of Portugal, other than the household gods in my backpack, was a couple of Bollingen Press mythology books by Carl Jung and Joseph Campbell, left behind by some tourist in the library of a little beach hotel in Lagos near where I lived on Piety Point. Reading Jung got me to dreaming so strongly about old Jean Heartstone that once again I had to quit writing my dreams down so they'd get less interesting. Without any dreams to record, I had more time to write my stories, which perked right up as my dreams got dumber, and also to read Campbell and company on the subject of the ground-myth of the wandering hero, which became more important to me than it would've become if there'd been more stuff to read in Lagos.

Okay, reader: Campbell says that your typical mythical wandering hero, whose biography corresponds to Jung's individuation-psychology and Erik Erikson's rites of passage and other stuff, at a certain point in his heroical career sets out westward on a night-sea voyage or what have you to his True Original Home, in the course of which he undergoes various initiation trials and sheds various ego trappings and dives down to the heart of mystery, et cetera. Among his typical adversaries, along with physical obstacles and father types like dragons and ogres and wicked magicians, will be assorted alter-ego figures: dark brothers, mirrors, tar babies—and doubles. When the time came for me to quit bopping around Europe and come home, instead of flying I took a Greek Line ship that happened to be sailing from Southampton to New York. I was all but broke, but I couldn't say no to a westbound homeward voyage on a Greek boat setting sail in the evening of the summer solstice. I was ten years under age; your proper mythic hero does his thing somewhere between thirty-three and thirty-six. But as it happened, the story I was working up at the time had to do with a latter-day marsh-country messiah who becomes as aware of this pattern of mythic herohood as an actor is aware of his script, and yet who feels authentically called to some kind of mythic herohood—he's not sure exactly what kind. This paradox reminds him of the New Testament Jesus, who for example healed the sick, Saint Matthew says, in order that Esaias's prophecy might be fulfilled: that the Messiah would heal the sick. Jesus knows the Old Testament messianic prophecies like the back of his hand; he also knows he's the Messiah. My tidewater webfoot hero knows the prophecies plus the Jesus story plus all the wandering-hero-savior myths of other cultures, and I myself had digested all those plus that heavy diet of Jung and Campbell plus my story-in-progress, which was threatening to collapse from sheer vertigo, plus my notes for its continuation. Wherein, having survived those initiatory ordeals and made his westward night-sea journey from Hoopers Island across the Chesapeake to maybe Washington, D.C., the hero must confront his mysterious destiny.

Now, then: Cocky as I was at age twenty-three and -four, I've never felt called to any vocation more heroical than making up English sentences about imaginary people. But there I was, circling homeward on a literal night-sea voyage and farther westbound yet, feeling truly summoned as a writer but still at sea and in the dark about every other aspect of my life. What was happening was happening in order that it might be fulfilled which was spoken by Heartstone the prophet, saying, Dreams are causes, not effects; what we write is not autobiography, but prophecy in disguise. I understood then that her restless ghost was playing the role of Hero's Helper: Venus to my Aeneas, Virgil to my Dante. As the boat left port, I poured a libation of Metaxa brandy over the taffrail, to Jean Heartstone, and waited to see what would happen next. Whirlpool? Sword bridge? Sea monster?

Half an hour later, I saw my double sitting across from me at a U-shaped bar just off the tourist-class sun deck.

He didn't look like my father or my brother, Kath; he was my clone, only older. He didn't look like what I look like now, seventeen yearsworth of stories later; he looked like what I'll look like another twenty-some yearsworth of stories from now, with luck.

I suppose with luck. My double looked physically fit for a man in his sixties, but not at all animated, and neither happy nor unhappy. He had curly gray hair and okay teeth and a moderate tan; he wore no glasses except to read, and his eyes were clear but tired-looking. Other than our age and clothing, the only difference I could see between us was our taste in nightcaps: his was Amstel dark beer; mine was Metaxa. It surprised me that neither the bartender nor the other passengers in the room nor either of us commented on our likeness, which was truly remarkable, but we didn't. We drank our drinks and went our ways.

Through the five days of our passage, I never saw my double smile or frown or for that matter speak to anyone. He dressed in ordinary conservative taste: light slacks and pullover sweaters by day—it was cool out there, even in late June—business suits in the evening. I'd see him strolling the decks and corridors, reading in the ship's library, or leaving the first sitting in the tourist-class dining room as I was going in for the second. He sat and walked very erect, shoulders back. He was always alone. I imagined him to be a professional man: maybe a doctor or a dentist; maybe a lawyer in estates and trusts. He seemed to me to be retired as well as retiring: a successful oral surgeon or orthopedist who'd made prudent investments and quit early. A widower, maybe, whose grown children had urged a change of scene upon their straitlaced father, still bereft some years after their mother's death.

He was as aware of our resemblance as I was, I was sure of that, and just as fascinated and mildly disconcerted from the other side of the years between us. Our eyes would meet; as we crossed the time zones, each of us would notice now and then that his double had been regarding him. Immediately we'd turn our eyes away.

He can't have found me prepossessing: one more blue-jeaned young American en route home from doing Europe on the cheap, and not much wiser than he'd been before he left. He himself, maybe, had been more of a man of the world at my age. He was a child of the century; his twenties had been the Twenties. What Cunard memories he maybe carried from the North Atlantic's heyday: his slim, small-breasted fiancée in cloche hat and knee-fringed dress; himself dolled up in John Held, Junior, drag; confetti and champagne at sailing time, and isn't that the Scott Fitzgeralds yonder across the bar?

Our situation could generate any number of stories—though I've read since that doppelgänger tales inevitably end in murder or suicide, if not both. But it generated none. As my double and his double avoided each other's eyes, we came soon to avoid each other's presence as well, insofar as that's possible in a five-day crossing on a large ship. A less myth-driven fellow and his double would quickly have made acquaintance; with a laugh and three clucks of the tongue, we'd have dispelled the spooky little co-incidence. One of us—probably the older one—might well have been unaware of any resemblance, as it turned out; he'd think it was all in the younger fellow's imagination. Then we'd have polled the other passengers at the bar, and some would have been struck by our strong likeness—one would even say she'd thought we were father and son—but some others wouldn't have noticed. By that time, however, we'd have discovered more things in common: He'd once aspired to write novels, for example, and he'd been Jean Heartstone's family doctor, of all things, out in Portland, Oregon! Or we might have learned that beyond some similarities of appearance and manner, we had little in common at all: a hard-nosed Republican stockbroker from Scarsdale or Teaneck and a vaguely leftist storyteller from Hoopers Island. Thereafter we'd have saluted each other across the ship's theater or promenade deck with a cordial small smile or a half-wave of the left hand.

But this was *my* double; we never spoke. Was he even American? I can't say for sure, though he looked it: an upper-middle-aged, upper-middle-class white Anglo-Saxon Protestant American male, unscarred but not untouched by the cataclysms of his century. I saw him last on the Greek Lines pier in New York, alone and baggageless, waiting erect and without expression for something or someone while we others milled about, collecting our bags and queueing up for customs, reminding one another that in this country one drives on the right, and that the word for "lost" is "lost."

My double is an old man now, if not a dead one, this many stories later. That many stories from this one, with luck, I'll be getting on to his age then. If I were back on that ocean liner, setting out on my night-sea journey, I would be less diffident; I'd be more friendly. Never mind the Myth of the Wandering Hero; to hell with the spell: I would strike up conversation with my old double. I'd explain Jean Heartstone's Magic Language Theory to him; then I'd ask him whether he'd read any good books lately. And years from now, when the situation is reversed—when I'm in Kennedy Airport at age sixty-five and see myself at age twenty-three alone and bemused among the families and the baggage and the purposeful and the sleek—I'll know the answer to that question.

Says Katherine Sherritt That kid will turn out to have been entranced by the later works of his favorite storyteller, Peter Sagamore, beginning with his Tidewater Tales. So are your children, Pins and Needles. See them listening?

YEAH, WELL.

Peter is in his story still. He asks his wife Where are we these days? Early on, before Jean Heartstone's second pregnancy and stoned suicide, sure enough the tale of her called forth a light southwesterly with promise of increase. Despite a twenty-percent chance of afternoon and evening thundershowers, we have weighed anchor and beat out of Rhode River, Katherine steering and navigating in her black beret *trouvé* while her husband tended sails and went on with the story.

I would say, says she, we're off the mouth of South River and done with our separate sex educations. I would say that that is the Thomas Point Light up yonder at eleven o'clock, to port of that old wooden ketch, and that we are probably headed for Slip Thirty-three of Beasley's Marina in Whitehall Creek, where we began our voyage together.

What she means, Peter learns over dinner in Annapolis that evening, is that whatever our original motives might have been, the emergent pattern of our ad-lib cruise, if not its organizing principle, seems to have become the touching of bases, personal and narrative. Even sailing whither listeth wind and tide, we need some chapter-by-chapter idea where we're headed; but knowing where we're bound requires knowing where we are, which like good navigators we reckon from where we've been. For four days now, we've taken fixes on the present from landmarks of our past: Howard "Huckleberry" Findley and Heather Foulke-Stoughton, Jean Heartstone and Poonie Baldwin and Marcie Blitz, the Gramercy Park Hotel and the Katherine Anne Porter party, Douglas Townshend and the Doomsday Factor. We now know, about as well as does the reader of these tales, where we are and how we got here. Inasmuch as Annapolis and the Severn River lay ahead when Peter asked his question, Katherine bets that if we'd lashed the tiller, *Story* would have sailed itself back to Slip 33 in the year 1970 and closed that particular circle.

Yes, well. Having told that story, however, it seemed to Peter (this was back there in the present, as we and that salty-looking beat-up ketch closed on Thomas Point Light together, lightfoot *Story* easily overtaking the larger boat), we were free to give our old slip the slip. Too early in the voyage, something told him, for closing circles. Says Kate in the Treaty of Paris Restaurant in the Maryland Inn in Annapolis that evening, I would have thought that according to old Jean Heartstone's Magic Language Theory, telling the story of Slip Thirty-three would guarantee our spending the night there instead of here. I was game.

So had been Peter. In his opinion, though, a chief value of recognizing what's pushing you, and how and why and where, is that it enables you to push back, or to use that push to go off in some other direction. That is some funky old boat, all right, he said back there at the Thomas Point Light, with its ratlines and baggy-wrinkled shrouds and jerry cans and patched-up sails and eyes painted on its bows like those on Iberian fishing smacks. What next? Its name was . . . P steadied his binocular elbow against the companionway hatch, but by the time we were close enough to resolve the lettering, we'd pulled abeam and couldn't read the narrow stern. A wiry, white-whiskered steersman in Greek fisherman's cap waved from the tiller. *ANTE IV,* Pete believes the name was or ended with: As in Time Before, K wonders, which is what our tales have turned and returned to? Or as in Raise the ante, muses Peter, which is what it's time our story did?

That is why, when time came this afternoon, we breezed sentimentally into Whitehall Creek after all, kissed each other's lips, and waved hello with the children to Beasley's Marina, sine qua non—but then sailed right out again on the same southwesterly (more bracing to beat against than to run before), across and into the mouth of the Severn to always-bustling Annapolis harbor. It is our fourth day out, fifth night: time for a proper shower and a meal ashore, we agreed; a room at the Hilton or the Maryland Inn. Both the track of our voyage thus far and Jean Heartstone's Magic Language Theory—by which nothing is, but dreaming, reading, or writing makes it so—indicate to Peter Sagamore that because we recognized, there off Thomas Point Light, the need for our story's ante to be upped, our story's ante will be upped.

The predicted possible thundershowers don't materialize. That weathered old ketch *Rocinante IV* does; drops its Herreshoff anchor out where Spa Creek meets the Severn, in front of the Naval Academy, as we tie up in a rental slip at Town Dock. The eye on her port bow is painted shut. Having winked at us, she swings her transom once just enough, before settling down to ride at anchor, for us to make out her full name from the town dock's end, where we're busy getting our land legs and watching with the 7 × 50s. Subdued Peter, grinning and sighing, says That does it. Let's go eat.

OVER TOURNEDOS ROSSINI WITH OKAY PÂTÉ, KATHERINE SHERRITT SAGAMORE EXPLAINS WHAT WE'RE DOING HERE.

Full many a sailor voyageth in quest of reasons for his/her voyage, is what Kath means by the emergent pattern of this cruise. She'll have the tournedos Rossini medium rare and house dressing on the salad, she tells the moon-faced young blond St. John's College philosophy or classics major who has just that minute handed us our menus in the Treaty of Paris and is retrieving the two spare place-settings at our booth for four. Says Peter The same only medium plus the fried potato skins with sour cream and a half carafe of the house red, and we hand her back the menus. My name's Debbie, the young woman now gets a chance to announce gravely, and I'll be your waitress this evening. Our special this evening is the prime rib with the au jus. Would you like a cocktail while you're deciding on your order?

K asks her husband to remind her to call Nopoint Point before we leave and then reminds him that his often-stated, unfulfilled-as-yet-in-his-opinion writerly ambition is to conjure an image larger and richer than any booksworth of sentences that sets it forth: Scheherazade yarning through the night to save her neck, Odysseus homeward-striving through the wine-dark perils of the sea, D.Q. and Sancho colloquizing across the Spanish plain, Huck Finn araft with Jim down the Father of Waters, et cetera.

Says Peter There is no etcetera; those are the north east south and west of it. Well, says the sober expression of Debbie bringing us our wine and rolls, what about such other cardinal compass-points as Rip Van Winkle snoozing while the world turns upside down and Ahab-and-the-whale and Robinson Crusoe and Alice-down-the-rabbit-hole and.

Two of the four we've already heard from, Kath continues, and have been counseled by the examples of. Huckleberry Findley down there on the Honga reminded us of the truths Twain tells and the ones he won't, as well as Sherritt's Third Law of Emotion, which she just now made up. The psychological physics (she will explain to her all-eared friend when that frowning full moon of a Debbie has retired into the kitchen clouds) that propelled Huck west into the Territory propelled Sam Clemens, as Pete pointed out, from Hannibal to Buffalo to Hartford and points ever east. Ditto P.S. to Portugal, Portland, and the 92nd Street Poetry Center. What she bets is that a corollary physics works the other way: that, the tide of his life having fetched him back to shoal-draft Maryland, when Peter finally clears his throat he'll people the page not with webfoot rednecks but with some finer-honed, less simple and less marsh-bound specimen than Huck Finn on the Honga, Parts One and Two.

Enjoy your dinner, Debbie orders us. Go on, says P to K: Ted and Deeahnah? Kath's been thinking about the Dmitrikakises, all right, all the while we spieled the reader with forest-green Crayolas and Doomsday Factors. Odysseus tells of wonders, is what has occurred to her, but deals in realities, except for his final fling with Nausicaa out of time. We know what Ted and Diana are in our story for, especially coming as they did on the ominous heels of Doug Townshend's death: Their job is to tempt us to *get out*, not à la Huck but à la them. Buy a secondhand world cruiser, Peter prompts; there must be a dozen in brokerage right here in Annapolis that we could afford. Let Willy and Poonie and the multinationals and the CIA and the KGB run the world and ruin it, K carries on; we can't stop them anyhow. The kids join in, AC and DC: Sail us around the world forever! Bring us up out of TV range! Well, we could, working here and there as necessary to pay the bills. No news; no careers; no civic responsibility. Whoopee. Hedonists really do have more fun, and time gets you anyway, as will the Doomsday Factor if push comes to button. The question is whether to ignore them or engage them in losing battle.

Reader, we could do it: shrug our family shoulders and seize the day. We have seen those salty households sailing by, their faery gold children perched on bowsprits, regarding the shore with clear-eyed wonder as they pass. But to go that route, Kate cautions, is, uh, to reject the community while feeding on its fruits: high-tech materials, gear, medicines; your royalties, unroyal as they are. Does Peter really want to be a nautical Thoreau? Well, she does make it sound appealing. The pâté on these tournedos, by the way, is okay, yes?

Yeah. See? There are your Balzacs and your Dickenses, in the thick of things, getting it all down. But there are your great isolates, too: Gauguins and Robert Louis Stevensons, reporting to their civilization from outside it. Sherritt's Third Law tells Kate that Pete's neither one nor quite the other; that he'll keep his distance figuratively, but not especially literally, from his material.

Tell him more.

Okay: A Sherritt has strong historical ties to citizenship: service to the region of her ancestors, et cet. Even Pig Willy feels those ties, in his crooked way: He may be the death of Talbot County, but Talbot County is his life. A Sagamore feels no such thing: Pete and Jake are immigrants by disposition. Look who's living in whose home county; look who keeps saying Let's touch base at Hoopersville but does so as seldom as decency permits. Yet it's Katherine, finally, who could bid bye-bye for keeps tomorrow to the Pratt Library and Nopoint Point and go bop around Bora Bora till the cows come home; and it's Peter, we suspect, who could hardly hack hedonism; who needs not only to tell tidewater tales to as many as will hear, but to keep one foot not far from Mother Marsh, whithersoever the other wander. And the reason for this paradox, we explain to Means and Ends (who, while less satisfied than we with Treaty of Paris pâté, are not too young to hear such things), is what we know about each other's heart of hearts: P's miniquasar deep in there; K's excuse the expression petite black hole.

In short, we decide (along with not to have the *Schwarzwäldertorte*, Debbie, just one American coffee, black), the lesson of *Mark One* is this: Odysseus put his house in order before he left it. Let's have these babies, I've Got It Bad and That Ain't Good, and let's clear their father's throat— and then let's see what's next. *L'addition, s.v.p.?*

Moon-faced Debbie's frown we read as a message from the reader that our bill contains at least one unpaid item: our nonchalance with respect to that extraordinary name (under the circumstances) of that funky sailing vessel out there off the U.S. Naval Academy parade grounds. The St. Johnnie all but stares P down as he fishes out wallet from hind pocket, Visa card from wallet—he registers wistfully that one gets out of this habit, sailing—while K uses the ladies' and the phone.

Yeah, well. We'd have thought it clear enough, after the cameo appearances as they say of Huck Finn on the Honga and Odysseus in the Little Choptank, that Jean Heartstone's ghost has become our cruise director. Out there on that beat-up ketch, somebody is tricked out as The Knight of the Doleful Countenance, ready to up the ante of our erstwhile-aimless odyssey for the third time. No need to dinghy out there to say hello; the bases we need to touch are chasing after us. Nonchalant Pete wouldn't bat an eye now if his wife found Shahryar's vizier's daughter in the Treaty of Paris loo. Hi: My name's Scheherazade, and I'm your bunkmate for this evening. May I tell you a story?

But he's still waiting for receiptful Debbie when, after an unusual while, Kate herds her belly back to our booth and declares Never mind Don Quixote. I've just had the strangest conversation in the universal world with my big pig brother.

I'll need your address and phone number on there, Debbie complains.

Asks grinning Peter How come you were talking to Willy? Take us out of this chapter.

Katherine's still amazed. He said he *loves* me, Peter. Willy Herpes Sherritt actually said those English words into a Chesapeake and Potomac telephone. She gives her strandy hair a shake. Pete pens our Baltimore address on the charge slip and removes the customer copy. Willy says he's really looking forward to being an uncle. The moon commands us to have a nice evening. Dazed Kate wonders to herself

WHETHER HERPES SIMPLEX CAN AFFECT THE BRAIN,

and aloud to Peter, five minutes later, as we stroll hand in hand down Duke of Gloucester Street to say good night to *Story* and Don Quixote before strolling over to the dockside Hilton for our night ashore, she wonders it again.

I mean, that was the single weirdest telephone conversation I ever did have in my one *life*. She'd scarcely said Hi to her mother and We're at the Annapolis Hilton and you're not a grandma yet but Rise and Shine are fine don't worry, when Irma had said in a peculiar voice Willy and Molly are with us, and a minute later Willy wants to say something, Katherine, and then Willy was on an extension saying Some things are hard to say, Kath, especially to you, but a lot of big changes have changed since you-all've been gone.

Peter wonders Since we-all've been gone? Did we cross some time-line like Ted and Diana?

Says K Me too: The world changed since last Sunday? So Willy goes It's damn hard to talk to you, Kath, and I say Give it a try, and next thing I know he's saying how his medical problem, quote unquote, has made him take a hard look at himself blah blah, and the fact is he's really come to understand what a wonderful person his wife is and things are going to be a whole lot different in their house from now on and he really appreciates me too, he just wants me to know that, he'd even say he loves me, but he knows I'd mock him if he used that word; anyhow he just wants me to know that he and Moll are really really looking forward to having nephews and nieces especially since it looks like they won't be having children of their own, and get this: He even wonders whether his medical problem isn't a blessing in disguise, coming right after Poonie's recent troubles and all—only he didn't say Poonie, he said Peebie!—and maybe it was all meant to straighten out his head about a few things. Then he goes I've said my say; now go ahead and mock.

Marvels Peter *Madre de Dios,* and Katherine Yup. This was on the extension in the little room off the foyer, and while I'm wondering whether herpes simplex has spread to Willy's brain and what's this Peebie business, Molly comes on teary-voiced on some other line and says Things really have changed in their house, and Willy says It's a whole new ball game, and they're both talking at the same time, like one in each ear, and I'm not believing a damn word of it but I don't want to stomp on Molly's feelings so I change the subject and say When did Poonie start being Peebie except to his parents and Molly? So Willy runs on how one of the things that's turned his head around is how Peebie's come to terms with his personal problems and accepted himself as being gay and his wife has too and other people will come around by and by, maybe even hardhearted me, and whether Peebie wins or loses in November, the whole experience will be a growth experience for everybody; he knows it's been an education for him already, et cetera.

The whole experience, echoes Peter. Kath says she gave Willy that one back, too; couldn't resist it, but otherwise held her fire if only out of mere flabbergastment. She took for granted her sumbitch brother was lying as usual, just talking up the vote; if not lying consciously to her and Molly, then lying to himself, or both at once as had been her ex-husband's wont. But so improbable a turnaround had no precedent in Big Will Sherritt's biography, and she wasn't after all one hundred percent sure that the man was an irredeemable swine; she was only eighty-five percent sure, and ready to give Molly Barnes Sherritt the fifteen-percent benefit of her doubt, though she feared the poor woman was riding for a harder fall than any in her wretched married life. She therefore confined herself to pointing out that it had never been Poonie Baldwin's gayhood in itself—gaiety?—she'd objected to: Gay shmay, witness May; some of her best friends et cetera. That's exactly right, had responded Willy, as if she'd affirmed rather than objected to his position; he had in fact remet her old friend May Jump at Nopoint Point last Sunday, and a fine upstanding person she was, too. But Kath had already begun protesting Anyhow, since when did Porter Baldwin, Junior, ever really own up to anything? What Porter Baldwin, Junior, did was get himself caught and then lie through his teeth to cover his tail until the lies wouldn't wash and then switch over to his Repentance-and-Reform mode. Let him acknowledge what and who he is; let him come out of the closet altogether and run on the truth, and maybe then she'll begin to forgive and even respect him. But that's just what he's doing, had trilled Molly as if into her starboard ear; he really is trying to be a new person, Kate. Come on, had scoffed Kath then: Poon doesn't even know who's really behind his campaign, much less who he really is, and sometimes I wonder the same about you, Willy.

She really said that, she groans to Peter as we cross the traffic circle to Town Dock, and she could've bit her tongue for letting that particular cat out of the bag. Sighs sober Peter, squeezing her hand, Oy. Groans sorry Kate I *know*. And Willy picked right up on it, too: What'd she mean by that crack? Look here, Willy, she'd said, she was sorry she'd come back at him like that; she was at the end of dinner at the end of a day in the middle of a cruise at the end of her pregnancy, and she guessed she was maybe tired. It was good to hear that the leopard had changed his spots and become a cuddly hubby and a prospective loving uncle, and she hoped his medical problem would go away, now that it had done him so much good. What do you mean we don't know who Poonie's backers are, Willy growled with an edge—not your easiest growl to growl. She didn't know what she meant, said Katherine. I'm being nice to you, Willy complained (to her relief) instead of pursuing the other subject, and you're being your typical bitchy self. That's true, Kay, Molly had agreed. Katherine apologized; was pleased to know that their marriage had suddenly turned perfect—There you go, went Willy—No, really, she didn't want to belittle his spiritual rebirth et cet if he'd truly changed his head; no doubt she was too wrapped up in getting Oil and Vinegar through their *first* birth to appreciate anybody's second.

Well, it's no joke, Molly had said staunchly. People *can* be born again; even Peebie. Gay Werewolves for Jesus, came back Kate, and heard Molly Barnes giggle for the first time since Deniston dorm days. I knew she'd mock, Willy grumbled to Molly across the Main House end of this trialogue, and to Kath Go ahead and mock. All I wanted to say is I'm sorry for the hard feelings between us in the past, and I forgive you and hope you'll forgive me. Affirmed Molly He does, too, Katie. K had got loud then: *He* forgives *me*? Thanks loads, Willy! Grunted Will gratifyingly Up yours, Sis, but then at once said No, I don't mean that; I take that back. Molly said There's no dealing with you sometimes, Kay. Who's dealing? Katherine wanted to know. We'll talk about all of that, Willy declared; I just wanted you to know that whatever you feel, I feel like I said before. We'll talk it all through when you're back here.

Like hell we will, Kate says she said to herself, but to Willy Yeah, well, and then Molly said The Deniston thing, too, Kay; Willy and I see eye to eye on that now. You what? had cried incredulous Katherine, but Willy declared they'd talk that all through later. Yall take care, now.

Isn't that a pisser?

You got your moneysworth out of that Treaty of Paris pay phone, Peter Sagamore agrees. Hank and Irma's VHF-radio gift to *Story* early in our pregnancy necessitated installation of a twelve-volt battery, an automatic built-in battery charger, and a 110-volt dockside power hookup, since our boat lacks an engine and a fortiori an alternator and indeed any electrical equipment at all except running lights with self-contained flashlight batteries. Taking advantage of our fifteen-dollar-a-night municipal boat slip, Peter rigs the shore-power cord to top off the battery charge; we walk out to wharf's end in case Don Quixote's waiting there to raise the ante on our story, though we'd as leave he put off that favor till tomorrow, Willy and Molly having raised it already. We think but are not certain we can make out *Rocinante IV* yonder among the other anchor-lighted vessels, and are relieved not to find her skipper standing by to buttonhole us, Ancient Mariner–style. Then we wander back to the dockside Hilton, soaking up the mild night, the salty-fancy town, the mere shore-room, before we go up to enjoy our room ashore, which we hired and showered in before dinner. Nightcaps on the balcony—That's it out there, all right, that weathered old ketch, and What in the world do we suppose is going on over at Nopoint Point? and Okay, it's too bad K let slip what she did about what Doug Townshend told us about Poonie Baldwin's anonymous campaign backers, but after all she really didn't let the cat out of the bag, just hinted that there was a cat *in* there; and Kath guesses she'll give May Jump a call *mañana,* since here we are in Annapolis. Maybe May'll explain how she happens to've become Willy and Molly's buddy in just the past five days; is that really only how long we've been out?—and then at *last* we end Day 4 in a king-size bed, *magnífico,* if we call last Sunday Day Zero, Nopoint Point to Dun Cove, and count Monday, Dun Cove to Dun Cove, as Day 1. At this rate, reflects pensive Peter Sagamore, it will take us a thousand and one nights to reach Ordinary Point.

Murmurs half-asleep Katherine Sherritt, half smiling: More Is More.

And you children, thinks P, won't get born till Nineteen Eighty-four.

Wide awake inside their sleeping mother, into each other's ears they whisper, chuckling. We'll just see about that, says Phylogeny; Ontogeny says We'll just see.

DAY 5:
LAY DAY, ANNAPOLIS

With heart-pang fit to kill, Kate realizes that of course she isn't married to any Peter Sagamore and thirty-nine and pregnant. Not at all. She's twenty still, still working the cataloguing department of Harvard's Widener Library, which however is also the library of The Deniston School for Girls. None of the foregoing in this account has happened, at least not yet, except the girlhood stuff. She's still engaged to Poonie Baldwin; no wonder she's so edgy, her stomach doing tricks.

Mrs. Florence Halsey schools her in the arcana of the Dewey Decimal System: the secret Tenth Category of the Tenth Classification, which a decimal master may reveal to but one protégée in her working lifetime. Dear Mrs. Halsey is nervous too, with excitement; she adjusts and readjusts her rimless glasses on her button nose. But she *is* a master; knows through and through not only her System but her girls. For forty years she's watched them blossom on Deniston's graceful grounds, and many have been lovely, many lively, many bright; several almost the one one waits for, and none quite. Then, just in time, along came Katie Sherritt, Irma Shorter's daughter by Sam and Dorothy Sherritt's son, and Florence Halsey knew she'd found at last what she'd been waiting for, but bided her time still, what little prime time she had left, teaching Dickens and Shakespeare as always—Charlie and Will, she calls them in the classroom—the love of language, learning, books. She waited for the System to speak to Katherine, for Katherine to come to her.

Speak they did and deeply, Melvil Dewey's Decimals, to that something-or-other under Katie's breastbone that wants experiences sorted out, given name or number, put each in its place and thereby made, you know, accessible. Newly published acquisitions come to Cataloguing with their Library of Congress call numbers already assigned; the department's Molly Barneses prepare the several catalogue cards, enter the acquisition on the main computer, type out and affix the proper call-number stickers for each item (we're at the Deniston–Widener–Pratt now) and add the book itself to the main library's holdings if it's not already there or send it out to one of the branches if it is. Even this routine work speaks to our Katherine: She does it errorlessly with half her mind while the other worries about her becoming Mrs. Porter Baldwin, Jr.; what *living* with Poonie will be like; *depending* upon him. But her special pleasure is the gift collections, thitherto undecimalized, in which occasionally will be found unusual, even anomalous items to challenge the cataloguer's acumen. All such Questionables are passed up to Mrs. Halsey's desk, where now Katherine and that elder lady laugh together over Lapsang souchong tea on a buffety deep November afternoon because the red light has just come on, signaling that their latest attempt to classify That Book has been, like all its predecessors, rejected. *El Misterioso,* they've come to call it:

THE MYSTERIOUS LIBRARY BOOK.

The new book-filing system, which the library is justly proud of having pioneered, senses when a volume has been reshelved incorrectly by the stack staff, mostly student part-timers, and signals automatically to the circulation desk its floor, stack, alcove, and shelf number so that someone more expert can be dispatched to locate, retrieve, and properly reshelve the misplaced item. For in a library of any size at all, Mrs. Halsey warns her girls, a book wrongly shelved might as well have been thrown into the Chesapeake, for all its chances of ever being found again when called for. She makes the Denistonians feel the plight of that luckless volume as if it were a child astray in forest or city, too frightened to call for help; not many books are lost by misfiling in the Deniston Library. But even the most conscientious of high school girls, and these are those, has a thousand things on her mind. Mistakes happen. The red light lights.

A refinement of this warning system—well beyond Deniston's means and needs, but not beyond the Widener's or the Pratt's—rejects with a similar signal, transmitted to Cataloguing instead of to Circulation, any book that has been miscatalogued in the first place: "throws it back at us," as the "Loggers" say, one of whom must then make her way against the black wind howling through the alcoves, follow the blinking red light to the offending item, and return it to the cozy shelter of her colleagues' office, where Kath and Mrs. Halsey, with sighs that fail to mask their eagerness, will reexamine, reclassify, and reshelve it, hoping for the best. Kate herself has effected this latest rescue (Florence Halsey has made ten thousand like it in her time, but is too frail now for such heroics); with *El Misterioso* clutched against her swelling breasts; now she shuts with difficulty the office door, grins at Mrs. Halsey, pushes clear of her eyes her wind-wild hair, and plops Their Baby onto the desktop.

Sent down like a riddling test from Dewey himself, *el libro misterioso* turned up like a foundling one morning in the library's night depository. Sans call number, charge slip, or library stamp on its page-edges, it was sent from Acquisitions to Cataloguing with a note from the "Ack" people in schoolgirlish hand:

Good Luck !!! ☺

A quarto volume bound in good though much-handled Morocco; marbled edges and endpapers; high-grade rag paper, clearly acid free; some pages still uncut—Haven't seen one of *those* in a coon's age, Mrs. Halsey said, fishing out her Toledo-steel letter opener to slit the folds. But no title on spine or title page, no named author, and the oddest text that anybody in the library had ever seen: a mélange of languages recognizable and unrecognizable, into which were mixed numbers and other symbols, white space, blank pages, snatches of verse, aphorisms (*What you've done is what you'll do* is the only one in English that Kath and Mrs. Halsey can understand, and they're not a bit sure they understand that), graphics of several sorts—including one pornographic, which Mrs. Halsey unhesitatingly cut out and destroyed, begging the pardon of the American Library Association and the Civil Liberties Union, before Kate could quite make out what was going on.

Well now, Mrs. Halsey asked Katherine that first time, semesters past, her ancient joke: Dewey do or do we don't? There are, it goes without saying, catchall categories in the system, but no Logger worth her salt will resort to those, and so began a series of trials and errors unprecedented in Kath's mentor's long experience. Their difficulty was compounded by the circumstance that (they would swear but could not prove it) the book's contents were somewhat different each time they retrieved, reexamined, and reclassified it upon the system's "throwing it back at them"—as if it were altered by their mistakes or—Kath's happy thought, which Mrs. Halsey kissed her on the forehead for—were carrying on a dialogue with them.

The old teacher could not have wished for a better problem at a better time. Carefully with her star pupil she would review the rationale for their previous classification, speculate upon why that classification had been red-lighted, log the interval between filing and rejection to see whether they were "getting warm," and plan their next move. Their joint frustration bridged the years between them; brought the two women so close that Katherine can smell Mrs. Halsey's pleasant powder now as the elder lady holds *El Misterioso* still, or tries to, like a squirming child at inoculation time, while Kate inks their newest trial call number onto its spine. They must bend forward together over the desk as wind shakes the whole library; Mrs. Halsey stands close behind her pet (Let them say it!), and they brace the strange book with their left hands while Mrs. Halsey guides Kath's calligraphy with her right. There are the age spots; there is her old Wellesley class ring. Her ample bosoms press just under Kate's shoulderblades; *There is no Mister Florence Halsey,* the girl suddenly understands. Had there ever been?

The job done, *El Misterioso* sent a-packing down the dumbwaiter to Filing, now they laugh: Take that, Melvil Dewey! Mrs. Halsey's English classes are frequently hilarious for all their rigor: a high-spirited, high-quality riot. But they've never before laughed together like this: two women with nearly half a century between their ages, laughing till the tears come. *El Misterioso* is out of their hands for the present, if not likely for keeps.

At least we've decided what the poor thing *used to be,* Mrs. Halsey sighs between their laughter, and for some reason that observation moves Katherine's heart. How she loves this ruddy little woman wiping her eyes now, her rimless glasses hanging from their black cord lanyard down upon her stout, befreckled chest like an official decoration: a silver-haired lady laughing like a schoolgirl! Heaven knows the situation isn't *just* funny; already the red light's flickering; K will have to go down there presently again, wind or no wind, find the thing and fetch it back, and her doing so will alter it yet further. The task is hopeless. Dewey do or do we don't? In the open neck of Mrs. Halsey's blouse, where her eyeglasses dangle, Kate sees now two or is it three underwear shoulder-straps: ivory, ecru, rose; brassiere, slip, what else. What I'll do, she understands with an inward groan, is what I've done: Drunken Poonie must inscribe my spine; there'll be an astonishing night in the Gramercy Park Hotel, Room One Seven Six; then Yussuf al-Din, Saul Fish, Jaime Aiquina, May Jump, the Katherine Anne Porter party—all to be beat through, dead to windward, before she gets. Back. Up. To.

The light is on.

Dead to windward is right, thinks Peter, and many's the hairy time like this he has wished us home in bed instead of slogging through what *Story* wasn't really built for. The characteristics of that light correspond to nothing on the chart in the neighborhood he reckons us to be in; to nothing in the Light List that he can find. Kath's more than a help; she is mothering indispensable; but it's his responsibility to know where we are and to make the major sailing decisions, and he has unaccountably lost track. Wind or no wind, he's in a sweat. Commands himself to wake up and does so. Does not in fact know for some moments where we are, whether he's not still dreaming one frame farther out. All right: We're in the Annapolis Hilton, and K is softly sleeping beside him, thank God. Black as the proverbial et cetera, our room, and the wind is piping up out there. He envisions whitecaps on the black Bay and thinks late-night thoughts: John Arthur Paisley; other corpses he has met. What is an "easy death by sea"? Child loss: How does any parent recover, especially when this crazy trip was our idea. Near misses from his own not especially daring boyhood: a seafood truck that backed into his bike and kept right on; a deerhunter's bullet that clipped through oak twigs ten feet from his head; a post-storm swim in the surf at the unguarded beach of Assateague Island, below Ocean City, where he learned that undertow really can tow under.

This whole idea was a mistake. We shall go back to Nopoint Point as soon as weather permits. Would we were home in our Stony Run apartment right this minute, so light, uncluttered, the awesome responsibility of parenthood not upon us. Friends, readers: The world is done for. Let's tell one another a few last stories to while away what time remains. A daughter, a son—who wants them now?

Well, *he* does, mightily, really. But!

Out on the sprit again, changing headsails in that evil chop. The bow pitches and plunges, Pete hates this part, carrying him wave by wave from near-zero gravity to half again his actual weight while he wrestles in the spray to douse a wet 150-percent genoa that seems that same percentage larger than its sailbag. Two hands for the ship, one armpit for himself, in which he clutches the bow-pulpit rail, and there's that light again, steady and clear now, at once a mile away and just a few feet before his eyes.

Wind snaps, wind whistles through the vowels and consonants of Annapolis and rattles the plate-glass balcony doors of our room. The red message light is on, on the telephone, on Katherine's side of our bed. Peter checks his luminous watchdial: 4:45. Naked in bed has been the custom in this relationship since Night 1 in the Gramercy Park: pj tops and uphauled nighties allowed in chilly weather, but nothing below the waist until we get up in the morning. That is the message light over there, and it is, oddly, on. P needs to pee. He slides over to Katherine, whose back is to him, snugs himself under her backside, parks his penis between her buns, gives it a flex to test whether she's awake, and lightly takes her upper breast. She moves his hand down to her belly, where Chessie and Peek are doing laps, breathing nicely underwater. K chuckles as she wakes the rest of the way up, thinking Well of *course* there is no Mister Florence Halsey!

Pete's asleep again already. In our house it's Kate who takes night phone calls, for example, because she wakes in full possession of her wits, able to weigh alternatives and make consequential decisions while Peter's still recollecting who he is. That is not *El Misterioso* calling, she understands now; it is the message light on our hotel-room telephone. If it were an emergency, the caller or the desk clerk would have rung us. It's merely a message of some sort, awaiting our pleasure. Let it wait.

THE MESSAGE LIGHT IS ON,

Peter murmurs into her shoulderblades two hours later, when we rewake; it's *been* on. Says Kate she knows, and explains why we needn't be concerned. Listen to that wind, one of us bids the other. We allow as how that wind blew through our dreams. That message light was in them, too. It will be P who says Sounds like no sailing today; Kath leaves such matters to him, as he leaves tactical-logistical ones to her. Bets Pete It's Scheherazade calling from the Islands of India and China, to tell the kids their bedtime story that they didn't get told last night. Bets Katherine It's Don Quixote on the ship-to-shore, reminding you that his author mainly futzed around till he was D.Q.'s age: in his fifties. Yes, well, Peter sighs.

He's still piss-proud down there, poking in. Kinky Katherine shifts a bit, lifts her upper leg, wets us with two fingersworth of spit, and bids him help himself while she takes the message; she finds such little incongruities a turn-on. Though he is not horny, P holds her by the hips and gently obliges, stuffing her but barely thrusting while she rings the front desk. There are flowers waiting for us, she is told, with love from the folks at Nopoint Point, wired in through one of those twenty-four-hour florists with instructions that they be delivered along with breakfast in our room when we're ready to order. Says Kath We're ready to order, and with erected nipples requests from room service one order of eggs Benedict, two grapefruit juices, two coffees, two plates, one Coke, and ketchup: our traditional hotel breakfast.

Sometimes the sweetest sex is by-the-way. Peter ejaculates thinking not really of his friend at all but of that wind out there, of his dream, also of death and Don Quixote. Inasmuch as we've never in our years together been obliged to use a condom, Katherine feels the warm squirt of him for the thousandth-plus time, but her mind is busy with Willy and Molly, with Florence Halsey, bless her heart, with *El Misterioso,* which reminds her now of something else. Back whispers They're at it *again.* Says little Forth Shh: That's how we got here.

To the bathroom. Then Peter slips into pajama bottoms in time to admit room service and sign for the order: a breakfast cart big as a hospital gurney, with a centerpiece of handsome Brandy roses. K comes from the bathroom in a sunshine-yellow cotton nightie, looking like a knocked-up schoolgirl. We congratulate Irma on her floral restraint—only nine roses, moderate of stem—and read the card: Mom, Dad, Molly, *Willy,* Chip, Olive and Lester Treadway, Bobby and Ruthie Henry. We slug fruit juice and divide eggs Benedict. We swap dream accounts, Peter censoring the darker footage of his: By sunny day, that wind's just wind, too rough for sailing in our condition, but not scary. He'll check the forecast presently. We'll see.

Kath's recounting of her *Misterioso* dream has reminded her of two other things entirely. If it weren't for Florence Halsey, she tells the children, sipping her Coke and seeing how they take to sauce hollandaise, you might have had a different daddy. Appalled, One and Only clutch each other. She quickly explains that Mrs. Halsey loved books as books almost as much as she loved literature, and that, in consequence, generations of Denistonians, whatever their social standing, wound up as book-drive organizers for any charitable purpose; as Friends of the Library, any library; as volunteer book-cart pushers in their local hospitals; as rare-book collectors or dealers; as neighborhood-bookshop owners or supporters. A fair number, like Katherine, went into library science or editing and publishing; a few became English teachers; at least half a dozen became writers—of children's books, mainly, but also of local history, of regional poetry and fiction. It's Katherine the oralist who's the bookish one in our house; she reads promiscuously, unlike Peter, who reads rather little but intensely. The final trouble with al-Din, Fish, Aiquina, and Jump was that they were in the wrong line of work—even Yussuf, who scorned the whole corpus of Western lit. To Florence Halsey goes part of the credit for Kate's profound initial and persisting attraction to Peter Sagamore, writer of books, is what she means, she says. And little skinny-assed stories don't do me, she reminds him: four pages here, three pages there, like Yussuf's mean little "switchblade poems." A *book* is what gets me off: something with heft to it, that you can take in two hands and spread like a woman. Mnyum!

Muses Peter What I've done is what I'll do. That sounds like death to us. What was the *other* other thing entirely that your Dewey Decimal dream reminded you of? There's no such thing as that secret tenth category and that red-light system, yes? Me and the kids think not.

Katherine Sherritt declares with professional dignity, while whapping ketchup onto the plate beside her egg Benedict, that the science of libraries is a vast and multifarious science, with its high technicians and its esoterics and its old guard and avant-garde. The guild secrets and ground mysteries of library science are not for bandying with the unborn and the uninitiate over breakfast. Says Peter Sorry there. But her other other thing entirely that K's library dream reminded her of, she says, slugging Coke as she did at our first breakfast together, in the Gramercy Park Hotel, is her celebrated Enoch Pratt Library Bookmark Exhibit, which Peter has heard about, and how it led to ASPS and ASPS led to HOSCA and HOSCA led the FBI and maybe the CIA into the margins of the story of her life before Douglas Townshend and Peter's Prince of Darkness ever came along.

BOOKMARKS

Kath thinks she's probably never told her husband this story in all our married life. It's coming on to nine. Do we want to catch WYRE?

But in this fancy hotel room there's no AM radio for tuning in the marine Accuweather forecast between pop recordings on the Annapolis station. Peter resigns himself to blowing a buck or more to ring up the Baltimore weather number and hear an odd-voiced lady tell him less than he wants to know, but Katherine points out that he can dial the big marine supply store right next door to the Hilton and get the detailed Chesapeake forecast from any salesclerk worth his/her salt, as it were. She's right, too, and while a buck is but a buck, this sort of imaginative quick good judgment is one of the things P prizes in the woman. The boy who answers at Fawcett's Boat Supplies Inc. has not in fact heard a weather report this morning, but at his elbow is one of those little weatherband jobs. He flicks it on and sets the phone beside it. A strong high-pressure system moving east from the Ohio Valley will keep the day fine, high-seventyish, and gusty; winds northwesterly at thirty-plus knots till evening, then westerly ten to twelve. Small-craft advisory in effect. A lay day, Peter declares. You were saying.

Kate says okay but remind her to call Mom and May Jump after this story, would he? Which is this: The American Society for the Preservation of Storytelling was founded on a chilly mid-October evening in 1969 around a campfire in Deep Creek Lake State Park in western Maryland by Katherine Sherritt and May Jump and a number of their library science and backpacking friends, half as a joke, in the following wise: The United States of America were in spectacular disarray just then by reason of our war upon Southeast Asia and the rise of our domestic "counterculture." Lyndon Johnson had vacated the presidency, Robert Kennedy and Martin Luther King, Jr., had been assassinated, the ghettos were on fire, the campuses were trashed, Richard Nixon had been elected—we'll explain all that to you guys when you're old enough. The McLuhanite reaction against poor old print-oriented, book-biased Western civ was also at its underwhelming peak: It was the era of mass poetry readings, street theater, the electronic global commune, oral history, anticopyrightists, the domestic samizdat, fringed miniskirts, macramé, lysergic acid, alfalfa sprouts, and the idea that virtuosity is a form of totalitarianism except maybe among rock stars. Between ourselves, happily, all this goes without reminding; otherwise that perfectly good room-service breakfast would go down the tubes.

Now, then! Librarians, despite their etymology, divide first into the book-oriented and those more attracted to audiovisuals, computers, oral ethnicity, and the like; second into the community service–oriented, who want to get the library out into the streets and countryside and vice versa, and the museum-oriented, who gravitate to Special Collections, Acquisitions—anywhere but Circulation. Young Katie Sherritt had been bibliophiliac if not from the first then at least from the second Mrs. Halsey got hold of her, as we have seen. In 1968, fresh from graduate library school, her black-militant poet and Hasid chamber-musician behind her, her Chilean Marxist just entering her life, she began work at the Pratt in Circulation, became fast friends with May Jump and friends with May Jump's fast friends, and threw herself ardently into the community-service camp. Her enthusiasm for books did not diminish, but she learned from May to appreciate the role of the oral in the library's services to the ill-lettered.

Among her new friends were several mostly young women whose shared interests went beyond library science to backpacking, canoeing, environmentalism, and feminism. Though a few were lesbian, most had, like Kate, male lovers, and some had husbands and children. Even the straights, however, enjoyed leaving their men behind for occasional camp-outs with the group, and it was at one of those, the following October, that Katherine mentioned the extraordinary bookmark she'd found that morning in Books Returned: a paper tampon-wrapper, marking the pages of Burton's *Anatomy of Melancholy*. Immediately a high school librarian rejoined that she'd once got the tampon itself, in a copy of *The Second Sex;* another, that she was still scratching her head over a secondhand condom she'd found years before in *Little Women*.

Since nearly all present had done time in Circulation, the list of remarkable bookmarks quickly grew: IBM cards, clip-on sunglasses, a single sock, dental floss, laundry and grocery lists, blank and canceled checks, parking and theater tickets. May Jump strummed her guitar: paper money, paper clips, love letters, business letters, pressed flowers, autumn leaves, postcards, greeting cards, playing cards, calling cards. Right 'round the campfire now, in turn. *Strum:* a Mason-jar ring, uh, hairpins, hair ribbons, prize ribbons. *Strum:* a broken drive belt, a black lace garter, a knitting needle, a 500-*lire* note. *Strum:* Band-Aids fresh and used, a dried strip of lean bacon, a *whole fried egg*.

Said Kath when they got hold of their mirth, We should make an exhibit, and found herself elected on the spot to do so. The group would pass the word around among their colleagues; the list would grow; they would assemble for display in the Cathedral Street windows of the Pratt either the items themselves—all but the X-rated ones—or duplicates and replicas. No exaggeration permitted; each item to be labeled as to source and, where possible, title of book thus marked. Pensive May Jump then wondered aloud What exactly is it we're laughing and shaking our heads at, sisters? What *about* these crazy bookmarks? One woman ventured It's a mad mad world out there. Thoughtsome Kate went further: Those bookmarks, she said in effect, remind us that beyond the orderly world of the library—the "book museum," as some of her higher-tech data-retrievalists scornfully called it—lies the disorderly world of the World, where, despite the age of electronics, books are yet read (at least opened, marked, and closed) by all sorts of people in all sorts of human situations. Her actual words were Those bookmarks are the people's loan to the lending library.

Growled May Jump Bravo, and more or less fell in love with Katherine Sherritt then and there. Bravo, says Peter Sagamore now, and would do likewise had he not long since done.

Three things ensued. First, back at the Pratt in the weeks thereafter, more and more involved with Jaime Aiquina, Katherine did indeed mount that bookmark exhibit (which came to include a whole windowful of "UFOs": unidentifiable flat objects). Subtitled "The Public's Gifts to the Public Library," it was such a hit in Baltimore that it subsequently traveled around the Maryland county library system and was much imitated by libraries in other states. Assembling it brought K and May Jump closer—they became apartment-mates—and led Katherine, in May's words, out of Circulation and into circulation: out of the bookstacks into the world of oral history and inner-city folktale-collecting, though she never lost her love of books.

Second, out there that night on the pine-girt shore of Deep Creek Lake, the women's talk turned from stories about extraordinary bookmarks to stories generally; thence to stories about women as traditional tellers of stories, especially to children (the bardic tradition, they acknowledged, was principally male, and the present-day professional Arab storytellers, like African grizots, are exclusively male; but then there is Scheherazade, there is Socrates's Diotima, there are Hawthorne's "damn'd scribbling women," who dominated the popular novel almost from its inception and continue to do so); thence to stories about women as story*keepers* (three-fourths of Katherine's newly ordained fellow M.S.'s in Library Science were Ms.'s).

Well. Among the group's other ties turned out to be a shared pleasure in sharing these stories, and so—third—before the weekend ended they'd invented the American Society for the Preservation of Storytelling, with Scheherazade as its proposed *patronne*. Right on, cheered one of May's girlfriends: Beguile the pigs and save our sisters. Replied nettled Katherine Scheherazade saved the king, too, and bore him three children and married him besides. Cracked May And look where Muslim women have been ever since.

In the event, they dropped both Scheherazade and Cleopatra (suggested by their acronym) as inappropriate totems for an American society; but a line was drawn already which only Kath's and May's friendship kept amicable for the next few years, and which eventually threatened to split the organization: the line between those who, like May Jump, wanted to keep things not only female but feminist, and those who, like Katherine Sherritt, wanted the society open to all storytellers, regardless of sex. In fact, the complexion of the ASPS (in whose organizing May Jump found her true vocation) was unmistakably feminist, from the name to the thrust of its leading spirits; but K's camp managed to keep its membership and most of its activities open to men as well. That original meeting was called DC-1, after Deep Creek Lake, and for publicity purposes each subsequent annual convention was similarly initialed and numbered.

In 1976, when May left the Pratt to become full-time director of what by then had become a genuinely national organization, she made the mistake, in Katherine Sherritt's judgment, of moving the ASPS central office to Washington (till then she'd been running it out of their old apartment and a cubbyhole in one of the Pratt's branch libraries) and herself to Annapolis. In Kate's view—particularly given that a number of current ASPS officers were also National Organization for Women people—seating the society in the capital would decisively shift its concerns from storytelling to sexual politics.

May had shrugged: Let it. Sure enough, by the end of the 1970s, ASPS was overshadowed by NAPPS (the National Association for the Preservation and Perpetuation of Storytelling), a purer outfit, with headquarters in eastern Tennessee and a strong Appalachian/Ozark flavor. See? had said Kate. Never mind, had said May, whose counterposition was that most U.S. storytelling in fact gets done in cities, because Number One that's where most people are, Number Two that's where most nonreaders are (May will not use the term *illiterates*), and Number Three that's where most oral-culture ethnic concentrations are, including previously rural blacks and hillbillies and excepting really only Amerindians and Eskimos. Katherine couldn't disagree with that argument, and in fact ASPS stayed alive and not exclusively feminist by emphasizing its urban/ethnic flavor. The charter members, it is true, are still inclined to get together around Blue Ridge and Allegheny campfires; but enough of those women are, like Katherine, happily bonded to their men—some of those men first-class storytellers themselves—to preserve a measure of hormonal balance in the society inspired by a tampon wrapper in Burton's *Anatomy of Melancholy*.

Humpty explains to Dumpty what tampons and, a fortiori, their wrappers are, though *she's* never seen either, either. Their mother wouldn't have imagined she could wax nostalgic about menstruation, but there she goes, prompted perhaps by that *SEX EDUCATION* playscript. Prompts Peter The FBI, and assures her we won't forget to call Irma.

Yeah, well, obvious enough, K supposes: When she and Jaime Aiquina were running up mileage on I-95 between Bolton Hill and Embassy Row to be with each other, and she and likeminded gringo Latinophiles founded Hands Off South and Central America, our various three-letter secret police outfits took a certain interest, as did those of their counterparts south of the border who maintained operatives in D.C. Even before President Allende was murdered in Santiago and his former ambassador Orlando Letelier ditto in Washington, the HOSCAs correctly assumed their telephones to be tapped and their organization otherwise monitored, perhaps even infiltrated. The American High Sixties were, after all, the palmy days of Operation COINTELPRO and other big-ticket domestic snooperies and harassments, when President LBJ entertained his friends with J. Edgar Hoover's tapes of Martin Luther King Jr.'s humping his lady parishioners, and the actress Jean Seberg was hounded quite to death by strategically circulated gossip that—but never mind, Pity, never mind, Terror: We'll initiate you into governmental reality when your little characters are formed and sturdified. What confounds the heart, but doesn't quite break it, is that college-educated American grown-ups in Silver Spring and Des Moines and San Bernardino, with salaries and schoolkids and mortgages and pension plans, devoted years of their mortal office lives and millions of dollars of the taxpayers' money to breaking the law of the land and the norms of common decency to intercept, transcribe, analyze, file, and report upon the high-minded, low-level, mildly leftish, essentially patriotic though frequently dissenting and above all not very effective grumblings of the likes of HOSCA, not to mention burglarizing, sabotaging, besmirching, and otherwise persecuting various of its membership. Oyoyoyoyoy, kids: Sometimes your momma hates the fucking facts of life.

So anyhow, then the CIA and ITT and General Pinochet made their big move in Seventy-three with Henry Kissinger's blessing, and the Chileno goon-squads literally got away with murder in our nation's capital, and Jaime Aiquina, who had been a gentle-mannered moderate Marxist, joined the Movimiento de Izquierdo Revolucionario and snuck back home in time to get his poor sweet body tortured and mutilated and *desaparecido*'d, and I went kind of crazy for a while, but good old May Jump not only kept my head together but saved me from forever despising my country, though not sundry arms of its federal government, by keeping me busy with those rafting trips and bluegrass pluckfests and bookmobile safaris into darkest Baltimore. She saved me for you and these several children, is what she did, and I'm going to call her up and thank her once again just as soon as we reach the end of this story.

Says Peter Me too. We three, say Tambo and Bones at least.

Which is, says Kate, that more out of friendship for me than out of her personal politics, May took a busy interest in HOSCA, and that interest earned her her very own personal file in our Federal Bureau of Investigation, which thereafter kept an undercover eye on ASPS as well, since some of our radical feminists were fairly radical on other questions too. So the chances are—and here's as much of a point as this story's ever likely to manage—the chances are that a certain number of entry-level white-collar FBI employees in Prince George's and Montgomery Counties, Maryland, and Fairfax County, Virginia—people morally no better or worse than my office staff at the Pratt or yours in the U. of M. English Department—have seen on their little green screens that the wife of the moderately noted writer Peter Sagamore and expectant mother of his children has slept around with niggers and commies and dykes, and goddamn it, honey, that's none of their smirking business!

She's crying; likewise Arm & Hammer & Sickle, in frightened sympathy. Peter comforts all as best he can. And do you think nobody else gets to those files? Kate cries. One day we'll be turned down for a bank loan, or our car insurance will be cancelled, or one of these children's third-grade teachers will have a certain shit-eating grin on her face, and we won't even know why. Do you think I want them to read in some future biography of you that their mother went to bed once with May Jump? It's an insult to everybody!

Peter comforts her. She'll wipe the fucking grin off that third-grade teacher's face! K bawls. What's the crime? Conspiring to debate and protest nonviolently the secret agenda of U.S. foreign policy in Central and South America, that's what, plus poor-mouthing our secret police. I'm so tired of being pregnant I could just shit!

Peter comforts her, and this time she lets herself be comforted. He mentions the Freedom of Information Act. Never mind the Freedom of

Information Act, sniffles Katie; it's by the Freedom of Information Act that May found out this stuff. But they censor what they give you anyhow. We need a Freedom *from* Information Act, is what we need. She blows her nose. Bastards. I'll call Mom now. No; I'd better call May first. But she'll be at work. What do we want to do with this goddamn lay day? When's checkout time in this place? Could you hand me the phone?

CHESAPEAKE & POTOMAC

is the Maryland telephone company, not another brace of names for our work in progress. P's relieved that K's experience of impudent wiretapping has not soured her on telephones; C & P therapy is a standby on her side of our house. He supposes that if she gets together with May Jump, he'll pick up some odds and ends at Fawcett's Boat Supplies Inc. and then spend the morning making notes on some of these stories. No drafts, Kath reminds him between Kleenexes. No drafts, he agrees. Or, if she can't get hold of May, we'll just stroll and window-shop and then check out of here and have lunch somewhere and think about packing it in. His wife declares We're not packing it in; we haven't even met Don Quixote yet. Her husband says Then maybe in the late afternoon, if the wind drops, we'll move out to the anchorage or sail up the Severn for the night.

He goes to shave. Kate's flypaper memory holds every telephone number that matters to her, but when a husky-rich middle-aged woman's voice answers, she wonders whether she maybe hit a wrong button on the touchtone. She hears what sounds like a man and another woman arguing in the background; before she can ask Is this May Jump's residence? the first woman says Hold on please and mildly asks the arguers Would you guys keep it down a bit? and then to Katherine Sorry there.

Is this Eight Oh Nine Five?

I'll check, the woman says, surprisingly. Yeah.

May Jump's residence? K's sure now that it isn't, but the throaty voice says You got it; who's calling, please? and a bit later May's on the line. Kiss? She's been down all week with a virus, May reports, but it's gone now, but she's staying out of the office till Monday. No, that wasn't her new friend that answered, the one she was coming home from Ocean City with last time she and Katherine talked. That was her new friend's mother, as a matter of fact: the maybe next president of ASPS and HOSCA both, whom Kiss has simply got to meet just as soon as possible. Where are you guys? It is quickly arranged that May will pick Katherine up in front of the Hilton in half an hour. Not to worry about the virus, Mama, May assures her; it's gone completely. I want you to meet my new friend . . . aaand . . . our son!

Maze?

May chuckles: Half an hour.

Peter shakes *his* head, too.

Now we call Nopoint Point, does Katherine, and gets her brother Andrew, the only one home just now besides Olive Treadway. Andy makes note of our lay-day intentions, accepts our thanks for the Brandy roses and the room-service breakfast, and relays to us his mother's reminder, who knew her daughter would be calling, that we are to double-check our bill to make sure that that breakfast doesn't get mistakenly charged to us. Says smiling Kath Okay. Now look here, Chipper: What's come over our older brother?

Okay, well. The boy confirms that Willy has done a one-eighty on a couple of things and adds the information that Mister Trippe (the ex–interior secretary) blew him away last Sunday on the matter of supporting the Baldwin-for-Congress campaign. Andrew doesn't even want to repeat what Mister Trippe called Poonie, to Willy's face, right there on the tennis court, not long after we sailed off. He'll maybe tell Peter in private, and Peter can tell Kath. But he doesn't know whether that set-down is connected to Willy's turnaround with Molly on the Deniston question or not.

Katherine Sherritt can detect high harmonics of emotion through microwave relays and kilometers of copper wire, as if a C & P telephone set were a $2K state-of-the-art stereo. What are you worrying about, Chipper?

What? Nah. Look, he really can't discuss stuff on the phone. Do we have any idea when we'll be coming home? Now, Kath says at once, if you need us.

No. . . . No.

Chip?

No. You guys take care. Have fun.

K's frowning across our hotel room to Peter, toweling his neck, who has caught her tone and stepped out of the bathroom to stand by. Well, she says to Chip. Kiss everybody?

Yeah. Bye, Kath.

The boy is twelve. Moreover, we consider, he is Andrew Christopher Sherritt, not some dork. In the matter of his needing us, if he had meant yes he'd not have said no, no? All the same we frown; we wonder; and we shall call again when we can.

Hum.

LET'S GET GOING ON THIS LAY DAY OF OURS,

all right?

All right. K will walk P as far as Fawcett's Boat Supplies Inc. and then stroll back. She washes, we dress; she takes the pretty roses with her to give to May and May's friend and May-and-May's-friend's son, whatever *that* may turn out to mean. In the down elevator, Peter reports that yesterday's sight of *Rocinante IV* with its odd hailport, *Montesinos,* has got him thinking about that most mysterious episode in Cervantes's novel: the one wherein D.Q. has himself lowered by rope into the spooky Cave of Montesinos in La Mancha and is hauled up sound asleep half an hour later and awakened only with difficulty. He straightway prays God to forgive Sancho Panza and their guide for having broken off the most delightful vision any mortal ever had: a vision so fantastic that not only does Sancho disbelieve it, as might be expected, but Cervantes pretends to quote a marginalium by the Moorish historian Cide Hamete Benengeli himself, complaining of the episode's implausibility; yet so compelling to the Don that later in the novel he offers to believe Sancho Panza's lie of flying to heaven on a wooden horse if Sancho will believe the story of what he saw and did in the Cave of Montesinos.

What is singular about the episode, in Peter Sagamore's opinion, is that of all the knight's encounters with the apparently marvelous, this is the only one unrefuted by reality. It is never accounted for, and though nothing in the plot turns upon it, Quixote clings to his belief in it to the end. Alas, however, neither Peter nor memorious Katherine can remember what it was Quixote claims to have seen and done down there. Maybe we'll pass a bookstore in today's wanderings and check it out; or May Jump might have a copy at her place. Maybe there's a Montesinos, Florida? Anyhow, it is an appropriate hailport for *Rocinante IV,* because in Peter Sagamore's judgment the Montesinos episode is as central to *Don Quixote* as La Mancha is to Spain and the Cave of Montesinos to La Mancha.

Katherine Sherritt says, crossing the lobby, that if the late Jean Heartstone's Magic Language Theory is worth the paper it never got printed on, then this much talk about Don Quixote ought to pipe him right aboard. We step out into the gusty sunshine—Hoo, what a breeze; good-bye, roses!—walk a quarter of a block, and there he is, leaving Fawcett's Boat Supplies Inc. as we approach. He squints and leans into the wind like Jacques Tati playing Monsieur Hulot, holding a faded blue Greek fisherman's cap onto his head. A wiry, gray-bearded, leather-looking old chap in lean worn jeans and long-sleeved workshirt, he carries a coil of light nylon line in his hat-holding hand as if he's about to noose his own skinny brown neck, and in his other a plastic shopping bag. Says Kath, who's in no shape to run, Go catch him and tell me all about it over lunch, but at that moment a silver Jaguar sedan honks and turns out of the traffic to and from the Spa Creek bridge; it pulls up onto the Fawcett's parking-lot sidewalk, blocking D.Q. from view, and the woman driving it calls from behind the wheel: Kiss?

Kath squeezes her husband's hand. As we stroll carward, May Jump pops out and around behind the car and trots to meet us.

GAY MAY

She's wearing khaki slacks and old running shoes and a too-small un-ironed tails-out short-sleeved madras shirt instead of a shredded greenish paisley flotation envelope; otherwise, that shot of "May" in that *SEX EDUCATION* playscript back there in Day 1 in Dun Cove is not far off the mark. May Jump is russet-cropped, big-boned, green-eyed, freckled, friendly; she is makeupless, outdoorsy-looking, sure-voiced, strong of grip; an easy pal, nobody's fool. Pete had a friend much like May Jump down in Hoopersville in boyhood days and thus knew the type before either he or his sister Sue-Ann or Charlie-for-Charlene Smart ever heard the word *lesbian* or could have imagined such a thing as women making out with other women. Charlie Smart was the daughter of a waterman who'd wanted a son; she was a tough and bluff and affable tomboy much attracted to Sue-Ann Sagamore in junior high but almost as close friends with Peter; she was the best all-round infielder and touch-football running back in lower Dorchester, a wondrous cusser, a precocious smoker of Camel cigarettes regular size no filter and drinker of Schlitz beer. Such young women as Charlie Smart in that innocent place and time had free and happy early high school years, perhaps more than usually confused dating experiences in later high school; they next went either to nursing school in Cambridge or to the state teachers college over in Salisbury, where they majored in phys ed and had certain new experiences that surprised them; they then returned to South Dorchester and, depending on the strength and clarity of their desires, either led celibate coaching or nursing lives or settled in like Charlie Smart with a similar soul and were occasionally looked askance at but never harassed by the hometowners—unless, in a moment of madness, one of them laid unequivocally amorous hands upon one of her charges, in which case a quiet fuss was made, and the offender left town without complaint or due process, like Charlie Smart, to butch it in the big city. Some years ago, reminded of Charlene Smart by his acquaintanceship with May Jump, Peter Sagamore asked his sister Did you sort of know, back in high school, that old Charlie Smart was lesbian? and Sue-Ann Sagamore Hooper, smoking a king-size low-tar filter-tip cigarette and drinking low-calorie beer straight from the sweating can, drawled D'you s'pose she was?

May Jump now reassures us Don't worry, shaking hands with Peter and carefully hugging Katherine, kissing her hair: My bug's all gone. Come meet my new family. Peter doesn't really want to, but chides himself for his ungenerosity. He truly believes that what still sticks in his craw is not Kath's having at a shaky stage in her life once gone to bed with this good-hearted woman, but Jean Heartstone's having been exploited virtually to death by that other dyke, that talentless ex-criminal procuress-poet. Katherine, in the middle, wants to know What's this son business, Maisie? as we move to the car. No sign of Don Quixote now; he has cut behind Fawcett's Boat Supplies Inc. and gone either into town or back out toward the docks. May chuckles Wait'll you hear, then steps in front of us, walking backward with her hands on K's shoulders. But you gotta be nonjudgmental till you do hear, okay?

Peter hums. May complains to Katherine He's humming. He hums, says Kath. Words like *nonjudgmental* make him hum. So hum, May says to Peter, but be nonjudgmental. We're at the silver Jaguar, on the passenger side. On the front seat is a fat boy the age of Andrew Sherritt, but with slicked-down short black hair, reflector sunglasses, and, improbably, the beginnings of a mustache; also a floral polyester long–short-sleeve shirt that Chip wouldn't be caught dead in, and shiny black slacks, blue socks, black shoes. He looks to Katherine like a miniature Central American right-wing general in Miami exile or a shopping-mall demonstrator-salesman of Yamaha electronic organs with pushbutton rhythm accompaniments. On the rear seat is a scared-eyed, lean-faced, punk-cut, twiggy-limbed, cigarette-smoking woman younger than Katherine, who reminds us both at once of a movie actress whose name neither of us can recall but who plays roles like that. The Jaguar is air-conditioned; the pair both push their window-down buttons, the man-boy later than the woman, as we approach.

Pete Sagamore and Kate Sherritt, May announces. This is my friend Simon, and this is my friend Marian, Sy's mom.

Owing to our respective positions on the sidewalk, Katherine says Hello to Marian first, wondering how so small and thin a woman ever squeezed out so gross a boy, and Peter shakes hands with Simon first, noting that the son, surprisingly shy in the handshake, must outweigh the mother twice over. The mother, he notes next when we switch places, is shy too, at least of handshaking, despite the orange-streaked hair and green eye shadow, and has next to no breasts under the sunny-side-up fried eggs printed on her Ocean City boardwalk T-shirt.

Old Sy here wonders if he can have a look at your sailboat, May informs us; his aunt and uncle are big-deal sailor types. The Marian woman says at once But he's not allowed to go on it. The Simon boy groans, but not loudly, Aw Ma, and we see that they really are mother and son. *Remarkable,* we suppose, would be a reasonably nonjudgmental adjective for that circumstance. Sure he can go on it, says easy Katherine. Why shouldn't he go on it? Is this your car, Maze? Oh: These flowers are for you-all.

For one reason or another, Peter Sagamore often wants to kiss his wife. Just now it's for the light quick way she has moved the attention off uncomfortable Simon, when P himself was in fact too mildly curious— about why a boy that age isn't allowed aboard a boat—to feel properly the lad's discomfort. May busses Katherine for the roses and explains that the car belongs to Marian's mother, the woman who answered the phone earlier on. She's back at May's apartment doing business: a real mensch of a woman down from Baltimore to manipulate some people on the governor's staff. We will love her. Katherine declares that Peter has got to get on with his errands in Fawcett's and all, and that our boat is parked just over yonder, so why don't they four ride around so Sy can have a look before they do the next thing. We two kiss good-bye and remind each other that we'll rendezvous back at the Hilton around checkout time or in the Annapolis hospital maternity ward should the unexpected befall the expectant. Peter politely declares he's glad to have seen May Jump again and met her friends. The Marian woman orders the Simon person to come on back there with her so that May's friend can sit up front, but Kath says No, nonsense, and climbs in back, though the large boy says, half a measure too late, I don't mind, in a way that—along with his certain shyness and, unless we're imagining it, an air of disappointment that Peter's not coming along with them—makes him seem to us possibly more likable than his unfortunate appearance suggests. Has May really adopted him, we wonder separately, or what? Katherine will soon learn, but Peter won't until later in this lay day.

They drive off, waving. P waves back and goes on into Fawcett's Boat Supplies Inc.

THIS IS OUR STORY,

not simply Peter Sagamore's, but we'll stay with the man just now because he's going into Fawcett's Boat Supplies Inc.: a Harrods or Bloomingdale's of retail marine supply stores, well stocked, pricey, and serious, specializing in sailboat stuff, which we both enjoy looking at. We buy at Fawcett's only when we need an item sooner than the big discounteries in New Rochelle and Philadelphia can mail it to us; also when we need to soothe our consciences for so frequently using the place to inspect and ask advice about what we're ordering from the cut-rate catalogues. This morning Peter admires a $610 two-speed self-tailing jibsheet winch, which we don't need at all but is a beautiful piece of British hardware; an $800 autopilot, ditto, though it must be nice especially in long calm stretches of motoring, but then we don't have a motor to motor us through such stretches anyhow, do we; a $900 roller-reefing-and-furling headsail system that reminds him of last night's sail-shortening dream and *would* be good to have if we had nine hundred free bucks and were going to be doing more sailing than we're used to rather than less; and three $3 nautical charts of portions of the upper Bay, two of which he buys to replace a pair of six-year-old ones aboard *Story*.

As he examines one of these charts to make sure it incorporates certain recent renumberings of the main ship-channel buoys above the Bay Bridge, he hears a sailboat-looking young woman salesclerk ask a sailboat-looking middle-aged assistant-managerial man about the skinny gray-bearded old gent with the Down East accent who looked to her like a cross between Uncle Sam and the Ancient Mariner and who just bought a bunch of quarter-inch double-braided nylon and stainless-steel self-tapping screws. The man replies That's Don Quicksoat, pronouncing the title Don as though it were a first name and the name as though it named an instant breakfast cereal. Everybody calls him Capn Don.

There are few customers in the store. The managerial-appearing fellow has put on half-glasses to look something up in the library of manufacturers' catalogues at the cashier's counter, but he doesn't mind pausing to tell the clerk and Peter (who has rolled his charts and joined the conversation) what he knows. Capn Don is regarded up and down the Intracoastal as a more or less engaging eccentric, one of many such migratory oddballs on that waterway: salty solitaries, usually late-middle-aged bachelors or widowers, usually singlehanding an old clunker as weather-beaten as themselves from winter in the Keys to summer Down East. Sometimes they're serious passagemaking sailors, even 'round-the-worlders, following in the wake of Joshua Slocum and Sir Francis Chichester; more typically they're make-do drifters, following the plane of the ecliptic, taking it easy on both their vessels and themselves. Some eke out their retirement income with spells of pick-up labor in the boatyards along their leisurely way; most prefer to get along on their pension checks. For that reason, one doesn't normally find their likes in list-price establishments like Fawcett's; they prowl the salvage yards for secondhand gear and buy their maintenance supplies from the discount houses. Sometimes they steal.

Capn Don Quicksoat is an exception: likes to talk; buys good gear for his weathered old boat, which is reported to be soundly built and well maintained except cosmetically. Those self-tapping screws and that double-braided nylon, for example, he could have picked up ten or twenty percent cheaper at the general hardware store just a block away; but he had a question about swaged terminals to ask of Fawcett's rigging specialists, and considerately purchased his other items while he was here. The man is said to pretend to believe that he really is Don Quicksoat, the old fellow in the book. He will explain to anyone who asks, the assistant manager has heard, that he and his boat have been blown by a certain magician all the way from Spain to the USA, and from the old days to now. People therefore reasonably assume Capn Donald to be daft, though the assistant manager himself has seen no evidence of daftness in him. He is also said to be rich and, if crazy, crazy like a fox. Others have wondered whether he's an elderly drug-runner, of whom the Intracoastal Waterway has a few. He has even been reported to be a famous writer living incognito, gathering material for his next bestseller. In any case, he pays cash; he doesn't shoplift; and he bathes more often than some others of his fraternity. The assistant manager sees him just about every spring and fall.

His boat, says Peter, says "Montesinos." Where's that?

The assistant manager looks over the tops of his half-glasses, pleased. I asked Capn Don that question once. He said if he knew where the hell it was, he'd go back there.

P gets directions to the nearest bookstore and beats up Main Street against the remarkable wind, clutching his rolled charts. Annapolis clinks like a giant wind-chime under sky as blue as bottom paint: thousands of unsecured halyards thunking hollow aluminum spars. The Crown Bookshop has the Signet Classics edition of *D.Q.* He finds the Cave of Montesinos episode and rereads it on the spot—chapters XXII and XXIII of Part Two—to check his memory, then buys the book in case Katherine wants to reread it too. Downhill and downwind to *Story,* straining lightly against its docklines like all its neighbors. P boards, disconnects the battery charger, which has done its automatic job, and opens ports and hatches to freshen the cabin. The little motion of the hull is so agreeable, the cabin so familiar and inviting, he decides to spend the rest of this lay-day morning aboard after all instead of back in our room. Later he'll transfer six years-worth of our annotations from the old charts to the new; just now he sets up the foldaway dinette table for a work surface and fetches out *Story*'s log to enter, let's see, Charlie Smart, our separate message-light dreams, as many items as he can remember from Katherine's bookmark exhibition, and what the Fawcett's man has told him about Captain Donald Quicksoat. Such a Heartstone overdose, he agrees with Katherine as he writes, must surely beam the old fellow aboard before checkout time.

PETER SAGAMORE IN THE CAVE OF MONTESINOS

He has recollected the episode pretty well, though not certain of its arresting details. It is a full hundred fathoms of rope—six hundred feet—that Quixote buys to descend into the cave with; he and Sancho and their guide are obliged to hack a path through thick brambles to reach the entrance; startled crows fly out of the underbrush at their approach—also bats, a sign that they are on the right track and that that track is pretty scary. In all, a daring bit of amateur speleology, well warranting Quixote's prayers to God and to his lady Dulcinea before he descends. The cave is real and deep: A translator's footnote remarks that local Manchegans believe it to run several kilometers, from its entrance-hole to the feudal castle of Rochefrías. The circumstance of that feudal castle, he supposes, together with the name Montesinos (a character from chivalric romance), inspired the episode. Cervantes has the retrieved and reluctantly awakened knight report that he came to rest upon the ledge of a cavity twelve to fourteen fathoms down, coiled the slack rope, and dropped off to sleep: not especially implausible for a man in his (seventeenth-century) fifties, exhausted by the strain of being lowered eighty feet down into a frightening black hole of unknown depth. He "woke," Quixote declares, to find himself in a beautiful meadow, within sight of a transparent crystal palace or castle. To make certain he wasn't dreaming, he tested himself carefully, as Peter often does in his own dreams, and satisfied himself that he was not.

The vision-adventure that follows, in Quixote's account, strikes P as only mildly interesting: Quixote is welcomed into the crystal palace by Montesinos himself, who at the battle of Roncesvalles five hundred years earlier, according to legend, cut out the heart of his mortally wounded cousin, Durandarte, at the latter's request, and delivered it to the slain knight's Lady Belerma. All three principals, much aged, are present in the palace under Merlin's ongoing enchantment: Faithful Montesinos has become a white-haired sage; noble Durandarte is laid out upon his own sarcophagus like a corpse embalmed, except that from time to time he repeats in verse his dying request, as if it had not long since been carried out. The peerless Lady Belerma, aged and ugly, appears in mourning, carrying her dead champion's pickled heart in a lace handkerchief. Montesinos explains to Quixote, who explains in turn to his "rescuers," that while the Enchanted neither eat nor sleep nor void excrement, much less die, they age, grow hair and nails, and—witness Lady Belerma—undergo the menopause.

They also suffer want, as the charming and unexpected end of Quixote's narrative-within-the-narrative attests. Montesinos and his visitor step outside the crystal palace into the meadow, where Quixote espies three peasant girls leaping and cavorting like frisky she-goats. One he recognizes to be none other than his own lady, Dulcinea del Toboso, under the Enchanter's spell with her maidservants like the rest. He calls to her; she flees from him—but then one of her maids comes saucily back to beg from him, on her mistress's behalf, a loan of six *reales*, offering Dulcinea's new dimity petticoat as collateral. The request astonishes Don Quixote, as this touch of Spanish realism astonishes and delights Peter Sagamore. Poverty, explains Señor Montesinos, extends even unto enchanted ladies of quality. The noble knight refuses the surety and gives the maidservant all the money he has: four reales, disbursed to him earlier by Sancho Panza to give as alms to the poor along their way. The mischievous maidservant takes the money and, in lieu of curtseying her thanks, capers six feet straight up into the air.

And that is the end of both Quixote's adventure (which he swears filled three whole days, not a mere half-hour) and his account of it, for at that moment in the former he awoke to find himself hauled up by Sancho out of cave and vision alike, and at this moment in the latter Sancho interrupts with protestations of utter disbelief. The knight's conviction remains unshaken: Another time, he patiently pledges, he will tell his squire such details of this cave-adventure as to compel belief. But he never does; at the novel's end, that pledge is still as outstanding as Quixote's loan of four reales to Dulcinea's saucy maid.

Peter Sagamore believes that he understands this curious story, not as a critic but as a fellow storyteller might understand it: fellow to both the enchanted Don Quixote who told it and the enchanter Miguel de Cervantes who dreamed it up and wrote it down. The realest parts of any dream are those strong details that waking leaves unexplained, or that no amount of waking explanation explains away. The sharp sensation of the double distance of that light in Peter's early-morning dream, for example—its being simultaneously two or three and two or three thousand yards away—he still feels in his nerves as clearly as he feels the present rocking of the boat and hears wind whistling through shrouds and stays; it is as real as they are. What pricks up the storyteller's ears about Quixote's Montesinos dream is not that business of three-day sojourns underground like Christ's and Dante's; not that chivalric baggage of crystal palaces, disheartened knights, weeping ladies. It is the combination of that homely beggary—hitting the old guy for four *reales* in mid-vision—and the fantastical detail of three women capering like she-goats in that meadow, bounding six feet straight up into the air! Peter's point, which he now enters in *Story*'s log, is that that irreducible, unforgettable detail goes as unexplained in Quixote's vision as the vision itself goes unexplained (and uncompleted) in *Don Quixote.*

Whatever his recent and current narrative hang-ups, Peter Sagamore is a professional. It would not be difficult for him to imagine endings to this story, even without the provocative presence in Annapolis Harbor of Capn Don and *Rocinante IV.* Indeed, without violating his pledge to Katherine, he permits himself a few lay-day notes. Seafaring is as alien to dusty *Don Quixote* (though not to its author, proud veteran of Lepanto) as landfaring to *The Odyssey,* its opposite number in other respects as well. P recalls hitchhiking across the Manchegan plains, en route from Granada to Madrid, over earth the color and texture of broken roof-tiles, through air as hot as a brick-kiln's and so dry that blinking actually scratched his eyes, as swallowing scratched his throat. Yet Odysseus ends his odyssey with an epic trek inland; and a central theme of *Quixote* Part Two is Sancho Panza's governorship of the Isle of Barataria: reality mimicking chivalric fantasy. . . .

He writes no further. Stung by imitators who leaped with Quixotes of their own into the ten-year breach between Parts One and Two of his novel, Cervantes not only kills his hero unequivocally in the final chapter of Part Two, supplying even a notarized death-certificate against spurious literary resurrections, but closes his book with the author's farewell to his pen, which he enjoins from ever writing again of Don Quixote. Where the master stopped, dare the apprentice go? Deeper yet into that cave, beyond the fourteen-fathom ledge, to the end of Quixote's rope?

Such must be P.S.'s future considerations, when the time comes for him to set down the story of Capn Don and *Rocinante IV.* What halts his pen now (that is, toward the end of the paragraph before the paragraph before this) is that word *mimicking,* which, the moment he writes its first three letters, reminds him where he saw once before, two years ago, that woman in May Jump's borrowed car, May Jump's new lover, that Marian, who looks to us like a punked-out version of Carol Kane in the movie *Hester Street*. I'M SO HAPPY I COULD JUST SHIT, her then T-shirt had declared, in that Fells Point bar where, following Douglas Townshend's lead, he had passed her on his way to meet the Prince of Darkness. Doug had spoken her name and courtly kissed her cheek: Mim. Her hair had been different then, teased out. She had glanced at Peter with those unhappy eyes of hers and gone her way, and he had gone his, upstairs to speak with Doomsday Factors in the pleasant room above . . . Carla's Cavern.

Carla B Silver. Franklin Key Talbott, that Frederick's brother, that CIA-exposer, that sailorman, and his wife, Somebody Silver, that sharp-looking American Lit lady, Leah Silver, yeah, at Doug's Georgetown dinner party a hundred years ago. That Simon boy's aunt and uncle, the big-deal cruising sailors, sure. Peter is out of the cabin in a hurry, blood ahum—Where's a pay phone? Way over there—hoping he has twenty cents change and that May Jump's number's not unlisted. He has; it isn't; *Jump, M.;* the phone bell rattles in some crosstown flat. Wind blams the booth. Our man unfairly curses all lesbians from Sappho through Willa Cather and Gertrude Stein to Carson McCullers and Charlene Smart. No way gay May could have known about the John Arthur Paisley connection, whatever it is, but screw that: That is his Katherine she's got in the clutches of her freako girlfriend's Gypsy-looking mother, whose missing common-law sonofabitch CIA spook of a husband once scared this Sagamore shitless with that poisoned mint-tea trick or nontrick. Peter wants to kill.

His watch says just past eleven. Amazing: He was down in *Story*'s cabin as long as Don Quixote was down in the Cave of Montesinos. Phone rattles on; wind goes blooey; P pounds back at it from his side of the glass, hangs up, steps out of the booth half frantic, wondering whether to run back to the Hilton or what. Remembers *Story*'s cabin is open; screw *Story*. Glances over that way anyhow and sees his great-bellied wife and that Carla B Silver person stepping out of that silver Jaguar down by the municipal transient slips! He *sprints,* then forces himself down to a jog toward them. Is that—Sure it is; let's hear it for Jean Heartstone: It's Donald Quicksoat standing on the sidewalk staring at *Story*, toward which the two chatting women stroll. Katherine holds her maternity skirt down against the wind: a dignified womanly gesture that touches Peter's heart. Where are May Jump and the others? The white-pants-suited Silver woman gesticulates with both hands. By when Peter reaches calling range, they and Capn Don are almost together.

He shouts his wife's dear name. She turns. He sees her smile at sight of him and say something aside to that Carla B Silver. Capn Don looks as if about to address them, but with so furious a rush does our man come on, the old fellow backs off a step.

Kate wonders aloud whether something's the matter.

Bursts back Pete 'Sthat Fells Point Doomsday lady! and thrusts himself between them as if wife and children were about to be physically assaulted, taking rough care not to bump the latter in his haste. Kate complains *Peter,* three dots and a period in her voice; the Carla B Silver person cocks a black eyebrow, but looks on approvingly. She's already *explained*, Katherine says. Says the Carla B Silver person Some things, anyhow. Donald Quicksoat approaches, smiling dolefully, one forefinger raised, his left eye winking and his eyebrows twinkling, as if to introduce himself. *Not now,* brusque Peter tells him. Begins Katherine That nice couple we met at Doug's first dinner party. P cuts her off: He knows, he knows; let him close up the boat and let's check out of here. Honey, you're being rude: Miz Silver's lost her son and her husband too. Rude Peter says pointedly to the Carla B Silver person I'm sorry about your son. The woman flinches, but says evenly Let me buy lunch for the three of us. No mint tea.

The skipper of *Rocinante IV* makes a final pass in our direction as, having gotten his wife's signal that he had better shelve his outrage and hear what Mrs. Doomsday Factor has to say, Peter buttons *Story* up and reluctantly helps K into the woman's car. We both sit in the back; Katherine takes Peter's hand to calm him. The old sailor calls Carla B Silver? Our driver lowers her electric window. Some other time, Don, okay? I got a fare and the meter's running.

I haven't seen you in two hundred years, Capn Don complains, shaking hands with her but looking also at us and winking like his boat.

Stop by Fells Point and catch me up. We got to run now, Skipper. Carla B Silver is cordial but firm; he's crestfallen; she raises her window and backs out of the parking slot, muttering Jee-*sus* to the backseat. Amused Kath asks Is his name really Don?

But her husband says We're not going to talk about that now and demands of the Carla B Silver person What are you in our story for? He doesn't know why his question came out like that, quite; it upped and did. Katherine protests She's *told* me, honey. Don't be so hostile. I'll explain it all later. Insists hostile Peter Sagamore—not hostile to Kate, mind—

I WANT EVERYTHING EXPLAINED RIGHT NOW.

The Carla B Silver person says Damn it, then, all right, and whips the Jag over to the nearest painted curb and turns to face us, resting her chin on the back of her hand on the back of the front seat. The long version takes sixty years to tell and isn't finished yet; I'll give you the short version.

And for the next some hours she does, beginning there in the car at the curb, then over club sandwiches upstairs in the Hilton restaurant after we check out—Peter is dehostilized already by that time, partly by reason of what his wife has told him alone in our room as we collected our stuff—finally back aboard *Story*, the three of us sitting in the cockpit, friends by then, Carla B Silver (as we shall now regularly call her, as she calls herself) holding in one hand a cigarillo in a cigarillo holder and in the other the spike-heeled pumps she has properly removed to come aboard. No sign of old C.D.Q. Sure, she knows him; Carla B Silver knows a lot of people; he ties up at Fells Point now and then and stops by her place for a beer, Dos Equis. She wishes her daughter Lee could meet him; Leah Talbott knows Cervantes and that crowd the way Carla B Silver knows the Maryland State Liquor Control Board, and Capn Don really does pretend to believe he's Whatsisname. There is more to it and to him, but that's another story. The main one told, C.B S. goes down into our cabin to pee. I'd get claustrophobia in one of these, she says afterward, meaning small cruising sailboats, but it must be something just to let go the ropes and sail off, the way my Lee did with her Frankele. Maybe one day.

Says Katherine, holding Peter's hand, It's the best there is.

We are subdued. Now that he can regard her with dehostilized eyes, Peter sees that May Jump's new girlfriend's mother is a mighty fine-looking sixty, trim and dark and seasoned, womanly and tough. A bit much for his taste in the makeup and jewelry way, but she wears them well. He says, and means it, I hope we'll cross paths again with your daughter and your son-in-law. Brother-in-law?

Carla B Silver says wryly Son-in-law by law and common-law brother-in-law, lighting another cigarillo downwind from Katherine. Fred and I never got around to marrying.

Fred is her name for Frederick Mansfield Talbott, we have learned: her disappeared Prince of Darkness; father of her disappeared grown son, Jonathan, but not of her daughters, Leah and Marian, a.k.a. Mim, the fruit of an early and short-lived marriage terminated thirty years since by auto crash. Carla B Silver, we have learned, was born in Europe of Rumanian Gypsy and German Jewish parents—unlikely match, but such things happen—both of whom died in the Nazi camps that she herself survived, she won't say how. The surname is her late American husband's, himself of German Jewish extraction. To him and to the non-Rumanian side of her own ancestry, Carla B Silver credits her head for business: Only twenty when Allan Silver died, she successfully managed his Baltimore row-house real estate interests, most unGypsy, and eventually opened her Fells Point bar, most unJewish, which now she hopes to expand ambitiously into Baltimore's Harborplace. Back in her row-house realty days, we have learned, she took in a Johns Hopkins undergraduate named Frederick Talbott, five years her junior, who subsequently joined Allan Dulles's CIA and became Douglas Townshend's protégé; by him she had the aforementioned son (whom Kath now remembers having met, in fact, at a Baltimore HOSCA gathering in '74!), and with her lover's loyal if peripatetic assistance, raised all three children while overseeing her business interests. She is, as afore-established, in Annapolis today not mainly to say hello to her currently lesbian space-cadet daughter (but wait till Peter hears, Kath cautioned him early in this history) but to lobby and dicker with some statehouse types concerning Carla's Inner Harbor. She may well be about to become a wealthy woman.

But none of this is why she's in our story. How her devoted-but-often-absent young common-law covert-operations husband grew up to be the veritable Prince of Darkness, Carla B Silver cannot herself quite say—other than that, as Doug Townshend once attested to Peter Sagamore, the chap found in himself a great natural talent for Prince-of-Darknessing, and great natural talent is not easily suppressed where there is ample inducement to its exercise. C.B S. herself, we have learned, is politically indifferent except on the subjects of free enterprise, upon which she thrives, and German nationalism, which not surprisingly gives her the heeb-jeebs. But her lover, whose politics were the Agency's, and her children, whose politics ranged from mild socialism (academic Leah) through Sandinista-style Marxism (blue-collar Jonathan) to countercultural commune-ism (frazzled Marian), all held one another and Carla in loving high regard despite their strenuous disagreements. Jonathan Silver Talbott, we have learned—outraged by our government's role in the subversion of Chilean democracy and by the likelihood that his father's team had been involved—went down there in 1977 to join the anti-Pinochet underground and, like Jaime Aiquina before him, promptly joined the *desaparecidos* as well. Frederick Mansfield Talbott took his son's disappearance even more to heart than did the young man's mother, if that is possible; so much so that Carla B Silver had been at first convinced that her Fred's Paisleylike vanishment last year from brother Franklin's sailboat in the mouth of the Wye River was a painful but somehow necessary cover for his ransacking Chile's political prisons in search of their son.

But none of *this,* too, either, is why the woman is in our cockpit, in our story. If from her German Jewish side came Carla B Silver's ability to carry forward her business successfully, not only in midst of these personal calamities but as therapeutic respite from them, to her Rumanian Gypsy forebears (we have learned) she credits among other things her dreams, which have the authority of revelations. Uh-oh, thinks skeptical Peter—or so thought when we learned this. For three years the family strove tirelessly in Washington to keep Jon Talbott's case alive, in case the boy should be. Well after Fred's disappearance—when Frank and Lee Talbott, exhausted by the search for information and convinced both men were dead, had set out upon a year-long sailboat cruise to restore themselves—Carla B Silver had clung still to the possibility, ever more a hope than a belief, that her son survived upon some wretched prison island in Chile's frigid southern archipelago, the mere map of which breaks the heart to contemplate, and that his devious and formidable father was down there, incognito, cunningly arranging the young man's rescue. In this loyal hope, though the circumstances of their son's loss had caused a breach between his parents amounting virtually to estrangement, Carla B Silver had put off, like Odysseus's Penelope, the advances of a Rumanian friend and business associate—until, on the anniversary of Frederick Talbott's disappearance into Chesapeake Bay, his ghost had imperiously come to her by night; had certified the fact, though not the particulars, of both his own death and their son's; had made his peace, mourned with, and comforted his widow; had commended her suitor, Lascar Lupescu, and advised her to accept him as her lover; and then with his own breath had blown out his Yahrzeit candle.

Ghosts have breath? asked Peter Sagamore. By this point in her narrative, we had sense enough already of Carla B Silver to ask such questions freely. At once, with a flashing Bizet smile, she replied How else could they talk? and informed us further that this particular ghost, at least, was also better in bed than some living men of her experience.

I *do* remember your son! said Katherine, touching Carla B Silver's arm. A short, heavyset fellow, but gentle-mannered, right? May called him Short Jon Silver. He hated Henry Kissinger and ITT.

Also Anaconda Copper, Carla B Silver affirmed. Jon was a plumber— a real one, not the Nixon kind. But installing copper pipe gave him political trouble. He was the only left-wing plumber in Fells Point, and it was a happy day in our house when PVC piping came along.

In any case (we have learned), she had followed Fred Talbott's ghost's advice; and the circumstance that ghosts, while real, are not infallible advisors, we have learned to be the immediate though not the final cause of her presence in our story. Her friend Lascar was a handsome and popular fellow, an able manager of her restaurant, and a capable lover, but given to drink and, in his cups, sometimes to inappropriate sexual overtures to other women. Just a short while since, fired by an excess of Premiat Cabernet Sauvignon, he had made one such to of all people Marian Silver, so spectacularly inappropriate that that young woman had renounced heterosexuality and moved in with her friend May Jump—another HOSCA connection—while Carla B Silver had not only dismissed Lupescu from her bed and business with a Gypsy curse, but threatened to put out a contract on him if she ever saw him in Fells Point again.

All very well: But why do we spend our lay-day afternoon, nearly the whole of it, sitting in *Story*'s cockpit at the Annapolis Town Dock with a virtual stranger, in the middle of our little cruise and our tidewater tales, and near the end of our pregnancy, tisking tongues at the spectacularity of the inappropriateness of the man Lascar's drunkenly embracing Marian Silver from behind as she scrubbed mussels for steaming in the kitchen of Carla's Cavern and grabbing the nub of a breast with his left hand while fishing down the front of her running shorts with his right and growling some Rumanian endearment into the nape of her traumatized neck? Not because his victim was his lover's (and employer's) daughter; not even because, as the fellow must have known, Mim Silver was uncommonly vulnerable, though that vulnerability merits a tongue-tisk, all right. Had he so seized her sister Lee, their mother attested, he'd have found himself sucking the mussel brush and clutching his Transylvanian crotch. But Marian, though a sexual activist from early high school days, an occasional bisexual for the past ten years, and the mother of a twelve-year-old child—

that is to say, though a woman far from inexperienced—had had a misfortunate psychosexual history, as follows:

Never as stable as her mother and siblings, in the druggy High Sixties Mim had dropped out of college and drifted about our troubled republic. In the late summer of 1967, we have learned, hitchhiking up the East Coast from Ocean City, Maryland, to points north, she had the bad luck to be kidnapped, raped, and otherwise mistreated for three full days by a large and hairy Pennsylvanian in a black Chevrolet van somewhere in the dunes above Fenwick Island, Delaware. The experience so scarred her, literally and figuratively, that when she subsequently found herself also impregnated by it, she was unable to muster the resolve either to abort the pregnancy, to relinquish its issue at birth for adoption, or on the other hand to mother it properly. The rapist was never caught. His victim delivered Simon Silver at a North Carolina ashram whereto she had drifted in May 1968, brought him back to Fells Point, and spent the next decade in and out of therapy groups and communes of sundry flavors. She worked for half a dozen liberal and radical causes—HOSCA included—and at the same time, by some logic, for antiabortion groups, leaving Sy's care largely to his inexhaustible grandmother.

Short Jon Silver's disappearance in Chile so discomposed Mim's psyche—both of his half-sisters adored him, we have learned—that she had to be confined to the Sheppard and Enoch Pratt Hospital for a year, to the end of recomposing it. In 1978 (not long before Peter Sagamore's tête-à-tête with the Prince of Darkness) she was released into her parents' care and made uneasy peace with her stepfather, who seemed truly to be turning inner Washington upside down in search of news of his son. Frederick Talbott's own disappearance, on the vernal equinox of '79, set her back into residential therapy.

It was under these among other clouds (we have learned) that Franklin and Leah Talbott cast off, late last June, upon the sailing voyage they had long been planning for Lee's sabbatical year. Exhausted by the serial catastrophies and concerned for Marian and Carla, they were inclined to cancel it, but Carla B Silver had prevailed upon them not to. There was really nothing further they could do for lost Jonathan and his lost father; Mim was in competent hands and wanted them to go; Simon would be looked after as he had always been, by his grandma; and with the help of her able new Rumanian assistant, it would be business as usual at Carla's Cavern. Moreover, they'd have to wait another seven years for Lee's next sabbatical leave (she was changing jobs); and the author of KUBARK was at a certain fork in his own road; and the couple had a certain problem of their own to come to terms with. So go, Carla B Silver had insisted: Maybe she and Sy and Mims would rendezvous with them somewhere in the Caribbean next spring. Maybe Fred and Short Jon too; she hadn't quit hoping.

Next year in St. Croix!

So they went, Leah and Franklin (we have learned), and Earth contrived yet another orbit without blowing up, and Marian Silver was once again discharged into her busy mother's care, and on the anniversary of the P.O.D.'s disappearance, his ghost advised Carla B Silver as aforetold. She agreed to take his advice under advisement and flew with daughter and mustachioed grandson not to St. Croix, quite, but next door to Charlotte Amalie in St. Thomas, U.S.V.I., thence to St. John, where Frank and Lee and their sturdy cutter, having circuited the Caribbean, were resting and reprovisioning for the long ocean passage home. The couple were all right, C. B Silver divined in two glances, but their great sabbatical questions— whether or not to beget children, and what exactly to do with the next part of their life together—had not been resolved by their year afloat.

She put forward to them her late Fred's dream-recommendations concerning Lascar Lupescu and herself. All hands approved, and after a short stay in the islands (during which Marian Silver seemed more nearly normal than at any time since her three-day rape a dozen years past) the Fells Point contingent flew home. Carla B Silver promoted her business associate to bedpartner and was glad, though thoughts of her missing son still tormented her. Marian struck up a new romance, almost normal, with the young West Indian bartender hired by Lascar Lupescu as his replacement, now that he was busy with higher-level work. C.B S. pursued her plans for Carla's Inner Harbor.

This was the hopeful scene (we have learned) that Frank and Lee Talbott found upon the successful completion, just last week, of their blue-water passage from the Virgin Islands to the Virginia capes and Chesapeake Bay. What was more, Carla's formidable intuitions told her that Professor Leah Allan Silver Talbott, now thirty-five, was pregnant at last, for the first time, by her strapping fifty-year-old husband! But as there'd been a cloud upon their childlessness, so C.B S. divined a cloud upon this belated early pregnancy, which she sensed had in fact not yet even been acknowledged between the parents.

With Joblike swiftness then (we have learned, back over those club sandwiches in the Hilton), there came to Carla's Cavern a new series of misfortunes. For private reasons that even her prescient mother could not quite divine, Lee Talbott had *aborted that pregnancy;* had done so, in Baltimore, on the very Friday 13th that Frank Talbott was attending Doug Townshend's in-house memorial service at CIA headquarters in Langley and we were attending the Alice Roosevelt Longworth lady's memorial cocktail party for him in Georgetown. C. B Silver, too, mourned her old friend's equivocal death, but her sorrow was overshadowed by concern for Frank and Lee's marriage and for Marian's horror at Leah's abortion (Mim looked to her healthier sister to turn out normal grandchildren for their mother, Jonathan being *desaparecido* and herself more or less non compos mentis). She reapproached the verge, did Marian Silver, of freaking out altogether, said Carla B Silver, and approached that verge more closely yet when her Barbadian lover now quit both her and his job on the unflattering grounds that Mim would neither use contraceptives herself nor permit him their use, and—a man of conscience—even though she had assured him that any consequences were hers alone, on the basis of her relation to Simon Silver he judged her unfit for motherhood and did not want her to bear his seed.

And at *that* spectacularly inappropriate juncture (supremely patient reader of this lay-day-long exposition)—Frank and Lee Talbott having returned, vacuum-aspirated, to their boat, to cross the Bay from Baltimore to Wye Island, the starting place of their year-long odyssey—Lascar Lupescu had made his drunken foray under the T-shirt and into the running shorts of mussel-scrubbing Mim.

So? So? What Peter meant, still up there in the Hilton restaurant overlooking the harbor, was that all that's a pity, for sure; more than a pity: a secondhand horror show. But so?

So, he learned, that is how Marian Silver became May Jump's roommate, just last Sunday, with Carla B Silver's weary blessing. The two had known each other casually from certain sapphic hangouts in D.C. during Marian's bisexual interludes; they had renewed their acquaintance through Jonathan Talbott's involvement in HOSCA, and had closened it in the three years since Short Jon's disappearance. May Jump had taken a kindly interest in unlucky Simon Silver, who one had to wish had never been born; she had become acquainted as well with Carla B, each appreciative of the other's strength. Declared Carla to Katherine At least May won't knock the poor girl up. She herself, she added, had profoundly had it with men for a while, though she couldn't warm up to the alternative.

All right! That is how May Jump came to be behind the wheel of that nifty silver Jaguar this morning with that Carol Kane look-alike in the backseat and that twelve-year-old mustachioed son of an anonymous Pennsylvania sadist in the front, and that's what Carla B Silver is doing in Annapolis besides stroking certain state officials connected to the Baltimore Inner Harbor development. And all right: Ms. Silver's friend Fred once gave the man of us as evil a quarter-hour as he has passed in his life to date, up there above Carla's old Cavern in Fells Point: a quarter-hour that put him off mint tea and Doomsday Factors presumably forever. But what are you back in our story for, C.B S., lumping the smooth sauce of our lay day with these flour-balls of exposition? Whatever happened to Less Is More?

The afternoon's half passed. The wind is moderating. We return to the HOSCA connection. After the murder of Salvador Allende Gossens in the Chilean coup of 1973 and the subsequent orgy of torture and killing up and down that attenuated country, Jon Silver Talbott had spoken calmly but bitterly to May Jump—perhaps even to Katherine Sherritt; Kate can't quite remember—of his father's senior officerhood in the Agency and likely involvement in recent Chilean history. May even recalls wondering whether the young man was perhaps an Agency plant, since both the ASPS and HOSCA were on our government's surveillance list. But she was persuaded by the sincerity not only of his indignation but also, paradoxically, of his respect for Frederick Mansfield Talbott: the same painful mixture of emotions she had encountered in Marian Silver. These were the early years of the Sagamores' involvement with Douglas Townshend; it is even possible that Katherine mentioned the sturdy Fells Point plumber to Peter. It is equally possible, in that period of our less-than-total secret-sharing, that she did not. When had Peter first spoken to her of the Prince of Darkness and of Doomsday Factors? 1975? 1977?

In any case, Kate spent this lay-day morning with May Jump and Marian Silver and Simon and Carla B remembering all these connections and remourning Jaime Aiquina and Short Jon Silver, while Peter lingered fathoms deep in the Cave of Montesinos. When it was established who all hands were and by what several paths they had fetched up at the same Annapolis apartment, tough Carla B Silver had permitted herself, briefly, to weep: not for the loss of her parents and the Six Million (and the five million who were not the Six Million), not for the loss of her first husband and her sort-of-second and their grown son and her latest lover (whom she really had quite liked) and her daughter Marian's emotional balance and promising new West Indian companion; but for the loss of Leah and Franklin Talbott's aborted child-in-the-womb, whereof K's full-blooming belly put her strickenly in mind. Such a wunderkind *that* one would have been! Such a mother, her Leahle; such a mensch, that Frank! Such a Friday Thirteenth, with poor dead Doug on top of all!

So you knew Doug? had asked rattled Kath up in May's apartment, adding at once Well of course you must have. The least superstitious of pregnant thirty-nine-year-old upperclass college-educated American women, she was nonetheless disquieted these days by any mention of abortion, miscarriage, or congenital defect; and her disquiet was as nothing beside little Chesapeake's and Potomac's down there.

Said Carla B Silver I should hope I did. And

HERE, READER, IS WHAT THIS WOMAN IS IN OUR STORY FOR:

Matter of fact, I killed him, I guess. Fred too.

Oy Ma, had complained Mim Silver, who was sharing a cigarette with her son. Replied unfazed Carla Oy Ma all you want; it's the Christ truth.

Quiet there, Amos; calm down, Andy. Syntactical Katherine queried— playing for time and looking to May Jump for assurance that she and our children shouldn't clear out of that apartment pronto—you killed Doug and your husband, or you and your husband killed Doug?

Said Carla B Silver levelly Both. Plus Fred killed Jack Paisley, and Doug and I each killed Fred, and I had some help with Doug, too. You start messing with Doomsday Factors, it's a regular can of worms.

Peter Sagamore agrees, in *Story*'s cockpit, It is that. Says Carla Well, you wanted everything explained right now. There it is.

But *now* by now is that second part of this afternoon, wind dropping, by when P has learned that what the woman meant back there in May's apartment, while May and Marian Silver and blackshod flatfoot Sy, at her suggestion, went for a nice walk outdoors, was that, as a practicing Gypsy, Carla had, upon her son's disappearance in Chile, laid a general mighty curse upon the Latin American branches of the covert operations wing of the U.S. Central Intelligence Agency, and more specific weighty curses upon then Secretary of State Henry A. Kissinger (who reads these lines at his peril, such is the operation of Gypsy curses) and upon her lover-husband, whom however she did not cease to love merely because she now also cursed him. To that contradiction in her heart, plus the circumstance of her being after all no more than half Gypsy, Carla attributed the fact of a whole season's passing before the curse came down upon Frederick Mansfield Talbott, and her hope even then that it had only *seemed* to work. As for Douglas Townshend: It was Carla B Silver's belief that it had been Doug's belief that Frederick Talbott believed John Arthur Paisley to have been a freelance double agent passing as a triple (do not ask us to follow such multiple inversions), and had arranged Mr. Paisley's termination with extreme prejudice off Hoopers Island Light to prevent his revealing to the KGB up at Corsica Neck the exact extent of the Keyhole-11 reconnaissance satellite's compromising by the loss of those technical manuals to the So-viets, as aforenarrated. Doug Townshend then, C.B S. regretfully believed, in *his* capacity as freelance neutralizer of Doomsday Factors, had regret-fully done in her Fred; the Paisley termination and the mint-tea caper had convinced Townshend that the Prince of Darkness had become a loose cannon on the pitching deck of the ship of state. This conviction Carla shared, and so Doug's hit of his erstwhile protégé and closest associate had been aided not only by certain of Rick Talbott's best enemies within the U.S. intelligence community (and covered by their counterparts on Corsica Neck to settle the score for their loss of Paisley) but by Carla B Silver's mighty curse as well. All the same, her Fred was her Fred, to whose memory she owed it regretfully next to lay a like curse upon the man she all but knew to have been his killer, dear as Doug had for decades been to her and her family. She imagined he would understand. Thus that rup-tured aneurysm on that Qantas Airways 747 on final approach to Sydney, Australia, which (the ruptured aneurysm) even knowledgeable, conserv-ative Franklin Key Talbott mistakenly suspected to have been induced by some Agency potion rather than the fifty-percent-Gypsy variety.

Mm hm. And why was she laying all this on Peter Sagamore's wife and children? And why do we sit together cordially, if not quite calmly, on little *Story* now, whiling our lay day into history and in no hurry at all to get on to Captain Donald Quicksoat, sooner or later no doubt to Sche-herazade, to the upper Severn maybe, and on to wherever else listeth wind and tide till our water break and our labor come upon us?

To have told so much and not yet told a thing! The *real* mickey in our man's mint tea (we here expostulate) was one he had got bombed on once before, with Douglas Townshend: We mean knowledge, secrets, the secret knowledge of What's Going On Around Here, particularly with respect to Doomsday Factors: a knowledge that Doug believed some American writer had better drink deep of, as of an elixir, whatever the cost, instead of hunt-and-pecking like all the other chickens in the python's cage. P.S.'s imagination is still hung over, still acrack from chugalugging that elixir. Get them out of our story, out of our Chesapeake, out of our heads, those triliteral curses: CIA, DIA, NRO, NSA, FBI, KGB! What has the art of literature to do (we here expostulate) with them? The motions of the human spirit, the passions of the human breast, the possibilities of human language—those are what your proper storyteller craves inside info on, not the back alleys of international pushiness. Leave *them* to the cloak-and-dagger groupies, the thrillerinos. Clear your head, Peter Sagamore!

But the Doomsday Factor is among other things a tar baby, reader, which, once brushed against, et cetera. To it, then: Why is C.B S. aboard our *Story*?

Because in the first half of our century the Russian revolution replaced czarist tyranny with Soviet tyranny (the Evil Empire, Carla calls it). Because after disposing of Nazi Germany, Eastern-bloc communism and Western-bloc capitalism perceived each other not only as natural enemies but as mortal ones. Because by the time both blocs regained their breath from the catastrophe of World War II, the phenomenon of thermonuclear weaponry kept the warfare between them cold instead of hot. Because the profound reciprocal distrust, not unjustified, of the U.S. and Soviet governments, together with the natural propensities of their military-industrial establishments, led in the second half of our century to the most ruinous armaments competition in history and, in consequence, to the gravest potential danger that human civilization has known since its beginnings and that life on Earth has faced at least since the pre-Cenozoic Great Death of 65,000,000 years ago. Because this grand wretched global competition between political-economic systems which in fact are natural rivals, and between peoples who have reason to be natural friends, manifests itself in a hundred thousand matters, of every magnitude, from Western civ's loss of Eastern Europe and the devastation of Southeast Asia and the butchering of for example Chilean democracy, down to the death or disappearance of spooks and counterspooks like Captain Nicolas Shadrin and John Arthur Paisley and Frederick Mansfield Talbott and Douglas Townshend, down farther to innumerable big and little pressures and counter-pressures: promises and threats and lies; baits bribes bugs and blackmails; sniffs, snoops, snares.

Because the "stagflationary" American economy of the 1970s happened to leave most minor U.S. private boarding schools, including The Deniston School for Girls, in parlous financial shape, in many instances kept alive only by the least admirable of causes: their students' parents' fear of racially integrated public schools, together with the indisputable mediocrity of most U.S. public education. Because, especially after the Paisley affair, the Soviet embassy in Washington craved even greater privacy from the local CIA for its local KGB, and desired therefore to expand its vacation-facility acreage on Corsica Neck, the estate of the late archcapitalist John James Deniston, where the tranquil Corsica joins the stately Chester, across and up the Chesapeake Bay from Washington, and, in pursuit of this objective, quietly offered to purchase contiguous wooded land from The Deniston School Corporation at top-dollar price and then some: top dollars badly needed on Deniston's bottom line. Because, given the grand demonology of our century, that quiet proposal was vociferously opposed by many of the few who got wind of it (e.g., Irma Shorter Sherritt and, at the outset, her son Willy), and reluctantly to positively favored by a few others of that same few (e.g., Katherine Sherritt Sagamore), and by others yet (e.g., Molly Barnes Sherritt, at the outset) viewed with mixed feelings.

Because while the staunchest of the opposers were your archconservative Sovietophobes and macho rednecks, not a few of whom would approve severing diplomatic relations with the Evil Empire altogether, among the staunchest though invisible supporters of the transaction, unknown to Katherine, was our CIA, for reasons startlingly set forth to Peter Sagamore by Frederick Mansfield Talbott over mint tea above Carla's Cavern in late '78, was it, just a handful of months before the Prince of Darkness Paisleyed out. Because Willy Sherritt now and then, in his own words, drank drinks and scouted pussy in the Fells Point bars, including Carla's Cavern, as well as in flossier watering-and-scouting establishments. Because Porter "Poonie" Baldwin Jr.'s desperate attempt at congressional comeback, after the homosexualcohol scandals that defeated him in '78, led his campaign treasurer to seek out and accept contributions without excessive scruple as to their source, so long as they were not directly from distilleries, gay-rights organizations, or the KGB itself. Because while Poonie and his campaign strategists routinely sniffed around the Corsica Neck question, along with many another question, to see whether it was worth taking a strident stand against, his campaign treasurer was being routinely watched and diddled by the Komitĕt Gosudarstvĕnnoi Bezopasnost'i, not for the first time, without his knowing who was watching and diddling him. Because the CIA in this instance knew what Willy Sherritt in this instance did not, and was not only watching the KGB watch and diddle Porter Baldwin Jr.'s campaign treasurer, but doing a bit of counterdiddling of its own.

Et cetera. Some hold the world to be a seamless web; we aboard *Story* find it seamy. But a web it is, wherein Byzantine centuries of czarist feudalism inspire a revolution that inspires a cold war that inspires a thermonuclear arms race that inspires high-tech snoopery and countersnoopery by and upon sundry Doomsday Factors, and which entangles—that web, we mean, in its common seams—Ivan the Terrible, John Arthur Paisley, and . . . Molly Barnes Sherritt.

Yup: old Molly there. What happened, see, was that among the several

Political Action Committees cautiously supporting P.B. Jr.'s reelection, even as we sit here in *Story*'s cockpit, is a sort of American Association of Eastern-Bloc Exiles and Defectors (not its actual name), who patriotically, if that is the right adverb, overlook Poonie's peccadillos in the light of his famous cold-warriorism, and originally pressed him, through his campaign treasurer, to oppose the Corsica Neck/Deniston School transaction (as they had opposed the original Soviet vacation establishment itself)—not knowing that the CIA supported it. Thus Willy's vain efforts to persuade his sister to soften her support of that real estate deal, and his astonishment at his own wife's late unprecedented opposition to his opposition to anything: an opposition that baffled us as—at first—it outraged him.

But what happened, see, was that after Jonathan Silver Talbott's disappearance in Chile and Frederick Talbott's into the Chesapeake estuarine system, Carla B Silver became a dedicated foe of all spookish huggermugger, as anti-CIA in this respect as she remained anti-Soviet in general. One of the last covert Agency suboperations she had wind of, via closemouthed Fred and Doug, was code-named BONAPARTE: the proposed deep-bugging of Corsica Neck through its Corsican neighbor, The Deniston School for Girls—especially that undeveloped acreage under quiet discussion of sale. With her own hands, Carla B Silver had poured scotch upon the rocks for Willy Sherritt in her Cavern, while Willy not only scouted pussy but was by pussy scouted: a KGB-paid puss who thought herself CIA-paid and would in fact have been, had not Frederick and Douglas known that the KGB was paying her already. Why waste the taxpayers' money? (That unwitting double agent deserved double time; she has by now, we presume, got galloping herpes simplex. But Willy will get the final bill, *com*plex, for what he gave her.) It did not please fairly decent Doug to see the brother of his young friend Katherine Sherritt (and brother-in-law of his literary repository, Peter Sagamore) become unknowingly ensnared in BONAPARTE; but Willy was in the unusual position just then of innocently opposing, on behalf of the Political Action Committee of that American Association of Eastern-Bloc Exiles and Defectors, a move that both the CIA and the KGB, for contradictory reasons, favored.

Carla herself, at the time, shrugged her shoulders and tended her bar: What *she* disapproved of was hired B-girls in her Cavern, no matter how classy; but her friend the Prince of Darkness suggested, in a way she understood, that she let this one do her thing. Even more, as we have seen, did it displease Doug to hear the P.O.D.'s half cynical, half serious mint-tea pitch to Peter Sagamore to recruit Katherine and Irma Sherritt in support of the Deniston land sale, which K already supported for nonpolitical reasons. At this suggestion too, when she later learned of it, C.B Silver shrugged her shoulders. Of what consequence to her were these goyishe-gorgio Gold Coasties?

Came then however down upon her Fred, belatedly, her curse; and whether or not Doug Townshend was, as she believed, its agent, and despite her extension therefore of the same curse to him, for a time those two in their sore sorrow were as close as old friends can be who are not lovers and who have between them, like the sword between Isolde and Tristan, a fifty-percent-Gypsy curse. In that peculiar intimacy, Carla B Silver learned from Douglas Townshend this detail: that in pursuit of BONAPARTE—his and Rick Talbott's last cooperative venture, having little to do directly with Doomsday Factors—and in lieu of that intractable young fellow Peter Sagamore, he had reluctantly recruited—*with her full knowledge*—Willy Sherritt's long-suffering wife, whom Doug had met in sunnier seasons upon his several visits with us to Nopoint Point. He had seen an opportunity, had demidecent Douglas, to do the Sherritt family a minor service in return for what troubles he had occasioned the crew of *Story*.

Kath had cried in May Jump's kitchen earlier today upon receipt of this tiding For pity's sake spare us favors from the CIA! Wait till Peter hears!

Yeah. What Doug knew, see, was that that AAEBED group, the exiles and defectors, was for obvious reasons substantially infiltrated by the KGB. Some of its members had posed as defectors for that purpose; others were bona fide seekers of political asylum who however had family back in Mother Russia and were thus exposed. Those infiltrators, Doug Townshend happened to know, would presently whisper into the ear of P.B. Jr.'s campaign treasurer (by now roundly laid and secretly photographed at his rutting, for insurance purposes) that the Association's leadership had, at the confidential urging of the Central Intelligence Agency, abdicated its stand against the Corsica Neck/Deniston School negotiations; they would appreciate it munificently if aspiring congressman Baldwin would do like-wise. In this whisper-to-come (Doug had told Carla, who had told Kath-erine, who had told Peter), the KGB was correct, but did not know itself to be. At least not for certain; their people took for granted the likelihood of Frederick Mansfield Talbott's deep-bugging scenario, but craved that acreage anyhow, and were as reasonably confident of their deep-debugging technology as was the Agency of its deep–anti-debugging technology.

So goes that wretched, that smug and sordid, that staggeringly expensive business, patient reader. But what Douglas Townshend knew was that the erstwhile apple-cheeked Molly Barnes Sherritt remained loyal to her un-deserving, herpes-blistered spouse, her more or less deserving country, and her pretty much deserving school, and might even be willing to risk Willy's initial displeasure by opposing his stand against the Corsica Neck deal: a stand, Doug gave her correctly to believe, which was leading her husband unknowingly into the clutches of the KGB. Her job was courageously to tip the balance saleward among Deniston trustees; at least to keep the issue alive. Her husband would be indignant; so Doug surmised and shud-dering Molly knew. But very shortly, decent Doug declared, as surely as the sun sets west and rises east, the man would do a one-eighty, for reasons Doug was not at liberty to disclose to Molly. He would even assist the transaction's progress, would Willy; lubricate its consummation with his considerable real estate savvy and plenteous connections. Moreover, he would then praise his wife for having shown him the path, Corsica Neck–wise; and she would have done him, her marriage, her alma mater, and her country all together a small but serious service, for which her country, at least, would make its gratitude discreetly known to The Deniston School.

Molly Sherritt!

These things Doug knew, see, reader, as he took off for Sydney, Australia, to address some other of the Big Bird's droppings, of a nature known to none of us here at the Annapolis Town Dock, on our lay day. What he did not know was that for one reason or another, as his Qantas 747 banked into final approach and he glimpsed from his window seat the glass-and-concrete sails of the opera house giving back the afternoon sails in Sydney Harbour, he would suddenly next see red and presently nothing again ever; or that Carla B Silver had by then become so anti-cloak-and-daggerish as to resolve, so far as in her lay, to expose expose expose, as Franklin Key Talbott's *KUBARK* book had done, everything she knew the Agency to be up to that in her judgment it should not be. The trouble was that about the only thing Carla knew that hadn't been somewhere exposed already was these nickel-and-dime details of BONAPARTE: Rick and Doug were not loose talkers. Even so, she resolved to seek out and apprise this Mr. and Mrs. Willy Sherritt, for example, of what has here been lengthily set forth. She had meant to speak of it to her best surviving friend (and brother-in-common-law and son-in-law), Frank Talbott, when he and Lee sailed into Baltimore from the Caribbean last week. But then, all in a few days' space, while decent dead Douglas was being memorialized, her Leah had chosen abortion; her Mims had refreaked and sought sexual asylum with May Jump; and Carla had had to dump genuinely remorseful Lascar Lupescu and somehow still get her Inner Harbor business done and manage Carla's Cavern and keep an eye on Marian plus poor gross Simon there and check out May Jump again in this new connection. A busy week. She had therefore put off her tattling expedition to the Eastern Shore, which on second thought she had little taste for anyhow—it was really not her business, was it, and it seemed, as such things go, pretty small potatoes and more or less benign on its bottom line. Bugs shmugs, as long as the KGB-girls stay out of her Cavern. But then to May Jump's flat had come this morning that call from Kiss Who? Kiss Sherritt: Katherine Shorter Sherritt Sagamore, May's good buddy from across the Bay—and two plus two achieved their customary sum.

Thus was our Katherine's lay-day morning eye-openingly spent. Despite her residual Episcopalian Gold-Coastity and Carla B Silver's *La Haba-ñeraismo,* the two women took a quick liking to each other. They rapidly found more in common, as May suspected they would, than either might have supposed. And thus was passed our lay-day afternoon, once Peter had climbed out of the Montesinos cave.

Thus too was sort of solved the Riddle of the Roses, posed only last night and delivered this morning by message light: Willy's one-eighty on the weightsome issue of The Deniston School's bridle-path-and-woodlot divestiture; his semidemidisingenuous sucking up to Molly and Kath. And here in June's late sunshine we three-and-then-some sit, the breeze really quieting now but *Story* still Annapolized, while in bleak gulags hopeless people suffer and die, in Pinochet's prison islands, in Khomeini's Evin Prison, bloody as the shah's, and there and there and there, enough to drive one shrieking mad. We tisk our tongues: tisk, tisk. We two, who have seen little; Carla B Silver, who has seen much (and Pulvis et Umbra, who have seen nothing yet)—we shake our several heads in wonder that the world does not between subject and predicate explode, or, with the tortureds' last groan, at any verb collapse.

There now, Peter Sagamore: It took a while, but all has been explained.

OUR NEW FRIEND CARLA B SILVER
FIRES UP A FINAL DOWNWIND SHIPBOARD CIGARILLO,
READS OUR MINDS, MAKES A SPEECH, UTTERS PROPHECY.

I didn't get out of Birkenau a virgin girl, but I got out. Wits? Guts? Dumb luck is what it mostly was. Where guts come in handy is in going on with it after.

I had my two baby girls before that semi trailer creamed Al Silver's Cadillac in Forty-nine, and I nursed and weaned them and watched them grow different as night and day. I still can't say which one I love more: my Mim that needs it or my Lee that deserves it. Never mind. Then I had my Jonathan, by the man I loved most and longest, and I nursed and weaned *him,* and such a mensch that one grew up to be! But did that save him from the butchers? Every morning I read the newspapers, I have to spit. Thff!

We know what Carla B Silver means, and Amnesty Internationalist Katherine has to spit too, neatly to leeward. Thff!

I know you want to get on with your sailboat ride, and you're right to do it, too. Look here: Relax and don't worry. It's going to be a girl and then a boy, with all their parts right and plenty upstairs. Don't I wish to Christ they were Frank and Lee's? But that's water under the bridge.

Well, she's not to feel guilty for turning it off, my Leahle. The world is wrecked and poisoned, friends: just about done with. But you guys are right to go on with it, all the same. Look at the pair of you! Look at that afternoon out there! So you'll be A-one parents, and they'll be dynamite kids! That can hurt the world?

Pretty soon you're going to meet Frank and Lee out there in some creek or other, and the four of you'll hit it off. Tell them Mim and Sy are okay; not to worry. Your friend May Jump has her head on straight and her heart in the right place; they shouldn't come running. For Christ sake don't feel sorry for their not having kids, Lee and Frank; but don't wonder about yourselves, either! It drives my Lee-Lee right up the wall when I talk like this. But what: You shouldn't have a Gypsy blessing with a little kosher sweet-and-sour? Besides, I *see* things, friends. Maybe I'll catch a ride up there and deliver you myself when your time comes. Who knows.

But that won't be tomorrow or the day after. So enjoy.

Stories. I could tell you stories.

Give me a hand off here, would you, skipper?

Drew and Lexie is what Frank and Lee were going to call theirs, if they'd had a boy and a girl: Andrew and Alexa. Sounds goyishe-chic to me, but that's why they make different-color neckties. You people behave yourselves now.

So today's the what: Friday the Twentieth? Last day of spring?

Hum.

I'll put my money on the Twenty-ninth.

DAY 6:
SEVERN RIVER TO
CHESTER RIVER

To let the world into your life is easy: Step ashore and stand still a minute. To clear your decks again . . . another story.

GET US OUT OF HERE,

we say to one another, not in words, while waving bemused *auf Wiedersehen*s to Carla B Silver's silver car. Out of here, off the madding land, away from Disasterville (we don't mean you, Annapolis), back to our *Story*.

She puts her money on the Twenty-ninth, Ms. Silver there? We are new to being prophesied at.

The purpose of Maryland's mainland, where one lives and works, is to yearn one toward its Eastern Shore, where one plays and dreams, makes babies, sails here and there gestating Irony and Pity and awaiting their delivery. Let's get over there ASAP.

So: *Auf Wiedersehen,* Carla B Silver; *au revoir,* May Jump & Co.; may things work out for you and your ménage. May's going to be good for that Simon Silver boy, Kath declares: our first, spell-breaking words after the Jaguar tools away. Peter doubts it, but agrees; she'll be a lot better than nobody. Who is he to say for certain what we both suspect: that that blackshoed, butt-smoking, mustachioed fatso child's a lost cause, the mother more so? Look what the likes of C. B Silver have survived, *con brio!* We look—and what we mainly see is the difference.

Then we demesmerize, we re-ice, we top up the ship's stores with this and that from the Front Street Market, and at afternoon's end we slip through Annapolis Harbor out into the mouth of the Severn on a ten-knot westerly. K's wearing her pet found hat. No sign of *Rocinante IV:* Capn

Don has given up on us. Were the wind from another quarter, the hour less late, we would bear some miles upriver to a proper parking place; there are one or two left on this still-lovely, far too crowded river. As is, we merely cross the Severn's mouth and poke into despoiled Mill Creek, behind the forest of U.S. Navy radio towers across from the Academy. Wall-to-wall houses and docks, Mill Creek, and talk about message lights! Every one of those giant towers is not only red-warning-lit but strobed; we imagine their twenty-four-hour traffic with the Pacific Fleet, the Mediterranean Fleet, the Caribbean Fleet; with satellites, nuclear submarines, aircraft carriers as big as islands and much faster.

But us, we're growing babies at 2100 hours on 1980's next-to-longest day; in the twilight of our century we're charcoaling ground-veal patties with rosemary and dry vermouth and chutney bananas in aluminum foil. Peter stands on the aft cockpit seat to mind the grill, flashlight in one hand, patent patty-turner in the other, water pistol at the ready to cool our coals. Grease-drips poof and flare like little bombs. The odd spark flies downwind, over the dinghy, and blinks out in Mill Creek. He thinks Doomsday Factor thoughts while checking the bezel of his watch: turning time. Kath sips Beaujolais Nouveau below, just a sip, and slices cucumbers, tomatoes, red onion. Life, she thinks, handing Pete pitas to pop onto the grille while he hands her down the patties and foiled bananas on a plate: Boyoboy. We eat indoors, not saying much, by the light of an amber-glassed patio candle netted like a fisherman's float. While in Chile's Dawson Island prison, down by Magellan's frigid straits, and in Moscow's Lefortovo and Lubyanka, and in other of Mother Earth's plenteous holes of Hell . . .

Waiting for the ten-o'clock Accuweather, we catch the headlines: Carter arrives in Europe for summit talks with Brezhnev. U.S. okays nuclear-fuel sale to India. Social Security's future called fragile. But tomorrow's Chesapeake weather's to be fine. We have anchored alee of that antenna city, not to be bothered by those strobes; through *Story*'s open companionway, all we can see are *beaucoup* house-lights across Mill Creek and the running lights of jetliners gliding up to Baltimore, down to Washington. The P.M.'s bugless. We'll get an early start, we agree, if there's any breeze to start with: up under the twin Bay bridges to the Chester, maybe, or whithersoever listeth et cet, but eastward if possible, over to the Shore. And we'll stay over there, we agree, until this cruise is cruised.

In fact, however, we sleep till eight, late for summer sailors, dreaming midsummereve dreams: P's back in the Cave of Montesinos, beside a stream meandering through grazed meadow that looks to us more like upland Pennsylvania or Turgenev's rural Russia than like La Mancha: black willows, rock outcroppings, vetch. K argues her older brother's case with a stolid but not uncivil officer of the Komitĕt Gosudarstvĕnnoi Besopasnost'i; she wakes with tears in her eyes, not for Willy but for the beauty of the tongue of Pushkin and Chekhov.

Gorgeous morning. Sweet-cool but going to warm up; fresh, delicious.

Pete's up; so are Rough and Ready. Kath dries her tears on her bedsheet, smiling. No sex this morning, just a buss on her buns as she peels off her nightie, a kiss in his hair as he primes the alcohol stove for coffee water. Says NOAA Northwest ten to twelve, full sun, air dry by local standards and eightyish: a perfect summer-solstitial day. Croissants. Pineapple juice. Rapid Soviet buildup reported, Afghanistan. Predicts Peter It'll be their Vietnam, but Katherine switches at once to Telemann on D.C. public radio. Let this be a day of delicious and/or entertaining matters only.

Up anchor and out, then, to a splendid, restorative sailboat ride. Once clear of the neighborhood and in open water, we confirm that the day's best course is exactly where we had in mind to go: a long morning's port tack up and across the Bay to Love Point and the Chester; a run and a reach then thereinto, to someplace snug and private enough to give birth in. We lay the tack, not quite close-hauled. *Story* takes the breeze in her bobstay (she's female this A.M.), leans into it, surges up toward hull speed. Good boatwright Charlie Bunting, in your grave now, who designed these planks and supervised their fastening; presumably good John Basel, now in yours, prior owner and meticulous upkeeper of our craft: Rest you well, chaps; the old girl still steps along.

Now that we know where we're headed, K radiotelephones Nopoint Point. BONAPARTE, we have agreed, shall not be mentioned via wire or wireless, nor shall any three-letter outfits nosier than the Environmental Protection Agency. The NSA just over yonder (don't mention it), may be presumed to monitor not only any but damned near all domestic as well as international traffic, its scanners programmed to prick up their computerized ears at every such cue. So it's pretty standard Irma–Katherine talk. We have been out for going on a week, and Irm and Hank have been being good about it. Don't we think we'd better mosey on home? Soothes Katherine Sure we do, Mom; Peter especially. He's just humoring me and the kids. We're going to park tonight somewhere in the Chester; if the breeze is right tomorrow, maybe we'll cut down through Kent Narrows and head home. We'll call. How's Chip? Olive Treadway's driving him in to Radio Shack for something that he needs to fix her CB; then he's racing his Sunfish this afternoon and tomorrow in the Oxford series. Does Katydid remember how she used to bring home the silverware in her canary-yellow Lightning, and in her Penguin before that? And in Irma's day, Stars and Thistles. Now it's all Sunfish and Windsurfers and Hobie Cats and Lasers, except for the old log canoes, and even some of those ancient craft are using Sunfish rigs for maintopsails. Sometimes Irma wonders.

Katherine assures her it's okay, this particular aspect of the march of time. We are privately relieved to hear that Chip is busy at such immemorial Sherritt pursuits as sailing regattas. Over and out, now; we're coming up on the bridge, and Kath wants to say hello to it.

Hello, Chesapeake Bay Bridge, always a tickler of the family adrenals to sail under. The erstwhile literary artist Peter Sagamore is having himself a mid-morning second breakfast of pepperoni Slim Jims and canned iced tea while stretch-exercising in the cockpit, steering *Story* through the Saturday crowd, and listening in on Kath's conversation. Now he lifts his Lipton's on behalf of the lot of us to the paired suspension spans as we head under them for the who-knows-how-manyeth time. But it's the kids' first trip; though they can't see, they feel their mother tingle and maybe hear the high roar of eastbound traffic headed for the ocean resorts. Katherine explains to them, not in words, that this four-mile-narrow place in our estuary, while actually three-quarters of the way up its 200-mile length, divides the Lower Bay (much larger, less polluted, and saltier, kids, but sea-nettle-infested and therefore virtually unswimmable) from the Upper (much smaller, more polluted, but fresher and therefore nettle-freer; plenty clean enough to swim in on the Eastern Shore side, and let's get over there and get you people wet). That to pass under it, therefore, in either direction, on a cruise, like passing either way between Bay and Ocean or for that matter between Sherritt Cove and Goldsborough Creek, affords one of your cruising sailor's two chief rushes: the thrill of leaving open for secluded waters and vice versa. In your parents' case (little Donner *und* Blitzen, little Port and Starboard)—as we summerly sail from the nettled Choptank and Tred Avon up to the Chester or the Sassafras, depending on the state of the season and the year's precipitation, till we reach the fatal threshold of five parts salt per thousand of water and can shuck our duds and go over the side—passing under these bridges from south to north means heading out for Hedonia, as the reverse means back to responsibility. To sail up under just now, on the year's longest day and one of its meteorologically jim-dandiest, through a troupe of spinnakers bellying our way like pregnant clown giants—about to give birth ourselves and as Irma said winding up a full week out, a week really quite full—is a high, children. As we look for more baroque, now that the bridges are astern, WGMS says Major heat wave sizzles Texas; U.S. to let Cuban boatlift people stay six months. Et cetera and enough: Today we're being carefree chickens on the python's back, cluck cluck. Here's something nonproblematically Caribbean: a little reggae to carry us—

Kath stops (she'd spoken none of this aloud), her left hand upon her breasts, her right upon her belly. She had been going to say Out of the Lower Bay into the Upper, out of springtime into summer; it has just now occurred to her that that also means out of Gemini into . . . Peter! she says, stricken, and his happy face flies. These children are Cancers!

That consideration carries us all the way up to Love Point, famous haunt of Chessie, the local sea monster, five nautical miles and a full hour later. Comforts Peter Sure, we'd hoped for Gemini, as we seem to be having more than one. But we hadn't really *expected* Gemini, had we, our median EDC being right where C. B Silver called it. Look here, hon, comforts Peter: Astrology, for pity's sake, it's just fun and games; and the, you know, precession of the equinoxes? has fucked up the zodiac since ancient times. Plus Cancer is the crab, right, not the tumor. What could be more appropriate? We'll name them Uca Pugnax and Uca Pugilator.

Says sort-of-comforted Kath That's who they feel like, all right. *Ucae.*

Two species of fiddler crab, reader, hereabouts. Keep an eye out for Chessie now as we round Love Point.

We duly do, and as always see nothing untoward. The tide does its usual queer stuff to us in that neighborhood, whose geography urges the current in several directions at once. Our plan has become to pop into Queenstown Creek, six or seven miles off, just around the Chester's great first bend, for late lunch and a swim, then to sail on upriver for a while if the good breeze holds.

No sea monster in this chapter. What, then? We're running downwind now, wing and wing, centerboard up and our biggest headsail whiskered out to windward; *Story* tucks up her skirts and scoots nicely down the warming air. But the better we move on this long leg, the less apparent wind we have to cool us. Off come our tops; we look forward to gybing, about four miles down the road, onto a cooler broad reach around the river's U-turn and over to Queenstown Creek. Katherine steers; Wing plays with Wing; Peter tersely tells our log about Carla B Silver, Marian and Simon and Short Jon Silver, also Whatsisname, Lascar the Transylvanian there. I dig these names, he says to Kath. If I were writing a story with these guys on the payroll, I'd call the Rumanian one Lascar Woiwod, which I think means "werewolf" in Rumanian or Slovenian. Maybe Lascar Woiwod kissed that Carol Kane person on the neck while he was handling her produce, and that's what tripped her circuit breakers.

But K's shading her eyes and looking over there toward Kent Island Narrows, at the bottom of the big U, where a tricky little channel like the drain in a sink-trap connects the Chester with the next river-system south. She says guess what *she* sees. Says Peter, not turning around, You see Chessie the Shoal-Draft Sea Monster, of course. Nope. Uh, you see Sindbad the Sailor with Don Quixote on his back. One more guess. Hum: You see Act Two of Sex Education colon Play.

You got it.

Come on. He looks where she points and sees nothing particular at first except, in the near distance off *Story*'s port bow, the radar-reflecting black buoy which happens to be our gybing mark and, in the farther distance, the red-and-black entrance buoy to Kent Island Narrows. Kath says Over by the red-and-black one, and he sees what she means: an orange float that looks to be moving with the wind and tide instead of bobbing in place like a crab- or eel-pot buoy. Yeah, well, he says, a float got loose, is all. Let's gybe.

Not till you check with the binocs. So we fetch up the 7 × 50s, and Peter says Yeah, well there, it's orange, all right, and it's loose, all right. And it's probably a crab float, but it really could be another one of those distress-flare canisters. He hands over the binoculars. Boyoboy; girlogirl: Let's go home like Irma says and have our little fiddlers and go back to Baltimore and back to work.

Katherine wonders whether God is a postmodernist or a CIA spook. We gybe per plan, but detour over toward that red-and-black entrance buoy and the crooked line of day beacons leading through the narrows. Both tide and wind are behind us here, but down there—for geographical reasons that we're used to—the tide will run powerfully against us, and that's fortunate; otherwise this monkeying around could fetch us into shoal water. It's an Alert-and-Locate canister, all right, just like the one we fished out of Knapps Narrows on Day 1. Are we ready for this? P takes the crabnet, K the tiller; we miss the thing on first pass, but get enough feel for its drift and ours to luff up on second try and lay it right against our leeward beam.

Your mother is a hotshot sailor, Pete tells Pugnax and Pugilator; wait'll you see. He dips the thing up, un-nets it, gives it a shake. Doesn't *sound* like flares and such in there, but it might be. So come on, says Kate: Open it already.

The idea that what we have here *could* be Act Two of that queer play-script, which it obviously is, is perfectly preposterous. The statistical improbability! The craziness of anyone's publishing his/her manuscripts by floating them off in casks, in installments, yet. Says Kate I love it; open, open.

Pete sits Turk-fashion on the cabin top, in no hurry, the canister in the space between his thighs. Maybe a genie will pop out et cetera. Do we know how to deal with genies?

Says Katherine Leave 'em to me. Maybe Scheherazade'll pop out and tell you stories enough to last you till the world ends. Her face flickers. How many would it take?

One, says Peter, if it's long enough. He's busy sailing now; in her condition, Kate can't winch the sheets hard without straining something. Queenstown Creek's just over yonder; let's go with this low-grade suspense till we're parked.

The big Chester's sprinkled with other sailboats, workboats, sportfishing craft; half a dozen more weekend sailors are threading up through the Narrows from Eastern Bay, the Miles, the Wye, and as many are threading down that way for the night. But the creek, when we enter it, is as we expected all but empty: too early for most folks to park. Just inside the entrance is an elderly black schooner from Toronto, heading home from down south, we guess: long, shapely overhangs, handsome teak decks, a fine transom cumbered by the ungainly contraption of windvane self-steering. Its crew sunbathe in bikinis, read under awnings, wave hello. Down by the funky public landing, which the cruising guide misrecommends as the creek's best anchorage, we spy a mast or two more. But in the upper end, snug and roomy, nobody's home; we beat up there, slowly, our breeze baffled by the walls of trees on either side, and drop our light anchor at the mouth of Salthouse Cove, our favorite spot in this neck of the woods. One Canada goose and seven white swans paddle in the shallow cove. Like that Toronto schooner, Peter remarks, they're in no hurry to get back home. Katherine observes that their ratio is the same as in the folktale, no?

Open the canister?

NOPE.

The post-noon is warm, the sky lovely, the creekwater clean and net-tleless. We're far enough off from our human neighbors not to bother with swimsuits, and those wild waterfowl won't mind. Let Act Two wait. Pete hangs the ladder, peels off his pants, and monitors his wife's painstaking descent—naked but for her black beret—before following her over the transom. Do not dive into these opaque waters, reader, until you've poked and paddled about the area first. Under that mild surface might just lie a sunken something not noted on the chart but waiting to fracture your reckless skull; or the tide might have swung you on your rode from the twelve-foot spot you anchored in to a three-foot shoal near shore.

Peter pops under to sound it while Katherine floats above; we're comfortably half again over his head. Silky on our skins, delicious: Queenstown Creek. Does our man have tears or tidewater in his eyes?

Both. Because when it's sweet, life is so sweet, and it is so miserable for so many so most of the time. A third of us, is it, more or less starving? Half? And more than that large fraction brutalized one way or another, exploited, harassed to the end of their Hobbesian days. And then the corruption, brethren; the pollution, poverty, crime, disease; the betrayal, deception, torture, derangement, and what else. Well, mere melancholy, which poisons even the rare ripe fruits of comfort and serenity. Pain pain pain! Plus, oh, the twin-edged blade of consciousness, which lets us know, as those eight waterfowl presumably do not, how privileged is an interlude like this—our floating lunch-break, our pregnant idle voyage—and thus at once keens its pleasure all but unbearably and makes us weep for the sorrows of, you know, the outraged world. Upon which the curtain bids to ring down anyhow.

Luckier than the reader, Kate gets told all this by one shoulder-touch at *Story*'s boarding ladder, up which presently we haul our dripping selves. Have we lost our appetite for lunch, she wonders, or are we all the hungrier?

Both. She parks her beret on the new canister, it having come from the old, and we *let the thing sit there,* honest to God, smack in the middle of *Story*'s cockpit sole, like a bright orange family Thermos, like a sign reading

IGNORE THIS SIGN, while we drip dry and relotion, make and eat lunch in high June sunshine tempered still with lingerings of spring.

Presently Peter sighs, says

OPEN THE DAMN THING,

and we do.

Tongue-tisking reader, what do you expect we expect? You're reading *The Tidewater Tales: A Novel;* we're telling our stories, which are our story, which we're living and have lived from moment to moment, creek to creek. No more than you do we really expect a genie, say, to roar like a smoke-flare out of this canister, or Act Two of *SEX EDUCATION: Play,* or any other astonishing, improbable thing.

So we merely hum and chuckle when out of the unscrewed canister Kate pulls nothing more nor less remarkable than a bundle of bright-colored rags. Next installment of the Emperor's Old Clothes? Well, not a bundle of rags, we now see: a bundle *bundled* in a rag. And not really a rag, right? It's pretty good material: a nylon or rayon or maybe even silk material in a swirly, slightly faded blue-brown print: a paisley kerchief or bandanna for Katherine, to go with what Peter now claims as his beret. God knows that is unlikely coincidence enough, whatever's in the bundle, which Kath a touch gingerly now unknots, and *voilà:* the rolled-up, rubber-banded sheaf of ruled $8\frac{1}{2} \times 11$ three-holers in its transparent plastic food-storage bag, and we understand that as with Captain Donald Quicksoat, there is no hurry at all; let's go sailing; it is too sweet an afternoon to waste. We could throw the thing back overboard, we half believe; take a turn or two up the Chester before parking again for the night, and it will be there waiting for us when we're ready to settle down and read it—at happy hour, say?

Humming uneasily, hum dee hum hum, we actually *do* put it back in the canister, the Baggie still Baggie-tied, and rescrew the orange lid upon our curiosity, and slip into our swimsuits and make sail and weigh anchor and tack out of the ungenerous channel of Queenstown Creek, out into the river, rich in sails now, the weekenders piling in from everywhere and the local fleet piling out. *Story* heels over with a sigh from tack to tack; Act Two of *SEX EDUCATION: Play* rolls around our feet till Peter pops it into a locker beside its twin lest we take a tumble. Kath's got her new scarf on already, not bad-looking at all (Pete's stowed the beret in a coaming box because it won't sit tight on his hair in a breeze). We gee-whiz as far upriver as Piney Point astarboard and Ringgold Point aport, and a little past; we consider Cacaway Island, up ahead somewhere in big Langford Creek, but decide not to park there, not on a Saturday; maybe farther up in one of Langford's forks or over in the Corsica, just up the road off to starboard, where now we can see the nearer of the two Georgian-style mansions of the Corsica Neck embassy compound.

Pete suddenly says Jesus: Paisley! Telepathic Katherine groans I'm gybing and pulls the helm hard up, cutting dangerously across the bow of a biggish sloop behind us. Its helmsman whips his wheel over to clear us as he's obliged to, but the maneuver collapses their monstrous Technicolored spinnaker, which the crew must scramble forward to rescue while the skipper gives us the finger and shouts strong language our way. Kate murmurs Sorry there.

Paisley/paisley/Paisley: We clap our collective figurative brow. Mixing Operation BONAPARTE with Swimmers and Floaters and Paisleys and Gay May in the merry month of June, we're not certain what we've got, but we're certainly ready for the second act. We could park for a spell right where we are or pop into the nearest creek—there's always one ready to hand hereabouts—but *Story*'s got her way on now, on almost as nice a reach down as the one up, and because so many careless sailors go aground at its deceptively straightforward entrance, Queenstown Creek is seldom crowded even on weekends. Back down the broad Chester, therefore, we broad-reach; we hang a left at the nun, another at the last blue heron to port in ankle-deep water at the entrance-channel's inner edge. Hello again, Toronto. We sail and scull through the flukey air inside, back up to Salthouse, where the seven swans and single goose have reserved our parking place, and though it's only late afternoon, we put the heavy hook down for the night and assure the Nopoint Pointers that we're an easy half-hour's ambulance-ride from the Easton hospital.

It is warm, even sweatsy, even under the awning in the nearly-no-breeze in here, and that water looks inviting, all right, and we'll dunk into it presently again for sure, but not before fishing out and having at that canister, opening that Baggie, stripping the rubber bands off that roll of loose-leaf paper, and (K first this time, passing on each manuscript page to P as she reads it) reading

ACT II: DOWNSTREAM.

Act Two, Downstream, she says. Not even a title page. If we had found this first, we wouldn't even know what it was Act Two *of*. Hey, you were right.

Come on, says Peter. Read it out loud.

Nontheatrical Katherine won't do dialogue except in folktales and children's stories, but she reads us the opening stage direction. What she meant by Peter was right was that after reading Act One back in Dun Cove, he'd predicted that in Act Two the plot would be thickened by the two ovas' encountering sperm, and under Act Two's title (we still can't recall ever

having seen chapterlike titles on the acts and scenes of television plays)
she reads

Scene 1: The Swimmer.

Says P What else is new? K reads

*(Somewhat farther downstream, somewhile later. The Mainstream is wide
here, the current steady but smooth, the space cavernous but less dark.)*

This is inside somebody's uterus? she asks, laying a hand on Minneapolis
and Saint Paul. Below the Confluence, Peter reminds us. May and June
had heard the first sounds of those Swimmer guys in the distance, coming
their way, but they shoved off anyhow, onward and downward. Read.

(Occasional background sound of THEM *the* SWIMMERS, *ever more frequent
as the scene progresses. From off-camera come the squeals and laughter of
the two* FLOATERS, *still calling "Onward! Downward!" as they work downstream.* JUNE *swirls into sight first, somewhat dazed but exhilarated, and
pauses in a shallow eddy below a large boulder.)*

Complains Peter She's always pausing in a damn eddy. Kath says Try
doing dialogue when you're shooting rapids. That's all I'm reading out
loud.

Boulders in a womb, Peter murmurs, but holds his peace while Katherine
reads on to herself.

JUNE *(Calls back upstream)*: Here's a place to rest, May! Whew!
*(*MAY *swirls into the eddy with a flourish, equally exhilarated; her envelope
is in tatters.)*

Paisley/paisley/Paisley, Katherine thinks, fingering her scarf and wistfully
recalling white-water adventures with May Jump in less pregnant days.

MAY: Look: It's practically *off* me.
JUNE: Mine too. That waterfall! *(She strikes a pose to display a revealing
rent in her own envelope.* MAY *whistles like one of* THEM.*)*
MAY: Wasn't that second whirlpool a bitch!
*(As they speak, they repair their envelopes, assisting each other in the
places difficult for the wearer to reach.)*

KATHERINE: Uh-oh.
PETER: Don't start uh-ohing. Hand it over.

JUNE: "Enjoy each stage, girls." *(They laugh.)* You're a terrific Floater,
May!

Here, says Katherine, passing him page one. That Enjoy Each Stage
stuff sure does sound like Florence Halsey. It's all too spooky.

MAY: *You* are. That last stretch of white water . . .
JUNE: I *majored* in White Water.

KATHERINE: Yay! White Water!

JUNE: But there isn't supposed to *be* any below the Confluence.

MAY: What isn't supposed to be would fill a book.

JUNE *(Grins)*: Maybe we'll write one.

PETER *(When he reads this far)*: A postmodernist self-reflexive lesbian menstrual comedy.

MAY: Why not? What's a book? Oh, right: book.

JUNE: We seem to *know* more things down here than we did upstream.

MAY *(Nods)*: More things that we don't know.

JUNE: For instance—Could you fix me back here?—I feel pretty sure now that I'm part of a . . . *woman* and not part of a horse or a hen. Don't you?

MAY *(Shrugs; she is enjoying her job.)*: Coach Lefkowith told us that a woman is nothing but a Floater's way of making another Floater. How do you know you're not a man?

JUNE: Ms. R said we're not *anything* until we merge.

MAY: Lefkowith said we're not anything afterward.

JUNE: So what do we know for sure?

MAY: I don't know.

JUNE: Too bad we didn't know about that second whirlpool, anyhow. Wasn't it there before?

MAY: *I* wasn't there before. The waterfall was as far as I got, last time down. *(She grins.)* From here on, it's virgin territory.

JUNE *(Grins too)*: For both of us. *(She takes* MAY'*s arm, impressed.)* You really *swam* all the way back to the Confluence from that waterfall! I can appreciate that better now, May.

Me, says Peter, I smell a dramaturgical rat. Shoot me that next page. Kate swears him to silence and does.

MAY *(Gratefully)*: I couldn't do it again. And it was certainly better coming down with you than going it alone. It was almost fun.

JUNE: It *was* fun. I'm glad you came with me. *(An especially conspicuous sound of* SWIMMERS *comes from downstream.* JUNE *shivers.)* They're getting closer.

MAY *(Points)*: What do you think? Can we make it to that ledge on that little island over there before the crowd arrives?

JUNE: So that's what an *island* is. Let's try it. It's a better place than this to watch them from.

MAY: Maybe we can throw rocks at their heads. Let's crab ten degrees starboard to compensate for leeway, wouldn't you say?

JUNE: Crab? Oh, right: Aye aye, ma'am!

MAY: *Ma'am?*

PETER *(Aside)*: Pretty soon it'll be Wham Bam.

(JUNE links arms with her; just as they plunge forward, a lone SWIMMER sweeps onto the scene, not from downstream, but from around the upstream boulder.)

K: Aha.

P: What does he look like?

K: What does *who* look like? I swear.

(He wears a black wet-suit, a white rubber cap, and wire-rimmed spectacles. From between his shoulderblades, a thin white tail runs down his spine and on for another several feet. He is swimming wearily upstream, croaking "Onward! Upward!" with failing breath—but the current sweeps him backward into the two FLOATERS. After a moment's tumbling consternation, they spring together upstreamward; the SWIMMER, equally surprised, cries out and springs downstreamward. The frightened FLOATERS backstroke carefully to hold position against the current and begin working warily sideways, JUNE toward the ledge, MAY toward the eddy. The SWIMMER, regaining possession of himself, pushes up his eyeglasses and crying "Love!" dives determinedly at JUNE. MAY cries out again and leaps back a few feet. JUNE deftly sidesteps. The SWIMMER tumbles past her.)

Katherine giggles. Peter hums.

SWIMMER *(Recovers himself, strokes his chin, straightens his tail. He is young and wiry, with a sensitive, somewhat drawn face.)*: Excuse me, ma'am! *(He adjusts his eyeglasses; squints now at MAY; dutifully shouts.)* Love! Love! *(He plunges at her. MAY shrieks, too alarmed to evade him properly, and he actually manages to catch hold, first of her envelope and then, as most of it rips free, of her leg.)*

KATHERINE *(Aside)*: May Jump would flatten him.

SWIMMER *(Sees that he has all but removed MAY's envelope)*: Oh, Father! I'm sorry, ma'am! *(But his right hand on her leg—his left is holding the torn portion of her envelope—galvanizes MAY. Much tumbling and crying out as she pummels him and he protects himself without letting go of her or the remains of her envelope.)*

MAY: Pig! Rapist! *(Etc.)*

SWIMMER: Ouch! Ow! *(Etc.)*

PETER: Yes. Well. Et cetera.

(JUNE has paddled over to help; she lays hold of the SWIMMER's tail with distaste and pulls. MAY is then able to free herself enough to deliver a wicked left-handed chop. The SWIMMER lets go of her leg and rolls about.)

K: Right on, Maze. But the poor wimp seems more confused than dangerous.

(JUNE, still alarmed but somewhat concerned for him as well, releases his

tail. Ever more belligerent, MAY *delivers a few well-placed kicks and would do worse, but* JUNE *restrains her. The* SWIMMER, *groaning and clutching his crotch, gets to his feet;* MAY's *paisley envelope has gotten wound around his neck like a scarf.)*

Get me *out* of here, marvels Katherine, pulling off her scarf.

(When MAY *tries to get at him, he retreats in freestyle terror. The* FLOATERS *pursue him—*MAY *ferociously,* JUNE *half amused—until he disappears upstream. They float back, laughing, to the ledge—*MAY *with some difficulty for lack of most of her envelope—and hang on awhile, comparing impressions, before hauling themselves up to rest and stand watch.)*

JUNE: You were terrific!

MAY: Thanks. The sonofabitch would've Fused with you if I hadn't been there.

JUNE: I don't think so. *(Teases her)* Anyhow, it was you he wanted to Merge with. I heard what he said when he went after you!

MAY: It wouldn't have mattered to him which of us he got. They all want the same thing.

KATHERINE: Come on, May: Knock it off.

(Again they inspect and patch their envelopes. MAY *has barely enough left to cover her.)*

JUNE: Seems to me he didn't know *what* he wanted, much less *which.* I think he was as surprised as we were.

MAY *(Not amused):* For the first time in history, We had Them outnumbered! I guess they can't take that.

PETER: Good point there, Playwright.

JUNE: Did you notice? He even said "Excuse me"!

MAY: Pig rapist. He attacked me!

JUNE *(Amused):* It was the most *tentative* attack I ever saw. We played rougher than that in the Right Ovarium!

KATHERINE: Oy, I'd forgotten about those Ovarium things.

PETER: The Saint Deniston School for Floaters.

K: Then the Park Schoolers down in Washington would be the Lefties. They always creamed us. Only Molly and me had balls enough to foul them right back.

JUNE: When you turned him off, he seemed almost relieved.

MAY: Faggot.

Katherine Sherritt opines that this anonymous playwright is making the May character into too much of a caricature; May Jump never went around saying "Macho pig rapist faggot." Peter Sagamore reminds her that life is life and art art, ideally.

JUNE: A macho pig rapist faggot?

KATHERINE *(Thinking of her first husband)*: It happens, honey.

JUNE *(Looks upstream)*: Why do you suppose he went on up? I thought *we* were supposed to be their destination. *(Excited)* Hey, aren't they funny-looking? Those tails! But I loved watching him *move*. Mustn't it be fun to swim like that?

MAY *(Appraises her companion candidly)*: Fusing with you is what would be fun. I can't blame him for trying.

Says Katherine There's our Maisie. Frowning Peter reflects that one of the pleasures of writing playscripts must be that stage directions needn't be socko prose. *Appraises her companion candidly:* fwuff.

JUNE: He certainly didn't seem to me to be *threatening*, May. Weren't you the least curious to see what it would be like?

MAY: Not with him.

JUNE: I wish we could have talked awhile before he swam off.

MAY: Talked! With a Swimmer?

K: Why not?

JUNE: Why not? All through school I kept wishing that. To find out what they're really like, and what's really downstream. (MAY *shakes her head;* JUNE *presses on.*) Don't you think *he'd* like to know about the Confluence, and the rapids up in the Branches, and what it was like in the Right and Left Ovaria?

K: Poonie sure wanted to.

(She breaks off as MAY *clutches her arm and points downstream. The sound of* SWIMMERS *is close indeed now; their splashing distinct. The* FLOAT-ERS *move back a bit on their ledge.)*

MAY *(Whispers)*: Mama Moon!

(Now we see what they see: the awesome spectacle of the SWIMMERS' ADVANCE GUARD *moving upstream. From their ledge, the* FLOATERS *can look and listen without being seen. Before and below them swim a dozen or more* SWIMMERS, *singing in rough male harmony "Onward! Upward!" as they stroke past in approximate unison. We see—and recognize better than* MAY *and* JUNE *yet can—several sorts: brawny "machos," all body and tail with tiny heads; "eggheads," some with tiny tails; effeminates and predators; self-flagellators and flagellators of others; and many quite ordinary fellows. Some surge forward, even pushing their comrades under; some lose ground and are swept back. Some wander off from the Mainstream. Some pause just under the ledge—the* FLOATERS *step back another step, not to be espied. Some merely drown and float off downstream.)*

This is not a bad effect, says Katherine: the Swimmers' Chorus. I see the whole thing more as a water ballet or an aquatic opera than as a TV play.

(The two FLOATERS *direct each other's attention silently to one Swimmer or another with expressions of amazement, amusement, alarm; with whispers behind hands and admonitions to silence lest they be discovered. Curiosity is* JUNE's *prevailing reaction; distaste* MAY's. *Both are inclined to draw about themselves what remains of their envelopes—but* JUNE, *in her interest and excitement, often lets hers go.)*

PETER: Of course she does.

(Soon the parade thins out. A final, ordinary SWIMMER *swims by, calling "Onward, upward" in a mild voice as if simply counting cadence, and disappears upstream. They watch him go, then sit some moments in silence.)*

PETER SAGAMORE: Not a bad effect.

JUNE: And that's just the Advance Guard!
MAY *(Shudders)*: So they say. A couple dozen out of millions.
JUNE: Did you see the one that was all head and no tail? He could have passed for a Floater!

P.S. *(Aside)*: There's a foreshadow.

MAY *(Nods grimly)*: It's the ones that are all tail and no head *I* worry about. Thank the Moon they didn't see us.
JUNE: That one we met earlier wasn't so terrible. Hey, look! *(She points upstream. Expecting another Swimmer,* MAY *scrambles to a posture of defense.)*
MAY *(Incredulous, as she sees what* JUNE *sees)*: Mo-ther!
(Bobbing idly down toward them is what appears to be yet a third FLOATER: *a spheroid body wrapped in a light green paisley Floater's envelope.)*

P.S.: Guess who.
K.S.S.: Ssh. Maybe it's the third act, rolled up in a Baggie.

MAY: It's another one of Us!
JUNE: But she's all tucked in, like a preschooler! How'd she ever graduate?
MAY: She's wearing my school's colors. . . . How she got through those Swimmers is what I'd like to know.
JUNE *(Touches* MAY's *arm)*: Do you suppose she's been . . . Merged?
MAY: It's your Identity you lose when you Fuse, Jay-Gee, not your arms and legs and head. *(The strange* FLOATER *is bobbing just past their ledge now.)* She's a mighty queer-looking Floater!
JUNE *(Moves to reach out for the stranger)*: All the same, a sister is a sister. Let's fish her in; she's not even steering!
MAY: If I fall in without my envelope, I might go under. I'll hold your legs while you lean out and get her.

Katherine, when she reaches this line, hums. Peter, when he reaches this line, hums.

(JUNE flattens herself prone on the ledge and reaches out for the FLOATER. MAY, prone also, happily embraces JUNE's legs to keep her from falling in.)

JUNE: Not so *tight*, May. Here she comes. . . . Just a minute . . . I've got her. . . . *(She has indeed drawn the new FLOATER to the ledge, and holds her with both arms to keep her from slipping downstream.)* Don't ask me how we're going to haul her up!

MAY *(Sighs)*: I'll lend you a hand. *(Reluctantly letting go, she moves to JUNE's side and also lays hold of the FLOATER. But their leverage is awkward; the two together are still unable to lift the newcomer from the water.)*

JUNE *(A little desperately)*: Where are *her* hands?

MAY *(Loudly, to the FLOATER)*: Hey, Dum-Dum! Can't you give us a hand?

K: Here it comes.

P *(A few moments later)*: Yup.

("She" does: In exhausted but rapid order, the FLOATER whips off the envelope—which we now recognize as the missing part of MAY's—

PETER: *Now* recognize?

—raises his head, uncoils his tail, wrapped around him like string on a ball, extends his legs, straightens his eyeglasses, and, his expression more desperate than triumphant, seizes both MAY and JUNE by the wrists. They scream and pull back; the SWIMMER—it is of course the one they first encountered—

P: Let us guess.

—holds on tenaciously. MAY slips and almost goes off the ledge. As the scene dissolves, the frantic FLOATERS are slipping nearer and nearer the water, while from downstream once again we hear the ominous sound of another host of SWIMMERS: no doubt the MAIN BODY.)

No doubt, says Peter; but the girls are perfectly safe. Katherine wants to know damn it how does he know, but she knows how he knows and answers her own question: because it's only Act Two of what is presumably a three-act play, and all protagonists are as invulnerable as Achilles until the last act. You can drop a protagonist off the World Trade Center in Scene One of Act Two, declares Peter Sagamore, and that protagonist will either bounce like a tennis ball or not hit the pavement until the end of Act Three. But Katherine worries about the May character.

Excuse P's expression, but the May character is more exposed, by reason both of her role as supporting actress and of the tendency of the plot. Supporting characters do not inevitably survive second acts, and in the case of supporting characters who are also foils for the protagonist, as May is for June, the actuarial picture is even more uncertain. But look, he doesn't want to spoil the story. Kath's got the other two scenes of Act Two there, right?

She leafs through the leaves. There's only one more. It's called

Scene 2: May Fuses.

Is that good?

Peter considers: three scenes in Act One, two scenes in Act Two. Act Three, then, when it floats our way, can be expected to be a single extended scene. And Act Two, Scene Two, is called "May Fuses." She's a goner, hon, he declares. Want to take a swim and read the bad news later?

Sighs Katherine All you Swimmers care about is one thing. Go dunk, she tells him; she and the kids are hooked. We'll just make tuna salad for dinner.

So our man slips out of his trunks and goes over the transom. He is *not* hooked, though he finds the conceit entertaining enough. And he is as spooked as is his wife by the several resemblances of this story to ours—not to mention our finding both canisters, in the right sequence, on a body of water as large and multifarious as the Chesapeake. Were the script not literally penned, he might suspect some crank of trashing the estuary with photocopies in distress-flare canisters: *Rejected by network television, distressed playwright signals for help.*

He does ten laps around the boat and then hangs onto the anchor rode to catch his breath. Kath's tee-heeing up in the cockpit. Downcreek he sees another dark-hulled cruiser, this one a salty-looking blue cutter, coming in under all plain sail, an inflatable dinghy in tow. The skipper must know the entrance well. It turns our way, the crew dropping headsails, and chugs up under power past the Toronto schooner.

Kath whoops *Testorium!* You're going to have trouble with this scene. Where are you?

Pete calls back his whereabouts and says to himself to the approaching cutter Not too close, friends; right about there. A husky, bearded, sun-browned fellow on the bowsprit signals the helmsman to stop—helmswoman, Peter sees now—acknowledges us with a wave, and lowers their anchor at a point politely halfway between us and the Canadians. It is about six in the afternoon, summer-warm, the sun still well above setting but about to drop behind the treetops just across the creek and give us shade. Though the newcomers have maintained maximum distance off for courtesy's sake, they are not far enough away for real privacy. P's pleased to see therefore that, like ourselves, they are neither prudish nor exhibitionistic: As soon as they're moored, the middle-aged-looking fellow drops first their swim-ladder and then, discreetly, his cutoff jeans and jockey shorts and lowers himself into the water. His companion—younger-looking, trim, similarly tanned—follows suit: another pair of sunbirds working north up the Intracoastal. Pete gets just flash enough of her on her way over their transom to observe that she's well put together and that her breasts and behind are almost as brown as the rest of her.

No *fair,* Katherine frets mildly, looking over there somewhile later through our binoculars: Look at her flat tum and those tight little buns.

Says reading Peter Shush.

(The same scene, a moment later. The FLOATERS *still struggle on the ledge, the* SWIMMER *clutching their wrists.* MAY *and* JUNE *give a last, frantic, concerted pull; he makes use of it, not to yank them in with him, but to heave himself, still trailing* MAY'*s envelope, up onto the ledge with them. Squeals and grunts as they tumble together. The* FLOATERS' *wrists are free. Tangled in* MAY'*s envelope, the* SWIMMER *falls face down, exhausted.)*

He's well hung, too, voyeuring Kate reports. She herself is back to paisley scarf and underpants; it is our first really sticky evening aboard. They remind me of somebody. Ted and Diana?

Theodoros Dmitrikakis wasn't bald, Peter reminds her, not looking up. We are finishing our cold supper and sipping Lancer's rosé and Perrier.

Says naughty Kate Not so: I bet Dee balled him every night.

MAY: Get him, Jay-Gee, before he Fuses us! *(She herself jumps with both feet upon his tail-tip, which happens to be nearby. The* SWIMMER *shouts in pain, but is too spent to move.* JUNE *piles on to straddle his waist and pummel his back, then bends one of his arms behind him. He cries out again.)*

MAY *(Kneels on the* SWIMMER'*s tail now, her back to* JUNE*)*: Farther up, or he'll whip around and bite us!

(Somewhat gingerly, JUNE *releases his arm and slides up to sit on the* SWIMMER'*s shoulders and seize his neck.)*

MAY: Throttle him!

*(*JUNE *begins to squeeze. Neither the job nor her position is to her liking.)*

SWIMMER: Don't!

MAY *(Pounds his tail on the ledge)*: Wolf in sheep's clothing!

SWIMMER: Ow!

MAY *(Pulls the wreck of her envelope off him and gives his tail a karate chop)*: Pervert!

SWIMMER: *Ow!* I wasn't trying to trick you! I was floating just to keep afloat! I won't hurt you!

MAY *(Jumps up and down on his tail)*: That's what they all say. *Throttle* him, Jay-Gee, for pity's sake!

SWIMMER: Please don't hurt me!

JUNE *(Eases up)*: They don't all say *that,* May. . . .

Katherine reports from the binoculars Their boat's called *Reprise,* pronouncing the second syllable "prize." Or is it Re*preeze?*

MAY *(Grabs his tail in a sort of hammerlock, grimacing at the feel of it)*: He pretended he was a Floater so he could pull us in and Fuse us both!

SWIMMER: I swear I didn't! I'm sorry about before. You're supposed to *want* us. . . . *(*MAY *wrenches his tail.)* Ow! Really, I'm not interested if you're not!

JUNE *(Less hostilely)*: Why did you swim on upstream?

MAY: You know why. He's after our kid sisters.

SWIMMER: I was trying to get away from *you!* Then I thought I'd might as well look around a bit, since I was up there with nothing to do.

MAY *(Sarcastically)*: "Enjoy each stage." *(Wrenches his tail)*

SWIMMER: *Ouch!* I'm sorry I tore your wrapper, ma'am. I didn't mean to. But it saved my life up there.

MAY: Transvestite.

JUNE *(Signals MAY to stop)*: How far up did you go?

KATE *(Sighs)*: Look at her neat little bazooms. Come on; have a look.

PETER *(Borrows the binocs)*: One on each side, the way I like 'em. What else is new? *(Returns the glasses to KATHERINE, who resumes her inspection, and goes back to SEX EDUCATION: Play.)* They're going to see us staring at them, hon.

K: That's okay; he's got *their* seven-by-fifties out now too. *(She waves hello with her fingers to Reprise. PETER sighs, sips, reads.)*

SWIMMER *(Recognizes JUNE's less hostile tone and replies earnestly)*: I got as far as the Grand Fork, I think. Where the Great Eastern Current meets the Great Western?

(MAY laughs derisively at this nomenclature.)

PETER: So do I.

K *(Sipping between views)*: So do you what?

P: Laugh derisively at this nomenclature.

(Even JUNE has to smile, but she shushes her companion.)

JUNE: Go on.

SWIMMER *(Pushes up his glasses; JUNE is startled by the motion, but does not attack.)*: I *couldn't* go on. The current was too strong, and I was too tired. So I tried just floating. But we're not very good at that.

MAY: You could have fooled us.

SWIMMER: I swear to the Sun I wasn't trying to.

(MAY wrenches his tail.)

SWIMMER: Ow!

JUNE *(Shakes her head at MAY)*: Keep talking, Swimmer.

Katherine says she might have to take the family for another dip. Says Peter Take, take; I'll clean up the galley after they've knocked May off. Up.

Kath vows she's going to swim over to that *Repreeze/Reprize* boat and ask for literary asylum. It's no fun sleeping with a chap who sees all the chess moves down the road. But before she jumps ship she wants him to know that she found the climax of II:2 quite moving, for all its farcical aspect. She straps a water-ski belt between her breasts and her belly for extra flotation, skins out of her panties, and goes carefully overside in the pleasant evening light, still wearing the paisley kerchief.

SWIMMER: I saw your friend's wrapper caught on something or other up there, where I'd let go of it before, and I found I could float much better with it.

MAY: So you put on my envelope and came looking for the ones that got away. For Moon's sake *throttle* him, Jay-Gee, and let's throw him back!

SWIMMER: No! Please! Our coach said you'd be just waiting for us to reach you. *(The* FLOATERS *exchange glances.)* I had no idea you-all *hated* us. . . .

JUNE: Well. Actually—

SWIMMER: I wouldn't blame you if you did. It looks as if we were taught some wrong things. *(The* FLOATERS *exchange a different sort of glance.)* And even if some of us didn't believe everything we were taught, I guess all of us believed *some* of what the coach told us. He certainly never told us there were *two* Shes at the She-Shore. . . .

(Both FLOATERS *are laughing despite themselves at his outlandish terminology.* MAY *gives his tail a twist to recall them to their purpose.)*

SWIMMER: Oh, Father: That hurts!

MAY: It's supposed to.

SWIMMER: I think you've broken it.

MAY: I hope so.

SWIMMER: Look: I don't blame you. I've learned a lot of things on this journey that we should've been taught and weren't. First you wouldn't let me Combine with you—

MAY *and* JUNE: Combine!

SWIMMER *(Embarrassed)*: You know what I mean. Then I nearly got Combined myself, just upstream from here. First by a couple of Gay Blades—did you see them swim by? And then later, when I put that wrapper on, a whole gang of Bruisers jumped me. I had to float underwater to get away.

MAY: Now you know how *we* feel.

SWIMMER: I really do, ma'am. Floating underwater raised my consciousness.

Peter calls Kath? She calls back from somewhere overboard, out of his sight. Just checking, he says. She reminds him she's wearing a ski belt. Maybe she *will* paddle over and say hello to *Reprise*. They obviously don't mind skinny-dippers any more than we do.

Bye.

JUNE: How did you float underwater?

SWIMMER: Do you suppose you could ease up a bit on my windpipe?

MAY: Don't do it, Jay-Gee.

JUNE *(Lets go of his neck, but keeps her hands at the ready)*: How does a person float underwater?

SWIMMER: What I did was just sort of . . . I'd have to show you.

MAY: Maybe we'll show you how to *sink* underwater!

SWIMMER: Damn it, ma'am, I'm innocent! I've seen a few brothers do some nasty things, here in the Night-Sea and back in the Right Testorium, too; but I don't consider such Swimmers as brothers, no matter what the coach says.

JUNE: The Right what?

PETER: You heard him.

SWIMMER: Where we passed our tests and trained for our Night-Sea Journey. I wish I were there right now, so I could tell my kid brothers what it's really like up here!

JUNE: If we let you go, are you going to try to Merge with us?

SWIMMER: Try to what?

MAY: Jay-Gee!

JUNE *(Resolutely)*: Fuse us. *Combine* us.

SWIMMER: I won't, I swear. Not if you don't want me to.

MAY: We don't, mister.

SWIMMER: The truth is, I'm not even certain how it's done! So many things we were taught have been wrong. . . .

*(*JUNE *is already climbing off him, warily but positively.)*

MAY: Jay-Gee! *(Seeing herself alone with his tail,* MAY *drops it like a snake and springs up and out of range, moving even farther back on the ledge as the* SWIMMER *painfully collects himself, examines his injured tail-tip, and begins to stand.* JUNE *too is awed as he rises to his full height—he is quite tall—shakes his head, and adjusts his cap and eyeglasses. But she stands her ground, and now they survey each other soberly from head to foot, even front and back.)*

PETER: Nausicaa on the beach.

*(*MAY *retreats another step, winding her rescued wrapper about her.)*

SWIMMER *(Carefully places his hurt tail over his shoulder, like a bandolier.* MAY *crouches defensively at this gesture, but* JUNE *stands steadfast. The* SWIMMER *laughs and shakes his head again, in admiring disbelief.)*: I can't believe this! If only my friend was here to see! *Were* here.

PETER: Discovery of Common Ground.

MAY: You mean to help you Fuse us, is what you mean. Just try it, mister!

JUNE: You have a friend?

SWIMMER *(Laughs bitterly)*: I *had* a hundred million of them. They all drowned in the Night-Sea, except me. *(He pushes up his eyeglasses.)* This particular friend drowned right at our launching. He was a cynical fellow with far-fetched ideas about our Night-Sea Journey—what it was really all about; what was waiting for us up here if any of us got this far. Everybody thought he was out of his head; Coach Mankewicz despised him. It wouldn't surprise me if some of my so-called brothers did him in. Even I couldn't take him very seriously, but I tried to keep an open mind. *(He sighs; shakes his head.* JUNE *is of course very interested.)* Now it turns out he was pretty much right! Except about your hating us. *(He sits, favoring his injured tail.)*

JUNE: If your whole . . . graduating class? *(The* SWIMMER *shrugs and nods.)* If they all drowned except you, who were those other Swimmers just now, and who is it we hear coming upstream?

SWIMMER: Another class entirely, I guess. Mind you, I'm not supposed to be alive, much less sitting here on the Shore chatting with a She! With *two* Shes!

PETER: With two Shes sitting on the salt She-Shore.

SWIMMER: We're supposed to either drown along the way or reach the Shore—one chance in zillions!—and then . . . Combine. Whatever that means.

MAY: Ugh.

JUNE *(Looks at* MAY, *but speaks to the* SWIMMER*)*: So: You're a survivor. From the last Lunation . . .

Peter Sagamore frowns, but not with disapproval. That this Swimmer should be a survivor too, May's counterpart, he hadn't anticipated. Since the plot cannot imaginably pair *them* romantically, their shared survivorship will be for the purpose of establishing enough wary rapport, between the rivals for June's favor, to motivate May's upcoming self-sacrifice. He thinks of himself and May Jump in time gone by, at that Katherine Anne Porter party.

MAY: Sounds to me as if their Lunations are about four *minutes* apart instead of four weeks. The place is crawling with them!

SWIMMER *(Shrugs)*: Sometimes as close as a few hours, I understand. Other times as far apart as weeks, months, even whole semesters. We call them Launchings. But when one class graduates this close behind another, they can't be from the same school. My friend claimed there were other testoria besides ours; millions of others! And millions of other Night-Seas, too, each with its millions of Swimmers. He didn't even know how he knew!

JUNE: But he seems to have been right. What else did he tell you? And how'd you stay afloat when all the others drowned?

SWIMMER *(Laughs despairingly)*: Where do I start?

PETER: Laughs derisively. Laughs despairingly. Laughs adverbially. *(Stops carping. Suspends judgment. Reads Act Two, Scene Two, to its end.)*

(He shifts position; MAY *makes ready to attack, but* JUNE *waves her down.* MAY *will, however, not sit, as* JUNE *now does.)*

SWIMMER: We're not supposed to be able to *float*, you see. We're supposed to swim, swim, swim, onward and upward—just for the sake of swimming, I suppose—without the faintest idea where we're headed or why, or what we're supposed to do if any of us should reach that mythical Shore. . . .

JUNE: And we're supposed to float, float, float, for the sake of floating, onward and downward to Mother Moon-Sea—

MAY *(To* JUNE, *sourly)*: Unless you find Mister Right.

SWIMMER: My friend called the whole idea absurd and nasty. He used to say that whatever that beautiful She-Shore turns out to be, if it really exists at all, it can never justify the death of a hundred million brothers.

MAY: Justify shmustify, as long as you all drown.

SWIMMER: My friend thought Coach Mankewicz's talk about "swimming for swimming's sake" was lunatic. Of course, the coach thought my friend was lunatic, too. And subversive.

MAY: You're *all* bonkers, if you ask me.

JUNE: I'm not so sure. What about us . . . Shes? What were you taught about us?

SWIMMER: You're going to laugh.

JUNE: You didn't laugh when I mentioned Mother Moon-Sea.

(The SWIMMER *smiles, looks away, adjusts his glasses.)*

MAY: He's our prisoner; that's why he didn't laugh.

SWIMMER *(Sighs and plunges in)*: We were taught that we Swimmers are made by a Maker, whatever *that* is, and launched on our Night-Sea Journey for reasons known only to capital-*H* Him. It's supposed to have to do with "Love" and with "Transmitting the Heritage" . . . . *(He puts quotation marks around these terms with his fingers.)* But nobody knew for sure what any of *that* meant! We heard everything from sermons to naughty jokes about it.

JUNE: Sounds familiar.

SWIMMER: This friend of mine kept asking "*Whose* Heritage? Transmit it to whom? Where's *our* percentage?" Then he'd say things like our Maker might not even be a Swimmer, but some sort of monstrosity, maybe even without a tail. Or that capital-*H* He might not even know we're here. Or that He might know but not care, because He makes thousands of Night-Seas in His own lifetime, each one filled with millions of Swimmers, like ours.

MAY: That's disgusting.

SWIMMER *(Shrugs)*: How about this? My friend used to imagine that our Maker might be stupid, or immoral, or drunk . . . or asleep and dreaming!

MAY: I believe it.

*(*JUNE *shushes her.)*

SWIMMER: Or He might know very well that we're here in the Night-Sea, swimming as hard as we can to reach the Shore; but for some reason or other He wants to keep us from reaching it and "fulfilling our destiny," even though He launched us Himself! Isn't that preposterous?

MAY: To me it makes perfect sense. We don't want you here, either.

JUNE *(Crossly now)*: *Will* you listen, May? *(To the* SWIMMER*)* Where do we Shes fit in?

SWIMMER *(Embarrassed, but determined to say it out)*: My friend liked to imagine that in maybe one Night-Sea out of hundreds and thousands, one single, solitary Swimmer—that's one out of hundreds of billions of us!—gets a chance at a very limited and peculiar kind of "immortality" . . . .

JUNE: Go on! It's beginning to fit what *we* were taught!

(MAY *rolls her eyes and nods sarcastically, mouthing to the viewer "Mister Right."*)

SWIMMER: My friend claimed that our actual destination was not a bright golden Shore, as everybody believed—which is just a place where we wouldn't have to swim in the dark anymore. He said it was something . . . not long and thrashing like us, but sort of . . . (*He gestures vaguely with his hands, in* JUNE's *direction.*) sort of smooth, and gently gliding, or floating. . . . (JUNE *nods.*)

MAY: And the big brave hero grabs her and tears her envelope off and Fuses her, bang!

SWIMMER (*Frowns seriously and adjusts his glasses*): Well . . . Combining. My friend used terms like "Consummation," and "Union of Contraries," and "Becoming Something Both and Neither." I had to agree with him that if what comes from all that is just another Maker—of future Swimmers or future Shes—at the cost of so many millions of dead brothers—maybe dead sisters too, for all we knew—then the whole business *is* very hard to justify.

MAY: To say the least.

SWIMMER (*Sees his chance to appeal to her*): He said that he himself wasn't even going to try. The whole thing struck him as obscene.

MAY: Bully for him!

SWIMMER: In his opinion, if that's the way things are, then the real heroes are the suicides. . . .

MAY: Bravo!

SWIMMER: And the hero of heroes, in my friend's opinion, was the one Swimmer in all that number who actually manages to reach a She, against those astronomical odds, and then *refuses to Combine!*

MAY (*Applauds*): Hear hear!

(JUNE *shakes her head.*)

SWIMMER: He said that that would put an end to at least one cycle of catastrophes.

MAY: That friend of yours had his head on straight. I'd like to shake his hand.

JUNE: I feel sorry for him.

SWIMMER: We all made fun of him. When he drowned at our launching, nobody cared except me. (*He is lost in his recollections.*) We were young and green and gung ho, impatient to be off and swimming! Never mind where or why; just to test ourselves against the Night, the Sea, the Journey itself. (*He pauses; looks down.*) What happened after that is too terrible to think about. (*He covers his face with his hands.*)

JUNE (*Reaches out impulsively, to* MAY's *horror, but checks her impulse*): But you survived.

SWIMMER (*Nods*): Massacres. Sea-quakes. Mass suicides. The strong drowning the weak. Gay Blades Combining with each other. Machos singing dirty songs and fighting duels with their tails. Eggheads making up rules and stories and connections between things, even as they went under. The horror!

JUNE: But *you survived.*

SWIMMER *(Shakes his head)*: Not because I'm the fittest, for sure. I've seen the best Swimmers of my generation go down. Stronger, wiser, worthier than me . . .

MAY: Than *I.*

*(*JUNE *gestures impatiently.)*

SWIMMER: Than any of us.

JUNE: What kept you going?

SWIMMER: I *didn't* keep going, ma'am; that's what saved me. I'd thrash along with the others for a while, thinking about my friend's crazy ideas and wondering What *are* we doing here? What's all this *for?* And I'd find myself resting and . . . *floating.* for a bit—which we'd never been told we could do—and thinking things over before I went back to swimming onward and upward. The others charged on ahead, to reach the Shore. . . .

JUNE *(Nods)*: But there *was* no Shore. And no She, either.

MAY *(Points to herself)*: Well, there was; but I was hiding out for dear life up there at the Confluence and teaching myself how to swim back home.

SWIMMER *(Ignores her, in his sad recollection)*: They all drowned: the fit, the unfit, the wicked, the good. Their bodies came floating back down to where I was swimming and resting, thrashing and floating, thinking about my crazy friend. And somehow making my way up past waterfalls and tidal waves and whirlpools. . . . Then the current got so strong that it carried me back no matter how hard I thrashed, and the time came when I just couldn't swim another stroke. I gave it up and waited to drown. That's when I bumped into you.

JUNE *(Moved)*: Oh, dear: And we thought you were attacking us!

(The SWIMMER *laughs shortly and shakes his head.)*

MAY: You did attack us! You hollered "Love" and tore my envelope off!

SWIMMER: I thought I was *supposed* to! My friend said that every She is waiting for her He to swim along.

MAY: He *was* bananas, after all.

SWIMMER: He certainly never imagined that Shes were strong and active and . . . uncombinable.

JUNE *(Her turn to instruct)*: Actually we're not. I mean, on the one hand we're not Little Goody Two-Shoes waiting for her prince to come. . . .

SWIMMER *(Admiringly)*: I can see that.

JUNE: Some of us might be like that, but not most of us. But we're not that other thing, either: uncombinable.

MAY: *I'm* uncombinable. Don't you forget it.

SWIMMER: No, ma'am. *(He strokes his injured tail.)*

JUNE: I'm beginning to think that despite all the hocus-pocus, there's nothing very mysterious about our situation. You Swimmers periodically come swimming up; we Floaters periodically come floating down—normally one of us at a time and millions of you. If you don't happen to run into one of us—and that's most of the time—you all die. . . .

MAY: *Tant pis.*

SWIMMER *(Points sadly to some of the earlier* ADVANCE GUARD, *now floating back dead)*: No question about that.

JUNE: And if *we* don't run into *you*—which is also most of the time—*we* die.

(The SWIMMER *nods sad agreement.)*

MAY: We do not! Ma Moon divides the Crimson Creek for us as She did for Grandma Moses, and we pass down to float forever on the Flat Sea!

(The SWIMMER *laughs.* JUNE *rolls her eyes. Even* MAY *is clearly no longer persuaded by this conventional wisdom.)*

JUNE *(Firmly)*: We die; I'm sure of it now. Even the three of us are only temporary exceptions. Our promised Moon-Sea is just like their Shore, May: another myth. You and I know there's no Shore up in the Right and Left Branches, and *he* knows there's no Flat Sea down where he came from.

SWIMMER: I know *I* didn't see any; and I could certainly have used one. *(He adjusts his glasses.)* So. Except on those extraordinary occasions when one of us actually *does* manage to cross paths with one of you . . .

MAY: Watch out, Jay-Gee. Here it comes.

JUNE: I suspect that *that's* a myth, too: your one-to-one idea. I was taught that we'd have *hundreds* of suitors knocking at our doors, so to speak, and that the only problem would be to choose the best among them. We've already seen quite a few go by, and it sounds as if even more are on the way.

MAY: I wouldn't touch any of them.

SWIMMER: But then what happens? I'm ready to agree with everything you've said so far. But let's suppose that the miraculous has occurred: There you are, surrounded by hundreds of us Swimmers—

MAY: Yech.

SWIMMER: You've looked us over; you've made your choice. Now it's time to Combine Identities . . . Fuse, Merge, whatever. . . . How do we do it? I mean you and your chosen one.

JUNE *(Embarrassed)*: Didn't they teach you?

SWIMMER: You've taught me to doubt everything I was taught!

JUNE: Well . . . It has to do with enzymes. The Floater actively constructs a Multicellular Physical Process in a very few seconds to accommodate the Swimmer of her choice, and at the same time she sloughs off her Vitelline Envelope to get rid of the other Swimmers. They're all hanging on, you see, like drowning sailors to a life raft. . . .

MAY: Or flies to a honey pot.

JUNE: And the Floater doesn't need her envelope any longer. She's done with floating, and he with swimming.

SWIMMER: Mm hm. What then?

JUNE *(Covers her eyes)*: It's not easy to talk about these things. Especially with you. *(She looks at him determinedly.)* But we *should* talk about them. It shouldn't be dark and dramatic.

MAY: *I* was taught that the next step is for us to bite off your head, spit out your tail, and go on about our business. *Thff!*

SWIMMER: I was taught that we're supposed to cry "Love!" and dive into you and get Transfigured. What you said about that physical process of accommodation helps explain the diving-in business, I guess; but I still don't know what Transfiguration means. Do you?

JUNE *(Shakes her head)*: Ms. R admitted that *she* didn't know, either; but she was pretty sure it had to do with enzymes. She said we'd understand when the time came. *(She pauses.)* I'm beginning to believe her.

MAY: Hmp.

SWIMMER *(Gently)*: Have you yourself ever Merged Identities, ma'am?

JUNE *(Merrily indignant)*: No!

MAY: It's something nobody does twice. Like drowning.

SWIMMER: Have you ever *seen* anybody Merge? I haven't.

JUNE *(Primly)*: We had excellent illustrated textbooks in the Right Ovarium, even though they were necessarily speculative.

MAY: In other words, the authors didn't know what they were talking about. *(The* SWIMMER *laughs and nods.)* In the *Left* Ovarium we had excellent illustrations on our lavatory walls.

SWIMMER: So did we. Also speculative.

JUNE *(Determined to be serious)*: Our textbooks agreed that there *is* some sort of physical . . . *combination* involved. But we don't *swallow* you, any more than you dive into us. *(She smooths her hair.)* We . . . *envelop* you somehow, with that Physical Process of ours, and from then on we're not us any longer. I mean we're *us,* but not you and I. I don't mean *you,* of course, or *me;* I mean Swimmer and Floater. Do you know what I mean?

SWIMMER *(Simply and admiringly)*: I was told that we die of love.

MAY: *I* was told that we die of indigestion.

JUNE *(To the* SWIMMER*)*: *Do* you know what I mean? I'm not even sure *I* do; but I *think* I do. Gametes . . . Zygotes . . . I don't know.

SWIMMER *(Gently)*: I believe I'm beginning to understand. Please forgive me for jumping you before. I was ignorant, scared, and exhausted.

JUNE: I forgive you.

(Sound of approaching SWIMMERS.*)*

The play's action having been for some pages at a virtual standstill—though not its plot and certainly not the development of its eschatological theme—Peter interrupts his reading here to check out the voices carrying *Story*ward from *Reprise.* Sure enough, Katherine has paddled over there and made friends, as she could do in ten minutes if you dropped her in the Gobi Desert. The murky water and fading light preserve her modesty; her scarfed head and bare shoulders held above water by the ski belt, she's chatting high-spiritedly with the couple aboard, who are clothed now against the No-See-Ums that pester Chesapeakers between sunset and dark. Time for Peter to get clothes on, too—but now he sees his wife apparently making ready to board the cutter!

The stocky fellow steps below, out of sight; the woman holds a large striped beach towel ready; Katherine pulls herself hugely up their ladder. Now Peter can just make out that the man has handed up a terry-cloth robe to his companion, who helps our woman into it. He returns to the cockpit with a tray of drinks, and the three resume their talk—Katherine, it seems to Peter, more animatedly than her hosts. At one point she waves and calls something to her husband across the water; the distance is too far for Peter to make out what she says. The man and woman, too, cordially wave to him. He waves back, slaps with the manuscript at a No-See-Um on his inboard calf, envies for the thousandth time his wife's gregariousness, and goes back to the about-to-be-beleaguered trio on their uterine verge.

JUNE: I forgive you.
(Sound of approaching SWIMMERS)
SWIMMER (To MAY): You too, ma'am. I'm very sorry.
MAY: Forget it. You'd better swim along, now; we've got things to do. (To JUNE) We've got to get rid of him and hide.
JUNE (Rises uncertainly): We hid before. We're not supposed to hide.
MAY: You go like a lamb to the slaughter if you want to. I'm hiding. (She starts toward the rear of the ledge.)
SWIMMER (Urgently, to MAY, as he rises too): You can't hide here, ma'am. This is the Main Body coming. There'll be so many that they'll swarm all over this ledge. (To JUNE) Don't you want to look them over, at least, before you choose—or get chosen?
JUNE: Now I'm scared.
SWIMMER (Tentatively but deliberately touches JUNE's shoulder; she looks at him sharply, but does not draw away.): Really, ma'am. If this group is like my group, you're not going to be choosing among suitors. You're going to be attacked by a horny mob.
MAY: I knew it. We've got to make siege preparations fast!
(JUNE begins to cry a little. MAY touches her other shoulder.)
MAY (To the SWIMMER): Get out of here now, Buster. You'll lead them to us.
SWIMMER (To both): Listen. Just down the channel and off to one side is a really safe harbor: It's an absolutely private cove, with an ideal vantage point for inspecting Swimmers without being seen. I stumbled into it on the way up, during one of my rest periods, and stayed there awhile to get my breath. There's a way to reach it without running into the Main Body, and the entrance is so tricky that only one Swimmer can come ashore at a time, so it's easy to defend. You'll be perfectly safe. (MAY is interested.) You can wait there till the whole crowd swims past and drowns, if you want to, and then float on down. (MAY is nodding assent.) Or you can look them over and choose a mate to Combine Identities with. . . .

MAY: Let's get going, Jay-Gee. *(To the* SWIMMER*)* What's the course from here to that cove?

SWIMMER: Two ten magnetic. But you'll never find it by yourselves.

MAY: We'll try. Two ten magnetic.

JUNE *(Really frightened now, to* MAY*)*: You can't float properly with what's left of your envelope, May!

SWIMMER *(To* MAY*)*: I'm really sorry about that. *(He examines his tail-tip.)* I can't steer properly, either, with this broken tip.

MAY: Who cares about you?

(The sound of the MAIN BODY *is nearer.* MAY *and* JUNE *clutch each other.)*

SWIMMER *(Earnestly)*: Look: Getting to this cove takes cross-current work as well as navigation. There's a breakwater and another whirlpool. I think the three of us together can do it.

MAY: Go away.

JUNE *(Quiets her. To the* SWIMMER*)*: How?

SWIMMER *(To* JUNE*)*: You can float and steer, but you can't really thrust. She can steer, but she can't float or thrust. I can thrust, but I can't float or steer. If you hold onto her and I hold onto you, she can steer for the three of us, you can float for the three of us, and I can thrust for the three of us, as well as tell her where to steer. *(He adjusts his glasses.)* I honestly think it'll work.

MAY *(To* JUNE*)*: He'll steer us right to Them.

SWIMMER: Damned if I will, ma'am!

MAY: You want our Identities all to yourself in that private little cove of yours!

SWIMMER *(Out of patience with her at last)*: I wouldn't have your Identity as a gift! *(The sound of the* MAIN BODY *grows.)* For pity's sake, let's get going; they're practically here!

MAY *(Links arms with* JUNE*)*: And here's where we'll fight them off. If we go under, we'll take as many of them with us as we can. We don't trust you.

SWIMMER *(Directly to* JUNE*)*: I beg you to, ma'am. Here they come.

JUNE *(To* MAY*)*: I think we should trust him, May. . . .

MAY *(Shakes her head; she has seen this coming.)*: Not me. You go with him, Jay-Gee: I think you've found your Mister Right.

JUNE *(Embraces her)*: I have not! *(*MAY *accepts the embrace, then stiffens as the* MAIN BODY *sounds again.)*

SWIMMER: Come on!

MAY *(Waves them both away)*: Go on. Here they are.

(The roar of the MAIN BODY *is now upon them, followed at once by a various throng of* SWIMMERS *from downstream, more densely packed than before, but otherwise behaving in much the same fashion as the* ADVANCE GUARD. *As the* FLOATERS *were forewarned, the* SWIMMERS' *very number thrusts a few of them willy-nilly up onto the ledge. Three of them now lie or kneel there, dazed, getting their breath and bearings; the three prior occupants crouch at the rear of the ledge. The throng in the Mainstream thrashes on.)*

FIRST MAIN BODY SWIMMER: Hey, guys! We've reached the Shore!

SECOND M.B.S.: Damned if we haven't! *(He points.)* Is that a She?

THIRD M.B.S.: Looks to me like a whole Shoreful of Shes!

(The original SWIMMER *has snatched* MAY's *envelope back, to her considerable dismay, and coiled himself as before. Now he rolls out onto the ledge before the newcomers, calling to them in falsetto.)*

SWIMMER: Here I am, boys! *(The three* MAIN BODY SWIMMERS, *shouting "Love!" and other things, jump him. As he fends them off, he calls to* JUNE *and* MAY.) Around this rock and two ten magnetic!

(While he wrestles with the three MAIN BODY SWIMMERS, MAY *begins to lead* JUNE *away as he directs. She resists. Now the attackers gleefully tear* MAY's *envelope off the* SWIMMER, *fling it away—in* JUNE's *direction—and discover their prey to be one of themselves.)*

SECOND MAIN BODY SWIMMER *(Holds up the* SWIMMER's *tail)*: Look what she's got!

FIRST M.B.S.: Fa-ther!

THIRD M.B.S.: Drown the faggot!

(They drag the struggling SWIMMER *toward the edge, over which now more* MAIN BODY SWIMMERS *are clambering onto the ledge.* JUNE *rushes to help him, ignoring* MAY's *cries to her, and leaps upon the* FIRST MAIN BODY SWIMMER. *He and the* SECOND *grapple with her as the newcomers pile upon the* SWIMMER.)

FIRST M.B.S. *(Grips* JUNE *from behind)*: Hey, this one don't have no tail! He's got other stuff!

SECOND M.B.S.: It's a She, egghead!

THIRD M.B.S. *(Jumps at once off the* SWIMMER *and dives at* JUNE*)*: Combine her!

(The fray now becomes general: JUNE *tears loose and defends herself energetically with the assistance of the* SWIMMER, *who has seized the opportunity to rush to her side. But more* MAIN BODY SWIMMERS *are swarming upon the ledge than the two of them can dispatch back into the Mainstream: It is a losing battle until* MAY, *who has retrieved her envelope, wrapped herself in it as in a sarong, and steeled herself for this moment, mounts a natural dais in the center of the ledge. She strikes an awkward pose in imitation of* JUNE's *earlier one and calls to the* MAIN BODY SWIMMERS *in what she hopes is an alluring voice.)*

MAY: Here it is, guys: the hottest Identity in the Mainstream!

(The MAIN BODY SWIMMERS *notice her, falter, and turn away from* JUNE *and the* SWIMMER—*who continue to get in their licks for a while, in particular shoving would-be new arrivals back into the Mainstream.* MAY *does a strip-tease to hold their attention: Singing "Onward and Downward" to a burlesque rhythm, she divests herself slowly of the retrieved portion of her envelope and tosses it over their heads, to* JUNE. *The* MAIN BODY SWIMMERS *gape, cluster, wave and thump their tails appreciatively, whistle and shout encouragement.* MAY *removes the bit of envelope that has been covering her breasts and looks imploringly toward* JUNE *and the* SWIMMER. *The* MAIN BODY

SWIMMERS *move in closer, surrounding the dais. The* SWIMMER, *understanding* MAY's *strategy, grimly and carefully leads* JUNE, *horror-stricken, toward the rear upstream corner of the ledge.*

The THIRD M.B.S. *now reaches out tentatively and touches, then seizes,* MAY's *leg at the calf. Her breath catches.* JUNE *would return to her, but the* SWIMMER *restrains her; more and more* MAIN BODY SWIMMERS *are gaining the ledge, attracted by the spectacle.*

MAY *shakily resumes her song. The* SECOND M.B.S. *seizes her thigh, just below the remaining scrap of envelope.* MAY *cries out, but forces herself not only to resume her burlesque "Onward and Downward," but to peel off the last of her envelope and throw it to the crowd. The two* MAIN BODY SWIMMERS *let go of her momentarily to thump their tails in lusty applause with the rest.* MAY *dashes between them to the ledge-edge farthest from* JUNE *and the* SWIMMER; *there she halts, turns, and—her back to the camera, her feet planted well apart and her head lifted proudly—opens her arms. With whoops and shouts, the* MAIN BODY SWIMMERS *throw themselves upon her from three sides, enwrapping her with their tails and burrowing their heads against her, while others just emerging from the Mainstream seize her legs from behind.* MAY's *tearful but defiant cries—"Do it, damn you!"—become screams as the flailing mass of her attackers tumbles with her over the edge, into the water, and out of sight downstream.*

JUNE, *still restrained by the* SWIMMER, *has been screaming after her. At the final assault, she hides her face in the* SWIMMER's *shoulder. As* MAY *takes her assailants over the edge, the* SWIMMER *curls his injured tail consolingly about* JUNE *and carefully leads her behind the rock and out of sight,* MAY's *envelope trailing forlornly from* JUNE's *hand.)*

Katherine Sherritt's entire yesterday morning in Annapolis we did by summary and recap, keeping the camera so to speak on Peter Sagamore, when in fact the real story line was across town, in May Jump's apartment, and all P did was read Don Quixote. So

THIS TIME WE'RE GOING TO BACK UP AND NARRATE KATH.

Plumply paddling some yards astern of *Reprise, Wye I.,* she calls up cordially from the creek Are you Repreeze or Reprize? The turbid water and failing light sufficiently veil her for the circumstances, she judges; if the guy gets a shot of her tits, *tant pis.* Were she to break her water, as they say, while in the water, would she know it? Queenstown Creek feels like a great LeBoyer bath.

The husky gray-beard nods howdy from their transom, leaning on a leg of the cutter's divided backstay and looking unself-consciously her way. Dryly from the cockpit the slim brunette says Dealer's choice, and Kath feels a sudden surge in herself as if the old amnion has indeed let go. But it is the surge of recognition.

Lee and Frank Talbott! We met you at Doug Townshend's once, a hundred years ago!

Says the fellow, surprised, So you *are* the Sagamores. We wondered. His wife says to Katherine Your memory's amazing. Their voices, unlike K's, are unenthusiastic. Okay: She understands why and feels creepy knowing what she really has no business knowing: that in addition to their several bereavements, the Talbotts have very recently undergone an abortion unilaterally decided upon. They are clearly not overjoyed to see pregnant us. Yet their tone seems not uncordial, only subdued, and Kath is too wowed by crazy coincidence not to splash on. You're not going to believe this, she chirps to Leah Talbott: We just met your mother and your sister and your nephew over in Annapolis! We spent all yesterday with them!

Frank Talbott says What?

Invite me aboard, merry Kath demands. This is too spooky!

The surprised woman says You saw Ma and Marian? Her husband says Come on up; I'll get you a beach towel. Katherine remembers having enjoyed his voice before: gentle, but resonant with testosterone. Get her my terry robe too, Lee Talbott instructs him, and asks Katherine hospitably enough Can you manage the ladder?

K does, slowly and carefully, and is handed first the towel and then the robe belowstairs. She apologizes for dripping all over their cockpit and feels like apologizing further for being so nakedly pregnant in their company, but doesn't. Unhitching her ski belt and wrapping herself comfortably, she catches Leah Talbott exchanging level glances with her husband as he returns upstairs. Too spooky! she laughs again, pulling off the paisley bandanna and shaking out her hair. Wait'll you hear.

But first the three shake heads together over Douglas Townshend's sudden death, and Katherine takes the opportunity to sympathize with the Talbotts' late other losses. She herself never met Frederick Mansfield Talbott, she tells them, though her husband in fact did, once. She's almost sure she met Lee's half-brother Jonathan, though, at some HOSCA meetings. What a terrible thing.

That it was, Franklin Key Talbott quietly acknowledges. He's looking at her scarf, which she's drawing idly between her fingers. Leah Talbott declares We're still wiped out. We've spent nearly a year sailing around in the Caribbean, trying to put things behind us. But we seem to have sailed right back into them.

K murmurs she's so sorry.

More to his wife than to her, Frank Talbott says Maybe Chesapeake Bay is spoiled for us.

Maybe.

From our one evening together, Katherine remembers Lee Talbott as having been a live wire. These days her brown eyes are not vivacious;

under her Caribbean tan, her face is drained; she seems now older in her trials than Katherine, though in fact she's four years younger.

K hopes aloud that the Bay is not spoiled for them; Jesus, she and Peter love it.

The man says kindly We've loved it, too, and his wife brightens up to ask how in the world we happened to meet Carla B Silver and company in Annapolis yesterday.

Frank Talbott opens cold cans of National Premium beer in Styrofoam sleeves. Kath declares It's just too weird, and understands as she does that this really is a sticky situation she has paddled herself into, where nearly anything she says is bound to add to her hosts' unhappiness. Have they even heard the news about Marian Silver and May Jump? For all she knows, she has barged in on a couple in extremis from accumulated misfortune; her great cheery pregnant presence could be their last straw. But there she is, and now she must hope that sheer goodwill will carry her through.

So she burbles on (You don't burble, Peter will tell her later tonight, when she retells all this. Insists K I burble): There we were in Annapolis, that being where the wind listed et cetera, and a lay day on account of its listing thither at twenty-five-plus knots, so why not call up her best friend in the world besides her husband, May Jump, and May said Come meet my new family, and then it turned out that we and Carla B Silver had even more to say to each other than Kath and May Jump did. Directly to Franklin Key Talbott, she says Peter was involved once with Doug Townshend and your brother, but *he* should tell you about that. We really admired your *KUBARK* book, by the way.

Frank Talbott winces his brown brow, but nods to the compliment.

I'm going to let him tell you, Kath repeats. Unless I do first. Isn't it too weird, though, all these connections?

The Talbotts agree that it is indeed, and Kath declares that that's just the beginning. May Jump's name seems to have broken some ice. The Talbotts turn out to have heard, by radiotelephone from Carla B Silver, of the blow-up at Carla's Cavern after they sailed away from there last Sunday: Lascar Lupescu's crazy pass at distraught Marian (a goddamn assault, really, Leah Talbott understands, who had truly *liked* the fellow; thought him good company for her mourning mother); and Marian's moving into a lesbian connection with May Jump. They had been going to return at once to Fells Point, to help beleaguered C. B Silver sort things out; but Carla had insisted they let things sort themselves out a bit first, in Fells Point and Annapolis and aboard *Reprise* as well.

Kath notes that Lee pronounces it Repreeze and that she perhaps said more than she meant to, there at the end. Her husband smoothly takes over: If we have met his mother-in-law and oldest friend, Carla B Silver, we understand that one takes her advice seriously. All the same, the Talbotts are mighty concerned about the Silver ménage. Leah Talbott says they have in fact met our friend May Jump once or twice. Lee's literary interests led her, two winters ago, to check out that ASPS outfit in Washington (she teaches in Annapolis nowadays, half an hour away); she was even ready to join it, and maybe HOSCA too, with which Marian was involved. But then Rick Talbott's disappearance, on top of young Jonathan's in Chile, preempted the family's energies; she took sabbatical leave from St. John's College and, with her husband (who was between careers, retired from the Agency since before *KUBARK* and doing occasional lectures and freelance political journalism), went a-cruising to restore their weary spirits. She and Frank did not know quite what to make of May Jump; she *seemed* okay. . . .

Kath does an enthusiastic character reference, relieved that Peter is not there to hmp. May Jump will do a world of good for the boy Simon, and no doubt for shaky Mim Silver as well. May Jump is the very Rock of Gibraltar, et cetera. Lee Talbott confesses that she has a tad of trouble with the lesbian thing. Frank Talbott wishes Simon Silver had a man to relate to. All the same, they are gratified by Katherine's high regard for Ms. Jump, and profess to feel easier in their minds now about Marian's move to Annapolis.

K is about to mention that as a matter of fact she herself is a cofounder of the ASPS and HOSCA. But in mid-testimonial to her friend, she has absently set down the paisley scarf, and Lee Talbott has absently picked it up. Katherine gets to grinning about the ovum "May's" self-sacrificial striptease in Act Two, Scene Two, of *SEX EDUCATION: Play.* Talk about unlikely coincidences!

To change the heavy subject, she chitters into the story (Says Peter You don't chitter; says Kath I chitter) of our finding not one but *two* floating orange Alert-and-Locate distress-signal canisters five days apart, one near Knapps Narrows on Tilghman Island last Monday and one right over yonder near Kent Island Narrows just this afternoon, the first with an old black beret in it, of all things, plus a manuscript of the first act of a really oddball TV play, of all things; the second, unbelievably, with this faded scarf here in it plus the second act of the same play. And wait till the Talbotts hear about that play: a comedy about sperms and ova which she thinks is funny enough and even somewhat touching in its way, but which professional Peter is having trouble with (he's over there finishing Act Two right now: Look over here and wave, Peter Sagamore). She very briefly outlines the plot thus far, with apparent success; the Talbotts shake their heads and smile. But it is impossible to judge the thing on its merits, Katherine declares, because she is so spooked by the coincidences: not just our finding of both canisters, against which the odds must be about a zillion to one, but the unsettling resemblances of both the "May" ovum to good May Jump (she's even called Lefty, and May Jump is left-handed!), and of the straight ovum, June, the "Right-O"—so Peter has declared— to herself: her gung ho preppiehood, her love of white-water canoeing, and some other stuff. Not to mention the general sperm-and-egg conceit— *two* eggs, one of which, the gay May one, just got herself massively fertilized in Act Two—when here Katherine sits, so full of babies she's about to pop!

Ah, she says shortly, reproving herself: I'm sorry, people.

Lee Allan Talbott languidly asks What for? K's cheeks twinge. She doesn't want to be a baby bore, she says; God knows it makes at least as much sense not to have any, particularly at her age and at this hour of the world. But she finds herself irrationally happy, however worried, and she burbles on more than she should.

Lee Talbott declares evenly, fingering an end of her hair, Ma told you I just aborted ours, right? Frank Talbott turns to her. Kath blushes, sees how transparent she's been being, and does not attempt denial, but says I hope you can understand that it was *right* for your mother to speak of it, in the particular circumstances. May I explain?

But Franklin Key Talbott says, in his quiet terrific voice, Carla B Silver is not a yenta, Katherine. If she told you about our decision, she did it for your sake, one way or another.

She really did, grateful Kate affirms. Peter and I have had a couple of problems to deal with too, though thank God no *desaparecidos*.

Firmly but not disagreeably, Lee Talbott changes the subject. So what's Katherine's famous husband working on these days? Or shouldn't she ask?

Why shouldn't she ask?

Lee shrugs. Some critic she's read says Peter Sagamore has painted himself into a corner with the Less Is More thing. Katherine's husband should surprise the shmuck with an eight-hundred-page picaresque novel.

K wonders: Tit for tat? But the woman's tone is friendly, despite some voltage still in the air from mention of the abortion. Touchy as the subject is, in our house, of Peter Sagamore's late difficulty and its several causes (Kath names them to herself: Vug, Crump, Fougasse, Dingle, Coomb, Cubby, Coign), instead of sorting out the protocol of confidence and counterconfidence, taunt and countertaunt, she follows a sure and luminous intuition and tells the Talbotts our situation in a nutshell: that P's aesthetic turn to Less Is More, many years ago, was subsequently aggravated by the coinciding of his CIA obsession (inspired and fueled by Douglas Townshend and enflamed by the John Arthur Paisley case), with our efforts to get pregnant, our miscarriage, and the rest. The man has in fact been all but blocked; we are scared shitless of possible connections between that block, our pregnancy, and this crazy Doomsday Factor factor, which K doesn't even want to go into.

She is babbling all this, mind, because she liked them at first sight, the Talbotts, and trusted them at second sight, and feels creepy about knowing of Lee's abortion before they knew she knew. Doug Townshend's sudden death was a kind of last straw for us, she blabs on (You don't blab, will say Peter Sagamore, and Kate I blab): We're out here bopping around in a little boat with no motor instead of safely home with car and telephone standing by for the big event, because et cetera. Finding this scarf and that funny-spooky playscript with the paisley flotation-envelope business in it was a touch alarming; it feeds our paranoia, which however steadfastly resists swallowing: Hence we go around wearing the scarf and beret, for example, and we are enjoying the Sex Ed play more than not, especially the idea of it. Coincidence *can* be crazy; no one appreciated that fact more than did Doug Townshend. We are determined to stare these matters down, see them through, even Operation BONAPARTE, which K hasn't mentioned yet—for all she knows, the Talbotts may know all about it—just as we have been addressing as best we can, calmly but unevasively, Peter's difficulties with the muse and with our imminent parenthood. There. Uh, we will pay but, um, not count the cost, you know? Fingers crossed, et cetera. There.

All through this speech, Lee and Frank Talbott have been exchanging wife-and-husband looks, obviously ready to say many a thing. Now Frank says Let's fetch your famous husband over here. You-all and we-all have some more things to say to each other.

What Leah says is that she'd like to read that Sex Ed play. Could they borrow it? How long are we guys staying in Queenstown Creek?

Says Kate No plans. Probably just tonight. You?

Says Lee No plans. After Baltimore, we sort of ran out of destinations.

Katherine suggests they three move over to *Story* (which name, she remarks by the way, was not laid on our boat by us) instead of Reprising Peter. It's time she got some clothes on, and we're well stocked with ice and drinks.

Franklin Talbott says so are they: Is she sure they can't bring something along? She's sure. He goes over the transom into *Reprise*'s dinghy first, to assist her. In the dusky near-dark, K carefully climbs down, wrapped in the white terry robe, and reaches back to Leah for the scarf and ski belt. Handsome Mrs. Talbott hands down the flotation belt and swings easily down into the dinghy; but she has rolled the paisley scarf into a headband, which makes her look like the Land O Lakes butter Indian maiden. Careworn or not, thinks Katherine Sherritt, this is one sexy-looking professor of American Lit.

Peter Sagamore has finished reading Act Two long since and considered rowing over to join the party aboard *Reprise,* but instead wound up sipping Dos Equis and logging notes on the curious play, its more curious echoes of May Jump and our pregnancy, and—most curious of all—our discovery, in order, of the two canisters and their contents. It is a splendid balmy first night of summer: no bugs at all in the still, mild air, now that the light is gone. His body feels to him first-rate; he is supremely comfortable in the cockpit in light jeans and short-sleeve sweatshirt, his bare feet in carpet slippers against the dew just forming on decks and cushions. Were the world to end tomorrow, he reflects, few of its inhabitants will have had a pleasanter final evening.

By penlight he makes a note not about apocalypse but about Very Extraordinary Coincidence: that in the patient plenitude of time and of astronomically large numbers, the most improbable will inexorably come to pass. What better illustration than the existence of even one grown fish in the sea or fertilized ovum in the uterus of Katherine Sherritt Sagamore?

The inscription of her name prompts him to check how fares that fine, beloved female animal. He cons *Reprise* with our 7 × 50s, lying near to hand: Their big objective lenses, wondrous gatherers of dim light, show him, through all the intervening dusky yardage, that K's new friends—the burly bearded one, anyhow—are about to ferry her home. Obliging of him. Ah, the woman's coming too, she of the perky breasts both port and starboard. Well, it is a night for rowing about Queenstown Creek; for anything but shutting the body up indoors.

That reflection prompts him to wonder what his old mother's doing: staring at a ceiling in Hoopersville, he imagines; racked with arthritis from stem to stern and too far gone in the memory, for better or worse, to recall delicious summer evenings from her own prime, of which even hard-bitten Fritz and rawboned Nora must have had their share. In the shallow yonder of Salthouse Cove, a great blue heron lets go a reverberating squawk. Some sort of owl replies; P's not sure which sort. To locate for the approaching rowers' benefit our own dinghy and boarding ladder, he fetches a more serious flashlight; he will invite the Reprisers aboard for a nightcap while Kath dresses and returns her borrowed robe.

She is in their inflatable dinghy's stern, he sees now, giving rowing directions to the fellow facing her amidships. The trim woman in the bow— is that a headband she's wearing?—looks over her shoulder and calls quietly

HELLO THERE, *STORY*.

We've brought your family back.

Says Peter Much obliged, and cleats their proffered painter. He has seen that face before: dark and seasoned, Mediterranean, attractive. Over the chunkle of shipped oars, Katherine sings out It's Frank and Lee Talbott, hon.

Smiling P replies Of course it is, and to himself makes the connection: Carla B Silver's other daughter, the unwrecked one, who knew his stories. And the Prince of Darkness's brother, who did too.

Come aboard.

He gives Lee Talbott a hand. She gives him a bright, serious smile and pulls herself up. Striking woman, our man's senses register; striking despite the clear toll, even in that light, of her and her husband's and family's late ordeals. Even more striking coincidence to remeet this pair so upon the heels of our Annapolis lay-day encounters, et cetera; no doubt Kate has run all that by them by now. The sight of Frederick Mansfield Talbott's brother stings him; but swart, sturdy, bald Franklin Key Talbott, standing in *Reprise*'s dinghy to steady K's boarding, says Good to see you again, Peter Sagamore, and grips our man's hand with a quiet goodwill that blows any misdirected grudges quite away.

Katherine kisses her friend hello and informs him cheerily We've been talking a blue streak, mainly about impossible coincidence. We decided it was time to let you join the conversation. What does everybody want to drink?

Everybody wants another Beck's or Dos Equis, including Katherine, who can't have either. I'm afraid we don't have any light, she warns; Peter drinks only the heavy. No matter, Frank Talbott says: Lee and I have a lucky metabolism that can put away brew without putting on pounds.

Boyoboy, Kate cordially complains; you should see me. We then drop what it occurs to us may be a touchy subject. P distributes fresh refreshment, and through half a Beck'sworth of mortal time K reports from cabin to cockpit, while changing clothes in the dark, that she has blabbed *everything* to our neighbor/guests, okay? P's connection with Doug and his meeting with Frank's brother and our subsequent miscarriage—

Was that mint-tea business a trick? Peter interrupts to ask at once of Franklin Talbott, who strokes his beard and says With Rick you never knew for sure. He went in for literary demonstrations, and his literary models weren't always the best.

—how much we both admired *KUBARK:* the writing as much as the inside dope—

Very kind of you to say so, Frank Talbott murmurs. I'm afraid I'll never be a real writer. His wife admonishes him quietly Don't say that.

—and what we're doing out here in my condition, K chirps up the companionway, and meeting Carla B Silver in Annapolis yesterday and hearing about Lee's abortion. When I blab, I blab.

Says Peter Mm hm. Kath hands up a lighted patio candle, in the glow of which he sees the Talbotts looking bemused but holding hands on their side of the cockpit. Mrs. T's headband, he now notes, is our paisley scarf. Where's our Sex Education hat? Katherine wants to know; she wants to show it to the Talbotts and also lend them that wacko play, which she has also already told them about.

On the shelf in my quarterberth, Peter tells her, and asks the Talbotts did they ever hear of such far-out coincidence? Of the estate of writers in general he observes that we are all Scheherazades, finally: only as good as our next piece. Lee Talbott says she'll drink to that, and does. Kath comes up wearing the beret *trouvé* and her light cotton-flannel pregnant night-gown; declares it's silly to put clothes back on at twenty-two hundred hours, no? and returns Lee Talbott's white terry robe. I guess that means you want your scarf back, the woman says wistfully, drawing it off her forehead and regarding it in the candlelight. Don't we wish we knew the story behind this scarf?

So that's the famous hat, remarks Franklin Key Talbott. Katherine offers it for inspection; he handles it like a sacred relic. Amazing. Lee Allan Talbott stretches her fine brown legs athwart the cockpit, slugs her beer, bets there's a story behind *that,* too. Of both men she inquires with amiable irony how any storyteller can possibly be hung-up, with so many stories floating all around. P understands how his wife and Frank Talbott's hit it off so easily; he is himself already enjoying that peculiar intimacy of people who, with unimpaired goodwill, have found out very personal things about one another: the necessarily trusting candor, a touch heady, of their being (excuse him) in the same boat.

In that spirit, K takes after all a healthy swallow of his drink and declares, vis-à-vis Peter's celebrated Block, that that's all bullshit. What's afoot, in her opinion, is a simple though heroic and anyhow ineluctable matter of driving through the Vanishing Point and coming out on the farther side. The sand in Olive Treadway's egg timer does it every morning. And oh Jesus, we forgot to call home; Hank and Irm will have the helicopters out!

Peter tells her he radioed Nopoint Point while she was spilling all our family beans to the Talbotts. He forgot to mention it. Things seem okay down there, but the folks are really putting the pressure on for us to get serious and come on home.

Olive Treadway's egg timer, Frank Talbott helpfully repeats. He has put our black beret upon his head; Leah and Katherine agree that it becomes him.

The Sherritts' Barbadian cook's, Peter explains, but the matter's *not* that simple, whatever else it is. Last time I counted, there were seven several dwarves upon our narrative back, or nine. Cries delighted Katherine I can't believe you said that! She means that image, those dwarves from our prologue, so to speak, which she recollected herself just a little while ago aboard *Reprise.* She swears to Christ we've become one person: Siamese twins, joined at the imagination.

Are we stoned? Lee Talbott asks of the four of us. What are these dwarves?

Kate also wants to know who are the extra two. Not little Onward and Upward in here, surely.

F. K. Talbott removes the beret, turns it thoughtfully again in his hands, replaces it upon his head, sips beer. Recites Peter Vug. Crump. Fougasse. Dingle. Coomb. Cubby. Coign. Plus maybe Uca Pugnax and Uca Pugilator, if you can remember that far back in this story.

See? says Mr. to Mrs. Talbott. That's how real writers and their spouses talk. Do we talk like that? No.

Base no literary generalizations upon us Sherritt-Sagamores, cautions Peter, and fishes into *Story*'s lazaret locker. Here's one of those canisters, by the way: the one that had Act Two and that John Arthur Paisley bandanna in it. The Knapps Narrows one is under your seat. Chimes in Katherine The scripts are in Baggies inside the canisters, each of which contains the key to the other.

She squeezes Peter's hand; he apologizes to the Talbotts for our talking house-talk: He'll explain. If we're stoned, it is Too-Far-Fetched Coincidence we're high on; Implausible Possibility.

This old hat here on my head, Frank Talbott declares authoritatively, is not in fact a beret, but a *boina:* accent on the "bo." Two sides of the same Pyrenee. He puts it on the flare canister. The Emperor's Old Hat, remarks K, and scarfs the same canister with our paisley.

He can deliver babies, too, declares Lee Talbott; so don't worry. He delivered his own daughter by his first wife.

In a Volkswagen camper in the public campground under the BBC transmitting tower on the old Crystal Palace Exhibition grounds in London, England, her husband acknowledges, looking his present wife in the eyes. And to us: Bloody battery wouldn't crank, and the folks camping next door were Australian obstetricians on holiday. Piece of cake. But that was the Nineteen Fifties; I'm out of practice. Another life.

READY FOR ANOTHER?

I mean Beck's or Dos Equis, Katherine adds quickly, but we're all chuckling. Peter kisses her hand; the moment is defused.

Leah Allan Silver Talbott says if Kath will give her back that paisley scarf, she can keep the terry robe.

Thinks Peter Sagamore Back? but says to Franklin Talbott If you'll tell me what really happened to John Arthur Paisley and Douglas Townshend, I'll tell you what's going to happen in *SEX EDUCATION,* Act Three, after you've read Acts One and Two, which you're welcome to borrow if you'll return them eventually, because the idea is pretty interesting, actually, and I might want to make use of it someday.

Says Franklin Talbott to Peter Sagamore If you'll tell me how it comes to pass that the author of a pretty famous and very good early novel whose characters sail around in a boat named *Story* is himself sailing around after the fact in a boat named *Story* but not so named by him, I'll tell you a not-bad CIA story but not about Doug or Jack Paisley or my brother.

Says Leah Talbott to both of us Sagamores If you-all will tell us who those seven or nine several dwarves with the funny names are, we'll get personal and tell you who Drew and Lexie were and why they went down the tubes.

Uh-oh. To get off that subject, Peter Sagamore says to Franklin Key Talbott If you'll tell us that not-bad CIA story, I'll tell all three of you plus Everybody and his brother there a story about improbable coincidence that even Katherine S. S. Sagamore hasn't heard, because I just now happened to remember it even though it was told me thirteen years ago by a more-celebrated-by-far American writer than yours truly.

Says Katherine Shorter Sherritt to Peter Sagamore If you'll tell us that story about improbable coincidence that even I haven't heard, I'll tell you who I think wrote *SEX EDUCATION: Play,* though not why it got put into Alert-and-Locate canisters and deep-sixed, let's say shallow-sixed, and not how it happened to be us who spotted both canisters, and not why there was an old beret in one and an old paisley scarf in the other, because I don't know those particular stories. I mean *boina.*

Says Franklin Talbott directly but not severely to Leah Talbott If you'll tell me why your having an abortion at age thirty-five means we're never going to have any children ever, I'll tell you why you didn't tell me you were pregnant until after you'd had that abortion, even though I knew it anyhow, just as I knew you'd had a look at my novel-manuscript that I'd rather you hadn't looked at till I'd proved to myself that I could write it.

Uh-oh. To the assembly at large, little Yon and Hither chorus If you four will tell us twain, not whence we babies come—for that mystery we have pretty well cleared up by observation, comparison of notes, and rapt audition of *SEX EDUCATION: Play,* Acts One and Two, and other tide-water tales—but rather wherefore we were conceived and are about to be launched into your world, which strikes us as we listen to you-all as being at best a problematical one, we'll tell you a tale of The Swan Prince of Queenstown Creek, which we just now made up with reference to those seven Whistling Swans and one Canada Goose up in Salthouse Cove there, and which we are not unhappy with, considering that it is our maiden effort in the storytelling way.

Okay.

Okay.

Okay.

Okay.

Okay.

Okay.

DAY 7:
CHESTER RIVER TO
WYE ISLAND

Sometimes these children get no bedtime story at all; sometimes they get Scheherazaded till dawn's early light, and it takes Peter Sagamore half of Day 7 to log (shorthand) Day 6's tidewater tales.

E.g.:

THE STORY OF THOSE SEVEN SEVERAL DWARVES OR NINE

upon our familial narrative back.

Vug, he declares for openers, taking that *boina* off that canister and perching it upon his hair like an oversize yarmulke, is your Doomsday Factor. I mean living next door to push-button apocalypse and more and more appreciating how imperfectly human beings and their governments control events. Vug teaches a fellow to stop worrying about the death of the novel and to worry instead about the death of all potential readers plus the earth whereon they dwell. For that instruction one is not ungrateful, but the guy is a real conversation-stopper and the very antidote to narrative abundance. That's Dwarf Vug.

Crump? Crump K takes to be her husband's personal pass and past. His coming on to forty, she means, with certain works and deeds behind him and not others. His particular trajectory as a man and um an artist. His arrival at what may be a mere and enabling pit stop or the Pit itself: very hard to tell which, while Crump there is riding on your shoulders with his warty hands over your eyes.

We know that Crump fellow, sighs Frank Talbott. An old acquaintance, his wife agrees.

Pleased P makes clear to all hands that these several dwarves' order of introduction is not necessarily the order of their clambering upon any citizen's narrative back. Fougasse, for example, is the slippery case of John Arthur Paisley, no? Peter's involvement with Doug Townshend's obsession that some U.S. writer of the non-thriller-diller sort be privy to the nitsy-gritsy of our hugger-mugger, if P may so put it. But Fougasse slips aboard well after Dingle, who is the petering out of literary modernism and the not-quite-petering-in of the Best Next Thing. All a chap can do, *re* Dingle, is scribble on and bear in mind the stockbrokers' maxim: One is buying not the whole market, but particular issues, which may well rise while most else falls.

That bear-market maxim, Lee Talbott sympathizes, may be bull; but she believes it to be the case that good artists are realer than the glue on the labels we use to classify them, and can do good work when those labels peel off. She encourages Peter Sagamore to regard Dwarf Dingle as an opportunity rather than a burden. But being an all-but-tenured professional academic, she sympathizes.

Thanks. Now who is Dwarf Coomb, if not our old friend Less Is More? Bane of bores, scourge of the gussied-up, astringent to logorrhea! But reticence likewise gets to be a bore, and it is the curse of overmuch so-phistication that as more and more goes without saying, less and less gets said. The welcomely spare and quiet voice peters into inaudibility; under-statement becomes unstatement. After the final word to the wise comes the silence we call Coomb.

Perhaps, Lee Talbott murmurs, Doctor François Rabelais can prescribe. But who am I to say.

Says Peter So can Doctor K. S. Sherritt, and gets his ear kissed by that physician. But the patient has to learn how to take the medicine.

Frank Talbott confesses it hard for the non–professionally literary—of whose number he counts himself one despite his acknowledged itch to perpetrate a novel—to follow this uptown blather. But he believes he remembers our mentioning, among those seven several dwarves or nine, one Cubby?

Cubby indeed. Dwarf Cubby Kate ventures to be our pregnancy: more exactly, the prospect of parenthood, as sobering in some respects as it is exciting in most, and not a truly weightsome dwarf except in company with Vug, who turns cute Cubby into a virtual black hole. If from such gravity not even light escapes, how then shall art? Ah, Cubby!

To Good and Plenty Peter says Don't take that personally, kids, and goes on to declare Dwarf Coign to be the mint-tea caper: one's encounter not only with the Prince of Darkness, but with Darkness's very Principle. Coign is likewise Kath's miscarriage, following shortly thereupon.

Frank Talbott says with dignity he's sorry. Kath says Don't be: You're not your brother.

And Dwarf Coign, Peter says, makes seven. If there are two more back there, they are Uca Pugnax and U. Pugilator, who may look to the un-trained eye like fiddler crabs, but who are in fact a brace of massy dwarves.

Pugnax was the sudden news of Doug Townshend's death, which hit us the harder for our having turned our back upon him after that set-to in Carla's Cavern. To mourn the equivocally dead while on the cusp of giving birth: one more dwarf upon the narrative back. As for Uca Pugilator . . . He closes his eyes. But I've run dry.

Soothes Katherine And no wonder, and massages her friend's shoulders. Uca Pugilator must be anybody's pent frustration, on Nopoint Point, at carrying Dwarves One through Eight: a dwarf for each month of Cubbyhood.

Despite which, Frank Talbott says, between the pair of you you've told another story: the story of those seven several dwarves or nine. My compliments, and

PASS ME THAT *BOINA,*

por favor.

Peter does. Lee points to where she just saw a star fall out of Lyra, but by the time we look up, it has fallen. When we look back, Franklin Talbott is wearing the narrative hat; it fits his strong bald head better than it fit Peter's strongly haired one. *Noch einmal Beck's, bitte.*

As an early-retired officer of the United States Central Intelligence Agency, Frank begins, it pains me to think that my former employer, my late elder brother, and one of my late best friends—Doomsday Factors every one—had even a minor role in the reduction of our favorite living American novelist to a good short-storyteller, thence to a questionable shorter-and-shorter-storyteller, finally to a man who worries that the world may end before his next sentence and therefore holds his tongue. That's damn sad, even though you haven't told me the whole story yet, and I haven't told you what I knew about it already.

One dwarf among seven, Peter Sagamore reminds him, or nine. It's true that once or twice I've considered taking up Doug's line of work: helping the world instead of telling stories about the damn thing. But I know I'd botch it.

Leah Talbott says Doug may have botched it, too. Her husband says We'll never know. But it completes the irony that an ex–junior-grade Doomsday Factor like me now wants to write a novel—and I don't mean a spy novel. Says Lee We hate spy novels; Katherine says Likewise.

The story he has donned the old *boina* to tell, Franklin Talbott goes on, is not about spies and Doomsday Factors, except indirectly; but while those subjects are sitting so to speak in *Story*'s cockpit, he may as well report that in his opinion our mutual friend Doug Townshend had got almost pathological about the DDF business. I agreed with Rick, he says, that

Doug had become capable of offing even *him* on those grounds, not to mention Paisley. His confiding in you to the extent that he did, over such a period, is more than just extraordinary; it strikes me as deranged, much as I loved the man. Didn't Doug realize who it was he was laying his load on?

Katherine's cockles warm at our guest's regard for her husband. But Peter says I asked for it. I fed on it. The more I saw, the less I spoke, et cetera. Anyhow, that was one dwarf among lots.

How Lee and I understand it is this, Frank Talbott declares: Rick believed that Doug believed that Rick did Paisley in, for either of the two classic reasons: Paisley was Supermole, or Rick was Supermole and Paisley got the goods on him. Carla B Silver used to worry that Rick was projecting his own capabilities onto Doug, and might do *Doug* in. In some moods, at least, Rick had called *Doug* a Doomsday Factor, ready to neutralize exactly the wrong people. She also worried that Doug might do *Rick* in, whether or not Rick had done in Paisley. The business had got that byzantine.

Right there, says Peter, is about where I threw up my hands.

As you would not have, Lee Talbott ventures, at comparable complexity in a novel. But of course, art isn't life.

Says Kath *Vive la différence.* But Lee then adds If Byzantium is where we live, we mustn't throw up our hands at byzantine complexity, right? and the three of us agree. Yet even in Byzantium, Frank Talbott imagines, some things were simpler than they appeared. In my retired but not inexpert opinion, Jack Paisley really did commit suicide in a spell of chronic depression over this and that, with which neither the CIA nor the KGB had a great deal directly to do. Two dwarves among nine, or eleven. I doubt he was even doing Company work with those fancy radios on *Brillig;* we've got better ways of sweeping Corsica Neck and Hoopersville. John just liked to sail around with fancy radios.

Thinks Peter Maybe.

In my opinion, Brother Rick drowned accidentally in circumstances unfortunately similar to those of Paisley's suicide, though it's not unimaginable that the loss of Jonathan and his estrangement from Carla put him under. Rick was not a careful sailor, and he had begun to drink a bit much. I had real reservations about lending him the boat—but he was my brother. In my respectful opinion, Carla B Silver's Gypsy curses may be lived with, though her visions are not to be sniffed at. And in my opinion, neither Doug Townshend's first heart attack nor his fatal second one was arranged by Agency people, though they certainly are capable of such arrangements. Nor was my own mild episode of last spring, which, along with other dwarves, prompted Lee's sabbatical leave and *Reprise*'s Caribbean expedition. But you're listening to the only man in Queenstown Creek who still believes that there was no sinister conspiracy behind John Kennedy's assassination.

Amen, cheers Katherine. That was not a bad CIA story.

Frank Talbott tips her his *boina*. But it's not my not-bad CIA story. I'll tell you that one another time. What I've put this old hat on to tell you is

THE STORY OF THIS OLD HAT.

Do you mind, Lee?

Lee doesn't. Frank Talbott therefore declares it to be a well-known bit of modern literary biography that when young Peter Sagamore went to Spain in Nineteen Whatever, he came back a capital-*W* Writer. Less well-known, deservedly, is that when Franklin Key Talbott went to live in Spain at just about the same time, with his then wife, for the express purpose of becoming a capital-*W* Writer, he came back a candidate for divorce, a prospective recruit for the CIA, and no more of a writer than he'd been before. Such things happen.

The main thing I picked up in España, he declares, was a fondness for *boinas*, which persists to this day. The novel I was trying to write back then was set in Madrid, where Rick happened to be stationed. It was about an American writer in Spain whose marriage is going sour and whose brother is a CIA man doing liaison work between U.S. military intelligence and the Franco government, with the objective of protecting our Spanish air and naval bases in the event of anti-Franco uprisings. The novelist in my novel admires Ernest Hemingway and hates Francisco Franco. His brother, whom he also much admires, claims half seriously that if Hemingway's side, quote unquote, had won the Spanish Civil War, Hitler would have occupied Spain in World War Two, controlled Gibraltar and the Mediterranean, and therefore won the war. The novelist's wife has an affair in Torremolinos with a young English bar owner, and the novelist himself gets so involved in his research into our efforts to protect our military bases at the possible expense of Spanish democracy that he comes to believe that the only way to undo what people like his brother are doing is to give up writing novels and join the Agency to help reform it from the inside.

Peter Sagamore sips, says nothing, but is impressed, though he sees what's coming.

Both my hero and I developed the habit of wearing our *boinas* at the typewriter, Frank Talbott continues. Just about when the novel got stuck, the marriage came unglued and our Spanish trip blew up. The author came home, got divorced, and joined the Company as a report writer under Doug Townshend, who laid much the same trip on me as he did on you. An early practice run.

The trouble with that novel, obviously, is that it wasn't fiction: It too was an early practice run, for *KUBARK*. But the point of this story is that the chap in that novel loses his *boina* at a certain point in *his* story and then gets it back in a way that changes his life. He loses it in the old city of Ronda, on the Ponte Nuevo; the wind blows it into the canyon under the bridge. You know the Tajo de Ronda? Never mind how he gets it back: The point is that that was almost the only invented action in the book, and not long after I invented it, something like it happened to me. My then wife flew home to Washington with our little daughter: trial separation. I stayed on in Madrid for another month to try to finish the book, but that book was finished before it started. Then I got word from Rick that Pat was filing for divorce—his lines of communication were faster than the post office—and I flew home in a hurry, leaving a lot of stuff behind for one reason or another. My books and typewriter and such I intended to retrieve eventually. The novel I left behind deliberately: didn't have the heart to just throw it out. The *boina* I thought I had with me and then found I didn't; I assumed it was lost, and I'd got so used to wearing it while I worked that I missed it surprisingly. I almost *grieved* for it, believe it or not.

When the smoke cleared a bit, Rick shipped my things home in three cartons aboard an Air Force transport from our base at Torrejón. The plane crashed on takeoff, and most of its cargo was lost, along with most of the crew. The only package salvaged with my name on it was a typing-paper box containing my manuscript and my *boina*. The manuscript was badly damaged by fire and chemical foam, and utterly ruined by failure of imagination: I chucked it for real this time, got divorced, and joined the Company. The *boina* was okay.

He takes it off. This isn't it.

Kate snaps her fingers:

SHIT: THERE GOES MY STORY.

Says Franklin Key Talbott with his crinkly smile Not necessarily. This hat here is the lineal successor to that one. He frisbees it over to her. If the *boina* fits, wear it.

She does, just long enough to say *You* wrote that *SEX EDUCATION* play!

A better hand at projecting plots than at intuiting situations, Peter Sagamore is startled. But he sees Lee Talbott smiling furrow-browed at her husband. Says Katherine to the pair of them After you tell us why in the world you packed it off in those two canisters with that scarf and this hat, I'll tell you why finding Act One was a turnaround moment in our story-in-progress. But even as she hands the *boina* back to Frank Talbott, she thinks Uh-oh: I guess I can guess why this hat was in there.

But Frank Talbott passes the thing along to his wife. She touches it to her lips, but doesn't put it on. You should hear Carla B Silver on the subject of sperm and ova, she tells us quietly. Ma says that no sexual animals actually reproduce their own kind, and our children are actually our grandchildren.

Oh?

What Ma means is that our sperms and eggs are our true children, and what we think are our children are really *their* children. To Peter she adds, surprisingly, It's the same with writers and readers, wouldn't you say? You generate your stories, and your stories generate your readers. Frank and I are your grandchildren.

Says Peter carefully, who is not *always* bad at intuiting situations, Nope:

A STORY IS NOT A CHILD,

and vice versa. But if stories *were* children, their readers wouldn't be *their* children; they'd be one of their parents, and the author the other. The Mother and Father of Invention. He gestures at the Alert-and-Locate canister. For God's sake, tell.

Frank Talbott seconds that motion.

Still turning the weathered *boina* in her hands, handsome, brown Lee Talbott allows as how she's not as sure as her husband is that his little heart attack last March was not a warning from his ex-colleagues not to do a sequel to *KUBARK*. Three nots. Anyhow, for her it is enough that it could have been: She hates the shit we're involved in—she means the U.S. us.

Me too.

Me too.

Me too.

Lifting it by its top-tab, she plops the *boina* onto her head. When Frank and Pat had Peggy back in Nineteen Fifty-two, Joe McCarthy was riding high and the cold war was red hot, but the Doomsday Factor hadn't really sunk in. Now it's worn us all out. I can't even look at a chart of the Chesapeake without tightening up: Edgewood Arsenal, the Norfolk Navy Yard, the fucking Pentagon. But let's don't talk apocalypse.

I got pregnant about six A.M. off the Club Med spiral pier in Buccaneer Creek in Martinique because I didn't think I was ovulating yet and we'd had a good time ashore and when we came back aboard after midnight I fell asleep in about thirty seconds without diaphragming or mentioning that I hadn't, and when Frank got up to pee at sunrise and came back to bed all horny, neither of us remembered. When I missed my period, we were working our way up the Windward Islands, and I didn't mention it because the subject was touchy because we'd pretty much decided that we weren't having children, but we hadn't quite upped and said so. That was one of the things this boat ride was supposed to clear up and didn't. Frank has done his bit in that line and has this terrific grown daughter and doesn't want to go through it all again even though he wishes I had kids. I want kids more than anything in the world but happen to believe I'd be a less than terrific mother for various reasons and that he'd be a grandfather instead of a father, so I'm not interested. I warned you I'd get personal.

Invites Peter Don't worry: I'll change all the names. Frank Talbott says never mind the names; he wishes he could change some of the facts.

When I missed my second period, we were standing watches on our first long ocean passage, from Saint John up to Bermuda and Chesapeake Bay, and I'd got to thinking doomsday thoughts about the world in general and Frank's myocardial infarct in particular. Plus I knew he half suspected what was up when I faked two periods and he didn't call me on it. Can you imagine trying to fake menstruation on a sailboat?

Nope.

Nope.

Then, when we finally clear the Virginia capes after this humongous storm such as I hope never to see at sea again, and we drag our tushes over to York River and put the anchor down for the first time since Cruz Bay Saint John, and we patch into Ma Bell to call Ma Silver up in Fells Point, the first thing we hear is that Doug Townshend has just dropped dead over Sydney, Australia, of a ruptured aneurysm. Remember, we were wrecked already when we *started* this cruise; it was supposed to un-wreck us!

So we pop the champagne that was meant to celebrate our safe return, but what's to celebrate, and the stuff is world-temperature anyhow 'cause we're long out of ice, and we're crying about Doug, and it occurs to me that just up the York River from where we're anchored is this place called ISOLATION, where Frank did his junior-officer training in the CIA before we were us, and I think Welcome home, Mister and Missus Talbott. Mind you, this was two weeks ago? It seems like a semester already! So after we've both gone through the Kleenex and the warm champagne over poor Doug, we pop over the side to take our first swim since the Caribbean and say hello to dear Chesapeake Bay, and something bumps my arm and I give a holler, thinking it's a skate or some Chesapeake version of a nip-plefish—Did you ever swim topless in the Caribbean, she asks Kath, and get your nipples nipped by a certain little fish that Frank and I call nip-plefish? No? Anyhow, it was a half-submerged orange flare canister that turned out to have nothing in it but some seawater and that paisley scarf there. Now, I'm a professional professor of literature, but I'm on leave, okay, and Frank is a real writer despite the story he just told you about not being one, but we must have both been on autopilot after that storm and the bad news about Doug, because after we finished wondering What the hell and went to sleep, I wore that scarf all the next day before either one of us made the paisley/Paisley association. By that time we'd sailed past the spot where *Brillig* went aground, and we were coming into the Patuxent past Solomons Island where one of the Company's safe houses used to be, and I was ready to turn *Reprise* around and head back to the B.V.I. Talk about spooky!

Talk about reprises, murmurs sympathetic Kath.

Says Lee Talbott You got it. We were back where we started last June, all the wounds still open, plus now Doug dead; all the big questions still open, too. So when we got up to Baltimore at last and Frank went down to Langley for the memorial service, I went and got myself vacuum-aspirated over in Cross Keys. In my opinion there were two distinct shlups: Drew and Lexie down the tubes. My gynecologist tells me it's a little-known fact that maybe as many as seventy percent of human conceptions are originally twins, but one of them normally dies fast, and nobody ever knows it was there. The Vanished Twin. He also tells me that some astronomers think our sun has a vanished twin—our s-u-n sun. It loops back our way once every twenty-six million years and knocks a few comets in our direction. Sibling rivalry. Its last visit caused the Precambrian Great Death, and its return is overdue right now, as a matter of fact, like the next big action along the San Andreas Fault. What time is it?

The woman is a coiled spring. Her husband touches her lean thigh-top; she flinches, then relaxes a bit.

TIME TO PASS THE HAT,

Frank Talbott says gently. She removes and kisses it; puts it on his head; fishes out a tissue to wipe her eyes with. On our side of the cockpit, Katherine squeezes Peter's hand.

KUBARK, Frank Talbott says, made us a little money and a lot of enemies and some friends. It also got me a literary agent (same one as yours, she tells me) and a trade editor in New York—though my real editor is my friend Lee Allan Silver. So last May, while we were going crazy over Rick's disappearance and Jon Silver Talbott's disappearance and Marian Silver's various problems, and planning our big cruise to collect our heads, I set to work on another novel. It was mainly about wyes.

Whys like the question? Wise as in wisdom?

Wyes like the wye in Wye Island and Wye River, which is just the letter before *z* spelled out in English.

Kath groans Jesus: I'm a damn *librarian,* and I never made that connection. She asks Peter Did you? He shrugs.

What I had in mind, Frank Talbott goes on, was forks and confluences in people's lives. The man has an unpresumptuous candor, innocent but not glib, in speaking of these things to Peter Sagamore, which pleases us. Like when the tide runs up the Wye River, he explains, one thing divides into two, your Front Wye and your Back Wye, and when it runs out, two things become one. Lee and I first bumped into each other at the literal fork of the Wye River, right down the road there, but that's another story.

At least I wanted it to be another story. What I was really thinking of was the way people grow apart, like Lee and her sister or me and my brother, and the way they sometimes come together, like Lee and me.

Sperm and ovum, Katherine Sherritt murmurs.

Murmurs Peter Sagamore Vanished twins.

And forks in the road, Frank Talbott says, where things can go either way in people's lives. So I made notes and outlines and maps, and I tinkered and diddled and fussed with the idea all the way down the Intracoastal and across the Gulf of Mexico and down to the Bay Islands and Belize, in between sailing.

We Sagamores squeeze hands and sigh: That has been our house daydream for years. Some season, in a bigger boat than *Story* . . . But professional Peter doubts he'd get real work done amid such flower-girt adventure— a hollow doubt, lately!—and professional Kate would have to quit a job she much enjoys and has shaped to her liking; and now we have a family, so forget it. In the year 2000, maybe, or 2010. Those dates will be here before we know it, no? If they get here at all. And after that we're dead, if not before, so On with the story.

Frank Talbott says Our understanding was that Lee wouldn't look at the manuscript till somewhere down the line, when I was ready for her reaction. At the risk of throwing good money after bad, I didn't want to nip the thing in the bud.

Excuse the mixed metaphor, says his editor, says Lee Talbott.

Yeah. The first major decision, believe it or not, was whether to wear this *boina* while I wrote. On the one hand, there was what happened in Madrid. On the other hand there was *KUBARK:* I wore the *boina* every day while I was writing it, to exorcise the demon, and once I'd done my homework that book practically wrote itself. So I put on the hat.

Peter nods but has his doubts: The art of the nonfiction exposé is not the art of the novel.

By Key West, Frank Talbott says, I was already in trouble, and by Cozumel I'd written myself into a hole as deep as the one Don Quixote went down into.

Montesinos, says Professor Leah Allan Silver Talbott. Professor Peter Sagamore squeezes the hand of his favorite library scientist, who says wistfully Cozumel.

I turned Rick Talbott into "Manfred Turner," because Doug Townshend called him the Prince of Darkness after Byron's Count Manfred. Lee and I were "Fenwick Turner" and "Susan Seckler." He smiles at her. Black-eyed Susan, right? My idea of the art of fiction was to make her and "Mimi" twin sisters and Fenn and Manfred twin brothers. You're supposed to nudge your neighbor and say, "Fen as in marshland, et cetera." Carla B Silver became "Carmen B. Seckler," for reasons even I am too embarrassed to tell.

Peter's done stuff like that too, Kath offers consolingly. Admits Peter Yup.

But your stories are *made up*. I even had Jack Paisley in mine, under his real name, and the story was actually just the log of our cruise: two people going down and coming back, trying to get their heads straight and make some hard calls at certain forks in the channel. Get this: My working title was *Reprise*. . . .

Sounds okay so far, encourages Katherine; I know a man who wrote a story with a boat in it named *Story*. Peter says nothing. F. K. Talbott says It wasn't okay; what it was was long-faced confessional melodrama. For example, would you put a spiel like this one into a novel? Of course you wouldn't.

Peter shrugs his eyebrows.

So after the Bay Islands I put the thing away while we did some hard passagemaking over to Jamaica, dead to windward: the most serious sailing we'd ever done. Then we shipped the boat by freighter from Kingston to Tobago while we flew on ahead for a week of R-and-R before starting north up the Windward Islands toward home.

Complains envious Peter Boyoboy.

Yeah, well. Anyhow, I was ready to pack it in again as a novelist, except for that *Y* business. You've seen *Reprise*'s hailport on his transom.

Lee Talbott explains that their cutter is male. Peter won't do the *she* thing either, Katherine says, except when *Story*'s in certain moods. Lee says Frank won't say "Hard alee" or "Ahoy" or "Gybe-ho." It makes him feel like Lionel Barrymore in *Captains Courageous*. We just say "Coming about, okay?"

Wyes and forks and reprises, Pete prompts Franklin Key Talbott, who passes a brown hand over his brown forehead.

Right. Choices and retracements. And conceiving children: sperm swimming up, ova floating down. Two things becoming one thing, which is both of them and neither of them.

Says Peter *SEX EDUCATION: Play*.

Sure. It came together one afternoon in Arnos Vale, in Tobago, while we were snorkeling naked and I was wishing that I wanted to be a father again so Lee could be a mother. I dived down deep to pick up a shell for her and looked up and saw her floating on her back, twenty feet above me.

Voilà, says Katherine Sherritt: Blam. Blooey.

Voilà indeed—all but writing it. The idea was to get as far from the other stuff as possible: nothing about us and Doomsday Factors and the CIA.

Hear hear.

Without telling Lee, I'm sorry to say, I dumped the *Reprise* manuscript into an ashcan in Scarborough, Tobago. But this time I kept the *boina,* because I was determined to write that play. Trouble was, I don't know squat about writing plays.

Among American novelists, Peter Sagamore reminds him, that ignorance is the great tradition. But it's not an advantage.

All the same, Frank Talbott tells us, while off-watch and during their stopovers in the Grenadines, Barbados, St. Lucia, Martinique, Dominica, Guadeloupe, St. Kitts, St. Croix, he drafted Act One of *SEX EDUCA-TION: Play* in longhand, and through his long solo watches en route home, while *Reprise* steered himself north by windvane, he revised and edited that draft. Given his inexperience of imaginative writing in general and playwriting in particular, he really had no idea whether he was onto something admirable or was perpetrating a soft-porn version of a girls-school senior class play. His wife, he knew, would know; but for reasons at once as obvious and mysterious to him as hers in not acknowledging her pregnancy, he did not tell her specifically what he was up to, much less show her the draft of Act One. On the contrary: He pretended to be plugging away at the novel *Reprise*—coming along satisfactorily, he reported to her, just as she reported to him two menstruations which in fact she did not have. That neither questioned the other's reports, while they lived week after week in the unprivate space of a midsize cruising sailboat, argues that each was more or less aware of the other's secret. Unprecedented dissembling!

And this despite . . . Frank Talbott's voice goes thick; he gives his head a shake, but does not dislodge the *boina.* Well, he says to Peter, you flirted with the Agency for a couple of years and got in almost over your head, right? Secrets from your wife; stuff you wished you didn't know. I was an officer for seventeen years, half of that time in counterintelligence and covert operations. When I married Lee and got out, I swore there'd never be a secret between us. That was partly what *KUBARK* was for: to clean out my head. Yet there we were. I meant to show her what I was up to just as soon as the air was clear. . . .

That first night back in the Chesapeake, I almost did, and she almost told me what was what with her plumbing there. We'd been out nearly a year, nothing was settled, and we had just about closed the circle. It was the right time. But then came the news about Doug, and then that scarf in that distress-flare canister in the York River, like a message from the Company.

Or from the muse.

Yeah, well. So we went on up to Baltimore—we tied up at Gibson Island, actually, as if we were still afraid to commit ourselves to the mainland—and we camped at Carla B Silver's in Fells Point while Lee did what she did in Cross Keys and I did what I did down in Langley. A semesters-worth of mail was waiting for us, too, at Carla's Cavern: Lee has to decide whether she's going back to Saint John's or down to a tenured job in Virginia; I have to choose between a senior archivist's job at the Aberdeen Proving Ground or some kind of freelancing. What to do with the rest of our lives, really. We've seriously considered just sailing right on, around the world.

Thinks Katherine Sherritt, with an inner wince of sympathy, They've also considered splitting. She can see that in their voices, she'll tell Peter.

Frank Talbott says *Faute de mieux*, what we more or less decided to do next is spend this summer at my father's farm on Wye Island, making the decisions we were supposed to have made before we got there. Last Sunday morning we set out across the Bay from Gibson to Wye—still island to island, and both of us about to pop. I pretty much knew Lee had paid a call on her gynecologist; she pretty much knew I'd scrapped the novel and done more in D.C. than just memorialize Doug Townshend.

You know the old Baltimore Light, at the mouth of the Magothy. Just as we left it astern, the floodgates burst. We were talking about poetry, of all things, or pretending to talk about it—a villanelle by Elizabeth Bishop that begins with the line "The art of losing isn't hard to master"—and suddenly everything got told: the pregnancy, the abortion, Lee's conviction that it'd been twins. I did my best to comfort her—and I told her that down in Langley I'd been pitched to take over Doug's consultancy under cover of my *KUBARK* reputation. That's the way certain minds work down there.

Katherine Sherritt says Uh-*huh* and thinks Poor Leah Allan Silver Talbott. Peter Sagamore thinks Aha: Operation BONAPARTE. Lee Talbott moves her long fingers on her husband's forearm. Rather to our joint unspoken surprise, we Sagamores do not find this particular long confession either creepy or, in this instance, implausible. The Talbotts appear to us to have worked some things out, and we feel as though we've been their close friends for years.

Then it was *her* turn to be shocked, Frank says of Lee, especially when I added that I'd scrapped the novel way back in Tobago and considered myself finished for good in that line. A failure. We sailed on, about as wrung-out as we'd ever been. I mean rock-bottom. I kept wishing something *amazing* would happen, out of the blue; something literally marvelous, unaccountable—don't ask me what—to disrupt the whole story. Like a sea monster: If old Chessie had suddenly risen from the deep, or a flaming sword had appeared in the sky . . . But the world went on being the world: sunshine and sailboats and problems.

Remarks Peter We were there. That's just about when I said to Katherine down on Nopoint Point For pity's sake set me a task, and she said Take us sailing, and here we are.

And there we Talbotts were, in the middle of the Bay, just above the bridge, and we ran out of wind the way we'd run out of plans. I couldn't even decide to start the engine: What for? Lee went below for a nap. I put up the awning and let the boat drift and sat and stared at the back of my eyelids for a while and then fished out the Sex Ed script and read through Act One, figuring that if anything about it looked good at such a miserable time, it would be worth saving and showing to Lee if the air ever really cleared.

It didn't pass the test. I'd have chucked it right over the side, but I didn't want to trash the Chesapeake. I'd have dumped it into our waste bin, but space is tight, and the story was so tied up with that vision of Lee floating over me in Arnos Vale. . . . Anyhow, we'd dumped enough things.

So: Back when Rick and I were growing up on Wye Island, we used to send messages out in bottles. . . .

Peter grins. Katherine too.

Rick's were spy stuff already: secret messages. Never mind what mine were. So there in *Reprise*'s cockpit locker was that empty canister that Lee had bumped into. I put Act One in a Baggie and put the Baggie in the canister, and at the last minute I stuck this *boina* in there too, for the obvious reason, and I floated the whole thing off down the tide like baby Perseus in his sea chest or Moses in his basket. Return to Sender.

Says Peter Alert and Locate.

Says Katherine, as much to Peter as to the Talbotts, Help.

Franklin Key Talbott doffs the *boina* and offers it to his wife.

WOULD YOU MIND WINDING UP THIS STORY?

We're wearing out our narrative welcome.

Peter Sagamore says Believe me, you aren't.

Believe him, echoes Katherine Sherritt.

They consider us. Lee Talbott takes the hat, kisses it again, puts it on, and tells us that since there wasn't any wind, they eventually motored on across the Bay—Frank did, anyhow; she stayed below, in her bunk, worn-out—and down into Chester River, intending to go through Kent Island Narrows and on down Prospect Bay to the Wye River and Wye Island. But as they cleared Love Point Light at the mouth of the Chester, NOAA declared a severe thunderstorm watch, and so, rather than get caught in the tricky narrows waiting for the bridge to open on the hour, they drove on up the Chester and anchored in the lee of Cacaway Island to ride out the blow. We could have ducked in here, she acknowledges, but since there was time to get up to Cacaway, and since nothing was settled, we stayed with our island-to-island thing. When the storm hit, as you probably remember, it was a humdinger.

We remember, all right. But you got more of it than we did.

Says Lee It suited our mood. I was still down below, licking my wounds. Frank got us anchored just as the shit hit the fan, and then came below saying that the wind had blown his famous *boina* right off his head and into Langford Creek. I told him no doubt it would come back, one way or another, as it had before, and he said This time it won't.

Do you guys enjoy storms as much as we do? At anchor, I mean; not at sea, thanks! This one threw *Reprise* around like one of those mechanical bulls in Texas bars, and flipped our dinghy right upside down with its painter cinched around it like a saddle girth. But we knew we were safe from anything short of a full tornado, and we've ridden out so many storms on dear old *Reprise* that we enjoyed it despite everything. When it was over, we felt cleaned out, and we made love for the first time since Black Friday.

We spent the next several days right there, on the boat and on the island, getting back together and deciding not to decide any of the big questions for a little while longer. It was like a mini-sabbatical at the end of our real one. Frank told me what had gone wrong with the novel project and why he'd scrapped it—I'd guessed as much clear back in Scarborough; it was a kind of foreshadow of what I did with Lexie and Drew. Then he told me what he'd been writing instead—I hadn't guessed that!—and what he'd done with *it,* and why. I didn't know what to say. I wished I'd seen it, but if I hadn't liked it, that would've been one more setdown for both of us, and we didn't need any more setdowns. He told me basically what the story line was, and an odd thing happened: Now that the script was gone, and in the wake of my abortion and all, that crazy idea more or less possessed our imaginations.

Over the next few days, when we weren't swimming and making friends with each other again and remembering the really good parts of our cruise, we each worked for hours on deck with our clipboards or down below at the chart table and the dinette table, scribbling away. I made notes for the new courses I'll be teaching if I take the Virginia job, and Frank went back to *SEX EDUCATION,* figuring he'd better write it out of his system after all to clear the pipes before going on to whatever next thing.

He found he'd all but memorized the first act without intending to. He sketched it all out in one day—last Monday, when the weather was so shitful?—

Katherine interrupts to say that that was the day we found the original, just inside Knapps Narrows, during some bad weather of our own. All the way down from the Bay Bridge to Tilghman Island in twenty-four hours!

Frank Talbott observes that the wind had been in the north and northwest, and strong at times: Two or three ebb tides could easily fetch it that far, with the wind to keep the flood tides from carrying it back. The miracle was *our* finding it instead of some Tilghman Island crabber. Peter Sagamore reminds him that a miracle is what he'd said they needed; be our guests.

Then he drafted Act Two, Lee Talbott declares. Like Sophocles after Aeschylus, he added a third character: that Swimmer. Then he sacrificed the second one, old May there, who had been inspired by your Annapolis friend. But the rape actually happened to my sister once, over in Fenwick Island, Delaware. Ma probably told you?

By the end of the week the rough draft was done, and he gave it to me to read. This was day before yesterday: last day of spring and exactly a week since my trip to Cross Keys. How could I be objective about it? The characters weren't *real,* but I felt I knew them, and I loved the idea that the sperm had survived by floating downstream like an ovum, and the ovum by swimming upstream like a sperm. Terrific.

The sperm-and-egg conceit itself is low comedy in Doctor Talbott's opinion, she goes on, but it's about as basic as a conceit can get. Theater of the Womb. Plus of course it was pretty obvious, after all that business of forks and confluences and wyes, that old June and her Swimmer friend are going to reach their secret cove at the beginning of Act Three by working *across* the current instead of up or down it, just as we'd crossed the Bay to Cacaway to get our own act back together. They're either going to get it on and make a baby or go their separate ways, right? Him upstream to nowhere; her downstream to nowhere. Aberdeen and Virginia.

Katherine Sherritt says warmly I say get it on. The Talbotts are holding hands, she's glad to see, but their expressions are not serene. The children wonder whether they've been renamed again. Peter says nothing.

Says Leah Talbott Well. I wanted more than anything to say This is terrific; you got it; dynamite; knock me up again quick.

Cheers Katie Yeah!

But the name of the game these days is honesty, right, as long as it's not aggressive? The fact is I just didn't know, and that's what I said. She looks at her husband. I just don't know.

In Peter Sagamore's professional imagination, Act Three of *SEX EDUCATION: Play* is as clear as if he'd just seen it in color on public television. But he holds his peace.

So we popped a bottle of Cordoniu Blanc des Blancs, Lee Talbott says, and we toasted our own sex education plus the Drama Thus Far plus our uncertain future, and then we launched Act Two into Langford Creek on the outgoing tide, but in a different spirit from the way Frank had launched Act One. For one thing, we both knew the story now—I guess I read it five times that day. Either one of us could reconstruct its main action, and together we could almost replicate the speeches word for word. It's in the Talbott family repertory, at least for a while to come. And this time we felt that we weren't so much throwing it away as floating it off, like a seed or a message. Like ourselves, for Christ sake. Maybe it would take root somewhere and bear fruit; maybe we'd get a response. Or maybe this really would turn out to be the end of things.

What we did this time was take the flares and stuff out of our *working* flare container and set them aside in a vinyl bag; they need replacing anyhow before we take another cruise, if we ever do. Then we put the script in, in its Baggie, and it occurred to me to put the paisley scarf in there too: back where it came from. We poured the last of the champagne over the transom, to the muses and the fates, and said *bon voyage* to June and her Swimmer friend.

She smiles, not animatedly, and gives the *boina* back to her husband. *Au revoir,* as it turns out.

Less wistfully, Frank Talbott says Then we popped another Cordoniu and watched the canister drift down toward the river, and we felt like firing off all the distress flares then and there. And yet we felt at peace with ourselves, too, full of goodwill, whatever might happen. The air really *was* clear, and the night was beautiful after that big high that blew in all day.

So that was Friday. Yesterday morning we upped anchor for Kent Narrows and Wye Island, where we started out this time last year. But it was such a perfect sailing day, and we'd been at anchor so long behind Cacaway, that when we got out into the river we decided to sail up to Chestertown, just for the ride, instead of down to Kent Narrows. Lee used to teach at the college up there; we thought we'd say hello to the old place and then drop down to Wye Island on the Sunday or the Monday. We're in no hurry! We've been half afraid for the voyage to end, and maybe we wanted to give *SEX ED* a good head start. So we spent a few hours after lunch yesterday strolling the town, and then we sailed back down in the second part of the afternoon.

We could have kept going and reached my folks' place after dark. *Reprise* could sail himself there, almost—in fact, he almost did, last spring, after Rick drowned. But it was another sweet evening, et cetera, and since the weekend fleet was piling up behind Cacaway, we decided to run down here to Queenstown Creek, which we hadn't seen for a while, and park up by Salthouse Cove, an old favorite of ours.

Says Peter But somebody had got there first.

I didn't recognize the design, Frank Talbott says, but the name *Story* was familiar. Lee reminded me it was the hero's sailboat in Peter Sagamore's second novel, which she teaches every year. We'd enjoyed meeting both of you at Doug's that time, and we'd often wished our paths would cross again, but we didn't imagine it was actually you-all on the boat; we assumed it was some fans of yours.

Sorry about that, says Katherine. The *Story* story can wait.

So we took a swim, Frank says to her, and I noticed you were looking us over, so when we came back aboard I got out our binocs and looked *you*-all over and saw one very pregnant lady aboard. I thought of moving, for Lee's sake, but she said no. Even so, the sight didn't exactly cheer us up, under the circumstances. Then we heard you guys laughing over here, and Lee checked with the binoculars and reported there's this good-looking curly-haired naked fellow wearing a yarmulke or a beret and reading some pages to the nifty pregnant lady, who's wearing a bandanna and nothing else, and they sure look a lot like the Sagamores to her, and if she's not mistaken there's a Day-Glo orange flare canister on their cockpit seat, and we thought Oyoyoyoyoy, of all the people in the world to find my poor old piece of a playscript; no wonder you're laughing. But even with the hat right there on your head, we didn't dream you'd found *both* canisters. The odds are too staggering!

He removes the *boina*. I'm surprised you didn't see me blushing like a red day-beacon from clear over here. He plops it down upon the cockpit seat and parodies the old song: Why oh why oh why oh, why did I ever leave Wye Island?

Well: In

THE OPINION OF US SAGAMORES,

which Katherine now offers both Talbotts, Homer was strictly correct in supposing that wars are fought so that poets will have something to sing about. Our woman's sentences, seldom terse, spread their wings at evening's end like great horned owls. Whether President Harry S. Truman established the CIA after World War II in order to provide Peter Sagamore, thirty-some years later, with a ground-metaphor for his next big novel remains in her opinion to be seen; but she declares to our new friends her suspicion that the reason why Leah and Franklin Talbott left Wye Island last June (to answer your question, Frank), shaken to their core by family bereavements, and then sabbaticaled around the Caribbean, endeavoring in vain to write a novel and to address large questions concerning their personal future, was in order to apparently fail in those endeavors, to reach a painful impasse with which we utterly sympathize, and in despair to cast over the side, in mid-Chesapeake, flare canister #1 and contents, which by the unlikeliest of hazards swam into the ken of dwarf-laden *Story* at a peculiarly volatile, suspended moment in our own tidewater tale, and in a manner of speaking catalyzed, goosed—Might as well say inseminated, says Peter—*inseminated* our onboard muse, though what she will deliver remains to be seen.

Hatting up, she tells them the story of Day 1, Dun Cove to Dun Cove, briefly synopsizing what led up to and what has followed our retrieval of that canister and our perusal, at first desultory, of its contents. In her considered, late-evening opinion, there is no justice: That Frederick Mansfield Talbott should presumably die, Marian Silver be raped and impregnated in a black Chevy van on Fenwick Island, Delaware, Frank Talbott's probably-okay-though-autobiographical novel go down the tubes, and a terrific couple like him and Lee get so strung out as to wonder even whether they'll stay together, not to mention have children, *just in order to maybe help Peter Sagamore's lazy muse get off her tush and tune up*, strikes Kath as little short of obscene—as if the purpose of the destruction of Dresden in World War II had been to inspire Kurt Vonnegut, Junior. But (she goes on) Dresden was destroyed in any case, and Act One of *SEX EDUCA-*

TION was jettisoned in any case, and we happened to happen upon it, and that odd happenstance set the tone for this oddball ongoing odyssey of ours, in course of the first week of which we have touched base with Odysseus and Nausicaa, Huckleberry Findley, Carla B Silver and company, and the Talbotts, and have had foreshadowings of Captain Donald Quicksoat and Scheherazade down the line, and have told and been told more stories than in an average year. So thanks, okay? If we were laughing over here on *Story* this afternoon, it was because your play is fucking *funny,* Frank, as it was meant to be, and because the additional coincidence of our also picking up Act Two is enough to make any self-respecting minimalist a touch hysterical. Okay?

Lee Talbott tells us gratefully It *is* okay, taking Katherine's hand across the cockpit. Frank and I are okay, too, somehow. Whatever happens.

Confirms Frank Talbott Yup, and with a gesture that could refer either to the twin flare canisters or to himself and his wife or to both, he says to Peter Sagamore If you can make any use of any or all of this, do it. We'll be honored. He grins and hands Peter his *boina.* And then old May there will not have died in vain.

In the latter end of this evening, Peter Sagamore like a certain bird in a certain oak has done more listening than talking. Now, however, he firmly presses the *boina* back upon its owner and says Absolutely not. Take these canisters home with you. Your script's inside, waiting for Act Three.

He considers, then adds May isn't necessarily kaput, you know; she's fertilized.

He considers further, then adds further The hat that comes back is not the hat you cast away.

He considers finally, then adds finally You've hardly even begun to wear that hat.

Lee Talbott asks Katherine Sherritt May I kiss your husband? Kath says If I get to kiss yours. Cross-cockpit kisses follow. K enjoys hers entirely; in her opinion this Franklin Key Talbott fairly exudes male hormones. Peter is more interested in than roused by his; sharp-looking Leah Talbott's afflatus is not estrogen, but some mixture of adrenaline and negative-pole electricity. All the same, she kisses him straightforwardly on the mouth, her lips slightly parted. He has a clear sensation that were he to slip his tongue-tip between them, some circuit breaker would let go.

Though by no means all of the tales promised have been told, we bid one another affectionate and interested but very tired good night. Our conversation is not over, we four feel, but our day sure is. We shall see what tomorrow's wind is and what the Sagamores and Talbotts feel like doing with it. For now (yesterday), good night, good night, good night, good night.

Complains wakeful little A.M. as her parents bed down at last (her alternate brothers, F and P, are long since asleep), We didn't get to tell *our* story: The Swan Prince of Queenstown Creek. *Mañana,* her mother promises. If you're good. Our unborn woman-child frets further And you neglected to tell us

THE END WHERETO ONE IS FETCHED FORTH INTO THE PARLOUS WORLD.

It won't be easy for a girl to sleep tonight, not knowing. A girl may have to wake her unborn brothers, for mere company in the dark, you know?

When *they* don't sleep, sleepy Kate reminds sleepy Pete, *I* don't sleep.

We two are saying good night down in the cabin, P's head in K's naked lap, *Story* as motionless as if aground in the silent creek. To our wakeful daughter in our woman's womb our man mutters Wumpf, little girl: As to that, our parents never told *us,* either, nor theirs them. But in your father's opinion, the end whereto one is fetched forth into the parlous world is neither more nor less than this: to hear or make up stories, and to pass them on. Night, now.

Thank you, Daddy, and good night.

DR. SAGAMORE PRESCRIBES.

Sunday, Day 7, dawns delicious, 6/22/80, a bright warm A.M. through which all hands sleep until near nine, though it's light at six, except Peter Sagamore, who cannot aboardship sleep in daylight no matter how late he gets to bed, and Leah Allan Silver Talbott over on *Reprise,* whom he sees lowering her brown slim self into Queenstown Creek as he steps up, naked too, into *Story*'s dew-soaked cockpit to check the day. She gives him a little wave and splashes off. Not to wake Katherine, instead of diving in he lets himself quietly over the stern and swims away through the balmish water into Salthouse Cove. As always in the Chesapeake, he swims eyes-open; as always he sees nothing but illuminated green. Presently he stands on the silty bottom in waist-deep water to pee and catch his breath. What a morning.

Mrs. Talbott swims his way with an easy, expert-looking stroke, pauses discreetly a *Story*'s-length off, calls What a morning!

Isn't it.

Your family still asleep?

Yup.

Mine too. She paddles nearer and stands, her breasts just under water. You two did us some good last night, I believe.

No harm, at least, Peter hopes, thinking a touch enviously of nipplefish.

Lee Talbott pushes her short hair back. I'm in love with your wife.

Me too; and your husband's a mensch. To himself he adds So let's fuck, and remembers agreeably his bachelor days, when such sweet windfalls as Katie-Sherritt-at-the-92nd-Street-Poetry-Center not only came along from time to time, but could in clear conscience be claimed and chomped. The beauty of women, Donald Barthelme somewhere proposes, makes of adultery a painful duty. Thinks Peter, standing hands on hips, Yes, well: And love makes of fidelity a manageable responsibility. Though it would be delightsome on so fine a June A.M. to get it on with sexy Ms. Talbott here in Salthouse Cove sans offense to either party's spouse, were such a thing possible.

She agrees, smiling: A mensch he is. Is he a writer too?

More candidly than he had expected he would, Peter finds himself saying Maybe not of plays. Maybe not of *that* play. But what do I know from TV plays? The stage-Jewish locution embarrasses him. Anyhow, Frank should finish the thing and then bring what he's learned back to the novel. This time it'll come out fiction. He gestures out toward their boats. Want to swim back?

In a minute. The woman's smile is beautiful. They're standing under an overhanging locust that has fallen most of the way into Salthouse Cove while retaining enough root-system to leaf out: a virtual bower, embowering an amphibian Eve and Adam. If I were that June person and you were that Swimmer, Lee Talbott hypothesizes, and this were that cove we were talking about in Act Two, the first question in Act Three would be whether we're going to make out, right?

P's scrotum tingles. Right. And if we were them, we would. If we were they.

Too bad for us we aren't, Lee Talbott says.

I guess so. But that won't happen till the end of the act. It'll *be* the end of the act, no?

Peter sees her see him admiring her breasts; she does not turn away, but settles chin deep into the turbid cove. It will?

Sure. Anyhow, getting it on isn't the larger question; it's only the presenting question. Upstream or downstream is the larger question. Separately or together. That's what they've got to decide.

Lee Allan Silver Talbott says Aberdeen or Virginia. What do you think? Pushing past into deeper water, Peter cordially reminds her that art is art and life life, by and large. Marital counsel is not his line. But as a doctor of dramaturgy, *honoris causa,* he prognoses that Act Three of *SEX EDUCATION: Play* will fall flat upon its moral-dramatical tush if the author elects for its principals any of the above.

You think so?

I know so. Take the word of an official doctor.

She says Hm and paddles beside him; they sidestroke leisurely homeward. On *Reprise*'s foredeck, Peter notes, Franklin Talbott is up and about in cutoff jeans, short-sleeve sweatshirt, *boina.* No sign of Katherine over on *Story*. Once again he reproves himself: this time for having slipped into Yiddish slang. Remembering Bernard Malamud's observation that if you ever happen to forget you're Jewish, some Gentile will remind you, he hopes Leah Talbott doesn't feel patronized or otherwise offended by his use of the word *tush;* his chapter with Marcie Blitzstein notwithstanding, he is no expert in such matters. Given the Y of *SEX EDUCATION*'s basic plumbing, he points out as they swim, there would seem to be *three* options for June and her Swimmer friend, not two: upstream left, upstream right, and downstream to the whatchacallit. . . .

Lee rolls her brown eyes: Don't remind me.

But in fact, says Peter, there's a fourth: the place they'll get to in the front end of Act Three. It's what Wye Island is to Wye River, or Cacaway to Langford Creek. Never mind that it's a kink in somebody's uterus; if I were a playwright, I'd plant that place with cattails and honey locust trees and throw in some blue herons and crabs and oysters. Then I'd fetch a full moon up behind those honey locusts and fly a few Canada geese in front of that moon while June and her pal are making out on the beach. I'd hold the camera right on that moon and freeze frame and fade right there: smack in the crotch of the Y. But what do I know?

They have reached *Reprise*'s boarding ladder. Frank Talbott comes aft to say good morning and offer coffee, which Peter declines. Lee Talbott unhesitatingly pulls herself up onto the ladder, displaying to Peter her splendid wet backside and to her husband her doubtless even more splendid front. If I weren't in love with you, Frank Talbott, she pleasantly declares, I would jump this man so fast his head would swim.

Unruffled Frank replies He'd be a lucky fellow, and hands her a towel. Orange juice? Danish? he asks Peter, who replies that he must go home now and do paperwork before we leave this creek for wherever.

Frank nods and taps his *boina:* Likewise. Shall we compare notes at lunchtime, if we're both still here? Sure. Lee Talbott busses her husband's beard. Has she got a note to compare with *him,* she says: Wait till he hears. She smiles beautifully at swimming P; he grins back and asks again, rhetorically, What do I know?

WHAT PETER KNOWS

Two-thirds asleep, Katherine Sherritt has dreamed something tiresomely uterine involving, what, crossed keys? She wakes groaning at the half-assed pun upon that pun upon that stylish Baltimore development where Lee Talbott's gynecologist vacuum-aspirated her. Nice and Easy have been awake for some while, considerably sucking each other's thumbs until their mother rouses. Wait till your father hears this new evidence for his pet hypothesis, K tells them: that the human unconscious is a ree-tard.

Can *we* have a pet hypothesis? they ask in unison. Thinks Kate (one-third adream) That's what it's going to be: Hartz flea collars and gerbil turds. She can hardly wait.

Nine o'clock! Has she ever slept so late aboard? Already it's quite warm in the cabin, but we went to bed naked; a sweet air licks the skin above her waist-high sheet. She is unsurprised to find Peter not at home; assumes he's swimming or socializing next door. But when she sticks her head up through the forward hatch to say hi to 22 June '80, she gets it kissed; he's perched in dry swimtrunks on the foredeck, logging last night's stories in note form. No kids yet, huh? he asks.

They're never coming out. Her husband lies back against the cabin trunk; she rests her chin in his hair and tells him about crossed keys and Let's remember to ask Frank Talbott about Operation BONAPARTE. He tells her about his little swim and how agreeable it would have been to fuck Lee Talbott standing up front-on in Salthouse Cove 'neath yonder honey locust tree, were there no such things as love and responsibility, which there are and so he didn't. Kathy says Much obliged, but what I don't appreciate about this piece of moral news is the pairing of successful writer with sexy hotshot lit prof, which leaves us pregnant librarians and failed playwrights sucking the mop. Peter objects: Frank Talbott's no failure; he's just getting started. And Lee Talbott is not quite Edmund Wilson with boobs. But you are unequivocally a pregnant librarian: my favorite one. Mollified Kate acknowledges that she too falls for women who are both smart and good-looking, not to mention men who seem wise, gentle, strong, well hung, and generally menschy. In another incarnation she would enjoy a dynamite affair with, e.g., Franklin Key Talbott. But our present incarnation, we remind ourselves with a squeeze of hands, is not bad at all; in fact, it's terrific.

Killer heat-wave continues in Texas through our breakfast; forest fires in Colorado. We pity everyone unfortunate enough not to be in good physical health, in love, and aboard a sailboat anchored in Queenstown Creek. The light morning northwesterly is usable for sailing; Peter's Hoopers Island savvy tells him that the afternoon will be airless. All the same, we decide to stay put till lunchtime, he scribbling, she reading and gestating like the pregnant librarian she is, and then see what's what. We've been being loners for a pleasant week, Katherine observes; cruising in tandem can be fun too. Maybe we'll see what the Talbotts plan to do next.

Peter explains why he believes they should do *nothing* next, in effect, though he acknowledges that to postpone certain decisions is a backhanded way of making them. Even so, his sense of human dramaturgy makes him wish that *Reprise* could follow *Story*'s lead for just a little while yet: whither the wind listeth, etc. But what does he know, outside the bailiwick of fiction? Whereto he will now repair, excuse him, mindful of our vow that he shall compose no actual sentences till Said and Done have seen the light.

Katherine declares You know a few things. Surveying the world, she observes that Lee Allan Silver Talbott, now demurely bikinied, is down in their dinghy sponging *Reprise*'s hull, and that her husband is evidently below, no doubt ascribble. The literary life. She thinks she'll swim or row over and spend the A.M. in female conversation, which she much enjoys and misses.

Men.

She slips a sunsuit on and makes a headband of our paisley scarf that sets off her beachy longish hair as well as it did Lee Talbott's dark short. We kiss good morning, and Peter Sagamore spends the next two hours bringing us up to where we narratively are. Our week has given him a possible idea for a book, he believes, but his practiced eye sees in it—he had been going to say snags and shoals, but the peril is more meteorological: between twin storms fore and aft, Horse Latitudes. The Doldrums. A novel in which next to nothing happens beyond an interminably pregnant couple's swapping stories?

WOMEN

Hi.

Hi.

Deft K ships her oars; the two dinghies tap. Lee Talbott is standing in *Reprise*'s inflatable, holding onto the cutter's bobstay with one hand and wiping anchorline mudmarks off the bows with a scrubbing sponge. Katherine Sherritt guesses that if *she* were a man or May, she'd want into that maroon bikini. We enjoyed last evening, she says, holding the dinghies gunwale to gunwale.

Frank and I did too. I guess it was an *important* evening, for us. Lee grins. I'd've jumped your husband this morning if I weren't so attached to mine. Plus et cetera.

Thanks for not. Peter felt the same way about you, but we think open marriage sucks.

Lee Talbott, scrubbing, says We think we think so too. But probably it's the chemistry of particular couples, no?

The Hispanification of North America, Katherine remarks, and knows that Leah Talbott understands at once that what she's referring to is that ¿No? habit (which the Sagamores too have picked up, through Kate, from her oral-ethnic expeditions into Baltimore's Latino community) and not anything to do with conjugal mores. With Peter, K bets aloud, she'd've had to clarify. Lee bets she'd've had to likewise, with her Frank—but listen to them sounding like a pair of stereotypes! You can scrub better if I steady the dinghy, Kate offers; Lee Talbott grants that, but points out that it would be imprudent for Katherine to stand in the dinghy and steady it with her feet while working it down the length of *Reprise*'s gunwales; the scrubbing, on the other hand, if K's willing, can be done from a lower center of gravity.

They end up tying the dinghies together and sponging first *Reprise* and then *Story* from cap rail to waterline stripe; then rowing over to that honey locust bower, not to disturb their husbands, and stripping and swimming; then sitting side by side in six inches of tidewater, leaning back on their elbows in a secluded sandy stretch farther up in Salthouse Cove. They talk until lunchtime. Katherine Sherritt tells Leah Talbott how it came to pass that our boat is named after that boat in Peter's novel, in which the characters themselves wince at that tacky circumstance. In course of that tale she fills her new friend in on Jean Heartstone's Magic Language Theory and sad death, Marcie Blitz's proposed public-television documentary of a few years back, our romantic encounter at the 92nd Street Poetry Center in June 1964 and our reencounter at the Katherine Anne Porter party in College Park in 1970. Lee Talbott tells Kate Sherritt about her husband's first marriage and divorce, her small problems and large pleasures with his daughter by that marriage—Lee's a step-grandmother at thirty-five—and her and Frank's Cute Meet (remeet, actually, since he had been her step-uncle for years) just below Wye Island in 1973, when she and scattered Marian had capsized their Sunfish and he'd come to their unnecessary rescue in *Reprise,* only then recognizing who they were.

She chuckles: Talk about jumping and getting jumped! Once we got each other alone on that sailboat, Frank and I went off like a pair of firecrackers. Chuckles Katherine So did we.

Lee Talbott then sits up and raises the confidential ante by telling Kate briefly about some important love affairs in her life, all pre-Franklin: A boy she really fell for in undergraduate days, whom on some principle or other—probably a reaction against her sister's early promiscuity—she would not screw but indefatigably blew. One of her graduate professors at the U. of M., who was both a brilliant dissertation-director and a sexual imperialist, yet who was so opposed to the idea of trading academic for sexual favors that she had to work half again as hard for an honors grade in his seminar than she would have had they not been lovers. Et cetera.

Katherine Sherritt sits up too and tells Lee Talbott a lot about her brief marriage to Poonie Baldwin, Jr., and a little about her intermarital affairs with Yussuf al-Din, Saul Fish, and Jaime Aiquina. Lee knows Saul Fish by musical reputation and says she has trouble with Hasidism, though she respects its influence on Franz Kafka and Isaac Bashevis Singer. So does Katherine, to whom the word *Hasid* always suggests hayseed. Next they talk for quite a while about Latin American politics; the common fate of Jaime Aiquina and Jonathan Silver Talbott chokes their voices. A horsefly roars through their neighborhood but does not pause to bite. Both women fear that if Jimmy Carter loses to Ronald Reagan in November, the U.S. is going to wreck Central America. Leah Talbott is pretty sure Carter will win; Katherine Sherritt, who moves mainly in nonacademic circles, is hopeful but less confident.

They swim again and then talk for a while about food: pesto, pâté, hoisin, sushi. About their parents and siblings. About having and not having babies. About contemporary writers they admire and do not admire. Lee enjoys being Jewish, but is uncomfortable except in an ethnic-cultural mix; Katherine enjoys being what she is, but seldom thinks of that as upper-caste WASP, though it is. Both women are temperamentally secular; neither believes in God or any literal afterlife, though Lee wishes she could, because she and Frank got a late start and because she misses her half-brother and her stepfather. There was more to Frederick Mansfield Talbott, evidently, than the unpleasant fellow Peter met. Lee is of a prevailingly pessimistic temper, not without reason: The actuarial prospect of a long childless widowhood so repels her that she assumes she'll take her own life not long after Frank dies—fifteen or twenty years at most, she reckons. *That* prospect so distresses her, when she thinks about it, that her irrational impulse at times is to end things now; hence her flirtation with the Virginia professorship and separation: a sort of trial suicide. Kath is prevailingly optimistic despite that black hole at her core: Though she allows notionally for very bad luck, she assumes as Leah Talbott would not that our children will be born healthy and normal and that we two will enjoy a robust longevity. *Her* fears are on the national, international, and global scale: She worries about the survival of the manatee, the dugong, the Chesapeake rockfish, and the world's rain forests; also human liberty, the dignity of the individual, the smog-eaten Parthenon.

They discuss clothes, San Francisco, G. F. Handel, diaphragms, Cimabue, D.C. dim-sum restaurants, Edgar Poe's *Narrative of Arthur Gordon Pym,* Portuguese *pousadas,* cellulitis, analogues of the Bitch-and-Pepper motif in contemporary urban folktales, breast-feeding as a natural form of birth control, Horace's odes, the flavor of human male semen, the preparation of fresh asparagus. And were either of them to be interrogated upon this conversation a year from today, she would remember nearly everything the other had said.

Asks Peter, coming up for air at half past eleven, So what did you and she talk about?

Oh, stuff. But can you believe it, I forgot Operation BONAPARTE. We're rafting up for lunch, okay?

BOMB IN ATTACHÉ CASE

Okay. As skippers of the smaller boat, we decide to unanchor *Story* and scull downwind to *Reprise.* Peter asks Katherine, who says Yup, whether she's been wondering about Molly and Willy and worrying a little about Chip. We think maybe this cruise of ours is about over. For one thing, we have pressed our obstetrical luck beyond all reasonableness. We'll maybe start moseying southward this afternoon, yes? With any breeze at all, we can be at Nopoint Point and in Jack Bass's hands by tomorrow evening.

K puts out fenders; P hoists anchor and sweeps us expertly alongside the cutter. Lee and Frank Talbott take our lines, and we make and share a light lunch under cockpit awnings. The air is low-eightyish, the sun bright, the breeze gentle but usable. The Talbotts guess they'll move on down to Key Farm on Wye Island, where Frank's old father lives alone, and close the circuit of their year-long voyage at last. Why not sail down together? *Reprise* can tow *Story* through the Kent Island Narrows if necessary, where the tidal current runs strong at the highway bridge.

Frank says to Peter I spent half the morning thinking over what you said to Lee about that cove in Act Three: making it less uterine and more estuarine. I might give it a try.

Says Katherine God knows this creek is uterine. And Salthouse Cove is downright vaginal. Just as she is about to bring up the subject of Operation BONAPARTE, Lee reminds Peter that he promised last night to tell them a story about coincidences even less likely than our finding *both* of those Alert-and-Locate flare canisters.

Right. Not to seem to be the moderately successful writer dropping names upon the moderately unsuccessful one, P omits the acknowledgment that he first heard this story from the author of the novel *Catch-22;* anyhow, it has been altered by much retelling. Once upon a time there was an IBM executive whose job involved frequent airplane trips. The time that this was once upon was the middle Nineteen Sixties, when there happened to have been a rash of commercial-airliner bombings by crazy-desperate people who insured themselves heavily and then blew up themselves and their fellow passengers with homemade bombs concealed in their attaché cases. No baggage inspection in those days. The IBM executive's wife was alarmed: Suppose her husband had the bad luck to board a flight with one of those crazies?

The IBM executive tried to jolly his wife out of her fears by telling her the joke about the rabbi and the priest who both survived the same airplane crash, but she'd heard that joke already. Therefore, more seriously, he had his office run a computer program to calculate the odds against there being, on any given scheduled domestic airline flight, one of those lunatics with a bomb in his attaché case. The odds were gratifying: Let's say about a quarter-million to one.

But the IBM executive's wife was not consoled. The odds against any given human spermatozoon's fertilizing an ovum, she pointed out, are tens of millions to one, and yet most people who want to get pregnant get pregnant, along with plenty who *don't* want to.

Ouch.

Sorry. Who's to say, said the IBM executive's wife, that you won't just happen to board that one flight in a quarter-million on which there is a lunatic with a bomb in his attaché case?

Well, the IBM executive sympathized with his wife's alarm, but he really couldn't *not* take his business trips. So after giving the matter further executive thought, he ran a program to calculate the odds against there being, on any given scheduled domestic airline flight, *two* people with bombs concealed in their attaché cases. The results were consoling indeed: hundreds of millions, maybe billions to one. In fact, unlike human conception, which happens all the time, or the finding of *two* Alert-and-Locate canisters with playscripts in them, which has happened at least once, the two-bomb coincidence had never happened in the history of aviation, so far as anyone knew.

Thereafter, therefore, in order to be perfectly safe, the IBM executive never boarded an airplane without carrying a bomb in his attaché case. Okay? Sorry about the sperm business; I was thinking of Frank's play.

Lee Talbott tells him he's forgiven. What she likes best about that story is the construction "Thereafter, therefore." These artichokes are spectacular, Kath.

May Jump gave them to us in Annapolis. These crab fingers are terrific, too. What *I* like best about that story is that it got told by my very own dwarf-infested husband without a hitch. You should have heard us a week ago, down on the Tred Avon.

Yes, well, says Peter Sagamore, but that's because this one's secondhand. All I added was the sperms and eggs, which I shouldn't've, and the business of the two flare canisters, which was the point. Plus "Thereafter, therefore," thanks.

We slide artichoke petals and crab fingers through our teeth and carpet Queenstown Creek with biodegradable discards; also sip iced tea. *Boina*'d even under *Reprise*'s awning, Franklin Talbott nods appreciatively but pensively. We wonder whether Peter's allusion to pregnancy has offended him; in fact, he will say presently, he admired the tie-in. Percipient Katherine, who also wants to lead our conversation to Operation BONAPARTE, says to him How about that pretty-good CIA story you owe us?

He smiles at her: It'll keep. Her insides tingle at the voice and smile. He then goes on to say, surprisingly—surprisingly even to his wife, it seems to us—I've got so much to tell you people that I hardly know where to start. Will you come down to Key Farm with us tonight? We'll all sleep aboard at our dock.

We check with each other. Why not? Kath can telephone Nopoint Point, and Jack Bass will be twenty minutes away by car. But why, exactly?

I didn't work on that play this morning, Frank Talbott declares, though I did think about it, and I might go back to it one of these days. There's a whole other book in the works that I haven't told you about, that I want to tell you about this evening. Nonfiction. I started it after KUBARK and set it aside for that *Reprise* novel, and I decided this morning that I'm going on with it. I was thinking of our conversation last night about Doomsday Factors and Operation BONAPARTE—

Katherine exclaims. Frank Talbott says We didn't mention BONAPARTE yet? Well, we will, tonight, at Key Farm. And many another thing. Bo-

NAPARTE has certainly been on my mind; it's what they pitched me for down in Langley after Doug Townshend's memorial service. But we're getting close to home, no? Peter's bomb story sort of went off in my head just now, 'cause I spent this morning making up what I guess you'd call a parable, which also involves bombs and airplanes.

Writers, Lee Talbott says: I swear.

Unlikely coincidence is what Katherine Sherritt swears.

Says Peter Shoot.

THE PARABLE OF THE AIRPLANE WITH TWIN BOMBS ON IT

Franklin Key Talbott strokes his beard once between brown thumb and forefinger.

There is a bomb aboard the plane. No: There are *two* bombs on the plane, as in Peter's story. The highly unlikely has after all come to pass.

So long as neither of the bombs explodes, the passengers and crew are normally safe. If either of them explodes, they're all dead. There is no intermediate state, and nobody can leave the airplane, 'cause it's in midair over midocean. Any attempt to defuse or otherwise disarm the twin bombs may very well set them off. . . .

Blam.

Blooey.

Yeah. Anyhow, the company can't agree how to proceed: Fly on? Turn back? Crash-land in midocean? Take a chance on fiddling with the bombs? There are serious and reasonable objections to every proposed course of action, as well as ignorant objections and bad-faith objections. Also ignorant proposals and bad-faith proposals.

So: Much gets discussed, and little or nothing gets done, with excellent reason. But in their anxiety over the situation, the passengers smoke cigarettes and drink alcohol and eat food laced with pesticides and artificial preservatives and radioactive isotopes, not to mention sugar, salt, and grease, and they drink water contaminated with Dioxin and heavy-metal residues, and they breathe air polluted with this and that.

The twin bombs don't go off. The plane lands safely after all, at John F. Kennedy International Airport, and the passengers and crew go home and eat and drink and breathe some more. Over the years, they get cancers and have heart attacks and give birth to defective children.

I guess I'll stick to nonfiction, Frank Talbott says.

There's still enough breeze to sail, Frank Talbott says, if we want to.

Frank Talbott shrugs. Want to?

OUR STORIES:
THE CLOTHES'
NEW EMPEROR

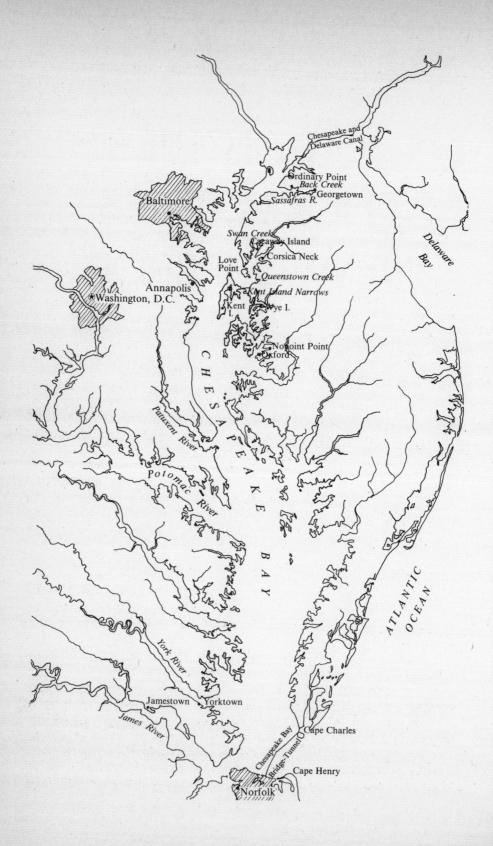

DAY 8: WYE 1.

A WHOLE NEW BALL GAME

In Katherine's belly in Katherine's berth aboard *Story* at the Talbotts' dock at Key Farm, Wye Island, Maryland, in the small hours of Monday, June 23, small Blam pouts to his sister It's a whole new ball game out there, and now we'll never get to tell our story of The Swan Prince of Queenstown Creek, which I think is as nifty a tale as some of theirs even though we haven't got it quite licked into shape yet.

Blooey counsels patience. Young as she is, she has remarked that in this neighborhood, stories have a way of getting told, sooner or later. That Franklin Key Talbott person, for example, has yet to come up with that pretty-good CIA story he's been promising; but no doubt he will, by and by. He has certainly been forthcoming on other fronts.

Blam wants to know Are *we* going to be born defective, like the children in that airplane story?

Bloo wishes she could reassure her brother on this point, concerning which, however, she is not entirely easy in her own unborn mind. In the prologue to our story, she reminds him, Mom made Dad promise we'd be okay when the time came: The Ordinary Point Delivery Story. But that was make-believe.

What's this Key-Key-Kepone they've been going on about between chapters?

You slept through the explanation. Kepone is the Allied Chemical Corporation's trade name for the pesticide they were convicted of dumping copiously, knowingly, and illegally from one of their manufacturing subsidiaries into the James River, down the Bay from here, through the Nineteen Seventies, effectively poisoning that once-noble estuary much more than not, our parents agree, and rendering its marine inhabitants unfit for human consumption—so it was ruled, for a time, over the protests of local watermen. The company was fined; the ban on fishing and shellfishing in the birthwaters of colonial America was presently lifted, over the protests of concerned ecologists; and the river—so toxified that scientists at first estimated its cleanup time in generations at least—dropped from the news.

Oh.

But we may assume that those Keponed fish and shellfish, unfit for human consumption and ignorant of human politics, were consumed in the natural way by other fauna, and that the poison thus accessed, as they say, the general Chesapeake food chain, of which you and I and Mom are high-ranking members.

Daddy too.

Dad too. That's what worries me, Brother Blam: Our parents love seafood. You and I are practically *made* out of seafood. So God only knows how we're going to come out. Stop sniffling.

I'm not sniffling.

Kepone was also the working title of that nonfiction book that that Frank Talbott fellow that Mom swoons over was researching before he switched to novels and plays, which he's now switching back from. That's where you woke up.

Says Blam Our daddy is a better writer than that Frank Talbott fellow.

Bloo loyally grants that likelihood, but thinks the comparison inexact: The art of fiction, she has heard, is not the art of the high-minded exposé. Blam says I've sure got me one smart sister, but then Blooey asks What's a ball game?

Her brother doesn't know either. He happened to hear his father say that: Boyoboy, it's a whole new ball game, et cetera. Do we think Mom and Dad are going to have recreational sex with those Talbotts?

Blooey primly opines that this is not that kind of story. Their parents she declares to be neither prudes on the one hand nor swingers on the other. Nor are Mr. and Mrs. Talbott, in her mom's opinion. They are all of them simply vigorous heterosexual adult human animals enjoying one another's physical presences along with other things. Anyhow, if things get sticky we can always push the Launch button and start our own story.

Blam eggs her: Do it.

Dare me?

He dee-double-diddly-die dares her.

Not yet. It's a whole new ball game out there.

K strokes her belly but does not waken. Her husband snores lightly in his quarterberth: deviated septum. The children soon rejoin their parents in sleep, the last easeful night any of us four will enjoy till midweek at the earliest.

Sleep, Tick; sleep, Tock. Peter Sagamore and Katherine Sherritt, sleep. Not least because our plot requires it, we are about to surprise ourselves with as sore a day as we have suffered in our decade as a middle-class American loving couple.

IT BEGINS SERENELY ENOUGH.

We breakfast early with the Talbotts—Frank, Lee, and Frank's father, George, a hale and wiry, half-deaf widower, eighty, who reminds us of the late Fritz Sagamore—on the screened front porch of the Key Farm farm-house. George's late wife, Virginia Key, inherited the place from her family; the Prince of Darkness dead, it must soon pass to Franklin Talbott. Lee is not keen on living here: She likes old George; she enjoys Wye Island in spring and fall; she understands Frank's attachment to his boyhood home—but except in summer she prefers cities, and through most of the summer the Wye River, like Sherritt Cove, is sea-nettle infested. The house, moreover, is what Lee calls a Grandmother House: white clapboard tidewater gothic, homely to view and costly to maintain, buried in over-grown spirea, hydrangea, lilac, wisteria. Yet it is prime Chesapeake water-front acreage and one of the very few houses on Wye Island; she'd like to sell it and buy on Cape Cod or Martha's Vineyard.

We chat about this over eggs scrambled and served by George Talbott's housekeeper. Cecilia Skinner's husband tenant-farms the corn and soybean lots, mows the lawn, and does light maintenance on the main and tenant houses, the outbuildings and machinery; Cecilia does the cleaning, cooking, marketing, and laundry, and sees to it that George takes his digitalis and folic acid. Lee Talbott wonders who'll be *her* Cecilia Skinner in her childless widowhood, if the courage to kill herself fails her upon Frank's death.

As Peter's father was, old George Talbott is gregarious, hospitable, good-humored, clear-minded, and much handicapped by his late deafness but unable to abide a hearing aid. Liver spots. Chronic sinusitis. On the strength of several terms in the county Orphans Court, he is called Judge, even by his housekeeper, though his trade was first farming and then dealing in John Deere farm machinery. Every day for the last forty years, regardless of the temperature and even in his retirement, he dons a fresh white long-sleeve shirt and a necktie. As Fritz Sagamore used to do, he tells anecdotes because he can't follow conversation; he makes a show of flirting with the women, but directs his talk to the men. Now he's telling Peter that he not only knows Katherine's father and mother but knew *their* parents, too; now he tells his son a version of the saga of Parker Pink and Shorter Point. Presently—though father and son had not seen each other for a year until last night—he withdraws to his Baltimore *Sun*.

The morning is fine and warm; a light southerly moves over the lawn from the willowed Wye, in whose fork Key Farm is nestled. Homely or not, the property must be worth more than half a million these days, we think. *Reprise* and *Story* lie on opposite sides of the old pier, their unequal masts visible above a wall of untended boxwoods. The four of us are subdued: yesterday's revelations; the Talbotts' having finally closed the circle of their cruise, with so many questions unresolved; the Sagamores' decision that we have pressed our luck far enough and had better head back to Nopoint Point and have our babies whether or not the wind thither listeth, as this morning it doth not.

Mainly, however, it is yesterday's stories and last night's confirmations of them that have left us somewhat dazed. We all slept well—sunshine, salt air, the working of the boats down from the Chester to the Wye—but we have much to assimilate.

THE POINT OF FRANK TALBOTT'S PARABLE OF THAT AIRPLANE
ET CETERA

that he laid on us yesternoon in Queenstown Creek is that in worrying about those Doomsday Factors down in D.C. and Langley—as every sensible citizen must, for they are short on integrity, virtually beyond control, and appallingly dangerous—we may be ignoring, fatally, the doomsday factors in our literal backyards.

OPERATION БONAPARTE?

Small potatoes, in Frank's opinion, though his late brother and our late mutual friend Doug Townshend, as Peter can attest, took it seriously enough. Both that bugging operation and its cryptonym (suggested by the Russians' location on Corsica Neck) were Rick Talbott's brainchildren. Not impossibly—though improbably, thinks Frank—the deaths of Rick and Doug, maybe of John Arthur Paisley as well, had somehow to do with their involvement in BONAPARTE; he did not mean to suggest that the game was inconsquential to its players. They need another Key to plug their Keyhole, had quipped Carla B Silver when Frank returned from Doug's memorial service in Langley and told her of being pitched to help with BONAPARTE. Witty dialogue everywhere, he had replied: The woman who'd pitched him (they have a few women senior officers down there these days; it's a very forward looking company) had quipped We don't begrudge your *KUBARK* book, Mister Talbott; down here we judge a book by its cover.

Said Kath Not bad.

Not bad. The woman then briefed me, in a general way, on the Keyhole Eleven story; all I knew was what I'd read in the papers. She told me why the Russians want more privacy on Corsica Neck and why the Company wants your Deniston School to go ahead with the sale. I told her I was slightly interested for Rick's sake, but that obviously I'd have to think twice before getting involved with the Agency again. The lady said Speaking of agencies, she understood that my New York literary agent handled some capital-*W* Writers as well as kiss-and-tell types like me: the Charming Candor gambit. She wondered whether I knew another Maryland writer who had that same agent: a fellow named Peter Sagamore.

Protested Peter Come on! Katherine was alarmed. Did that mean that the CIA knows about Doug's telling Peter all that stuff?

Frank Talbott imagined so (Lee declared They know every damn thing about everybody; I hate their fucking guts); they could be assumed to know at least about Rick's and Doug's pitch to Peter in Carla's Cavern in 1978, which of course Frank himself hadn't known of last week. Doug would routinely have reported it, whether casual Frederick did or not. But it turns out, Frank said to Peter, it wasn't you the lady was interested in. She wanted to know whether I happened to know your wife.

Groaned Katherine Could we please aim these boats at Polynesia right this minute?

Well. You heard all this in Annapolis from Carla B Silver, right? The Deniston Connection. I told my pitch-lady I didn't really know you two. She said they'd want me to develop that connection.

Said pensive Peter So here we are. He's wondering whether certain extraordinary coincidences in our story maybe weren't so coincidental after all.

Not yet, replied Frank Talbott. That had been as far as his recruiter had gone; he had agreed to consider the proposition and get back to her. That night he'd mentioned the matter privately to Carla B Silver—

Privately, Leah interrupted to explain, because this was our Black Friday.

Black Friday it was; our air wasn't clear. Then Carla told me about Rick's and Doug's pitching Peter Sagamore there in that room where we were sitting. And she told me more about Operation BONAPARTE, including the KGB girl down in her bar who'd been put there as bait for another guy that both outfits were fishing for.

Said Kath Oh Jesus.

Yeah. But the irony was, Frank was ignorant of Katherine's maiden name—Lee could have told him; she remembered such details; but Lee didn't hear of all this till later, at mutual-confession time out in mid-Bay—and so when old Lascar there, Carla B Silver's Rumanian bartender and new boyfriend, had supplied *Willy's* name and, next evening, pointed him out in the bar, Willy having become a frequent patron of Carla's Cavern and a buddy of its bartender, Frank Talbott did not make the Sherritt/Sherritt association. Carla herself could not have made it until she met Katherine at May Jump's. Only Lee Talbott might have connected the several names, but she didn't get *all* this information even when her husband later told her of his being pitched by the Company. Their air, you see, was not clear.

Sitting there in *Reprise*'s cockpit over lunch yesterday in Queenstown

Creek, we four agreed that the withholding of information between husbands and wives is not only bad marital policy but cheap-shot dramaturgy, and makes for lumpy exposition farther on. E.g.:

That was all Frank Talbott had known about BONAPARTE until one calm day in his and Lee's Cacaway Island interlude—last Wednesday or Thursday, he guessed it was—when, for something to do in that calm impasse, they'd put the little outboard on *Reprise*'s inflatable dinghy and motored the flat four miles from Langford Creek across the Chester to the Corsica, to have a look at Corsica Neck and The Deniston School; had even gone ashore and strolled the wooded grounds in question, chatting together about Frank's old *Kepone* project and the Natural Recycling Research scam, of which the patient reader is still ignorant; and Lee Talbott had remembered that Sherritt was Katherine Sagamore's name, too—the writer's wife's—and wondered whether that Willy Sherritt fellow and Katherine Sherritt Sagamore might be related.

And then—cheap shot!—a day or so later the Sagamores meet Carla B Silver in Annapolis and hear chapter and verse, not only about BONAPARTE, but about *Reprise*'s Caribbean odyssey and its aborted climax, pardon the expression; and the day after *that* the Talbotts meet the Sagamores in Queenstown Creek, reading *SEX EDUCATION: Play*. Get us *out* of here!

Not yet, said Katherine Sherritt, yesterday: Wait till you guys hear *this;* and she laid on them

THE MYSTERY OF THE BRANDY ROSES,

laid on *us* in the Annapolis Hilton by among others an improbably sweetened Willy Sherritt: more precisely, the mystery of Willy's one-eighty concerning the great Saint Deniston Soviet sellout, which on Poonie Baldwin's behalf he had so vigorously opposed, and the subsequent clarification of that one-eighty by Carla B Silver, who had informed us that a CIA/KGB infiltrator of the American Association of Eastern-Bloc Exiles and Defectors had given aspiring Congressman Baldwin's campaign treasurer to understand that the Agency had persuaded the Association that the patriotic thing for the Association to do was to cease its lobbying against the Soviet Union's dealings with The Deniston School for Girls, never mind why.

But before *that,* inexorable Kate explained, according to Carla B Silver, Doug Townshend had recruited my sister-in-law, Molly Barnes Sherritt, to save her husband from the snares of the KGB by standing firm against him in favor of the Russian deal. Molly is also a Deniston trustee, see. So when that KGB girl and that CIA/KGB Eastern-bloc–defector infiltrator persuaded Willy to do a one-eighty, they probably saved his marriage. Another count against secret agents, in our opinion.

It was then Leah Talbott's turn to marvel Get us *out* of here! and Frank's to shake his handsome head.

Said P Not yet. *He* then proposed, on the basis of no real evidence whatever, that unless life is as impenetrable by art as is the KGB by the CIA, that Eastern-Bloc Exiles and Defectors Association CIA contact who assisted Willy's one-eighty will have been Carla B Silver's Rumanian barkeep, Lascar Woiwod. All the rules of Dramaturgy for Minor Characters demand it. Then the Company paid him off, and he drank too much Premiat Cabernet Sauvignon under the full moon, and his werewolfly aspect got hold of him, and he laid lecherous hands upon Lee's sister a-scrubbing mussels in Carla's Cavern's kitchen.

Said Lee I could throttle the bastard. Poor Mimsi! But his name isn't Woiwod.

Woiwod is his wolf-name, Peter spun on. The other one's his human cover.

Frank Talbott said Lupescu. He worked for Rick now and then before he worked for Carla. You may be right. Anyhow, it's a damned shame. Carla liked him; we liked him.

Ma warned us he was an ass-patter, Leah explained to Katherine, but supposedly that was just Transylvanian high spirits. I hope he gets herpes.

Kate assured her that he very well might, if he beds the bargirl who baited her brother. Shall we all up anchor and head for Bora Bora, while there's still time?

Franklin Key Talbott said Not yet. Now I have to tell you about

KEPONE AND *KEPONE,*

the former trademarked by Allied Chemical and the latter almost copyrighted by me. The story leads back to your brother again, Kath, I'm afraid.

Talk about dwarves on the narrative back, said Lee. One more reason for our getaway cruise.

The afternoon advanced; the light breeze flagged; but *Story* and *Reprise* were not about to go their separate ways. On with the story, the Sherritt-Sagamores bid the Silver-Talbotts, and, spelling each other at the helm of it for the next hour, what that couple told this couple was this:

These waters upon which we yarn and float, reader, are our birthwaters: Katherine's, Peter's, Franklin's, America's—Leah's, too, though she came to know them somewhat later than we others did. We are morally obliged therefore to despise the directors of the Allied Chemical Corporation and its relevant subsidiaries, among a lengthy list of others, responsible for knowingly and intentionally polluting, despoiling, and otherwise contributing to our Chesapeake's ruin in the interest of higher profit. . . .

Cautioned Kate We mustn't be sanctimonious: *Story* doesn't have a holding tank. The Sagamore poop goes right into the Sagamore birthwaters. She raised her right hand. But we never park in marinas or pump the head in busy harbors. Lee said same with them.

Said Frank Anyhow, what he really wanted to write after his CIA exposé, as aforetold, was that novel called *Reprise;* but his appall at that pesticide-dumping case, and a professional pleasure in investigation, led him to imagine a successor to *KUBARK* called *Kepone.* There was no CIA connection, as far as he knew: The Agency's chief poison-supplier was not Allied but Dow Chemical, whose herbicide Dioxin (from the folks who brought you napalm) was the active agent in Agent Orange. But the further revelation in 1976 of the massive toxic dumping at Love Canal in western New York State—carefully concealed from its potential victims in a manner Frank knew well from numerous Agency and Pentagon experiments—suggested a book that would use the Kepone case as illustrative of the enormous general scandal of illegal toxic dumping.

It was a problem not then large in the public mind—but in itself too large by far, he soon discovered, to be dealt with effectively in a book. The Kepone story, on the other hand, monstrous as it was, seemed too particular for his purposes: one company, one river. How to bring the problem truly home to the average middle-class American, whose backyard is neither a fragile estuary nor a former military-industrial dumpsite?

Key Farm (one of whose chief crops, Frank Talbott declared, has been the keys to sundry puzzles and problems in his life and work) gave him the answer and his subject.

A year or so earlier, George Talbott had mentioned to his sons in passing that he had leased a few wooded acres of the property, complete with a gooseblind, a simple cabin, and a dirt access road, to a small New Jersey firm interested in using it as a hunting retreat for its executives. Such arrangements are common among Eastern Shore farmers. The lease fee offered was unusually high, but Judge Talbott had shrugged his shoulders; everybody knows that Delawarians, Pennsylvanians, and New Jerseyites are made out of money.

What presently aroused his suspicions was the traffic to and from those woods: the occasional Jersey-plated Cadillac or Mercedes, yes, but locally licensed pickup trucks, too, small closed six-wheelers, once even what looked like a septic-tank-pump-out rig, unmarked. Well, live and let live was George Talbott's philosophy. The rental property was a back corner of Key Farm, its access road not readily visible from the house. The small New Jersey firm had asked for and received his permission to renovate the cabin somewhat, at the firm's expense, into a proper little cottage; no doubt the vehicular traffic had to do with that renovation. But next they offered him a startling sum for year-round use of the premises: Some of their people wanted to fish and crab as well as shoot Canada geese. And could they fence off the woodlot with chain-link fencing, for general security and privacy?

George conferred with his sons and said no to both requests. The officials of the small New Jersey firm were unhappy: Look what they had invested already in the place! But they had not been asked to do so; the property was not theirs; when Franklin and Leah Talbott were in summer residence, they sometimes put friends up in that cabin; even Frederick Mansfield Talbott and Carla B Silver used it on occasion. So: No. The small New Jersey firm did not renew the lease; it seemed Key Farm had got a spiffy guest cottage for free.

But in 1977, a distinguished fellow Wye islander, former U.S. Interior Secretary John Trippe—

We know John Trippe! cried Katherine Sherritt. I know you do, said Franklin Talbott.

—had called upon his near-neighbor with alarming news. Among Mr. Trippe's several business interests in his retirement from public life was a firm called Environmental Research Corporation, which contracted with Maryland's Department of Natural Resources and the U.S. Environmental Protection Agency to detect and clean up "spot" pollution in the Chesapeake estuarine system. ERC had cause to believe, John Trippe reported, that that small New Jersey firm (with the innocuous name of Jersey General Hauling) was an arm of a *larger* New Jersey firm in the refuse-disposal business; that the parent firm had created Jersey General Hauling to transport and covertly dispose of particularly noxious industrial wastes. To do so legally is expensive; Jersey General Hauling disposed of a certain amount of its cargo legally, for appearances' sake, but its profit came from other methods, principally the "minidump": an out-of-the-way spot where a certain quantity of dangerous material could be covertly buried, spread, drained off, or otherwise surreptitiously gotten rid of over a relatively brief period, literally covered up, and abandoned. One of Trippe's own woodland holdings, in particular its duck pond, had been thus abused under false pretenses, and ERC was fairly certain that Key Farm had been as well.

Investigation proved him right. We remembered the case: Owing to the pristine character of Wye Island, in the heart of the Eastern Shore's Gold Coast—also to the irony of the former interior secretary's innocent involvement and of Key Farm's connection with Francis Scott Key—it had gotten brief national and considerable local media attention. A surprising quantity of carcinogenic PCBs (polychlorinated biphenyls, from the oil used to cool certain electrical transformers) had been dumped right into a drainage ditch leading to the river itself; drums of modestly radioactive waste material had been buried in the excavation for an extension to the little cabin, and considerably more in the excavation for its improved septic system. That system itself had been supplied with auxiliary solid-waste tanks, leach fields, and dry wells for the purpose of draining toxic matter into the ground—and similar small dumps were subsequently found elsewhere on the peninsula by Environmental Research Corporation, particularly in the large woodlots and remote marshes of the lower Shore. The term *minidump* entered the ecological vocabulary, and Frank Talbott had the subject he was looking for, for the book he would write if he didn't decide to try a novel instead.

As for the Key Farm minidump, it and the one on John Trippe's property proved so particularly toxic, and their cleanup so problematical, that Trippe's ERC formed a subsidiary called Natural Recycling Research to investigate ways of containing and detoxifying such minidumps without expensively wrecking and restoring the landscape. Government funding was secured through the ex-secretary's connections, and both Trippe and George Talbott sold their affected acreage to NRR for the worthy experiment. The little company hired additional specialists in chemical detoxification, built a discreet metal work-building on each of the two properties, and fenced off the areas after all, to protect the unwary from what lay under the ground or in process of experimental neutralization in the buildings.

The NRR staff became a chief source of technical information for Frank Talbott's *Kepone* project, which he carried forward through 1978. With their aid and much legwork of his own, he began to piece together a dismaying picture, not of isolated large-scale insults to the environment like the poisoned James River and Love Canal, but of hundreds and thousands of minidumps in the Middle Atlantic states. Industries uninterested in disposing of their dangerous waste material contracted legally with firms like Jersey General Hauling (whose directors were themselves presently hauled into the state and federal courts) to relieve them of that chore. JGH's parent company was alleged to be Mafia-controlled, an offshoot of the mob's general involvement in refuse dumping in the Garden State; its teamsters' directive was to lose as much as possible of their freight in transit, to "divert" a great deal more, and to deliver the remainder to legal (and expensive) dumping sites. "Losing in transit" meant literally leaking and dumping the poisons along rural roadsides and drainage ditches; "diversion" meant more elaborate repackaging of the contents into smaller, innocuous-looking drums and dumping them cheaply in public disposal areas or offshore from small leased barges—or burying them in minidumps.

Frank Talbott had felt on uncomfortably familiar ground, especially when his investigations led him to the mafiosi, with their alternate bribing and bullying of truckdrivers, disposal-site superintendents, barge captains. We were reminded of Doug Townshend's comparison of the criminal and the political undergrounds, and their not infrequent dealings with each other. In this instance, the industrial corporations were like the executive branch of the federal government; JGH's parent company was in effect their covert-operations division; Jersey General Hauling was like the proprietary airlines and other dummy companies to whom the CIA farms out its dirty work; and the estate caretakers, rural trash collectors, excavation contractors, and off-season watermen who often did the final dumping were like the hitmen and other cut-outs employed ad hoc by those dummy companies.

Caretakers? Off-season watermen?

Frank Talbott would get to that. We should understand that the more his *Kepone* researches (as he still called them) came to resemble his *KUBARK* researches, the more his feelings about the project were divided. Here was a book he knew he could write and which his citizenly conscience, as well as literary ambition, bid him pursue. But his probing was a little dangerous, and bid to become more so as he pressed on; after *KUBARK,* he had promised both himself and Leah not to expose himself to further such risk. And his real literary ambition lay elsewhere.

Early in 1979, an occasion presented itself to set aside *Kepone* for *Reprise.* The breakup of Jersey General Hauling broke also, at least for a while, the link between Mafia-influenced waste contractors and the Delmarva minidumps whose detection and cleanup had been the chief business of Natural Recycling Research, Inc. Restless John Trippe therefore sold NRR to another company and turned his attention to Eastern Shore grainland speculation, establishing with several cronies a firm called—

Breadbasket! Katherine cheered. Let's hear it for Breadbasket Inc.!

Home turf, Frank Talbott acknowledged—though he had not known at the time that the Henry Sherritt who organized Breadbasket Incorporated was the writer Peter Sagamore's father-in-law. In any case, the new management of Natural Recycling Research redirected the firm's energies toward the ecologically sensitive but potentially beneficial and lucrative project of using activated sludge from municipal waste-treatment facilities for agricultural fertilization. Its minidump activity they scheduled for phase-out, though NRR maintained its Wye Island monitoring station. It was a good time for Franklin Key Talbott to redirect his own activities.

And that he did, especially when his brother's disappearance from *Reprise* in late March, into the mouth of the Wye River, reprised John Arthur Paisley's from *Brillig* off Hoopers Island Light the previous September. The blue cutter went ashore almost within sight of Key Farm; the body must have been carried out into the wider and deeper waters of Eastern Bay, for it was never found: a most unusual though not unprecedented circumstance among Chesapeake drownings.

The Talbotts divided that sore spring between Key Farm and Baltimore. They consoled George Talbott, Carla B Silver, and each other; they chased down, in vain, all possible clues to Rick Talbott's demise, while still pressing reluctant State Department people to keep open the inquiry into Short Jon Silver's disappearance in Chile two years earlier. Addressing the question of their personal future, they decided upon a sabbatical from responsibility: the extended cruise aboard *Reprise* that they had half planned for years but never quite got around to. Frank set aside *Kepone* and began making notes toward a novel.

At least he set aside his more extended investigations: no more expeditions to New Jersey and New York and the D.C. offices of the Environmental Protection Agency. But an NRR department chief whom he had come to know remarked to him in April that while her minidump-detection staff had been halved by the new management's venture into sludge-recycling research, there was alarming evidence that the dumping itself had been vigorously resumed. With fewer people on the lookout, her office was nevertheless turning up danger signs *everywhere,* faster than her processing crew could stay abreast of them. It looked to her as if the link broken by the exposure of Jersey General Hauling had been reestablished by someone with much more local knowledge than the original leasers of Judge Talbott's and John Trippe's gooseblinds. The Key Farm operation, she informed Frank, was now no more than a passive monitoring station and a depot for materials in process of detoxification elsewhere. She thought she might look around for a different job.

The place looked little changed from the summer before: a brown metal prefabricated building on a concrete slab, fortunately screened by white oaks, ashes, river birches. Padlocked olive metal cabinets on small concrete pads presumably housed the monitoring devices. The rust-stained loading dock was lined with black fifty-five-gallon drums in wooden cradles, under the girders of a loading hoist. The chain-link fence was now grown with and disguised by wild honeysuckle and Virginia creeper, the No Trespassing sign on its gate perforated by bullet holes like all such signs in rural America. Back to *Reprise* and *Reprise:* both the boat and the novel had to be gotten ready for the voyage ahead.

But George Talbott had complained that traffic in and out of the place these days reminded him of Jersey General Hauling's goose-hunting department. Trucks came and went even at night—checking those instruments, George supposed—and now that he'd sold that part of the property, he couldn't prevent them. All the same, Wye Island was zoned strictly agricultural and (just barely) residential; a variance had been granted John Trippe's NRR solely for ecological research and cleanup. The judge wondered whether the new management mightn't be using the shed as a storehouse in its sludge-recycling operation, which, while essentially of a research nature, had a commercial aspect too, and would thus be pressing if not quite overstepping the limits of its zoning variance.

Good old Wye Island, sighed Peter Sagamore yesterday. Down in waterlogged Hoopers Island, where he comes from, every waterman's backyard is residential, agricultural, and light-commercial at the same time: A man takes his ease among his half-acre of Big Boy tomato vines while repairing his trotlines and his crab pots.

Out of professional habit, Frank Talbott that June did a bit of monitoring of his own. Without telling Lee—

Uh-oh, said Katherine Sheritt, yesterday.

Yes. That habit has a long half-life, and is as contagious as herpes simplex. Without telling Lee, not to worry her, he kept a mild surreptitious eye on the comings and goings from that sheet-metal building. In three days he saw as many vehicles: an unmarked half-ton pickup driven by an elderly black man whom he recognized as the rural private trash collector whose clients included Key Farm; a midsize tank truck marked "MT"; a smallish six-wheel closed-body truck marked "Easton Air Freight." The dusty pickup was accompanied by a shiny Mercedes driven by a white man; it arrived with three fifty-five-gallon drums in a wooden cradle, which the driver exchanged for three others from the loading dock. The white man, well dressed, assisted the black man with the hoist. The tank truck connected its large-diameter hose to a pipe cap on one side of the building: its pumps pumped for a quarter-hour—in or out?—and the truck left, its driver padlocking the gate behind him. The closed-body vehicle drove up one night at eleven, but by no means secretively; the driver, with a companion, unlocked the large loading doors of the building, turned on the lights, backed the truck inside, closed the doors, and left at midnight.

This is traffic? had wondered Frank Talbott. Well, yes, for a virtually abandoned building on busyless Wye Island. And none of the visitors seemed interested in those little freestanding olive-painted instrument boxes. Summoning his long-unused "tradecraft," Frank had one night scaled the chain-link fence and, seeing no sign of burglar alarms, let himself into the building through a side door locked only with a push-button door lock, easily picked without damage. The air inside smelled damp and oily. His flashlight showed more rows of metal drums, stacked vertically along one wall and horizontally along the other, together with an overhead chain hoist like the one outside. In the rear of the building, opposite the loading doors, were two long tanks from which pipes ran out through the walls, down through the concrete floor, and up through the ceiling, replete with valves and electric pumps. There were overhead fluorescent fixtures, gray switchboxes, several empty cardboard barrels and corrugated cartons. No desks, chairs, tables, file cabinets, phones. Frank's tradecraft did not extend to the picking of the padlocks on the instrument boxes outside.

With the Key Farm telephone he was more successful. All the while scolding himself for not mentioning this little adventure to Lee (and for not working on his novel instead of mucking around in activated sludge), he quickly learned that "MT" stood for Marshyhope Transfer, a small hauling and vehicle-leasing company down in Dorchester County. Its modest fleet included, besides several trucks, one air boat, the sort used in shallow marshy waterways, and one "buy boat," a small freighter like those to which oystermen sell their catches. The company's principal customer was Natural Recycling Research, for whom (said the genial fellow on the phone) they provided the air boat for tracking down illegal dumping in the Dorchester marshes and their other vehicles for hauling this and that from here to there.

Settle down, children, said Katherine Sherritt, yesterday.

So also did Easton Air Freight, a two-man company whose total hardware was one vintage DC-3, one helicopter, and one biplane for spraying pesticides. The first two, sometimes even the third, were frequently hired by NRR for aerial spotting of minidumps.

Back to *Reprise*: a novel about a former CIA case officer who etc. But it turned out that Frank had gone to high school with one of the pilot-owners of Easton Air Freight; in renewing their acquaintance by telephone, he happened to learn that both EAF and Natural Recycling Research were in fact owned by a local odds-and-ends conglomerate called Sherbald Enterprises, Inc.—

Oy gevalt und veh is mir, groaned Katherine Sherritt, yesterday. Lee Talbott said Me too. But did he tell me? No.

—with offices in the village of Queenstown, right over there. Did Sherbald Enterprises own Marshyhope Transfer as well? It did. And who owned Sherbald Enterprises? Their telephone receptionist would not say, but John Trippe would: The "Sher" in Sherbald was his Breadbasket partner Henry Sherritt's eldest son; the "bald" was ex-Congressman Porter Baldwin, Jr. Both sons' fathers, in John Trippe's opinion and phrasing, were as fine a gentleman as you'd ever want to meet; but he wouldn't give you fi' cents for either of the boys.

Neither would I, said Katherine Sherritt, yesterday. May we get out of here right now?

We could take up the slack on the anchor rode, declared Franklin Key Talbott, for all that remained to be told just then in Queenstown Creek was that this was the first time he'd heard the name Willy Sherritt. Also, that while he was a touch surprised to find ex-Congressman Baldwin involved with NRR—until his defeat in '76, he'd been the consistent enemy of federal regulatory agencies like the EPA—still, a profit was a profit; howevermuch it seemed a contradiction of values, the venture could scarcely be called a contradiction of interests. John Trippe declared he wouldn't trust the bugger with a ten-foot pole; he had demanded a cashier's check for the sale of NRR to Sherbald Enterprises. But NRR's new activated-sludge operation did not surprise him, for both Will Sherritt and Poonie Baldwin were just as full of you-know-what as they could stick.

SHIT APPROACHES FAN.

Mm hm. And that was that, friends, expositionwise, both in Queenstown Creek yesterday and at Key Farm late last spring. Time for *Reprise* to set out for southern waters; for Frank Talbott to set aside *Kepone* for *Reprise,* and *Reprise* in turn, eventually, for *SEX EDUCATION: Play.* Time for *Reprise* and *Story* to make their way yesterday, as we had by then agreed, from Queenstown Creek over to Kent Narrows and down to Key Farm, where the Sagamores would meet Judge George Talbott and go on with their story. Were our new friends sure we wouldn't be underfoot? Much as there was yet to get said (and now it was *Story*'s turn), Lee and Frank were after all completing a twelve-month voyage and must have one million things to do.

As we had seen, Lee Talbott said, she and Frank were in no great rush to declare this voyage ended, pressing as were the decisions to be made ashore. We were welcome to tie up with them at the Key Farm dock until we felt like moving on.

Therefore we said so long to the seven white swans and single Canada goose, tied *Story* behind *Reprise* (There's a switch, said Peter Sagamore) and the two dinghies behind *Story,* and motored down *à quatre* in the cutter's cockpit through the calm mid-afternoon. Once our caravan cleared the Kent Narrows Bridge and was aimed due south toward the Wye, Frank Talbott said So: That was where things stood, *Kepone*wise, last June. No reason at all, beyond professional suspiciousness, for him to imagine anything amiss about Natural Recycling Research. Okay, the name buzzes; but no more so than John Trippe's Environmental Research Corporation, which was one hundred percent legit. George Talbott's trash man had acknowledged to Frank that he hauled and dumped trash for Mister Sherritt both "reg'lar" and "extry," as he did for Judge Talbott and anybody else along his route; trash removal was his line of work. He no more cared what was in those drums and cartons than he cared what was in Frank's father's garbage.

So that *was* Willy, Peter said. On that loading dock, with Lester Treadway. Ice-blue Mercedes, right?

Kath declared gloomily It's like Willy to help old Lester with the hoist.

And so Frank had put by the *Kepone* project right about then and set to work on the *Reprise* novel en route down the ICW, as aforetold; and in Scarborough, Tobago, he had dumped that novel; and en route home he had scribbled Acts One and Two of *SEX EDUCATION: Play;* and latterly he had been pitched for Operation BONAPARTE and had learned from Carla B Silver about the Willy Sherritt/Porter Baldwin, Jr., involvement in *that.* But so what, after all? Frank had not one shred of hard evidence, and only one shred of soft, that Sherbald Enterprises was involved in anything improper at all. The direct application of activated sludge to agricultural acreage, for example, has its vigorous proponents among the ecologically knowledgeable; there are established experimental programs in its use not only at a number of agricultural colleges but in several rural Maryland counties. Reviewing last week in Carla's Cavern what he knew about Doomsday Factors and minidumps, Frank had felt like one of those KH11 reconnaissance satellites: sharp-eyed, much-seeing, but stupid. Something was missing from the picture; BONAPARTE and NRR (or, as one might say, *KUBARK* and *Kepone*) were like, oh, two locked caskets, each of which perhaps contained the key to the other. All they had in common was ruddy, ubiquitous Will Sherritt.

Katherine covered her face with her hands. Peter patted her shoulder and asked Frank Talbott what was that shred of soft evidence he'd mentioned.

Old Lascar Lupescu there, without knowing it, gave it to me, Franklin Key Talbott quietly replied. In my last conversation with him before Lee and I left Fells Point to go back to *Reprise* and sail over here, Lascar happened to mention that that BONAPARTE fellow he'd pointed out to me the night before gets his money from New Jersey, quote unquote. I was supposed to know what that meant. It turns out that a friend of Lascar's in the Baltimore mob had complained of his New Jersey colleagues' muscling in on the Maryland waste-dumping racket; he and his outfit had kept them out of the city so far, but thanks to that fellow sitting right over there, the Jersey crowd had the whole Eastern Shore in their pocket. I'm sorry, Katherine.

Her face still covered, K only shakes her head.

There was the key he'd needed, Frank Talbott told us finally. But before he could turn it, the shit had hit the family fan—abortionwise, confessionwise, musewise—and he had dumped those orange flare canisters and most of his literary aspirations over the side. Then *Story* and *Reprise* had crossed wakes in Queenstown Creek, and here we were.

And there we were, reader, yesterday, and pretty silent for the next half-hour. Anon we reached the lovely Wye. Lee pointed out grimly, as we turned upriver, the shoal below Bennett Point, near Black Can 3, where *Reprise* had been found aground last year sans the Prince of Darkness; more spiritedly, as we approached the fork, the spot where her Sunfish had capsized in '73 and Uncle Franklin had come to her and Marian's rescue. We sighed together at new construction in evidence since either of us had last been there; no season went by without more woods cleared, more waterfront houses built, more docks run out—in these instances, mainly tasteful half-million-dollar items with hundred-thousand-dollar yachts moored in front, but where would all these wealthy new sailors sail to? Who, other than they, would not rather have the woods that used to stand here? And who could keep his/her mind upon such trifles in the face of what we had just learned?

We separated our train of boats and docked. Judge George Talbott, white-shirted, necktied, balder than his son and lean instead of stocky, made his smiling way down the lawn to greet us as we tied up; alerted from Baltimore, he had expected the homecoming for some days, but was wise enough in the ways of wind and tide, evidently of his son, perhaps also of the world, to wait without impatience. We Sagamores shook his hand and busied ourselves aboard *Story,* to stay out of the family's way and begin the labor of assimilating what we'd heard.

Unnecessary, the former, and the latter impracticable. The deaf have small conversation. Father and son and daughter-in-law embraced and shouted close-range greetings. How was their boat ride? Fine! How're things at Key Farm? Can't complain; storm last weekend took out two trees. And to Lee: Are you prettier than ever, honey, or am I just a year older? The Henry Sherritt relation was established: as fine a gentleman as etc. Judge George had even heard of Capn Fritz Sagamore, and looked at *Story* with an appreciative eye. Though he was no sailor, he could see the design's tidewater lineage. He reckoned with a wink at Katherine that we'd be in the market for something bigger next season. Next *weekend!* Kate called into his starboard ear.

Et cetera, all which we could no more than half attend. Though George Talbott insisted that unannounced guests were no problem for Cecilia Skinner, we four insisted in our turn on making dinner aboard for five and eating with him at the picnic table down by the pier. But first, glad to stretch our legs, we took a short tour of the immediate grounds. Blam's two victims—aged, half-dead white oaks—were pointed out where they lay, partly dismembered by Lew Skinner's chainsaw. Back yonder was Natural Recycling Research, Inc.: more traffic than ever, George declared, and no wonder: Minidumps were popping up all over the Shore like pimples on a high school boy. We did not pursue the subject, then.

Okay: We saw what Lee meant about the house. We wouldn't choose it either, though it is a far cry from Sagamore Flats, which Peter doesn't much mind having grown up in.

Over cold rosé and lamb kabobs rolled in cumin, as Judge Talbott inevitably tuned out, we finished the day's exposition by retailing to Frank and Lee what we knew about Sherbald Enterprises and Breadbasket Inc.: a tale briefly told, as we knew very little. That on behalf of Sherbald (which we'd understood to be no more than a holding company for his real estate and other interests), Willy Sherritt lately made a bid to join his father's grainland investment program, not only for simple business reasons and, as he declared, to keep the A-rabs off the Shore, but in hope of using some portion of the tilled acreage for Natural Recycling Research's Frankly Controversial sludge-spreading experiments, and certain of the marginal woodland for other Carefully Monitored Research in the natural detoxification and recycling of dangerous wastes. That John Trippe, still rankled by Poonie Baldwin's betrayal, as he saw it, of their past political connection, was steadfastly opposed to the proposal, about which Henry Sherritt had mixed feelings and Jack Bass, the other major Breadbasket partner, was shrug-shouldered. As of Blam, last Sunday, that was where things stood.

So what in the world were we four to do with what we now suspected? Nothing, we agreed, till we had slept on it.

Speaking of Jack Bass and telephones: After cleanup, Kath went to the house to call Irma, report our position, and discuss the logistics of an obstetrical checkup sometime the next day: Dr. Jack's place is one long day's sail from here, but only half an hour away by car. Frank Talbott and his father lingered at table to speak briefly and amiably, at high volume, of Key Farm matters. Peter, his imagination fast-idling, swam from the dock in the velvety late-evening light. One would have expected a flurry of unloading and unpacking from *Reprise,* but Leah Talbott changed into her famous maroon bikini and joined him in the river. Too much to be done for her to know where to start, she said; that, too, she would think about in the morning. Franklin likewise; he presently joined the swimmers. Kate came down in the last light with Lew and Cecilia Skinner, whom she had of course befriended in short order up in the house: a weathered white couple in their late sixties. No fair, she complained, and changed outfits and came into the water too. Moon and Sixpence, cued by their parents, cavorted in *their* birthwaters, too, like a brace of young otters. The older trio lit cigarettes and regarded us benignly from the dock, as if we were teen instead of middle-agers. Giddy. Carefree.

Would *you* swim in that water, Judge? Lew Skinner loudly asked George Talbott, who replied that he sure used to, once upon a time. Dag if *he* would, Lew Skinner chuckled, nowadays. But he never was one for swimming.

You didn't hear that, Katherine said to Alert and Locate. But they did.

HITS

So we agree over Monday breakfast, there on the grandmotherly porch of Key Farm, that it is a whole new ball game. Our civic responsibility, clearly, is to blow the whistle on Operation BONAPARTE and to assist Frank Talbott quietly in the further investigation of Natural Recycling Research, Inc., should he decide to resume his *Kepone* project. Katherine, for one, declares her conviction that not even Willy would sink so low as to—but her declaration rings hollow in her own ears. Is she against the Soviet–Deniston deal, then, Peter asks her, now that we know it's tainted by the CIA and the KGB? Suppose the little transaction were quashed: Won't the two superpowers go on with their wretched deadly jockeying and counterjockeying on 1001 other grounds and fronts? Of course they will; all the same, the whistle must be blown and the proposal reconsidered in that light: the light of the . . . sound of our blown whistle.

Lee Talbott in shorts and T-shirt wonders what, after all, blowing the whistle consists of, exactly. Katherine can report to the Deniston board of trustees Carla B Silver's BONAPARTE story, and Lee's mother will no doubt readily pop over from Fells Point to confirm it; Molly Sherritt can affirm or deny her connection; Willy likewise. The CIA will routinely disavow any involvement or interest in the transaction; the KGB will say nothing. What the school trustees will have is a far-fetched–sounding, secondhand report from an admittedly maverick member of the board, substantiated by a more or less eccentric-looking witness. No doubt Frank's testimony will help, if he is prepared to make public the Agency's pitch; but it is to be remembered that the Agency can go to some lengths, overtly and covertly, to discredit Frank's testimony, as they did upon the publication of

KUBARK: Lee imagines that the average Deniston trustee is a patriotic conservative inclined to believe the U.S. Central Intelligence Agency more . than its detractors.

You said it, K acknowledges. But the board's feelings have been mixed about the deal from the beginning. The combined testimony of Carla B Silver and Frank Talbott and Molly Barnes Sherritt—if Molly can be persuaded to speak out—ought surely to carry *some* weight. Anyhow, our objective is by no means necessarily to quash the sale, which Kath herself supported until our lay day in Annapolis; it is simply to let all hands, including Willy, know what's going on.

Peter raises the question whether there is danger involved. He detects in Lee's tone some concern for Frank on that score. Frank Talbott thinks not; as he does not clearly know the stakes of the game, however, he cannot be certain. Messing with New Jersey minidumpers, he imagines, is probably riskier than messing with Langley, Virginia, on this matter.

That unsavory business—NRR's New Jersey connection—Kate is inclined to go home and raise a shout about at once, whereas Peter thinks it ought to be investigated from outside the family. We presently agree to poke no farther into it, from our side of the table, at least until Sturm und Drang have been safely delivered: not a very long moratorium.

On the obstetrical front, we Sagamores agree, the prudent and responsible course is now to stay put at Nopoint Point until Birthday. Indeed, the sensible thing would be to leave *Story* where it lies—in nobody's way, the Talbotts reassure us—and ride on back together to the First Guest Cottage with Irma after K's obstetrical inspection (all set for 2:00 P.M. today at Jack Bass's old stand in Easton), and move the boat down a week or so after Birthday, when K & Co. are home from hospital.

That idea once broached, no other course seems reasonable. We have more than once shaken our heads at what we've been up to this past week: our voyage into the teeth of common sense. Now that we're ashore—we mean aShore, unlike our Annapolis lay day—our folly retrospectively astonishes us. Irma is bringing Chip along; we had considered briefly his and Pete's daysailing the boat home and rejoining Kate tomorrow evening. But even that separation now seems reckless to us: What if K commenced her labor and P were unable to get to her side for six hours? Time to pack it in.

Accordingly, breakfast done, we all return to the pier. The Talbotts desultorily set about the large work of cleaning out and cleaning up their vessel; the Sagamores (after morning exercises) the smaller labor of deprovisioning ours and offloading what doesn't stay aboard.

At least Katherine sets about these chores, and Frank Talbott. Peter sits at *Story*'s dinette table for a few minutes to log mnemonic cues to yesterday's huge exposition: *Kepone, KUBARK, Jersey General Hauling, Natural Recycling Research*. His sitting there, and the pleasurable kinetics of pen upon paper, put him in mind of yesterday morning in Queenstown Creek and that earlier forenoon in Annapolis, spent making long notes in those agreeable circumstances. Be with you directly, he says to Kate, and makes a sketch of the cove he imagines that ovum and her spermatozoon friend swimming into in Act Three of Frank Talbott's unfinished play. In Peter's fancy it is now conflated with Salthouse Cove, except that it needs a sandspit at its entrance and a high bank behind its bit of beach, with cattails and spartina to one side and, let's see, a couple of abandoned apple trees up on that bank.

Offshore from it should be a stone jetty or breakwater . . . with a flashing light. Be right there, hon. A message light. Now it occurs to him, irrelevantly, that if Scheherazade on the 1001st night presented the king with three sons—"one walking, one crawling, one suckling," as the text specifies—then her pregnancies must have been spaced about equally through the 1001 nights. 3 × 266 = 798 from 1001 leaves 203 nights before after and between; he wonders whether the number 1001 has a gynecological-obstetrical aspect in addition to its other aspects, and, if so, what the significance of that aspect might be. Arab storytellers, he understands, tend not to wear their formal cunning on the sleeves of their djellabas. Why does Scheherazade stop telling stories exactly when she does, rather than sooner or later? Is there a story in that question?

Peter, Katherine carefully complains.

Be right with you. But though the day bids to stoke up, just now a pleasant light air is moving down the companionway. Leah Talbott, splashing off the pier, calls merrily to Franklin I'm never coming ashore! Come on in here and Merge!

Don Quixote is the least nautical of novels, but Peter remembers that somewhere in it the hero comes across an empty rowboat and immediately presumes, on chivalric precedent, that it is there to fetch him magically to his next adventure. He boards it (With Sancho? Where is the horse Rocinante?), casts himself off but does not deign to pick up the oars, and is carried downstream to . . . the fulling mills, as P recalls. And there is a later interlude aboard a proper ship—¿No?—in harbor at Barcelona, involving Moorish pirates and their Christian captives. Where is Rocinante then?

Have you packed *Don Quixote* yet? he asks Katherine. I've got an idea for a story.

Pregnant as I am, says K—less carefully this time—I've packed *everything,* single fucking handed. But you've got to do the lifting, and it's time to do it.

Says Peter I'll lift, I'll lift. But he's leafing back through *Story*'s log. He has a problem, only now coming clear. Good Franklin Talbott, he understands, is not an artist. Though the chap might well write a creditable novel one of these days, or a nonfiction book that will do more practical good than all of Peter's stories put together, the muse is simply not in him; he has not *vocation.* Whereas vocation is about all Peter Sagamore has, lately, even under that freight of back-dwelling dwarves. Well, it's not quite all, but . . . *He is not ready to get off the boat,* he realizes, and helplessly tells Kate. Cannot in fact bring himself to haul himself ashore just yet.

So don't, our woman says, trying unhappily to be cheerful. We'll come back and sleep aboard tonight, and you and Chip sail down tomorrow. We've pushed our luck this far; she guesses we can risk a day's separation.

But we have already scratched that idea, at breakfast. P will not hazard being absent on labor day; we must stay together, or within very close reach. At the risk of offending good Hank and Irma, however, he cannot go back to that state of affairs in the First Guest Cottage until his own labor not only commences, but gets vigorously under way. He has just now realized that, to his own surprise; dismay, even.

Katherine sits. What exactly does he mean, "within very close reach"? Uneasy Peter twirls his pen; tells her (pleasantly, but never mind that) that if she really feels it's best for her to be at Nopoint Point starting today, then unquestionably that's where she should be. He'll stay on here at the Key Farm dock and get down to work, a phone call and a half-hour ride from the hospital. He simply cannot yet close our circle, he realizes, as the Talbotts have closed theirs.

Hurt Kate says softly I can't believe what I'm hearing. Then she gets a touch annoyed. We have humored that tight-ass muse of his for an entire *week;* at some expense of her comfort and even some risk of safe delivery. This piss-ant cruise was her idea: She set him the task he set her to set, for both our sakes but mainly for his. By sheer good luck, we have come this far unscathed, and the risk looks to have paid off: That logbook there is as loaded as she is. Any minute now, Ding and Ling will push the old button—she almost thinks she just now felt them do it—and this low-level suspense will be done with. In two weeks we'll be back in our Stony Run apartment if we want to be; never mind Mom's fancy nursery. Meanwhile, Bobby Henry can tow this boat around *today,* for God's sake, behind his johnboat, and we can live aboard in Sherritt Cove, if Peter insists, or just behind Shorter Point if he wants to be out of Hank's and Irma's view. Could anybody be readier to go the extra kilometer than she is?

Wait: She's not done yet. Katherine respects her husband's deep feeling that while something positive has happened musewise in the past few days, something else has yet to happen: as if . . . as if the sex has taken place, ovulation and ejaculation have occurred in the right firing order, sperm and ovum are separately launched and under way on collision course, but *their* connection hasn't yet been made. All the same, she can't help feeling that now it's time *he* gave something up for *her,* for the kids, for us— above and beyond what we've each gladly given up already in the way of individual liberty for the sake of capital-*U* Us. God damn it, Peter!

Miserable P agrees, agrees—but he can't go back to Nopoint Point.

K turns up the volume: Read *won't!*

Okay: won't. No, damn it: *can't,* any more than Kate can run four miles just now. Why not come back to *Story* after her checkup?

Kath's eyes are wet, but she's really pissed. She calls out the companionway to Lee Talbott, toweling off on the dock, Do you hear what this man's saying? Nope. K climbs out to declare to the whole Eastern Shore of Maryland that if we happened to be up in the Chester River, all we'd be doing today is sailing this damn boat around, whither the wind listeth, not writing the Great American Nothing. But now the sonofabitch won't even ride down to Easton with her for her checkup! Protests mortified Peter That's not true, Kath. Something got going yesterday, and he needs to follow it up: He'll be ready to ride down to Easton after lunch. But he's coming back here afterward, and he wishes she'd come too, but he has no right to insist. . . .

See? See?

The Talbotts don't want to be involved in this—Neither do we!—but with due respect to Peter—and they *do* respect him, duly and more than duly—they tisk their tongues. Of course, says Frank, his dad's old Dodge is ours to use—or Peter's to use, if Peter's really going to stay here—when it's not already in use. They sold Frank's Volvo before they left for the Caribbean, and Lee's Toyota is decommissioned in the garage. And we really are not in the way here, both or either of us. . . .

But it's clear they agree with Katherine that our man is being awfully unreasonable. They excuse themselves as soon as they decently can. K won't stay on the boat another minute; goes with them, up to the house, leaving Peter wretched among our duffel. The thing he has ever hoped wouldn't happen is suddenly happening: his having to choose between Katherine and what we're calling his muse, and though it's clear to him he'll lose either way, he seems stubbornly to be choosing the latter. Does he follow his aggrieved mate up to the farmhouse? He does not. Appalled at his own ability to *write,* of all things, in such sore circumstances, he makes furious notes till near noon upon the subject of *Rocinante IV,* about which who can care at a time like this?

Lunch: P takes two apples from *Story*'s icebox up to the house, but Cecilia Skinner has already dealt Katherine in on a cold-cut platter. Lee Talbott has fetched her father-in-law off on some errand in the Dodge; Frank has eaten already and is out back recommissioning the Toyota so there'll be two cars available, just in case. Kath has said her good-byes to them all. Cecilia Skinner stays out of our way, but she agrees P's being a hard-nosed bastard, K lets him know, and won't eat his apple.

That's not true, Pete complains. I can't defend or explain myself, except to say I feel very strongly—Oh shit: I hate this whole scene.

Change it.

No. Stay here.

Damn it! Damn it. She won't say Damn *him,* or even Damn his damn writing: Look how reasonable she's being, even in her distress! Nor will she forbid him to ride with her down to Easton, though she certainly feels like doing so. She's going to be reasonable all the way, damn her.

And even her reasonableness she doesn't make a great fake show of, to get at him, does she. When the saddle-brown Cadillac noses up at half past one and all hands have kissed one another hello, she explains to Irma and Chip with minimum fuss and no histrionics that a serious disagreement has unfortunately come up between us, namely et cetera, which we're sorry to visit upon them, but et cetera, so let's get on down to Easton, and we'll be cheerful some other time. She puts it all so fairly that there is nothing for Peter to add. Dolled-up Irm doesn't get to meet a single solitary Talbott. Shocked Andrew clearly has as hard a time believing what he's hearing as we do. I'm not going to say a thing, says sensible Irma. Andy doesn't either. Off we go, on a mighty quiet ride, all windows down because Kate hates air-conditioning and the afternoon is, as it bade to be, steamy and still. She sits up front with her mother; the two males share the backseat, each unhappier-looking than the other.

As partner emeritus of Easton Medical Associates, P.A., Jack Bass covers for his ob/gyn colleagues when they're ill or on vacation. K goes into his office-du-jour to get inspected; her retinue sit in the empty waiting room, not reading magazines. Chip picks at his knee. Don't pick at your knee, Chip, Irma instructs him. I've got stuff to tell you, he tells Peter when his mother goes to use the toilet; not now, though. Peter nods: What his mother-in-law must be thinking, he hates to think.

Jack Bass summons Peter into his office to say All's well, though Kate's wet eyes belie him. We're dilated about a centimeter already. Two strong heartbeats. Tomorrow, next week; no telling. Peter nods.

Says Katherine They're both scared shitless, and it's all your fault. Peter wonders What happened to Reasonable?

You did well to call an end to your sailing cruise, Jack Bass says. Katydid's healthy as a horse, but why take chances?

Peter nods.

Doctor Jack looks from mother to father over his half-glasses. Now: Let's go back to Hank's and Irma's and sit tight till we're home free.

P looks at his wife but asks Jack Bass Will it be any riskier if we stay aboard the boat tied up at Wye Island with a car right there?

Unsurprised Jack Bass replies at once Ten minutes riskier. That's insignificant. The point is that if Katie wanted to spend the next few days in the hospital *parking* lot, you ought to go along with her. As it is, she's asking nothing unreasonable, and her psychological comfort is important.

P nods: Of course it is. All the same, he happens to know that unfortunately he needs to work on board for a while, mornings, and to keep away from Nopoint Point, for a while. Stay with me, he says to Katherine.

She shuts her running eyes and pummels her belly with both fists, pummel pummel pummel, to make it happen now, and gets noisy when Peter grabs her forearms. He can do what he damn pleases; she is *not* going back to Wye Island; she's going home.

No less dismayed than she, Peter Sagamore digs in his heels. We can't believe this, but it's happening. No pussyfooting around now, Jack Bass and Irma Sherritt make their positions clear: They've never heard of such unreasonableness as this of his—clearly it isn't callousness, or maybe it is—at such a time, on the part of a sensible man who supposedly cares about his wife. All tears in the waiting room, Kate whams her gut again, with just her left fist this time, as she's wiping her eyes with the other, and not as hard. Alarmed Chip springs to stop her. Terrified Diastole cries We'd better do it *now*, Sis, clutching his head and her foot. She's trembling too, but says Not yet, Di, if you can *possibly* hold out.

Slightly calmer Katherine says now to her mother Let's go. That slightly calmer upsets Peter no less than the child abuse: She isn't coming with him! And—unbelievable!—he's not going with her, not even so that Bobby Henry or whoever can drive him back to Key Farm. Certainly he won't let Irm haul back there first to drop him off before she ferries Katherine home. Anyhow, Irm doesn't offer to do so; her mind is decidedly elsewhere. Very well, damn it: He'll stick out his thumb for the first time since Europe seventeen years ago.

Splitting! Sort of. And now, of all times! Nobody is on Peter's side, not even Peter—at whose core, however, perversely pulses that cold quasar. Only Chip, who so adores his sister, nevertheless wants his brother-in-law not to be alone in this sticky wicket. He gets his mother's hesitant permission, and Katherine's less hesitant, and ultimately Peter's most hesitant, to go with him back to Wye Island. No hitching, though, says thick-voiced Peter. We'll call a cab.

Splitting! Cheeks wet, he makes at least to kiss his wet-cheeked, scared-eyed wife good-bye. Nothing doing.

Jack Bass complains I can't believe this. You two, of all people. You and me both, marvels Irma; really, Peter. Give us a ring when you come to your senses.

Out on shady Aurora Street, as the two women climb into the car and the three men do not—as the Coupe DeVille *drives off,* carrying Mother from Father, us from each other—panicked Tuck makes a dive for the button; Nip catches his arm just in time and hugs him fast, bawling with him.

Thus salted are the tideless waters of Amnion.

Splitting!

And not much later,

SPLAT.

Stunned Peter sits in *Story*'s cockpit with worried Chip, who despite this alarming turn of events has tentatively told what he had to tell. The late-afternoon air is still and wet, half hazy but unoppressive. Busy with their

business, the Talbotts come and go from *Reprise,* but except for the odd
nod or little wave of hand, leave *Story*'s crew alone.

They have spoken little, Peter Sagamore and his young brother-in-law,
but are as comfortable with each other as the situation permits. Peter would
rather be alone, if he's not to be with Katherine; on the other hand, he is
touched by the boy's gesture (which he understands better now), and never
displeased to have him aboard. Green-eyed Chip has predicted an early
embassy from his father, who with the excuse of bringing his son a few
overnight necessaries will try to mediate P and K's differences. Peter doubts
that. About six, however, as the two eat beans and franks off paper plates
like a brace of Boy Scouts, the brown Coupe DeVille slides into the drive
and up to the farmhouse, and Chip, who has been checking out a green
heron with the binoculars, reports untriumphantly that it's Hank, all right.
Solo. With, sure enough, Chip's ten-speed on a bike rack on the trunk.
Does Pete want to bet on the backpack?

Henry Sherritt takes his time: socializes with Judge Talbott, who has
come off the porch to say hello; shakes hands with Franklin and Leah,
ditto. Andrew and Peter see declined the Talbotts' invitation to come
inside; they see *Story* pointed out, where Hank will have espied it already;
they see him wave away Frank's offer to unrack the bicycle.

He won't unrack it yet, Chip predicts from the binoculars, because we
might have decided to sail the boat home after all. Or I might not want it
here, for some reason. Come on, Dad: backpack.

What? But as Peter watches, Henry Sherritt reaches into the car and
fetches out a small russet nylon backpack; says something genial to the
Talbotts; closes the car door; heads down toward the dock. Yay, Dad! his
son murmurs, and dutifully goes to meet his father halfway. Mindful of
his distance from his own father, Peter regards for the thousandth time,
with ungrudging envy, the easy goodwill between Henry and Andrew Sherritt, who talk quietly down the rest of the path.

No Sherritt ever steps uninvited from dock to gunwale. P nods hello and
says quickly Come aboard, Hank. Chip guesses he'll stroll up and get his
bike, okay? Not just yet, his father bids. He glances appreciatively at
Reprise, steps lightly aboard *Story,* and shakes Peter's hand.

Serious-looking cutter, he declares. Henry's wearing a lime-green Izod
shirt, cream chinos printed with tiny mallards, light suede deck shoes, socks
to match the shirt. I'd miss the big genny, though.

He accepts a paper cupful of the Almadén red in progress; sits; says So.
Inspects and sips the wine. Pete will not prompt. Chip stands uncomfortably
by, backpack in hand. Peter senses him anticipating dialogue-lines as he
had anticipated his father's movements: a new development in the boy.

Holding the wine cup in both hands and leaning forward to rest his
forearms on his thighs, Henry Sherritt observes that a man ought to be
with his wife at this important time in both their lives.

Jesus, Hank; we all know that.

Well, then. He winces quickly. I can't help being offended by your attitude toward Nopoint Point and our hospitality, Pete.

Bear with me. It must be clear that I'm closer to you-all than I ever was to my own parents.

Henry considers; says he doesn't pretend to understand art and artists, but to him this looks a lot like a damn *whim*.

Unruffled Peter guesses it does. But since you know me pretty well and have some idea what Kath and I feel for each other, it must not be what it looks like.

Henry guesses he accepts that. Sips his wine. Hopes this sort of thing doesn't happen often between us.

First time. Will you call, Hank, if her water breaks or her labor starts? Telephone Key Farm, and I'll be there in no time.

Henry strokes his nose and turns his handsome gray eyes Peterward. Katydid made me promise not to. You want the news, you're supposed to come on back with me. She's crying, Pete, and she's pounding on her stomach. Peter leans his face into one hand; exhales through his lips. Marvels Henry Sherritt So those little stories you make up are really that important.

P nods. Says he's sorry. Says No, he's not sorry: They're that important. But he's sorry anyhow. He wishes Katherine were here.

Henry considers, then declares he'll tell Kate he can't keep that promise. But you'll have to make this up to her some way, Peter, if you can.

I know; I know.

Chip asks from the dock, where he's still standing by with his backpack,

MAY ANDREW "CHIP" SHERRITT PLEASE SAY SOMETHING?

Surprised Henry says Sure. Sure, says interested Peter.

Okay. Andrew "Chip" Sherritt guesses he cares about his sister about as much as anybody can care about anybody, but if you ask him, Kate's being a little dorky on this matter. She has made a crisis where none was called for. Peter's love for her and his regard for the Sherritts are beyond question. To Chip it is evident that our sailing trip in the first place, and Peter's current declared need to stay aboard *Story* and away from where he set out, are anything but whims; rather, they are deeply felt if only half-comprehended artistic . . . uh, pressures in a mature professional approaching the peak of his career, okay? Pressures which, to P's own great distress, set his responsibilities as an artist against his feelings as a loving husband and first-time expectant father. But all that happened only because Katherine forced the issue! Is Peter demanding that they go to sea or otherwise put themselves out of touch and reach? Key Farm is ten minutes farther from the hospital than Nopoint Point is; Doctor Jack himself has called the difference insignificant. A car can be parked right here at the dock, ready to go. There could even be a cordless telephone aboard, though one isn't really necessary. No: The whole problem, in Chip's opinion, is that his sister wants Peter to love her *more* than he loves his writing, and to prove his love at his work's expense at a critical time in his career, when she knows very well that the last thing he wants is any conflict between those absolute commitments. That's exactly why he put off getting married in the first place, right? What Kath ought to be doing is everything possible to avoid such a conflict, the way she normally does and Peter too; but the tail end of her pregnancy has crashed her system. If you want to know Chip's opinion, she ought to be *ready* to go to sea, if her husband felt that going to sea just now was necessary to his survival as an artist. At least she ought to be right here at Key Farm, where Chip's nieces and nephews would be ninety-nine percent as safe as they are on Nopoint Point. At very *very* least, if she feels she has to be home, she ought to be there cheerfully and ungrudgingly, instead of carrying on like a hysterical high school girl. That's Chip's opinion.

It is, huh. Henry Sherritt nods. Glass of wine, son?

No thanks, Dad.

Well, Hank's unconvinced, but he sees Chip's point. Maybe Katydid *is* being just a wee bit stubborn. There is a streak of that in the family, from Henry's mother's side: Willy has it the most, but they've all got a touch of it. He'll let Kath and Irma know there's another side to the story.

But Peter bids him hold on and speaks seriously to Chip. He has a strong *feeling,* he declares, that he shouldn't take *Story* back home until he has found and fitted a piece of the puzzle that he wasn't particularly aware he'd been assembling. That feeling, however, is no more than a feeling— albeit one based upon considerable professional experience. It is perfectly possible that he's mistaken: that he won't find the missing piece; that there is none, or that it's right back at Nopoint Point, all covered with bluebird shit, excuse him: the missing Maeterlinck, excuse him. The point is, he may very well be raising a fuss about nothing, whereas Katherine *knows* that anytime now she'll go into labor for the first time in her life, at age thirty-nine, to deliver twins at least: as consequential a business as we'll ever do in our lives together or separately. It may indeed be that she'd be as safe and almost as comfortable here as at Nopoint Point; but inasmuch as she is the one who must do the delivering, if she feels easier in her mind at Nopoint Point, who has the right to challenge that feeling? What are a few stories, or one novel more or less, compared to two live Sherritt-Sagamores and their mother? Why should his strong inclination, which amounts to no more than a bet, take precedence over hers? Why shouldn't he be with her one hundred percent of the way, while she's putting her body on the line to have our children?

Hank claps him on the shoulder. Let's get going.

Says Peter Nope. He simply doesn't want Chip to lose sight of the other side of the coin. Kath and he are both being unreasonable, but neither is wrong, and neither wants what's happening to happen. How's the Bread-basket business?

Henry Sherritt will be damned if he has ever in his life heard such ping-pong soap-operatics as he has heard this afternoon: everybody talking themselves out of their own positions as fast as the other one talks them back in, and vice versa. Give him another splash of that jug wine: The Sherritts hold considerable stock in National Distillers, who own Almadén Vineyards. Come on aboard this boat, Chipperino.

The fact is, Breadbasketwise—and what relief, for Henry, to talk plain old *business*—John Trippe is out and Willy's in.

Oh?

John has simply been being unreasonable: If he wants no truck with Sherbald Enterprises, that's one thing; but for him to reject on principle any dealings with Willy at all, Henry takes as an affront to himself. Himself as a businessman, mind, not as a friend; he and John are still bridge and tennis partners, but not business partners.

Muses Peter with a glance at Chip So Willy's in, but not Sherbald Enterprises.

Chip examines his russet backpack without opening it, no doubt predicting its contents.

Well, says Henry, it was only John who objected to Sherbald. Jack Bass and I don't have any trouble there, and their grubstake was a helluva lot higher than Willy's alone. We're not talking marriage, Pete; we're talking business.

But Peter remarks with raised eyebrow that that means that Poonie Baldwin is in the Breadbasket too. He can imagine what Katherine will have to say about that.

Henry points out dryly that Peebie's not a partner; Peebie's Mercantile Bank blind trust is. And Katydid doesn't advise her father on business matters any more than he advises her on library science. Anyhow, he adds with his brilliant smile, Sherbald Inc. has made him an offer he can't refuse: Somehow, they got hold of that old granary up on the Sassafras River that he's been trying in vain to buy for the past ten years, and Willy's signing it over to Breadbasket to sweeten the deal. When John Trippe said no to *that,* Breadbasket said good-bye to John Trippe. Truth is, Henry's pleased to have his elder son in on the business; there is more to Willy Sherritt than his sister cares to acknowledge. Once our children are safely delivered, the Bassess and the Sherritts mean to sail up in *Katydid IV* and have a look at Breadbasket's new showpiece from the water; Henry hopes that Willy and Molly will come along.

As for himself, he'll be getting on home now. He has done his best. PJs and toothbrush in the backpack, Chipper, and a change of socks and underwear. Come get your bike if you want it. We two are being a pair of obstinate characters, if Peter wants Hank's opinion; but true love, he guesses, seldom sails the rhumb line. He remembers once years ago when he and Irm—but he winks and says Never mind. He will phone Judge Talbott when the action starts, promise or no promise.

WHAT WE'VE DONE IS WHAT WE'LL DO.

The prevailing Chesapeake summer southerly is back in business now, refreshing the P.M. A fine evening for a sail, Henry Sherritt observes, were it not for et cetera. The three walk through the bugless air back up the lawn, Chip to fetch his bicycle (once it's reestablished that Peter will not undock without Katherine), Peter to telephone Nopoint Point. He leaves the Sherritts and Talbotts chatting good nights around the Coupe DeVille and follows Frank's directions to a phone. Irma answers. Peter tells her that Hank is en route home; apologizes again for what must appear to be both ingratitude and stiff-neckery but isn't; asks to speak to his wife.

I doubt she'll talk to you, Irma reports, not incordially, then says across a space Will you talk to your husband? She says she doesn't have a husband, Peter.

P asks his mother-in-law please to aim the instrument at her daughter and shouts Kath, you get on this telephone now! I want to apologize!

You do not, K calls back. Neither do I.

You do, too! Peter calls. I ought to be there, and I'm sorry! But I'm not coming!

Then what's to talk about? She's on the phone now, to everyone's relief, and thick of voice. What are we doing and why are we doing it, honey?

That's what her husband would like to know. Also our children. Literally and Figuratively.

Maybe she's being headstrong and willful, Kath grants; if so, she's sorry. But she's the pregnant one, and she's staying here. What's happening to us?

What's happening indeed. Maybe our story needed a crisis, but our life didn't.

One of the kids won't stop crying, K reports. The boy, I think.

He probably has a headache. A splitting headache. Get it?

You're making it worse.

Let me talk to him.

Our man quietly does: assures Tippecanoe and Tyler too that their parents' love for each other and for them is not in question in the current squally weather. The boat of our marriage, he declares, may pitch and roll a bit, but our ground tackle is secure. We'll ride it out, little Tip; never you fear. His sister tattles that her brother keeps going for the button, but she won't let him push it; and what a crybaby! Her father advises Be gentle, honey: little boys are emotionally younger than little girls. But *keep his hand off that button.* Don't worry, Dad: But you'd better cheer Mom up so she'll stop pounding us, or we'll be Black and Blue, ha ha.

Marvels Peter to his wife That's some daughter you've got in there. She's twenty-three already.

Kate sniffles We talk a lot; you know me and women. I may call her May.

I might call her Might. Might and Main.

Come here to me.

Come here to me.

K thinks about it. The nothing at her center feels just now even larger than the people in her belly. I guess not, hon. Go write your stories.

Does Peter tell her to go have her babies? They're *our* stories.

Says sad Kate They were going to be.

They still are! And I've got Chip stuff to tell you; he's in on the plot.

K doesn't reply.

But the phone won't do. I *hate* talking to you on the telephone, Katherine.

K doesn't reply, says K; she says further K doesn't *need* to reply. What we've done, she echoes, is what we'll do.

DAY 9: WYE I.

Chip in on the plot? Why not?

Neither Katherine nor Peter quite forgot, in our late long conversations with the Talbotts concerning BONAPARTE and Breadbasket and *KUBARK* and *KEPONE*, Andrew Sherritt's anxious telephone-voice in the Annapolis Hilton on the morning of the Brandy roses. It even occurred to Peter Sagamore later, up in Queenstown Creek—call it masculine intuition; call it a dramaturgical mind-set—that the boy might possibly have overheard some quarrel at Nopoint Point between Willy and Molly Sherritt concerning the Deniston School/Soviet Embassy transaction and Molly's courtship by the CIA. But in the Whole New Ball Game of Days 7 and 8, our concern for the boy got sidetracked. Then yesterday, as long-faced Chip and shaken Peter waited for the taxi to fetch them from Jack Bass's office out to Key Farm, the boy said again I've got stuff to say, Pete, but this is a dorky time to say it. When you're ready, okay?

Say, say, said Peter. And so there on the sidewalk, then in the cab, later in *Story*'s cockpit over canned beans and franks prior to Henry Sherritt's gray-eyed visit—all tentatively, the lad realizing that he faced a problem in dramatical priorities but understanding as well that dramatical priorities are not always the highest priorities—

WHAT CHIP SHERRITT TOLD PETER SAGAMORE YESTERDAY

was effectively this:

That he had pretty well decided to be an artist instead of a computer theorist when he grew up, though probably not a writer, though probably some other kind of a storyteller, not a painter or a sculptor or an architect or a musician. Maybe he would get into movies or theater, but not as an actor; he didn't care to be any kind of performer. Maybe he'd write for serious public television.

Well now, Chip, drowning Peter managed to say.

That while working with Peter two Sundays ago on Buck Travers's No-point Point audiovisual intercom installation, and studying the system manual later that evening aboard *Katydid IV* in Dun Cove with his parents, he'd observed that a fairly simple bit of recircuiting could defeat its privacy-protection feature so that the audio output of any "remote" station could be monitored from the "master" station in his father's study, even when the remote station was switched from Monitor to Off. As scrupulous as he is curious, Chip had experimentally diddled only the unit in his own bedroom; once he'd proved his reasoning correct by hearing his stereo play Scarlatti over the intercom master downstairs, he restored the wiring to normal and went back to reading Joseph Conrad and improving his tennis backhand against his father.

A few days later, however, Olive Treadway had asked him to have a look at her CB transceiver before she took it into Easton for repair: Several times her husband had tried to call her from one of his trucks and had failed, though he could raise his other drivers without difficulty. Examining *its* owner's manual with the other still fresh in his mind, Chip believed he saw a way to interface the systems so that the intercom remote station in Olive's room (where she sometimes spends nights when her services are needed late, and to which she retreats from time to time during breaks in her day) could monitor her CB radio in the kitchen. Should her husband call during one of her breaks, Olive could return to the kitchen and call him back.

The procedure for *this* experiment (in which Chip's interest far exceeded Olive's) involved, for reasons not followable by Peter while worrying about the crisis in his marriage, the defeat of the no-snoop switch on the *kitchen* intercom station—and thus Chip happened to overhear a conversation not meant for Sherritt ears though conducted in the Sherritt kitchen, beside the principal Sherritt fridge.

Doctor Jack Bass and ex–Interior Secretary John Trippe had repaired from the Sherritt tennis court to the nearest patio for refreshment after a set of doubles, while Henry warmed down by hitting a few more with his eldest son: the second or third time since Day Zero that that foursome had combined business and pleasure. Finding neither Irma nor Olive about, they had moved from patio to kitchen, which Chip had just vacated, to help themselves and fix drinks for the other players as well. In his father's study, Chip was surprised to hear John Trippe's voice declare Nothing against queers, Jack. They disgust me, but that's their business. And it don't matter (Chip's reproduction of the ex-secretary's speech) that I wouldn't trust Baldwin with a ten-foot pole, 'cause we're not about to trust the sumbitch with anything. But you let Sherbald into Breadbasket, you're setting the fox to mind the henhouse.

Chuckling Jack Bass had replied You burnt your mouth on the soup, John; now you blow on the milk. See any lime there? Willy's talking big bucks, Doctor Jack had said further, and it means a lot to Hank to have his son on board.

Had grumbled John Trippe The bucks had better be big, 'cause they got to buy me out if they're buying Sherbald in. And then God help the Eastern Shore of Maryland.

Under Peter's questioning, Chip acknowledged that actual dialogue, eavesdropped upon or not, is seldom if ever so convenient and efficient as the above—whose substance, however, he stood by. At this point the men had moved out of intelligible range, except that Chip thought he heard Mister Trippe say something like You take your Bobby Henry and your Lester Treadway, and you multiply by a couple thousand. . . . But that ominous arithmetic meant nothing to Andrew Sherritt; embarrassed to have eavesdropped even unintentionally, he had as soon as possible thereafter restored the intercom to normal and contented himself with repairing Olive's CB, which needed only a replacement jack at the transceiver end of the antenna lead. As he understood already from outspoken Katherine that neither their brother nor her first husband was held in universally high esteem, Chip was not especially dismayed to hear John Trippe's sentiments. But he was and remains troubled by the insinuating references to Bobby Henry and Lester Treadway—is *insinuating* the right word?

It is, Chipper.

—and he wonders how it is that letting Sherbald Enterprises buy into Breadbasket Incorporated would be like setting the fox to mind the henhouse. Moreover, it bothers him to know stuff that his father and mother apparently do not, and it makes him sick to his stomach to think that his brother is, evidently, an *evil man.* He'd hardly thought before about what *evil* means, really. Do evil people think of themselves as evil? Do they, you know, *enjoy* eviling? He'd wondered about that the night Willy did his famous one-eighty on the Deniston School business and got all syrupy with Molly; everybody but her saw how phony the whole thing was. But this new trouble between Katherine and Peter makes his stomach sicker yet. Between the two, a boy can hardly hack his beans and franks. He has decided to remain a bachelor when he grows up: a bachelor writer, as Peter used to be, but in some other medium than prose fiction. He allows, however, for his being currently a twelve-year-old virgin, who may change his mind.

Henry Sherritt's arrival at this point, yesterday, rescued pained Peter from the obligation of speaking to the general phenomenon of evil while adding the franks of Chip's information to the beans of what he knew already, in the . . . oh, in the saucepan of his professional problems, bubbling on the fire of his personal ones, fuck it. Hank now gone (yesterday), phone call to Nopoint Point completed, sun down on the daytime portion of Monday, 23 June 1980, the pair redescended Key Farm's dew-soaked lawn, lump-throated P recollecting the evening-wet swards between the

Sherritts' Main House and First Guest Cottage, where swallows swoop like Stealth aircraft around the statues Cathode and Anode, Less and More. Now that Chip's bike was parked on the farmhouse porch, anytime the boy felt like returning home, he could be there in under an hour. But he was of no mind to do that, yet. Did Pete see what he meant about his hating to know things, at his age, that his father didn't?

Sure. But we really know nothing, Chipper, except that Mister Trippe is no fan of your brother's. Let's take a swim.

They did, off the pier, yesterday, under the Gouda-colored moon, among phosphorescing noctilucae and sea walnuts glowing yellow-pale and large as lemons, which is what Katherine calls them. Where was she? Peter as usual simply dropped his shorts and drawers on the pier-end and climbed in, cautioning Andrew (as we once again caution the reader) not to dive into water he can't see through, at least until it has been walked around in. He rather expected Chip as usual to change modestly into swimtrunks in *Story*'s cabin; was pleasantly surprised to see the boy follow his example, merely turning hind-to to shed his Izods and Nikes. Painfully our man missed his woman: What was she doing just then? Sitting glumly all by her lonesome (at her own insistence) in the gazebo on the pointless point of Nopoint Point, under the smoked-Edam moon; sipping more brandy-and-Kahlua than is good for little Beans and her sorrowing brother; staring out at the slack low tide in Goldsborough Creek; wishing she were swimming naked off *Story*'s transom with her best friend.

Kath and I believe that Willy's involved in some illegal waste-dumping, Peter told his young in-law, considering his words carefully as the pair paddled about. His Natural Recycling Research outfit and maybe Sherbald Enterprises too are doing stuff they shouldn't do. We hope not, but we think so, and there's more to it. What the connection is with Breadbasket Incorporated, exactly, and just where Bobby Henry and Lester Treadway fit in, we don't really know. But let's not forget the presumption of innocence, Chip. You know what that means, right?

Sure.

And it's not necessarily our place to try to prove your brother guilty.

The boy considered, swooshing his arms on the water-surface to make the noctilucae flash. It is, isn't it, if Willy's doing bad stuff to himself and the family and the environment?

Yeah, well. But your father is a smart man as well as an honorable one, Chip; nobody's likely to pull a fast one on him. And there are people looking into the case. If they find out anything real, the whistle'll get blown.

Do you-all know things about Willy that Dad doesn't know?

Maybe. Maybe not. We-all aren't together just now.

Now and then, here and there (Where are you, children?), Peter felt along his skin the tiny stings of the first small sea nettles in the Wye, not present the night before. The Choptank/Tred Avon, therefore, next river-system down, was by now unswimmable, as this would likely become within the week. If K and Alpha and Omega were afloat just then, which they weren't, they were in the Sherritt pool, which they weren't.

Uh-oh, Chip said, in the Wye, yesterday: We've got company. From the moonlit dock, Frank Talbott called May we join you fellows? We're bare-assed, Peter warned for Andrew's sake. Understanding Leah reassured them at once We're not, and promised not to peek; Hey, we want Katherine! Game Chipper called back So do we, and a quarter-hour later, when he was ready to climb out, simply announced I'm climbing out now, Lee, and climbed, and casually retrieved his clothes and strolled aboard *Story* to dry and dress. Good man, remarked pleased Leah. Pleased Peter reflected that Katherine would be pleased.

A PRETTY-GOOD CIA STORY

Says Kath via Chesapeake & Potomac from Nopoint Point next morning I *am* pleased. Chip's a mensch. Has he grown any pubic hair?

That's none of our business. How are By and Large these days? Up and Coming?

Seek and Ye Shall Find.

Ask and It Shall Be Given Ye. I'm asking you to come back here right now this morning, please?

No. How come you're calling? You're supposed to be working.

I'm going to work. I've run five miles and swum for fifteen minutes, and now I'm going to sit down in that Sagamore Twenty-five of ours and make notes for part one of a three-part story about Don Quixote's further adventures in the Cave of Montesinos. Did those children get their bedtime story last night?

Hah. Their mother got one-quarter-sozzled on brandy-Kahluas and gave us all hangovers this morning. That's what happens in broken homes. So what'd you-all do after you had your gorgeous swim amongst the sea lemons, which only you and I are supposed to swim naked amongst?

We told bedtime stories.

What was Lee wearing?

Nothing worth reporting. Chip had a nightcap with us in *Reprise*'s cockpit, and there was a mosquito or two but no Katherine. I'd already told Chip in a general way about our worries about Willy, after Chip had told me what I told you he told me. I told him that Frank was quietly looking into the NRR thing, and that we weren't particularly out to get Willy in trouble—

We aren't?

—just to blow the whistle on the poisoning of our birthwaters et cet before we all start shining in the dark. You should've seen those lemons. Lee kept her bathing suit on.

Okay.

They're working things out. They seem more worried about us than about them.

So am I. So is Lumière.

So is who?

Your bright little daughter. *Et Son aussi, sans doute,* but he's off crying his heart out in a corner and won't talk even to her. So what got said up there in *Reprise*'s male cockpit, with my cool kid brother and Lee with her clothes on and sexy Frank, while we're down here drowning our sorrows? Did you see that moon?

Not the same one you saw. It's a physical impossibility that the same moon could shine on the Tred Avon and the Wye when you're there and I'm here. Lee told us Frank's pretty-good CIA story.

How was it? Never mind. Okay, we're listening.

Once upon a time there was this erratic North African dictator, like Colonel Muammar el-Qaddafi. Probably it *was* Colonel Muammar el-Qaddafi, in wherever. Algeria?

Jesus, Peter.

Libya, Libya. So a team of Rick Talbott's P.O.D. types manages to penetrate the guy's regime under deep cover the way Israel's Mossad penetrated Idi Amin in Uganda, by leasing him a fancy private airplane through one of Mossad's proprietary companies. The company, I believe, was Zimex in Switzerland, and the airplane was a Grumman Gulfstream Two, although they also leased him a Boeing Seven Oh Seven, if I remember correctly. God bless details.

Peter.

I was looking at that moon and missing my family. For all I know, it was the Israelis who got to Qaddafi and us who got to Amin. Anyhow, the shtik was—

The shtik? You were looking at Lee Allan Silver Talbott, is what you were looking at.

The shtik was that the lease agreement called for the suppliers to provide pilots and flight crews for the airplane, and a certain number of those people were our Prince of Darkness people, and so the equipment was exquisitely bugged, and the quality of our information about some of the guy's plans and operations was unusually high. We were even able to thwart a couple of his hairier schemes, like buying bootleg nuclear weapons, without his ever knowing how we found out about them or how we messed them up.

Good for us. But.

Right. To maintain this unusually privileged intelligence, we have to maintain the dictator. So while this one P.O.D. team is bugging his Gulfstream Two, some of our other P.O.D.'s—P.'s O.D.?—are supplying him with stuff he needs for his terrorist operations. They even help him set up his own intelligence service. These were Company agents whose cover was that they were rogue agents, but who we believed or hoped weren't really or mainly rogue agents. It gets that tenuous. So we permit at least some of the guy's overseas operations to succeed at bloody cost, even though we know all about them in advance, and we don't interfere in his domestic nastiness at all. We not only countenance his suppression of his enemies but in a few cases assist it, because if he's overthrown, the new regime is going to be at least as anti-CIA as he is, and it will have to be penetrated from scratch, whereas we already have this character in our pocket without his knowing it. What's more, the operation is a very profitable one for several of our suppliers and agents, and a good career move for three or four of our people, and the quality of that information is really high: a case officer's dream.

So.

So the team's job becomes not to help undermine the dictator for the sake of a government better for the country's people or even better for our own government's interests, but just to acquire higher-and-higher–grade information about him. The crux comes when one of our key people over there gets wind of a truly serious plot to overthrow the sonofabitch. In order not to disrupt our lines of intelligence, he makes policy and sees to it the plot misfires.

I hate this part.

"Key People" is *my* term, mind you, not Lee's; I don't think Frank was directly involved. This particular key person knew his American history: He cited the precedent of George Washington's administration's secret dealings with an Algerian pasha whose pirates had hijacked a U.S. merchant ship off Tripoli and made slaves out of its crew. Washington ransomed the American sailors by presenting the Algerian pasha with a brand-new, fully-armed frigate, ideal for piracy. The case officer in that case happened to be the poet and diplomat Joel Barlow, author of *The Columbiad* and *The Hasty Pudding*. Nowadays our writers teach in our universities.

I *know* what our writers do nowadays. How does this pretty-good CIA story end?

This not-bad CIA story ends with the key case officer's rationalizing his exposure of the coup, all of whose participants are tortured and shot, by saying to Franklin Key Talbott Okay, so we gave the bloody bastard this one. But we can do him in anytime we want to. To which Franklin Key Talbott replies You're never going to want to.

Will you come home to me now, honey?

That isn't where you are. Please come hither.

No. What did Chip think of that pretty-good CIA story?

I suspect it gave him a little handle on the Problem of Evil. This morning he's helping Frank Talbott install a beeper on the delivery gate of Natural Recycling Research.

Dear God.

Perfectly safe and ninety-eight percent moral. Frank's out to improve the quality of his information on the minidump industry. What are *you* doing this morning?

I'm having babies without my husband's assistance and support. You?

I told you. I'm making up

PART ONE OF A POSSIBLE THREE-PART DON QUIXOTE STORY.

It's called quote Rocinante Two unquote.

The whole three-part story is called that?

No. If you need me, I'll be aboard *Story*.

That's right.

Huckleberry Findley on the Honga River; Odysseus Dmitrikákis on the Little Choptank; Captain Donald Quicksoat outside Fawcett's Marine Supply store in Annapolis Harbor—musing upon their splendid originals, Peter Sagamore remarks to *Story*'s log (not for the first time) that whereas the first of them lights out for the territory and the second escapes from time, noble Don Quixote, armored in his delusions, tilts with the real world around him. Though he most often ends up on his back, that armor remains unshaken even when the man himself is knocked breathless, and in time (i.e., in Part Two) it is reality that yields; that cooperates in the sustaining of his fiction. His own quixotic aspiration, P.S. notes not for the first time, has been to leave behind him some image as transcendent as his favorite four: Odysseus striving homeward, Scheherazade ayarning, D.Q. astride Rocinante and discoursing with Sancho Panza, Huck Finn rafting down the Big Muddy. His fortieth year near run, his narrative career half done, P. Sagamore finds himself neither famous nor unknown, unsure of his accomplishment but absolutely certain that nothing of his invention approaches that ideal. Dwarfed septuply into silence (he writes), I am a Quixote windmilled flat. Unhorsed early and sent home. Coomb'd. Crumpt.

Let Don Quixote rest in peace, Cervantes warns in his last chapter: Do not presume to resurrect or disinter him. But it is fact, not fiction, that *Story* overtook a few days back off the Thomas Point Light: *Rocinante IV*, her curious skipper and winking bow-eyes and provocative hailport, all as real as that Phaeacian 35 in Madison Bay. By what chart, P asks his logbook, does one sail from the Cave of Montesinos in central Spain to Carla's Cavern in Fells Point?

For there, surely, is where Capn Don's voyage begins: in that cave wherefrom the aging knight so laments his having been withdrawn; which in another sense he never leaves. "God forgive you, friends," he cries to Sancho and Sancho's cousin when he awakes; "you have snatched me from the most delightful vision that any human being has ever beheld!" Had they not hauled him up and waked him, Peter notes, he might have completed his adventures underground: some consummation, surely, involving capricious Dulcinea, to whom he has loaned the last of his money. His retrieval leaves that debt outstanding; it also leaves his enchanted self, the one in the vision he now recounts, back down there in the crystal palace of Montesinos.

Yes. The Don Quixote who ascends from the cavern after "three days" by his own reckoning (half an hour by Sancho's) and goes on to complete Cervantes's story, including the story of his interrupted sojourn in the cave—that Quixote is not the same who went down on a hundred-fathom line to that ledge, opening onto that golden meadow and transparent palace. While the real Don Quixote dreams on, bound by enchantment like Dulcinea and all that subterranean company, his reemergent self is "wakened," does this and that, suffers final disenchantment, dies a proper Spanish death at the novel's end—and therewith sets free his still-enchanted self to commence its voyage.

Voyage?

From a restless sleep like Durandarte's, the knight awakes and stirs. His half-century-old joints complain. God be praised! white-headed Montesinos cries: One *encantado* in the palace is enough.

How long has he slumbered? There is neither clock nor calendar where he is, yet time does not stand still. His nails and beard are longer; Montesinos reckons that the four *reales* his visitor bestowed upon Dulcinea through her serving-maid, if loaned out at five-percent simple interest per annum, would by now have earned half again the principal amount. But he has seen no sign of those frisky ladies since the loan was made; nor does he expect to, until they need to borrow more.

There is no more, says Don Quixote, carefully stretching his arms and legs. If there were, you may be certain I'd never lend it to Dulcinea del Toboso.

Montesinos once again praises God and declares this to be the first evidence he has seen that the enchanted can actually learn from experience, instead of merely aging. But Don Quixote goes on to make clear that his lady can no more borrow his money than she can borrow his heart: Both are hers outright, in fee simple.

At the word "heart," the knight Durandarte rolls over and groans. In the house of the hanged man, Montesinos warns Don Quixote, don't mention rope. The battlefield at Roncesvalles, where my cousin fell, was a noisy and fearful place, and I was a young soldier in those days, not a sage. How was I to know, when he bid me fetch his dying heart to the Lady Belerma, that he was speaking in figures?

This talk of hearts (and ropes) reminds Don Quixote not only that the Cave of Montesinos is in the heart of La Mancha, but that he himself is in the heart of Part Two of his own history, as he knows from having read Part One several chapters back; also that Sancho and his cousin and faithful Rocinante must be waiting for him at the mouth of the cave; at the bitter end of that coil of rope. He therefore bids good-bye to Montesinos and his odd household, leaves the crystal palace, and sets forth across the golden meadow, looking for the place where he first woke upon being lowered to the cave ledge. He wishes too late that he had marked the spot, taken bearings on the palace, or at least looked back from time to time as he first crossed the meadow. Nothing he sees now looks familiar: The erst-while-golden meadow is an ordinary field of gorse; the palace is already more translucent than transparent; presently it is opaque.

Where by his best guess ought to be a hundred-fathom line hanging from the sky, he finds instead a small winding creek, which he does not recall having seen before: the headwaters, he supposes, of the Guadiana River. He follows its meanders downstream for a kilometer; it widens from the size of a drainage ditch to that of a modest canal. No sign of the rope. Is he lost, he wonders? Or have Sancho and company long since hauled up their empty line like luckless fishermen, presumed him dead, and gone their ways? He is tempted to despair—but then, under a black willow tree around the next bend of the creek, he sees a battered, flat-bottomed skiff with its stern in the water and its stem nosed into a mud flat. It was once gaily painted in the style of Portuguese fishing boats, but the paint is chipped and flaked and faded except for the great eyes staring from the bow. Even before he makes out the name *Rocinante II* behind those eyes, he assumes the vessel to be there for his use. The absence of anchor, oars, mast, or sail confirms his assumption.

Picking up a dry stick from the creek bank to steady himself on the slippery flat, he unhesitatingly steps aboard and is astonished to find, on the stern-seat, two one-*real* coins: the only sign of human presence besides the aged skiff itself, whose frayed painter is coiled idly in the bow. For a moment he wonders whether they are, after all, enchanted interest on what he never meant to be a loan, or Dulcinea's shy repayment of half the principal. Then Montesino's words come back to him—that not even the enchanted are free from want—and he joyfully pockets the coins. He has not a *centavo* on his person; surely the two *reales,* like the skiff, are a sign and token from the Enchanter himself: not wicked Merlin, but (as he has already remarked aboveground to Sancho Panza) the all-seeing Moorish historian Cide Hamete Benengeli, author of *The Ingenious Gentleman Don Quixote of La Mancha.* The Moor has published Part One; Quixote himself, like all of Europe, has read it. He will now be in midst of setting down Part Two, whereof the knight's every present action is, as it were, a sentence.

Don Quixote strokes his beard. Don Quixote steadies himself with his stick. Don Quixote seats himself in the skiff's stern and waits to see what Don Quixote will do next. His aftward movement lifts the bow from the mud flat, and off he drifts in *Rocinante II:* now stern-first, now bow-first, now beamwise, but always downstream. So be it, he says contentedly to himself: Whither the current of the story fetches me, thither shall I go in this enchanted boat, with these enchanted two *reales.* A further happy thought occurs to him: He gave Dulcinea's serving-maid four *reales* because, though she had asked for six, four was all he possessed. Now he has the other two.

Author of my adventures! he cries: ¡Muchas gracias! not only for providing me with this splendid vessel and these twin coins, but for plotting my course through this episode! He stands unsteadily, the better to con the creekside for Dulcinea, and is pitched to his knees in the bilges when the skiff bumps a rock in the shallow stream. There he prudently remains, though his hose and doublet are soaked through, for the skiff is far from watertight. Your knight-errant, however powerful and benevolent his Enchanter, is more at ease on horseback than afloat. Even in the Cave of Montesinos, gravity is gravity; best to keep the center of it low.

But his stomach soon grows uneasy from the skiff's random spinning. Much as he trusts his author to navigate Rocinante II expeditiously to his next encounter, he discovers that the course thereto can be more comfortably negotiated with some assistance from himself. First he experiments with using the frayed painter as a halter, and learns that what steered the first Rocinante well enough is of no use whatever on the second. Further trial and error reveal, however, that dragging his walking-stick astern tends to keep the skiff's bow aimed downcurrent and to prevent its spinning in the eddies. He even contrives narrowly to avoid the next rock in his path by poking to starboard a bit with that same stick; the rock after that he dodges rather more adroitly.

After a few kilometers, he has the hang of it. Between maneuvers he bails the bilgewater with his barber-basin helmet. In the more placid stretches, he is able to enjoy the passing scenery and the bright sunshine—if that is the word for a clean light that seems to come from everywhere and nowhere, like the glow of lucid prose. Though his kneecaps in the leaky bilge complain, so exhilarating does he find adventuring by sea that he is not at all disappointed when by "sunset" he has seen neither Dulcinea nor any other human being, only the odd egret stalking minnows and the splash of startled fish. The creek has widened into a proper río, presumably the Guadiana. Ahead, the scrubby plain through which he has been winding gives way to low hills pleasingly greened by stands of almond, olive, oak. Without doubt he could put his life in his author's hands and float securely through the night. All the same, he dexterously steers Rocinante II ashore, makes fast her "halter" to the nearest tree-root sticking from the nearest bank, and beds down high and dry near that same tree, a wild olive. How can there be stars, he wonders, in a cave? Yet the sky is spangled from horizon to horizon, as if instead of mid-Spain he were in mid-ocean. The gentle motion of the skiff, which he can still feel in all his body, reinforces that illusion: an enchantment within an enchantment. Somewhere in Part One of Don Quixote, he remarked to Sancho Panza that the road is better than the inn. Can it be, he wonders now, that the river is better than the road? He falls asleep in pleased anticipation, not of overtaking Dulcinea del Toboso, but of voyaging all day tomorrow down the Guadiana.

Guilty Peter leaves off making narrative sentences. He has broken his pledge to us both, and in imaging Don Quixote he has forgotten Katherine Sherritt and Either/Or; also Chip, the Talbotts, minidumps, the Doomsday Factor. Stirred by the wake of a passing powerboat, *Story* tugs lightly at its lines; the Wye chortles along its hull. Quixote's dream, were our man to continue writing, would be of adventuring on in *Rocinante II,* no longer alone but with Sancho Panza, discoursing toward Portugal. He would awake next morning, startled to realize that it is not Dulcinea at all whom he needs to find, but indispensable Sancho. If he "owes" Dulcinea two more *reales,* what does he owe his faithful squire? The fact is, he does not know quite what he would do with Dulcinea should he find her, beyond pressing upon her those coins; he cannot imagine truly conversing with her, whereas he has a thousand things to say to Sancho. Dulcinea is for invoking and saluting; she is the inn at the end of the road. But for going down that road, or this or any river . . . give him Sancho Panza!

To find Sancho, however, he must find the rope that lowered him into this story, and to find that rope he must go back to the palace of Montesinos. Though Peter Sagamore makes no more sentences, he cannot resist sketching the rest of *"Rocinante II."* When Quixote goes to the skiff this morning, as if to confirm his new understanding he discovers not only two more *reales* on the stern-seat (discharging Dulcinea's debt to him, he is now pleased to believe, and his to her—as well as enabling him to repay what he borrowed from Sancho), but also a sturdy pair of oars, unnecessary for going on downstream, but essential for going up. So be it: All that day he alternately rows and tows *Rocinante II* upstream. Once he gets the knack of keeping his oars in their thole-posts, he becomes as adept at rowing— and at judging the stretches which must be waded through, his stick in one hand and the skiff's halter in the other—as yesterday he became at downstream steering.

But the river he retraces is not the river he came down. Its course is straighter and more swift, through wooded hills, under a cooler sky. As he ascends, the rapids become more numerous. The skiff is not only of no use against them; it is an ever-greater impediment to his progress. He stumbles, almost falls half a dozen times. In one rare rowable stretch, despite his new dexterity, an oar slips from its tholes; he pitches backward (that is to say, bowward) into the bilge, wrenching his spine and losing the oar. The other by itself is useless for upstream work; now it is pull, pull, pull, like Sancho his sometimes recalcitrant Dapple. Toward evening, all his muscles sore, he rounds one more slight and unfamiliar bend and is gratified to see ahead, not the crystal palace, but a small walled town on a low stony island in the river, which forks to encircle it: a miniature, low-profile Toledo, sidelit in the last of the sun. He decides to rest there for the night and tomorrow make inquiries after his squire, of whom the inhabitants may have heard if Hamete Benengeli's book is circulated here underground as it is throughout the rest of Europe. At very least he will learn where in Spain he himself is, what river he has ascended, and whether it leads out of the Cave of Montesinos. Surveying the moated town before him, he thinks wryly of Sancho's ambition one day to govern an island. He presses on, encouraged, reheartened, into the last obstacle between himself and the end of his day's work: a short stretch of rapids so swift and steep as to amount almost to a waterfall. As he picks his way through an agitated pass between two cottage-size boulders, *Rocinante*'s frayed halter parts. Quixote springs too late to catch hold of the stem; the skiff swirls away downstream, fetches up broadside against a rock, and swamps; it spins again and is pinned against another, only its stem and gunwales above water. Where its port bow scraped the first rock, the paint is gone; the eye there seems now to weep, or wink.

The knight scrambles three more steps downstream, loses his footing on the mossy pebbles, falls hard on his right side. His basin-helmet strikes with a clang the same stone that closed *Rocinante*'s portside eye. His last image, as the waters sweep over him, is neither of Dulcinea del Toboso nor of Sancho Panza: It is a sudden vision of the Moor in whom he has so misplaced his trust, now calmly inscribing—in beautiful, heartless Arabic—the sentence *Thus ends Part Two of* The Ingenious Gentleman Don Quixote of La Mancha.

And thus could end, notes Peter Sagamore, Part One of a possible three-part Don Quixote story, the general outlines of whose next installment, like a walled town rising from a river, one can already begin to discern.

WHAT PREGNANT-FANCIED, GUILTY-CONSCIENCED PETER SAGAMORE
DID WITH THE REST OF DAY 9

Damn near nothing.

Ate light lunch with Chip and the Talbotts up on the Key Farm farmhouse porch: a lunch toward which he was permitted to contribute only the last of the fresh fruit we laid in in Annapolis: half a dozen ripe pears. He's going to have to borrow Chip's bike or the Talbotts' car and go buy provisions if he really means to stonewall it there on Wye Island, as he guesses he does.

Listened to Chip's sober-but-excited account of what he and Franklin Key Talbott accomplished that morning while Peter worked Captain Donald Quicksoat down and upstream and Leah Allan Silver Talbott made notes for the lecture course on Postmodern American Fiction she means to offer at that northern branch campus of the University of Virginia come September. She has accepted that tenured associate professorship, and the decision has energized her. It is not a terrific job, she and Peter agree, but in a tight market it will do; anyhow she hopes to publish her way out of it in two or three years. She appears relieved, even happy, to have taken the step, Peter will report tonight to Katherine, and to let the marital chips fall where they may.

Frank Talbott, for his part, is pleased both by his wife's decision and by his own remounting of the *Kepone* project, now tentatively titled *Minidumps* and subtitled *The Doomsday Factor in Your Own Backyard*. Besides installing that primitive monitoring device next door—no more than a remote signal that the NRR gate has been opened, so that he can keep a log of what comes and goes—he has confirmed by telephone that the state health department's hazardous-waste inspection division can manage no more than thirty percent of the monthly routine inspections required by Maryland law for the 2200 licensed by-producers of hazardous waste material in the Old Line State: a circumstance well-known to most of those businesses and industries. A committee of the state legislature, he has learned further, is drafting a bill to encourage the treating and recycling of hazardous wastes instead of their burial. Among those openly lobbying for that bill is Willy Sherritt. Frank has not quite decided yet where he will spend the next three seasons, or what exactly he'll be doing for money if his and Peter's agent can't swing a substantial advance on *Minidumps*. The campus lecture-circuit, maybe, though he's not yet well-known enough to command good fees. But he sees no reason why he can't do his homework in northern Virginia about as well as at Key Farm, if he digs up enough stuff this summer. The NRR beeper, needless to say, is the most preliminary of research aids, soon to be followed by fancier hardware: just a little tradecraft exercise, really, like Peter's filling his fountain pen or sharpening his pencil.

If you were here, sad Katherine says, I'd sharpen your pencil.

Peter observes that the Talbotts' problems seem to be bringing them together after all, though the big one is still up in the air. They seem okay. Says Kath They *are* okay, and wonders whether our problem isn't maybe that we haven't had enough problems. We hit one wretched little rock in the *río* of our life, and the skiff of our marriage goes the way of *Rocinante Dos*.

You don't believe that.

Of course I don't. But here we are: Here and There. What else did you do.

Swam. We've got baby nettles here now.

Preteen ones here. What else.

Drove into Easton with Chipper in the Talbotts' car and reprovisioned *Story* with enough for the two of us to last until Hide and Seek touch base. Safe and Sound. I mean the two of *us*.

What else.

Called you from the Acme Market in Easton to make sure you weren't in labor with Fourth and Goal. I talked to Olive Treadway instead. You were out.

Yeah.

Read some more in Part Two of *Don Quixote* and got to thinking about

Carla B Silver as a postmenopausal Scheherazade. Wrote a letter to Mother that she won't be able to read. Cooked out with the Talbotts: zucchini and cherry tomatoes *en brochette* and soyed chicken breasts and Sebastiani Eye-of-the-Swan Pinot Noir. Ran and swam again with Chip. Called my estranged wife. And you?

Says Kath Sorry: My mind wandered.

WHAT DID KATHERINE SHERRITT SAGAMORE DO
WHILE HER ESTRANGED HUSBAND WAS DOING ALL OF THE ABOVE?

Oh. Plenty. If we lived under the same roof, you'd know.

That's right.

Talk to your daughter now, okay? Things are worse down there than they are in that Cave of Montesinos. Here's your biological father, Lox.

How goes it, honey? Over.

With a catch in her muffled but still-brave voice, our daughter reports that everything is a touch more desperate than it was this time on Day 8. In fact, it's a whole new ball game down there. Her brother stopped crying sometime this afternoon, when she told him Joke 39½: If a seagull flies over the sea, what flies over the Bay? But he still won't talk to her, and his silence bothers her more than his bawling did. She is afraid, says Here Today, that he may have decided to turn himself off altogether; to become the Vanished Twin.

Come on, now, sweetheart! Over?

She means it. There used to be about three of us down here, you know, she declares surprisingly, until you guys got into this thing of making up funny pairs of girl-and-boy names like Arts and Sciences and Wash and Wear and Renaissance and Reformation. Today we're just Tomorrow and Tomorrow. By tomorrow . . .

Live! Let live! What are you telling me? Over!

The third one got discouraged out of existence: Whatserface's Magic Language Theory. If you and Mom don't hang it up soon, I'm going to be an only child.

Good lord! Katherine?

We *should* hang it up, Peter. *I* certainly want to.

I want to too! Come on back here!

I guess not.

You guess not. I guess I guess not, too. *We guess not, honey.* Not quite yet, anyhow. Over? You still there, honey? Over?

Over and Out.

DAY 10: WYE I.

To *Story*'s log Peter Sagamore says *Wednesday 25 June '80: Sky hazy, air humid, breeze SW light but steady. Texas still frying, Countdown begins for trial release of radioactive gas from Three Mile Island, Maryland wetlands law suffers setback, blah blah blah. Where's K, and what am I doing here? Leave me alone, Muse.*

But she will not. Instead, this morning he doesn't even telephone Nopoint Point or do his A.M. workout, but after breakfast says to Andrew Sherritt—who is more concerned now about K & Co. than about Peter, and has decided to bike on home—See you soon, pal; thanks for the company; and, grim-mouthed at what he's doing but ridden now by a rider who dwarfs even those seven several others, without so much as a howdy-do to the Talbotts he forges through the forenoon through

PART TWO OF THAT POSSIBLE THREE-PART DON QUIXOTE STORY,

namely, *"Rocinante III."*

Wake up, Dee Kew, he urges his hero, last seen concussed and drowning in an unnamed river. No response. He repeats the invocation as a command *en español: ¡Recorde, Don Quijote de la Mancha! ¡Arriba!* The third time he puts his words into the authoritative mouth of Don Carlos de Barja, Duke of Villahermosa, the alleged original of that duke who entertains Don Quixote and sponsors his illusions through much of the middle of Part Two of Cervantes's novel.

The old knight stirs, opens his eyes, lifts his head, and looks around as if expecting to find himself in heaven or hell. Seeing instead a well-appointed bedchamber in a noble seventeenth-century Spanish household, he falls back upon his pillow and presses his fingertips to his temples.

God and El Cide be praised! he says, as much to himself as to the elegant couple standing by his bedside. I thought my story done, but I see I've begun another chapter, with an aching head. To whom do I owe my rescue, please, and where am I now in the errant plot of my adventures?

Taking a cold compress from a serving-maid, the duchess herself applies it to Quixote's brow and declares that he is the welcome guest of two enchanted admirers of the Knight of the Rueful Countenance and his squire, Governor Sancho Panza; admirers also of Part One of *The Ingenious Gentleman Don Quixote* et cetera, by Miguel de Cervantes Saavedra. That he is doubtless presently somewhere in the course of Part Two of that history, in which she and her husband are honored to play a small role— not too far along in it, they hope, as they look forward to sharing his company for many a chapter to come.

More particularly, adds the duke, you are on the Island of Barataria, fetched here by two fishermen who happened to be chatting on the riverbank when they heard a great clang and saw you carried under by the current. They fished you out: That is their métier.

I must reward them, Don Quixote declares, though it's to my Moorish enchanter that I owe both my peril and my rescue. In my purse, sir, are four *reales;* kindly divide them between those fishermen.

The duke replies with a smile In your purse there is at the moment nothing, my friend, and nothing is what you owe your rescuers. I've clapped the pair of them into jail until the return of Governor Panza, who will judge their case again as he has done before.

This second mention of *El Gobernador* reminds Quixote of the first, which he was almost too dazed to register, and of the object of his upstream trek. He craves explanation: How did Sancho's ambition come to be fulfilled? Where is the fellow now, and where in Spain for that matter is this Island of Barataria? How is it that his rescuers are in jail, and what happened to his four *reales*? But the duchess insists that he rest: Time enough tomorrow for exposition.

In the seventeenth century, a man in his fifties bordered upon old age. All those chapters on the road, however, and lately upon the river, have so toughened the whimsical old bachelor Alonso Quijano into Don Quixote that by midday, after another short nap, the Knight of the Rueful Countenance is on his feet, his head no less clear than before his accident, and his curiosity no longer to be put off. Very well: His hosts explain to him that "Barataria" is one among several villages under the duke's hegemony, and that he and the duchess were pleased to bestow its administration, some chapters ago, upon the illustrious Sancho Panza, whose practical wisdom had been made manifest to the world by the Cide Hamete Benengeli in *Don Quixote, Part One*. Nor was their confidence misplaced: All afternoon they regale their new guest with such anecdotes of Sancho's executive good sense as may be found in Chapters XLV, XLVII, XLIX, and LI of Part Two. His sagacity in these matters is the more admirable, they agree, inasmuch as he took office grieving sorely the loss of his master.

I should very much like to know how I was lost, says Don Quixote, and the duchess explains that, having lowered him at his own insistence into the infamous Cave of Montesinos, Sancho and his cousin waited as long as they dared and then drew up the rope, which they were horrified to find had nothing at the end of it. They lowered it again; they called down into the cave-mouth; they lowered a lantern, in case Don Quixote was groping about lost down there. But their calls went unanswered; the lantern came back up extinguished time after time, the rope slack. They considered lowering one of themselves into the cave; but neither of them was strong enough to raise the other unaided. Besides, in the squire's opinion, for either of them to go down into that fearful place would be like throwing a copper coin into a well to retrieve a gold one dropped accidentally.

Says Don Quixote That is Sancho Panza's very voice.

And so after three days of lowering and raising the rope in vain like luckless fishermen, the pair abandoned their vigil as hopeless, returned to Sancho's cousin's village, and announced the sad news. Your squire then said good-bye to his cousin and went his sorrowing way, which led eventually to us and to his distinguished governorship of this island, in which, were it not for his bereavement, he would have rejoiced as much as we. Thus the weeks and chapters passed, during which we have faithfully recorded his wise sayings and judgments, in case there should be a sequel to Hamete Benengeli's famous history. But after the publication of Part One of that history, your career was so unfortunately brief that we could scarcely imagine its being padded out to fill a second volume, even with the Annals of Barataria thrown in.

Just two days ago, however (the duke went on), a local fisherman complained to His Excellency the Governor that his boat had been stolen from the riverbank some distance downstream from here while he was relieving himself in a wild-olive grove nearby. So great had been his natural need, he said, he had not bothered either to tie the boat up or to pocket the four *reales* he had just earned by selling his catch. As he stepped out of the bushes, he saw the thief poling away downriver with his boat and his money. Governor Panza asked the fellow to describe the stolen property. The fisherman declared that it was a spanking new vessel painted in the Portuguese style and named *Rocinante Two* after Don Quixote's famous horse, about which he and his companions had heard such tales from the governor himself. The boat was fitted with a magnificent mast and sail, he said, fully equipped in all particulars, and worth a hundred *reales* at the very least.

Hearing this, Governor Panza at once pronounced the fellow either a liar or a fool: A fisherman with such a splendid new vessel, he declared, would have shat his breeches rather than leave it unsecured.

That is quite so, says Don Quixote. No offense to your lordships intended, but Sancho might have added as well that the fish of this river are of famously poor quality and would not have fetched the two *reales* I found in that leaky old skiff, much less four. Moreover, there was neither sail nor mast aboard, not even oars, and no fishing tackle of any sort.

As to the fish, declares the duchess, you're mistaken: The fish of the Ebro are as fine as any in Spain. But as to the rest, you're right. Governor Panza then asked for a description of the thief, demanding that it come closer to the truth than that of the missing property. The fisherman acknowledged that in his vexation he had perhaps improved the vessel a bit; as for the thief, he bid God strike him dead if the rascal was not a lanky gray-beard in outlandish armor more suitable for tilting at windmills than for angling after trout. And having stolen the boat and pocketed the money (the fisherman guessed it was three *reales* after all, not four), the old thief shouted a prayer of thanks to the Moor El Seedy Something-or-other, proving himself to be an infidel as well as a pirate.

On your life, Governor Panza threatened him (says the duke), tell me what sort of helmet this thief wore on his head, and whether the infidel he prayed to was the famous enchanter El Cide Hamete Benengeli or some other Moor. That was the very name, the fisherman swore: As for the thief's helmet, it looked like nothing so much as a brass spittoon or a barber's basin, such as they say the famous Don Quixote used to go about in.

So affected was Governor Panza by this news (the duchess continues), he prayed my husband to appoint a vice-governor at once to take over the administration of Barataria, so that he himself could set out that very day in pursuit of this alleged thief, who was either his late master come back from the dead or a shameless impostor. If the former, then no crime had taken place, only a miracle of resurrection; for Don Quixote of La Mancha could no more be induced to steal than Rocinante to fly. If the latter, then very likely the rascal was a thief as well as a fraud, whose neck the governor himself would wring with pleasure.

We offered him a boat for his search (the duke declares), very like the one described by the fisherman; but Governor Panza distrusts all conveyances except his faithful Dapple. He set out upon her that same evening, leading Rocinante behind him and following the banks of the Ebro downstream; and very sorry we were to see him go, for his government has been as merry as it was wise.

Then yesterday (says the duchess) those two fishermen fetched you here, half drowned, claiming they had caught the thief and recovered the stolen boat, much the worse for wear, but not the three *reales*. My husband ordered them searched, and found on one of them—the same who claims to be the master of *Rocinante Two*—a purse with four *reales* in it, whereupon we bound them both over on suspicion of theft until Governor Panza returns to try their case. And we dispatched a messenger after the governor to tell him that the man he seeks is our honored guest. There is our story thus far.

Don Quixote, who has followed this narrative like a tennis match, thanks his hosts for their care and prays the duke not only to dismiss all charges against his rescuers, who are guilty of nothing worse than the sin of all fishermen, exaggeration, but also to give the boat owner those four *reales,* of which two indeed were in the vessel when he set off in it, thinking it put there by the Enchanter for his conveyance. He presumes the other two to have come from that source as well, and hopes the sum will cover what damage he has unintentionally done the boat. He then thanks God and Hamete Benengeli for leading him from the Cave of Montesinos to the Island of Barataria and so nearly to a reunion with Sancho Panza himself, the very object of his search. Having observed how that latter enchanter works, he does not doubt that in this chapter he must overtake his squire, who is searching for him, so that they can proceed together to the consummation of their story.

But how is it, he wonders, that the duke and duchess speak of the Ebro, when it was the Guadiana (known for the poor quality of its fish) he went down upon from the palace of Montesinos, and whose course he retraced the next day, which led him here?

His hosts assure him that he is mistaken. The Guadiana rises in the plain of Montiel, in the heart of La Mancha in New Castile; it flows westward through Extremadura to Badajoz, where it turns southward to become for half a hundred kilometers the border between Spain and Portugal. It then strays through the cork-oak and olive groves of Portuguese Alentejo, after which it empties into the Atlantic at the Gulf of Cádiz, between the rocky Algarve and the Coast of Light. The Ebro, on the other hand, rises in the Cantabrian mountains in northern Spain, flows eastward through Old Castile and Aragon into Catalonia, and empties into the Mediterranean. The two systems are divided by mountain ranges; there is no navigating from one to the other.

No matter, says Don Quixote: Such is his faith now in the Cide Hamete Benengeli, it would not surprise him to be enchanted in the space of one paragraph from the Duero to the Nile or from the Guadalquivir to the waters of heaven, to say nothing of the Guadiana to the Ebro. Nor does he imagine that the duke's messenger will reach Sancho Panza before he himself does, even with a day's head start. *What is best for the story* is what the great Moor causes to come to pass, and it were best for the story that the searcher be found by the one he seeks.

He then begs from their lordships the loan of that vessel they had offered Sancho; for he has learned in *Rocinante II* that a mere skiff poled downstream can cover more kilometers in one day than Dapple and the first Rocinante can cover in three. Amused at the prospect of further comedy in the reciprocal pursuit of knight by squire and vice versa, the duke and duchess oblige him with one of several trim and gaily painted pleasure craft maintained for their household. They insist only that he permit them to provision the vessel modestly, lest his enchantment wear thin to the point of hunger and thirst, and to cause the name *Rocinante III* to be lettered upon its bows and transom.

The knight agrees; though he still takes Montesinos's word for it that the enchanted require neither food nor drink, he found in his previous voyage that they are not therefore exempt from craving both. He even permits one of the duke's staff to demonstrate the raising, trimming, and furling of the boat's sail and the operation of its tiller, he having learned that his enchanter's navigation is too direct in its accuracy to bother avoiding rocks and rapids. But so steadfastly does he refuse their offer of some money as well, they are obliged to conceal a purse of six *reales* among the loaves and water casks, the baskets of dates and olives and fine Manchegan cheese aged in oil.

They then send him off with much ceremony from their pier—well below those rapids that were the undoing of *Rocinante II*—down the Ebro toward the sea. Crowds of townspeople, including the duke and duchess themselves, follow his progress for a while in boats of their own, in carriages along the riverbank, on horseback, and on foot. One by one then they salute him and return to their usual pursuits; by nightfall *Rocinante III* is unaccompanied but for a pair of the duke's mounted men under orders to follow the knight unobtrusively, both for his protection and to report his adventures to their master and mistress. These scouts remain some distance behind, keeping the vessel just in sight, until at afternoon's end Quixote steers the craft behind a small wooded island and, instead of drawing up to shore and sleeping under a tree as he did before, anchors *Rocinante III* in midstream and beds comfortably down on deck, under the stars.

The scouts make camp in an almond grove alongshore, and next morning—though they wake dew-damp and muscle-sore at first light—find their quarry flown. They gallop a long way downstream, certain of overtaking him; they see other vessels, more and more of them as the Ebro widens into a busy waterway in its lower reaches, but no *Rocinante III*. Presently they meet the duke's earlier messenger on his way back toward Barataria with Governor Panza, whose joy at that messenger's message turns to vexation now at theirs. A brace of proper ninnies, he calls them, for not standing alternate watches through the night! Did they suppose the duke sent a pair of scouts to keep each other warm in bed? He dispatches one of them, with the messenger, to search back upriver as far as Barataria while he and the second return downstream; the team that first espies *Rocinante III* will send word to the other as well as to the duke and duchess.

But though they carry out this sensible plan—Sancho and his companion all the way to Cabo de Tortosa, where the Ebro meets the sea—neither party crosses paths again with Don Quixote de la Mancha. They cannot believe him lost at sea: How could he reach the Ebro's mouth without their seeing him? That he might have turned off, upstream, into one of the river's tributaries, seems unlikely; they scout those tributaries anyhow, in vain, and have finally to conclude that the Knight of the Rueful Countenance has redisappeared as mysteriously as he reappeared—the more mysteriously in that the duke's boat has disappeared along with him.

Baffled, they return to Barataria and their daily lives. How Sancho's ingenious administration of that island ended may be found in Chapter LIII of Part Two of *Don Quixote;* for the rest, as the duke remarked earlier, a Part Two without the main character is scarcely worth recounting. Sancho Panza, the scouts, the messenger, the two fishermen, the duke and duchess, the burro Dapple and the old mare Rocinante—all live until they die. The seventeenth century becomes the eighteenth, the nineteenth, the twentieth. As surely as its stony rivers run to the sea, Spain's hard history becomes the history of Spain.

Where is Don Quixote?

A light easterly stirs *Rocinante III*'s standing rigging. The anchor rode creaks in its chock as the boat swings; wavelets lap the hull. From a confused dream of America, the knight wakes to find a bright moon setting astern, downriver. Eucalyptus scents the air; he does not recall seeing or smelling any along the Ebro. And how is it that the moon is about to set downstream, when the Ebro flows southeastward?

He strolls the dewy deck. Already it comes naturally to him to move from cockpit to foredeck, steadying himself with grabrail, shroud, or spar— whatever comes to hand. The river is wider than he remembers; he looks vainly through the near-full moonlight for that wooded islet. Perhaps the boat has dragged around some bend? He is new at such matters, but the anchor appears to be holding, and the breeze and current seem to him far too gentle to drag even an ill-set hook.

He admires his little craft's sheer, her high bow, the glinting dew on her well-joined deck and graceful tiller. If it was agreeable to drift and pole down the Guadiana on *Rocinante II,* how much more so to feel the breeze lift *Rocinante III* (as happened once or twice the afternoon before, when he accidentally got her sail trimmed right) and surge her along with only the lightest hand on her tiller. How must it be, then, to leave land astern altogether, like those true knights-errant Cristoforo Colombo and Prince Henry's *Descobridores*?

Comes again the perfume of eucalyptus, and he understands this night to be literally enchanted, the river to have once more metamorphosed, as did the Guadiana into the Ebro. Though he can have slept only a few hours, he feels refreshed. Full of calm purpose, he hoists the lateen sail; lets it luff while he weighs and secures the anchor. Unhurriedly, as the boat gathers sternway, he steps to the tiller, brings her bow around, trims the sheet, and glides down the track of the moon. He does not yet care what waterway this is; that it flows westward is enough. Somewhere aboard, he divines, is a purse of six *reales,* maybe eight. He need not even look for it.

There are heights in the Serranía de Cuenca where an unlikely portage of two dozen kilometers—from Cella on the Jiloca to Orihuela del Tre-medal on the Gallo, for example, or from Medinaceli on the Jalón to Sigüenza on the Henares—might fetch an intrepid white-water canoeist from a headwater of the Ebro system to one of the Tagus, whereon he might then make his rocky way west to beflowered Aranjuez, past improbable Toledo, on and on to where Tajo becomes Tejo and flows green and Portuguese to Lisbon and the sea. No matter. Here are no rapids, boulders, spillways, snags. The sun rises astern and sets ahead, day after Iberian day; the breeze seems always on one or the other quarter or abeam, never forward of the mast.

As with *Rocinante II,* the knight presently grows adept at managing its larger and abler successor. Not for a day at a time, but for weeks on end he navigates downriver, becoming ever more expert both at handling his craft and at subsisting by himself. Weathered already, he scarcely minds the occasional rough wind or rainshower, once he knows how to secure the boat. He discards his makeshift armor, as unnecessary as it is cumbersome. On the river's more open stretches he teaches himself navigation and piloting from a book he finds among the jugs of Valdepeñas and the several purses of coin. He begins a log of his journey: observations of the changing weather and the passing scene; notes of his infrequent stops and provisioning transactions, which he makes as brief as possible. He works the log back to include the voyage from Montesinos's palace to Barataria.

In time he comes to understand a new order of enchantment: not crystal palaces and magical swords and fire-breathing dragons, but brisk or mild southeasterlies, the language of clouds, the working out of compass courses, current sets, and time/speed/distance calculations, the inexhaustible charm of a dozen simple knots, each with its uses. From a map of Iberia, which he finds among rolled nautical charts and boxed navigational instruments in the forepeak, he eventually infers his location and identifies the villages he sails past—seldom, however, stopping to verify his identifications. He learns the stars; he practices with sextant and chronometer. He forms the opinion that two smaller sails, on separate masts, would be more manageable than his single large one, and that an optional squaresail on the foremast might be better offwind than a lateen, just as the lateen is better than the square for upwind work. He does not know that Prince Henry's caravels revolutionized sailing with that discovery two centuries earlier. In time he reckons himself to be approaching the Sea of Straw and the city founded by Ulysses.

What of Sancho Panza, the object of his seaborne search? Not until he anchored *Rocinante III* behind that little island on the first evening out of Barataria did Don Quixote realize that in his busy pleasure with learning to steer and trim sail, he had neglected utterly to keep an eye out for his squire, for Dapple, for Rocinante. By when he weighed anchor on that transformed river some hours later, repaying his debt to Sancho was scarcely even his official goal. He told his logbook, when it occurred to him weeks later to begin one, that it was his enchanter he was now in search of, to repay—but not in coin—his greatest debt of all. But even as he penned those words, he somehow understood that the Cide Hamete Benengeli is no less a fiction than Don Quixote de la Mancha, the Knight of Doleful Aspect.

No: He is presently looking for Lisbon, which his chart tells him he will find about twenty-five kilometers down that widening of the Tagus called (for its amber reflection of the afternoon sun) the Sea of Straw. He will then seek the port of call after that, and the one after that, and along the way perhaps come to understand where and why he's voyaging. Or it may be that, like the river, those questions will transform themselves into others, with other answers.

There is the ancient city on its seven hills. Reluctantly he stops to have his little ship refitted for coastwise cruising. Appraising the local craft with a now less innocent eye, he modifies his preliminary sketches and discusses with a number of boatwrights yet further alterations. In many particulars, he yields to their experienced judgment; where they disagree among themselves, he makes his own decision. On a few matters (the optional square-sail, for example, which they all deem not worth the expense and bother except on larger craft, for long passagemaking), he stands his ground against their concerted opinion. Given the enchanted accrual of "interest" on his unspent *reales*, he reckons that paying for these alterations will be no problem; all the same, he bargains with three builders before settling on a price, and becomes more knowledgeable in the process.

No one along the Lisbon waterfront regards his appearance or behavior as unusual. Eager as he is to cast off for wherever, he enjoys moving through the city unarmored and unremarked. When not dealing with the boatwrights, he spends much time in the Torre de Belém, staring out to the Foz do Rio Tejo and the sea beyond. He also shops for a few items not included in the duke and duchess's extraordinary provisioning, though he has no clear idea where he will go next. At a bookseller's in the Bairro Alto, in course of looking for a better manual of celestial navigation, he picks up and puts down a number of chivalric romances, wondering mildly what about them had ever interested him. He buys a Spanish translation of *The Odyssey* and an edition of Camoëns's *Lusiads,* which he means to attempt in the original Portuguese. While paying for these, he observes that the clerk himself is reading a Portuguese translation of *El Ingenioso Hidalgo Don Quijote de la Mancha,* Parts I & II—not by the Cide Hamete Benengeli, but by someone he now recalls having heard the duchess mention: Miguel de Cervantes Saavedra.

Without declaring his own identity, as in chapters past he would have done, he reproves the clerk for thus abetting imposture or literacy piracy: The circumstance that Benengeli is not a Christian does not license his history to be sold under false authorship or imitated and extended without his authorization. The clerk, amused, replies that there have in fact been such imitations and false sequels; indeed, that it was the true author's indignation at one such that prompted Part Two of the book in hand, a full decade after the great success of Part One. But the perpetrator of that false sequel was not Hamete Benengeli, for that admirable Moor is as much a figment of great Cervantes's imagination as are Sancho Panza and Don Quixote himself.

Quixote resists the temptation to prove the fellow wrong. Instead he remarks, ironically, that a true Part Two of Don Quixote's history must recount such matters as the knight's reading and approving Part One; his setting out on the road again with Sancho Panza; his fateful descent into the Cave of Montesinos, and Sancho's governorship of the Island of Barataria. That is a book he would pay much for, if only to learn where Don Quixote sailed to from Lisbon.

For jumbling fiction and fact, the clerk responds, you take the prize. He shows him the book's table of contents, from which Quixote infers that its first part is the same he read in La Mancha, and that its second does indeed include the episodes mentioned, followed by others unfamiliar to him. None involves a voyage to Lisbon, much less beyond it. The chapter headings conclude with his chastened return to his home village . . . and his peaceful death there.

The knight (he scarcely now thinks of himself as one) is perplexed, the more so because, unaccountably, those unfamiliar chapter titles seem *right* to him, even the mention of his death. But now he hears the clerk speak of the book as the greatest *novel* ever written, and concludes that its second part must be a work of fiction extrapolated from the true history of Part One: an ingenious if somewhat high-handed idea. Remembering his long and painfully consequential enchantment by novels of chivalry, he pronounces it a reckless thing indeed to confuse the boundary between life and art. All the same, he buys the book in order to see how this Cervantes fellow measures up beside the errorless Moor.

For the next several weeks, however, he is too busy studying celestial navigation, coastwise piloting, and the finer points of sailing, both from his books and in conversation with seasoned mariners along the waterfront, to look into his alleged adventures after the Cave of Montesinos. For experience, he sails out several times with fishermen, and picks up useful pointers not only about light- and heavy-weather sailing, docking and mooring and navigating, but also about catching and preparing fish. Two or three of his new companions have voyaged in larger vessels to Brazil and Mexico, even to the vast, scarcely colonized new world to the north of those fabulous territories. Could one sail there alone, he inquires, in a boat much like this? They advise him that if he is so eager to end his life, it would be quicker and less expensive to throw himself off the cliffs of Cape St. Vincent, or over the side. Not one of them would set out from Lisbon down the coast of Portugal to Sagres singlehanded, much less across the ocean; a sailor without a shipmate, they agree, is Don Quixote without Sancho Panza, or vice versa: unimaginable.

He reads *The Lusiads* and resolves, despite the fishermen's advice, to try *Rocinante III* alone down the Portuguese coast to Cape St. Vincent and the Sagres headland, from where the Discoverers set forth in their caravels. His refitted vessel is ready. After several trials on the Sea of Straw and adjustments to the rig, he provisions her and, one sharp blue morning, sets out.

A fifteen-knot westerly whips straight into the mouth of the Tagus; he has his hands full tacking the ten miles out from Lisbon past Belém to the ocean, where for the first time he and *Rocinante* must deal with sizable waves as well as wind. Five- and six-footers they are, white-capped and dismaying even under a brilliant sky; but he finds that with her shortened sailplan and versatile rig, *Rocinante III* rides them like a seabird. He is too busy and excited to feel ill. With his heart in his throat, he turns south around the Island of Bugia, off the Foz do Rio Tejo, and lays a compass course for Cape Espichel, about twenty miles ahead, keeping the curved, rock-skirted shore always in sight. Four hours on a galloping beam-reach puts him there—and there, he knows, he should stop for the day.

But though his route, like the Discoverers', is southerly, toward Africa, the breeze he's reaching on blows straight from North America. He holds his southward course; it will now carry him for the first time out of sight of land, past the Capes of Sines and Sardão to Cape St. Vincent, if he is lucky, one hundred miles ahead: to Sagres, the southwesternmost tip of Europe. The sun is past the meridian; it will set in the empty west, rise over Iberia, and set again, he calculates, before he sees the St. Vincent light, if he ever does. Should he stray to leeward during the night, he will pile up on the rocky palisades; should he stray too far to windward, he will miss the cape altogether and wander toward Africa in fact, but never reach it in that boat. So large and sturdy-seeming in the Ebro and the Tagus, *Rocinante III* is a cockleshell out here, and the afternoon wanes. Turn back, old fellow, every reasonable voice in him implores. His inspirers now, however, are no longer Amadis of Gaul and Palmerín of England, but the equally improbable Columbus, Magellan, Melgueiro. More knowledgeable, they, and vastly more experienced than he, in larger vessels with larger crews—but then, he is not bound for the Cape of Good Hope or the Capes of Virginia, only for Cabo de São Vicente. He does not even cross himself; he simply presses on.

Remarkably, he gets there, and in better time than he estimated. The wind veers aft, northwest; he deploys his squaresail to advantage. The breeze holds through the night and all the next day. *Rocinante* sizzles along. Only once, in a moment more of euphoria than of exhaustion, he lets the boat broach to, takes green water aboard, and tastes what the terror of his final moments will be like, when they arrive. But the little craft struggles to its feet, as does its skipper; the seething water finds the scuppers; the sails refill; the voyage proceeds. Everything above and below decks is soaked (Camoëns is drowned; Cervantes, merely baptized). No matter. He has taken harder falls from the first Rocinante; he and her successor have come through.

And there it rises, just toward sunset: the high promontory of Cape St. Vincent. He is unspeakably relieved to see it heave into view—and he has still to get around it and find harbor for the night. But even as he admires the play of last light upon cliffs and lighthouse, and the surf pounding against Portugal, his heart turns to where that light comes from: dull red, descending into blue haze westward.

Part Two of this possible three-part Don Quixote story (Peter Sagamore notes) should leave its hero there on Europe's tip, bounded on three sides by the sea, no land in sight except the spectacular cliff he stands upon, among the ice plants and the blowholes, beside Prince Henry's old navigation school with its great stone compass-rose. *Rocinante III* rides in a nearby harbor on the Lagos coast. Her skipper (and only passenger) lives aboard. Now and then he sails out beyond the jetties to fish for his dinner, but he plans no further voyages in her. From the Sagres headland, he has seen terrifying storms blow through and well-manned ships carried under; she cannot take him where he wants to go.

Part of every day he spends out on that windy headland, before the abandoned buildings, reading and rereading *Don Quixote.* Formerly he marveled at how accurately, in Part One, "Hamete Benengeli" recorded his and Sancho's early adventures. Upon first reading Part Two, he is enchanted by how skillfully, from the Montesinos incident on, this Miguel de Cervantes spins out a convincing alternative to the truth: as if he really had been hoisted out of that cave and gone on with that story. So seamless is the transition from history to fiction, so persuasive the narrative, that those later adventures of "Don Quixote," ending in his death in La Mancha, come to seem to him the real story, far more plausible than what has actually happened since Chapter XXII. Indeed, after several rereadings, Part One also strikes him as a splendid and amusing fiction; he reads it neither more nor less spellbound than any other late-middle-aged reader— and identifies neither more nor less with its hero.

He does not want for money. Though the enchantment that once virtually exempted him from hunger and thirst seems to have worn off like his old romance with chivalric novels, his material needs are small, and the *reales* (which he has deposited in the Bank of Portugal) patiently accrue. He stares mesmerized out to sea and rereads *Don Quixote.* How much time passes? The ships rounding the Cape change design, as do the costumes and vehicles of sightseers out on the headland and, to a much lesser extent, those of the fishermen.

One afternoon a lean and beardless young fellow, whom he has lately often noticed alone out there like himself—reading, writing in a notebook, running the footpaths for exercise—salutes him in heavily accented Portuguese and remarks amiably that he looks rather like the hero of that novel he's always reading, which the fellow declares to be his own favorite in the world. Don Quixote does not immediately reply that in a sense he *is* the story's hero; like many another solitary, however, once the conversation has begun (and they have shifted to Spanish, with which both are easier than with Portuguese), he finds himself telling his whole story, just as Peter Sagamore will one day set it down.

So you're Don Quixote, the chap marvels—merrily, but not sarcastically. ¡Well met, *amigo*! He too, he declares, has strayed improbably to Portugal out of a great novel, as it were: one with which his celebrated new acquaintance may be unfamiliar. Having put his native village behind him and rafted chapter after chapter down a certain North American waterway, at a certain pass he lit out for the Territory, so to speak, rather than return to his starting place at the voyage's end. Thereafter he sharply missed those downstream days and nights, which came paradoxically to seem to him an island in the flow of time, rather than time's flow itself. Inspired by the memory of them—and by the images of such other wayfarers as Odysseus and Don Quixote, he embarked upon a voyage far more erratic and uncertain than his first: a voyage which, for reasons he himself has yet to discover, has fetched him here to Saint Vincent's Cape, where he means to stay until the next leg of his journey is clearer, and the nature of his vessel as well.

As to the former, says Don Quixote, my advice to you is not to wait overlong. At your age especially, if your craft is able, you need only the most general notion of your destination. Weigh anchor, fellow: Test the wind, lay an approximate course, and leave it to your destination to clarify itself as you go along.

The young man replies that that is more or less how he got to Portugal. All he knew when he left America was that he hoped one day to cook up a story as memorable as those of Odysseus, Scheherazade, Don Quixote, or Huckleberry Finn. That ambition led him somehow from the Capes of Virginia to Cape St. Vincent—but he cannot say that he feels any closer to his destination.

Don Quixote professes himself no great hand at allegory, but believes he understands: as if, enthralled by the novels of knight-errantry, he himself had set out, not to be a knight-errant, but to write a great novel of knight-errantry. He does not know this Scheherazade (though her name sounds Moorish, and he yields to none in his respect for Moorish storytellers) or that oddly named fourth personage, but he shares his new friend's admiration for great Homer—in particular that part of the *Odyssey* between the hero's loss of ship and shipmates and his final landing in Ithaca. In short, his singlehanded voyaging.

The American (he will identify himself no further) agrees that if any part of that splendid story can be called more admirable than the rest, it is that part: the interludes with Calypso and Nausicaa; the encounter with gray-eyed Athene herself on the beach at Ithaca. But what of such other great scenes as Odysseus's reunion with Penelope?

Don Quixote, however, prefers to talk of seafaring, especially solo seafaring. Over the next days and weeks he searches out the young man's company nearly every afternoon or evening, and hears from him astonishing stories, which the American swears to be true, of people who have done the very thing that Quixote aspires to do: people who have sailed alone not only across the ocean, but around the globe. He hears of Joshua Slocum in the little boat *Spray* and Francis Chichester in *Gipsy Moth IV,* both men in late middle age. On a map such as Quixote has never seen, his friend traces the thirty-seventh parallel of north latitude directly from Cape St. Vincent west to Capes Henry and Charles, the entrance portals to his home waters. That coincidence, the American says, perhaps accounts for his presence in Sagres, though his route to Portugal was by no means so direct; and perhaps it is to those birthwaters he'll eventually return, when his craft is ready—but not by sailing the thirty-seventh parallel. Admirable as are those literal solo voyagers, he still regards Miguel de Cervantes as the noblest singlehander of them all: he who in the sea battle at Lepanto lost the use of his left arm to the greater glory of his right.

After providing Don Quixote with many more particulars both about the author of *Don Quixote* (who, like "Alonso Quijano" and the present Don Quixote, came to his best identity late in his career) and about the kinds of sailing vessels best suited for singlehanded passagemaking—as well as about the republic on the far side of the ocean before them, more rich and dangerous these days than Spain in the *Siglo de Oro*—the American presently bids his elder friend good-bye. It is spring; he has spent a long winter immersed in his four favorite stories, in his own practice, and lately in conversation with his estimable fellow voyager. Now he means to follow Quixote's advice and move on, he scarcely cares where, with no other Rocinante than his thumb, taking note of everything, before making his solo return to where he came from.

I know now why I came to Sagres, he declares: It was to meet you, on neutral ground.

Salud y suerte, says Don Quixote: success and godspeed, quixotic as your project is. Who knows? Perhaps our paths will recross, maybe even in those waters at the western end of our parallel. It is not often, he declares, that a young man inspires an old. But he is resolved now to equip himself to do what until meeting the American he would scarcely have dreamed possible: aboard some fourth Rocinante, in quest of nothing but the having done it, to sail alone from the old world to the new.

Their handshake turns into a proper *abrazo,* and then—first apparently from the American's far-off birthwaters, then as it seems from right inside his narrative head—comes an insistent beeping that the young man realizes he's been hearing for some time: Beep-beep-beep, beeeep beeeep beeeep, beep-beep-beep. Beep-beep-beep, beeeep beeeep beeeep, beep-beep-beep.

IT'S YOUR FUTURE CALLING.

Peter Sagamore has not written the foregoing sentences. But shamelessly, possessedly, he has logged long notes upon this unfinished possible Don Quixote story all through the sticky morning into the forepart of the afternoon, with scarcely a frontal thought for his other responsibilities until they rouse him from the Don's *abrazo* with a Very Very High Frequency Mayday.

Stop here, Dad, his potential daughter calls. Sorry to interrupt.

That's okay, Stop. It's okay. What's up?

I've tried to keep my eyes open every blessed minute, she declares, in a tone indistinguishable from Peter's conscience's. But I dozed off back there for just a second, and your potential son got his finger on the Abort button.

Dear God, Stop!

Not for both of us; just for himself. He did it while Mom was sort of sobbing down here by the pool and you were up there working on your story. Now he's cried himself to sleep, but I can feel the machinery starting up.

Ai yi!

Right. Request permission to push the Launch button right this minute, Dad, to try to salvage us both before Go aborts. Over?

PUSH! PUSH! PUSH!

pleads her father: Go, Stop! Oh, Go! And he springs in one bound from Portugal to Key Farm, Wye I. He races from dock to porch; Judge George Talbott is napping in a wicker chair there, white-shirted, necktied, looking dead but comfortable, and doesn't stir when P crashes past and explodes through living room into kitchen. Nobody home. He tears upstairs, hollering Frank? Lee?

Leah Talbott gets up from typing a formal letter of acceptance, as it happens, to the Commonwealth of Virginia, confirming her earlier telephoned yes to the job down there. (Her Selectric sticks in Wye Island humidity; once she's on salary, she decides, she'll buy both a word processor and a food processor.) She steps wondering into the hallway, T-shirted, short-shorted, from her makeshift office. Kath's delivering and aborting at the same time, Peter explains; I'm pretty sure. Where's your car keys?

Let me drive you, she says; then Oh my: Frank took the Toyota down to Easton for more electronic stuff, and Cecilia Skinner's gone marketing in the Dodge 'cause their Chevy died. Who knows when they'll be back. . . .

Ai yi yi. Chip's ten-speed? Nope; Chip's already back home. Cab from Easton? Too slow getting here, but let's call one. Shit shit shit.

Not to question your masculine intuitions, Lee Talbott says, but shouldn't we phone Nopoint Point first, just to make sure?

He does, twice, from the kitchen: Busy. Oy, Lee, I've been being such an asshole!

Well. Call your cab, and then try Nopoint Point some more while you're waiting.

He does, then dials the Easton Hospital: No Sagamores or Sherritts registered. Nopoint Point again: Busy. It's happening, and he's not going to be there, and it took a Mayday to wake him up. So why didn't Hank call? But who knows whether Hank's home just now, and why should Hank *have* to call? The beeper goes off again, but this time it's upstairs— in the bedroom Frank's using for *his* office, in fact. Lee explains that it's the signal Chip and her husband rigged to let them know when there's company out back at NRR. She's supposed to stroll over, if it's not inconvenient, and note what's coming and going from that driveway.

Peter commands or begs her to ring Nopoint Point until she gets through and to tell Katherine he's been being a deep-dyed shit but he's finally on his way. He dashes to the porch (old George is stirring); considers jogging Eastonward (there's only one road off Wye Island; if he meets Frank Talbott or Cecilia Skinner or the Easton taxi, he'll turn them around); sprints, finally, as if set off by the insistent beeper, around behind the house, across the long front yard, which as on most waterfront properties is really the backyard, over to the line of woods and the chain-link fence, through which he now sees, hot dog, an idling black Cadillac limousine with, yup, New Jersey plates. He is prepared to scale that fence, pound on the rolled-up windows, and pay (with what?), even threaten (with what?) the driver, if necessary, to fetch him to Nopoint Point. But the bugged gate is wide open. He charges through, realizing among other things, as he sees the driver reach inside his jacket, that he himself is walletless, weaponless, topless, and barefoot, wearing only cutoff jeans and a pukka-shell necklace.

Slow down, Peter Sagamore. Put your hands up; open them, anyhow, and smile as you approach, to show the two men in the backseat plus the driver in front that you're harmless: a maker of sentences, brief ones at that; a sometime inventor of imaginary personages; an abandoner of your nonfictional dearest friend. As he trots around to the driver's side—tough-looking hombre, that one, and Peter knows but can't name the face regarding him through the window behind—the rear door on the far side opens, and big florid-faced sport-shirted cigared Willy Sherritt heaves out of it, grumbling Peter Fucking Sagamore. What can we do for you.

His manner is . . . guarded but not incordial. Peter says Kath's in labor, Willy. Can you drop what you're doing and get me to Nopoint Point?

Mm? In Willy's face, as he mouths his cigar, P sees painfully his brother-in-law's awareness of our opinion of him. All the same (as a ragged monarch butterfly, en route to Mexico, flitters across the Cadillac's black roof for no other purpose, just now, than to emphasize this pregnant pause), one large hand on the open door-top, one on the raingutter, Will ducks his head to confer for two sentences with his backseat companion, then says to Peter Cmon around here and opens the front passenger door for him. Our man starts to say, for example, I really appreciate this, Willy: We're tied up at a friend's dock here, and Kath went on to your parents' while I worked on some stuff, and wouldn't you know it, there was no car available when the time came. But Willy says This is Paul, and to the driver: Paul, this is my brother-in-law, and, irrelevant to this introduction, Peter now realizes who the fellow in the backseat is.

Great-brown-eyed, sallow-faced, blue-jawed, sleek-haired Paul removes his right hand from his presumable pistol but does not shake Peter's hand, only twitches his eyebrows hello and starts the engine. Take her out, Willy tells him; I'll get the gate. The amiable other backseater offers his hand over the seatback and says as the car rolls out I guess you and I have never quite met. Porter Baldwin.

Sheepish Peter—Why sheepish, will ask indignant Katherine? Well, the guy was being so amused and civilized; it was like meeting Mephistopheles at last after all the bad notices and finding him a charming fellow. Plus he was so spiffy in his beige linen jacket and his blue forty-dollar shirt and his twenty-dollar club tie and his black mustache and his silver-gray hair, and me begging a favor in my beach-bum drag. It made me feel creepy. *Creepish,* then, K will insist; not sheepish. Creepish Peter shakes his wife's first husband's hand. Willy locks the gate and heaves into the car and tells Paul Go out the way we came in and take Fifty south and I'll tell you from there. We'll be back inside of an hour.

Quips Porter "Poonie" Baldwin, Jr., No robbing Paul to pay Peter. He quipped no such thing, Kath will protest, but Peter will swear that that was the fellow's very quip. And he's a nice-*looking* guy; much more attractive in person than in the media.

He never cornholed you with a forest-green Crayola.

Well, that's true. Anyhow there I was, expecting Uca Pugnax and U. Pugilator, and okay, they're villains, but they were anything but villainous, is my point. Cool and relaxed and good-humored and decent about the situation. I felt creepish. So the big moment is at hand, says the first man ever to insert penis into beautiful young Katherine Shorter Sherritt of Talbot County, Maryland, and Vinalhaven, Maine, before he went on to other sexual interests. Congratulations to both of you.

Katherine here spits upon her ex-husband's congratulations. The Devil is always a charmer, at first.

You get a call? Willy wants to know. P says he got a message. Awfully good of you-all to interrupt your business and taxi me in.

She at the hospital or home? Peter doesn't really know; acknowledges that his message might be garbled. Smooth Poonie says Why don't we find out? And to Willy You'd better do the calling. Already they're off Wye Island, speeding through the green corn and soybeans toward the main highway south. You're docked at Judge Talbott's? Poonie mildly asks Peter while Willy punches buttons on a phone he's fished from somewhere back there. Before our chap can reply, the black Cadillac swooshes and is swooshed by an ice-blue Mercedes going the other way in a powerful hurry with, what was it, two ladies in front? Says Willy What the fuck; that was mine. He punches up a different bunch of buttons and asks Vi, is Molly there? In accents that even from up front Peter hears to be unreconstructed

Eastern Shore black female, it is declared that Miz Sherritt is over to Nopoint Point with Miz Sagamore. Ex-Congressman Baldwin smiles brightly at Peter and at the ceiling of the automobile, now turning onto Route 50 south. His expression does not change when Willy says he'll be buggered if that wasn't Molly and Kate in his car, headed where present company's coming from. He rings Nopoint Point; Olive Treadway confirms that Miss Molly is driving Miss Katherine out to Wye Island to meet Mist Peter. At 60 mph, impassive Paul gives Peter a 150-yard level look. Says blushing Pete My message must have been garbled.

Turn us around, Paul, Willy recommends. Ex- and aspiring Congressman Porter Baldwin, Jr., holds the smooth tan point of his chin between his thumb and two fingertips. Dizzy broads, Will mutters, but it's pretty clear that in his judgment, dizziness crosses gender lines. Peter admits that his summons to Nopoint Point was more urgent than clear. Poonie observes helpfully that the girls were in an obvious hurry, all right. Maybe they meant to pick Dad up en route to the hospital?

Our party passes the Wye Oak, a national park consisting of a single white oak tree bigger than can readily be believed (Except, adds Kath— if we're going to sully our Tidewater Tales with tourist-guide stuff—by them as have sat in that town park in Lahaina, Maui, consisting of a single banyan tree even bigger, no?), and zips back through the beans, over the Wye Narrows bridge, and through more commercial agriculture to just within sight of the unlabeled gate of Natural Recycling Research, Inc., where they see the ice-blue Mercedes retracing *its* way, too. In one fierce motion, impassive Paul hits the brakes and whips the black limo sixty degrees to port, blocking both lanes and putting Peter at the mercy of Molly Barnes Sherritt's reflexes.

They are sufficient, just. Willy whoofs and chuckles. Porter Baldwin, Jr., perhaps begins to say to Peter affably If your wife wasn't having a baby before, I'll bet she is now—but Peter's out of the car already, *springing* to Katherine, who's fumbling with her seat belt and her door latch at the same time. We do not see Willy step over to have a word with his alarmed wife, or Paul straighten out the New Jersey Cadillac and withdraw with Poonie some discreet yards up the road; we'll reconstruct that business later. All momentum one moment ago, P now halts, almost in doubt; holds his hand out to the open window, fingers spread. K almost shyly puts out hers. As electrically as at that Katherine Anne Porter party so long since, our fingers interlace. Now our man pulls open the ice-blue passenger door and joyously thrusts in; our woman gives up trying to unbelt herself and joyfully receives his arms and chest and back, his wet face in her hair, hers on his bare shoulder.

For the expectable while we go on like that, with the expectable muted interjections, protestations, apology—until now, which is when Franklin Key Talbott drives up in his wife's chocolate-mousse Toyota fraught with electronic items and Andrew "Chip" Sherritt. From his Radio Shack errand Frank has made a spontaneous embassy of reconciliation to Nopoint Point, only to learn from Irma that Katherine has taken leave of her senses—at about the same moment, it will turn out, and as precipitately, as Peter put by his willfulness—and sped spouseward, pride be damned. The right move, Irm guesses, but Frank thinks her unconvinced. Sure, Chip can come along back to Key Farm, if he wants to catch the next chapter of our story. Why not?

Why not, indeed? Everybody's out of automobile now except Paul and Poonie, up the road. Willy Sherritt has actually kissed his sister in the hair and grunted Did Molly tell you our good news? Before Kate gets to reply, Peter with his arm around her says to Frank Talbott This is my brother-in-law Willy Sherritt and his wife, Molly; Frank Talbott. Pleased to meet you, red-faced Frank declares, shaking hands with the object of his research. To his wife and everyone, Peter explains I got this really urgent message, and Willy happened to be here on business. . . . So did I, K murmurs. It was garbled, but never mind.

Brother Andrew, Willy says to Chip for no particular reason as we stand about. Self-conscious Chipper waggles two fingers hello. Improbable brothers! Frank Talbott glances up the road. Inspired Peter Sagamore (flipped-out Peter Sagamore, in his wife's opinion, but never mind; we're back together) waves the New Jersey black limousine usward, saying to Katherine and to Franklin Key Talbott Guess who was good enough to give me a lift to Nopoint Point?

We bet Molly's looking nervously toward Katherine just here, Willy having spoken with her in low tones, but we are so full of our reunion that neither of us happens to be looking Molly's way. Upon reflection, we find it surprising that dour Paul would respond to Peters's summons—Who is Peter Sagamore, to order that one about?—but at the moment our man feels so much the dramaturge that he could summon spirits from the vasty deep, and they would answer him. Why else would Leah Allan Silver Talbott—having at last got through some while ago via C & P to Nopoint Point and reported to Katherine that Peter was attempting frantically to reach her side before she gave birth, and been told that she, Katherine, wasn't *giving* birth yet, if ever, but was on her way out the door with Molly en route to Key Farm to put this foolishness behind us, pride be damned and maybe good sense too, and hurried out back (Leah did) to tell Peter that, only to see the black limo tear off, and gone back inside to let Kath know, but found as she feared that Kath had also already set out, and then stood by until, sure enough, in roared the ice-blue Mercedes an appropriate number of minutes later, got the news brief, did a one-eighty, et cet—why else would Lee just then stroll down from the house and out to the road in time to join the party and meet (as does hard-swallowing Frank Talbott and *appalled* K. Sherritt Sagamore) Porter "Poonie" Baldwin, Jr.?

Says introductory Peter: Frank Talbott, the writer. Poon remains in the car but shakes hands through the window. Frank says politely Congressman, and quickly and pleasantly Poonie says Former and Future, thanks; hello to your father from his ex-representative. Professor Lee Talbott, our master of ceremonies announces, and Lee says Hi, just ducking down a bit to have a look at Kath's celebrated and controversial ex there in the flesh, though she knows nothing of our woman's forest-green recrayoning in 1963.

Peter pauses; he has gone far enough. Everybody pauses. I guess the rest of you know one another, he says then lowly. Much obliged for the lift, Paul, Willy, uh, Porter.

We have not described old Poonie's face, have we, framed now in the limousine window and regarding swollen Katherine with grave benignity. The baby-blue eyes; the trademark black eyebrows and mustache below the waved trademark hair, once ash-blond but now a distinguished silver-gray; the sensitive-looking chin, on which, politically, Peebie Junior has more than once taken it; the delicate mouth—

In which ditto, grudging Kate says later, but holds her tongue when at the time, earnestly, he says My best wishes to both of you, Katherine. Glad to've met you all. Willy?

Business, Willy explains to the assembled. Tells Paul he'll get the gate. Goes and gets it while Cecilia Skinner drives up with a Dodgeful of groceries and Judge Talbott wanders down to see whether he can see where everybody went. The taxi from Easton—which we expect to see driven by one Stavros Petrakis of NYC, but it isn't—rounds the bend.

BEEP

goes Frank Talbott's beeper then for the next half-hour up at the house, whereto we have all repaired except Molly Sherritt, who guesses she'll head back home unless she's needed here, and Chip, who guesses he'll let Molly drop him off now that things seem to be going to be okay with us, and the taxi man, whom Katherine pays for his trouble, and the driver and original passengers of the New Jersey Cadillac, who are at their business, the beeper tells us, at Natural Recycling Research. Beep. Beep. Once per second, like Peter's now normal pulse, Beep, till Frank turns the damn thing off; but then he can't help switching it back on every few minutes to confirm that they're still over there, all right, doing what wouldn't he give to know exactly what.

We shake and shake our heads at the thing that so surprisingly seized the pair of us by our relationship (but heedless love, we note, fetched K back to P; mere emergency P to K; our man will not soon forgive himself that); at the unassimilable but after all not so surprising coincidence of Peter's catching Willy and Poonie and the Garden State Mafia red-handed at damned if we know just what—Why doesn't Frank just stroll over there and ask for a tour of the plant?—followed by P's and K's respective impulsive simultaneous automobiling eachotherward. Beep. Katherine says

Molly says Willy says in his cups that there's a couple hundred drums of PCBs right smack in the foundations of the North Ocean City high-rise where their own condominium is, right next door to the one where Hank's and Irma's is, stashed there by the building contractor by arrangement with NRR. You trying to tell me they're doing any harm down there under all that sand and cee-ment with a twenty-story building sitting on top of them? Willy demanded of Molly, who wasn't trying to tell him anything. Baloney, her spouse declares, in his cups: They're our friggin' ballast! Used to be sturgeons in the Bay? Used to be shad? Used to be dinosaurs, too, once upon a time.

Beep.

Somewhere toward this chapter's end, a merry Key Farm dinner gets made and eaten—rockfish: They'll be the next to disappear, we reckon— and then the couples go down-lawn to savor the filling moon, the sweet southwesterly that breathes through our standing rigging. Katherine Sherritt keeps covering her face with her left hand and saying Poonie! I can't believe it! But she's laughing with the others now. Peter has been being so happy to have his friend back, so self-reproachful for having breached us, that only now he remembers to ask her what that good news was that Willy mentioned, when we were all standing around back there in the road. K groans Oh Jesus: Molly told me Willy's humping her for the first time in a hundred years as part of his big one-eighty, and she's letting the sonofabitch in, herpes and all, which he says is in remission, and now she's missed her period. She knows it's probably menopause, but she won't get a test 'cause she wants to think she's pregnant for a while.

Poor poor Molly.

Franklin Talbott steps aboard *Reprise* to silence a clinking staysail halyard; we'll follow and sit pensive about the dewy foredeck. Frank declares himself pleased with Lee's job decision. Today's crazy encounter with both the Sher and the Bald of Sherbald Enterprises (Your ex-husband's cute, Lee teases Kath) has geared him up all the more for his minidump book. He means to crash forward on the investigative work between now and Labor Day and then commute to wherever from wherever to be with Lee. Happy Katherine, her fingers linked with forgiven Peter's, asks Leah Did you telephone Carla B Silver to tell her your news?

Says Lee Are you kidding? She told *me*. Ma intuits stuff. So I asked her what else is new, and she told me to remind Frank that this coming weekend the moon's full and I'll be ovulating. Plus she says hello to you guys and thinks you ought to have a little talk with your daughter in there.

We have in fact already had one, gentle but serious. She is cool and indisputably precocious, is Pepper Sherritt Sagamore, but inexperienced and after all quite young. She simply got the story wrong, her mother now explains: Little Salt was frightened and discouraged, for sure—as who wasn't—but not last-ditch desperate, and certainly not self-destructive. Yes, he cried himself to sleep; presently, however, he's sleeping peacefully, sucking his thumb. He missed his daddy, is all. I missed me, too, says

Peter; where in the world was I? We conclude that Jean Heartstone's Magic Language Theory is only that: a theory. Or, if a principle, not the only principle. Rest in peace, poor Jean: *Amor omnia vincit,* now and then.

All the same, says Peter, I'm glad I got the message. Good night, Leah; good night, Franklin. We're sleeping aboard. Tomorrow we'll see.

Says Lee Us too, leaning her head on her husband's portside upper arm. Okay? she asks his shoulder.

Okay. Frank fishes from an aft pants pocket his old black *boina* and frisbees it to Peter. Wear this for me, okay?

Lee wonders: Honey?

It's okay, Frank assures her. *I'm* okay.

P regards it; puts it on. Okay.

OKAY,

he declares to his family a short while later, snuggled together in *Story*'s forward berth. We're going to do whatever suits your mother: either go back together to the First Guest Cottage and let the chips fall where they may, or wait here together till the action really starts. He tells Katherine I'm working now. Ready to get started, anyhow. I'm okay, I think, sort of. And the world's not likely to Vug out before next weekend.

Immeasurably happy K considers, not for awfully long, those alternatives. What we've done is what we'll do. Take us sailing.

You've got to be kidding, says astonished P, and hears she's not. Well! Well. We'll see what we think in the morning. Settle down in there, *niños.*

But they're both wide awake now, Fore and Aft, playing madcap ring around Mom's rosy. Says sleepy Kate For Christ sake tell them a story, would you? A *short* one. Less Is More. With authoritative hands upon her belly, their stirred father quiets them and, their mother's fingers deep in his hair under the *boina* that's all he's wearing, whispers through her navel

THE KEY TO THE TREASURE,

guys, may *be* the treasure. Night.

Night.

Night.

Night.

DAYS 11 & 12:
WYE TO SASSAFRAS

THE PLOT THINS

Before daybreak, the wind over Maryland shifts northeast; from splendid sleep we wake to a cloudy, cooler, sprinkly Thursday, June 26, rich in confidence that Candidate Reagan will never be president of the United States of America and that when, despite our confidence, he is overwhelmingly elected to that office in November, he will not rape our federal regulatory agencies, kill Soviet/American détente, rearm and unleash the CIA, plunder Central America, put the nation on a war footing, and spend spend spend on armaments until our federal deficit bankrupts half the world. Also that our concern with Breadbasket/BONAPARTE/Natural Recycling Research/Sherbald Enterprises can be put on hold for a semester or two while Franklin Key Talbott accumulates his minidump/Mafia evidence, and that Carla B Silver's Annapolis prediction (that Kate will deliver on 6/29/80 and not before) can be depended upon at least as much as these others. What a very good night's sleep. In family council over breakfast, we therefore resolve neither to stay on at Key Farm nor to retreat to Nopoint Point; we will, after all and by golly, reset sail, no longer whither listeth wind and tide but out of the Wye and straight upstream, upBay. Destination: Ordinary Point on the Sassafras, Blooey!, and the rest of it. ETA: *mañana,* or the day after: a little margin for prematurity.

We reasonably inquire of ourselves whether we have lost our motherfucking minds. Regained them, we prefer to imagine: Before donning our slickers and bidding the reasonably surprised Talbotts *au revoir,* we spend the mild, dripsy morning effecting certain changes in our and *Story*'s way of going.

From the treasure trove of Nopoint Point (specifically, from the hind end of *Katydid IV*'s tender), Bobby Henry drives up with a 9.9-horsepower electric-start outboard engine to clap onto the long-unused bracket on

Story's transom. It comes complete with an alternator for topping up our battery and two six-gallon fuel tanks, filled. We now have a calm-weather cruising range of at least a hundred miles at better than five knots. Hefting the thing into place, Peter sighs Sorry there, *Story,* but it's late in the action, you know?

Winking Bobby also brings us Andrew Christopher Sherritt, seabag packed, to help with the boat handling, and Andrew Christopher Sherritt's citizens-band radio transceiver to back up ours and our VHF. We propose to radio position and status reports and float plans to Nopoint Point not once, not twice, but thrice daily: before weighing anchor each morning, again at noon, and upon anchoring each evening. Welcome aboard, Chipperino.

So far from protesting, we agree in telephonic conference to rejoice at the proximity, as it may occur, of *Katydid IV* and/or the Basses' sloop *Off Call,* their owners and crews. The elder Sherritt and Bass appetites for a Chesapeake go-round of their own have been whetted by our reckless small adventure; they mean to sail up in one or the other or both yachts to Back Creek on the Sassafras to take official possession for Breadbasket Inc. of that old granary, gift of Sherbald Enterprises—a business in which the crew of *Story* hereby defer their concern, yes sir, for the present.

We arrange to be pleased, and in fact are, that Doctor Jack will carry aboard a bit more than his usual medical-surgical kit, and that Joan Bass is a veteran R.N. who could in a pinch deliver rings around your average midwife. Recommends Kath Put that in our catalogue of what Ma Non-troppo helps Whatsername deliver: rings around your average midwife.

Does Irma want to redo *Katydid*'s captain's cabin into an emergency delivery room? Stirrups, rubber sheets, high-intensity lights, sterilizer? Go to it, Irm—but we're setting sail at 1100 hours this morning, noon at latest. We *like* it that *K IV*'s electronical hardware (and its master's clout) can summon and coordinate ambulances, rescue boats, helicopters, obstetrical frogpersons, who knows what. We promise not to hesitate to call for such aid as may be called for, and we mean it.

Willy Sherritt even offers (via happily choked-up Molly) to station Easton Air Freight's chopper on standby alert in our daily neighborhood; it has business up that way anyhow. Says grim K, but politely, No thanks, Moll. Bye. We love you.

Reprovision? Um, no need to: P already did that on stiff-necked Day 10 or 9. He did, did he, says Kath, and looks the larder over while Peter stows stuff. Jesus, honey: canned beans and franks? Yes, well; sometimes a chap regresses. She negotiates better stores from Cecilia Skinner's Key Farm pantry; Irma sends up better yet with Chip and Bobby Henry and the 9.9, so much that *Reprise* has to stock the surplus. Finally, at P's request (but don't ask, he warns his crew), Chip delivers from his seabag the battered three-ring binder in which Peter has first-drafted everything since college days. Don't ask. We re-ice, re-water, rebid *auf Wiedersehen* and good hunting to Frank and Lee Talbott, thanks to the Skinners, good-bye to old Judge George, whom we shall not see again in this life, much obliged to Bobby Henry and Irma and Hank, peace on earth to men of goodwill, and we cast off (under sail, having tested the outboard and shut it down), Chipper at the helm in the light air, from Wye Island. Bye-bye. Beside themselves with excitement, By and By romp and giggle and wave. K rolls her eyes; puts one hand to her mouth, one to her belly; sits down.

Could you and I chat for a minute? Peter Sagamore hears Franklin Key Talbott off-handedly ask Bobby Henry as *Story* slides stern-first away from the dock into the Wye. Chip puts our helm over; Peter holds the jib aback until our bow swings across the wind. Kate then deftly trims the main, Chip the jib, while Pete coils docklines. His sheet made fast, young Andrew sounds our conch.

We're under way.

THE TOWN QUEEN OF SWAN CREEK'S PRINTS

Texas heat wave continues; candidate Reagan calls for tax cuts now; House okays peacetime draft registration; *Story* broad-reaches down stem of Wye on light northeasterly through cool drizzle like suspended dew, hoping to turn the corner under Bennett Point and port-tack up Prospect Bay to Kent Island Narrows. The wind fizzles, however, and the tide's contrary; the men douse sail, rig our awning against the wet, fire up the outboard. Ears and nose offended, Kate says Blah and goes below to build lunch. Through water roiled now only by our wake and the occasional swirling school of skates, we chug up the chart while green-eyed Andy dutifully radiotelephones home base.

He gets to report that we are west of Wye River Can Three heading zero zero zero magnetic toward the Kent Narrows Bridge at five point five knots before his mother says That will do, Andrew. Are you an uncle yet? Chip says You're supposed to say Over, Mom; over. Says Irma I am not about to say Over into a C and P Princess telephone standing here in my bedroom packing my suitcase. *You* say Over, honey; I'll just chat. Did you remember to pack your you-know-what?

Boyoboy, Mom; the whole Chesapeake *Bay* listens in on these conversations! How insensitive can a mother get? Over.

Equable Irm coos I know that, sweetheart. That's why I said "you-know-what" instead of you know what. Is your sister there?

She happens to be on board.

Agrees Katherine, taking the microphone, Low blow, Mom. Does Chipper remind you on the public airwaves to pack your Geritol? Anyhow, his zit's under control; we're monitoring it. Over.

Groaning Andrew escapes to the cockpit, where Peter smiles sympathy. The lad had been going to be the first young North American since the invention of Clearasil to navigate from one end of adolescence to the other without a single facial blemish, but in the space between Days 9 and 10, after beans-and-franks night, his maiden pimple purply popped at the lower left lip-corner, and though he has never consciously touched the thing with unmedicated hand, he's sure it's going to leave a pock.

Irma tells Katherine Your father and I are setting out, probably with Jack and Joan Bass. He says one o'clock latest, but it'll be later. Where do you think you'll park tonight?

K looks up the companionway to Peter, who checks his wristwatch, says Swan Creek, and asks Chip please to reckon nautical mileage and estimated time of arrival. The boy has already done so, to assorted waypoints and likely destinations. Eight point five nautical miles from Kent Narrows at five point five knots puts our hook down in Swan Creek about fourteen forty-five, he is pleased to announce, if we make the one-o'clock bridge, which we should despite the adverse tide if we throttle up half a knot or so.

Says Peter, twisting the throttle, You want half a knot, you got half a knot.

Katherine tells her mother Swan Creek. Irma doubts *Katydid* will get that far today; she's hardly started packing. Probably just Dun Cove, though she guesses Hank will push for Tilghman Creek at least, once they're under way. Driving at night reminds him of his Annapolis-to-Bermuda days. Go with it, Mom, Kath recommends; it stays light till all hours now.

Irma says she's noticed that: Summertime, she believes it's called. What do we think of Willy and Molly's news?

K says she thinks Molly Barnes Sherritt had better get herself to a gynecologist fast, but she doesn't want to talk about it, okay? Get yourself packed; we'll call on channel sixteen around happy hour. *Story* out.

Chilled artichokes vinaigrette, salmon salad, Perrier. In the fickle air, we motor and sail and motorsail by turns, up through the tricky narrows, back into and up out of the Chester, past the Love Point Light—where Andrew scans the world in vain for Chessie the Shoal-Draft Sea Monster, and Peter wonders whether such an implausibility might be successfully surfaced in an otherwise realistic novel, not at the beginning (anybody's credit is good at the beginning), but as late as the climax, and Katherine muses duly upon love's point and is awfully pleased that we two are under way together again, motor or no motor, and that we're we and not Molly and Willy or even Lee and Frank or her parents, and Toil and Trouble put their heads together on a revised version of that swan-prince story they've been gestating ever since Queenstown Creek—briefly into the Chesapeake itself, its western shore shrouded in this weather. Hello there, Chesapeake Bay, we say, you long-limbed, formidable, slightly poisoned beauty. On up the Eastern Shore to the funky old villages of Rock Hall and Gratitude and into Swan Creek, our shelter for the night: spoiled at the bottom end with moorings and marinas, unspoiled because shallow at the top; no particular gem, but properly snug.

Got it, the kids agree: The Swan Prince of Queenstown Creek.

We park in the upper middle. While Chip takes a swim in the chilly rain (to give us some privacy, we bet, on his mother's orders), Peter hats up and talks to our log about Sex Education and Scheherazade, Katherine to her obstetrician's wife about where everybody is. Reports Joan Bass, who has taken Kate's call at *Katydid IV*'s navigation station, *Off Call*'s off call with a sprained gizmo from last week's race, so we're all on *Katydid*, headed out the Choptank. Here's your father. Hi ho, *Story,* calls Henry Sherritt; hello there, Katydid. Over. It takes a while to sort out this traffic, as Katherine's father keeps using her nickname while Joan Bass uses his boat's name. Presently, however, it is established that we are where we are— twenty minutes or less to the Rock Hall Volunteer Fire Company ambulance, with whose crew we promise to have a readiness chat before bedtime; another fifteen or twenty minutes to the Kent and Queen Anne's County Hospital in Chestertown, should push come to shove, over—and that *Katydid IV* will be parking this evening in Tilghman Creek, at the mouth of Eastern Bay, whence by less convenient logistics Jack Bass could get to that same hospital in, oh, two hours or less. So you may fire when ready, young lady, says Doctor Jack, but don't hurry through your labor when it starts. Relax and tell the kids a story.

It is, however, their turn to tell us one, using their mother as their mouthpiece. *Katydid* out. *Story* out. After a dinner agreeably cooked and eaten indoors for a change as in early spring and late fall cruising (Those are sauteed softshell crabs, little Push tells Shove, and this is the feta cheese in their Greek salad. The wine is something Rhenish: a Piesporter, I'd guess. Our mother does well to go very easy on the wine, for our present and future sakes; at the same time, she does well to sip just a bit, for the education of our palates. Piesporter Goldtröpfchen Seventy-eight. This is pita bread. . . .), we stow the table and lounge about our cozy cabin, the five or so of us. With the aid of a flashlight—but listening carefully at the same time—Andrew Sherritt watches spiders spin their nightly snares here and there among our lifeline stanchions and standing rigging, and silently identifies most of the species. Peter Sagamore relaxes from invention, perches Frank Talbott's *boina* on Kate's belly, and rejoices that the world is at least temporarily reassembled. Katherine Sherritt wishes May Jump were with us to judge how much she's speaking and how much being spoken through; May's good at that.

Queen Anne's County and Queen Anne's lace, she hears herself say, and Queenstown Creek and Queenstown town, home of Sherbald Enterprises, are all named after You Know Whom of England, late-seventeenth, early-eighteenth century, so that gets queens on the table, all right? Now, then: Any unborn child can tell you that when a boat named *Story* sails into a creek named Queenstown and sees seven white swans rafted up with one lonely Canada goose, either that goose or that child's mother is Mother Goose. If that unborn child has a twin to discuss things with and a brain in their two heads, they'll soon figure out that since Mother Goose is in Queenstown Creek, at least one of those swans has to be a handsome young prince in drag; therefore the goose must be a princess at least, and that leaves old Mom to do the dishes and tuck everybody in with a bedtime story.

Except you guys already *did* the dishes, thanks, and Fish and Chips here are calling the narrative shots, not me. So this young prince, we guess, had been princing along very nicely on the family spread, which we'll call Prince George's County, Maryland, though his name was Bruce. Bruce? Bruce. Fourteen hundred–plus SATs and three varsity letters at Choate or Hotchkiss, plus he's a decent chap, not to mention gorgeous and from old southern Maryland money, first tobacco and later real estate and banking but lately just dividend collecting and public service. Princing. The whole Ivy League's after him, not to mention half the debs in the East, but he's cool; he's in no hurry. After a year's backpacking around Europe on a Eurailpass like everybody else, he settles in at Princeton to study . . . international studies. Is that the way to say it?

Our storyteller breaks unexpectedly into tears. Alarmed Peter assures her that "study international studies" is perfectly okay to say in first draft; we'll maybe neat it up later. But it turns out K has got Molly Barnes Sherritt on her mind: not the herpes business; she doesn't know what, exactly, and she doesn't want to sit around in male company being simultaneously pregnant, intuitive, and weepy, but she *knows* poor Molly's in deep deep trouble, and not from Operation BONAPARTE or Willy Sherritt's penis. Excuse her.

Chip says Hey, Kate, and gets Kleenex. Kath blows her nose and kisses his cheek and readjusts the *boina* and says So, anyway, old Bruce's mom there gets galloping cancer and good-bye, and the family's floored 'cause they all loved one another, but anon King Dad finds himself a new consort who certainly isn't older or worse-looking than his dear departed. The kids agree that life has to go on, and they're happy their father's not alone, but one thing leads to another—maybe à la Hippolytus, maybe not—until one day in his sophomore year, blam: The prince finds himself turned into a whistling swan and stuck out with six others in the royal bird sanctuary, which happens to be the Eastern Neck National Wildlife Refuge just over yonder.

Praises Peter (wondering what's what there with his wife *re* Molly Barnes Sherritt) This story sure has profluence. It proflows. He and Chip split a National Premium beer. No, thanks, says Kate; Spit and Image say Thanks, Mom, and go on with their story: There's Bruce out there with the migratory waterfowl, feeling mighty sorry for himself and for his father, who has no idea why the boy dropped out of Princeton or what happened to him. But once a prince always a prince, we guess, 'cause when he sees this poor bedraggled female Canada goose being driven away from the park ranger's corn by half a dozen whistling ganders, he lets them know who's the boss swan in these parts and invites the young Cahnahdienne—she's from Quebec—to help herself.

Which she does, okay? And thereafter Bruce sees to it she gets her share of the action despite grumbles from the other swans. Their gripe is that he's subverting the ancient and established Eastern Neck National Wildlife Refuge pecking order, probably of divine origin. Georgette—that's the Quebecoise, and you're saying it wrong, kids: It's not Jor-Jet; it's Zhor-*zhet*-tuh, okay? Let's hear that *tuh*.

Georget-te feels in her gizzard that the swans are right, but dinner is dinner, and her benefactor keeps telling her Don't be a goose; we're all birds of a feather, under the skin. Fact is, Bruce knows zilch about waterfowl ethology, 'cause his Princeton curriculum didn't get to Whats-isname's studies of the greylag goose until junior year—

Konrad Lorenz's, says Andy Sherritt. This guy went to Hotchkiss? I doubt it.

Anyhow he's pretty much in despair about what's happened to him: Eastern Neck Island is not Princeton Station, and swansdown's fine in an L. L. Bean vest but something else again when it's what you have instead of hair and clothes. So when Georgette, not surprisingly, falls hard for him, he doesn't give her a tumble, even though now that she's eating regularly and preening herself a bit, she is one good-looking bird. Bruce grants her that; he even likes her, especially by comparison to those pushy swans. But when he thinks of the human girls back at Smith and Vassar and for that matter Saint Deniston's just across the river, he can't help choking up, even though his sobs come out like whistles. Remember to call the Rock Hall Volunteer Fire Company, honey, when this story's done.

So: If he'd been a natural-born bird, maybe he'd have returned poor Georgette's feelings. Or maybe not: Those other swan types are ready enough to make it with her, now that she's all fledged out, but it's clear enough they're just wolf-whistling till their own kind comes down the flyway. In any case, Bruce keeps things on a big-brother/kid-sister level, and Georgette sadly concludes that despite his protestations of ornitho-logical egalitarianism, in his heart the guy's a snob.

What next? Well, the fall migration gets up steam, and all the sunbirds come down the Intracoastal, and Georgette there flirts with a couple of arriviste Canada-goose ganders to see whether that scores her any points, but all Bruce does is advise her in a kind way to look the singles scene over carefully before she makes her choice, since geese mate for life. If she weren't in love with him, she'd wring his neck! Her only consolation is that *he* doesn't pair up, either, with any of the lady swans that come along, the way the other whistlers do. To smooth her ruffled feathers, she wishes she could agree with those spiteful ganders that the guy is gay, but all her hormones tell her he's anything but. So she thinks he must be even more of a snob than she thought, if his own kind aren't good enough for him either.

All right: I am now instructed to report that back at the palace at this point in our story, King Dad of Prince George's County and his presumably wicked step-queen total their Bentley on the D.C. Beltway in a royal exit-ramp misunderstanding with a Mayflower moving van, and despite lap and shoulder restraints, the gentleman is paralyzed for life and the lady is skished. Who knows whether air bags might have saved them? The minute she kicks, Bruce and possibly other of her victims elsewhere find themselves restored to their prior estate. Fortunately for him, it's only late September: The water's still warm, and there aren't too many sea nettles that season. Georgette sees the lonesome apple of her eye suddenly turn into a naked and very surprised young man splashing ashore in Salthouse Cove, Queenstown Creek, where the Eastern Neck flock has bivouacked for the evening. Don't ask our children how he gets himself to the nearest telephone or explains himself to the constabulary; Georgette's last sight of him is in a warm-up suit doing stretching exercises on the pier at Queenstown Landing. While waiting for a taxi, maybe? Yes: The narrative committee has decided that she sees a taxi drive up and hears this beautiful human young fellow tell the driver My name is Bruce; take me to Prince George's County, please.

Alas and alack . . . right: Alas and Alack now divide their narrative perspective in order to declare that while Bruce takes his rightful place as the prince of Prince George's County in his father's incapacity, poor Zhor-*zhet*-tuh languishes in Queenstown Creek and would no doubt starve that winter, were it not that the six remaining swans are too preoccupied with their new girlfriends to enforce the pecking order, and the arriviste geese are as always decimated by the hunters, whereas *she* knows all the local blinds like the back of her webbed feet. So she survives, but she is one lonesome cohunk, believe you us, and more hopelessly in love than ever, now that she can tell herself it wasn't snobbery that made Bruce so stand-offish but rather the circumstance that he wasn't a bird at all. He was holding off for *her* sake, right?

On with the story: Along about Groundhog Day, a certain lecherous old gamekeeper on Bruce's family payroll goes out hunting with a young female assistant gamekeeper on whom he intends to put the moves before the morning's over. To keep himself warm and to soften her up, he puts away more Jim Beam than he should, and because at his insistence and to the girl's dismay they're shooting illegally over corn right smack in the middle of the Eastern Neck National Wildlife Refuge, even Georgette is lured into range, and that will be the end of our female lead if the old rake doesn't stumble in his cups as he rises to shoot, and trip and fall and experience fatal cardiac arrest when his Remington lets go about one foot from his ear. Happily, however, all that happens, *et voilà:* Georgette finds herself standing bare-ass naked in a Kent County cornfield, metamorphosed back into the sharp-looking young assistant park ranger with a master's in wildlife management that it now turns out she herself had been before her immediate superior turned her into a clipped-wing Canada goose for threatening to charge him with sexual harassment in the workplace plus shooting over corn, of which offenses he was as guilty as was the dead man now cooling off before her, being in fact the identical same sumbitch.

Well! The two women size up each other and the situation, and while the authors of this story try to figure out why Bruce the swan knew all along he was a prince, but Georgette the goose didn't know till just now that she'd been a royal goose-girl junior grade, her successor in that post helps her strip enough warmies off their mutual harasser to keep her from freezing and explains that she herself had every intention of reporting the rascal too, once she was out of his goosing range, if only to get a private audience with that hunk of a prince whose private bird-sanctuary this is. Yeah, right, says Georgette.

So back they go to Prince Bruce's palazzo in Prince George's County, after ringing in the Maryland Natural Resources Police to tidy up the scene and take the appropriate depositions. Georgette leaves out the metamorphosis part in her account, because the officers are suspicious enough as it is of one woman smelling to heaven of Jim Beam and the other half-dressed in the dead trick's camouflage suit. Darlene herself, the Jim Beam one, can already hardly believe she saw what she saw, and Georgette now encourages her to imagine that she didn't; that it was the booze, or something in the booze, and that what she's just made up for the cops is the truth: i.e., that she, Georgette, just happened to be strolling by when the old guy was about to put the moves on Darlene, and that as he was forcing them both to strip at gunpoint, his ticker gave out from overexcitement. Yeah, yeah, says Darlene; I guess that's how it was. Yeah.

Our goose-girl doesn't even mention to Darlene that she knows Prince Bruce already, much less what she knows about him. The prince himself has cooled that story, for a couple of reasons that we'll soon come up with, like, um, to spare his father's feelings about the late step-queen, maybe, whom the old king really had had a passion for and is still mourning the skishment of; also, we guess, because the whole whistling-swan episode sounded so dopey on the face of it that he came almost to believe what the rest of the family suspected: that like some other overprivileged kids he'd dropped out of the Ivy into Cokesville for a while. Junior year in outer space kind of thing. Don't *you* dare get mixed up with that stuff, Chip Sherritt! Chipper?

Okay, Sis, okay. Finish your story already.

It's not my story; I just work here. Molly's got cancer, Peter; I *know* she has!

Jesus, Kath . . .

Why'd you ever have to know that Jean Heartstone person? I'm killing poor Molly, and I can't help it!

Peter Sagamore really wonders whether this is what a nervous breakdown looks and sounds like; he has never observed one. He puts an arm around our storyteller and explains to Andy that he once had a girlfriend a hundred years ago who believed et cet, and to Katherine that even if, as Dr. Oliver Wendell Holmes guessed correctiy of Nathaniel Hawthorne in 1864, the shark has got its tooth into Molly Barnes Sherritt (a speculation based on no evidence whatever, that Peter has heard of), the big C is not as uppercase nowadays as it used to be: At the first real symptom, folks nowadays go over to Johns Hopkins or up to Sloan-Kettering and get themselves diagnosed and in a great many instances fixed, you know?

K knows; she knows. Excuse her.

As for Georgette, she shakes Darlene after their official short interview with Prince Bruce, who is even more gorgeous than she remembered his being and who exonerates them both of any culpability in the death of horny Claude the gamekeeper. Claude? I'm just reporting the news. She manages a private couple of minutes to discuss the question of getting her old job back and then asks the guy directly whether he remembers a certain lonely little Canada goose hen who used to swim around with seven whistling swans in Queenstown Creek last year, and six of the swans chased her off, but the seventh used to see to it she didn't go hungry? Old Bruce fidgets like he's got a loony on his hands and says he doesn't get out to the royal blinds lately as much as he wishes he could; princing takes up all his free time. In fact, he's behind in his appointments as it is, and he's got to get back up the Amtrak to Princeton that same afternoon and study some more international studies. As to her job, no sweat; what with Claude gone, there's room for her and Darlene both. Maybe she could draft him an official report on swan-goose interaction in the Eastern Neck Refuge and what if anything should be done about it.

So by golly she does, crestfallen as she is. Between her regular gamekeeping chores she writes out this story we two have just told—We *three,* you little turkeys!—called "The Swan Prince of Queenstown Creek." It ends with the Canadian goose-girl junior grade writing out her story and sending it Express Mail up to the prince in Princeton, wondering whether he'll dispatch a car for her at once from Prince George's County or rush down the flyway himself to Eastern Neck Island and marry her on the spot with Darlene as her maid of honor, or whether maybe the human pecking order is finally even stronger than the bird one, and tenderly as he remembers his petite Canadienne from Salthouse Cove, he's engaged now to Heather Foulke-Stoughton of Wye Landing and Saint Croix and *c'est la vie.*

But the truth (say Tried and True) is that just as Georgette in her goose days had no memory at all of ever having been human, while Bruce's was total and exquisite, now that they've shucked their feathers and got back into their clothes the reverse is true, no matter what we might have said before: Bruce believes that he just lost a semester somewhere back there, OD'd on some Controlled Dangerous Substance. He writes Georgette a really nice rejection letter, telling her that while he's no authority in literary matters, he thinks she definitely has a way with words and maybe ought to send the piece to Joyce Carol Oates for possible publication in *The*

Ontario Review on account of the Canadian connection, and he really wishes Georgette good luck in her writing career, which she ought to be able to combine nicely with the job of chief gamekeeper, which he's promoting her to in old Claude's place, because no doubt there's a lot of privacy and quiet time for writing down there in the refuge.

Kate goes to bed. We all go to bed, after making sure by CB radio that there is indeed an ambulance and driver in Rock Hall. Peter tells our children pretty much what Bruce told Georgette, except that his judgment is at once a lot more professional and, in this instance, a lot less disinterested: It's their first time up at the narrative plate. He kisses Kath's forehead, chin, neck. She squeezes his hand. She'll be all right tomorrow, she promises. It's just she had this dreadful flash about Molly.

Says Chip from his settee berth after lights-out I guess if Sherbald Enterprises Inc. were here in Swan Creek instead of over in Queenstown, and Poonie Baldwin, Junior, had some photographs taken of himself and his friends doing gay stuff around this anchorage, and the KGB got hold of those photographs and threatened to circulate them if Poonie didn't play ball with them, some smart-ass political columnist could call those pictures "The Town Queen of Swan Creek's Prints."

In order to shine her flashlight, of which we have one for each bunk, full into Andrew Sherritt's blushing face, Katherine hauls all the way out of her V-berth and into *Story*'s main cabin. Her husband is breaking up in his quarterberth. Little Balls and Strikes don't get Chip's labored joke. In the morning, their mother promises, your Uncle Andrew will explain to you the principles and practice of human homosexuality. Right now he's got to get out of bed and apply his you-know-what to his you know what.

IN *STORY*'S LOGBOOK TABLE OF CONTENTS FOR THIS NOVEL, WE DON'T EVEN AWARD SEPARATE-CHAPTER STATUS TO DAY 12, THOUGH BEFORE IT'S DONE WE HEAR AT LEAST TWO NOT-BAD TIDEWATER TALES

It begins with physical exercise, does Friday, which we feel we've been neglecting lately. Kate does those Kegels and the other pregnant stuff. Waking to find themselves still unborn, Time and Again do submarine aerobics until Mom goes swimming to settle them down. Peter and Andrew do stretchies on the foredeck and then swim laps around the boat, whose waterline they also scrub—the dinghy's, too—before coming in for breakfast. Chip agrees with us over coffee that humor at the expense of homosexuals is not as entertaining as it used to be and may in some instances reflect a degree of sexual insecurity in the would-be humorist; at the same time, he asserts his entitlement, as a twelve-year-old virgin, to some degree of sexual insecurity. The FM's A.M. news is that as we slept, the French government revealed that it has already built and tested its own enhanced-radiation "neutron" bomb (Score one for Vug the Doomsday Factor, sighs Peter Sagamore), and a poll indicated that seventy percent of inadvertently pregnant Baltimore County teenagers get abortions. Complains Chip Pregnant teenagers? Abortions? I thought the stork took care of all that.

You're but a one-zit preteen, Kate consoles him. After you're bar mitzvah'd next year, we'll let you read Franklin Key Talbott's *SEX EDUCATION: Play,* Acts One and Two, and you'll know two-thirds of the facts of life.

Our daughter signals that she'd prefer we-all not talk about abortion and the Doomsday Factor, if we don't mind; those subjects make her brother uneasy. Can't we do the weather or something?

It bids in fact to be a stinker, declares the VHF weather channel: We may thank Zeus we're not in Texas, where the murderous heat-wave perks along, but hereabouts we're in for a sunny, low-ninetyish and humid day, winds on the Bay southwest ten to twelve, waves one to two feet. Says *Story*'s skipper Sassafras River, here we come. He'll catch the dishes while Chip gets the sails up and Katherine checks in with the grown-ups. We bid *hasta la vista* to Swan Creek, power out past the Rock Hall fish traps into the blue-gray Bay, and run wing and wing seventeen nautical miles on the steady, warm southwesterly, up past Fairlee and Worton Creeks to improbable Still Pond. In these upper-Chesapeake latitudes, in the long stretch between the Chester and the Sassafras, the Eastern Shore looks like the Western down where we come from: high wooded banks broken not by rivers but by a series of snug creeks with alarmingly narrow entrances, typically S-shaped and fortunately well markered, through which the tides boil in and out. The large-ship channel swings almost to the beach up here; we move out of it to let a Toyota-fraught Japanese freighter steam by like a metal cliff toward the C & D Canal, bound we guess for Philly. Large yachts pass us, too, power and sail, headed north from Florida waters for Long Island Sound, Narragansett and Buzzards Bay, Marblehead, Maine, Nova Scotia. Katherine asks, as always, Can we go? Says Peter Sure, some day, and wonders whether we ever shall. There are also Greece, Grenada, Pago Pago, he forgets what else—all to be inspected.

Chip takes lots of bearings and keeps a running plot of our course; never since he was last aboard has *Story*'s position been fixed with such exactitude. *Katydid IV* wonders what's our hurry; their plan is to sail from Tilghman Creek as far as Fairlee or Worton and go ashore for dinner at the marina restaurant, of which there is at least one on each creek. Kate explains that that's exactly why we're not stopping there, even for lunch; we'll push on up to Still Pond, which won't be spoiled by marinas and moorings for another couple of years yet. As of Friday, 27 June '80, there's a Coast Guard Search-and-Rescue station at the sigmoid entrance to that creek and almost nothing beyond it but woods and water; K bets the USCG could get her to Chestertown hospital even more quickly than the Rock Hall Volunteer Fire Company could have, should our lunch be interrupted by her labor. Should it not, we mean to go yet another dozen miles up and into the Sassafras for the night. There, she promises, we-all will rendezvous *mañana*.

Well, they guess they would prefer we wait for them in Still Pond; but as we'll be there noonish, and they not till day's end even should they forgo dinner ashore and push on, they guess they understand. Saturday at Breadbasket's granary, then. But we will call at noon, yes? And again at five or six, when we're anchored.

Through the sultry morning's run, with Peter's all-but-unprecedented permission (he's still feeling plenty guilty about Days 8 through 10), Katherine reviews his log-notes for Parts One and Two of that possible three-part Don Quixote story, asking decipherment as needed, but trying for imaginative exercise to ask as seldom as possible. The thing makes her itch for Iberia. Toledo! The Tajo/Tejo/Tagus! Dear Lisboa! Does Peter remember the cast-iron Eiffel-looking Santa Justa Elevador that you take to get up to or down from the Bairro Alto unless you ride the little funicular on the Calçada da Gloria instead? Peter does. And the Alfama! Turn this tub around and take us there!

P sets her the task instead of following out the dramatic trajectory of the possible story into Part Three. Given the several escalated themes— D.Q.'s quest in turn for Dulcinea, for Sancho, and for the Cide Hamete Benengeli; the changing nature of his "enchantment"; his increasing nautical skill and ambition—how and why and to what end do we get him from Cape St. Vincent to Capes Charles and Henry? From the Sagres headland to Fawcett's Marine Supply in Annapolis? Needless to say, we can't use Odysseus and Nausicaa's trick; Ted and Deeahnah already copyrighted that one in their Phaeacian 35 Mark I.

Kate says she'll work on it, and does as we surge along. Chip at the tiller thinks it's a fairly cool story, so far. Should he read *Don Quixote* this summer or when he's a little older? Says Peter Both, and reminds us, himself especially, that it's a lot easier to toss chestnuts into the narrative fire than to fish them all out again, excuse the mixed metaphor. We have made an end-run around the mechanics of the voyage through time by soft-focusing the passage of centuries as Quixote lingers on the Sagres cliffs; we have yet to commission *Rocinante IV* and give its voyage a point, a climax, and a conclusion.

Story's crew agree, passing Fairlee and Worton, that the compounded interest on those two *reales*—which Andrew Sherritt considers a neat symbol but wishes he knew the approximate monetary value of in current dollars, so that he could calculate D.Q.'s gross income for 1980—will pay for the design, construction, and outfitting of *Rocinante IV*. We agree further, approaching Still Pond Creek (I don't see any entrance at *all*, Chip marvels, who has never sailed into it before. Advises Peter from the helm, as he appears to steer us smack into the shoreline, Have faith), that Part

Two sets the narrative stage for a voyage to America. But in search of whom or what? And does he find what he's after, or does he go into gracefully decaying orbit like the handsome Dmitrikakises?

I don't *believe* this, Chip declares from the bow; it's Crab Creek!

Indeed, like Crab on the South River (and Fairlee just below us, and Turner up on the Sassafras, and Grove on the Chester, and half a dozen other jim-dandies here and there about the Chesapeake), Still Pond Creek must be entered to be believed. A few yards from the sheer and driftwood-littered bank, Pete hangs a hard left around a buoy into a sandspitted entrance channel that appears from nowhere; he powers through it against a two-knot current funneling between beaches we could almost touch with our boathook, hangs a hard right after the green day-beacon off the Coast Guard station, and here we are in six to eight feet in capacious Still Pond, rightly named, the Bay and the creek entrance already out of sight astern. What's more, the only other boat inside, riding at anchor just ahead, is a hefty old ketch half again our length and more than twice our draft, by the look of her, which—

I don't believe *this,* says Kath, but the binocs confirm it: *Rocinante IV, Montesinos.* Capn Don Q.'s already waving us over with his Greek fisherman's cap, unsurprised. *¡Hola, Story!* Come raft up. Got a friend of yours aboard here!

Wonders Andy What's going on?

Peter promises we'll explain, when we know. Let's put out fenders and lines portside. *Rocinante*'s port bow now winks our way. Binoculared Katherine's giggling; looking smart if not quite at ease in white ducks, scarlet halter-top and bandanna with plenty of necklaces between, brown shades, bare feet, and cigarillo, Carla B Silver accepts the coil of sternline Kath hands her and grumbles *Muchath grathiath, theñora;* now tell me what to do with the mothering thing.

WHAT IS CARLA B SILVER DOING IN STILL POND CREEK?

She's tying this damn rope to this thingumabob and making such a job of it you'll never get loose. Who's your young friend there, skipper?

Introductions and handshakes all around. Andrew Sherritt. Carla B Silver, a new old friend of ours. Donald Quicksoat, an old old friend of *hers;* just call me Capn Don, sir. Like Peter, the man is wearing only cutoff jeans; he looks fit and brown and wiry, more like a seasoned desert prophet than an errant knight, with his short white beard and craggy brows, bright eyes and eagle beak, and more like the ancient mariner than either. So here we are in Still Pond Creek, some of us.

And the rest to follow, we expect, growls cordial Carla, her cleat work done. Either here or up the road. How's that?

Kath says It'll hold. Hey, you look great!

You look great. The women embrace across two gunwales. Damn boats make me nervous, declares Carla B, especially since Fred. What'm I doing here? Want a beer, Mister Sagamore?

And a swim, says sweatsy Peter. Hold your story for a minute, okay?

Kate says she'll just split a Perrier with her brother. The three men take a short dip in Still Pond Creek. Carla B Silver says Gypsies don't swim, and Kath's not in a ladder-climbing mode; all she wants, please, is an entire bucket of water poured over her from head to foot on *Rocinante*'s ample, bulwarked foredeck. Capn Don admiringly does the honors before going over the side.

What they're doing together in Still Pond Creek, C.B S. and C.D.Q., and why they're not all that surprised to see us, comes to this, told over a long and light but dark-beered lunch under *Rocinante*'s mizzen-boom cockpit awning: After crossing her path and ours a week ago in Annapolis, her old acquaintance Capn Don sailed straightway up to Baltimore and sought her out in Carla's Cavern, a favorite haunt of his, which he hadn't happened to visit in his past couple of runs up and down the Intracoastal. There he learned for the first time of Frederick Mansfield Talbott's presumable demise and of Lascar Lupescu's abrupt dismissal. That latter chap he'd never met, but he got the idea if not the whole story, and being himself a knight-of-all-trades in no particular hurry, he volunteered to take Lascar's place as barkeep and kitchen helper till Carla found a replacement.

That was only last Saturday or Sunday, she declares. By Tuesday he's already upping the ante.

With a wink at Chip, Donald Quicksoat cheerfully acknowledges Singlehanders get horny. And just look at her, lad, would you now?

But she wasn't yet ready for anything further in *that* line, was Carla B Silver, we gathered; the Lascar lapse was too fresh, and she was still assimilating daughter Marian's alliance with May Jump—which, by the way, seems hunky-dory, but she'll come back to that. A little sailing weekend, then, C.D.Q. was proposing by, say, Wednesday. Some sunbird pals of his were to rendezvous this weekend before they mosey on north for the summer—where he expects to mosey himself, sooner or later, as usual. But he's in no hurry.

Sailors do it at hull speed, cracks Capn Don: one point three five times the square root of their waterline length. Chip murmurs One point three *four*.

No thanks, said I, says C. B Silver. Sailboats give her the heeb-jeebs. But in her daily chats with daughter Leah, whether by C & P or by ESP, she'd followed the story of our meeting *Reprise* in Queenstown Creek, our remarkable chancing upon the text of Franklin Key Talbott's play, our visit to Key Farm, our separation and reconciliation—

Complains Peter Jesus, it's as if we've been living on channel twenty-six.

When it comes to omniscience, Donald Quicksoat says proudly, this lady has got your NSA beat all to hell.

Carla says no, it's just she and Lee are on the same frequency. When she heard the good news that we were back together and bound for the Sassafras to have our babies, she advised Frank to take the weekend off and go sailing too and get her daughter pregnant again, please, before settling down for the summer. What had happened had happened, water under the bridge. Hearing then yesterday from Lee that they might just do what Mama suggested—

Cheers Katherine Yay!

—and further that Kath's parents and obstetrician and *todo el mundo* were casting off for the weekend, she told Mister Captain Donaldo about her vision of K's going into labor up at Ordinary Point on Saturday or Sunday or Monday, most likely Sunday (a vision that involved, by the way, a lot more than just a brace of human babies, but never mind that). . . .

Now this is one pregnant coincidence, D.Q. tells us he told Carla B Silver when she told him all that, yesterday: Ordinary Point is where my *amigos* are rafting up this weekend, before they hit the C and D. He winks at Katherine: And I don't mean D and C.

Says Carla B Silver *Oy gevalt.* Says unfazed Quicksoat So I propositioned my boss to take the weekend off and let's poke on up and watch the show, and here we are, almost.

Kath says *Olé,* but is pleased to hear our not entirely Gypsy friend say *Almost* says it, too. I looked him up and down the way I'm doing right now and double-entried him a bit: how he'd sure as hell bailed me out by taking Lascar's place downstairs, but before he came *up*stairs we'd have to have it out about this cutesy-creepy Dee Kew business, you know? I told him I'd sleep on it.

Grins Capn Don And I told her—

Never mind, says Carla, smiling at Chip, who sighs I guess I'll go write a play called *SEX EDUCATION,* but doesn't.

So I talked to Mims, Carla says, on the telephone, and found out that she and May Jump and Simple Simon are meeting Lee and Frank at Kent Narrows today at lunchtime for a weekend on their boat, so I said to my colleague here Okay, you're on—but tomorrow morning, not tonight. So we had a nice whatyoucallum over here from Middle River—beam-reach?—and I didn't get seasick after all. She shows us her copper-braceleted forearms. Shall I lift my curse on General Pinochet and Anaconda Copper?

Says Kathy Nope, and Capn Don declares that what *he* thinks is, C.D.Q. and C.B S. have both singlehanded long enough. He wishes she'd declare a whole season's holiday and cruise with him clear on up to the Maritimes.

Not likely, says Carla B Silver. I'm a working girl. Anyhow, one step at a time, no? If people are going to live in sin, they have to be able to sin to each other's satisfaction.

Says Donald Quicksoat Sailors do it at an angle. Sailors do it with buoys and gulls. I'll tell you the story of Singood the Sailor, that was told to me by Scheherazade herself.

Wonders Peter aloud, who can't quite get a handle on this odd duck: Scheherazade?

In Kitty Hawk, North Carolina, nods Capn Don, last Columbus Day weekend, at the ASPS wingding down there. He lifts his beer glass in salute to surprised Katherine. The one you weren't at, so I've been told.

Says Carla B Silver You tell that one, and I'll tell another that that very same A-rab told our friend down in Annapolis. It's called What in the World Am I Doing Here? and sometimes I wonder.

Captain Donald tips his cap. You show me yours, and then et cetera.

The crew of *Story* have followed this ping-pong conversation. Sorely wishing she hadn't missed that Eleventh Annual ASPS Convention (but we had our reasons), Katherine holds Peter's right hand in her left, Andrew's left in her right, as if to steady her reception and assimilation. Her younger brother must be baffled, though he seems entertained enough; her husband watches for yet another orange Alert-and-Locate canister to fall from the sky or pop up from under, with Frank Talbott's third act inside. Giving those hands a sudden squeeze, K says

I'LL GO FIRST.

Brow furrowed, eyes flashing, D.Q. nods. C.B S. smiles. Peter Sagamore wonders, proudly. Chip just wonders. Hers wakes His to hear Mom's tale. To the skipper of *Rocinante IV,* Kate says I happened to have spent this whole A.M. reading Peter's notes for Parts One and Two of a possible three-part Don Key-*ho*-tay story that he started when we first saw you in Annapolis last week. It takes you from the Cave of Montesinos in La Mancha in maybe Sixteen Hundred to Sagres, Portugal, in maybe Nineteen Sixty-three—where I gather you were?

Right next door, young lady, says Capn Don. I crossed solo from Lagos to the Virginia Capes in this boat right here, seventeen summers ago. First time for me, third time for old Rosy. I bought this boat off a Cornishman in Albufeira who'd already singlehanded her across the Atlantic twice before he took sick and ran out of money. She needed refastening and repainting and a new set of sails and an engine overhaul, but what caught my eye was he'd already named her *Rocinante* and painted fisherman's eyes on her bows. All I had to do, once I'd fixed her up, was add the numeral and change the hailport. Let's hear that story.

K consults its potential author, who says Go ahead; it isn't written yet. And so she does, Katherine Shorter Sherritt Sagamore, fearlessly improvising upon her memory of Peter's notes in *Story*'s log: tells us all the tale of the knight's descent into that fateful cave; his vain search for a way back out, then in turn for Dulcinea, for Sancho Panza, and for the Moor his chronicler; his step-by-step transformation, abetted by the duke and duchess of "Barataria," from landsman to seaman, and from enchantment by chivalric fantasy to enchantment by fantastic reality; his roundabout voyage from Montesinos's palace to Sancho's island to the outermost tip of Europe, and from the opening of the seventeenth century to the closing of the twentieth. It is by far Kath's most extended venture in the way of oral narrative; when its hero finally bids farewell to his young American friend on the Sagres headland, she sits back winded and perspiring.

Bravo! her audience applauds—all but Captain Donald Quicksoat, who nods his head, fingers his whiskers, but says nothing. Chip is wowed; likewise his unborn kin. Carla B Silver declares that just as Scheherazade's stories saved their teller's skin, Katherine's story has saved at least one listener's lunch; she was too entranced to remember to get seasick. Peter declares we'll record that story postnatally in our Tidewater Tales just as Kath has told it, or as closely thereto as can be managed. He is even moved to wish aloud that May Jump were with us, to share his pride in her narrative protégée. Our woman's pregnant heart glows.

In a way, declares C.B S., May Jump *is* with us. I'll let her know you've reached brown-belthood, Missus Sagamore.

P's prepared to second that promotion; also to ask in *what* way, other than the obvious and attenuated, Kath's former coach may be said to be with us. But his wife says to him Unfortunately our story didn't please its main character. I guess we got it all wrong.

¡NO NO NO!

insists the grizzled skipper of *Rocinante IV,* reaching across the cockpit to reassure Katherine Sherritt's left knee. You've more than pleased me—a whole sight more. Like Mister Cervantes before her, he declares (Englishing the name: Sir *Van*-Tease), Katherine has definitively told his story. More accurately, he supposes, Peter in the role of Miguel Cervantes and Katherine in the role of his narrator, Hamete Benengeli, have together told, about that particular part of Don Quixote's career, so much more authoritative a story than the one he himself is in the habit of retailing, that just as the novel *Don Quixote* has become the story of his life up to the Montesinos episode, and just as the rest of Part Two of that novel came to seem to our Don Quixote rather more believable and even truer than his actual adventures aboard *Rocinante* II and III, so our story of those adventures now strikes him as more believable and true than what he would have told us, if asked, about his life up to Sagres in 1963. Do we follow him?

We do.

Therefore, with our permission, he proposes to let that part of his story stand exactly as we've imagined it. By God, he further exclaims, from now on that *is* the story of those chapters of his life! All that remains is for him to brief us on

PART OF PART THREE OF THAT POSSIBLE THREE-PART
DON QUIXOTE STORY

—that is, how he came from Iberia to Still Pond Creek on Chesapeake Bay in the Free State of Maryland. It is a story briefly and simply told, but, he warns us in advance, sans denouement, unless our combined powers of enchantment wind it up for him here and now.

Says grinning Chip, not quite to himself, Here and Now, and is burbled at by his nepotes in the works.

Donald Quicksoat's final enchantment, Capn Don declares, directing his story mainly though not exclusively to Carla B Silver, was neither with chivalric romance nor with unchivalrous reality, but with the enchanted story of Don Quixote as written by the grand enchanter Miguel de Cervantes Saavedra. Just as poor Alonso Quijano, in middle age, was so bewitched by the novels of chivalry that he declared himself Don Quixote de la Mancha, the Knight of Doleful Aspect, so the skipper of *Rocinante Cuatro,* in his own middlescence, was led by his passion for Cervantes's novel to identify himself with both its hero and, eventually, its author. Enough said, no?

Sí.

How I came by this boat, I've told you already. *It* came by *me,* I guess.

So did ours us, puts in Peter, relieved as ever to have it known that *Story*'s name is not directly our doing. Captain Donald winks his port eye our way and asks Carla What was I doing stranded and alone in Sagres, Portugal, at Alonso Quijano's age? These two have really explained that to me for the first time: I was looking for some way out of a cave I'd got myself lost in chapters before. When I saw this boat up for sale in Lagos and read the name on her transom, I decided like Dante in the Dark Wood that the long way around might be the only way out. In the course of getting to where I was, I'd logged many a mile with one mate or another; now I figured I'd singlehand it to the end of the story, like Cervantes himself.

Says Carla B Silver I'm with you, and adds quickly You know what I mean.

You know what you mean, beams C.D.Q. Now, if our friends here were telling this part, they'd have me set out in search of Cervantes himself this time, to square my biggest debt of all. ¿No? Maybe look for him in Jean Lafitte's Barataria, down by New Orleans?

Peter Sagamore shrugs his hand to allow that possibility.

But even in Sagres, says Capn Don, I reckoned that Cervantes owed me as much as I owed him. Anyhow, we characters sometimes get loose of our authors.

C. B Silver meaningly clears her throat. Pardon the professor-talk, says our host. Let me just say that before we were three days out to sea, me and Rosy here, barreling westward straight across the thirty-seventh parallel, I understood that I was my own goshdarn Cervantes. *The passenger who is also the skipper,* he says directly to Peter Sagamore—who nods and at once replies, also in italics: *The skipper who is also the passenger.*

You've got it, says Capn Don.

Murmurs Chip Gosh darn.

Now, then: Self-steering rigs have come a long way since Nineteen Sixty-three, but I'd learned a trick or two about steering myself: I gave *Rocinante* her head—as long as she went more or less where I wanted her to, which was true west.

To Carla B Silver he declares I've heard this and that said about me, and some of it's true, and most of it's not. I'm well enough off. The initial investment, you might say, was Mister Cervantes's, and the interest is paid by readers of *Don Quixote*—but that's more professor-talk. I've been sketching up a *Rocinante Five,* to maybe sail back to wherever I decide I came from. How 'bout up the Guadalquivir to Seville's cathedral, where Cris Colón dropped his final hook? If you asked me what I'm looking for these days, I'd say *Nada* whatsoever, thank you—except maybe, out of the side of my eye (he winks), a certain hundred-fathom line, hey? Let down by Sancho P into the Cave of Montesinos, where you tell me I still am. When I find that line, *compadres,* I'll give 'er a tug and be hauled up in a bosun's chair back into Part Two of *Don Quixote.* They'll tell me I've been away 'bout half an hour, and we'll go on with Sir Van Tease's story. I know for a fact I won't try to tell them what I saw and did in the here and now, 'cause if I did, it would say so in the book. Which it don't.

So I ask you: Is that the end of my story? You bet it is. But we ain't there yet, 'cause I haven't found that final line. Closest I ever came to it was in another cavern, just across this Bay just a few days back—but I guess it's me that's paying out *that* line, hoping this lady here will take the fall of it.

¿PREGUNTAS?

Good show, says Peter Sagamore.

Agrees Carla B Silver Not bad. Don't mix me up with Whatsername, though: that Dulcinea. If I grab hold of this line of yours, you'll as likely get roped into Carla's Cavern as me get shanghaied aboard this boat. But neither of us hog-ties the other, *comprende?*

Donald Quicksoat nods Fair enough.

Kath has a question: Did he really meet a certain aspiring young American writer in Sagres, Portugal, in the winter of 1962/63? Laughs Capn Don Did I meet one? Honey, I *was* one—only not so young by then. And on that *particular* solo voyage, unlike your friend here, I sank without a trace.

Next wonders straight-faced Peter: In your travels up and down the ICW, have you happened to cross paths with a couple that could pass for Odysseus and Nausicaa? They sail a thirty-five-foot Phaeacian with a squaresail.

Ten point six six eight meters, murmurs Chip. His sister hugs him and says Murmur murmur.

Know 'em well, grins Capn Don. Likewise Huck Finn and Lemuel Gulliver . . . aaand Aeneas and Candide and Robby Crusoe and Roddy Random and the other old salts, including Sinwell the Sailor there and his old lady Scheherazade. He smacks both his knees. Hell, boy, you can set by the window this time of year up in Schaefer's Canal House Restaurant and watch 'em all go through the C and D! Wouldn't s'prise *me* to find half the gang up back of Ornery Point this evening!

Now he smacks Carla B's knee and stands. Which it's time we struck our tents and aimed our camels at, nessy pah?

Growls wincing Carla Nessy *pah?* Get me *out* of here.

CARLA B SILVER STANDS HER TRICK AT THE NARRATIVE HELM.

But he must be doing something right, we guess, old Donald Quicksoat there, for when he and his pal dinghy over some three hours later to bid *buenas noches* to the crew of *Story* in Back Creek on the Sassafras, C. B Silver is so at ease with her weekend that she neglects to kvetch about sailboats and seasickness; just says to Peter Hand me up out of this dingbat, would you, and I'll tell you guys a bedtime story.

Punch and Judy clap each other's hands. Says Katherine Ouch.

Chip had asked us, as we threaded out of pretty Still Pond after lunch, Who's Roddy Random, and Is this how Chesapeake cruising always is? No wonder we went out from Nopoint Point and didn't come back. Poker-faced Peter assured him that that narrative lunch had been just another meal, and Katherine wondered how come Captain Donald there didn't mention Edgar Poe's Arthur Gordon Pym along with Smollett's Roderick Random; also Jason the Argonaut and Chessie the sea monster and Ahab and the Flying Dutchman, whom-all she certainly expects to say hi to before we hang up our Tidewater Tales.

Peter then remarked that C.B S. had been done out of her narrative turn and that that was a pity, as she'd said something more or less cryptic about his second favorite woman and storyteller in the universal world. But even Andrew Christopher Sherritt could see that the way this cruise is cruising, Ms. Silver's tale—and Scheherazade's—will not likely go untold. There followed a slow run up to the last good sailing-river on the Bay and then an even slower broad reach into it, *Story* moving with the hot wind in apparent airlessness. Some miles up, where Ordinary Point all but crosses the Sassafras from its north shore, the breeze gave out, and P consulted sweating K as to whether we should park and have our babies.

Not yet.

So we kicked in the outboard, scouted the anchorage—two dozen yachts riding there already and more moving down from the Georgetown marinas to begin their weekend, but no sign of Odysseus and Nausicaa Dmitrikakis or other literary-nautical luminaries—and decided to poke on two miles farther, to Back Creek: roomy but uncrowded because very easy to run aground in. Hello to the Breadbasket of the Revolution; hello to Breadbasket Inc.'s new old granary, handsomely preserved, on the creek's north shore. We made our way past it, Chip in the bow feeling out the shoals with our telescoping boathook, and anchored in five feet of water not far from shore in the pretty wooded bight to starboard. The occasional water-skier zipped by from a public landing farther upcreek, rocking us with his/her wake; couple of fishermen in aluminum skiffs worked a water-lily patch across the way. Otherwise the place was ours.

Two-thirds of our already-born crew members shucked their clothes pronto and skinny-dipped in the creek's sweet water; Chip joined us in his Jantzen and brown-bead necklace after radioing our position to the folks, themselves at cocktails in Fairlee Creek before going ashore to dinner. We Sagamores found ourselves embracing: Here we were, by golly, where we'd sort of set out to go, so unexpectedly many chapters since we'd set out to go there. Chip offered to swim the other way, but no, no: We embraced him, too, and despite our nudity he allowed our hug. This isn't sex, Andrew; it's the being here together at last—where we'd no more than half-seriously wished the wind would fetch us—full of stories and babies and the knowledge that our time is all but upon us.

Reader: May the world not soon end, for this life is sweet, here and there, and Back Creek is beautiful. God's curse upon the Doomsday and the Sot-Weed Factors; upon all who leach and taint and subdivide, coerce and bully and kill. But upon the peacemakers and the conservators, thy blessing and ours, amen.

Said Chipper then On with the story: Here comes *Rocinante Four*.

We doubted it, though there she stood, just off the granary, sails furled and engine all but idling: Boats that size, with ocean-crossing keels, seldom venture into these unmarked shallows. We had followed *Rocinante*'s following us out of Still Pond Creek and had waved good-bye to her out on the Bay, where with her larger sailplan and longer waterline she soon left us behind. Not seeing her at anchor behind Ordinary Point, we assumed she'd gone on up to Georgetown, maybe dinner ashore and a marina slip for landlubberly Carla's sake. Turns out they drove up there, just for the scenic ride, but that Carla wants to try a night at anchor: something she never did even with Frederick Mansfield Talbott, former Prince of Darkness. Give her first class on the *QE2* any time, but if she's going to do this sailboat thing, she'll do it right.

So she tells us after *Rocinante,* to our surprise, powers gingerly past the granary after all, runs aground, backs off, pokes a fair way farther usward into Back Creek, runs aground again, backs off, and sensibly anchors where she is in the unmarked channel, a few hundred yards away. We wave; captain and passenger wave back. Over dinner we wonder among other things how they're hitting it off, and what that amalgamation of Popeye the Sailorman and the Knight of Rueful Countenance must be like in bed. Kate's inclined to respect Carla B Silver's judgment in such matters, but agrees with Pete that in this instance Carla too seems not quite to have made up her mind.

We see them fire up their barbecue grill as we have fired up ours, and then disappear below. Says Chip I think she's making up her mind. He puts down the binoculars and sighs Sex.

A while later, Capn Don comes up alone, wearing fresh Bermuda shorts. He puts meat on the grill, returns below, comes back up to mind the cooking. Then Carla emerges in a white pants suit—the day is welcomely cooling down—with her hands full of dishes, and they dine in the cockpit, as we're doing. Afterward they dinghy over to say good night.

Standing now arms akimbo in *Story*'s cockpit, Carla looks around her at the long light quivering in the trees and acknowledges This does beat working. Are you okay? she asks Katherine closely, who smiles and says Sure. You?

Never mind me. There is fine perspiration on her lightly mustached lip; the sun fires her bracelets and gold earrings. A very together woman, in our opinion. Ask me tomorrow, she suggests.

Says Capn Don Ask *me* tomorrow. She makes a damn fine vinaigrette; we've established that.

But can she tell a story? asks Peter Sagamore, having taken nightcap orders. She promised us one by Scheherazade herself.

And she'll deliver it, says Carla B Silver, though not as expertly as our friend May Jump, who told it to me.

May! cries happy Katherine. I should've known.

Nods Carla There's a storyteller for you. In fact, I'm going to let May tell that one herself: the What Am I Doing Here story. May Jump swears she met Scheherazade in person last September in Annapolis and took her to that ASPS thing in Kitty Hawk.

Laments K The one I missed. . . .

Capn Don affirms that that's where *he* met her, all right, and Miss May Jump, too: damn fine storytellers both. And he joined their little club, *amigos,* and hopes he gave one-half as good as he got.

Touching Kath's shoulder, Peter says proudly We have here that society's founder: the Mother of Invention. But it's Carla B Silver's trick at the helm, no?

That it is, skipper, says C.D.Q. That it is.

Says Carla B Silver to Andrew "Chip" Sherritt, once our refreshments are in hand, This is an R-rated story, comrade, but I guess we can assume your parents' consent. Quips Chip We're outside their three-mile limit; all I need is the captain's consent. Peter declares We're all consenting adults, sexually educated and dramaturgically mature. Chip knows that denouements don't come from distress-flare canisters.

Talk like that, says Carla B Silver, is over her head, but never mind. Her story's not sexually explicit anyhow, just gynecological—and latently statistical. *¡Olé!* cheers Donald Quicksoat. Carla regards him over imaginary reading-glasses and says I'm calling it

THE STORY OF SCHEHERAZADE'S FIRST SECOND MENSTRUATION.

Kath groans. Another menstruation story! This Bay is nothing but menstruation stories.

Says aplombful Carla No wonder, all these moons and tides. To us all she announces I'm going to dedicate this story to Katherine Sherritt Sagamore. Here's to her safe and speedy delivery before this weekend's done.

Says Capn Don Hear hear.

That realization thrills us; we sip to it. But Chip wonders aloud First second?

Attaboy, says Carla seriously. Now then, we hear you're good with numbers. Let's check out your statistical sex education.

Quick Chip, who is being permitted half a Molson's ale as well as the impending story, gamely grins and touches his sister's belly: One on one makes two? He gets himself kissed, hissed, and groaned at.

Still to blushing Andrew, Carla B Silver declares The normal human female menstrual cycle is a lunar month, right?

Those were the days, sighs K. C.B S. agrees and turns back to Chip. Now, my friend: Do you remember exactly how many days the so-called nine-month normal human pregnancy averages out to?

Yes'm, Chip answers at once, upon whom our familiar arithmetic has not been lost: Two hundred sixty-six, plus or minus fourteen. *Pour le sport* he adds That's nine and a half lunar months exactly, or . . . buzz buzz clickety click . . . eight point seven two of *our* months, if we call the average month thirty and a half days long. Thirty point four four something, actually.

His sister and brother-in-law look at each other, as we are wont to do in prodigy's presence. Cool Carla says Right you are, I bet. You like the story so far? Now: Does anybody happen to know how long it normally takes a lady to get back into the ovulation/menstruation business after she's given birth?

Chip passes. Me too, says Peter Sagamore, but whistle a few bars, and we'll fake it. Capn Don confesses that if he ever knew that particular fact of life, he has forgotten it. Queries Katherine Doesn't it depend on whether she's breast-feeding?

It can, says Carla, and in certain times and places *that* depends on whether she's a lady. Scheherazade told May Jump that upper-class Muslim women where she comes from—which is someplace called the Islands of India and China—don't do their own wet-nursing. Couple of months, isn't it? Damn if I can remember that far back.

Katherine says Six to eight weeks if you're not lactating. She imagines, correctly, that Peter is wondering whether this so-called story has a plot or is all Pampers and Kotex, numbers and nursing pads. It is late in the day, friends, late in the cruise, late in our Tidewater Tales and our pregnancy for a shaggy-menstruation story.

Okay, says Carla B Silver: What Scheherazade told May Jump last fall was the story of how and why she got herself involved with King Whatsisname in the first place, King Shahryar there, just exactly at the time she did. I mean, for years the guy'd been popping a virgin every night and then killing her in the morning so she'd never be unfaithful to him, and young Scheherazade was not one of your Shiite kamikazes: She wanted to straighten the king's head out and save her country, which was going to ruin, and protect herself and her kid sister too. Turns out she had good reasons for making her move exactly when she made it and then for hanging it up one thousand and one nights later, instead of a hundred and one or two thousand and two or any other number.

The parents of Pete and Repeat exchange another, different glance, remembering our *Nights* talk on Day Zero and our recent dizzy conviction that where Huckleberry Findley, Odysseus Dmitrikakis, and Captain Donald Quicksoat have crossed wakes, Scheherazade must in some guise soon sail by.

Once upon a time, says C.B S. (in a new tone now, behind whose resonance we imagine Rimsky-Korsakov's solo violin transcribed for cello), there were two kings, brothers, both of whom considered themselves happily married. But the younger brother, Shah Zaman of Samarkand, comes across his wife one day smack in the act with a minor member of the kitchen staff. Not even the chef! He draws his scimitar and skewers the pair of them on the spot, but he's so shocked he can't cope. He turns the government of Samarkand over to his prime minister and takes what

I guess you'd call psychological refuge in his brother's palace over in the Islands of India and China, wherever *they* are.

Ceylon and Taiwan? Chip wonders. Quemoy and Matsu?

Long Ago and Far Away is how May Jump puts it, says Carla B Silver. Our children perk up their ears.

So Shahryar, the older one, sees that his brother's wrecked, all right, but can't persuade him to say what his problem is, until one fine day when *he*'s out of the house on business, Shah Zaman sees his sister-in-law go to it in the palace courtyard with a low-class blackamoor that she actually calls down out of the trees. Lots of racism and classism in this story, no? Which, so far, is right out of the book, but who remembers the book?

All hands' hands go up, in fact, except Chip's and Chip 'n' Dale's. But this is a tale we don't mind rehearing, we assure her.

Carla says Hmp. The version *she* read to Short Jon Silver a hundred years ago must have been a spayed and dehydrated one with pictures by N. C. Wyeth, 'cause all this adultery is news to her. Anyhow, she says directly to Chip, when young Shah Zaman there sees what he sees, it cheers him right up: Misery loves company, you know? He doesn't tattle on the queen right away, but when his brother comes home he tells him the whole story of what went wrong back in Samarkand and what he did about it. And here's the next number for your data base, Mister Chip: King Shahryar hears Shah Zaman out and shakes his head and says Is *that* all you did? Just blew away the guilty parties? By Allah, man, he swears: If my wife did a number like that on me, I'd kill a thousand women in revenge! Got that?

And you've got us, says Peter Sagamore. On with the story.

Says Carla May Jump says Scheherazade says Be careful what you up and swear when you're playing the lead in an old-time tale, 'cause the gods have got the whole scene wired.

And Scheherazade's right, affirms Katherine Sherritt, taking her husband's hand. That's how we got here.

Um hum. So naturally Shah Zaman sets it up for his brother to see what *he* just saw—and there was more than I'm telling here, but we don't want to lose our R rating, okay? Evidently the queen and half the house staff used to go to it every time Shahryar stepped out the front door. Now, here's a nice touch for you: Despite his macho swaggering, when Shahryar sees that orgy in his own backyard, he's too wiped out to do what Shah Zaman did. He doesn't even *confront* his wife, much less butcher her and her apeman friend; he just turns the administration over to his grand vizier, the way Shah Zaman did, and gets the hell out of there. The two brothers go off together incognito to wander the world, shaking their heads and tisking their tongues.

And that would be the end of their story right there, if it weren't for a little X-rated adventure that they happen to stumble into on the very next page. We're going to skip that one, too, alas, to get on with the arithmetic;

also to encourage the innocent bystander here to go read the book for himself. The moral of this episode—for the two brothers, anyhow; not for me and May Jump and Scheherazade—is that their wives were no exception to the general rule, which is that *all* women are promiscuous.

Capn Don, to our pleased surprise, drops his rubery to observe it's not Rigoletto who sings "*La donna è mobile*"; it's the horny Duke of Mantua.

Bravo, says Carla B Silver. But there they are in Ayatollah Khomeini Land, so they decide to go back to their separate kingdoms, take a virgin to bed every night, and have her head chopped off in the morning before she can be unfaithful. Young Shah Zaman takes off for Samarkand, and we hear no more from him till ten volumes and Allah knows how many virgins later. Shahryar goes home and puts his wife and her group-sex crowd out of business for keeps and gives his grand vizier the same orders: a virgin a night or else, and off with her head before breakfast.

So it goes, for the next three years. Can you do the body count, Mister Chip?

His wheels already spinning, Chip asks Islamic years or Gregorian?

Chuckles Donald Quicksoat Both, lad, both!

Uh one thousand ninety-five virgins Gregorian, says Chip; ten ninety-*six* if one of those three years was a leap year. And um clickety buzz ten sixty-two Islamic, I think. I forget how Moslems do leap years.

So do we, Katherine marvels.

Says satisfied Carla B Silver Anyhow a thousand or so, right? So file that little datum away, 'cause here comes Scheherazade into the story. Turns out the prime minister there has two virgin daughters himself. All we know about the younger one is that her name is Dunyazade and she hasn't reached puberty yet, though she will by the end of the story. As for the older one, she's got it all, like excuse me Miss Leah Allan Silver back in high school and college days. She's as good-looking as Princess Kate here; she's as brainy as Mister Andrew Sherritt; she's talented every which way. And her name is Scheherazade, which doesn't hurt either, 'cause if it doesn't mean "Born in the City," it means "The One Who Sets the City Free," and by this time the town is in an uproar, as you might imagine. So many of Shahryar's taxpayers have voted with their feet—especially the ones with unmarried daughters—that toward the end of Year Three there's not a virgin left in town fit to go to bed with.

Except You Know Who, the pearl of the city, and now the plot thickens. We find out that the king has deliberately passed over this particular pearl out of respect for his prime minister. On the other hand, the P.M. is still under the ax if he doesn't come up with the nightly morsel, and after three years the cupboard is bare.

Now, *amigos,* what do you think: Has Scheherazade been sitting on her hands all this time? Her father's the grand fucking vizier, excuse my French; she knows very well what's going on in the king's bedroom and in the Islands of India and China. She sees that the guy's been driven right 'round the bend by his late wife's misbehavior and that his crazy revenge is wrecking the country, and early in the game she hatched an idea how to save the show. In fact, she's been in training for a long time already; she knows more songs and poems by heart than Miss May Jump does, even, and she's got herself a private library with guess how many books in it, Mister Chip?

Andrew is puzzled, but Peter Sagamore is delighted: A thousand books of histories, he recalls, quoting Sir Richard Burton's English. I hadn't noticed that little echo, Carla.

Declares Carla B Silver Scheherazade told May Jump that that's what gave her the idea. She was counting her collection one day back in Year Two, and the number of her storybooks reminded her of what her father once told her about the king's vow to Allah just before he learned he was a cuckold. That's when she set to work reading all the stories in the world, and practicing on little Dunyazade how to tell them.

Peter Sagamore observes that that circumstance is not in any text of the *Nights* that he can remember. Text shmext, replies Carla B Silver; this is from the horse's mouth. So the day her father comes home pissing and moaning that the jig is up 'cause he's out of virgins, young Scheherazade floors him by volunteering herself. She has a plan to end the massacre, she tells him, but she won't say what it is: only that if it works, they'll all be out of the woods, the king included, and if it doesn't, they won't be any farther in than they're gonna be anyhow, unless Pop's planning to join the boat people with her and Dunyazade that same day.

Well, my friends, a father is a father. He tries to talk her out of suicide, as he sees it, by telling her a story with a certain moral to it. But not only does his story not change her mind; she plays the old guy like an accordion. If he won't give her his permission, she says, she's going to go straight to Shahryar and tell him she'd love to go to bed with him, but her father won't let her.

That *is* in the text, recollects pleased Peter.

An offer he can't refuse, remarks Donald Quicksoat.

Says Carla Papa's back is to the wall. He shakes his head and gnashes his teeth, but at last he goes in to his boss and tells him frankly the whole story of this hassle from start to finish, including his daughter's threat. Now, then: Crazy as he is on the subject of women, Shahryar's not out of his tree altogether where his self-interest is concerned. This is his faithful prime minister here, and his faithful prime minister's prime daughter. Does Miss Scheherazade understand what she's volunteering for? Does her father? I'm afraid we do, says Mister Grand Vizier, and I hate to think what the girl's mother would say if she were alive to say it. But this is one determined young lady we're dealing with. So Shahryar claps his hands, or whatever it is sultans do, and says Amen, my friend: Let her will be done. Your daughter is one prize package, and I've been looking the other way for your sake. But don't either of you imagine that I'm going to change the rules tomorrow morning.

The grand vizier acknowledges that there is no god but God and goes to fetch his crazy daughter, who told May Jump by the way that the closest she came to panicking in all this was just a couple of paragraphs ago, when she realized that her father's story hadn't changed her mind. Do you get it, Mister Chip?

Andrew shakes his head and apologizes; he was doing numbers.

Smiles Carla Were you, now. What'd you come up with?

Nothing, particularly. I just wondered whether Scheherazade was keeping count, or whether it's just coincidence that she made her move right about when the king finished killing his thousand women in revenge. I guess it wouldn't matter unless the king was keeping count too.

Give that boy a Pee Aitch Dee, commands Carla B Silver. What does your text have to say about that, Peter Sagamore?

Says Peter Not a word. But there it is: The king's at least a thousand days into his vow.

Katherine says she's going to have to read that book again; she doesn't remember Scheherazade's worrying that since her father's story didn't change *her* mind, her stories might not change the king's mind, which is what her life depends on.

You won't find it in the book, says Carla. But as Doctor Sagamore says, There it is—and wouldn't *you* worry? What Scheherazade told May Jump is that your A-rab storytellers don't bother to say what goes without saying: They give the man in the souk enough action to keep him happy, and the rest they leave for Mister Chip to figure out for himself. As I told you before, this Scheherazade is no crazy-lady. The book calls her the Savior of Her Sex, but she had to stand by and let a thousand virgins go to the chopping block before the time was ripe for her to make her move.

And the time is ripe, ventures Captain Donald, when these two things come together, no? He's killed his thousand women, and about the same time he's used up his supply of virgins.

Plus the country's a wreck, Kath reminds us, as the king must know. If the vizier told him the whole story of his argument with Scheherazade, you can bet he threw in the news that she's the last item on the shelf. When Shahryar kills her, the jig's up anyhow. I hadn't thought of that.

Donald Quicksoat adds that if Shahryar then kills the grand vizier for not bringing him what there isn't any more of, he's *really* scuttling his own ship. *He* hadn't thought of *that*.

Peter Sagamore says he himself hadn't thought of *any* of this stuff, and he believed he knew the story backward and forward. Backward and Forward say It's all news to us; we're only two hundred sixty-four nights old.

Chip wonders what the quote man in the souk unquote is. Says Peter You're looking at him, but then defines the term.

And none of this is in the book? His brother-in-law assures him it's *all* in the book—between the lines. And he sure wishes he could say hello to this Scheherazade lady.

Now, then, class, says Carla B Silver, who has in this interval lit herself a cigarillo: Was it the thousandth night, or the thousand and first, or what?

We don't know, but we bet it wasn't some random number like the nine hundred second or the ten seventy-fifth. And was it pure coincidence that the vizier runs out of virgins right about then? Maybe so, for story purposes, but we bet the supply had been short and the quality down for some time, and that all hands knew the clock was running out. Plus there was one more item on the young lady's checklist, maybe the most important one of all, though you won't find it mentioned in the official version any more than those others. It's what this story's finally all about, and that's the only clue you get.

Okay? So everybody knows what happens next: Scheherazade gives her kid sister some careful instructions and then presents herself to the king. He whisks her off to bed, and she starts to cry. What's your problem? the king asks her, and if he expects her to say she's changed her mind about dying and could she please be excused, he gets a surprise, 'cause all she says is she can't bear to be separated from her little sister on this last night of her life. Just let her have Dunyazade to keep her company, and it's on with the show.

Well, Shahryar's no prude: He shrugs his shoulders, fetches Dunyazade in to sit at the foot of the bed, and then takes Scheherazade as he's taken at least a thousand before her. No big deal by this time, right? Pearl or no pearl. When he's had his fun, he rolls over and maybe even says good night—though that would be a touch much, I guess, wouldn't it.

Anyhow, sometime after midnight Scheherazade quietly wakes Dunyazade, who's sound asleep, and Little Sister goes into her act: says she can't sleep, and would Scheherazade please tell her a story, the way she does back home? Shush, says Scheherazade; you'll wake up the king. You won't wake me up, says Shahryar; I can't seem to get to sleep tonight either. Let's hear your story.

So why can't the king get to sleep, friends? Scheherazade told May Jump that she wouldn't bother to say what goes without saying.

Say, say, urges Peter Sagamore: It never occurred to this particular man in the souk till now what an odd request that is of Dunyazade's: to ask for a story from a person who's about to die.

Says Carla They set it up that way to pinch the man's conscience. As if the kid hadn't been told, right? And they cross their fingers that the king's been counting nights instead of counting sheep, and putting two and two together: That Night Number One with the Fairest of Them All happens to be at least Night One Thousand and One of his crazy vow. But whether or not Shahryar's doing the numbers, Scheherazade knows he knows that the girl he's just deflowered was not only the most eligible nubile virgin in town, but the last one; and that ordering his prime minister to kill his own daughter might just be the last straw for what's left of the taxpayers out there. What's more, this beauty has got to be his first playmate in a thousand and one nights who actually volunteered for the job! Who knows what she's got up her sleeve? No wonder the poor sucker can't sleep; he's humped himself into a corner, pardon my French.

Says Captain Donald, shaking his head, *L'homme du souk, c'est moi.*

And I'm another, says Katherine Sherritt. And we're at least two more, say Oui et Non.

P.S. declares he's going to turn in his union card and go back to Writers' Kindergarten; he has read this story a thousand and one times, and now he sees he hasn't read it at all. He'd thought himself a pretty clever fellow for noting that the first story Scheherazade tells is just close enough to her own story to make its point without exactly writing its moral on the king's eyeglasses. . . .

The Tale of the Merchant and the Genie, Kath remembers, and explains for Andrew's benefit that it's about a merchant who, in imminent peril of being killed by an imperious genie, stalls for time like Scheherazade by telling his would-be executioner a story.

Three stories, actually, if Peter Sagamore's memory serves: stories told by the characters in the merchant's story, to give the guy more time, and each one very pointedly applauded by the other characters as being even more marvelous than the one before.

But on this critical first night, Carla B Silver reminds us, all she tells is the front end of the Merchant-and-Genie story and two-thirds of the first of those three stories in it—a story that *also* happens to be about an innocent man on the verge of execution. Then, just before she gets to its punch line—you can imagine how many times she's been over this with Dunyazade, to get her timing down perfect—smack in the middle of a *sentence* she says Uh-oh: I hear the roosters crowing, or the muezzin in the minaret, or something; my time's up, I guess. And before the king can even react, Dunyazade says that that's about the best story she ever heard in her life—*two* of the best, in fact, and she can't stand not knowing how they end. To which of course Miss Scheherazade says Pish tush, child: You call *that* a good story, before I've even got its chestnuts out of the fire? That story can't fetch tea for the ones I'd tell you tomorrow night, if I were here to tell them.

And there she stops and holds her breath, my friends, 'cause numbers or no numbers, last straw or no last straw, her life is on the line, and the hombre she's in bed with is not Donkey Ho-Tay dee la Mancha, but a meshuga A-rab sultan who for all she knows might be perfectly ready to commit national suicide over her dead body.

And that's where we should end this story, no?

NO FAIR!

cries Andrew Christopher "Chip" Sherritt.

Show of hands, says Carla B Silver, and gets a unanimous mandate to proceed. Nevertheless, she declares she's done with it: not the story of

Scheherazade's first second menstruation, but the story of Scheherazade's stories, which any crew member can go read off the shelf, just as she herself means to do one of these years. Needless to say, the king thinks carefully for all of two seconds about the pros and cons of Scheherazade's indirect pleas for a stay of execution—mostly pros, inasmuch as the only con he can imagine is losing his image as a capital-B Badass where women are concerned. Happily, there occurs to him a way to have it both ways: how to save face with his grand vizier after swearing he'd make no exception of Scheherazade, and how to save his political hind-end as well, which is as much on the line as his new friend's neck.

So declared Scheherazade herself to May Jump in Kitty Hawk, N.C., declares Carla B Silver, reminding us that nowhere in our printed version of *The 1001 Nights* do we hear the king decide to mend his ways before the sky falls on his head; much less that the coolest way to go about that might be to declare a tacit moratorium on further executions before he goes public with his change of heart. Now, Mister Chip: Just how *long* a moratorium do you think he'll tacitly declare?

Says Peter Sagamore You've just answered a question I asked on Day Zero. Why should *The Thousand and One Nights* be a thousand and one instead of some other number? Somebody *has* been talking to the horse's mouth!

(Not us, swear Chick 'n' Little.)

Kath admits *she'd* thought the number meant simply plenty and then some, if she'd thought about it at all: a taleteller's number.

And that it is, says Carla; but that's not all it is. Nor is it just a playback of his vow, you know: the time of his sex-murders played back as the time of his penance. It's both of those things plus another big one—and the person who has it from the horse's mouth is your friend May Jump.

Hold tight now while we skip to the end, which is what May did when she told me this story, 'cause that's where Scheherazade began it: a thousand nights after the morning when the king made another vow to Allah, that he'd put off killing the vizier's daughter till he'd heard the end of her story. That first morning, you understand, he didn't say Boo to her; when the sun came up, he just climbed out of bed and went to work. The prime minister showed up with a shroud under his arm to fetch his daughter off to the guillotine, and the king didn't say Boo to *him,* either; he just went on with business as usual, leaving the poor guy to wonder what's going on. Then back to bed for another shot of sex with his new roommate, who you can bet has been turning cartwheels and polishing her act all day. She knows she's not out of the woods yet; so on Night Two, when the time comes, she gives him the rest of her first story-within-the-story, plus the whole second and third one, plus all but the very end of the one that frames those other ones: the Merchant-and-Genie story, which she breaks off right before the punch line with her crack-of-dawn routine.

Et cetera, okay? Because a routine is just what it gets to be over the next nine hundred and ninety-nine nights: First comes the sex; then all hands grab a nap; then Dunyazade says On with the story, et cetera. Now and then Scheherazade gives him a clutch of quickies all in the same night; another time she spends a hundred nights spinning out the same story, just to see if she can get away with it.

By that time, needless to say, she's pretty sure where she stands. But in Magic Carpet Land, tacit means tacit: Her stories run from G to triple-X, but no matter how explicit they are, the things that go without saying never get mentioned. One of those things, I don't have to tell you, is that it would not have been very smart of young Scheherazade to do Night One with Shahryar at a time when she happened to be menstruating, no? Even if we leave aside the old Muslim suspicion that sex during menstruation is what causes leprosy, it would've been suicide for her not to wait till the coast was clear. Right?

Well (we agree), we'd never thought of that; but yes. For sure.

For that matter, says Carla B Silver, if you were Scheherazade and you'd managed to survive Night One, you'd really feel like a dummy if you got your period on Night Two, wouldn't you? Or Three or Four or Five, when your position was still pret-ty delicate. Seems to me that along with the body count you'd've been keeping tabs on the moon and your menstrual calendar before you made your big move, and that once you'd cleared the first hurdle by surviving Night One, you'd want as much time as possible to firm up your position before the night comes when you have to make it on art without sex. Don't you think?

I think, I think, murmurs Peter Sagamore; but I never thought of it before. Where've I been?

You've been reading the lines, Carla assures him, like the rest of us. Scheherazade told May Jump that good readers read the lines and better readers read the spaces. Why should she have the scribes draw a picture of what any shtook can figure out for himself? No offense intended.

So when we shtooks put our heads together, Captain Donald Quicksoat sums up, it turns out that Night One is Night One for three or four different reasons, of which the only one mentioned in the book is that the vizier can't find any more young women for Shahryar to play with. By happy Arabian coincidence, a thousand sacrificial virgins just about uses up the supply, maybe give or take a weeksworth of C-minus specimens—

Andrew Sherritt remarks surprisingly A couple weeksworth, I bet. Carla B Silver taps her cigar ash over the side and beams.

A couple weeksworth, Capn Don shrugs: to give her time to clear the monthly decks before she goes into action. I guess she'd choose the first night after she was finished, if she could, to allow herself a solid three weeks before she's off limits again.

Unless! Katherine says suddenly. Don't I remember that she has three children by the end of the story?

Carla smiles. Does she or doesn't she, Professor Sagamore?

She does, remembers Peter. On the thousand-and-first night they go through exactly the same routine as on all the other nights, and then on the thousand-and-first morning-after, Scheherazade finishes her last story. Instead of starting another one, she asks for a favor in return for her thousand-and-one nightsworth of entertainment. The King tells her she can have anything she wants, and then she calls for her children—the first time they're mentioned in the book. The nursemaids bring them in: three sons. . . .

Rhyme and Reason gasp as one.

Triplets? Carla wants to know.

No; different ages, I believe. Yes: One's walking, one's crawling, and the nurses are carrying the third one.

Wet-nurses or dry-nurses? Carla demands further.

Capn Don declares he'll bite: What difference does it make to the story whether Scheherazade breast-feeds her children or farms them out?

What story? asks Carla B Silver, palms up. The story's over. Scheherazade parades the kids in and asks their father to spare her life—not because of her storytelling, but so the boys shouldn't grow up motherless. The king says sure, even though a few hours ago he was still doing his old routine: By Allah, I won't kill her till I've heard the end of her story, et cetera. We get the idea he changed his mind a long time ago and that she and Dunyazade probably knew it, but it's been a matter of saving the old face again not to make it official till now. So Shahryar sends for his brother to come over from Samarkand, where all this time he's been doing the virgin-a-night thing—Samarkand must have a lot more virgins than the Islands of India and China—and he tells Shah Zaman all about what a prize this Scheherazade is: how she's fixed his head with her stories and her good looks and her character and general smarts. Then he orders the scribes to write down all her stories in thirty volumes, plus the story of his craziness and how Scheherazade cured him better than any shrink and saved his kingdom at the same time.

Peter Sagamore, professional writer, can't help saying If she borrowed all those stories from her thousand volumes, I hate to think of the paperwork involved to get permission rights for the new anthology.

Katherine Sherritt, professional librarian, says Think of her having to tell her stories all over again, to the scribes! But maybe she and Dunyazade wrote them down each morning, after the king went off to work.

Anyhow, says Carla B Silver, little Dunyazade has reached legal age herself by this time, and with her and Shah Zaman it's love at first sight—despite the blood of how many virgins on his hands, Mister Chip?

Two thousand and two minimum, Chip says at once. Not allowing for travel time between Samarkand and the Islands. But excuse me now: I'm counting something else.

Says Carla I bet you are, and while you're working your way to the bottom line, I'll just ask your classmates here Where do you suppose the king gets the idea to do the next thing he does, which is to marry Scheherazade in a double wedding with Shah Zaman and Dunyazade? I mean aside from the general situation.

None of us remembers, until now reminded at third hand by Scheherazade herself: that just as her first story pointedly dealt with a person very much in her position (and the first story within that story with a person very much in *that* person's position, lest Shahryar miss the point as we did), so her last story—no doubt by this time to their mutual though tacit amusement—deals with a cobbler whose shrewish and unfaithful wife meets the fate she deserves, and who subsequently becomes king of the country and marries . . . that's right: his grand vizier's excellent young daughter.

So okay, says Carla B Silver. So now we ask this Muslim story a Jewish question, the Passover question: How is this night different from all other nights? You say 'Cause it's the thousand and first, and I say What else is new?

Peter Sagamore declares that whatever else is new, it had not till this evening occurred to this particular shtook-in-the-souk that there are a thousand and one nights of love and life-engendering narrative because there'd been the same number of murderous defloration, following Shahryar's reckless vow. Each morning that he hasn't killed Scheherazade is a kind of penance for his having killed one of her predecessors; the morning that that penance is finished is as fit a time for her to make her plea as was Night One for her to make her play. Hats off to Arab formalism! says Peter Sagamore. I don't deserve Frank Talbott's *boina;* where's my dunce cap?

Carla B Silver asks for a refill—we're *all* ready for a refill, though some of us have been too engrossed to remember to drink—and remarks portentously that Franklin Key Talbott's unsinkable *boina* (it's in Peter's seabag, but she doesn't know that), will no doubt soon float by. But dum-de-dum-dum, she says, drumming her fingertips on Donald Quicksoat's knee: We are making what I believe you chaps call sternway. *One walking, one crawling, one suckling,* mates, and How is this night different from all other thousand-and-first nights?

She's pregnant again? Captain Donald ventures. Nah: That'd be nothing new.

Three times two hundred sixty-six, begins Peter Sagamore, trying to remember his log-note of a few days back. No: a thousand and one nights divided by three sons? Math isn't my long suit.

She's *not* pregnant again? Kath wonders. I'm remembering what you called this story. . . .

You're getting warm, Carla tells her. Then we all sit silent in *Story*'s cockpit in warm Back Creek on the lovely Sassafras, under a moon that only the calendar can tell is one night shy of full, watching Chip Sherritt, his eyes closed, clickety-buzzing his chin and fingers, now and then rejecting something with jerk of head or wince of brow, until at last he pauses, opens his eyes, and lights up like that moon.

I think Mister Chip has got it, says C. B Silver.

Yes ma'am.

ANDREW "CHIP" SHERRITT CRUNCHES THE NUMBERS ON SCHEHERAZADE.

But first I need to know the average age when a Moslem child begins to walk.

Grins Carla Muslim shmuslim: Kids are kids. Lee was ten months; Mimsele was closer to a year. Their brother was nearly one and a half. Call it a year.

Doctor Spock says twelve to fifteen months, Kath confirms, who is closer to such scriptures. Did you happen to see him out by Ordinary Point, by the way, just in case?

How about crawling? Chip asks next. When does that usually start and stop? The women consult: Carla's daughters by her late husband were both crawling like mad by six months; her missing son by the missing Prince of Darkness skipped crawling altogether and went tardily from flailing on the rug to walking sturdily upright. Kath remembers Andy's crawling at, oh, between six months and a year—and she trusts her memory, because she used to hop over from College Park to Nopoint Point every chance she got, to spend time with him. Six months to a year, say?

All right. Clickety buzz. Chip blinks a long blink. To begin with, I guess Scheherazade would schedule Night One not just for when she's finished with her menstrual period, but somewhere in the two weeks—I mean the ten days or so between when she finishes her period and when she ovulates. 'Cause if she's already ovulated, she's going to have her period again in less than two weeks, but if she gets pregnant right away, she won't have her next period for nine months, plus or minus two weeks plus six to eight weeks more—assuming she doesn't, you know, lactate, and assuming she doesn't get pregnant again right away at her first ovulation after the birth of her first son. Which as a matter of fact we know she doesn't. Okay?

We are accustomed to Andrew Sherritt's feats. Captain Donald, on the other hand, gives his head a shake as if a genie has foamed from his beer bottle. *How* do we know she doesn't, young fellow?

Chip nods in his direction. 'Cause if she got pregnant on Night One and had her baby on Night Two Sixty-seven, which would be her median EDC, and then got pregnant again on Night Two Eighty-one or so and had *that* baby on Night Five Forty-seven, he'd be fifteen months old by Night Ten Oh One and walking like his older brother. Then if she got pregnant for the third time on Night Five Sixty-one, which is fourteen days after Five Forty-seven, and delivered Number Three on Eight Twenty-seven, *that* one would be nearly six months old on Night Ten Oh One and probably crawling while his two older brothers walked. The walking son has to be nearly a year old at least, right? But since he has two younger brothers, he's got to be at least eighteen to twenty months old. The crawling son is probably between six and twelve months old, since he's crawling, but since he has a younger brother, then he's going to be more like ten to twelve months old. And if the third son is nursing but not crawling yet, then he's probably less than six months old. Could I have a Pepsi, please?

Donald Quicksoat commands us to give that boy a Pepsi.

That's not all, is it, Mister Chip?

Chip Sherritt replies politely that that's not *anything,* yet: It's just what *isn't* the case. He doesn't believe Scheherazade to be pregnant again on Night 1001, by the way, but that opinion is dramaturgical, not mathematical. If she were, and knew it, he believes she would mention that fact as part of her plea: one walking, one crawling, one nursing, and one in the works.

On with the story, gently coaches Peter Sagamore: So we think that Ms. Scheherazade's pregnancies were spaced about evenly through the thousand and one nights, with the first one probably beginning sometime between Nights One and Ten, and the third one late enough so that the child isn't crawling yet at the end, but probably not so late that he's premature. . . .

Clickety buzz, Chip replies: Third conception no earlier than Night Five Fifty-two, and no later than Night uh Seven Thirty-five.

Which means she almost certainly wasn't breast-feeding them herself, observes Katherine, who intends to if she can handle Betwixt and Between at the same time. Otherwise she wouldn't likely have turned them out so fast. Breast-feeding is a famous method of birth control.

Not to be an *absolute* dummy, Peter says, I here point out that as far as we know, the king had no children by his fickle first wife. So it would be doubly smart of young Scheherazade to get herself pregnant as early in the game as possible.

Katherine Sherritt, greenish-brown-belt raconteuse and collector of stories, bets the girl got herself pregnant on Night One and delivered exactly nine months later, since she's the sultan's girlfriend and a character in a Persian/Arab story. But what does all this arithmetic have to do with Scheherazade's first second menstruation, she'd like to know, whatever that odd phrase means, and with the Other Reason why there are a thousand and one nights instead of some other number?

Chip Sherritt raises one forefinger and quietly fanfares: *Ta-da!* We give him the floor and his head, knowing the lad to be, while anything but a show-off, as thorough as he is prodigious.

Looking over the spreadsheet, he tells us, and bearing in mind the constraints of "one walking, one crawling," et cetera, and assuming that Scheherazade got pregnant at her first ovulation after um losing her virginity, it seems pretty clear to him that she must have ovulated and men-

struated once after each of her three babies was born, and that she then got pregnant again at the very next ovulation after each of those menstruations—at least after the first and second of them. Otherwise the kids come out to be the wrong ages at the end. So-o-o . . . he guesses that whatever Moslem taboos apply with respect to coitus during menstruation, the king was pleased enough with Scheherazade by the time their first son was born to do without for a while and just listen to stories. Now, then: Assuming for the sake of simplicity and, you know, symmetry, that she first got pregnant on Night One, as Kath has suggested, and that all three of her pregnancies were of exactly average length—two hundred sixty-six days—and that the interval between each childbirth and her next menstruation after each, uh, postnatal ovulation was the exact average forty-nine days for . . . non-nursing women (Kath said six to eight weeks, right? So let's make it seven weeks on the button), *a-a-and* remembering that Scheherazade isn't pregnant again on Morning Ten Oh Two and that Ms. Silver called this story The Story of Scheherazade's First Second Menstruation . . .
     Yes?
     Chip grins. Lost and Found hold hands, understanding little of this but dazzled by their favorite uncle. She delivers Number One on Night Two Six Seven. That makes him two years and four days old on Night Ten Oh One; he's been walking for maybe a year. Seven weeks later, on Night Three Sixteen, she menstruates, having ovulated two weeks before. Two weeks after that, on Night Three Thirty, she gets pregnant for the second time, and she delivers Son Number Two exactly two hundred sixty-six days later, on Night Five Ninety-six. That'll make *him* thirteen months, ten days old on Night Ten Oh One: not too late to be crawling still, right? Seven weeks later she menstruates again, on Night Six Forty-five—you could call that her second *first* menstruation—and two weeks after that she gets pregnant for the *third* time. On Night Nine Twenty-five she delivers her third son, so he's just two and a half months old at the end of the story: nursing, but not crawling yet. Seven weeks later she menstruates again, just as she did after her other two pregnancies—and if things kept on going as they'd gone before, she'd get pregnant again on Night Nine Eighty-eight and be two weeks into her fourth child at the end of the story. Which of course would be too early for her to know for sure, and that could be why she doesn't mention it. But the thing to notice is that if she ovulated right on schedule on Night Nine Eighty-eight there and *didn't* get pregnant— which would be the first time such a thing ever happened in her three years with King Shahryar—then she's going to menstruate again on Night Ten Oh Two. As a matter of fact, since she always tells her stories just before daybreak, Night Ten Oh One is really Morning Ten Oh Two, and it could be that she ends that cobbler-king story the way she ends it and then calls in the children and pleads for her life because she realizes that for the first time in a thousand and one nights she's having a normal twenty-eight-day menstrual period. The king hasn't made her pregnant again on schedule: It's her first second menstruation.

Dear gawd, whispers Capn Don, and not in awe of Scheherazade's position. Chip sips Pepsi from the can. Dun & Bradstreet applaud; they're not sure what, but they rate it Triple-A. Carla B Silver gives her narrative assistant an enormous hug and prophesies This fellow here is going to make some difference in the world. What prompted Scheherazade to tell May Jump this story in Kitty Hawk, North Carolina, she then declares, was that some shmendrick at the ASPS convention asked her whether she'd stopped telling stories on the thousand-and-first night because she'd run out of gas, the way some storytellers do.

We Sherritt–Sagamores do not exchange glances.

Says Carla She wouldn't dignify the shmuck with an answer. She assumed the main reason went without saying: that at the end of Night Ten Oh One, Shahryar had been a good boy for exactly as long as he'd been a bad one. It was the right time to make her move, even without the private extra reason.

But that extra reason, says Captain Donald, is pretty important, no? Shahryar's expecting business as usual tomorrow night—tonight, actually—a roll in the hay and on with the story. But he isn't going to get it for nearly a week.

Katherine declares, neutrally, that she's relieved to hear it wasn't a case of Storyteller's Block. Knowing the Arabs' fondness for formal design, she finds Chip's numerical exercise both appealing and persuasive. What she's wondering now is how it happened that the pattern broke down: What went wrong on Night Whichever, when the king was supposed to get her pregnant again and didn't? Had the man lost interest? Become impotent? That impertinent person in Kitty Hawk wondered whether Scheherazade had run out of gas; Kath wonders whether maybe *Shahryar* did.

Chip declares that that's not his department—but for what it's worth, he remembers our saying that the story ends happily with the double marriage of the two brothers and the two sisters. . . .

Carla B Silver nods. We have Scheherazade's own word for it that the king was no more out of gas than she was out of stories. She was pleased enough not to be pregnant again right away for a change, but she was still a healthy and good-looking young woman, and she fully expected that Child Number Four would come along sooner or later. She and the king were particularly looking forward to having a daughter somewhere down the line, now that they had three sons in the bank. . . .

PETER SAGAMORE SAYS NOTHING.

Well, then, excuse me, says Captain Donald Quicksoat presently, but I guess I'm wondering why you've told us this particular story. With all due respect to Mister Chip's mathematical fireworks, what's the *point* of Scheherazade's so-called first second menstruation?

Carla B Silver pats his knee. That is exactly what she herself asked May Jump, she declares. But did May Jump ask Scheherazade the same question? She did not. And why not? Carla flourishes her cigarillo, straightens her back, and looks directly at *Story*'s skipper. *Because,* Mister Sagamore: May Jump says that every real storyteller will get the message for him/herself. *¿Buenas noches* time, Capn Don?

DAY 13:
WHY TO SASSAFRAS?

Over breakfast next morning, Peter Sagamore levelly asks or declares to Andrew Christopher "Chip" Sherritt

LET'S EMULATE THAT WISE OLD BIRD.

Chip frowns at his pound cake, at his instant coffee, at his orange juice, at his glass of milk. What?

Let's emulate that wise old bird.

Capn Donald Quicksoat?

No. That owl we heard hooting last night in one of those white oak trees right over yonder. Let's emulate that wise old bird.

I didn't *hear* any owl hooting last night in any white oak tree right over yonder. What's going on?

You didn't hear that owl, says Peter sagely, because that owl quit hooting early. That owl sat in that wise old oak, and the more that owl saw, the less that owl spoke. Owls have good hearing as well as excellent night vision.

Katherine's grinning. Hoot 'n' Anny nudge each other and her as if they understand. But she decides that that's enough teasing and explains to Chip that over the bar of the Owl Bar in the Belvedere Hotel on East Chase Street in Baltimore, where she and May Jump used to spend time in days gone by, is a locally famous stained-glass triptych, the first panel of which reads *A wise old owl sat in an oak,* and the second *The more he saw, the less he spoke,* and the third *The less he spoke, the more he heard,* and that May Jump had included that three-quarter quatrain along with other uncompleted verses in Katherine's brown-belt exercise book in First-Level Invention.

Oh, says Chip, and, contented, eats.

K confesses she'd been going to say *That's why he's such a wise old bird.*
Wrong tense, Chip points out immediately. Right you are, Peter agrees.
Kath kisses them both and says she sure misses May Jump. Carla B Silver's
story has got her thinking about her old friend. What's the point of Peter's
finishing up that poem just now?

What's the point of Scheherazade's first second menstruation? Peter asks
in return. He's filling in the blank in May Jump's Belvedere Owl Bar poem,
he declares, because this morning is Day 13, 28 June '80, full moon tonight,
and *tout le monde* is converging upon the Sassafras, May Jump no doubt
included, to watch us have our babies at last. Things could start popping
any minute, any minute, and we have so many plot-chestnuts yet in the
fire that it's going to take a narrative miracle to fetch them all out by closing
time. He thought he'd knock that little one off now, before things get busy.
Wasn't he a wise old bird?

Goes without saying, in Chip's opinion.

I should've gone to that ASPS convention in Kitty Hawk! Kath laments.
It's the only one I've missed in eleven years. Wait till I see that Maze: She
didn't say a word to me in Annapolis about Scheherazade!

We all swim. Then the born men swim some more while Katherine and
the unborn radio their immediate ancestors. Today bids to be another bona
fide Chesapeake summer item, maybe less hot than yesterday, but just as
damp and hazy-sunny, with another light southerly to dry the sweat and
move the action along. Definitely a clothes-off, dunk-in-the-river day; maybe
even an awning day, if the breeze doesn't pick up. We note with satisfaction, but know better than to mention, that Chip Sherritt is going native:
This morning, for the first time in mixed company, he piles over *Story*'s
stern sans swimsuit. Pubic hair just sprouting, like Five-O'Clock Shadow.

Katherine presently announces to those in the creek that the *K IV* people
are having a long English-style breakfast down in Fairlee Creek. No Sara
Lee pound cake for them: scrambled eggs with cream cheese and chervil,
toast with rough-cut marmalade, Canadian bacon and fried tomatoes and
tea. They expect to reach Ordinary Point by late lunchtime; they hope
we'll join them for dinner.

Says expansive Peter from the water Maybe we will, if the stork hasn't
struck by then. What else is new?

On the doomsday front, K reports, the House of Representatives is
expected to approve funding today for the MX missile.

Tick tick tick, worries Chip, floating so as not unduly to expose his
crotch. They're going to blow it up before I get to see it. His sister reminds
him to put his he-knows-what on his he knows what, once he's dried off.

Isn't the logic of that owl poem all mixed up? the lad now wonders to
his brother-in-law. The second and third lines imply that the owl's wisdom

came from talking less and looking and listening more; but the first line establishes that he was wise already, before he did that.

Peter Sagamore regards his remarkable young relative, cups one hand behind one ear, says nothing.

THANK GOD IT'S SATURDAY,

Captain Donald Quicksoat calls from his companionway a short while later as, Chip having sounded the conch for anchor aweigh, we glide by *Rocinante IV* on our way out of Back Creek. Low on ice and water, we have decided to poke upriver to Georgetown for a pit stop and then—unless etcetera et cetera—sail back to see what's doing at Ordinary Point. A satisfied-looking hombre this A.M., Capn Don reports that his shipmate is sleeping in after a comfortable night, thank you. Their agenda is a daysail out on the Bay if the breeze permits, after which they too will probably return to the Sassafras to see who's here and what's what. Did Peter figure out what Scheherazade's first second menstruation is supposed to mean? Be damned if *he* did.

From the bow, where he's dipping *Story*'s anchor clean, Peter calmly calls back Sure.

Says Chip at the jib halyard winch You did?

So tell me! hollers Capn Don, but we've already moved too far apart for talk. So tell *me,* says Katherine Sherritt at our tiller. She has banded her forehead with Lee Talbott's paisley scarf *trouvée;* she looks like a pretty, pregnant pirate. Her husband reminds her, however, that while only a prodigy like Andrew Sherritt can crunch the numbers (at least in his head), we have May Jump's word for it that every real storyteller will get Scheherazade's message for him/herself. He *him*self got it, belatedly, just minutes ago, as he was hauling up our Danforth anchor; if they'll excuse him now, he has writing to do. Let him know if any babies start being born.

Kath's heart hums. You're making notes for another story?

Nope. He kisses her bandanna en route downstairs. Fact is, my water just broke. I'm delivering.

Round and Round do a maypole dance. Their mother's eyes brim. *The Tidewater Tales?*

Not yet. Just a little warm-up exercise.

Thus is it left for our woman to observe to *Story*'s log that while the day stokes up and *boina*'d Peter Sagamore scribbles away at who knows what in his old faithful three-ring loose-leaf college binder (which he uses *never* for mere note-taking, only for serious sentence-building) with his old faithful British-made fountain pen (K didn't even know he'd stowed it aboard!) bought back in apprentice days in honor of great Boz in a stationer's shop in Rochester, England, alleged to be Mr. Pumblechook's premises—an

English pen for penning English, says P—it is left to her able young brother and her equally able though terminally pregnant self to sail us all on a slow easy reach the pretty miles to Georgetown. By 1000 hours, the Sassafras is festively abustle: Ultralight aircraft, bright as spinnakers, wheel overhead; yachts of all sizes, power and sail, swarm down from the Georgetown marinas—at least four and a half million dollarsworth, Chip casually estimates, assigning a median value of $30,000 to, say, 150 yachts; waterskiers, Windsurfers, Sunfish zip through the swarm; ospreys protest the traffic from their nests on every beacon; herring gulls dive and kvetch. A splendid spectacle withal, sailing through which (*Story* seems to be the only vessel headed upstream) requires Chip's and Katherine's unremitting attention to helm and sail-trim and right-of-way rules—but scribble scribble scribble goes Peter Sagamore, only now and then popping his bereted head out to check and smile upon the world.

We park at the first commercial fuel-dock—not *we,* Kath corrects her log entry: Chip and I do it, Himself being at it belowstairs—and a tidy bit of seamanship it is, given the congestion and the circumstance that she and her brother dared each other to try it under sailpower alone, and took the dare, and made a perfect eggshell landing in the slot between a forty-foot Concordia yawl and a mighty sedan cruiser, both of whose skippers were sure they were about to be rammed by a pregnant lady and a pubescent boy—and re-ice and re-water. Who shleps the ice blocks? Andrew Sherritt. Who tops off the water tank? Herself. Lunch? Just an apple for Himself, thanks; scribbledy scribbledy scribble.

Who's Mimi? she'd like to know, resting her chin on his *boina.* Lee's sister? Who's that Fred?

Tapping her tum with his pen-top, topless Peter says Them right there, probably. Stop peeking, okay?

OKAY, OKAY.

So: Sixty-six point seven percent of our crew raise main and genoa again and join the Bayward-headed fleet but get sweaty in the petering air so drop the sails and kick in the outboard and take the next exit-ramp off that nautical expressway into Woodland Creek, says the chart, where they don't even bother to anchor but let *Story* drift in the no breeze while they cool down the kiddies and themselves with a nice little skinny-dip. Well well well, look who's here: His now bottomless but still *boina*'d self deigns to join the party, if but briefly. Then it's scribbledy scribble, under power under cockpit awning, back down past Back Creek to Ordinary Point, where *Katydid* isn't yet but soon will be; Hank's already turning the corner at Howell Point, Chip reports from our radio: seven miles downstream, out of the Bay and into the river's underslung mouth. How long has it been since Katherine Sherritt last spoke with her parents? Oh, six hours. How long since she last saw them? Just three days. But she's as pleased at their approach as if we'd been a season abroad. And now, further excitement: When Chip switches back to channel 16 and dutifully notes the above transmission in our radio log, a woman's voice says *Story, Story,* this is *Reprise, Reprise.* Come in?

Lee? cries Katherine. Proper Chip says *Reprise,* this is *Story;* go to sixty-eight, please, over, and switches to that working channel.

Cries Katherine *Lee?* Leah Allan Silver Talbott chuckles from somewhere on the multifarious Chesapeake that she happened to pick up our transmission to *Katydid IV* while she was showing Simon Silver how to work the VHF. So how come we haven't had some babies yet. Over?

Says Kate 'Cause it's only the next-to-last chapter. Peter's working on the last chapter now, but he won't let me look.

Without looking up, Peter says This isn't the last chapter. And *this* isn't the next-to-last-chapter.

Katherine says Scratch what I just said, Lee, and sees her husband scratch out a line of whatever that is. So where are you?

They are off Worton Point, Lee Talbott replies, between Fairlee and Still Pond Creeks, and headed north. They parked in Swan Creek last night and plan to park in the Sassafras tonight, but not early; right now they're heading into Still Pond for a swim. Maybe we can get together this evening, if Kath's not in labor? They have some friends of ours aboard.

It's Peter that's in labor, Kath declares. He's wearing Frank's hat and breaking his promise not to write our stories until after B Day, so it must be serious. Who-all's with you? Did you know your mother's here?

A grave boy's voice says Hi, Missus Sagamore; this is Simon over.

Hello there, Simon Silver. Is your mom with you?

A mock-male voice replies gruffly So's his old man. Ahoy there, Kisses, and over we go.

Maze? Hey, Maze, what's this Scheherazade business?

May Jump says in her natural voice Everything in its place, Katydid. We'll look for you tonight if this thing doesn't tip and sink.

By Godfrey there's a wise old bird, remarks Peter: Everything in its place. I'm not breaking my promise, by the way.

You're not?

Leah Talbott now calls from our loudspeaker Kath? Lee again. So Frank and I decided to follow your example; I'll explain when we see you. So we picked up Mims and Simon and May at Kent Narrows yesterday and took off for a long weekend. Sy's been a little bit seasick, but he's getting his legs now, aren't you, Sy? So Kath? Ma really took the plunge, and you guys ran into her and Whatsisname on his boat?

Affirmative, *Reprise.*

Lee giggles. What's he like? He sounds like a kook. Over?

Everything in its place, says Katherine. You can judge for yourself tonight. Look behind Ordinary Point for an old ketch called *Rocinante Four,* with lots of baggy-wrinkle on the rigging and eyeballs on the bow.

We'll be there late, Lee reminds us. Sy really needs to get off this boat and into the water for a while. So we'll look for you, okay? *Reprise* out.

Chip hopes the crew of *Rocinante IV* didn't have their ears on. Who's this Simon? He logs the transmission and goes swimming himself.

SCRIBBLE SCRIBBLE SCRIBBLE

goes Peter Sagamore, at anchor behind Ordinary Point. Katherine and Andrew dinghy ashore to stroll the beach and make certain that the old Atlas automobile tire with the locust tree growing through it is still there. Kate delights in the prospect of seeing May Jump and the Talbotts again; she makes Full and By promise to hold on for one more chapter if they possibly can. Chip wonders how anybody could get seasick in three knots of wind; his sister reminds him that not everyone takes boats for granted. She is tempted to enlarge upon the May Jump/Marian Silver/Simon Silver ménage, but decides not to; she enjoys watching her brother size things up for himself. There's Mom and Dad and the Basses, Chip says, pointing out to sea. Without binoculars, K sees an undifferentiated mass of sails stretching to the hazed horizon, but she doubts neither Chip's discernment nor his estimation that *Katydid IV,* if it holds present course and speed, will round Ordinary Point in about thirty-nine minutes. He sets the bezel on the Seiko Sports 100 we gave him last Christmas.

About thirty-nine minutes? grins Peter when they're back aboard and Kath reports this news. That's like saying it's about fourteen minutes and twelve seconds after one o'clock.

Replies Chip, checking his bezel, About seventeen minutes now, if they've held course and speed. But he further predicts that despite the wind-shadow of the river's south bank, which *Katydid* must move through in order to clear the point, his dad will not turn on the engine to maintain speed, but will round the point under full sail, even at one knot. So add . . . a quarter-hour.

At (about) 1344 plus six seconds, Chip blows a great note from our bow with *Story*'s freon signal-horn, and Peter takes a break from his labors to join the reception committee. The Sherritts' big ketch has just slid into view at maybe two knots under all plain sail—main, mizzen, and 150-percent genoa—and turned to where Chip now signals again our location among the anchored yachts. Way to go, Dad, the boy says proudly. If *he* were aboard to help instead of Doctor Jack, he declares, *Katydid* would be tooling along under mizzen staysail and reaching spinnaker as well, and would not be eight minutes late; Dr. Jack's a racing skipper, but too old to be a racing crew.

Even without his young foredeck hand, Hank now pulls off a spectacular bit of macho seamanship. Having waved recognition and roller-furled the jib, instead of starting the engine and readying the anchor, he and Jack Bass rig bow and stern lines and starboard-side fenders while Joan Bass stands bow lookout and Irma, no slouch in these matters, threads downwind under main and mizzen through the already busy anchorage, shaving just below this boat's transom, just above that one's anchor rode, between dinghies, sailboards, swimmers. Are they serious? Chip wonders happily. They're going to raft up under sail? We'd better believe it, says Peter, and makes haste to hang *Story*'s portside fenders. We stand by then to take lines when the moment comes. With Hank at the wheel now, simultaneously monitoring water depth, headway, wind speed, and the other vessels both moored and moving, *Katydid IV* slides massively past us almost at boathook range. Admiring Peter says conversationally, as Irma goes by in the bows, Hello there, Mother-in-Law. A coiled line in her left hand, she blows a little kiss with her right and says, just as conversationally, The beret becomes you, Peter. Jack and Joan Bass waggle their fingers; Henry Sherritt turns his head for no more than a second to wink at his children—two knots seems swift indeed in these tight quarters, for a fifty-foot, two-masted object with no brakes—and then makes a short U-turn through disbelieving dozens in the last stretch of six-foot water at his disposal, maybe three of his boatslengths astern of us.

Now comes the dicey part: rafting up under sail alone, which Peter Sagamore is an expert at in little *Story* but would never attempt with a twenty-ton ketch. Having swung around dead to windward, Hank aims at a slight angle for our port side, lets all sails luff, and banks on his intuitive estimate of how far *Katydid* will "shoot" of her own momentum through the crowd, against the tiny breeze. Five seconds after his father turns, Chip announces He's got it. Just a tad fast, Pete predicts, but no problem; if he'd waited any longer to make his turn, he'd be aground. Chip says You should've seen Kath's eggshell landing this morning. That he should have, P acknowledges, though he could tell from downstairs that it was A-plus.

Almost so too is *Katydid IV*'s: a more considerable maneuver because the object at risk is another boat, not a wooden pier, and because the forces involved are larger by an order of magnitude. Be it credited to Henry Sherritt's good sense that in any real breeze he would never have chanced banging up his and other folks' expensive toys with a piece of show-offery. The last of his steerageway fetches him neatly alongside us; as the hulls kiss fenders, Irma tosses Chip the bow line, and Jack Bass hands Peter the stern. Both are quickly snubbed down, for as Peter foresaw, the ketch still has enough way on to shoot maybe another twenty feet, given her heavy displacement. The pull pulls *Story* half that distance forward on her anchor before the two boats settle back, rafted.

Cheers Kate Bravo! Peter tips Frank Talbott's *boina;* Chip says All *right!*

and piles across the mated gunwales to visit his folks. There is even scattered applause from the relieved near-missed in the neighborhood. Henry Sherritt acknowledges us with a smiling short nod . . . and *now* ceremoniously starts his engine, to charge the fridge, top off the batteries, and heat water for the galley and showers.

Peter kisses the ladies, shakes hands with the gentlemen, helps serve and eat a communal lunch aboard *K IV,* and then—having demonstrated to the family's satisfaction that we are indeed again one person—excuses himself to get back to work. Chip helps his dad with a couple of boat jobs; boys his size are in especial demand for going aloft in bosun's chairs to do this and that at the masthead. Then he breaks out *Katydid*'s Windsurfer to entertain himself for the rest of the afternoon. People swim. And Katherine Sherritt, happily spoiling herself, bathes both in the Sassafras and in the bosom of her family. Though no one, least of all Peter, has forgotten his late intransigence, all hands are relieved to see that we are quite okay.

To give our man maximum privacy, the party remains under *Katydid IV*'s ample center-cockpit awning, though Katherine assures them that once her husband's juices are flowing, he could work standing up in the concourse of Pennsylvania Station. What's new with Molly Sherritt? she wants to know. There is no news, because for reasons unknown, Molly has abruptly changed gynecologists: some young Cuban in Chestertown, whom mildly miffed Jack Bass hasn't even met yet. She and Willy are to drop in by Easton Air Freight helicopter tomorrow noontime for a little ceremonial presentation of the Back Creek granary to Breadbasket Inc.; maybe we'll learn something then. Kate wants her parents and the Basses to meet our new friends Carla B Silver and Captain Donald Quicksoat, who'll be sailing in shortly; also the Talbotts, ditto, whom Hank has met but not Irma. And guess who's with them: May Jump!

Says Irm That's nice. Kath's folks don't *know* about May Jump and their daughter, any more than they *know* about their son-in-law's professional-aesthetic difficulties; but though relatively innocent in some respects, they are neither blind nor stupid. So: That's nice. Kath looks forward to introducing them, as she does Chip, to clumsy Simon Silver, his strung-out mother, and his potential foster father. . . .

A landing party of six, plus Ark and Dove, piles presently into *K IV*'s Boston Whaler (on which has been hung a bigger outboard engine than the one we borrowed) to go have a look at Breadbasket's new showpiece, appropriately backdropped by green cornfields also now owned by the corporation. Peter really would like to join the expedition—but no: The muse summons, sort of.

Katherine worries: Sort of?

He thought he'd told her: What he's scribbling at is, per promise, not the real thing yet; just a warm-up, a stretching exercise. Don't ask; she'll see it presently.

Cheer Scratch and Scribble, whose Uncle Andrew has already become their model: Way to go, Dad! Give us a scribble! Give us a scratch.

SURE.

At tide-turn the southerly catches its breath and settles in at a welcome five knots to ventilate evening on the Sassafras. About cocktail time— later than usual, since lunch was late and nobody except Chip is the least bit interested yet in dinner—Peter comes up for air and in for a swim and over for company, announcing with satisfaction that that's that, muse- wise: enough new American literature for one day. Also (he's climbing *Katydid*'s portside boarding ladder now and kissing his wife hello, who has missed him) that that looks to him like *Rocinante IV* across the river there, sails furled, motoring not our way but into Turner Creek, on the farther shore.

Right you are, affirms Chip. Aboard *Katydid IV,* except under way, one does not drink beverages from their containers as one does aboard *Story.* The older foursome are sipping Jack Bass's dry martinis; at his father's instruction, Chip goes to the galley now to pour his brother-in-law a chilled glass of Dos Equis, of which Hank Sherritt has laid in a supply for Peter's sake though he can get it only in fridge-inefficient, trash-intensive bottles. P raises his defrosting glass in toast to his parents-in-law and to Breadbasket Inc., whose involvement with Sherbald Enterprises we do not bring up on this agreeable occasion.

K raises hers—Perrier only—in tacit toast to the unlamented memory of Less Is More, R.I.P., and borrows the binocs to watch *Rocinante* pick her way through the distant creek entrance: another of those tricky S-turns, with not a channel marker in it. She sees the old ketch go gently twice aground, back off, try again, and finally disappear behind a stand of mixed hardwoods into Turner Creek proper. That's where *we're* supposed to be, she suddenly remembers. And why are they parking over there instead of over here? Maybe Carla B Silver needs to use the pay phone in Turner Creek Park, Peter offers. Maybe they want to get off the boat awhile and picnic ashore. Maybe Donald Quicksoat's friend Odysseus is anchored over there. Maybe there are thunderstorms in the forecast, and they want a snugger anchorage than this. Maybe they're meeting Scheherazade and Sindbad at the public landing. Maybe their weekend isn't working out, and Carla's lighting out for Fells Point with Huckleberry Findley.

Katherine explains to everybody that when he's writing, her husband and father of our children can dream up seven reasons for anything.

Chip points out that that's only six. Peter adds, obligingly and at once, Maybe they're not parking over there; maybe Capn Don's just showing his friend Turner Creek. As for our supposed to be being over there ourselves, he assures his wife (as imagined in our prologue): Let us never forget that the late Jean Heartstone's Magic Language Theory is fiction's sport, not nature's law. To thy rest, dear doomèd Jean, may flights of angels sing thee! But it is enough and more that here we are, safely on the Sassafras on Day 13 of our reckless, random, pregnant cruise; we are no more obliged to park in Turner Creek instead of snugly rafted with our obstetrician than Katherine is obliged to give birth to a south Italian midwife named Ma Nontroppo and the rest, or Blam be followed by Blooey this time tomorrow.

He gets like this, happy Kath explains, when he's writing. Lean Joan Bass, on her second martini, says she thinks it must be a wonderful wonderful thing to make up stories out of thin air and write them down on paper in a book, you know? *She* couldn't any more do it than fly to the moon. Binoculared Andrew Sherritt says Number Seven wins: They're coming back out.

He passes the Fujinons to his sister. Sure enough, in the lengthening light she sees *Rocinante* winding out of Turner Creek as carefully as she wound in, this time without incident. Peter lifts his *boina,* whose provenance he has briefly explained over Dos Equis (and Katherine, less briefly, earlier in the afternoon as they toured the old granary). We look for the ketch now to head our way; to our surprise, C.D.Q. aims west again instead, behind the point, Bayward.

Uh-oh, says K. Says P Not necessarily, but declines to run through the half-dozen alternatives. At Irma's suggestion, Chip checks the forecast; if there is even a slight chance of thunderstorms, we'll unraft after dinner and anchor separately instead of swinging two boats from one rode. There is none, NOAA/Baltimore assures us. All the same, while there's still light we follow sound nautical practice by setting out *Katydid*'s main anchor in place of *Story*'s; the raft now swings from its largest member, with the heftiest ground tackle.

While the four men play this game, the three women review our combined larders and set to building dinner. The remains of a wild-mallard pâté, served first with cocktails as hors d'oeuvre, now reappears with seedless red grapes and iced rosé as an appetizer; Olive Treadway made this pâté out of ducks shot down on location from the Shorter Point blind last December and now at the end of their shelf-life in her Main House freezer. The entrées are swordfish and salmon steaks, grilled on a pair of taffrail braziers to keep the heat outdoors and served simply with lemon, sliced tomatoes, ripe olives, and Pouilly-Fuissé. There follows a salad (*Story*'s contribution) of Belgian endive vinaigrette, and another round of the same wine for the nonpregnant. As the sun sets over this last course, we touch fortunate glasses across the big stowaway cockpit table—clink clink clink clink clink clink clink—and toast a number of things at once: Jack and Joan and Irma and Hank the good long life behind them: decades of successful work and harmless play, and who knows how many first-rate duck pâtés and white Bordeaux?—maybe five years more, ten at most, of sailing these agreeable waters before their bodies' aging puts such sport behind them. To these agreeable waters, P proposes: May they remain so for our kids to enjoy, even when their parents can't. Chip bets they won't; he bets the twentieth century will be the last real one. Andrew? Irma wonders. Katherine smoothly hugs her troubled brother and proposes On with the story.

Now it's deep dusk. Having corrected for our meridian of longitude the Greenwich Mean Time given in the tide tables, Chip scans the east with the 7 × 50s to watch for moonrise. A few boats are still coming in, under running lights; those of us already moored raise anchor lights on our head-stays. Cabin lights are going on, too; the anchorage glows like a little city. Here comes *Rocinante*, Chip announces. They're following another boat. A cutter. It might be *Reprise*. It is.

We hope they'll come this way, though there isn't room left in our neighborhood for two more yachts to swing at anchor. The three skippers rapidly agree that, given the clear forecast, it will not be unsafe to add the pair to our raft, one on either side, if we can hail them and if they care to join us; *Katydid* will simply let out more scope. Peter goes below to try to raise them by radio; not surprisingly, all channels are achatter with friends calling friends round about the Sassafras and the upper Bay. The calling channel, 16, is free only for seconds at a time. In a clear moment P tries it, without response; either the Talbotts are monitoring another channel or, more likely, they're too busy single-filing through the fleet in the dark to bother with their radios. He goes around the dial again (*Katydid*'s fancy VHF can do it automatically, pausing at each channel in use), returns to 16 for a final try, and hears what must be young Simon Silver's voice calling *him*—and not from *Reprise*, but from *Rocinante*. Story, Story, this is *Rocinante Four, Rocinante Four*.

Rocinante, this is *Story*, Peter replies, though it isn't. Try Seventy-two, Simon. Over.

After only a little confusion the boy gets the link established, along with the information that his Uncle Frank and Aunt Lee have been in radio contact with his grandma and Capn Don through the latter part of the afternoon; that the two boats had been going to join up behind Ordinary Point, but—*Reprise* being delayed in Still Pond Creek by Simon's seasickness, and the daylight running out—they rendezvoused off Betterton instead, in the river's mouth. There he boarded *Rocinante*, to lend Grandma a hand, and she and Captain Donald fixed his seasickness, and now they're following Uncle Frank in because he knows the waters better at night. They're looking either for us or for a place to park, whichever comes first. Uh, over.

Roger, *Rocinante*. Peter instructs the boy to instruct his skipper that we have them in sight; to look for a blinking flashlight on a raft of two boats. . . . Off their port beam now, Chip helpfully calls down. Off your port beam, Simon. I'm going to turn you over to my friend Chip Sherritt here; he'll talk you in.

Chip takes the microphone, and in the fifteen minutes it requires for Capn Don to get the word to Franklin Talbott and for the two boats to circle to us, the boys become sort of friends. We decide, and pass the word along, to put *Rocinante* on *Katydid*'s port side and *Reprise* on *Story*'s starboard. We also bring the Boston Whaler up behind *Story*'s stern for the night. Should Katherine's amnion burst or other imminent birth-sign come upon us, Hank will speed Jack Bass and Irma and us to Georgetown: a twenty-minute Whaler ride at an easy fifteen knots. Assuming prompt ambulance connection, his passengers can be in the Chestertown hospital forty minutes later or, if there's no emergency, in Easton Memorial in another hour. In the morning, Bobby Henry will come up by car, returning Jack Bass if his work is done; the Goldsborough Creek flotilla will then either make its way home with available crew (Chip is already lobbying to manage *Story* singlehanded) or lay our boat up in a Georgetown transient slip to be retrieved later.

Says Kate, correctly, That's about what we had in mind. Boyoboy, are we trouble.

Perfectly cheerfully, her father, mother, and obstetrician agree. We have also the genuine option of delivering aboard, on a rubber sheet on the queen-size berth in *Katydid*'s aft cabin. Barring complications, all would probably go well. But if he has to do a cesarean, as is quite possible, Dr. Jack prefers a proper delivery room and a few trained helpers besides good Joan. We shall therefore agree, shall we not, that tomorrow—our nominal D Day, our EDC—will be the last of our cruise in any case? That if we are still pregnant after the granary ceremonies, say, we shall move on up to Georgetown, berth our boat, drive home with Irma and the Basses in the car already scheduled to be driven up by Bobby Henry, and stay uncomplainingly put on Nopoint Point till the end of the chapter? Says Irma smoothly, and mostly to Katherine, It's all arranged. Your dad and Chip will bring *Katydid* back on Monday, and Bobby Henry will drive *Story* home.

Chip reminds the world politely that *he* could bring *Story* home single-handed. That Bobby Henry doesn't even know how to sail, and would have to motor the whole way.

Katherine looks to Peter; he to her. We tuck in our lips. We smile. Sure.

WHY TO SASSAFRAS?

The moon is up and splendid on the Sassafras. Except for the dead and missing and the otherwise unfortunately engaged, we are all here now, snugly rafted for the night. Round about us the anchorage throngs with sociability: Japanese lanterns and fish-pennants, burgees, windsocks in the rigging; radios and guitars; laughter, splashes. Folks dinghy here and there; a raft of streetwise mallards paddles from handout to handout. Among our raft, too, once lines and fenders are secured and all hands introduced around, people settle out in amiably shifting groups to enjoy one another's company. In all the period of their awareness, our children have never seen such a party. This is what they do, Behold explains to her brother: They have fun. We shall, also. Lo wonders whether everybody does.

Between May Jump and Katherine Sherritt, grand *abrazos*. Holding K's belly briefly like a beachball, May grumbles I wish to God they were mine, Kiss. And then, to Peter, Since they aren't, I'm glad they're yours. May's looking nifty in white flared jeans, red polo shirt, white headband, brown bare feet. Peter both shakes her freckled hand and busses her freckled cheek. If Chip Sherritt is taken aback by the corpulence, precocious mustache, black Bermuda shorts, and plain white T-shirt of his radio pal Simon Silver, his good breeding and natural friendliness conceal the fact. He shakes the boy's shy hand, introduces him around *K IV*'s cockpit, and takes him below to show him the yacht's fancy electronics and engine room. In half an hour they're motoring off together in *Reprise*'s inflatable dinghy to check out the whole anchorage. Captain Donald Quicksoat and Carla B Silver meet the Basses and the elder Sherritts, as do Leah and Franklin Talbott, whom we hug as friends now old and close. C.D.Q. is at his ease with sailors of any sort; C.B S. at hers with people of any sort; the Basses and the Sherritts share the admirable trait of being, with people quite outside their circle, at once entirely themselves and entirely disposed to cordiality. Peter Sagamore's parents had not that gift. He sees his wife's eyes shine, not for the first time, with love for her progenitors; he feels his glisten with love for her.

Lee Talbott looks happy and terrific in short shorts and faded blue workshirt, tails knotted. Sturdy brown bald gray-beard Franklin kisses Kate's lips lightly and once again stirs her hormones. Hi, Frank.

You are hatted, he remarks to Peter, who replies equably I am, and want a word with you.

Says Franklin Key Talbott Likewise. Tonight, if we can get to it?

Tomorrow morning if we can't.

Things are popping.

Yup.

Odd fellow out is Marian Silver. Though her mother, sister, and lover are all more than mindful of her, Mim doesn't know what to do with herself, with the little party, with the full moon. Her skintight khaki shorts crease deeply between her labia; she cannot move without announcing in effect *Voilà ma funfunette,* and she moves often, self-consciously crossing and uncrossing her white legs. Her baggy orange T-shirt is lettered WYDIWYD. Says friendly Katherine Don't tell us; let us guess. Marian fiddles with the silver prow of her punk cut; lights a cigarette; murmurs May gave it to me, day before yesterday. No: Wednesday. It's a thousand times too big.

She crosses her legs.

The latecomers have snacked but not dined. Rather than make dinner now, Lee and Carla retire to *Reprise*'s galley to build eight tuna-salad sandwiches: two for Simon, whose mal de mer spoiled his lunch but has been quite cured. Katherine helps, in order to be with her women-friends.

May Jump crosses *Katydid*'s deck to join them, leaving Capn Don, Frank Talbott, Peter Sagamore, and Marian Silver in *Rocinante*'s cockpit. Marian stretches her arms, yawns, says Excuse *me,* uncrosses her legs.

In answer to Peter's question—Why to Sassafras?—Frank Talbott says For six or seven reasons, I guess. To give Mim and Sy a little outing and get to know May Jump better. (We like her, he assures Marian, who wanly smiles and shrugs and crosses her legs.) To ease our withdrawal-pains after four whole days ashore after a year afloat. To have a look at that granary ceremony tomorrow. . . . Does *ceremony* come from *cereal?*

Nope. Wax.

Pity. To swim without standing sea-nettle watch. To help you guys have your babies. To celebrate our new life, I guess: Lee's and mine. Our new lives. Things look okay on that front. How many's that?

Six or seven, Peter guesses.

To talk to you about a thing I might try to do after *Kepone.* Sort of a novel, actually.

Sort of?

A novel. When do I get my *boina* back?

Says Peter Everything in its place, my friend. You may have to take the long way around, back to where you first lost it.

Marian Silver asks Captain Donald Quicksoat Is there a toilet on this boat? Sure, and he'll show her how it works. But he's also listening to what's getting said.

Franklin Talbott wonders: back to Wye Island or back to Spain? If you ask him, he and Lee have already taken the scenic route to Wye I.—via Tobago.

Says oracular Peter I mean the Tajo de Ronda. Donald Quicksoat pauses at *Rocinante*'s companionway, down which he is escorting Marian Silver. He whose *boina* falleth into the Tajo de Ronda, P declares, or whose protagonist's *boina* doth, doth not simply stroll down and bring it back. Doth he, Capn Don? No more than Dante takes a shortcut out of the Dark Wood, or Quixote climbs right back up the rope from the Cave of Montesinos.

Captain Donald winks. That is the truth, amigo. Come with me, young lady.

Hopes Franklin Key Talbott You'll explain.

Yup.

IN THE GALLEY OF *REPRISE,*

and then in the cockpit, also on the foredeck, and here and there about the rafted foursome, as our company eat and drink and move about and mingle under the moon:

Marian Silver thanks Captain Donald Quicksoat for reminding her how to work a marine toilet. As he does not then promptly leave the cabin so that she can use it, she thanks him additionally for fixing her son's earlier seasickness. Did Simon give the copper bracelet back? The boy can keep it, says C.D.Q., leaning easily against the pillar of the mainmast. It's just superstition, but it seems to work. Then it's not just superstition, Mim declares, and for some reason adds that she really likes and appreciates May Jump, all May's doing for her and all. But it's not the same, you know? Capn Don smiles.

Katherine Sherritt tells Leah Talbott that she's looking more than merely terrific, dot dot dot. Carla B Silver agrees; her eyes meet her elder daughter's. Laughing Lee sets down her sandwich to kiss her mother's forehead.

Taking May Jump's hand, Kath says Let's emulate that wise old bird? And what else rhymes with *crossed* besides *frost tossed mossed* and *lost*? May promises to work on it and confides to Katherine—also, later and separately, to Carla—that in her opinion, Maid Marian is ready for another man, alas, whether she herself realizes it or not. Carla sighs and lays a hand on May's forearm. That's a pity. Thanks, says May; I think so, too. You're good with her and good with Simon, Carla declares further. Thanks, May says; I suppose Sy needs a man in the house, too. You should've seen him hanging onto his Uncle Frank. But thanks. She pats Carla's hand on her arm and grins: Forearmed is forearmed?

Says Katherine Who wouldn't hang onto his Uncle Frank?

He was hanging onto Captain Donald, too, Lee points out. We like your new friend, Ma, what we've seen of him.

Yeah, well, says Carla B Silver.

Out on *Katydid*'s bow pulpit, Simon Silver confides to Andrew Christopher Sherritt that Marian Silver is not his real mother. That his Grandma Carla and his Grandpa Fred found him floating in a lifeboat from a sunken ocean liner in Baltimore Harbor when he was just a baby, and that they all pretend he's Marian Silver's son so people won't think she's nothing but a goddamn lesbian. That's interesting, Chip says. I've got cigarettes hidden, Simon says; you want a cigarette? Chip guesses not. His Grandpa Fred, Simon says, was the biggest spy in the whole CIA. Just before he disappeared off Uncle Frank's boat there, he gave Simon this special CIA bracelet? His Uncle Jon was tortured to death with chili. His mother was once kidnapped by a Hell's Angel and tied up and stripped naked and burned with cigarettes and fucked for three whole days, and that's why she's crazy, but she's not really his mother. He hates her guts. May Jump acts nice to him because she's queer for his mother. When he grows up, he's going to fuck a hundred naked women, but he's never going to have any snot-nose bratty kids. How about Chip?

I probably won't either, Chip says politely.

Mister Simon, May Jump calls from *Reprise*'s cockpit: Ask Mister Chip if he'll have a tuna sandwich.

Says Simon lowly She fucks my mother with an artificial cock that she straps on her hairy old pussy. I saw it in her dresser drawer.

If there's a spare one, May, Chip calls back. Thanks.

Carla B Silver tells Leah and Katherine When I see a moon like that, I miss Fred Talbott so much I could howl. Lee kisses her mother's left hand. May Jump rejoins them, bringing drinks to order from *Reprise*'s icebox, and asks Where's our Mim?

Our Mim, says Carla grimly, is where the boys are. The *big* boys.

Peter Sagamore misses his wife. He and Frank Talbott having finished the first installment of their private conversation, he excuses himself, goes looking for her, meets her on *Story*'s cabin top coming to look for him. She has redonned Lee Talbott's paisley scarf *trouvée,* again as a headband. The Basses and the Sherritts announce that they're going for a moonlight swim. Franklin Talbott comes over to see whether Lee and May and Carla are in that mood. May's game; Lee and Carla want to talk. We too decide to sit this one out. Katherine notes that Capn Don, two boats over, has managed to make Marian Silver laugh at something. So let's swim, Frank says to May Jump. Andrew Sherritt says he'll join the party. Coming in, Big Sy? Frank asks, laying a hand on each boy's shoulder. Simon says Nah; he doesn't feel too good in his stomach again.

On *Katydid*'s afterdeck now, Katherine tells Peter that Lee Talbott has told her among other things that our twin-naming habit has got her thinking about a new scholarly-critical study: twins, doubles, and schizophrenia in the American literary imagination, from say Hawthorne through Mark Twain to say Nabokov. Cracks P In two volumes, right? and asserts that if he were setting about to write the new novel that Franklin Key Talbott has just been discussing (also among other things) with him, inspired by *Reprise*'s Caribbean cruise, he would turn both the Silver sisters and the Talbott brothers into twins: twin twins. And he'd shorten the voyage from a year down to nine months, for obvious reasons but also because that's a school year, and sabbaticals are for learning new things. But he'd begin the story in the last two weeks of the ninth month, when the couple reenter the Chesapeake Bay. And he'd frame it with the loss and recovery of the magic *boina*. Shut me up, Kath! It's not my novel.

Wonders Katherine warmly When *does* Frank get his hat back? He's got it back, says Peter; I just haven't given it to him yet.

She squeezes his hand. Soon, okay?

Very soon.

Should I return this scarf to Lee, or keep it? I kind of like it, and she gave it to me in Queenstown Creek.

P considers. Neither. We'll see.

Without bothering to change into a swimsuit, Marian Silver now joins the bathers. Carla B Silver goes by, en route to *Rocinante IV* to have a little chat with Captain Donald Quicksoat.

Simon Silver's stomach's sore. He has gone below, on *Reprise*. His Aunt

Leah presently comes down to check on him; finds him lying in a settee berth, facing its back. She can't at first get anything out of him. To discourage bugs, the cabin is lit by a single citronella candle in a netted orange glass container. She leans over him in the flickering light, sees he's wearing his reflector sunglasses and turning the copper bracelet on his wrist.

Sy?

He sniffs. She touches his forehead. You okay, honey? The boy lets go a weeping caterwaul; rolls over like an anguished manatee and desperately flings his arms around her waist; buries wail and wet face together in her shirt.

Frank says he's got the goods on Willy and Poon, Peter tells Katherine. What I've heard so far is pretty amazing. How're you doing?

We're back aboard *Story* now, just the pair-plus of us, holding hands in our cockpit and admiring the pockèd moon. I'm fine, she says. I've got so much stuff to tell you! What's that sound?

We shall be another fortnight sorting all these conversations out, and that night's subsequent several dreams. Just now Leah Talbott sticks her head through *Reprise*'s companionway and says across to us Kath? Peter? Ask Ma to come over, would you? We've got ourselves a little problem here.

SPECTACLES TESTICLES WALLET AND WATCH,

Peter remarks through *Story*'s moonlit cabin to Andrew Christopher Sherritt maybe three hours later, when the three of us, at least, are at last in bed.

What?

In her berth up forward, though her heart still stings with sympathy for Simon Silver and May Jump—for poor flakey Marian Silver too, for that matter—Katherine giggles.

It's about four minutes and thirty-seven seconds after midnight, Peter says from his aft quarterberth. Today is Birthday, Chipperino; no time to waste.

K agrees: Got to get the plot-chestnuts out of the old fire.

Repeats P Spectacles, testicles, wallet, watch.

Chip gives up, though *testicles* reminds him of some of the extraordinary things he has heard Simon Silver say.

Convert? said the rabbi to the priest, Katherine prompts: *What do you mean, convert?*

Chip tries harder to concentrate, but doesn't get it.

Peter says *I could swear, said the priest to the rabbi, that when they pulled the two of us from that wrecked airplane, I saw you cross yourself.* Good night, all.

Nighty-night, says Kath. What an evening.

After a silent while, Andy Sherritt says I *almost* get it.

On behalf of offended rabbis everywhere, Katherine Sherritt murmurs *Cross shmoss, replied the rabbi: I was just taking inventory.* So's Peter. Cross yourself once, Chipper, while you say the punch line.

She is asleep already when sleepless Peter, his motor still racing upon (among other fuels) poor Simon's outburst and May Jump's new unfinished Scheherazade story, hears sleepless Andrew whisper aft Do all Jewish rabbis wear pocket watches and carry their billfolds in their coat pockets? Or only Conservative ones?

Everything in its place, P whispers back.

What an evening indeed; but all seems well enough now. Khomeini censures Iranian government for softness on hostage issue. U.S. to rush tanks to Thailand. Texas heat wave breaks at last; leaves twenty-one dead. *Jewish rabbis* is redundant, he reminds Chip softly; but the boy is asleep.

We are ready.

DAY 14:
ORDINARY POINT

Port to starboard through the raft, fore to aft aboard each vessel, in Sunday's small hours, 29 June '80,

ALL HANDS DREAM.

Laid out for singlehanded passagemaking, *Rocinante IV* has but two berths: an ample portside foldout double, to which Captain Donald treats himself at anchor, and, for use at sea, a narrow starboard settee with attachable lee-cloth to prevent his rolling out. In the double, Carla B Silver sleeps alone, conversing with Frederick Mansfield Talbott and Short Jon Silver. Upstream through her lower reaches, into which their generator Capn Don introduced them not long since, millions of spermatozoa thrash purposefully to no purpose. Their sleeping hostess, safely past the menopause, lets them paddle undisturbed and unobstructed toward their deaths. Through the four-decades-plus of her sexual life, these have been preceded by tens of billions of their fellows, intromitted by perhaps three dozen men in various circumstances. Of those tens of billions, just three individual sperm achieved their biological Cathay. Each of C.B S.'s twin ovaries, in the years between her menarche and her menopause, faithfully in turn launched an ovum every second lunar month: four hundred plus between them. All went the way of those tens of billions of hapless swimmers— save one who, on D Day afternoon, met and chose a spermatozoon of Al Silver's with whom to become Leah Allan Silver; a second who did likewise not long after to coauthor sister Marian; and a third who, years later, took unto herself one of Frederick Talbott's doughty swimmers to the end of forming Short Jon Silver.

So go the stupendous odds, Jon explains now to his mother, against anything's happening the way it does at all. Yet the world proceeds. He and his father, though dripping wet, are at their ease, like Franklin Key Talbott and Peter Sagamore in *Reprise*'s cockpit a few hours past, just after their retrieval of Simon Silver from the Sassafras. They smell of brine and cold sea-wrack; they are drowned men. But in death there is a living peace between them such as never was in their lives' last years. Not even the cruel marks of the torturers on Jonathan's sturdy naked corpse dismay; his mother views them with the gentle pain of parents registering old scars upon the precious bodies of their children. It is to comfort Carla B Silver that her men have swum together into her sleep. The tale they tell her is not true: that, for complicated Prince-of-Darkness reasons, Fred Talbott faked his Paisleylike disappearance from *Reprise* in order to work his covert way clear down to the Straits of Magellan and effect the spectacular rescue of his son from one of General Pinochet's prisons—on Dawson Island, Ma, laughs Jon, in Tierra Fucking del *Fuego*!—only to drown with him and two others when their little launch capsized in stormy night waters en route back to Punta Arenas. The facts are that Frederick Mansfield Talbott committed calm suicide in the mouth of the placid Wye upon learning from Douglas Townshend that Jonathan's DINA torturers (some of them trained at a CIA establishment on the Chesapeake) had accidentally killed him sooner than they meant to in the course of "yellow-submarining" him: holding his head down in a toilet bowl full of urine and feces. He never even reached the Dawson Island internment center. How do we know? We know.

The fiction does its job. It *is* tisk-tisky, Carla's men acknowledge, that, of the products of her three successful ova and the Ishmael sperm they coupled with, one (Rick Talbott's only one) will carry the line no farther; that another did, but inadvertently, via rape, and with problematical issue; and that the third—a sterling Silver indeed, mated to a better Talbott— saw fit to pluck and chuck their union's fruit before harvest time. But the tale's not done, they tell her, smiling: Even as she sleeps, the avant-garde of Frank Talbott's recentest have attained Lee Silver's newest. Before this sentence ends, the biochemical election will have been made; he and she become we. And this time, unless the world go bang, John Frederick Silver Talbott will ensue. Rest therefore from your labors, mother and wife! Neither mourn us any longer nor rush to join us. One of us feeds the earth; one the water. But we're together; can wait; shall embrace you soon enough. Sleep.

Carla wakes. Remembers where she is; understands that she's alone in the double berth though not in the moonlit cabin. She is grateful to her lank companion for having moved to the lean settee, where she hears him breathe: They're done with each other, but will part friends. Now the dream surfaces, at first to scald her eyes and heart, then to commence its calming work. True or not, what they said soothes through; her tears are of a sweeter flavor, and presently put by. She's glad she let old Quicksoat in after all; made her little peace with him as she has made her large one now with Frederick Mansfield Talbott. She's glad for this whole weekend, poor Sy's outburst notwithstanding.

Men: God knows she's loved them. Beloved bastard Rick. Bullheaded darling Jon.

She guesses she'll go pee.

May Jump is camping out with her son along an empty stretch of barrier beach above Hatteras; just the pair of them in a sky-blue pop-tent with a nylon fly for shade. He's, oh, four and blond, brown and sturdy, a down-right edible kid, eager for the world. May shows him knobbed and channeled whelks, how to recognize their egg cases on the beach, like necklaces of dried sponge, and the black hooked hardened ones of skates, called mermaids' purses. These are ghost crabs, Mackie; those are sand-diggers. Nothing here will hurt you.

Now the Outer Banks become Maryland's end of Assateague Island. A solitary gaunt white horse—one particularly poor specimen of the wild Assateague pony herd—plods into sight far down the beach, just at the water's edge, walking head-down toward them through the spume. Sand-pipers comically advance and retreat with the surf, but the ancient nag is heedless of the waves that now and then foam her fetlocks. On and on she comes, and at first May's son is excited, and then he's amused, she's such a plodding old Rocinante, and then he grows just a touch afraid, so inex-orably does that bag of bones come on. May hunkers on a beach blanket in a square of shade before the tent, where the pair of them have been building a fantastic castle. The lad leaves off working on his parapet, stands beside her for reassurance, puts a sandy arm across her shoulders. That is one tired old horse there, Mackie boy, she tells him: a candidate for the glue factory.

At last the animal passes, thirty feet in front of them, never giving them a glance. Remarkably, she pauses just there, for the first time since she hove into sight. She lifts her tail; she pisses and pisses and pisses! May watches her son's reaction. The boy is wide-eyed, almost shocked. He looks to her to see whether it's all right to laugh; sees it is, and lets go that wonderful belly-laugh of his, one of God's dear sounds upon the earth. The antique mare plods off.

Where in heaven, May wonders when she wakes, did *that* one come from? "Mackie"?! Her eyes well up; she can almost smell the Coppertone on that little boy's sweet brown body. A far cry from Simple Simon Silver! Well: Poor Sy is what she's got, or had, and he's going to take some bringing around. She and Carla will manage it somehow.

But what the damn hell is she talking about? Her friendship with Marian's ma is real enough: one mensch of a woman appreciating another. She felt a true bond with Carla B Silver through the evening past, when Sy went over the edge and Marian flaked out altogether; it was that felt bond that encouraged her, for the sake of the general peace, to leave *Reprise* after

Simon's rescue and accept Captain Donald's invitation to join *Rocinante*'s crew for the night. But when she bid the couple good night and lingered up in the cockpit to sort out her thoughts *re* Marian (*that* little affair was done with, clearly and alas), she'd heard them having quiet sex below; and not long after, when Capn Don had come up and urged her to turn in, declaring his preference for the cockpit on summer nights, she had actually smelled their heterosexual juices in the cabin.

So what on earth is she talking about? Now she realizes, amused, that Carla B Silver is using the toilet. Dreams: boyoboy!

No auditory privacy on a small sailboat. After pumping the thing as quietly as she can, Carla steps out of the head compartment in a caftanlike nightgown and makes her way down the space, no more than eighteen inches wide, between the two berths. Impulsively, May reaches both arms up to her in the faint light. Seeing who it is, Carla chuckles and takes her hands, interlacing her strong fingers with May's; squeezes them firmly for some moments; bends over to kiss just the tops of both her thumbs.

So, she says.

Despite his having lately fired a flaccid charge into his recent employer and weekend shipmate (he is after all on the far side of sixty, and has made love with her both that morning and the night before), wiry Captain Donald Quicksoat gamely *soixante-neuf*s a very young woman in a large wet T-shirt and not a stitch else: a young woman not unlike Marian Silver, who has followed through on her earlier, pretty obvious flirtation. Crazy or not, she is her own woman, and he's his own man, no? With both hands in her strangely cut, strangely colored hair, he guides her head down on him. Her thighs and hams, two inches from his eyes, are goose-pimpled, sea-wet, lean; he thrusts his face into them as into a basin of cold salt water, and at once the situation changes from oral sex to foul weather at sea, with which in fact he has had more considerable experience. He is where he knows he is, in *Rocinante*'s cockpit, in black and heavy though not frigid going. He must back the staysail, harden the mizzensheet, and lash the helm down so that the boat will heave to and he can ride out the blow under the battered spray-dodger. It is not a particularly frightening storm; just routinely life-threatening. He has neither need nor wish to make head-way, only to survive at minimal cost to himself and *Rocinante*. He proceeds with his customary care: Missteps mildly serious for other sailors can be fatal for singlehanders, especially at his age. But his left sleeve snags on something that won't let go; the mizzensheet has got itself fouled in a winch override that he can't unjam with his one free hand; and there's a new sound in the darkness to leeward that could be surf breaking over Johnson's Reef, just above Trunk Bay on St. John in the U.S. Virgins.

As he has done dozens, maybe hundreds of times while passagemaking alone, he prudently wakes himself at this point instead of waiting for the kitchen timer to awaken him. He's wet with dew and perspiration in his old single bedroll on *Rocinante*'s port cockpit seat, where he has spent many a mild night in many a harbor. The anchorage is quiet. He is of course relieved not to be in the pickle he was dreaming; all the same, he wouldn't mind finding himself in Trunk or Caneel Bay again instead of the Chesapeake. *Rocinante* rides secure and motionless under the white moon descending now over Ordinary Point; it is a serene and splendid Maryland midsummer night. His left arm's numb, ah, from his having pinned it against the coaming in his sleep. Now it tingles back into feeling. His weathered penis, standing piss-proud like Quixote's lance, reminds him of the earlier portion of his dream. He chuckles to himself and shivers; chastizes his old tool *en español* for not having risen as well to reality as it has done to dream.

An all-right weekend, anyhow, this, and there's a moral to it: He and good Carla B are done. Back to singlehanding for C.D.Q., and the odd windfall in *Rocinante*'s double, if there are any. No more daydreams of putting down roots or taking a permanent mate aboard. May they part friends.

He hauls up to whiz over the portside lifeline and winds up whacking off as well, surprised at himself, but nowise displeased. Hi ho, Mim Silver, who was certainly sending signals his way earlier that night, till her ma barber-hauled the pair of them and young Simon made his move. He spurts through Marian's clothesless image into the Sassafras. Small fish rise to the droplets; his sparse spermatozoa are straightway swallowed.

How do we know? We know.

At the nurses' station on Floor Three of the Union Memorial Hospital on Thirty-third Street in Baltimore, to which she frequently returns in sleep, Joan Evans's shift is done. She is too bone-weary to look forward to her 2:00 A.M. Thanksgiving dinner date with the new obstetrical resident, who has promised or threatened a rabbit stew of Wasserman-test sacrifices in his Calvert Street basement apartment. It is past midnight already, and she has yet to get back to her own place to shower and change, if she's really going to dinner. But her replacement is late, and the forty-one-year-old in 312 who on Monday delivered a Down's-syndrome daughter is shrieking again. Damn you, Schneider, Joan sighs to herself, swearing not at the luckless patient but at the tardy relief-nurse, and relapses into deep sleep. When she wakes some hours hence in the ample forward cabin of *Katydid IV*, she'll remember Suzie's name with pleasure; it has been maybe twenty years since she last thought of the colleague who almost scotched her first date with her future husband. But Obstetrics was not on Three, and that poor Down's-syndrome mother who suffocated her baby was in Easton Memorial just after the war, not Union Memorial in '41. Dreams get things wrong.

Suzanne Schneider!

Doctor Jack, beside his wife, steams toward the Coral Sea aboard the doomed aircraft carrier *Yorktown*. In a ship's officers' lounge which is also somehow the Fleet Reserve Club in Annapolis, he plays bridge with Rear Admiral Arthur A. Ageton, author of the Navy's sight-reduction tables for celestial navigation, and argues amiably with him and two other former midshipmen the relative merits of sundry Chesapeake yacht harbors. A fellow medical officer, trained like Bass in gynecology and obstetrics, remarks apropos of nothing that the nearest human vagina is probably some 300 nautical miles to the east, in the New Hebrides. The admiral, whose declared postwar intention is to retire to Annapolis and write a novel or two based on his wartime experiences, jokingly requests permission to record that observation. Fuck vaginas, says Jack Bass, arranging his hand. What's trump?

Knock it off now, Willy, Henry Sherritt chuckles in *K IV*'s aft cabin, where he and Irma sleep feet-sternward in their queen-size berth. Across the nursery, their first-born is banging his crib against the wall again, a habit he picked up some weeks ago. The sturdy ten-month-old likes to get on hands and knees in his blue Dr. Dentons and lunge heavily back and forth, going *unh, unh, unh.* His parents can move the crib a foot from the wall and put rubber cups under the casters, but when Willy Sherritt decides to "chunk himself to sleep," as they call it, his motion inevitably inches the crib along until its headboard hammers the wall. Knock it off, Big Will, his father chuckles through the dark.

Irma touches his arm. She has just waked from good-humoredly chiding her daughter-in-law, who in the interval between Easter and Flag Day has become a sudden "chocoholic." This time next year, Irma prophesied beside the pool at Nopoint Point, you'll weigh a hundred eighty-five. Replied morose Molly This time next year I'll weigh less than I do now. Awake, Irm wonders what's come over Molly Barnes Sherritt, but that concern gives way to a leisurely inventory of others, from that poor unfortunate fat boy who tried to drown himself, through what to get Olive Treadway for her upcoming fortieth birthday and fifth anniversary in their service, to the approach of her and Hank's old age and inevitable infirmity. She does not omit her daughter and son-in-law's reckless recent wardship of her grandchildren, which (the recklessness), thank God, seems at an end. Her husband chuckles again in his sleep; she kisses his pajama'd shoulder and does in fact, politely, thank God.

In an unsuspected alcove under the bed in our Stony Run apartment in Baltimore, Katherine Sherritt Sagamore finds Tawney's edition of Penzer's translation of Somadeva's eleventh-century tale cycle, *The Ocean of Story*, in ten sea-green folio volumes, of which the first (containing the "Kathapitha," or "Story of the Story") is conspicuously missing. Relieved, she squeezes her burden into the slot. But Florence Halsey, glasses down on her nose, eyes twinkling over the rimless lenses, is already shaking her head. I know, sighs Kate, I know. Behind the cubby she senses another secret space, opening upon vastness like the keyhole to a closed planetarium. She grips the retrieved volume momentarily between her knees; *that* won't help for long! *Ma-ay,* she chides. Her underpants feel wet. *¿Qué pasa?*

(Of the lot of us, only Night and Day make no distinction between waking and dreaming, even when awake; but they feed upon, filter, and flavor their mother's dreams. Her shudder now alarms them; they clutch each other and themselves. About twelve hours, eleventy-nine minutes and counting, they agree, though they have no timepiece; it's just a way of talking they've picked up. Declares proud Rock: Daddy's writing all this in a book. His sister says So's Mom: *El lee-bro meesterioso,* and we're in it. About twelve hours, eleventy-eight minutes and counting.)

Andrew Sherritt, directing the number-two cameraman to dolly in tighter, is surprised at the husky male sound of his own voice. It is himself at his present age, in the bed of his bedroom at home, on a green and tender late-May morning. But the smiling woman beside him—tawny-haired, brown-eyed, brown-skinned as a Coppertone model sans bikini, across whose nakedness the sweet air moves as over his—is his wife. Her head is propped in her right hand; her left rests lightly on her upthrust hip. Her face, also her body, is of a surpassingly *friendly* beauty; Chip will remember that phrase, the ease of his lying there with her, the air on their skin, the feel of their being husband and wife. He'll recall her face exactly; it reminds him of no one's he knows, nor any composite that he can sort out. He'll wish he had gotten her name, at least, and wonder why in the world he was filming them in bed together. He'd never do that! His eyes and nose will sting: His first real wet-dream, and they were such good friends!

In Limbo Straits, between Lower Hoopers and Bloodsworth Islands—so named by Captain John Smith in June of 1608 after squally sailing there—the writer Peter Sagamore lies becalmed. His committee is still in conference aboard the Committee Boat nearby; he awaits their judgment in his College Park office. He has for example not paid enough attention to his old mother: Where has Nora Sagamore been, these many pages? He does not care as much as he ought for his sister and brother, better human beings in several respects than himself; surely they think him snobbish, too good for them with his Gold Coast bride and in-laws. That's not the *point,* Sue-Ann, Jacob!

What is the point, then?

Okay: He does not expect to fare so well as Dante Alighieri, welcomed in Hell's First Circle as one of themselves by Homer, Horace, Ovid, and Lucan, together with his sponsor, Virgil. Homer will dismiss him as too narrow, among other failings; Cervantes and Sam Clemens as too fancy. No matter that he has worked honestly and hard, year after year for above two decades, at his art: The committee rightly cares nothing for effort, only for accomplishment.

His friend in court, if he has one, is Scheherazade, an amalgam now of

May Jump and Carla B Silver. Yet even she seems to admonish him, not in person but in a caption that rolls by as on a Trans-lux: YOU NEED NOT LOVE THE WORLD. . . . YOU NEED NOT EVEN APPROVE OF IT. . . . BUT RELISH IT YOU MUST.

Probation, then: an Incomplete. Fair enough. What he'll do, muse willing, is what he'll have done when he's done, and he is not done yet.

Aboard *Reprise,* all hands in sleep replay the evening's ruckus, each in his/her personal key. How do we know? We know. Bid by Peter at Leah Talbott's request, Carla B Silver made her way across the rafted boats to see what ailed Simon, who was by then howling in the cutter's cabin. Kath offered her services, but stayed put when Lee advised her it was a family matter. Captain Donald tagged along, but stopped with us aboard *Story,* for the same reason. By the evidence, we agreed, the trouble this time was not seasickness. Where's his mother? Kath wondered. Swimming, aft of *Katydid,* along with May, Chip, Frank Talbott, the Basses, and the Sherritts. Probably couldn't hear Simon's voice for their splashing.

To his grandma, Sy now shrieked curses upon his mother and May Jump: wild imprecations that even we could hear, of a tenor with his earlier confidings to Chip Sherritt. Oh, the poor boy! Kath commiserated. And poor May! We shook our three heads, tisked our three tongues (Pity and Terror, praise God, were napping, and missed this scene). Lee came out and called sharply into the dark for Marian and Frank; the other swimmers paddled usward too, wondering now. Hearing her name by Simon hoarsely screamed, May Jump hauled herself up *Reprise*'s stern ladder behind the other two. I do believe I'm being summoned, she remarked in our direction. Capn Don warned her that the boy sounded clear out of control; May said Yup and went dripping on down to see what was what.

The sight of his irritated mother, soaking wet in her now-translucent orange T-shirt and skintight shorts, proved Sy's last straw. He bellowed a foulness at her; she yelled right back You little shit! and whacked him upside the head. Sy snatched a sharp pair of British one-handed stainless-steel dividers from the chart rack beside *Reprise*'s quarterberth and lunged at her. Wet May caught his arm and expertly restrained him, at the same time urging him calmly to cool off. As gently as he could, Frank Talbott retrieved and stowed the dividers; his wife, less gently, moved her dripping sister back out of range, toward the forward cabin, scolding her. Well I've *had* it with him! Marian wailed. I can't do *anything*! Growled Carla B Silver For Christ sake *can* it, Mims.

To sunglassed Simon, thrashing now in May's strong grip like an animal in a trap, Frank proposed moving upstairs to talk things over. By an agreement of eyes, May seconded the motion; she was the wrong one to be restraining him. The instant she let go, however, and before Frank or Carla could recatch him, the boy bolted up the companionway they were nudging him toward, out into the cockpit, up and over the starboard lifeline. Had *Reprise*'s dinghy been rigid fiberglass like ours, he would in all likelihood have hurt himself; it was secured on that side to clear the boarding ladder. As was, he landed heavily but harmlessly upon its inflated outboard side, splashed into the black Sassafras, lost his reflector sunglasses, and proceeded to drown.

Frank Talbott and May Jump, already in swimsuits and still wet, piled up the companionway right behind him and into the river. Peter Sagamore, standing barefoot in shorts and shirt in *Story*'s cockpit, dived in a moment later over the head of Chip Sherritt, who was en route up our boarding ladder (his parents and the Basses were already toweling off on *Katydid*). In the event, the two men did most of the rescuing—without great difficulty, for the shock of the water and of what he'd done frightened Simon into nauseated helplessness. May Jump, every bit as able and probably as strong as they, kept clear at a little distance, not to provoke the boy into resisting. Katherine Sherritt, Leah Talbott, and Donald Quicksoat manned flashlights, horseshoe rings, and boathooks from *Reprise*'s cockpit; Hank and Chip Sherritt, instead of joining the rescuers in the water, prudently stood by in *Story*'s dinghy; Jack Bass hurried down to his cabin to fetch his bag; Joan and Irma sensibly stayed put in *Katydid*'s cockpit, as did Carla B Silver in *Reprise*'s, saying things to herself in various tongues. Marian Silver, still in her wet clothing, closed herself up in the cutter's forward cabin, bolted its folding louvered door, and flung herself onto the V-berth.

That's where she is now, in dry underpants and a shirt borrowed from Frank Talbott, sleeping on the berth's port side because she wet the starboard—May's side. Captain Donald Quicksoat's leathery hand is in her crotch; she put it there. He's sort of cute, and Mims has never made it with a guy old enough to be her father. It occurs to her to wonder whether she even needs to bother with her diaphragm; she's heard old guys can't keep it up, but she can't remember whether they're still fertile even when they're impotent. It's late in her month; she'll take a chance; it's semigroovy to have to think about such things again. But there's Sy, bawling in his crib. Feeding time already? Her nipples are still raw and swollen from before! Let the little bastard holler, she frets to her mother; I'm wet all over.

Lee Talbott sees him still—sick, scared, embarrassed—pulling himself up the boarding ladder and vomiting at the same time (Sy swallowed some Sassafras). The men in the water below moved aside but encouraged him, as did she. Attaboy, Sy; good man, Sy; here's a towel. She and Captain Donald took his arms and steadied him over the transom. But it was his grandma he needed, and Carla B Silver was of course right there to envelop him: water, vomit, and all. All right, now, Mister Simon; time to dry off and hit the hay. Down we go, sir, and no more swimming till tomorrow. Doctor Jack came over with his kit, but agreed there was no call for his services. Half a Dalmane, maybe, to help the boy sleep through, but the less embarrassing attention, the better. One for the mother, too, if she needs it? My sister needs more than Dalmane, Leah said; thanks anyhow.

Once he'd splashed the transom clean, sighing Frank came up and aboard; kissed his wife, toweled off, and went below to change. Carla B Silver had Simon's wets in a bundle to hand up to Lee for rinsing in the river and hanging out on the lifelines; the boy himself was in the head compartment, cleaning up and getting into his pajamas. The adults simply shook their heads. Where's Mim? Frank wondered. Muttered Carla Where indeed, indicating with her head the closed cabin door, and went upstairs to let the man dress. Uncle Frank? Simon called quietly from the head compartment. Right here, Sy. I'm sorry. Forget it, fellow; I'll tell May you apologized.

But Lee Talbott dreams he's drowned: lost like her stepfather without a trace. She holds the unavailing life-ring, the flashlight lighting nothing. All the swimmers come out of the water. Frank embraces her from behind: We'll just have to start over, is all. That's *not* all, she knows. All the same, she's stirred; she slightly shifts position to let him enter.

In bed at last after things had settled down and all hands except Simon— thirteen of us!—gathered in *Katydid*'s great center cockpit for nightcap and bedtime story (Lee or he occasionally checking to see that all remained quiet aboard *Reprise*) and eventually said good night, Franklin Key Talbott gratefully embraces his wife from behind in the dinette settee double that we much envy them. To his surprise—they've been abed less than ten minutes—he discovers she's already asleep, as, thank God, are Simon in the quarterberth and, presumably, Maid Marian in the forward cabin. What an evening. Like us, the Talbotts sleep naked in warm weather and bottomless in cool, except when there's company aboard. Tonight he's in cotton PJ bottoms, through the fly of which his erection thrusts, and Lee's in a combed-cotton top like a long T-shirt that comes nearly to her knees when she's standing, but rides above her hips when she's in bed.

From long custom, her body responds to his, even in three-quarter sleep. At the feel of his hands upon them under the bedsheet, her buttocks tuck into his lap. The light poke of his penis between them lubricates her. She shifts position just a bit; he parts her lips and, steadying her firmly, slides in—to the hilt in three gentle thrusts, on the third of which he comes, a drowsy, happy man. At once he deliquesces into sleep, even as, stirring, Lee slides her right hand back to *his* hip, holds him in place, and squeezes the last drops from him. Though he doesn't know it, his hands move now to her breasts, under the nightshirt. His face is between her shoulderblades. His first dream of the night, when presently he dreams it, will have nothing to do with her or sex, at least not overtly, though he'll still be in her: He'll lean far out over *Reprise*'s gunwales with the boathook, trying unsuccessfully to fish his old *boina* out of the water as it slides by. Aha, he has it. Nope: got away. His next try pushes it farther under. Yet when, in their wake several boatlengths aft, he sees a large sea-mammal leisurely surface, roll, and gulp—Manatee? Sea lion?—he recognizes that *that's okay*. In fact, it is what their long voyage has been about. They may now get on with it: They'll just start over, is all.

Lee wakes briefly, feels her friend inside her, and understands that after the awful drowned part, what she was dreaming was also taking place. She can't recall that's having happened to her before and hopes she'll remember it in the morning. She puts her hand atop the sleeping hand upon her right breast, presses, and tightens her vaginal sphincter. As his penis squirts out, Frank looses his embrace without waking; their limbs disengage, and she rolls comfortably onto her stomach. She has a quick image of May Jump, after Simon's rescue, discreetly climbing *Story*'s boarding ladder instead of theirs; conferring with that Donald Quicksoat person while Katherine Sherritt fetched her a towel. For the good of the order, May decided, she would bed down elsewhere than with Marian Silver that night; she asked Lee, via Katherine, to send her backpack over to *Rocinante IV*. Marian, reemerging from her hideout without a word to her son, made no objection. Leah Talbott herself has never made love with a woman; has no interest in ever doing so, though the general idea does not repel her; and is unaware of Katherine's brief affair with May, though not of their long-standing friendship. She didn't see Kath blush at her remark that, much as she loves her scattered sister, May Jump deserves a better friend. Agreed Carla B Silver She does that. Well, they'd see which way the wind blew in the morning and work out the best logistics for getting all hands home under the circumstances. Meanwhile, Kath's lovely parents and their friends, who seemed to take anything in their stride, were inviting everyone to have a good-night drink with them, to unwind before turning in. As she drops back to sleep, Lee remembers her mother's accepting May's hand-up onto *Katydid*'s gunwale and bussing her cheek when she got there. Two good people.

What an odd story May Jump then told!

Lee drifts off, half smiling, and at that moment—about 0117 hours, thirteen seconds EDST, 29 June '80—becomes pregnant again.

And of what does Simon Silver dream?

Silver Simon dreams of hymen, 'cause the world's unfair.
Fat, unlovely bastard boy, your father didn't care
how young hitchhikers whimpered when he grabbed them by the hair
and held his pistol on them till they dropped their underwear
in the grubby rear compartment of his Chevy van. He'd swear
to shoot them if they didn't close their mouths and open their
behinds for buggering, if boys; for humping everywhere
if girls.
    Thus did your mom, in Fenwick Island, Delaware,
become your mom: because she hitched one time too often there
along the beach and climbed into that Pennsylvanian's lair;
because he forced her fore and aft, but reached one climax where
his uninvited sperm could go the natural route and snare

their natural prey—just then, alas, available.

                                        A pair
of options yet remained; but Mim was shocked into a rare
intransigence (for her): Your mother found she couldn't square
away the fetus early, on the one hand, or forswear,
on the other, maternal rights to you at birth. She would declare,
"I hate the little shit, but he's the cross I have to bear."
So here you are, your father's son: unloved and made aware
(against your grandma's wishes) of your history; forced to share
your father's guilt—your mother's, too—with every breath of air
you breathe. No wonder you dream dreams now dark enough to scare
yourself awake:
                          "Aunt May" and Mom play double solitaire;
you sneak into the room and smash May's head in with a chair.
You bind and gag and blindfold Mom and then proceed to tear
her clothes and underclothes off, layer by motherfucking layer.
(She taught you that word early; now she's going to pay the fare.)
You tie her wrists and ankles to the bedposts and prepare
to take revenge upon her with your belt upon her bare
bazooms, backside, and belly till she's redder than a flare,
after which you'll make her eat you like a chocolate-cream eclair
until your putz is bigger than that rubberized affair
"Aunt May" straps on to fuck her with.
                              "Now, Simon, *don't you dare!*"

Bullshit, you'll say: too late for that; she'd better say a prayer.
You're going to split her open just the way your unknown *père*
once did. (Aspiring rapists of their mothers should beware
comparisons like that, for which poor Simon has a flair.)
You'll hump her like the van-man—and your issue will compare
with his: another wretched Simon Silver, with a pear-
shaped body and a twelve-year-old's mustache that folks will stare
and laugh at; one more loveless, unloved bastard. . . .
                                 In the glare
of this flashforward, lust and anger melt into despair:
Unmanned by tears, you kiss your mom good-bye, run up the stair,
climb the rail (the dream-scene's changed), and—since you can't repair
the hurt done either to or by you—jump.
                             Here Sy's nightmare
ends, before Katherine Sherritt can work *pare, player, mère, sayer, mal
de mer,* and other available rhymes into this intermediate-level exercise in
the retrospective invention of what, knowing what we know, we can imagine Sy Silver might have dreamed, had he dreamed in relentless Simple-
Simonian. In fact, exhausted by his P.M. wring-out and sedated by fifteen
milligrams of Dalmane, he sleeps pretty soundly through the night, wakes

refreshed though basically miserable and worried about what's to happen to him next, and reports through the cabin to his Uncle Frank that he dreamed last night that the taut wire rigging on *Reprise* must be like a giant bowstring, and the hull the bow, and the cutter's mast the full-drawn arrow, ready to be shot through the bottom of the boat to the bottom of the river. In his dream he could *feel* those forces, cocked and ready to let go. That's not a bad image of the actual case, Franklin Key Talbott will reply from his berth, wondering what kind of mood mercurial Marian will treat them to this morning. But you can also think of those forces as balanced in tension, instead of ready to let fly. His wife places his hand upon her lower belly, between her navel and her crotch.

Good morning, everybody.

WYDIWYD BEGUN: THE UNFINISHED TELLALONG STORY
OF SCHEHERAZADE'S UNFINISHED STORY,
AS PUT TOGETHER LAST NIGHT BY THE SEVEN WOMEN IN OUR RAFT,
AS RECORDED THIS MORNING BY PETER SAGAMORE IN THE LOG OF
STORY

Peter Sagamore wakes with a headful of good ideas for the novel Franklin Key Talbott ought to write, inspired by *Reprise*'s sabbatical sailing cruise to the Caribbean and back: what to keep of the actual experience, what to discard, what to alter, what to invent. Further such ideas crowd upon him as we swim, breakfast, and bid one another good morning up and down the raft. There ought for example to be some literal marvel at the story's climax, P believes: some flabbergastment surfaced from the tale's dark depths to echo, sea-changed, those who earlier sank and disappeared: John Arthur Paisley, Frederick Mansfield Talbott, Douglas Townshend. And he has a better name in mind for the couple's boat: one less portentous. But he keeps these ideas under his *boina,* which this morning he wears even into the Sassafras, maintaining it carefully above water.

Have it back? Frank asks him from *Reprise*'s ladder. I had a dream last night about old Chessie and that hat, and this morning I've half a mind to give fiction another go. Fresh start. No autobiography.

Says Peter Soon. Let's get together later this morning, the four of us, if Kath's still pregnant. I have something for you.

Frank says he'd like that, but they'll have to see. It's time they headed homeward. Marian and Simon, however, aren't out of bed yet, and it's not entirely clear who's going where with whom. Nine-thirty? Ten?

Says Peter from the river More like eleven. Our house.

Kath's already visiting her parents and the Basses, who-all are merrily exchanging dreams. Lee Talbott now leads her sulking sister across the whole raft to *Rocinante* and into deep confab with May Jump and Carla B Silver. Captain Donald Quicksoat, odd man out, visits F. K. Talbott aboard *Reprise*. They summon Simon Silver up to join them in a gratifyingly messy male mechanical project: the dismantling, degreasing, relubrication, and reassembly of the cutter's manual anchor windlass, salt-fouled from a year of blue-water sailing. Today, says the National Weather Service, will be even more subtropical than yesterday—mid-ninetyish air, steamy sunshine, little or no breeze, evening thunderstorms likely—a day for awnings and air-conditioning, for swimming and sipping iced drinks, not for sailing, sentence-writing, or sweaty childbirth. From Tehran comes the radio news that Prime Minister Bani-Sadr, under pressure from the Ayatollah Khomeini, is hardening his line again on the American hostage issue. The disposal of toxic agents in the United States, declares *The New York Times,* is insufficiently regulated.

Well, yes. As P goes down our companionway to work, he sees Carla B Silver literally brow to brow with her wayward younger daughter, their hands upon each other's shoulders. He sees Frank Talbott glance over there from his windlass-work to be smiled at beautifully by Leah, three yachts away. He sees the woman of us send a kiss down in his direction from *Katydid*'s high cockpit next door, consult her wristwatch, smile, and raise nine fingers. It is in fact about nine o'clock now, and she has been in the ninth month of our pregnancy for what seems like nine hundred pages, but none of those is what she means.

God's blessing be upon these characters, thinks Peter Sagamore, himself included. Remembering suddenly last night's dream, he then instructs our logbook RELISH IT YOU MUST. Jorge Luis Borges writes that Moses Maimonides writes that when the words in a dream are distinct and clear, and the person uttering them cannot be seen, they are from God. But subtitles on Trans-luxes?

Under it he enters *WYDIWYD,* by way of a short version of the long unfinished story told at the end of yesterevening—mainly by May Jump, but chorused out by the other six women in our four-boat raft, not excluding Marian Silver. Then he puts the log away and returns with relish to the finishing of what he's been up to since this time yesterday at least.

Nobody's going anywhere, Marian Silver insisted last night when Captain Donald Quicksoat suggested that Simon join his grandma and himself aboard *Rocinante,* to ease the post-rescuary tension on *Reprise.* That thoughtful suggestion got its maker later laid, but Marian declared The little bastard made his bed; let him stew in it. I'm finished with *everybody.* That was when May Jump, at C.D.Q.'s further invitation and Carla's warm seconding, shifted berths instead. We were all of course concerned for the boy, dismayed by the mother, sorry for May. Hank and Irma, bless them, came through splendidly, insisting first that May and then that all of us smooth out the ragged evening in *K IV*'s cockpit and environs before we turned in for the night. Lee and Carla lingered awhile aboard *Reprise,* calming Marian, soothing Sy, while the other ten of us sipped things and changed the subject. In time, Marian agreed to let her son switch boats and go back to Baltimore today with Capn Don and Carla. She might even do the same, she thought: move back to Fells Point, if her mother would have her; try something else. But by that time Sy was mercifully asleep in his berth. The three women therefore joined us—Marian Silver conspicuously avoiding her erstwhile lover, and Frank or Lee Talbott slipping back from time to time to check on Simon's slumber as might anxious parents a one-year-old's.

We have not mentioned, have we, that May had as always brought along her guitar: a weathered Gibson, dear to Katherine's memory. When Lee Talbott brought it across *Story* to *Katydid* en route to *Rocinante* with the exile's backpack, it was Katherine who received it with a little cry, kissed its belly, propped it on her own to run her thrumb across its strings, remembering half a hundred ASPS camp-outs. She then presented it to its owner—whom also she kissed, on both cheeks—and announced that May was going to sing us a good-night song. Hear hear, said the rest of us, except Marian.

May Jump frowned and strummed three or four quick but pensive chords. What a difference (even among southpaw guitarists, who have a problem) between the expert and the inexpert hand! Then she smiled, first at Katherine, next at Marian, and said All righty. But first I want to tell you an unfinished story about an unfinished story. She tuned a string or two: strum strum strum. This is a tellalong story—like a singalong song?—and it's for all the wives and mothers in this anchorage. You ladies join in whenever the spirit moves you, okay?

Strum. Now: You gentlemen all noticed Mim Silver's T-shirt earlier this evening, first dry and then wet. . . . Strum. W-Y-D-I-W-Y-D, right? With a little emphasis on the two Y's and a little cleavage at the I.

Said Marian I'm leaving. Said May No need, hon, 'cause this story's not about you or me or any present company. Strum strum strum. It's about the first owner of that particular T-shirt.

Said Kath suddenly Scheherazade! May Jump fixed her with a look of serious long wonder. If they gave black belts for intuition, she said, dot dot dot and strummy strum strum. How in the loving world did you guess this was going to be a story about Scheherazade?

Kath was darned if she knew but said Carla B Silver told us the story of Scheherazade's first second menstruation, when was it, just the night before, over there in Back Creek; and Kath certainly wished she hadn't missed that eleventh ASPS convention down in Kitty Hawk, and how come May hadn't mentioned Scheherazade last week in Annapolis, if not before? Who *was* this person claiming to be Scheherazade? What'd she look like? What'd she wear?

Me, said Donald Quicksoat, I never did get the point of that second-menstruation story. Must be 'cause I'm neither wife nor mother nor storyteller.

My friends, wondered Henry Sherritt: What on earth are we talking about?

With a wink at Carla B Silver, May Jump invited us all to tell along, tell along as the narrative spirit moved us: the women especially, since Scheherazade's is a woman's story, but the men among us, too. Who's to say who's a mother and who's not, till the chicks are hatched and the chips are down and all precincts heard from?

I'll second that, said Leah Allan Silver Talbott, taking her husband's arm.

From professional habit, Jack Bass inquired First second menstruation?

Asked Peter May I? and May Jump said be her guest. In a commendable feat of abbreviation then (His long suit, no? May teased), he distilled for those who hadn't heard it the tale of Scheherazade's gynecological arithmetic as narrated at second or third hand by Carla B Silver in Back Creek, tabulated by Andrew "Chip" Sherritt, and now certified as plausible by Jack Bass, M.D. But nursing, Nurse Joan reminded us, could sure mess up those numbers.

I will not milk a moral from that story, Peter said, and handed Frank Talbott's *boina* to May Jump. But I have drunk its message, friend.

Me, said Katherine, I'm going to kiss you both. She did, much touched by this rapport between her husband and her old friend, and settled the *boina* on May Jump's head. Kiss, strummed May, is always kissing. Tell along, Lee Talbott urged. Declared May I will if you-all will, and set her guitar aside. More exactly, she thrust it upon Mim Silver, who, startled, took it, maybe blushed, and dutifully stood it like a child between her knees while her ex-lover—with a little help from friends old and new—went on with the story:

She had first been introduced to Scheherazade, she said, one evening last fall in a certain Annapolis gay bar, in the straight company of a certain Maryland novelist (not Peter Sagamore) and his wife (not Katherine Sherritt), who had telephoned ahead to arrange the meeting.

For his parents' sake, Chip Sherritt asked Is this story G, R, or X? Said May PG. That particular bar was my idea, to give our visitor a shot of twentieth-century America. It didn't much faze her, 'cause she'd done time with odalisques in harems, but we'll leave that bar now and go to my place, the four of us. Scher and my novelist friend are wearing these widdy-wid T-shirts, okay? W-Y-D-I-W-Y-D. And Missus Novelist has got one on reading *T*-K-*T*-*T*-*T*-I-*T*-*T*: accents on the K and I—May winked at Katherine—and more T's than McCormick's warehouse.

A real teaser, cracked Kath, that T-shirt. Asked May But did I ask? Said Donald Quicksoat I'm about to, but Carla B Silver patted his pate and bade him wait. Marian Silver said she herself has a T-shirt that a Road Vulture gave her that says KILL 'EM ALL AND LET GOD SORT 'EM OUT. Said

Irma You do? Frank Talbott remarked he'd heard it's an axiom of the theater that an audience will sit still for just about anything for thirteen seconds, but that after that they want the action to start making sense. I second that axiom, said Henry Sherritt, checking his wristwatch.

Said May I guess I'm going to need my Gibson girl after all, and retrieved her guitar from between Mim's legs. Strum strum strum and here we go: The first night after that, when I'd got to know her better, Miz Scheherazade told me that on the thousand-and-second night, out of habit, she told Shahryar the story of Night Ten Oh One, which Mister P.S. has just now abbreviated for us. She was twenty-one years old back then, and the mother of three children, and the teller of four-hundred-plus tales in those ten hundred and one nights; but she was no more out of stories than she was out of ova, or her audience out of sperm.

Drawled Joan Bass Four hundred plus? That happens to be how many eggs a woman lays between puberty and menopause. Irma said she herself forgot to count.

She could've gone right on telling, strummed May, and turning out children too. With three sons to her credit, she'd hoped to have a daughter somewhere down the road. What's more, the genie who'd slipped her all those stories over the past three years had let her know that there were seven volumesworth of Supplemental Nights in Burton's Eighteen-eighty-five edition, over and above the ten volumes they'd just reached the end of. More about this genie later.

Aha, said the literarios in our raft: Katherine and Peter and Lee Talbott. What was that T-shirt again? The one with all the T's?

Another story, May declared, and she'll tell it later, as Scher told her. Just now she's telling the king on Night Ten Oh Two how she'd said to herself on Night Ten Oh One that every morning he hadn't killed her was a kind of penance for his having killed one of her sisters in the thousand and one nights before she'd come into his life. He had done exactly what he'd sworn he'd do when his first wife did that number on him; then he'd paid his penance for the same length of time; and there she was, about to menstruate twice in a row for the first time in a thousand and one nights. In fact (strum) her period comes on while she's telling him this story on Ten Oh Two—and like a word to the wise, my friends, that first repeated message of her blood let her know that it was time for a change.

Hear hear, agreed Carla B Silver, an arm around each of her daughters. Tell along, May.

Time for a change, Scher said, May said, in the circumstances of her production. She quoted a quote her genie had laid on her from Johann Wolfgang von Goethe, Seventeen Forty-nine Eighteen Thirty-two: *In the morning, study; in the afternoon, work; in the evening, enjoy.*

Henry Sherritt stretched out his legs and said he was enjoying the evening more than before. Kate kissed him. Remarked her mother, smiling, You *do* kiss, don't you.

Through the morning of her green- and brown-belt basic training, declared May Jump—which was the three years of Shahryar's virgin-a-night period—young Scher there had studied storytelling like young Peter Sagamore in College Park and Portugal. Those thousand books of stories she collected; all those poets she learned by heart. She had boned-up in her library on the art of telling stories like Doctor Jack Bass in med school on the art of delivering babies, and Nurse Joan in nursing school on the art of registered nursing. She had gone at her apprenticeship like Mister Henry Sherritt—whereabouts, Mister Henry?

At my father's pin-striped knee, said pleased Hank promptly, patting his son's bare left one, where I learned some things they don't teach you in the Wharton School of Business.

May strummed and nodded and bade Captain Donald Tell along. Like Don Quixote studying the novels of knight-errantry, said C.D.Q., and like yours truly studying *Don Quixote* till I couldn't tell me from him.

Kiss?

Like me learning Dewey's Decimals from Florence Halsey in the Deniston library, said K, adding to herself And other things in other places from Yussuf al-Din and Saul Fish and Jaime Aiquina and May Jump and even Poonie Baldwin, so I'd be ready for Peter Sagamore when our time came.

Like Carla B Silver, May proposed (Don't ask, growled Carla), and most or all of us on this four-boat raft of ours, young Scheherazade had spent the morning of her life a *studying,* okay?

Marian Silver confessed she'd spent hers mainly in the sack. Tell on, Mair, May invited her, but Mim said Nope, 'cause she hadn't learned diddly-squat.

Strum. And in the afternoon, said May—I mean the thousand and one "afternoons" of a night-shift worker—hadn't Scher worked? She'd turned out stories like Jack Bass babies, and she'd turned out babies, too.

Like Jack Bass stories, cracked Joan. He's got some would curl your bangs.

Concluded May Like every one of us near or past forty in his her way: We've studied through our morning and worked through our afternoon. And the storytellers present have had their necks right on the line like Scheherazade, 'cause every time we come to bat, excuse my metaphor, it's a whole new ball game.

(Hear hear, said Block and Tackle, hearing and remembering: Tell along.)

But there comes a time, said May—and for Scheherazade it had come the night before, with a twinge down here and a tenderness up here, half a headache on top and the blues on the bottom line—there comes a time when Publish-or-Perish turns a girl off instead of on, if you know what I mean. There comes a time when removing the ax from the narrative neck is not only the fit reward for stories told and babies borne, but the best insurance of more to come. I mean maybe she'd tell and maybe she'd swell, but she'd earned the right, Scher figured, to tell no more stories *ever;* to bear no more children *ever.*

Affirmed the three older women of us Hear hear, Hear hear, Hear hear. Strum strum went May Jump's Gibson. Will Scheherazade go on with the story? We may certainly hope so. Given who she is, we may even bet she will. Has Doctor Jack stopped delivering babies? Has Miz Irma turned her back on Saint Deniston's School for Girls, and Mister Hank taken up thumb-twiddling? Not yet. *But*—

But after that first second menstruation, put in Peter Sagamore, not even Chip Sherritt is allowed to *count on it*. Amen, May Jump, and good show.

AMEN. AMEN. AMEN. AMEN. AMEN. AMEN. AMEN. AMEN. AMEN. AMEN.

Amen, said Marian Silver last, then stood with her hands in her green-and-silver hair and guessed she'd go make sure Sy hadn't sleepwalked back overboard. You do that, hon, strummed smiling May. And you, said Marian (of whom we saw no more till morning) . . . you tell along.

May did. That had been Scheherazade's first story to her, she declared, on the first night May'd really come to know her. And it was the last one she'd told the king for twenty-one years—which we remember was her approximate age when she told it. The main stages of Scher's career, like those of many another woman's, had been marked by changes in her plumbing. The day she'd reached puberty, just a tad late, happened to be the day Shahryar had skewered his fickle first wife. A thousand and one nights later, on her eighteenth birthday, she had volunteered herself, had put her apprenticeship behind her with her maidenhead, and for the next almost-three years had done her number, as set forth by Andrew Sherritt. At circa twenty-one, that first second menstruation aforenarrated had prompted her pitch for marriage, which the king granted. Did we expect she'd go on as before, telling stories and giving birth? So did she—but she did not. The next two decades after that thousand-and-second night she devoted to being queen of the Islands of India and China and her husband's closest advisor, especially after the death of her father, the grand vizier; also to raising her three sons (that hoped-for daughter, May was sorry to say, never came along); and to transcribing, editing, and publishing in thirty volumes the tales she'd told, plus the story of her telling them to Shahryar.

Those twenty-plus years passed more swiftly, it seemed to her, than had the thousand and one nights of her storytelling. At the end of them, her boys were men (one a father himself already, one a bridegroom, one a fiancé); her husband was at the end of middle age and all but impotent; and Scheherazade herself was forty-three or -four and ready, though she scarcely realized it, for her next great change of life.

Don't we remember, said the chorus of Irma Sherritt, Joan Bass, and Carla B Silver. Thought Katherine Dear God: I'm almost that age now, and look at me.

Her menopause, said May, came on that same year: even earlier than her menarche had been late. She and Shahryar were still friends, but their *mariage* had gone *blanc*, pardon my French. Old before his time, the king had abdicated the throne to his eldest son and spent his days reading the thirty volumes of Grandma's tales to his infant grandson, who couldn't understand a word.

Those volumes had appeared at the rate of one every nine months, and they'd established their teller and editor as the absolute boss of Islamic storytelling. Her readers called for more, more, more. But when she put the final period on Volume Thirty—the story of her marriage to Shahryar and her sister Dunyazade's to Shah Zaman of Samarkand—and closed the final period of her menstrual life, she found herself as weary of writing stories as she'd become of telling them. Weary as well of advising and administering; weary of wifing; weary of mothering. Her number-one daughter-in-law, already pregnant again, said Come live with us and make up stories for your grandchildren. No doubt she would, Scheherazade replied, with love and pleasure, one of these days. But *pas encore*. Stories? She had hundreds more, for stories breed stories the way money breeds money.

However, she was tired of all that, at least for the present. Pure vacation was what she craved: a thousand-night leave from responsibility, after which she would take stock and perhaps settle down to grandmotherhood and the rest. Well, said Shahryar and their three sons and two daughters-in-law: If that's what you really want. . . . That's what I really want, said Scheherazade. Do you remember my stories about Sindbad the Sailor? His seven several voyages?

Do we ever! They gathered around and shushed the baby, eager to hear those famous stories told again. All Scheherazade said, however, was that she wished she could voyage like Sindbad to parts unknown. But Sindbad's motive, more than mere restlessness, was to make his fortune, or increase it; hers was simply to hazard forth. And Sindbad, though he was resourceful in the matter of surviving one peril after another, was essentially the pawn of chance. Every one of his seven adventures began with his accidental separation from a ship on which, even if he owned it, he was merely a passenger; his aim thereafter was nothing more than to save his skin, recoup his losses if possible, and get home to Bassorah. If she were to attempt such a voyage herself, she'd want to be captain of her fate, and she would seek no further treasure than the tale itself of her adventures.

But she knew better than to imagine that a Muslim woman—who happened also to be queen of the Islands of India and China—could sail off at the helm of her own vessel like some anonymous merchant mariner or simple fisherman, especially as she understood nothing of the arts of seamanship and navigation. Even if she could and did, her fame had so spread that she would quickly be recognized in every port, for better and worse: Pirates would be on particular lookout for her; she'd have to go surrounded by armed security guards, as she must every time she left the palace. Moreover, her craft's chief cargo would be the very responsibility she craved vacation from: Wherever she sailed, she would carry a freight of guilt for leaving husband, children, and grandchildren behind.

In short, she concluded, what I want, not even Your Excellency the King can give me; yet nothing else will do. I just thought I'd tell you. Now I'm going off to Samarkand, *faute de mieux,* to visit my sister. Like a good girl, I'll go by first-class caravan, heavily escorted, and at every stop along the way I'll discharge my obligations to our subjects and to my audience as queen and famous storyteller, as well as carrying the obligatory gifts to Dunyazade and my other hosts en route and writing faithful letters home and shopping for souvenirs to bring back to you all, because I really do love you very much indeed, and I'll miss you enormously. Okay? But don't think for a minute that this is the vacation trip I had in mind when I said what I said before.

They promised not to.

WYDIWYD CONTINUED: *TKTTTITT,*
OR,
A MONTH OF MONDAYS

Dunyazade's marriage to Shah Zaman had not gone well.

In their separate kingdoms, back before Scheherazade entered Shahryar's story, the cuckolded royal brothers had each deflowered and decapitated a thousand and one virgins in revenge for the infidelity of their wives. Through the thousand and one nights thereafter, unaware of Shahryar's narrative beguilement and moratorium, Shah Zaman had carried on—2002 deflorations and executions before the news reached him of his brother's change of heart—and not one of those victims had charmed him enough to be granted a second night in his bed, much less commutation of her sentence. Shahryar had set aside his policy because his murderous vow had in fact been carried out; also because his kingdom was in revolt and his supply of victims all but exhausted; and finally because Scheherazade, both in and out of bed, happened to be the most appealing woman he'd ever known. Shah Zaman had made no vow, only followed his elder brother's lead. His supply of sacrificial virgins lasted longer because he kept his practice a state secret, giving out the fiction that maiden refugees from his brother's kingdom were welcome in his, on condition they agree to be resettled far to the west in a newly established colony of women called

Amazonia. And he abandoned his practice not because he was repentant but because he was bored (the last few hundred virgins he had actually sent west as promised, after defloration; the last few dozen he had packed off unmolested) and ready once again to follow Shahryar's lead.

Dunyazade (when Shah Zaman came at his brother's bidding to meet and marry her) he had found attractive and by no means untalented in her own right: Those thousand nights at the foot of her sister's bed had been an extensive, though vicarious, sex education, and Scheherazade's stories had made Dunyazade similarly wise, though similarly unpracticed, in the ways of the world. She had never concentrated her energies upon any one thing, as had Scheherazade upon storytelling, and had therefore become adept at several. In the arts of singing, dancing, needlework, yoga, and calligraphy, to name only a few, she was her sister's clear superior.

After the double wedding ceremony, the kingdom of Samarkand was bestowed upon Shahryar's grand vizier, father of the brides, in reward for his long-suffering patience. The royal bridegrooms retired each with his bride, and while all went satisfactorily in Shahryar's chamber (where Scheherazade, out of action, entertained her old bedpartner with the story of her first second menstruation), the other couple's troubles began. After quite satisfactory foreplay and defloration, followed by a postcoital nap, Shah Zaman had said Story time, and Dunyazade had sung him a little song instead. Bravo! her bridegroom applauded. Now let's have the story. Dunyazade obliged him with an extraordinary yoga position called Bandha Padmasana, from which contortion she recited a risqué limerick concerning two lesbians in a tub. First-rate contortion and risqué limerick, cheered Shah Zaman: The last line especially, of the latter, tested the very limits of the genre. Now: a story. His bride sighed, untangled her limbs, fetched out her manuscript copy of Volume One of Scheherazade's transcription of *The Thousand Nights and a Night,* and launched into Tale One: "The Merchant and the Genie." Shah Zaman interrupted her: Don't *read* it, hon; *tell* it.

Well, she tried. It turned out, however, that she had no knack at all for telling stories, nor any particular wish to acquire that knack. Much as she admired her older sister, she was altogether satisfied to be herself. Her bridegroom, on the contrary, wished only what his brother wished; admired only what his brother admired. If she couldn't spin yarns like Scheherazade, he pouted, they might as well go back to sleep.

They did. But the second problem surfaced on Night Two: the first night in six years that Shah Zaman had gone to bed with the same woman he'd waked up with. As Dunyazade undressed for his pleasure, he could scarcely pay attention; he had *seen* already what was under her sari. Her yoga positions could perhaps have been enticing if each had been assumed by a different virgin, but he was not fooled; copulating with a woman he'd already once mounted and deflowered was like hearing the same risqué limerick again and again. By the third night he felt as if they'd been married for three years. On Scheherazade's advice, Dunyazade acted out stories in pantomime, drew them in watercolor panels, embroidered them in silk— all to no avail. By the end of the week, Shah Zaman was impotent. By the end of the month he had switched to young boys, and by the end of the season he had young boys switching him. Before the year was out, he died of acute inanition.

Dunyazade shrugged, went to visit her father in Samarkand, and arrived to find *him* dying as well, from uncongenial responsibility. Many a first-rate concertmaster fails as a conductor. On his deathbed, the former grand vizier confessed to his daughter that the most satisfying days of his career had been those terrifying thousand when, shroud under arm, he would appear each morning before Shahryar, expecting to be ordered to lead Scheherazade to her execution, and the king would say nothing, and they would proceed with the business of the day. *There,* he said with his dying breath, was diplomacy.

As there were no male heirs, and Dunyazade had no interest in politics, the government of Samarkand was taken over by those Amazonians whom Shah Zaman had victimized incompletely or not at all, and who now re-turned in force to rejoin their parents and/or claim reparation. To her surprise (she had not thought to flee the country), Dunyazade herself had been briefly arrested as the dead tyrant's consort, and all her property confiscated. Knowing her limitations in the field of oral narrative, instead of pleading her defense in person she wrote an account of her thousand nights at the foot of Shahryar's bed and her half-dozen or so in Shah Zaman's. What was irrelevant to the point of the narrative, she omitted from it; what was relevant, she included; what happened to be out of most effective place, she artfully rearranged; what was missing, she boldly invented—but so far from exaggerating her effects, she understated them, letting eloquent details speak for themselves. And because she knew the Amazonian junta to be women of action, not given to such lei-surely pastimes as reading or listening to stories, she kept the thing terse: more like thirty pages than like Scheherazade's thirty-volume work in progress.

The result was so lifelike, convincing, and moving a story that it gained its author not only a full pardon from the Amazonians and the restitution of her confiscated property, but the love of Samarkand's new chairperson, with whom Dunyazade cohabited for several years thereafter, and a certain literary notoriety. Samarkandians, like the citizens of the Islands of India and China, were accustomed to hearing stories to which they were accus-tomed, told typically at considerable length and enlivened with genies, rocs, flying carpets, and talking fish. The idea of a story written out, not to be memorized and told with appropriate embellishment to a circle of listeners but rather to be read silently by individuals word for word from the page, and dealing moreover in ordinary language with the intimate but ordinary life-details of characters rather like the writer and the reader, in a few pages devoid of both grandiloquence and marvels—it was caviary to the millions, but much admired by a discriminating few. So much so, in fact, that Dunyazade had followed that first story with a slender volume of others, similar in style and substance but more or less *made up*: narratives as unastonishing, as marvel-less, as fact . . . presented as fiction!

Fan-*tastic*, marveled her lover and a few others: few not only because the novelty of Dunyazade's art itself put off a people disinclined to innovation but because the novel method of production and dissemination—where literacy was rare and printing unknown—limited even her potential audience. Undaunted, Dunyazade pressed on: At the time of her sister's visit, twenty years later, she was just winding up an almost superrealistic little piece about two women making slow love in the bath while one reads silently a story that the other is writing. Fan-*tastic*, the reader character marvels at the climax, though the story is programmatically devoid of fantasy. The author character is left, in the last line, wondering at what exactly her reader marvels.

I wonder the same thing, Scheherazade confessed. But I didn't really come to Samarkand to read stories, Dun; I came to tell you one.

Dunyazade shrugged and set aside her work in progress. Wouldn't it have been easier to write me a letter? But go ahead; tell along. It will be good regressive fun to sit and listen to you again, as in the old days. Just let me call my friend Kuzia Fakan; she knows all about you, and she'd love to hear you perform.

No Kuzia Fakan, said Scheherazade, for the same reason I didn't send you a letter. This is not only an ears-only story; it's an only-*your*-ears story. Put your pen down now, and listen:

Once upon a time, you may remember—back when *I* was the one who was menstruating and you were the one who wasn't—I saved the day in a thousand and one nights with the help of the only bit of literal magic I've ever personally experienced before or since.

I was there, Dunyazade reminded her. The key to the treasure, et cet.

Right. But since Kuzia Fakan *wasn't* there, when Dunyazade writes this story out for her latest bed-and-bathtub partner to read, she'll include the following retrospective exposition, dialogue and all:

It is one thing to resolve, as young Scheherazade did, to save the virgin daughters of the Muslims and rescue a revenge-maddened, sexist king from his madness by going to bed with him herself and beguiling him postcoitally with some sort of magic charm to make him change his ways. It is quite another to know what magic will work and how to practice it. After nearly three years of researching the literature of the known world in vain, Scher cried out in despair one afternoon to her sister, "We need a miracle, Dun: a literal miracle. And the only genies *I've* ever met are in these made-up stories, not in Moormen's-rings or Jews'-lamps. It's in *words* that the magic is—'Abracadabra,' 'Open Sesame,' and the rest—but the magic words in one story aren't magical in the next. It seems to me that the real magic is to understand which words work, and when, and for what. The trick is to understand the trick."

"If I understand you correctly [Dunyazade will say she said], you're saying that if for example this whole situation here were fiction instead of fact, and if in this piece of fiction you found the right way, after the king deflowers you, to make him want to go on sleeping with you night after night instead of cutting your head off in the morning—that whatever magic trick you found, it would come down to particular words on the page of the story of you and the king, right?"

"You've got it: words made from a couple dozen letters we can draw with this pen. Squiggle squiggle squiggle! These dumb little ink-marks are the key to the whole puzzle, Dun. If I knew exactly which ones to make, our troubles would be over."

"Not only that," observed shrewd Dunyazade: "Since your reward for saving king and country would also be described in particular words in the story—like 'happily ever after,' et cetera—those little ink-marks might be said to be the treasure as well as the key. Do you follow me? The key to the treasure *is* the treasure."

Nothing happened. But then Scheherazade, musing upon her precocious sister's aperçu, repeated it with a slightly different emphasis—"The *key* to the treasure *is* the treasure . . ."—and Wham! A tall, bespectacled genie materialized right there in the library stacks.

The rest of the story is well-known. He was no genie, the fellow declared when he'd collected himself, but a storyteller—and not only from another place and time, as his appearance testified, but from another order of reality, where he happened to have been thinking for the thousandth time about his favorite storyteller in the world, Scheherazade, and the book of her thousand and one nights with King Shahryar.

The young women had no idea what he was talking about.

It had occurred to him, he explained, that the stories with which she beguiled and cured the king were not only the solution to the problem—hers, the king's, her father's, the country's—but also her reward for having solved it, as was made manifest by the king's ordering them published in the same breath with which he revoked his decree of death and proposed marriage. In more ways than one, the genie had said to himself, the *key* to the treasure *is* the treasure—and immediately upon saying those words he had found himself transported from his writing room in the United States of America to the Islands of India and China and the presence of two very consternated young women.

Well, it didn't take sharp Dunyazade long to realize that if their visitor was truly from the future, where there existed a book with a happy ending about herself and Shah Zaman and Scheherazade and Shahryar, then et cetera and *voilà*. The genie not only told Scher what to do—which is to say, he reported to her that what she had done in the story was tell the king stories—but told her as well which stories she told, and in what order, and where to interrupt them to best dramatic effect by the dawn's early light. At Dunyazade's suggestion, he and her sister repeated the magic formula together exactly at noon (local time) every day for the next thousand and one days. The genie would then appear for half to three-quarters of an hour in Scher's library, read her the next installment of *The Thousand Nights and a Night* from Richard Burton's 1885 edition, and dematerialize back to his writing desk in Genieland, where he had problems of his own to deal with when he wasn't helping Scher with hers on his lunch break. The story goes that he wound up writing a story about the *key* to the treasure's *being* the treasure, which not only solved his problem for the time being, but demonstrated the proposition itself.

End of flashback; on with the story.

Scheherazade herself mightn't have told it just that way, but never mind. The point just now was that when all that was done with and the country was saved and the sisters had married the brothers and *The Book of the Thousand Nights and a Night* was in transcription, she and the Genie (as she still called him, out of affectionate habit and because she couldn't get his real name right) had ended their daily tête-à-têtes. Each was beginning a new life-story, so to speak; at least a new chapter in his/her ongoing one. But they agreed to repeat their magic formula once every thousand and one nights, in order to say hello and see how each other fared.

And so they had done, the first two or three times. But an "anniversary" that recurs only once in nearly three years, and never at the same time of year, is easily lost track of when one is busy raising three children, managing a palace, advising a chief of state, and supervising publication of a thirty-volume opus, all at the same time. On one occasion, Scheherazade forgot until the thousand-and-*second* noontime, which was too late; she recited the formula, solo, and nothing happened. The time after that, she remembered but was absolutely too busy at the key moment even to stop and say the magic words, not to mention have a half-hour conversation. The time after that, she was neither forgetful nor particularly busy, but she felt so ashamed of herself for having missed their previous two dates, so to speak, that she guiltily let this one go by as well.

The truth is, Scheherazade told her sister in Samarkand, Djean was always rather more interested in me than I in him.

Djean?

Short for *genie,* which is how they say *djinn* where he comes from. It's as close as I can come to his real name. I don't mean to sound snobbish, Dun, but you and I are vizier's daughters who married royalty and also happen to tell stories, or used to once upon a time. I don't know what your social calendar looks like, but mine is so full I can't keep up with it, and every day (till Shahryar Junior took over) I used to make decisions that affected all the Islands of India and China—which owe their political stability to the stories I once told Shahryar. Djean, on the other hand, as far as I could gather, did nothing but scribble away all morning at his stories, sail around in a little boat with his wife in the afternoon, and sit home nearly every evening, reading books and sipping beer.

That sounds like me, said Dunyazade, except for the wife and the boat and the beer. Kuzia Fakan likes to dance, but I'll take a hot tub and a good book over your whole social calendar.

No criticism intended, Scheherazade hastened to say. I'm here because I've put all that behind me. Anyhow, I'm confessing, not defending myself. Another thing was that I'd always felt there was something romantic, or at least erotic, in Djean's interest in me, you know?

I question that, Scher, Dunyazade objected, if it's the *Nights* days you're speaking of. He never made a pass at you, either physically or verbally, and the way he used to go on about his girlfriend sounded convincing to me.

Scheherazade agreed. He had married the woman, by the way, she added, not long after the sisters' own wedding, and she understood the marriage to be a good one. Nevertheless, his interest in her had a prurient aspect, in her opinion, along with its more innocent and flattering aspects, that made their interviews a touch uncomfortable. At their third anniversary rendezvous, for example, he barraged her with questions about her menstrual cycle, of all impertinent things, back in her storytelling period!

So ask him about his erections, Dunyazade advised, or the regularity of his bowels: tit for tat. Anyhow, if he loves his wife a thousand out of every thousand and one nights, but wouldn't mind jumping into the tub with you every thousand-and-first, what's the big deal? But of course, if you're simply not interested . . .

Well, she simply wasn't, Scheherazade declared: At least she hadn't been, back then. After all, it was Shahryar's insane jealousy that had caused all the trouble in the first place! Which is why she'd never told him a word about her genie friend. But not so long ago, it happened that one of those thousand-and-one-night "anniversaries" almost coincided with her forty-second birthday, and from the perspective of her new restlessness—and the early termination of her menses—she'd found herself thinking about her former comrade in a different way.

Aha.

Yes, well. Djean did more for me—for both of us, Dun—than I've ever done for him, though he gallantly claims the opposite. He's hardly what you'd call handsome, as you remember, but he isn't bad-looking either. The last time I'd seen him, ten or twelve years ago, he was still tall and trim, whereas Shahryar was going to fat already . . .

Mm hm.

I admit it: As the day approached, it was more and more on my mind how shabbily I'd treated the fellow while I was busy being Superwife and Supermom. But all that was done with now, and when Shahryar retired from the throne, he retired from one or two other things, too—jealousy included. Though of course he had his reputation to think about, and so did I.

Of course. But it occurred to you that a little fling with a genie from another order of reality might be something else, as we say in Samarkand:

more interesting and less risky than a roll in the hay with the prince next door. You have my attention, Scher.

Remember, I'd stood him up three times in a row: Four thousand and four nights had gone by since we'd seen each other! I had no reason to imagine that he was still sitting by the phone, as they say in his country. And even if he were, who knew what he'd be like so many years later?

I'm on the edge of my silk-embroidered cushion.

For that matter, who knew what he'd think of *me* at forty-two? Standards of female beauty are different where he comes from.

In my opinion, said Dunyazade, you and I are graced with a timeless beauty that transcends cultural differences and laughs at years. But on with the story, please. You decided that if the guy was still faithfully watching the calendar after all that time—and if he hadn't turned into an absolute scarecrow—you'd give him a different kind of lock to turn his key in. I'm with you.

You're ahead of me. Maybe you're an old hand at these things, Dun, but I'm strictly an amateur. When the morning came (it happened to be a Monday), I must have changed clothes and hairdos half a dozen times. Would he like me better in madras or paisley, or maybe just a simple solid color? Should I unbraid my hair or leave it for him to unbraid if he wanted to? Maybe I should pretend I didn't think he'd show up, and let him catch me wearing nothing but harem pants?

Ai yi, said Dunyazade. How old did you say you are?

That morning I was about fifteen, going on sixty. At eleven A.M. I told everybody in the house that I had three hours' homework to do on our budget for the new fiscal, and I hung a big DO NOT DISTURB sign on the library door. At eleven-thirty I decided that the whole idea was change-of-life madness, and that if Djean really appeared, we'd just salaam and have a cup of tea and catch up on each other's lives. At a quarter till twelve I realized that I was wearing the wrong earrings *entirely* to go with the white smock I'd decided at the last minute to wear instead of the harem pants. . . .

White smock!

Wait till you hear. I'd decided that instead of dressing sexy, I'd pretend it was just another morning and that I'd been working as usual in the stacks when I happened to remember what day it was and gave our magic key another turn just for old times' sake. But get this: Under the white smock? Nothing.

Ten till twelve, said Dunyazade. Five till twelve. High noon.

Sit or stand? asked Scheherazade. Legs crossed or uncrossed? Pretend to be reading you-know-what or stop playing games? And suddenly I really *really* needed to use the chamberpot! When I heard the muezzins start their noon prayer-call, I was standing in the middle of the room in that frumpy-looking smock, on the verge of tears, with an earring in one hand and a book in the other, one braid up and one unbraided, wishing I were up in the nursery giving my grandson his bottle. I wondered whether I'd even remember the words.

But you did.

I did.

Scher?

Hey, Scher?

The *key* to the treasure *is* the treasure, Dun. It really is. There he sat—even his desk chair had got transported somehow this time, and a strange-looking object it was. But Djean wasn't strange-looking at all, not to me. A little older, sure: more lines around his eyes, more wrinkles on his brow, and as much gray as brown in his mustache. But he was my Djean, all right, still trim and fit as he'd been at my age, when I first met him. He was more surprised than I was! He told me later he'd all but given up on me. But whereas *I* felt like sinking through the floor, he wasn't flustered a bit, just surprised and pleased. He *sprang* to his feet, Dun, and if you could've seen the delight in that man's face! I told him later—

Later later, smirked Dunyazade. Tell me later what you told each other later. What'd he say *then?* What happened next?

What happened next was that he held out his arms and said *Scheherazade,* and it didn't matter in the least whether my hair was up or down and what I was wearing or not wearing. No comments, Dun, please.

Who's commenting? I'm envious. Tell along.

I know very well you're going to write this all down as one of your stories and pass it around, so all I'm going to say about what happened next is that the *key* to the treasure *is* the treasure, period and Amen. Also that language is a more amazing thing than flying carpets and crystal palaces, but wordlessness can be eloquent, too. When we got around to talking, we got a lot said, Allah be praised, before the spell wore off. But we also said a few things before we talked, and Allah be praised for that as well.

There is no god but God, said Dunyazade, and he is an incorrigible romantic. On with the story, Scher; don't hold back.

Well. Since these visits never lasted as long as a full hour, and we had so much to say to each other, we met regularly for a while, till we got things more or less said.

The Thousand and One Lunch Breaks.

I wish. But there were scheduling problems on both ends, for one thing. For another, we couldn't abide the idea that inevitably, sooner or later, one of us was going to want to break off the connection. We were middle-aged people, basically satisfied with our lives—Djean especially, but me too, despite my itch for something very different, and I don't mean just him. The fact that we were important to each other in a special way didn't mean that either of us was kicking over the traces. What's more, we didn't want to wear out the specialness of our connection. So we decided to meet once a week, at noon on the Monday, for an arbitrary period, say half a

year, and then to end the affair absolutely except for our thousand-and-
first-night anniversaries, which weren't liable to cause any problems on
either end. Djean is more of an Arab formalist than I am; he proposed a
lunar month of Mondays: twenty-eight Mondays, starting with that first
one. But I had learned from him that the calendar in his place had months
as long as thirty-one days, and so I persuaded him to make it thirty-one
Mondays, *not* counting the first one. That gave us four extra times together.

To me, said Dunyazade, the whole program sounds like coitus inter-
ruptus on the larger scale. Tell me more.

Not about that part. But it really was like a quick daytime replay of the
Nights, except that nobody's life was on the line, and the stories we were
telling were nonfiction.

But you did make love, no? Or was the sex on some other plane of
reality too, like Sahib Djean there?

Scheherazade stood fast: Storytellers don't *always* kiss and tell. What
we did or didn't do before we talked (and *while* we talked: something
Shahryar never thought of) is between Djean and me. It has nothing to
do with this story, which concerns a different key, to a different treasure.
I told him all about my situation and my crazy ambition to do something
like what Sindbad had done, but for a better reason, and to do it *myself,*
not as a first-class passenger in a deck chair, even if I had to disguise myself
as a man to do it. But I didn't know where to start, and in all of Islam
there was nobody to teach me what I needed to know. Anyhow, I wanted
to do the thing alone, not in charge of a crew of rowdy sailors who would
take charge of the ship and me as soon as we were out of sight of land,
and do the usual things with both of us.

Djean said that *he* didn't find the idea crazy; it was simply impossible
where I was. His wife, he said, sometimes took their boat out by herself
for a short sail; in his place and time it was not unknown, though it remained
unusual, for women to cross oceans singlehanded, even to circle the globe.
But their doing so depended upon instruments and materials so exotic as
to seem magical, though they were not, and they went in vessels far sea-
worthier and easier to manage than anything currently available in the
Islands of India and China. There was no way for him to provide me with
such things; even his desk chair never "came over" with him after that
first Monday, nor did several books he tried to bring me about women
solo sailors. It was only Djean himself who materialized, pen in hand, as
the Mondays flew by. That pen itself, I should say—which had become as
familiar and dear a sight to me as its owner, was in fact as peculiar a gadget
as those nautical ones he spoke of. We have nothing like it here.

No comment, said Dunyazade.

With it, Djean told me, he had begun another story about me, inspired
by our Mondays . . .

Tell along.

. . . in which he swore to be exactly as discreet about us as I'm being
right now. Its plot was the situation and problem I've just described, and

Djean's reasoning was that what had worked once before, in our thousand and one nights, might work again before our month of Mondays ran out. Since we were coming together from different orders of reality, if he could invent a story in which my problem was solved, that invention might somehow solve it in fact. What I couldn't quite tell him, out loud, was that as those Mondays approached their end, my problem had changed.

I could see that coming, said Dunyazade. Don't forget, I'm in the story business myself.

So am I, said Scheherazade, but *I* didn't see it coming. And I never told him, either; not in words. We nattered on about *sailboats,* for God's sake, and what he calls high technology, as if I cared at all any more about Sindbadding around by myself. On my end, at least, the whole voyage idea had become a code word for what I really wanted—but I didn't want it if *he* didn't want it. Our time was almost up, and I heard no suggestions from Mister Djean that we open-end our Month of Mondays ad infinitum.

Anyhow, declared Dunyazade, *that* wasn't what you wanted either, by then. You wanted more than just more of the same. I wish Kuzia Fakan could hear this.

She doesn't have to hear it; she'll be reading it soon enough. You'll write it up to the point where Djean had written it by our twenty-ninth Monday. We'd agreed the week before that there was no way I could quote Do What I Wanted to Do close quote in my place and time and order of reality—PTOR, as we came to call it. I would have to resort to a higher technology yet, of a sort that his PTOR lacked altogether, but mine was rich in: magic. With *that* hi-tech, he said, I should be able to cruise the world by rug or Roc-back, or (what was closer to the mark than he knew) contrive to cross in reverse not only the time barrier, but the fact/fiction barrier, whichever one wanted to call which. In short, come over to his PTOR as he'd come to mine.

Now we're talking, cheered Dunyazade. But I see trouble in the next paragraph, Scher, as we scribblers say.

Yes. Because that's what he said *in short,* and I seconded the motion, heart soul and body. But what he said in long was to come over to his PTOR and—Are you ready, Dun?—join him and Mrs. Djean on Chesapeake Bay, in the USA, in the year Nineteen Seventy-nine of the Common Era. Don't ask me! They would take me to a place called Annapolis, he promised, in a place called Maryland, and put me in the hands of cruising sailors as knowledgeable as any on the planet: far more so than he and his wife, for whom sailing was by no means a way of life but merely an agreeable recreation rich in metaphors. The hands of cruising sailors! What's more, he would introduce me to a group of mainly female storytellers called the ASPS, who would embrace me as their tutelary spirit and see to it I lacked for nothing.

Hey, I'm interested, said Dunyazade. But I know how you must have felt. Is the man oblivious, or is a month of Mondays really all he wanted?

I truly don't know. I have to think it was the second. But either way, I lose.

Maybe if you told me more about the nonverbal part.

No: That part will remain nonverbal. I went along with his idea, hoping that *he* was speaking in code, too, and that it was the same code. In the talking part of our next-to-last Monday, I pointed out to him that the magic in the *Thousand and One Nights* book is all in my stories, not in the story of me and Shahryar—what Djean called the frame story. How could we break through that frame? The only truly magical thing that had ever happened in my real-life story was him, I told him.

That's putting it plainly.

I thought so. And he told *me,* not for the first time, that the same was true for him. We agreed that this story couldn't go any farther unless one or the other of us found a different kind of magic by next Monday: a new key, to a different treasure.

But here you are, said Dunyazade. I therefore sadly gather, dot dot dot.

We tried, Dun. We lost a lot of that Monday experimenting with our old formula—reversing it, rearranging and reemphasizing the words—to see whether that might take me to his place. *The key to the key is the key; treasure the* is *treasure the to* key *The.* Nothing. At twelve-fifty, when Djean started to fade, I literally jumped him; I hung on with my arms and legs, with everything.

Good girl.

But by one o'clock it was myself I was holding onto. Empty air. Imagine how I racked my brains that last week! My family had no idea what had come over me; I think they chalked it up to change of life. I was frantic; all the more so because I sensed Djean wasn't. He cares about me, Dun; I know that. (Look at me using the present tense!) I can't really believe he's unaware of my feelings for him, or indifferent to them. But to Djean, finally, this really was just a more than usually poignant problem in an uncompleted story that he was involved in. He was concerned. He was sad. But he wasn't holding onto me the way I was trying to hold onto him.

So.

I didn't even want to call him up that last Monday noon. But I called. I didn't want to see in his face that he hadn't come up with the magic new words we needed—*I* needed—and that it wasn't killing him that he hadn't, sorry as he was. But that's what I saw. I'd half hoped he'd take the coward's way out and not come over at all this last time, so that I could hate him while my heart broke. But he did come over, and my heart melted instead. I was wearing that same plain white smock I'd worn on our first Monday— but this time I had the rest of my clothes on, too, and my hair was braided up tight. . . .

Earrings?

No earrings, and no makeup. The first thing I noticed, after I'd seen exactly what I didn't want to see in his face, was that this time he'd left his pen behind.

I should think so.

Of course. All the same, I missed seeing it so much that my eyes watered. So many times he'd smiled and set down that pen and reached out to touch me, and after he'd faded I'd find ink smudges on me from his fingers. . . . I guess he saw my eyes fill up, because he said my name with his foreign accent, just the way he'd said it on our first Monday, and he came across the library to where I was sitting—I wasn't going to meet him halfway that day!—and he hugged me so hard that I felt something break against my chest.

Scher.

Wait. He held me like that for a long time, lifting me right up off my cushion. I didn't push him away, but I didn't respond, either. After a while he moved back from me a little without letting go, and we saw a black stain on the front of his shirt and the front of my smock, just over my breast: the same mark on both of us, where we'd pressed together. He hadn't left his pen behind; it was just out of sight, in his pocket, and we'd broken it. We laughed and cried. I didn't hold back then.

But there was nothing to *say*. Halfway through our last hour together, we actually dozed off in each other's arms, on the old Bokhara on my library floor that we called our magic carpet. There: I've told you more than I meant to, in that line, and you can put it in your story. I woke before he did, with my back turned toward him. We were still . . . connected. His arm was under my head; I watched our last minutes run by on his wristwatch. At the very end, he pressed up tight behind me. Then I felt him disappear.

That's the end of the story, Dun, even though it's no way to end a story.

It certainly is not. How long ago did you say this was?

It's been a year and a half since that last Monday, and I've never felt so *unfinished* in my life. For a while I went a little crazy. I would send the help away and clean the whole palace in one day. I threw out the ink-stained smock and then turned the city upside down to get it back, and wept when I did. Sometimes I'd curse myself for ever having gone past the storytelling stage with him. Other times I'd lie down naked on our magic carpet on a Monday noontime and . . . pretend Djean was there. At my worst, I'd get weepy and kiss the ink stain on my smock and wish I'd been able to get pregnant by him, at least, before our time ran out. A little daughter . . . Please don't say anything.

Change of life, my family said; change of life. They were patient and understanding, and I tried to get back to normal, for their sake and mine. But they were like strangers, even little Shahryar Three. And I'd thought I was restless *before*! So I decided to trek over here and tell my little sister all about it. Not because I think that you or anybody else can prescribe for me; there isn't any medicine for my condition. But I hoped that telling the whole story to somebody might take the edge off, you know? Maybe help me come to terms.

Has it worked, I hope? asked Dunyazade.

No. I feel worse than before. And *that,* May Jump told us all late last night in the great center cockpit of *Katydid IV,* is the end of the first story Scheherazade ever told yours truly in Annapolis, Maryland, U S of A, after I'd come to know her well enough to trade stories of that kind. Now, then: Let's hang it up and turn in. It's tomorrow already.

WYDIWYD UNCONCLUDED: WYDIWYD

I guess we should, Henry Sherritt agreed. We old guys, anyhow. We thank you for the story, Miss May: quite unusual and quite entertaining.

And quite unfinished! Irma Sherritt said strongly, to her daughter's pleased surprise. You turn in, hon; I'm going to hear the rest of this story if I have to make it up myself.

I'm with you, Joan Bass declared. That genie fellow doesn't get off that easily while Irm and I are awake.

And I'm with Hank, her yawning husband said, much as I'd like to hear you tell along. My eyes are closing—not from your story, young lady! And Captain Chip's are already closed.

Sure enough, Andrew Sherritt was asleep, his head on Katherine's right shoulder. So by now was most of the thronging anchorage. Doctor Jack and Hank Sherritt kissed their wives good night and went below, Hank first gently waking his son to suggest that the boy get himself horizontal next door. I guess I will, Chip said; I missed the last few Mondays anyhow. You'll tell me tomorrow, Kath, right?

If I have to make it up myself, Katherine promised.

Frank Talbott stretched his arms and legs and guessed he too was about storied out. What did Lee think? Lee Talbott thought she was as ready for bed as she'd been since they'd reached the Chesapeake after standing watches from Bermuda to Norfolk, but she had to hear what happened next. Captain Donald Quicksoat said *he'd* storied out in 1616; what's more, he'd heard his colleague Scheherazade spin what he imagined was the next and final episode of her still-unfinished yarn at the ASPS jamboree in Kitty Hawk, just before she took off for parts unknown. But he guessed he'd hang in there and listen—if that's what his shipmate planned to do—to hear whether the story had grown a proper tail on it since then.

Am I going to hang in there and listen? asked Carla B Silver. I'm going to help Miz Irma tell along, if she needs any help.

Irma said she'd just been joking; that she was no storyteller. But if somebody called Scheherazade had actually told stories at the last get-together of her daughter's storytelling club, and already before that had told May Jump in Annapolis the story she'd told her younger sister Whats-ername—the story we just heard—then for better or worse she must have found some way to get from there to here, right? Irma would certainly like to know what that way was and what happened next.

So would Irma's daughter, Katherine said: Half asleep is half awake.

So would Irma's son-in-law, said Peter, if men are allowed in this next installment. I can't leave my favorite storyteller lying alone on that rug, kissing her ink stains.

You're allowed, my friend, May Jump declared: This is the story of a woman, but it's not just a woman's story, any more than the ASPS is just a woman's club. Right, Kiss?

Well.

Okay, so it's mainly. But not exclusively. Irma Sherritt has got us off to a good start, if you ask me. What would Carla B Silver say happened next, back in Samarkand?

To the eight of us who remained (Frank Talbott yawned a few times, but stayed), Carla B Silver said Carla B Silver would say that when Scheherazade told her sister how she felt worse now than she'd felt before, 'cause the story was so damned *unfinished,* old Dunyazade there said something like I know where you're coming from, Sis, 'cause I've more or less been there myself.

I can hear her, Lee Talbott declared: I won't pretend I have any advice for you, Scher-babe, but I affirm my solidarity with you one hundred percent in this exemplary mid-life crisis of yours.

She doesn't want solidarity, Joan Bass bet. She wants Djean-Boy. But she knows that *that's* over and done with. We've all kissed our share of ink stains, right?

Cracked Kath You might say the magic had gone out of their relationship. And magic is the only thing that can come to her rescue, other than time.

Which we all know is the final medicine, said May Jump. Don't we. But the trouble with time is that it takes too long.

And it has bad side effects, added Irma. Like old age. I'll take magic anytime.

But who can write that prescription? May Jump asked. Not Miss Dunyazade, for sure. I pride myself on being realistic, I can hear her telling Scheherazade, in my life as well as in my stories. If you want my honest opinion . . .

What you've done is what you'll do, declared Carla B Silver.

Katherine Sherritt gave a little gasp, waking Dichtung. Relax, Wahrheit whispered: I'm on watch, and it's only about eleven hours, seventeen minutes and counting.

Now how in the world, May Jump pretended to marvel, all the while thumbing her guitar, did Miz Carla B Silver know that that was what Dunyazade said?

For one thing, said C.B S., I've been down on some rugs myself, in my time: magic and otherwise. For another, I had a spy in the audience at Kitty Hawk.

What you've done is what you'll do, Donald Quicksoat affirmed: That's what the lady said. And it's true, too.

Whatever it means, Peter Sagamore put in, remembering our musings upon those words when Kath happened to dream them in the Annapolis Hilton early in the morning of Friday before last. I have more trouble with that bit of wisdom than I do with first second menstruations.

So did Scheherazade, said Carla B Silver: all the way home from Samarkand. And I think Miss May had better tell along from here, 'cause she was closest to the action.

Closest of those bodily present, May supposed, though she certainly was not on the scene at either end when Scheherazade's story took its next leap forward.

She'd been disappointed by her sister's words, Scheherazade told May Jump in Annapolis early last fall: disappointed, but scarcely surprised. Time *was* your only ink-stain remover. But time was the problem, too, in more ways than one: Dunyazade's dark prophecy itself, depressing as it sounded and whatever it meant, was time-soaked from start to finish. In Scheherazade's words, it presupposed both a past and a future, while denying their difference in the present.

What you've done is what you'll do. At first the saying seemed as clear as it was chilling: She should forget about any really new direction; her future would be Business As Usual. But in major respects, that was literally impossible: She had been young, and was no longer. She had borne children, but (once that desperate wish for a love child had subsided) she would bear no more, even if she could. She had recounted stories at a prodigious rate that she could not expect to match again, under circumstances that would strike her speechless now. She'd been a virgin girl, a concubine, a wife, a mother—those roles were all behind her.

Then did Dunyazade's prophecy mean perhaps that what she had accomplished was all she ever would accomplish, of any significance? Nonsense! Forty-plus is not twenty, but it isn't eighty, either. Those Mondays on that magic carpet had picked her up and then let her down for sure, but even homeward bound from Samarkand she knew she had begun to get over that affair and would soon be ready again for some large, novel undertaking before she settled down to late middle age and grandparenthood—if she ever did.

What you've done is what you'll do. What had she done? She had helped a catastrophically embittered king to become a gentle and humane one. Though not a radical like Dunyazade, she had introduced a few modest but real improvements in the lot of Islamic women: nothing miraculous, but a genuine beginning, or a high-water mark to be remembered, should things backslide in the current administration. Moreover, so Djean had often told her, she had embodied the storyteller's condition in such a way as to become a symbol; she was not sure of what, but gathered it was something hopeful, of positive value. Finally, and no doubt most important—the key to all the rest—she had come truly to understand that both in human intimacies and in human language, the *key* to the treasure *is* the treasure.

A pause here for fresh tears, truly less salt-stinging than their forerunners. (She's back in her library, having home-come and distributed souvenirs of Samarkand—just another place—and news of Aunt Dunyazade. It is a blue Monday—but she's not kissing ink stains; she's not down on that Bokhara.) By Allah, she and her genie friend had defeated time, or at least got 'round it, when he'd supplied her from the future with exactly those stories from the past that she'd needed in the present—and had supplied them from his copy of the *Nights*. Prophecy be damned: What she wanted to do was as unlike what she'd done as anything could be: Once again (but no longer to the same end as in her Month of Mondays) she craved to *cross over,* from her PTOR to . . . some other.

Did she really think he might appear when she repeated their words, in their special place? Did she really want him to? Not really, no. Yes, of course (Admit it, Scher: You've got that white smock on); but no. No doubt he was busy turning that key upon his present treasure: his life-in-the-works, his story-in-progress (in which she hoped parenthetically, if she was in it, he would maintain the reticence he'd pledged, and make her no unhappier than she was in fact). *He* seemed content enough to go on doing what he'd done, in however different company and circumstances from when she'd first met him: scribble scribble scribble, to the end of the story. Isn't that why he'd not held on, when their arbitrary time was up? Now she *did* truly wish she could see him—innocently, innocently—before their next thousand-and-first-night anniversary, just to ask whether he perhaps knew the key to her sister's prophecy, apparently so clear, actually so cryptic: *What you've done is what you'll do.*

Ka-*pow!* cried Captain Donald Quicksoat at this point in May's retelling, for he had been among the listeners around a certain bonfire on a certain famous sand dune near Kitty Hawk last October.

Blam blooey, added Peter Sagamore, who had not been there but didn't need to be. Various of the assembled looked startled indeed at that brace of male startlers; but Carla B Silver said Yup; Katherine Sherritt said Oh my! and Baroque said Dad's not calling us, Rococo; those sound effects have to do with the story they're telling.

In which the original narrator suddenly found herself no longer in her tranquil library of a thousand-plus volumes in her and Shahryar's quarters in their first son's palace, formerly theirs, in the Islands of India and China, but on the low side of some sort of sailing-boat such as she had never seen before and was likely never to see again, as it was tilted terrifyingly far over onto one side—*her* side—in a stiff wind on some choppy sea, and obviously about to capsize and go down like one of Sindbad's clunkers, with all hands. Which was to say, herself (holding for dear life onto a shiny stanchion down there on the boat's low side, almost in the water, and in fact getting soaked with spray as they crashed through the waves); another woman, somewhat younger than herself, dressed in what looked to Scheherazade like nothing but the briefest of undergarments and, incredibly, perched up on the vessel's high side as much at her ease as if she were sunbathing instead of about to drown; and—equally at ease the first moment she saw him (he hadn't yet seen her) at the vessel's helm (a wheel that he steadied with the toes of one bare brown foot)—her old friend Djean. He was dressed only a touch less scantily than . . . *his wife,* Scheherazade realized: bleached-blue trousers cut off at mid-thigh and a short-sleeve white combed-cotton pullover shirt with what at first glance she took to be ink stains on its front but then saw was some lettering, in his alphabet and presumably in his language.

Within the space of this paragraph, they'll see her—and hear her, too, for her alarm is already in her throat—and be properly astonished. Before they do, it is important to get said that while Scheherazade could no more decipher her friend's alphabet and language than he could decipher hers, speech between them had never been a problem, in this sense: Everything Djean said sounded like "Arabic" to her; everything she said sounded "English" to him. Magic. What she now cried out was pure fright in any language. Mrs. Djean replied with a smaller cry of pure alarmed surprise. The helmsman bolted up, put both hands on the wheel, did a double-take (his eyes had been upon the sails, the windvane, something), grinned with almost pure delight, and exclaimed, in the perfect "Arabic" of which he swore he knew not one word: Scheherazade! How in the world? Welcome aboard!

Inshallah! Scheherazade cried back. There is no god but God! Allah spare us!

The near-naked woman now said dryly *Shmah Yisroel* et cetera, and held out her hand. Since you're here, come on up where the view is better.

What had happened? Where was she? And was it possible that these people were actually *enjoying* themselves? They were. The vessel was theirs, she would learn presently, and they would have her believe that it was in fact not about to sink or even tip over; that it sailed safely and normally at that dismaying angle when "beating to windward" in a good breeze; that they were out there doing what they were doing, not to reach any port of refuge or deliver some precious cargo or accomplish any other riskworthy mission but simply for the sport of it. They found what they were doing *fun!* For their new passenger's sake, however, they took in some sail and changed course homeward (they were not at sea, they assured her, but in a branch of water just before their house). Once the wind was behind them, as if by magic the day turned suddenly warmer and calmer; Scheherazade's terror subsided, if not her consternation.

Well, now, said "Shmah"—that was not Mrs. Djean's name, any more than her friend's was "Djean," precisely, or her own was "Scheherazade"; but it sounded plausibly Arabic, it was close enough, and it stuck in Sche-

herazade's head as the first word she'd heard the woman say—I've heard
so much about you, I almost feel as if et cetera. Do you want to slip out
of that wet thing? I've got another top that might fit you.

Once up on the boat's high side (but there was no high or low now,
Allah be praised), Scheherazade had put her hand to her chest to cover
the telltale ink stain. Now, when she said No, thank you; this will soon
dry out, she saw with relief that either the sea spray or her sudden transportation to Djean's PTOR had removed the blot entirely. She saw *him*
see that, too, and smile.

So! they all more or less said, and more or less sized one another up,
and began more or less to relax. Somehow or other, she had managed to
make the journey that she and Djean had so often speculated upon (Shmah
knew at least something about it, too, evidently, from her husband's stories
of what he called his Metaphorical Excursions in the other direction). That
meant that Scheherazade had a little time with them before she faded back
to where she'd come from. It's terrific to see you again! Djean said, and
seemed quite to mean it. And *here!* We've got to figure out how you did
it, so Shmah and I can show you around a bit in the future.

As they addressed this question, Djean politely asked her permission to
remove his shirt, for comfort; the day was unseasonably warm. Scheherazade colored and said Of course, understanding that customs differed.
He peeled it off . . . she was sure his wife was reading her mind. . . . But
Shmah said Me too, and actually bared her breasts! Which were, obviously,
as accustomed to the sun as was the rest of her. The woman was attractive,
even by Thousand-and-One-Night standards; also cheerful, cordial, energetic, and rather more trim and fit than Scheherazade was. Feel free,
Shmah said, if you change your mind.

Djean said nothing.

Well, going smockless would have been more comfortable, certainly,
though the wet cotton felt cool on her skin. But beyond the fact that she
was still a modest daughter of Islam and somewhat stunned by what had
happened to her, Scheherazade was particularly disinclined to undress
before either of those two, not to mention both, and especially to shed
that particular garment in nonpassionate circumstances. Again she de-
murred, and as they sailed "homeward" (Djean now and then checking
his wristwatch in a familiar way that made her heart catch), she told them
a suitably abridged and seemly version of what had led up to her transportation: her visit to her sister in Samarkand—no mention of its motive—
and Dunyazade's ambiguous, oracular remark, with whose sense she had
been wrestling when she found herself with them.

To her surprise, she saw Djean and Shmah smile more and more merrily
as she spoke. Now they took each other's hands and declared the mighty
mystery solved. The key to the treasure, said laughing Shmah, is my husband's T-shirt. Holding it up, she explained that the bold blue letters across
its front—WYDIWYD—were an acronym for an anonymous, unpostmarked

message that had come to Djean in the mails after the publication of his last book. (Another one about you, Shmah told her candidly. Infidelity with fictional characters doesn't give me any problems, by the way; I get crushes on Djean's male leads all the time.)

Nothing really indiscreet in there, smiling Djean assured her. There's a copy waiting for you on my desk. Now I understand that that letter must have been from your sister, though God knows how it got from Samarkand to here. It's hard enough to get my royalty statements from New York.

Wherever it came from, the message had been the same: *What you've done is what you'll do.* And at first it had depressed him, for professional reasons, as Dunyazade's had depressed Scheherazade for personal. Nothing ahead but repetition or silence? But he was so far from finished saying what he wanted to say—even about Scheherazade; maybe *especially* about Scheherazade—and so determined to tell along, tell along, whether with or against the winds of fashion, until the Destroyer of Delights crashed his Macintosh for keeps, that what had initially sounded like the knell of doom had come in his and Shmah's house, and on their boat, to be a slogan of encouragement. So much so, they had abbreviated it to a kind of catchword, which Shmah had caused to be lettered upon what in their PTOR was called a T-shirt, as a surprise gift for him: WYDIWYD. Just a little while ago, when in the course of their afternoon sail (he having spent the morning tapping away at his latest yarn, into which he could not promise that present company would not materialize) they had turned into the wind, he had called down to his wife in the cabin to fetch him a shirt from his seabag when she came on deck, and Abracadabra! The moment he'd recognized the acronym and pronounced the sentence aloud like a wry mantra, Scheherazade had appeared, white smock and all. Clearly they'd said the same words at the same time, as had happened with certain other words before. It was a hypothesis, in any case, easy enough to test.

As they approached their dock, the broad river narrowed, and the traffic of other boats increased: some pleasure craft like theirs, some obviously workboats, whose crews had the no-nonsense look of working watermen everywhere. Shmah stepped below to cover herself more properly, by their standards. In her brief absence, Djean and Scheherazade spoke volumes to each other with one long glance—his eyes smiling, questioning, and serious, hers merely serious.

Shmah emerged wearing a T-shirt of her own—TKTTTΠT—and now Scheherazade was at ease enough with them, with the situation, and with herself to share the joke. Once the boat was secured at their dock and she dared to move, they showed her around it: one of the sort Djean had described to her, more or less, and in face of its exotic, complicated reality, Scheherazade dismissed her solo-Sindbad fantasy forever. Nowhere in the Islands of India and China did such materials exist, or workmen to fashion them into such astonishments. (Check again, Shmah advised: Half of this stuff comes from Japan and the other half from Taiwan.) In any case, she began to believe, it would be quite enough for her to make *this* voyage, from her PTOR to theirs and back . . . a number of times . . . to supply her with a busy old-ageworth of new stories for her grandchildren.

Next they wanted to show her their little country house: No servants, Djean warned her, but wait till she saw the gadgetry! In particular he wanted to demonstrate for her the device he'd bought to replace his old fountain pen, which after decades of faithful service had taken to leaking all over the page. . . . But he declared with a glance at his watch that all that would have to wait for another visit. Fifty minutes had passed already since Scheherazade's appearance; it was a wonder she hadn't begun to fade home. I've enjoyed meeting you, Shmah said, shaking her hand. You do want to come back, don't you? Djean asked. If so, we'd better make arrangements fast. There's so much for you to see!

Scheherazade considered. I'd like to try it once more, anyhow, if you're willing.

Friday at five P.M., Djean said positively. We're both here then, and our week's work is done. This coming Friday at five sharp we'll do what we've just done and take it from there.

Scheherazade agreed. Making these arrangements (whose unspoken voltage was more amusing now than painful) had taken several minutes; she was pleased they'd gotten things straight before she left, and not a little surprised to be with them still, on their boat, at their pier, as substantial as ever in her slowly drying smock. Had Djean's visits to her ever lasted so long, back when they'd both have given much for a quarter-hour more?

One o'clock passed; their conversation thinned. One-fifteen.

Well, said Shmah: It seems that Wydiwyd's got more staying power than Tikittity-Titty ever did. I'm going to say good-bye now, Scher, and catch a swim. You two probably have things to say before you split.

Not really, they both assured her. But please go on with your afternoon, said Scheherazade. Both of you. I can't imagine why I'm still here.

As Djean's watch approached one-thirty, she grew uneasy indeed. He wouldn't hear of leaving her to fade alone; on the other hand, their talk was strained under the circumstances, neither party confident of finishing any given sentence. Djean's wife stepped onto the pier and, to Scheherazade's astonishment, peeled not only out of her T-shirt, but out of that scanty swimsuit-bottom as well, and dived naked into the water. Nobody here but us, she called back when she surfaced, and the river's still warm. You'll have to try it next Friday.

Your wife is both attractive and friendly, Scheherazade said when Shmah swam off.

Thank you, said Djean. She's also smart, high-principled, firm-charactered, and other good things. He smiled and took her hand: A friend. You'll get used to our ways, Scheherazade. I had the advantage of having read the *Nights* before I came to visit.

She much wanted to ask him, apropos of Shmah's earlier remark, not only whether he had in fact told his wife, if not his readers, the whole story of their Month of Mondays—as it certainly appeared he had—but (more important to her) whether she herself really had seemed to him, even at the time, not a flesh-and-blood woman but a *fictional character,* insubstantial as Tawaddud the Slave Girl or Fatimah the Turd in the stories she'd told Shahryar. If so, little wonder he'd not held on! Yet such insubstantiality ought to cut both ways, and except in the moments of his fading, Djean had never seemed fictional to her. Was it a fiction who once had . . . But if such questions were to be raised at all, this was not the time to raise them.

At one forty-five, Djean asked Would you like something to drink? There's beer and Coke and iced tea in the cooler.

No thank you, Scheherazade murmured to her fingernails. You go ahead.

At two, Shmah climbed from the wide river and rinsed herself in the spray from a long, snakelike tube that produced fresh water at her wish without anyone's pumping or pouring. Then she wrapped herself in a towel and rejoined them, saying brightly It turns out we could've showed you the house after all. Shall we give it a try?

Allah help me! Scheherazade wailed. Is this my punishment, never to return to my children and grandchildren? What have I done? What shall I do?

Shmah took her arm and said firmly You'll come inside with us, to start with. You'll get out of those wet clothes and into something comfortable: I've got two caftans and a djellaba up there for you to choose from. You're to stay for dinner at least, and for as long after that as you need to. There's plenty of room.

Scheherazade wept.

We'll take an extra Cornish hen out of the freezer, Shmah went on, and I'll bet you anything that just when it's thawed and we put it on the barbecue, you'll take off.

Her manner was joking, as usual, but her sympathy and hospitality were seconded by Djean, and abundantly implemented. Shmah demonstrated the marvels of showerbath, flush toilet, underarm spray, and electric hair dryer. To make their guest feel more at home, she and Djean donned caftans too, which they had picked up in their travels. Djean caused authentic Arabian music to sound from a remarkable music-machine; also a piece composed in her honor and bearing her name, the work of some Tatar. Shmah, who did her own cooking, even produced a creditable harira to precede the lamb kabobs and pita bread (the Cornish hens, she said, can wait), and persuaded Scheherazade to bend Islamic custom enough to take a glass of wine with them in honor of Omar the Tentmaker—who, if Shmah remembered correctly, did *not* say A loaf of bread, a jug of mint tea, and thou.

But how could Scheherazade savor their food and hospitality (and Shmah's wit); how could she assimilate the astonishments of dials, keyboards, lighted screens, automobiles, and airplanes, while hoping every moment to transmigrate from their patio or porch back to her library? Maybe if you held your breath and *pushed,* Shmah suggested over dessert—but who could tell when that woman was being serious?

She did not fade; not that night or the next day or the day after that. What she'd done, it began to appear, she could not undo: The passkey WYDIWYD admitted one into the treasury of wonders that was Djean and Shmah's PTOR, but not out again. She despaired: never to see her sister, whom she still prized despite the changes in her! Never again to be with her husband, the father of her children, whom she had scarcely imagined she could so much miss! Her hosts tried to console her, and she for her part tried to be consoled: It was not a foregone conclusion that her translation was irreversible; they simply didn't know how long it would last. We've had houseguests like that before, said Shmah.

Scheherazade was used enough to her manner now to understand that she was only teasing again, and not to doubt her and Djean's concern and their assurances that she was welcome. But she knew too that no guest is welcome indefinitely, especially one who once had a very special relationship with one of her hosts. Accustomed to a palaceful of servants instead of a houseful of labor-saving machines, she couldn't really pull her own weight. Djean and Shmah were both working people, schoolteachers, busy with their new semester; Djean moreover spent all of every morning at his word machine, printing out stories that, like Dunyazade, he made up in his head, to be read silently off the page. No matter how they protested otherwise, she knew she was in their way.

On the fifth evening, as they dined on those Cornish hens that Shmah had mentioned earlier, Djean speculated seriously that the difference between his visits to Scheherazade's library and hers to Chesapeake Bay were perhaps related to the difference between past time and future time, though he could not say quite how so. Certainly the two were very different things. For the reality of the past, there was abundant empirical evidence: We infer from Burton's 1885 edition of *The Book of the Thousand Nights and a Night,* for example, that there once was a year 1885 and a brilliant odd fellow named Richard Burton, though neither exists presently; from the *Nights* themselves we infer that in another PTOR there once was a king named Shahryar, et cetera: merely inferences, but reasonably well grounded. The future, in Djean's view, was a camel of another color: Though he was no philosopher, it seemed to him that there was no empirical evidence for its reality at all, only a reflex expectation. Fallible and insubstantial as memory might be, it struck Djean as much solider stuff than anticipation; he had more confidence in the reality of yesterday than in the reality of tomorrow. Besides, he concluded, I've *visited* the past. And a nice place to visit it was, though et cetera.

It's a matter of perspective, isn't it? Shmah suggested, though she too disclaimed any philosophical expertise. From Scher's point of view, you came from the future—a real piece of empirical evidence, by the way, for the future's reality. Your little get-togethers were in the present, at the time, though we all presume they're in the past now, don't we. When Scher gets home again, this scintillating conversation and her whole visit will be in the future, from her viewpoint, not in the present—though in another sense I guess they'll be in the past, since she'll be remembering them. I say to hell with it. What do *you* think, Scher?

Scheherazade admitted that she *had* read the philosophers—though from her present perspective they were ancient philosophers indeed, and in a different order of reality besides. But now that she'd been with Shmah and Djean a few days, it seemed to her that motions and emotions in the islands of Chesapeake Bay were not very different from those in the Islands of India and China. Here as there, night followed day; people smiled when they were pleased and fretted when they were not . . . *et cetera,* as her hosts were fond of saying. She therefore imagined that what she'd read long ago in her library might be as true now as it was then: namely, that past and future are like the world above the sea's surface and the world beneath it, or like fact and fiction: really different, but not really opposite, and both of them really real in their very different ways, as is their . . . meeting place.

She burst into tears.

Thank God, Shmah said dryly, but hurried to comfort her, as did Djean. Give me tears over metaphysics any time.

Today is the day I was supposed to come *back* here, cried Scheherazade, and I can't even leave! I want to go home! I *hate* this situation!

Djean sighed: We all do, more or less. We're sorry for us, much sorrier for you—but we're stuck with one another, and we'll see it out. Listen: I've got something to confess.

Shall I leave the room? Shmah asked. Or is the confession for me?

I should leave the room! wailed Scheherazade. I don't want to come between you two! I don't want to be in your way! Where can I go?

Please listen, Djean said to both women. I think I'm more responsible for all this than I thought I was, and I'm not sure what's to be done about it. Here's the story:

The story he had been in process of inventing last Monday, he now revealed (the one in which he'd hinted Scheherazade might once again appear), was literally that: a story in which a man who once magically visited Scheherazade now wishes that she could visit him, so that if what he's done must be essentially what he'll do, it might be done at least as spiritedly and wholeheartedly as before. In short, that story was this story, and, like this one, it was not only unfinished, but stuck.

Sighed Shmah I should have known: postmodernism. Boyoboy.

Yeah. When me and the guy in the story were trying to think up a way to bring Scheherazade here, I came up with the WYDIWYD trick, and Blam! There you were, in the story. That same afternoon, Blooey! There you were, in our boat. Then you didn't fade, and it occurred to me that that was just the right complication for the story, so I put it in: how the novelty wears off, and the problem gets to be not only how to get you back home but what to do with you in the meantime. You know what I mean: what you're to do with yourself till your time's up.

If it ever is! cried Scheherazade.

Now look here, said Shmah: This is serious. I could let my feelings be hurt, but I'm not going to. . . .

Please don't, Djean urged her. There was nothing romantic about it, except the romantic idea of inspiration.

Now you're hurting *her* feelings, his wife pointed out. But better hers than mine. Let me see if I have this right. The WYDIWYD trick happened in your story first and then in our lives, but the no-fade problem happened to us before you put it in your story. If cause and effect are being passed back and forth, the ball's in your court.

Scheherazade wiped her eyes. You're very sharp, Shmah.

She is that, Djean agreed.

Oh, I can analyze to beat the band, Shmah acknowledged. But invent? Forget it.

I can't do either, said Scheherazade. I only tell, tell, tell.

Well, I *invent,* Djean declared, and so does the fellow in my story. Believe it or not, I invented him, too: We don't have much in common besides Scheherazade and this problem. And the ball *is* in our court, evidently. The trouble is, it's stuck there. You don't just write WYDIWYD or T*K*TTT*I*TT or *Go away* and make it happen; I've tried that, for all our sakes.

He touched Scheherazade's arm. In my opinion, WYDIWYD got you here because it was dramaturgically appropriate, excuse the expression. And your nonfading went into the story because *it* was appropriate, dramaturgically. But WYDIWYD pure and simple won't get you home, because that isn't good dramaturgy. He looked from one to the other of his listeners. We're prisoners of dramaturgy.

Do you mean to say, appalled Scheherazade began.

Exactly. And they've thrown away the key.

PRISONERS OF DRAMATURGY,
OR,
SCHEHERAZADE'S UNFINISHED STORY UNFINISHED

At this point (Peter Sagamore says to *Story*'s logbook), May Jump said to us last night in *K IV*'s cockpit "At this point, Scheherazade said to me in Annapolis *At this point.* . . ."

No need to say on, because the et cetera is clear: Until the fellow in "Djean's" story, which is to say Djean himself in effect though not in fact, comes up with a dramaturgically appropriate return ticket, he and "Shmah" are stuck with their distinguished visitor, she's stuck in their PTOR, and the story's stuck period, or dot dot dot. No mere fiat or god on wires will save them, Q.E.D.: A bona fide, "inevitable" key, forged by the whole Story Thus Far, is the only thing that can turn the trick.

Allah knows he tried, poor Djean, Scher told us that night at Kitty Hawk, May Jump said. The burden was on him, not simply because he was responsible for the situation, or felt himself to be, but because Shmah and I were out of our element. He begged my forgiveness; I said Forget it: I'd wanted to make the trip even more than he'd wanted me to. What's more, he must see that I had failed *him,* too. Need I explain?

Anyhow, as he kept reminding me, this whole prisoner-of-dramaturgy idea was no more than a working hypothesis, and work at it he did. To verify it, he would have to come up with the key and make me disappear; if I suddenly found myself back home, I could presume he had regained his powers of invention, which would mean that I had regained mine of inspiration, whether or not I ever learned what I had inspired him to.

Meanwhile, there was no reason for me to go on camping in their laps until that happened, if it ever did, and there was good reason not to. So I reminded Djean of that storyteller's group he had once mentioned to me. I wondered whether they might take me in for a while, and whether I could somehow pay my way by telling them my stories.

The ASPS! said Shmah. That's a terrific idea! She explained to me that they were not exactly an ashram or other sort of community, just an association of oral storytellers in which Djean had taken some interest since its founding, and to which he'd been elected an honorary member even though his medium was writing. They had no clubhouse, only a small central office, but they were a most hospitable group—whose annual fall get-together was scheduled for the weekend after this one. She and Djean would introduce me to their chief executive officer; I would tell her my story, and we would see what happened next.

What happened next? Nothing. As storytellers themselves (Scheherazade declared at Kitty Hawk to her last audience), they must understand the distinction Djean once made to her, as valid in talespinning as in physics, between effort and work. Things went on, things went on, but nothing *happened,* dramaturgically speaking. The next day, for example, Saturday, Djean and Shmah drove her to Annapolis to meet the executive secretary of the ASPS, as well as to do some shopping and sightseeing. So responsible did Djean feel for his role in her predicament, sometime in midweek he had established a checking account in her name with the money paid him for a story he'd invented about the birth of her three sons. Shmah promised to show her, in Annapolis, how such money is used. To calm her apprehension during the hour's drive—the longest she'd made in their machine, and across an impossibly high bridge over Chesapeake Bay—they made up endings to the story-in-progress, half hoping one would work. Suppose for example the ASPS turned out to have just acquired an anonymous new sponsor: an Arab oil sheik, who supports the organization as a tax write-off on his American interests as well as in honor of Islam's most renowned storyteller. Word reaches him of Scheherazade's miraculous presence-in-the-present, and of her plight; he comes forward and reveals himself to be . . . not the Aga Khan, Jr. (patron of *The Paris Review*), but King Shahryar, transmigrated here by some magic of his own. Embracing his lost companion, he declares: "Treasure is the key to everything."

Et cetera. Nothing happened. They toured the United States Naval Academy and the old town; then Djean went off to inspect some new sailboat designs, and the women shopped for a few simple items of clothing to supplement Scheherazade's white smock and to replace the borrowed caftan. She could not bring herself to wear knee-length skirts, not to mention shorts, but consented to white corduroys and blue denim jeans like Shmah's, two blouses, a hooded sweatshirt, and, as a lark, a freshly printed, bright orange WYDIWYD T-shirt. To step forth publicly in such garb, even among people all similarly costumed, required all her courage. What I'm doing, she said to Shmah, I've never done before.

Nothing happened. At afternoon's end, May Jump reported last night, they donned their various T-shirts and went to my favorite bar in Annapolis, as we'd arranged by telephone, to meet the executive secretary of the American Society for the Preservation of Storytelling—that's me—and we hit it off right away. To make Scher feel at home, the bartender and I had invented a drink called the Flying Carpet—hot mint tea with vodka—and over two of those, Scher updated her story, which I'd heard the main part of from Miz Shmah. I never doubted the truth of it: Would we storytellers make up stories? I proposed that she move in with me, at least till after our eleventh-anniversary fest in Kitty Hawk. She could help me with the last-minute conference arrangements and then tell her Story Thus Far to the ASPS in plenary session. If a whole congress of storytellers couldn't come up with the right ending—which maybe they couldn't, I warned her, 'cause they're really tellers, like Scher herself and yours truly, not inventors like Mister Djean and Mister Peter Sagamore—then at least they might come up with the next move: some kind of a job, someplace to live.

We four moved on then to a proper restaurant for dinner; not even two Flying Carpets could make my friend Djean feel at home in that particular bar. Over oysters Rockefeller, he seconded my Kitty Hawk proposal, but said he still suspected it was up to him to unlock the door he'd never meant to lock. More than once, in time past, he had been uncertain of his next narrative move: Witness those first visits of his to Scheherazade, years ago. But never since the day he first took up his professional pen had he really been stopped cold, stymied altogether, as he felt himself presently to be. His mistake, he believed, had been to work this time from life: to put *himself* into the story, however transmogrified. Be that as may, what he'd done was what he'd done; he couldn't chuck the thing now without turning his back on Scheherazade, and that he would never do.

Nothing happened. Dinner proceeded. Djean himself could not attend Kitty Hawk Eleven, as the ASPS conference was called; he planned to spend that weekend at his word processor, searching for Scher's return ticket. Shmah hadn't planned to go, but began to think she might, if she could find a ride. I invited her to come with us: I was flying down with a friend who has her own plane. At the end of the evening, Scheherazade thanked Mister and Missus Djean for their kindness and declared again that Djean's responsibility for her predicament was no greater than her own. Then she took from her wrist a terrific gold bracelet set with gem-stones and gave it to Shmah by way of special thanks for her understanding and her hospitality. The bracelet was the work of Shahryar's chief gold-smith, she said, and the stones were opals, sapphires, and carnelians. The king had given it to her on Night Two Hundred Sixty-seven, when she went into labor with their first child: The opals stood for fertility; the sapphires and carnelians insured a safe delivery. She hoped Shmah would have good use of the bracelet's powers someday, as she had had.

Yes, well, said Missus Djean: It's a knockout, all right. But I only analyze, remember? Neither conception nor delivery is in my line. She accepted the gift, which really was a magnificent piece of work, but she wouldn't put it on her arm. She would safekeep it, she said; if things worked out in Kitty Hawk and Scheherazade took off for home, she would prize the bracelet as a souvenir of her visit with them. Otherwise, when Scher's little bank account ran dry she'd arrange to sell the bracelet and deposit the proceeds in that account.

All "effort," Scheherazade reported to her listeners; no dramaturgical work. In the week after that dinner meeting, she and May Jump became close friends. Scheherazade was able to help with the thousand and one details of the conference arrangements, and on the Friday, which happened to be Columbus Day, Shmah joined them for the flight from Annapolis down to Kitty Hawk. Now Scheherazade learned how Sindbad must have felt, carried aloft by Roc! More frightened than she'd been aboard Djean's sailboat, she was at the same time as exhilarated as if truly carpet-borne. The Bay below spread out like the map on Djean's study wall: In her free-speaking way, Shmah had called it the Vagina of Virginia, or the next thing to it, and had demonstrated what she meant by comparing that map of the Chesapeake to Figure 570 of Gray's *Anatomy*. The little plane rose higher, over yet other waters and along the seacoast, climbing for the sake of the view to the very limits of its safe altitude; the pilot then brought it down in one terrifying swoop—much enjoyed by all except Scheherazade—to the sandy birthplace of powered flight itself, where the ASPS were assembling in their multitudes.

But though she had flown faster than any wind (Scheherazade would tell them presently), covering two hundred miles in less time than it takes to relate her story thus far, that story moved forward not an inch: She was as solid there on the dunes of Kitty Hawk as she'd been in the cockpit of Djean's boat. Effort, but not work; motion, but not progress. She would have despaired, but for May Jump's confidence in the ASPS and Shmah's in Djean. They walked the dunes and beach together; her friends spoke of the evolution of flying machines from Leonardo da Vinci through the brothers Wright to great rockets that will more likely destroy the Earth than carry people to the stars. As Scheherazade listened, shaking her head at such progress, she idly picked up souvenirs: seashells from the beach, a sea-bird feather from the dunes. Djean had urged her to keep him posted, and so she literally did: To show the ASPS how writing was done in her PTOR, she sharpened the feather into a quill, and on a picture postcard of the Wright Brothers Memorial she wrote in Arabic *Much glorious motion, dear fellow prisoner, but as yet no progress.* Below this inscription she drew the curve of her flight: that low, flat glide over his home waters; the slow, exhilarating climb; the precipitous descent and last-minute landing. She then asked Shmah to take the feather (which May Jump identified as an osprey's) and a single small shell (which Shmah identified as a kind of sea snail's, called the oyster drill) back to Djean at the conference's end, without explanation. To her, the feather stood for high-flying effort that accomplishes no work; the shell, their mutual hope of real progress even if at a snail's pace. But let him figure them out.

What happened next? Nothing. All that evening and next morning, more ASPS arrived; before their first plenary session on the Saturday evening, they foregathered in small, shifting groups to swap songs and stories. They were mostly women, Scheherazade observed, though a substantial minority were men. They were of diverse races—not, apparently, including hers: The ones called Indians, as they themselves made clear, were miscalled. Their costumes were even more various than their skins, and their stories more various than their costumes. She began rather to hope that she would not disappear at once.

That evening, after sundry preliminaries, May Jump publicly introduced her, declaring that even as they wondered how Scheherazade got to Kitty Hawk, North Carolina, *she* was wondering how to get back home to *The Thousand Nights and a Night:* an unfinished tale whose telling May would leave to its principal character at evening's end. On with the stories!

There followed a grand narrative hoedown on Kill Devil Hill itself, governed by the ASPS's conference-competition procedure. The public address system was plugged into an automatic timer; each storyteller was given one minute of introduction by May Jump and nine minutes to tell or sing a story. At the end of that time, a bell rang, the microphone clicked off, and the next teller came onstage: six tellers an hour for two hours. Some were cut off in mid-denouement; others told two or three quick ones and had time left over. The best came right down to the wire; the winner, by acclamation, told a story about the winning story in a storytelling contest, whose final word and punch line, delivered exactly on the beat, was the sound of the timer's *ding*.

Then all hands called for the timer to be disconnected so that Scheherazade could tell her story. But that lady (who had borrowed Shmah's TKTTTİT-shirt for this occasion) reminded them that throughout her narrative career she had told against time, one eye ever upon the king, one upon the bedroom window for the first sign of dawn's early light. She'd feel more at home, she declared, with the timer running, and home was where she hoped her tale would take her. A full two hours, then, May proposed. No? An hour at least! Make it fifty minutes, said Scheherazade.

She then told a version of Djean's Key-to-the-Treasure story: the secret history of *The 1001 Nights.* In her telling, the tale divided into three parts, each shorter than the one before, in a certain proportion: The first set forth, in half an hour, the reign of terror in Shahryar's kingdom; Scheherazade's dilemma; the Genie's magical visitation, and his proposal to assist her by reading to her, each afternoon, her story-of-the-evening. The second (in twenty minutes) carried forth that program through the story of Ma'aruf the Cobbler and his wife Fatimah the Turd; the Genie's announcement that that was the last story in his edition of the *Nights;* and Scheherazade's consternation at that news—compounded by unmistakable signs of her impending first second menstruation and her realizing that she was not pregnant again on schedule, as she had assumed she would be. Part Three of the story would have taken exactly ten minutes to tell—but at the very period of Part Two, as Scheherazade had planned, the timer rang, the microphone went dead, and, though she was a Muslim, she bowed to her audience Hindu-style, her palms pressed together as if in prayer.

Such applause! May Jump reported. If any were skeptical of their guest's identity, their skepticism no longer mattered to them: If she was not who she said she was, she deserved to be! Scheherazade's hope had been that they would demand the story's continuation tomorrow, like Shahryar in years gone by, so that she could wind it up in her first ten minutes and launch into the one that mattered: WYDIWYD, the Genie's second round of visits (she had a version that would spare Shmah's feelings), and her inadvertent transportation to late-twentieth-century America. But these were the ASPS, not a sleepy sultan: All Sunday morning she heard them, in their little groups, working over her Story Thus Far, and that afternoon, at the rate of six per hour for a full three hours, she was presented with one-and-a-half-dozen endings to it. Several she liked even better than the truth (which also turned up in a couple of versions); at least one she thought not inferior to Djean's own, in which the Genie himself simply steps onstage and makes a brief, affectionate farewell to her and Dunyazade, concluding with the maxim *The* key *to the treasure* is *the treasure.*

That evening, in the first ten minutes of her allotted fifty, she thanked the ASPS for their ingenious efforts and declared that inasmuch as they were convened not to confess life histories but to tell stories, she would not disclose which of their endings happened to be the "true" one. What difference would that disclosure make? Nor would she presume to judge which was the "best," dramaturgically speaking (though like any storyteller, she had her opinion), since in this case nothing followed from that accolade.

But tonight, my friends, she declared, much follows indeed. My life is not on the line, as in nights past, but my happiness, perhaps even my sanity, depends upon my finding exactly the right ending for an unfinished story that you see suspended before your eyes. I pray to Allah that one of you will hit upon that ending, so that I can return to the order of reality I recklessly forsook in pursuit of further stories. Never since my first night with Shahryar have I felt the stakes so high. But whereas if the king had been able to end that first story of mine for himself, I'd have been lost, now I shall be lost if you *cannot* end this one for yourselves and for me.

Turning upon her wrist the gold-and-gemstone bracelet that Shmah had insisted she borrow back for the successful delivery of her story, Scheherazade here unzipped her hooded sweatshirt to display the new orange T-shirt beneath and launched into its legend, WYDIWYD: her change-of-life restlessness; her yearning for a voyage of some certain special kind. Her unsatisfying visit to Samarkand (at considerable expense to the dramaturgical integrity of her tale, she made no mention of her Month of Mondays with the Genie), which issued in Dunyazade's dismal dictum. Her mulling upon those words, and her sudden transmigration to Genieland, USA. Her expectation of returning after the customary fifty minutes and of revisiting for the same period at sundown on a series of Fridays thereafter—perhaps weekly for a while, perhaps once or twice a month—to carry home with her more stories from and about this world.

She glanced at the timer: fifteen minutes to go. Her finding herself stranded here, and her growing alarm that WYDIWYD might prove a one-way ticket. The Genie's confession and hypothesis: that she is a prisoner of dramaturgy. His thus far vain attempts to unlock that prison, for all their sakes, with the aid of his word machine . . .

Five minutes left. Her move to Annapolis and alliance with May Jump, to whom she rehearsed her whole story thus far. Their hope—desperate now on Scheherazade's part—that the ASPS assembled might be able to accomplish what neither she nor Djean nor the society's executive secretary had been able to. She spoke faster: her decision not to take what would perhaps have been the more prudent course of telling them this story all at once, yesterday, to give them time to ponder it, but rather to bet all her chips on dramaturgy, dramaturgy, by coming to the end of her Story Thus Far exactly-at-the-moment-when-the-past-overtakes-the-present-*ding*.

Ding?

May Jump put down the old guitar with which she'd been strumming an occasional soundtrack to this tale. High G is as close as my Gibson girl can come to it, she declared.

Damn, I wish I hadn't missed that conference! Katherine pinged her middle finger at Wear and Tear, who were, however, sound asleep. You guys had better be worth it. It must've really been something else to see the woman go Bingo right before your eyes!

Lee Talbott agreed: Frank and I have got to join that outfit. I've made up our mind.

Carla B Silver puckered her black brows. Captain Donald Quicksoat fingered his beard. Peter Sagamore said Hum.

That's right, Mister Sagamore. May patted our children. The lock on the door of the prison of dramaturgy is not to be picked with Technicolorful gizmos and distractions. Babies aren't brought by storks, and denouements don't come from automatic timers. That dinger dinged; the dune fell silent on both sides of the microphone—but Queen Scher was just as much with us as before. I happened to be standing just beside and behind her, and sorry as I'd have been to lose my famous new friend, I was sorrier yet to see her still there. I put a hand on her shoulder and said Hold on, babe; maybe it takes a second or two, like satellite transmissions. We're all with you.

But after a *very* long minute we were indeed all too much with her, and she with us. Her shoulder under my hand was as solid as my hand on her shoulder. The tears came then, from more than one pair of eyes, and I got her off that podium.

There ended Kitty Hawk Eleven. The ASPS dispersed, with many a headshake, handshake, and murmur. Plenty of *them,* like Princess Kiss here, thought the moment had been A-plus; they'd been on the edge of their dunes when that dinger dang. They promised to keep on trying, telling Scher's story around the republic till somebody hit the jackpot. Most of them headed out that same night, in their campers and cars and pickup trucks. Shmah said good-bye to us and caught a ride home with a group headed over the bridge-tunnel to Cape Charles and the Eastern Shore; she promised to explain the feather and the shell to her husband if he couldn't figure them out for himself. Scher was too wrought up to remember to give her back the bracelet, and neither Shmah nor I had the heart to remind her.

That night, my friends, I held one mighty unhappy lady in my arms, and hoped every time I woke up that I'd find myself in bed alone; but such good bad luck was not to be. On the Monday morning, all the stragglers went their ways, as we-all here will do *mañana*. Scher and my pilot friend and I hung around to clean up the loose ends of the conference. A few others pitched in: some who were going on with late beach-vacations on the Outer Banks; one or two new or prospective members still auditioning for their green belts or just reluctant to let the story go. While we cleaned up camp, they tried farther-and-farther-fetched endings, hoping they might just score and see Scheherazade disappear before their eyes.

But she didn't. Toward lunchtime, the work was done, and we joined the handful of diehards at the monument on Kill Devil Hill. They were telling along, naturally, and I hoped a few good stories might distract Scher from her problems. They were tactful enough to lay off *her* story for that last hour together, but her example had inspired them to a clutch of stories about other travelers out of time. The fellow just then holding forth claimed to have met Odysseus the sailorman and his mate Nausicaa sailing up the Intracoastal Waterway, which they said they'd reached by crossing the Atlantic east to west so fast that time went backward and then stood still. Like Scheherazade, they were stuck in an everlasting Now, and they'd been stuck in it for three thousand years. But luckier than she, they were shipmates in an endless summer, where Limbo is just the name of a Caribbean dance.

Sit tight there, Sagamores. The teller of this tall tale then declared himself to be another such traveler out of fiction into fact: not so young as Odysseus, and not so lucky as to have Nausicaa for a shipmate. Matter of fact, he hadn't started out as a sailor at all, though he'd ended up as one. Like our friend Scheherazade, but a lot less urgently, he was looking for the way back to where he came from: not a key, in his case, but a dangling line. . . .

And that, declared Captain Donald Quicksoat, is as far as I got, mates, 'cause at that moment a bright orange T-shirt and a jeweled gold bracelet fell kerplop into the sandy middle of our circle. We all turned 'round to see what was up; whether our famous unlucky visitor had decided to hell with it and was shucking her duds for a swim. *Perdóneme* for interrupting, Miss May.

De nada y pues nada, said May Jump, which is what this story comes to. Scher had been standing beside me, wiping her eyes with the neckband of her T-shirt, and then she stepped a step behind me, not to distract Mister Capn Don here from his story with her sniffling. Just as I was turning to put my arm around her, the shirt and bracelet dropped out of the sky, so it seemed. Where was Miz Scher? Gone into thin air. Not faded, as we'd first expected and later hoped, but blinked out like a soap bubble. Not even a poof or a click! Presumably topless, presumably back with her husband and family in the Islands of India and China. But since nobody we know of has heard a word from her since, who can say?

I hung around Kitty Hawk for as long as I could that afternoon, until my pilot friend flew me home to Annapolis: one sad executive secretary. Capn Don Q., I'm told, took his new green belt back to his boat and made his way down the ICW. Not so long ago, I gave that orange T-shirt to Marian Silver, to pick her up when she was down, and I found that it must've changed sizes in flight: It had fit Scher like a second skin, and she was a trim enough little number, but as has been seen, it's *way* too big for our Miss Mims. The bracelet Miz Djean told me I should keep, since I'd been closer to the Prisoner of Dramaturgy than she'd been. *Her* souvenir of *l'affaire* Scher was her husband, thank you—who she said had put aside his fancy word-machine and gone back to his faithful though leaky fountain pen, but was otherwise mum on this whole subject.

And that, comrades, is the end of the unfinished story of Scheherazade's unfinished story. No questions, yes? 'Cause I've got no answers.

Whoa, now! complained four of the six of us who still sat up (Irm Sherritt and Joan Bass had reluctantly packed it in just before Kitty Hawk; Donald Quicksoat had been there, and Carla B Silver seemed privy to the tale). Late as was the hour, we couldn't quite let go of a story so undone. No one actually saw the woman disappear?

Nadie, said Capn Don. She couldn't have faded, Q.E.D. She couldn't have peeled off her shirt and bracelet and run away, or we'd've seen her. We say she blinked out like a light, but nobody saw it happen or heard a sound, except the plick of that bracelet on the sand and the pfft of that T-shirt fluttering down. They *dropped down,* you understand: as if she'd thrown them over our heads or lifted off like Wilbur and Orville when she went.

Protests disgruntled Peter That prisoner of dramaturgy wasn't released; she broke jail. If that ding wasn't enough to spring her, that pfft of an ending never would have. Some ASP on the way back home to Appalachia must have hit the right ending at just that moment.

We don't know for sure she's back where she came from, Lee Talbott reminded us, and her husband said Maybe she's waiting for Capn Don in the Cave of Montesinos.

If I ever get back there, C.D.Q. promised, I'll send a postcard. I don't like an unfinished story any more'n you do.

I'll tell you what Carla B Silver thinks, that lady declared. If we all agree that the story as is—or the lady as isn't—is as whatyoucallumly unfinished as a story can be, then maybe the woman didn't really disappear. Maybe she only *appeared* to disappear.

Yes! said Katherine Sherritt Sagamore. She changed persons the way her shirt changed sizes. She turned into Maisie Jump, and by Allah, we won't let her go till we've heard the end of her story!

Grinned May Don't count on it, Kisserino.

Peter Sagamore seconded his wife's first proposition. As to the second, however—for Katherine's sake, mainly, but for his sleepy own as well—he asked When did Scheherazade ever finish a story the same night she began it? Tomorrow, friends, tomorrow.

Do not count upon it, May Jump rewarned, and we dispersed to our several dreams.

NOW IT'S TOMORROW: TODAY,

well into the forenoon of Sunday, Day 14, which we reckon to be Day 266± a couple. P closes these log-notes with May's injunction, goes over certain passages of his other manuscript once more, tucks it into the orange distress-flare canister he has earlier emptied for this purpose, tucks the canister under his arm, and sticks his head into the other world, the real one, to see whether Step 'n' Fetchit have turned into Get Up and Go.

No. There being no wind, Chip Sherritt has rigged his Windsurfer on a long line off *Katydid IV*'s fat transom to give Simon Silver Lesson One: how to stand up on the thing and pull the rig out of the water without capsizing. Sy's doing badly and much enjoying himself, loudly encouraged by May Jump and Katherine Sherritt in the Boston Whaler, Chip in the water, and the crew of *Katydid* here and there. Splash! he goes again, copper bracelet and all, and May calls Yay for Simon! and he laughs with them as he clambers walruslike to try again.

Well, now, thinks Peter.

From above and to his right (*K IV*'s high awninged cockpit), his mother-in-law says Look who's come up for air. From behind and to his left (*Reprise*'s awninged cabin top), Lee Talbott says There he blows; get a line on him before he sounds. Kath hears all such references to Peter as a mother hears her baby's breath; she turns her paisleyed head *Story*ward and lights up.

P taps his wristwatch; raises the Alert-and-Locate canister in his left hand; removes the borrowed *boina* and crowns the canister therewith; points to *Reprise*'s cockpit. All concerned parties get the message.

But first go say good-bye to Captain Donald, Katherine instructs him across the water. He and Mim Silver are ready to leave, but he waited for you.

He and Mim Silver?

Says Franklin Key Talbott We'll explain. Go on over—and then come back fast.

What they'll explain, presently, is that while Peter scratched and scribbled, and Frank/Sy/Captain Donald overhauled the Talbotts' anchor windlass, and others of our raft pursued other pleasures through the sticky morning, significant crew-changes were worked out between *Reprise* and *Rocinante IV*. Though Carla B Silver and Donald Quicksoat understood themselves to be no longer a couple, they were still friends; Capn Don had assumed, over pawls and springs and ratchets, that he'd be ferrying her back to Middle River and Baltimore, where he'd ferried her from— and Simon with her, for the general peace—after which, at his leisure but not long hence, he would bid them all *hasta la vista* and head on up the "D and C" Canal, as it lately pleased him to call it, in pursuit of his legendary and missing *amigos*. Marian Silver, still pouting about last night's ruckus, three-quarters wanted to go with them, rather than back with rejected May to Annapolis to pack up her and Sy's things for moving to Fells Point; her fourth quarter busily nursed that grudge against the child she had once nursed.

No problem, May Jump volunteered: Let Frank and Lee drop her off at Kent Narrows to collect her car and go home alone. Let Maid Marian go back to Baltimore on *Rocinante* with her mother and her son, and come down when she pleased to retrieve her stuff and Sy's. She was going to miss them, all right; she'd had big plans, no doubt cockeyed ones. But what she'll do is what she'll do. Don't worry 'bout May.

Me, said Capn Don, I keep my stuff with me; that way I don't have to go back and retrieve it when the story's over. Only things *he* ever left behind, he said, were Sancho Panza and the last three *Rocinante*s; only thing he'd consider going back for is a certain rope in a certain cave.

May Jump agreed: Traveling light is traveling right. Maybe she'd just let her old Volvo rust there on Kent Island and hitch a ride with him up the ICW. Swap a few lies? Play Sancho to his C.D.Q.? Declared Captain Donald *Rocinante Cuatro* is a nag you'll never be unwelcome on. Then added gallantly But you've got more knight than squire in you, says I.

Damn straight, and enough of this, then objected Carla B Silver and Leah and Franklin Talbott, with Katherine Sherritt's strong silent second: The tail of solicitude, it seemed to them, was wagging the dog of common decency. Sy Silver's feelings, made explosively plain last night, are of course important; meshuga Marian's are not to be disregarded, either. But good May Jump must not be treated so cavalierly! Miss Mim will damned well go home the way she came (her mother, sister, and brother-in-law resolved as one); Simon too: to Annapolis, damned well behaving themselves en route, and will pack their own duffels and move themselves out of May's apartment pronto, if that's the way things stand. No jumping ship in this raft on such ungenerous grounds! Well, considered Carla, but perhaps she'd go with them, as insulator and supervisor, if *Reprise* could hold them all and if Capn Don didn't mind going it alone—whether back to Carla's Cavern or on his way. To hell with rushing home to Fells Point in time to open shop tomorrow: Let the winos miss a Monday. Let'm miss a month of Mondays! Okay, May?

Well: Frank Talbott had been about to propose, only half jokingly, that Marian Silver keep May Jump's apartment and May and Sy move in with Carla to help her run the Cavern (Simon, by the way, has properly apologized to May this morning, and sincerely: His mother's final rejection of him seems to have cured his animosity in that quarter. In his grandma's company he likes May fine; he now directs his grievance toward his aggrieved mother only). You following us, Peter? Simon's being bigger about things than Mim, who really wants to get the fuck away from Tidewaterland and head for parts unknown with . . . somebody new, however old.

At about this point—mid-morning, maybe, windlass reassembled and Sy off splashing with Andrew Sherritt—Señor Capitán Donaldo Quicksoat said Shit, *amigos,* here's how we'll do it: You folks go down to Annapolis and square things away—Carlissima included, who can oil anybody's troubled waters. I sail this tub back to Baltimore solo, as is my custom. I open the old Cavern for business as usual tomorrow morning and mind the store till all smoke's cleared and all bags are packed. After which, *adiós*: say, Wednesday?

At which proposal Marian Silver then mustered enough something to declare, surprisingly, she was going with him. She could run the kitchen again—as she had in fact done with some competence till Lascar Lupescu put his Rumanian paws in her pants while she was scrubbing mussels—and Mister Captain Don could run the bar, and obviously Sy's happier with his grandmother and even with May Jump nowadays than he is with his mother.

You know, doll? here said May: That is not a half-bad proposal you just proposed there. C. B Silver gave her younger daughter and her weekend's date one lengthy look-over. Poker-faced Quicksoat shrugged, but reminded all hands that he really was going to weigh anchor within the week, aurora-borealisward, as soon as he located his fellow migrants.

To her parents and the Basses, to whom communiqués of this casuistry were from time to time relayed, Katherine Sherritt remarked Bit of an education for you folks, no? Come come, said Doctor Jack Bass: We obstetricians weren't born yesterday. Added Joan Your mom and I were just debating whether to swap husbands or run off to Key West together, just she and I. All in all, said Irma, I find the soaps more interesting. And Hank, disappointedly, We just got word from Willy that their chopper's down for service and he can't get here till five, five-thirty. Shall we cancel the granary show or just postpone it?

No reason to cancel, they decided. With no breeze for sailing and no place to get to in a hurry, they'd as well stay put: read, swim, and play bridge till cocktail and granary-presentation time; then move up to Georgetown for dinner ashore in the cool of the evening—after which et cetera, as we Sagamores had agreed.

Says Peter Mm hm, and, all this exposition assimilated, crosses *K IV* to bid *buen viaje* to a curious character indeed.

BUEN VIAJE,

he bids, hunkering amidships on his in-laws' portside gunwale and stretching out a hand to the skipper of *Rocinante IV*. Her old diesel's puttering, her lines are singled up, her new crew stands fetchingly at the tiller in crotch-cleaving shorts and a fresh T-shirt whose legend—OVAL RIGHTS!—Pete's not even going to ask her about. Her lank-leather captain steps aft from coiling a bow line to take our man's hand, squint smiling up, and say Good voyage to you too, pal, and to yours.

You have a new crew. P waves his left-hand fingers at Marian, who wanly smiles and adjusts a silvered spike of her hair. His right is retained by Donald Quicksoat, who acknowledges I do. Durn near as nifty as her ma.

You can't hang around for the obstetrical punch line?

Still squeezing Peter's hand, C.D.Q. shakes his head. As I understand it, that line could still be two weeks off delivery. I hope to be in Nantucket by then, with Queequeg and my other buddies.

Thinks P We're never going to know for sure about this hombre. And it occurs to him we'd sort of forgotten that by golly those EDCs *are* ±two weeks—even though, in K's case, more likely minus than plus. Two more weeks!

His hand is still gripped. It's a four-, five-hour motor ride from here to Middle River, Capn Don is remarking, and your usual *tronadas Chesa-*

peakas are on the evening menu. So off we go. How old did you say you are, boy?

Startled Peter Sagamore answers Thirty-nine years and nine months. Plus or minus two weeks.

Donald Quicksoat nods and squints. And how long is it old Menos Es Más has had you by the scrotum?

Oh, a dozen years. Thirteen. Seven. But I have an idea that particular dwarf is losing his grip.

Captain Donald does not loosen his. Listen, lad, he says, almost confidentially: Break his hold on you, but *keep your hold on him,* is my advice. You worry maybe you're *terminado* at forty? Maybe you are. Or it could be you're just astray in the funhouse and taking the long way home.

He is not done. Me and Alonso Quijano, he declares, didn't know who the fuck we were till fifty-plus, and our author didn't find out who *he* was till he found out who *we* were. *Cincuenta y ocho,* my friend, when he published Part One! Think about that. And ten years older yet when he published Part Two! Up till then it had all been diddling around.

He is not done, though Peter nods acknowledgment. *Paciencia,* the old man says, in perfect Castilian: Very possibly the world'll go bang; prob'ly it won't. Prob'ly you won't *ever* do anything really world-class, but very possibly you will. Not many blokes can say that.

He actually said blokes, awed Peter will report to Katherine Sherritt presently. *Y paciencia, paciencia.* Eat yer spinach, he told me. Lose not thy nerve. And *keep your hold*—but relax your grip, once you've broken Its. Yer prob'ly choking up Miz Kate's delivery!

He said *that?* will wonder Kath. Verfuckingbatim, will swear Peter, more or less. All those mixed-up "yers" and "thys"—the Delphic oracle as Popeye the Sailor. Plus *Hasta la vista,* pal: Here's to lead in yer keel and yer pencil, but not in yer ass and yer gas tank. You're welcome to raft up with Huck and me and Capn O. D. Seus anywhere you find us, from Belize to Halifax. As for that landlubber Scheherazade, he says, wherever she may be: She'll lay her mitzvahs and baruchas on you in personal private, I daresay, ere this tale is told. So cast off my breastline, bub, he says, there's a good hombre, and off I chug—get this—all Mimsied, to Fells incensèd Point. Mighty apposite, hey? Back to Montesinos, via, you know, *una otra cuevita de Carlita.*

SEX ED

¡*Una otra cuevita!* growls C. B Silver in *Reprise*'s cockpit when this mighty *buen viaje* is retold: Watch if I don't cold-cock that horny old buzzard.

To Fells incensèd Point, mighty apposite? Lee Talbott giggles, and that is no easy line to giggle.

All Mimsied? marvels Frank, thinking also of J. A. Paisley's *Brillig*.

Wonders Katherine, in her turn, Mitzvahs and baruchas from Scheherazade? And your grip is choking up my delivery?

For that matter, puts in Peter—crossing his heart that he has reasonably approximated that long handclasped farewell—Oval Rights?

Oh, those, says Lee. Mims was going to have it say "Ovarian," but it's the eggs she's lobbying for, not the organs. I asked her Aren't the sperm entitled? and she said Write your own T-shirt.

The sisters had kissed each other good-bye and exchanged some private sororal sentences. I know you're going to ball him, Lee had said to Marian; won't you feel creepy, when he's just been balling Ma? I can handle that, Mim declared: It's not much more than a ride home, and Ma and May together'll be terrific for Sy. Together? They're not *together,* Mims! They will be, Marian had calmly predicted, and then suddenly embraced her sister. I'm finished, Lee; I'm just too tired of it. As *Rocinante IV* pulled away from the raft, she waved faintly at her son in the water, who waved faintly back; she blew a kiss to Lee and to head-shaking Carla; even to May Jump, who by now seems more bemused than hurt at the weekend's sorting out.

Astonishing, how Sy's hostility has dissolved in this new solution! He and May Jump and Chip Sherritt are now porpoising all about the rafted boats. Henry Sherritt and Jack Bass are experimenting with the Windsurfer. Carla B Silver guesses she'll go talk dreams and do Tarot cards with Irma Sherritt and Joan Bass, as she sometime promised, after which another joint lunch project will be mounted. *Rocinante IV* turns Ordinary Point and heads Bayward, Marian Silver at the tiller with Captain Donald Quicksoat standing close by to instruct.

Well.

Frank Talbott says to Peter Sagamore Would you kindly unscrew Act Three now, boss? We're on tenterhooks.

Okay. Peter unhats the canister, hands Franklin Key Talbott his *boina* back (Frank accepts it, but does not yet put it on), and tells Carla B Silver that she and May Jump are welcome to audit the contents, though they haven't read Acts One and Two of Frank Talbott's abortive seminal television script.

Says Carla I'll pass, and kisses each of the four of us atop his/her head before climbing over *Story* to *Katydid IV*. I know how it ends.

May Jump, though, accepts our invitation, leaves Simon and Chip to their play (they're aboard *Story* now, taking turns diving off our bowsprit), climbs aboard *Reprise,* wraps her sturdy tanksuited body in a striped beach towel, and waives synopsis of the drama thus far. No reflection on you, she assures Frank Talbott: If you did your job and Pete's done his, any black belt worth her sash can fill in the blanks.

Remarks Katherine Sherritt, against whose side her solid old friend and coach has damply snugged, I've hardly said a word in this chapter, and yet I bet I'm the only one here who knows what literal tenterhooks are.

She is, too.
Reads Peter

ACT III: THE COVE,
OR,
SEX EDUCATION.

Here's the opening stage-direction, in italics:

(We are yet farther downstream, a short while later. The waters here are open, devoid of "boulders," islands," and the like, as well as of waves. In the near distance, the MAIN BODY OF SWIMMERS *can be heard still passing.* JUNE *and her* SWIMMER *friend swim into view, doing a sort of sidestroke:* JUNE's *legs are locked about the* SWIMMER's *chest; her envelope provides their main flotation, and she steers them both with movements of her arms and upper body. The* SWIMMER *propels them with his arms, legs, and tail. The remains of* MAY's *paisley envelope, knotted around his waist, provide some additional small flotation.)*

Lee Talbott explains to May Jump that this May is a Floater from the Left Ovarium who died in Act Two.

She didn't necessarily *die,* Frank reminds her. She got gang-fused, is all. It was a diversionary tactic, to protect her friend June.

Was I asking? asks May Jump. Black belts don't ask; they *infer.*

Sorry.

I forgot to mention, Peter says offhandedly: I can't do plays, so I wrote this as a dialogue without a real narrator. The Swimmer guy adjusts his eyeglasses with one hand and says in a loud whisper Sideways! A touch more to starboard, if you can.

June says Like this?

Swimmer says Perfect.

June says That's two *twenty* magnetic. You said two ten.

Remarks May Jump The current, dummy. Says Peter, glancing over at her with professional respect, the Swimmer says We have to allow for the current. . . . You should see a low breakwater, too, with a flashing light.

I see it! says June: Dead ahead. Thank goodness!

We can thank May's goodness, says the Swimmer.

My pleasure, Kiss, says May Jump, giving Katherine a small hug. K sighs I'll never be black belt. Presses Peter June says Poor May!

They reach the breakwater, indistinguishable from a "real" one. Swimmer says We go over it. June says We can't get over that!

Sure they can, declares Frank Talbott, taking his wife's hand. Peter nods approval; Lee Talbott too.

Together we can, says the Swimmer: Here we go, now: one, two . . . *up!* June catches her breath as the Swimmer, with a mighty thrust, propels them both up onto the narrow wall, where they rest, disconnected. Both are spent. Several Random Swimmers from the margins of the Main Body pass by, too intent upon swimming upstream to notice them. In a loud whisper, June says Can we go on?

The Swimmer adjusts his glasses wearily. Sure. We have one nasty little whirlpool to get around. . . . See it, over there?

Dear God.

Leave it *very* close to port, the Swimmer tells her: Its current will give us a boost toward the cove. He points farther right. If we go too far to starboard of it, we get swept back by the countercurrent. He smiles at June. Scylla-and-Charybdis sort of thing, you know?

June nods. Katherine can't help explaining to May Jump This is all taking place in somebody's uterus. They say things they don't know how they know. May places a vertical finger upon her friend's lips. K groans Sorry.

June says I sure can see your whirlpool, but I don't see any cove.

The Swimmer points: Just beyond it; two ten on the button. Look here now, he says in a businesslike tone: If you feel us going *into* that whirlpool, you're to kick free and make for the cove by yourself. You can swim that far alone, and you'll be absolutely safe there. Here we go.

June does not acknowledge this final directive. They link up as before, slide off the far side of the breakwater, and stroke toward the maelstrom.

Farther to port! the Swimmer urges her. June says We'll go under! The Swimmer says But we need the push. . . .

The whirlpool current threatens to draw them under. June cries out. The Swimmer says Kick loose!

She does not let go.

Attagirl, Lee Talbott cheers.

Gripping him firmly with her legs, June rolls over into the crawl-stroke position she invented in Act Two and flails ahead furiously. Push, damn it; *push!* she hollers at the Swimmer. Harder! You can do it!

Katherine squeezes Peter's forearm.

Face down in the water, the Swimmer manages a few final, grunting thrusts of his legs and tail, and they are out of the whirlpool. He then hangs on, exhausted, as June, aided now by the favorable current, both propels and steers them. After a while she says I can see our cove!

The Swimmer very weakly says Swim on along, then. I'll follow after a bit. He slips her legs free of him; June collars him in a lifesaving hold with her left arm. Come *on,* now! Onward and sideways!

One last tail-thrust from the Swimmer, though his eyes are closed and his arms limp; one last sidestroke from June; and they haul up onto a deserted strand, fall exhausted upon it side by side, and lie half in the water and half out.

Ordinary Point, predicts K.

Carlita's *otra cuevita,* predicts Lee.

Sherritt's Cove, predicts May Jump, smiling at Katherine's lap.

Somewhile later, June's eyes open. She stirs, disengages herself demurely from the Swimmer, and sits up. He wakes and does likewise, clearly reluctant to let go of her. She looks about; the Swimmer looks at her.

June picks up a stick of driftwood nearby and says huskily Well. She stands, wrings out her hair and envelope. I'll scrounge up some more of this for a campfire, and we'll look for something to eat.

Little Goody Two-Tits down to the wire, May Jump teases. Protests Kate This is Franklin Key Talbott's play, not ours. June was like that when Frank hardly knew us. Smiles Peter If the T-shirt fits, et cet, and reads on:

The Swimmer reluctantly rises, brushing sand and water from himself: Later, okay? June looks at him sharply.

So does Katherine Sherritt, says Kath.

He smiles and says It might be unwise to build a fire until the rest of the Main Body swims past. One or two Swimmers are bound to stray in here as it is.

What do we do when that happens?

The Swimmer shrugs at that unpleasant prospect. We . . . deal with them, he says, before they can deal with us. Let's climb this bank and see whether any of those trees are whatyoucallums . . . fruit trees.

Fruit trees, June says after him. The meaning dawns on her; she touches his shoulder. Oranges! Apples!

Pomegranates, says May Jump.

The Swimmer laughs, nods: Breadfruit! Coconuts! We'll be regular Robinson Crusoes!

June laughs with him. Bananas! I'm dying for a banana!

Let's find you a banana, says the Swimmer.

Frank Talbott puts the *boina* firmly upon his head and says I'm going to cut that line, Pete. Lee Talbott kisses that *boina*. Peter Sagamore looks up at him, grins, reads on:

As they scramble up the low sandy bank toward the grove of trees, the sound of the Main Body of Swimmers increases. June and the Swimmer pause and look soberly out over the water they've just emerged from.

June says I can't believe we covered all that distance!

The Swimmer's still admiring her. We're a long way from where we started, he says.

June shades her eyes. It's so bright now!

Swimmer says There's to be a full moon, isn't there? That's your department.

June nods. Shivers. It was warmer out there than here.

Use this. The Swimmer takes May's paisley envelope from his waist and drapes it about June's shoulders.

May Jump ceremoniously acts out this direction. Kath lifts a corner of the beach towel to her lips.

June touches a corner of it to her lips, reads Peter, then to her eyes, and shivers again as the sound of the Main Body increases. Poor May! June says: Brave May!

May shmay, says May Jump: On with the story.

The Swimmer shakes his head: That *can't* be the way it's supposed to be. Then his eyes narrow as he observes and hears his own kind dying en masse in the distance. But who knows how anything is supposed to be? Look at *those* poor devils going under.

Appalled, they forget their errand and themselves. As before, there are multitudinous confused male shouts, whistles, drinking songs, martial commands, cries for help. So many! June says.

At a far-off male scream, her eyes widen. The Swimmer briefly covers his own eyes and touches her arm as if for moral support. June flinches, then takes his hand. They watch and listen.

June says Why do they *do* that to one another?

The Swimmer shakes his head. God knows why, when they'll soon drown anyhow. What they're doing is what they've always done.

June turns away and says I've lost my appetite. Swimmer says Me too, and then Uh-oh. He has glanced back down toward the sandspit where they beached, just below them.

Nick of time, observes May Jump. Frank Talbott nods agreement. Bets Katherine Interloper, right? May pats her knee. Reads Peter A stray Random Swimmer, the First Interloper, is wearily hauling himself ashore. Over his wet-suit he wears a club necktie and two-thirds of a three-piece business suit: the jacket and vest. He carries a slim leather attaché case.

Lee Talbott claps her hands. Okay!

Leaving June where she stands, the Swimmer springs upon the newcomer, who is too spent to struggle, and unhesitatingly drowns him in the shallow water. The job is easily done, but it leaves the Swimmer retching. June joins him where he kneels in the shallows beside the drowned one. She touches her friend's shoulder; thumps him lightly on the back to help him recover.

I'm all right now, the Swimmer says.

Do you have to drown them? K protests. P looks at her levelly and says It says right here that June says Do we have to drown them? Can't we just hide till they leave?

The Swimmer shakes his head and coughs. Once they got their breath, they'd get wind of you and whistle for the whole crowd. There won't be many, and it won't be hard to deal with them, as you saw. You can do it, easily.

June says Me!

Sure, you, says Katherine Sherritt before anyone else. Get your hands messed up. Agrees Lee It's her oval responsibility.

It has to be done, the Swimmer says, but I feel like a traitor doing it.

Okay, says June. But could you sort of stand by?

The Swimmer gestures toward the bank. I'll be right up there, where I can hear you if you call me. Let's get rid of this one.

They push the First Interloper's body out into the current. It drifts away, case still attached.

Peter half glances to see whether Frank Talbott appears troubled by suggestions of his drowned brother. If you can find you can't manage it, he quotes the Swimmer, still speaking to June, or can't stomach it . . .

It's all right, Frank assures him.

Peter nods. The Swimmer pauses, about to climb the bank. On the other hand, he says, it goes without saying that if your Mister Right should swim past. . . .

Oh, him, sniffs Lee.

June frowns. I told you I don't believe that stuff.

There is a splashing nearby. Uh-oh, she says.

Don't be afraid, the Swimmer tells her. Climb up here and jump him.

June's earlier self-confidence returns. I'm not afraid, she says. They both climb the bank. June stands poised to spring upon the newcomer; the Swimmer withdraws just behind her as the splashing comes nearer. But don't go too far, she whispers. Can you hear me?

The Swimmer's voice-off says I can hear you, June.

Now the Second Interloper hauls up into the shallows: a beefy, hairy fellow, rigged out in fancier motorcycle leathers than his predecessor's in Act Two: reflector sunglasses, iron crosses on his crash helmet, even a studded black leather sheath for his tail. But he too is exhausted from the swim: He plops himself wearily down in the shallows, breathing hard, stroking his beard, looking back out to seaward. From a pouch somewhere he draws a can of beer, pops it open, guzzles, burps, sighs . . . and then begins to sniff the air.

We're glad Marian's not here, Lee Talbott observes. It was a guy like that in a van on Fenwick Island that messed her up.

June glances into the trees for reassurance, takes a breath, gathers herself, and, holding May's envelope like a garotte, leaps upon the Interloper from behind, as the Swimmer did earlier, just as he rises to investigate what he has dimly sensed. With a grunt he topples face-forward into the water, holding his beer can high and dry. June straddles his back and throttles him with May's envelope. To the end he holds the can aloft. She waits a few moments till the can, then the hand, fall; then she dismounts, drags the Interloper out into the current, and returns with the empty beer can and May's envelope.

This is getting too violent to be the Saint Deniston senior class play, Katherine remarks. P reads on, undeterred: The Swimmer's voice-off says Good work, June!

Good riddance, says June. She buries the beer can in the sand. That was for May.

You're welcome, Kath says to May Jump. Frank Talbott commends the ecological tidiness of the violence so far: Drowned swimmers are biodegradable, but aluminum beer cans aren't.

The Swimmer says appreciatively You were ferocious!

Says June I was terrified.

Get ready, he warns her: Here comes another one.

June scrambles back into position. This is no fun.

Fun or not, declares May Jump, where there's two interlopers there's got to be three. Predicts Frank Talbott But this one will be a seahorse of yet another color. A tellalong playscript, remarks Katherine: That's pretty front-edge, no?

Says Peter If you want to risk letting them come ashore, the Swimmer says to June, it's your choice. But I hope you won't.

A Third Interloper appears, pulling himself up on the sandspit like his predecessors. But this one is a remarkably handsome fellow: a curly-headed young Adonis wearing only swimtrunks, who, once on his feet, stretches his splendid body and looks about with a radiant, wondering smile.

Good move, all hands agree. P holds up a forefinger:

Poised to leap upon him from her concealment, June is arrested by his beauty; she regards him with astonished admiration, pressing her knuckle against her teeth. Her Swimmer friend steps from the trees behind her; appraising the situation quickly, he tightens his lips and withdraws. The Interloper does a few leisurely, graceful exercises to loosen his tired muscles; he sniffs the air, puzzled, then with a sigh wades back into the shallows. Over his shoulder, he takes a last, quizzical look toward shore (June has stepped behind a tree trunk); then he shrugs and dives wearily back into the swim. June starts out as if to stop him. Her friend soberly watches her.

Mm hm, Frank Talbott says, and turns the *boina* in his hands. Lee gently puts it back upon his head. From the Mainstream, reads Peter, the sound of the Main Body is beginning to diminish. As June still stands in stricken wonderment, a Fourth Interloper staggers toward shore: a puny, obviously frightened fellow, alarmed by his own tail, which he mistakes for an attacker as he stumbles over it. June steps out before him, cries "Boo!" and snaps May's envelope at him like a towel. He leaps back, trips over his tail, falls, and conveniently floats away. In the background, the Swimmer smiles grimly. Says Peter aside, not particularly to Frank, All these "smiling grimlys" and "watching soberlys" will have to come out: "astonished admiration," all that dreck. I was working fast. Frank gestures for him to go on.

Against the fading sounds of the Main Body can be heard now the approach of what sounds like yet a Fifth Interloper. Sighing, June makes ready; but the splashing subsides, as does the background sound of the Main Body. In the silence, June sits pensive some moments on the bank, the Swimmer still observing her from behind and slightly above. Suddenly she makes a pained sound and springs down to the beach, where a drowned Swimmer is now seen floating ashore, faceup. It is the handsome Third Interloper. Grieving, June pulls him in. She cradles his head in her lap; touches his face and hair; closes his eyes; wipes his brow with May's envelope. Her Swimmer friend moves nearer, to the edge of the bank.

Aloud to herself, June says Now I'm afraid. I'm afraid.

The Swimmer joins her, pushing up his glasses. Together they consider the beautiful drowned young man. The Swimmer squats beside June and puts his arm around her shoulders.

He's . . . beautiful! June says (I want her voice to choke up on that line).

The Swimmer nods. Fine-looking chap.

June's voice is thick: He's magnificent! You'd think that if *one* of you were going to survive . . .

The Swimmer sighs. They just won't learn to float with the current now and then. They swim till they sink.

June's holding back tears now. *He* didn't whistle for the others!

The Swimmer agrees: All he could think about was getting back into the swim.

June puts the drowned Interloper's head gently down and stands. Whatever *fittest* means, it must not mean beautiful.

Lee Talbott says softly Ouch.

Realizing that this is no compliment to her companion, Peter reads in agreement, June looks at him now for the first time in this interlude. His arm is still loosely around her shoulders; she puts hers lightly around his waist. I'm sorry, she apologizes; I didn't mean that you—

The Swimmer nods. Let's ease this poor fellow out to join his teammates.

They do, and June casts May's envelope after him, as a kind of tribute.

Odysseus! Lee exclaims, less softly. With Whatsername's scarf—Iris's? Ino's! I'm sorry, she says to the group: Academic reflex. Her husband tells her Don't apologize; you're a professional. But Lee insists School's out, and I'm getting interested in this pair. Let's all try not to interrupt for a while.

Kath has removed her paisley headband; she draws it thoughtfully through her fingers.

Interrupt, bids Peter: You're entitled. The Swimmer chap goes on to say There'll be millions of drowned ones floating back now: It's not a pretty sight to watch. But it should be safe for us to build a fire and make some dinner. He smiles: No bananas up there, but I found us some apples. Look. He takes an apple from inside his wet-suit top, polishes it on his sleeve, and hands it to her. And maybe we can catch a fish somehow, or some softshell crabs.

June pensively examines the apple. And then what?

The Swimmer stretches. Then we'll turn in. *I* shall, anyhow; it's been one long night.

June still turns the apple in her hand and looks out sadly to where the beautiful Swimmer drifted off. You go ahead. I'll stand watch.

The Swimmer smiles seriously. They're all dead now, June. There's nothing to watch for except the moonrise. He looks to the horizon. Half an hour or so, wouldn't you say?

June clasps her arms distractedly about herself and says She's rising right now. She points off, with the apple.

A huge, tawny, gorgeous moon begins to rise where she points, though

June is still looking toward where she cast away May's envelope. Ah, says the Swimmer: Incredible! He takes her hand. They sit on the beach, their backs to the embankment, and watch the moonrise. In her left hand June still holds the apple.

After a few moments the Swimmer says carefully Shall we review our options?

June nods thoughtfully. Sure. She bites into the apple and speaks around it: Mm. Red delicious.

It is Katherine Shorter Sherritt, not Lee Talbott, who says *Oy veh*. But pats Peter's leg.

June offers the apple to her friend, reads unabashed P. He takes a bite. They pass the apple back and forth during the following:

Andrew Sherritt approaches with *Story*'s conch-shell horn, which he has fetched out to show Simon Silver, and asks in a whisper may he listen with us? Sy, we see, is with his grandmother and the *Katydid* ladies, apparently content. Says Peter Sure, but no questions till the end, okay? It's that play by Frank Talbott called *SEX EDUCATION,* that I sketched this third-act scenario for yesterday. Frank'll show you the front end sometime, if you're interested. I'm interested, says Chip. Peter says The Swimmer says carefully I feel very . . . strongly for you, June.

It's her turn at the apple. When you call me June, she says, it doesn't sound right.

Oh? Sorry.

No, no, June says: I mean it's as if *June* isn't my right name any longer. The Swimmer wants to get back to the subject. What shall I call you?

I don't know yet. June glances at him sidelong. So let's review our options, she says, as you suggested. She holds up the apple core. This is biodegradable, right? Not like that beer can.

Sure. More food for the fish and crabs, along with our friends out there.

June chucks the core out into the water. And us, too, eventually.

The Swimmer looks at her. Yup: We're biodegradable too. And so's this script, of course, Peter interjects, but everybody shushes him. June says to her Swimmer pal What about those options?

More businesslike now, the Swimmer says Well: Upstream is out, much as I'd like to meet your teachers and see where you grew up. Can't be done.

June nods: What a shame. She laughs and boldly picks up his tail-tip. (These guys have wet-suits and tails, Chip.) Look what I brought for Show and Tell, Ms. R!

Ow! says the Swimmer: That's still tender.

June touches his shoulder instead, still laughing. I'm sorry. The Swimmer puts his hand atop hers, on his shoulder. June regards their hands. So, she says: Upstream is out.

We could go our own ways, the Swimmer suggests: down and out, separately. . . .

No! cries Katherine Sherritt Sagamore, clutching her scarf in both hands. June too is startled at the suggestion. No!

The Swimmer is pleased by her reaction. Or we could go down together, he says, once my dead colleagues are all flushed out. I think we could make it safely as far as the delta—unless another quarter-billion Swimmers happen to come along.

Could that really happen? June asks him. So soon after this batch?

I've heard of such things, the Swimmer says. But it's not *very* likely.

June says thoughtfully I'd like to see where *you* come from, too, I guess. If it were safe.

The Swimmer laughs shortly (you'll have to cut these adverbs, Frank): It wouldn't be safe. But that can't be done either, as we know. Bear with this next part, requests Peter Sagamore: The Swimmer says After the Whatsit—what was your name for it?

June smiles and blushes: *La Rivière Rouge.*

We called it the Wine-Dark Sea, says the Swimmer. After that, it's anybody's guess.

June leans back against the embankment, takes his hand, looks out to sea. It doesn't sound so awful, actually, she says: floating along downstream together like . . . The name occurs to her: Huckleberry Finn and his friend. She looks at him. You wouldn't miss swimming?

The Swimmer considers. It really is what I'm mainly designed for. But I could paddle us to one side or the other if we saw something to explore. That would be enough swimming for me. We could take our time; poke around the creeks and rivers; get to know the whole Night-Sea. And each other.

June sighs, shakes her head. But then it's all over! You cruise along and cruise along . . . and then it's over and done!

Well, says the Swimmer: You're right about that. There's no second ride down the river.

They consider this truth for some moments. So do the assembled aboard *Reprise*. After which the Swimmer says matter-of-factly Then there's the other option.

Right, says June (same tone): Two options, actually.

Two?

I mean, it's certainly not unpleasant right here, June says, just as we are.

The Swimmer agrees: Not bad at all.

Talking together, June says seriously. Exploring the differences between Floaters and Swimmers. Breaking down the walls between your kind and my kind.

Could we call it lifting the veils, the Swimmer wonders, instead of breaking down the walls? Anyhow, you're quite right: We could just go on like this. . . .

You being you, says June, and me me.

Lee Talbott makes a small sound.

Pleased at that sound, the Swimmer repeats it: "Me me." There's a pretty name for you: Mimi!

June's also pleased. You may call me that, if you like it.

I do like it: *Mimi.*

June laughs: It feels like my real name already! What shall I call you?

Bemused, the Swimmer shrugs. Let's go 'round, says Peter Sagamore.

Lee Talbott: Ishmael?

Frank Talbott: Man-o'-War?

Katherine Sherritt: Lieutenant Pinkerton?

May Jump: Rodolfo!

Chip Sherritt: Uh . . . Rin Tin Tin?

Okay, says Peter, and the Swimmer says Call me what you called me before, Mimi.

I didn't call you anything before. I don't know your name.

Peter glances again at Franklin Talbott. I don't either, says the Swimmer: But on the beach a while ago, when you said you needed me . . . you called me *Fred.*

Fred? June's puzzled. I called you Fred?

Frank frowns.

I liked the way you said it, says the Swimmer: "Ah Fred . . . ah Fred . . ."

June laughs and puts her hand on his leg, which is beside hers. *Afraid!* I said I was *afraid!*

The Swimmer holds her hand gravely there upon his thigh. From now on, my name is Fred.

June still smiles. Okay, she says: Fred it is. Fred.

Mimi.

Moved by the same impulse, they tentatively kiss; draw apart to regard each other's faces; lightly kiss again.

Chip Sherritt examines the conch shell's coral-pink mantle. Lee Talbott holds her husband's hand. Peter pauses as if to check with him before proceeding. Grave-faced Frank Talbott nods.

Fred pulls his swim cap off, revealing a handsome head of hair, which Mimi admires, even touches, as he speaks: We really could just live out our time here in this cove, Mimi. Not a *couple,* exactly, but a sort of team.

Mimi says Not like Sun and Moon, though, right? Fred grins: No, no. Nor Sword and Scabbard, nor Plow and Furrow. (These are all metaphors from Act Two, May. You said it, says May Jump. Sounds like they're naming your children.)

Plow and Furrow! says Mimi: I should say not! I hate those metaphors.

Fred shrugs his eyebrows. How about Bow and String, then? Or Finger and Thumb?

Our kiddies whirl: Chutes and Ladders! Dungeons and Dragons!

Those are better, Mimi says: I like Finger and Thumb. She makes a circle with hers.

What about Right Hand and Left? Fred takes her right hand in his left. Mimi squeezes it and nods as if to say Done.

Peter checks. Frank seconds Mimi's nod.

Then there's the other thing, Fred reminds her. Mimi looks down. The other option, yes. Now she looks full at him: Suppose we *were* to do the other thing, Fred?

Fred looks seaward: Merge. Fuse. Combine. He turns to Mimi. I've been thinking about that, Mimi.

So have I, Mimi admits. Plenty.

Coincidentia oppositorum, Fred says: the union of contraries.

We're not contraries! Mimi objects: We're partners. Fred says My late friend used to talk about the transcension of categories. (That was back in Act Two, Chip.) But I don't think of you and me as categories, Mimi: You're Mimi; I'm Fred.

That's now, says Mimi. But if we were to Combine and Merge Identities . . . no more Mimi; no more Fred.

"Something both and neither . . ." Fred looks at her. What kind of thing would that be, Mimi? What would we become, that's both of us and yet neither of us?

Mimi shrugs and says it straight out: A Baby, I guess. Then she laughs. But a baby what? Baby sea urchin? Baby prime minister?

How about a baby poet, Fred suggests, or a baby coloratura soprano? His voice goes grim: Baby dictator. Baby purse snatcher. Baby alcoholic, schizophrenic, drug addict . . .

Mimi takes his wrist, to stop him. Maybe we'd turn into Odysseus, Fred, striving home from Troy across your Wine-Dark Sea. Or Don Quixote, riding through Spain with Sancho Panza.

How about Scheherazade? says Fred: I see us as Scheherazade, telling stories for a thousand nights and a night.

Mimi grins. A baby storyteller! She sighs, then smiles briskly. Let's think about it awhile.

Fred nods: There's certainly no need to decide right now. The danger's past. We've had a bite to eat. He stands, still holding her hand. Want to take a little swim before bedtime?

Mimi's astonished: A *swim!* Fred laughs, draws her up. Not out in the Night-Sea. He gestures toward the sheltered water on the other side of the sandspit. I mean in our private little cove here, that we've hardly even looked at. The air's balmy now; I'll bet that water's delicious to float around in.

Mimi gently resists his drawing her there. Maybe in a while, Fred. I'm worn out from the trip down. And I keep remembering poor May, and all those drowned Swimmers. . . . She looks sadly back toward the beach where the handsome Third Interloper came ashore, and clutches herself as if for warmth.

Fred understands; says Some of them especially, I guess. Mimi takes his hand again, her eyes still averted.

Fred brightens determinedly: So, he says: Then let's just watch the moon sail by. We'll eat some more fruit if we get hungry; we'll talk when we feel like talking.

Mimi nods. They sit as before, but this time on the point dividing the Mainstream from the cove, where willow withes arch from the bank behind and droop toward the moonlit water. From the silence now comes suddenly the late summer sound of crickets. A whippoorwill calls out; a blue heron squawks. For some while the two listen, enthralled and pensive. Presently they resume their dialogue, speaking huskily, somnolently.

Mimi says It should have your hair, Fred.

What? Oh. No: I like your hair better.

Your brown eyes, though.

Your breasts.

Surprised, Mimi cups and inspects them candidly, comparing her chest to his. Well, she says: If applicable.

Fred nods: If applicable.

The same goes for *your* particular parts. Mimi gestures toward his lap. Your tail . . .

If applicable, Fred agrees. Anyhow, your cheerfulness, your bravery—it should have those. Your spirit.

Impulsively, Mimi kisses his hand: *Our* spirit.

Fred nods. Pauses. What a moon, Mimi!

The camera moves to where the moon now gleams through the willow-limbs, its track glittering across the calm Mainstream and the distant break-water with its winking beacon. There is a far-off sound of migrating geese. The voices of Fred and Mimi continue, off camera.

Can those be geese I hear? asks Fred.

Geese, definitely, Mimi says: Canada geese. Flying south to Chesapeake Bay for the winter, I'll bet.

Our first Canada geese! Fred pauses. A while ago . . . you mentioned storytelling, Mimi.

One of us did. *The Thousand and One Nights*. Scheherazade.

Well. Suppose we were to Combine . . . and suppose that what we turned into really *did* turn into a storyteller instead of into a snow leopard or an oyster tonger. . . .

A little drowsily, Mimi asks What's an oyster tonger, Fred?

You know: chap who tongs for oysters?

Oh, right: oyster tonger. Boyoboy, I'd *love* some half-shell oysters, right this minute! Wouldn't you?

We'll hunt for some in the morning.

With champagne! says Mimi. Extra dry, to celebrate our first Canada geese.

Katherine Sherritt can't help saying This is some womb, all right. Womb service, even. Excuse me, hon.

That's what Mimi says, too, says Peter Sagamore: Excuse me, she says to Fred: You were talking about storytelling. And Fred says What? Oh.

If what we turn into turns into a storyteller, Mimi reminds him, instead of into a clarinetist or a Freedom Fighter . . .

Right. Mind, Mimi: I'm not against clarinetists and Freedom Fighters. But I'm thinking about *us* now: our story.

What story? Mimi wants to know. Fred says Well, I mean, a good schoolteacher, say, or a good biologist—he or she might *do* something in the world besides just make more Floaters and Swimmers. But what I'm wondering is this: Would a good first violinist, for example, or a sea porpoise—I mean even a really *smart* sea porpoise—would it remember all this, and what we've been through together? Would it remember *us*?

Ah, says Mimi: Shooting the Tube. (They did that in Act One, Chipper.) Meeting May up there at the Confluence and learning that I can actually *swim*! And your learning that you can float, sort of . . .

And meeting you, Fred says. Mimi giggles at the memory. That was no joke, Mimi! And May: amazing May . . .

Katherine squeezes her hand; Peter's too. The headband's perched atop our posterity. May says nothing, but squeezes back. Mimi, after a pause, says And us: how we swam and floated. And this cove, that I love. She calls out *You'd better remember this cove, storyteller!*

Sure, says Fred. But any rockfish, any Canada goose might remember this cove. I want our *whole story* remembered, Mimi: beginning, middle, and end.

Sighs Katherine Right right right; so do I. Right is right, agrees Lee Talbott. Mimi says Mm: But we don't *know* the end yet.

Then let's try to imagine it, Fred says to her: What do you suppose would happen if you and I were to *concentrate* on our story; concentrate very hard on it together, the whole time we were Combining. . . .

Oh, Fred, Mimi sighs: Do you believe it might remember us then? Our friendship?

Maybe it would, says Fred, if we concentrated together. You know: "Once upon a time" and the rest.

Hm, says Mimi. And then, seriously, after a pause: I guess I doubt that, Fred.

So do I doubt it! But if it's even possible . . .

Mimi shakes her head. Whatever we turn into will have to die too, she says.

Well . . . sure.

Well I *hate* that idea! Mimi cries. This is our baby we're talking about! It's *us*! What can it leave behind, besides more of us to die?

Fred considers: Maybe that's not so bad: a little Mimi, a little Fred. Hundreds of Mimis! Billions of Freds!

Mimi's not amused: All to die. So much dying! And then that's that: The End.

Hold on, says Fred: You're forgetting about the *story*, Mimi.

No I'm not. Stories die too, Fred. I just now realized that.

Fred just then realizes it, too. Wow, he says, very soberly: You're right. Oh, Mimi. All of them, do you think?

Mimi nods. Some a little sooner, some a little later. I suppose the odds against a story's surviving must be about the same as the odds against *our* surviving, and meeting, and reaching this cove together.

Fred whistles out his breath: Pretty grim, huh. But then it occurs to him to say Yet here we are.

Here we are, Mimi sighs. And the terrible Night-Sea's like a warm bath now: a quiet anchorage on an Indian-summer evening. She yawns. Excuse me, Fred. Let's listen to the geese till we fall asleep, okay?

Sure, says Fred: Maybe take a little skinny-dip in the morning, when we hunt for oysters and champagne.

Drowsily again, Mimi asks What's a skinny-dip, Fred?

And now, friends, we come to the close of this floating opera: Fred says You know: swimming and floating without our wet-suits and envelopes, just for the pleasure of it. Bare-assed. Mother-naked. . . .

Hey, says Mimi mildly: We *are* naked!

Says Fred I just now noticed.

Well!

Fred chuckles: Must have been something we ate.

Mimi pauses. It *feels* okay, to me.

It feels terrific, Mimi.

Another pause. Mm, says Mimi.

And another, after which we hear Fred's voice say Oh, my, my, my.

Then all we hear are the crickets, the tree frogs. Our camera remains unswervingly upon the moon. Geese we hear, too, in the background, and see their silhouettes now and then as they cross the moon.

Very quietly, Mimi's voice says Wait. She pauses. *Softly,* she whispers: *Don't wake the baby. . . . Now.*

There, says Fred. Together, says Mimi. And together, ever more softly, their voices repeat as the scene dissolves:

Once upon a time . . .

Once upon a time . . .

Once upon a time.

SUMMER AFTERNOON CELLARDOOR THEOPHANY B♭

As Katherine Sherritt will tell it next fall, when we're home in Baltimore and she's back at work (part-time) as Consultant in Folklore and Oral History to the Enoch Pratt Free Library, upon that triple incantation of her husband's (by oval Mimi, spermatozoic Fred), the starter-locks on all the Talemobiles and Storycycles of the library's Narrative Extension Service unlocked as one, and those dramatic vehicles ran unsputteringly thereafter to their inevitable denouements. Seven several dwarves at least (will swear awed Peter Sagamore to his College Park apprentices) slid singly from his narrative shoulders into the empty signal canister, like a troop of djinns back into their bottle. Vug! Crump! Fougasse! Dingle! Coomb! Cubby! Coign! He nodded respectfully to each (Fougasse and Vug, in particular, flashed him a look that said You've not seen the last of us)— then quickly clapped atop them the manuscript in hand. As if left hand to his right, K stuffed with one sure motion the paisley scarf atop that script; right to her left, P capped that canister. Way to go, team! cheered Left and Right.

No hocus-pocus, reader, removes such malign forces from the world or even long contains them; but for their mere remission, Muse be thanked.

That orange container itself—lead-heavy now with the thing contained, as P's fancy is helium-light—we do not chuck into our waters for some hapless future voyager to take aboard. The burden's ours. But we'll stow it, ballastlike, low in *Story*'s bilge, where such weighty matters stabilize instead of merely cumbering. Just now we merely cap it, and Peter says to Franklin Key Talbott So much for *that*. Now you go home and write your next thing, and I'll go home and write ours.

Do Homer, Scheherazade, Cervantes, and Mark Twain then and there embrace our P as their peer? Not yet, and no matter: They're stars he steers by, not his destination. Anyhow, he has work to do: Once upon a time is only the beginning. Leah Allan Silver Talbott, however, crosses the cockpit of *Reprise* to kiss him solidly upon both cheeks. Her pensive but now firmly *boina*'d husband says I have something for you downstairs, friend, and goes to get it. May Jump, her left arm around Katherine's shoulders, nods *yes* to the script's conclusion and shakes P's hand. Kath herself leans over Fred and Mimi to kiss their father full upon the mouth. Who needs the committee of immortals?

Frank calls up to Lee Where'd Mims put Wydiwyd, hon? saying the acronym as a word. It belongs to Peter Sagamore.

Kath's still kissing. Lee Talbott begins to say Maybe that last "Once upon a time" sent it back to its original owner? But at the word "time," a magnificent B♭ sounds from next door, and Katherine feels a movement in her belly so distinctly different from what she's used to (like twin cellardoors, she'll say, opening up and out) that she goes Oof into her husband's mouth and stands right up.

The sound's just Chip, paying his tribute to the tale on *Story*'s conch and announcing, at his mother's bidding, lunch. Hey! calls Simon Silver from *Katydid:* Let me! Frank Talbott comes up grinning with a different T-shirt in hand in payment for his hat, saying Marian must've taken old Wydiwyd with her and left this one behind. Or else we've had company.

He shakes it out; holds it up. It's man-sized, long, crew-necked, plain white, unmottoed, clean combed cotton—except for a palm-sized, amoe-boid inkblot over the heart. If it fits, declares Frank to Peter, it must be yours.

As we laugh, the conch resounds: Sy this time, his copper bracelet glinting in the sun, a high-volume triumph on his maiden try. Now? asks Blam; says Blooey *Now,* and Katherine Sherritt's amnion bursts at last.

ANCHORS AWEIGH!

Twice upon a time, at the time we tell of, twin thunderstorms struck Chesapeake Bay at the same hour two weeks apart and fanfared our de-livery like harbor cannon. Where went this summer afternoon, 29 June '80? Down time's tubes, like its eventful spring counterpart two Sundays past; like our storied fortnight since; like K's birth-fluid now through *Reprise*'s cockpit scuppers: into the Sassafras, the Chesapeake, the mingling waters of the world.

She stands before her seated spouse, laughing, leaking, her hands upon his dwarfless shoulders. Uh-oh, says May; says Lee Ai yi. Peter calls calmly Doctor Jack? Jack Bass responds from *K IV*'s afterdeck, where he and Hank are tethering the Windsurfer for their lunch break: Yo!?

Lunchtime, everybody! Irma sings up from her galley. Carla B Silver, who, bringing up a full bowl of fresh fruit salad from that same galley, turned toward us at the second conch-blast and in one unsurprised glance assessed the situation, corrects her: *Launch* time, Bubeleh. Your grand-children have smashed the champagne already and started down the ways.

Says May *I've* got something to deliver, too; excuse me. She pats K's tush and goes below.

Frank Talbott puts a tentative arm around Katherine's shoulders. You all right? Her hands still on Peter (who is steadying her by the hips), she smiles and touches her forehead briefly to Frank's chest. Joan Bass and Irma Sherritt have surfaced from *Katydid*'s downstairs; Chip and Sy stand awed upon *Story*'s cabin top; Jack Bass and Henry Sherritt are already making their way across the rafted boats. Kath's forehead's pressing Peter's now; our four eyes are closed; we're back-and-forthing as if in joyful prayer.

Here you go, guys, says May Jump: little labor-saving device. She lifts K's right hand off P's left shoulder and slides onto that wrist a finely worked gold bracelet with three several stones. Have a safe one, Kiss.

Oh, May! Hugs, busses. Katie? wonders Irma. Katydid? calls Hank: You okay, hon?

Peter Sagamore, standing now, grinning, assures them: We are okay. But our time has come.

Patient reader! So!

Hank and Peter busily wonder now, of Jack Bass: Scrub up? Put water on to boil? Crank up CBs, VHFs? Helicopters! Ambulances! Move and shake! Chip Sherritt announces, on his and Sy's behalf, We'll stow the Windsurfer! It is the best he can come up with, and not bad.

Tut tut tut tut tut tut tut, says our unexcited obstetrician, patting Kath's head (she's still standing there) and verifying with one plump forefinger along her left calf that she has not in fact simply peed with anticipation. Easy does it, mates. Grandpa, he says to Henry, I want you to chop me a cord of firewood while Dad runs forty laps and Grandma rigs a gantline to the bosun's chair. But first let's all sit down and have a nice lunch.

He is serious! It is not the rule, he tells us, for amnionic/chorionic sacs to break before even preliminary labor commences; but it isn't all that extraordinary, either. Chances are, he tells us, we'll go spontaneously into labor . . . within the next twenty-four to forty-eight hours.

Where's Ma Nontroppo? Kathy frets. Where's Walter Cronkite?

And that's only latent-phase labor, Doctor Jack reminds us. Things don't get serious till the grunts get regular, and we haven't started our *ir*regular contractions yet.

Declares wide-eyed Katherine, squeezing his elbow, Whoops: Yes we have.

Time for lunch then, prescribes Jack Bass. After you wash that champagne off. Then we'll mosey up the river and down the road. Once she really gets started, he reminds her further, she's got eight or ten hours' work to do, and his guess is she won't really get started before happy hour.

Lunch, then! A happy hour in truth aboard *Katydid IV*, under the big blue and white awning, where last night's long stories got told. We narrators are too dizzy to register what we're eating; we bet it's good. Real Mumm now: just a sip for us and our physician. Katherine turns and turns Scheherazade's charmed bracelet upon her wrist; she smiles, shakes her head, sniffles over the—yes, it is ambrosia, fresh coconut and all. She leans her head upon her mother's shoulder (Irm's calmly delirious); tries to change the subject; cannot. There's another contraction! Neither Joan Bass nor Irma Sherritt nor Carla B Silver wants to be a birth-bore, but how can they be expected not to recollect and compare their own first and subsequent deliveries? Chip Sherritt asks earnestly It's really eight to ten hours of second-phase labor? That's a lot of hard work. Eight to *twelve,* Doctor Jack assures him, on the average, the first time out. Later ones are shorter, on the average.

This one, Carla prophesies, will be shorter; but there's no hurry. Jack Bass raises his benign black eyebrows and regards her over his half-glasses. Here's to it, toasts May Jump. Henry Sherritt instructs his wife Don't let me forget to call Willy and cancel. We've got more important things to take delivery of than that granary.

We toast that granary; also Breadbasket Inc. Even Willy: Here's to Willy, proposes Katherine. Here's to *Poonie,* even. God bless us every one.

Says Franklin Key Talbott, his arm around his wife, And here's to Fred and Mimi.

A and P, chimes Chip, who got left out of last night's go-round; Sol *y* Sombra, Hollywood and Vine. He grins: Over the River and Through the Woods? Til Eul and Spiegel? Winks his father Wheel and Deal.

We're not drinking, reader, just lifting our champagne flutes in toast after toast. To Truth and Consequences, says Lee Talbott. Even Simon, new to our game, tentatively comes up with Night and Day? *Night and Da-a-a-ay!* May Jump sings to him—but Chip thinks we've used that one already. Fly Now and Pay Later, chirps Joan Bass. Her husband proposes Benedictine and Brandy. Peace and Plenty, predicts Carla B Silver. Uh, says Peter, Shem and Costello?

Katherine leans back against his new T-shirt; closes her eyes—another contraction! Says Come and Get It.

Time to go: Such a lovely lunch, so high-spirited an interlude, the afternoon's advanced before we're done. Good-bye to *Reprise*! She'll follow us upriver toward Georgetown to top up water tanks and icebox at the first marina we pass, then get going Bayward and homeward. Frank Talbott promises Peter, aside, to keep us posted, minidumpwise; we owe it to the Great Mother to nail Willy & Company, and Frank shall do his level utmost in that line. But the Talbott–Sagamore connection, and this weekend especially, has him feeling corner-turned: He's getting novel ideas almost as fast as he can log them. Lee bids us warmly Have a good life, you all. Chip and Simon have stowed the Windsurfer very securely along *K IV*'s portside bow lifelines. They shake hands; then Sy surprisingly goes the rounds of *Katydid* and *Story,* manfully shaking hands with each of us, thanking Irma for lunch, expressing polite gratification at having met Mr. Sherritt, Dr. and Mrs. Jack (nobody smiles at this little slip), us. May Jump and Carla B Silver exchange a Would You Look at That look.

I've got it, Chip then announces: Pete and Kath ride up on *K Four* in case the babies come early, and Sy and I drive *Story* together till *Reprise* makes its pit stop. Then I drop him off and catch up with you. Okay?

Simon Silver can scarcely believe what he's hearing. Hey, yeah!

Peter checks with Hank. Done. Scout the slips at the Sassafras Boat Company if we get separated, and monitor sixteen in case we need to confer.

So long to May Jump and Carla B Silver, who together board *Reprise* now, looking couplelike. For being in our Tidewater Tales, our thanks!

Simon's standing by already on *Story*'s bow to unraft. Chip asks Peter Flags?

P thanks him for reminding us. Fly the whole wardrobe! So the boys run up on our port and starboard flag halyards the nautical Stars and Stripes, the Maryland state banner, two varicolored windsock streamers, a red crab on a white field, an orange Chinese carp, and a white seagull on a blue field reading SAVE THE BAY. *Reprise* obliges with the USA, Maryland, the old green and white ecology flag of the 1960s, a yellow quarantine flag, assorted national courtesy flags from the Caribbean and the Bahamas, an even larger Chinese carp in blue and white, and a polygonic radar reflector. But as Jack Bass at the helm of *Katydid* idles up toward its anchor, and Peter on the bow takes in the slackening rode, and *Reprise* and *Story,* unrafted, circle in attendance, Henry Sherritt runs up the big ketch's full-dress regalia: an alphabet of signal flags from the tip of the bowsprit up the headstay to the mainmast truck, aft to the mizzen truck, and down to the outboard end of the mizzen boom. Nor is he done—

But ta-*roo!* goes Simon Silver on our conch, and May Jump answers him with *Reprise*'s freon signal horn: ta-*roo! K IV*'s anchor's aweigh; Peter secures it in its bowsprit roller and sluices the mud off while Dr. Jack shifts to Go. Chip drops *Story* neatly astern of us; Lee Talbott swings *Reprise* into line smartly astern of him; Joan Bass pops *Water Music* into *Katydid*'s stereo cassette player and turns the volume up high. As if in response to G. F. Handel, Kath's uterus joyously recontracts, and our flotilla steams out of the anchorage at Ordinary Point. Is that smirking Howard Huckleberry Findley among those cheerers on the final raft we pass? Is that an outbound Phaeacian 35 just clearing Back Creek as we leave Knight Island to port en route to Georgetown? Sy'll swear he saw Chessie the Shoal-Draft Sea Monster tip us a flipper off Old Field Point, unless it was a sperm whale. Hardly enough water over there to float a sperm, chart-minding Chip will remark to himself, much less a whale. But for Simon's sake he'll pretend he thought *he* saw something, too. The anchor work done, Peter rejoins contracting Katherine in her parents' cockpit and shows her the calendar date on his wristwatch. Sixteen years to the day, he reminds her, since our night in Room One Seven Six of the old Gramercy Park Hotel. Replies sky-high Katie in his arms You'd better set that bezel, hon; I think I'm getting regular.

And up to *Katydid*'s starboard main spreader Henry Sherritt now runs

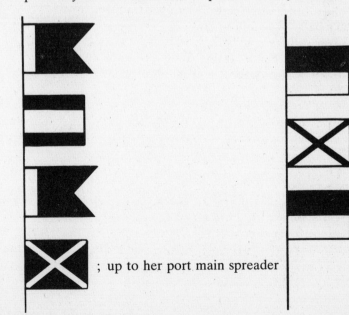

; up to her port main spreader

(But they're going to be born in the other order, predicts Carla B Silver aboard *Reprise* when her daughter decodes those flags from Chapman's *Piloting, Seamanship, and Small Boat Handling.*)

<pre>
           A   E
Sturdy little D! Bright-eyed V! Welcome to your garden!
           A   E
           M
</pre>

THE
ENDING

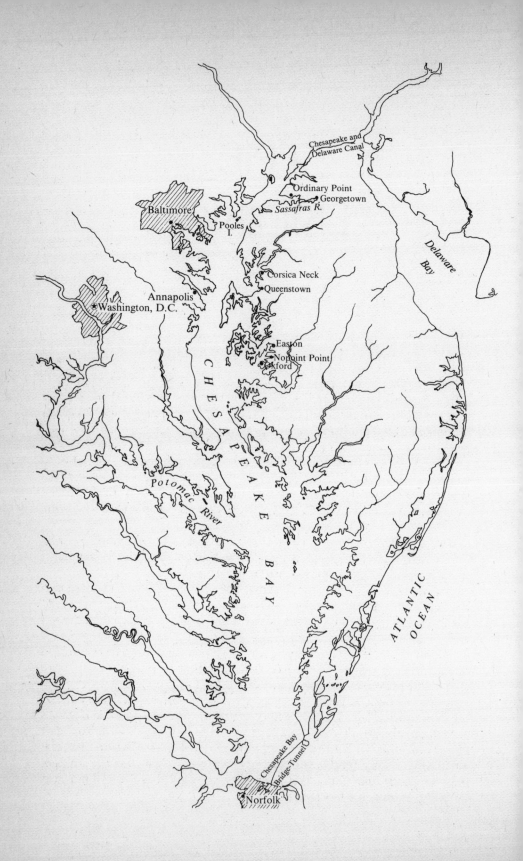

SCHEHERAZADE TUCKS US ALL IN.

SHAH BETTER, SADAT SAYS.
Shahryar's been perkier, too, since his wife rematerialized nine months past on the Persian carpet in her library in their son's palace in the Islands of India and China. (There, as on the Chesapeake, this Monday evening—last day of "June 1980" by "Djean's" calendar—is mild and fresh behind the high that blammed and blooeyed us late yesterday afternoon, to which blooeying we shall duly orbit back.) Look who's here, Shahr said when Scher showed; we were wondering. So was I, said Scheherazade as soon as she'd got her breath. I'll tell you the whole story—starting tonight.

But at their age and stage, the old formulas change. No more "retiring to his harem at midnight and doing his will upon the vizier's daughter"; they split a cozy nightcap and turn in before eleven.
OLYMPIC SECURITY PERVADES MOSCOW. She'll explain. What sex there is in the old-folks' wing of the palace—Once a week? Twice?—happens usually in the morning these days, when husband and wife are at once both drowsy and refreshed. Frisking at bedtime riles them up, blows their sleep. So it's a glass of red at ten, ten-thirty; then off to bed, and Shahr tucks behind Scher or Scher behind Shahr like two forks nestled in Shmah's flatware chest, and she takes up where she left off till one or the other of them drifts away. Usually Shahryar ticks off first. No literary criticism there; they're old friends now at the end of their day, and sex is nice and stories are fine, but both will keep—and if they don't, *tant pis*: They've had a fair share. Sometimes it's the teller conks out in mid-sentence, before the told; not at dawn's early light these days, but on the crest of a night-wave stronger than her story line. *Later that same evening,* she'll be saying—and next thing she knows, it's morning.

Down to breakfast then with the grandchildren, and on with their personal denouements.

So: She's told him what she's told him, has Scheherazade, *re* her Month of Mondays and her expedition on the Chesapeake with Djean and Shmah, and her stay in Annapolis with Ms. May Jump, and what happened at that ASPS convention, Kitty Hawk Eleven. Shahryar chuckles and clucks his tongue; hopes she had herself a time; gives her a squeeze or a *potch in tuchis* and dozes off: the man before whom once all Islam's daughters trembled.

But then about eleven P.M., if it happens Shahr's asleep and Scher's in a mode between this and that, where distances go strange and she could as well be an eye in the sky as a bag in a bed, she gets a burst transmission from C.B S. that sorts out later in her dreams and that she then re-sorts in her notebook after breakfast, what she can still recall of it. May Jump's involved in these; so is Djean, she's ninety percent sure. Though it's still our story, somehow Djean's the source; M.J.'s the voice (if you're getting this message, it's May you're hearing, at the end of June); and the indispensable medium is C.B S. (Call Back, Scheherazade!), who adds items of her own to the signal. SHAH BETTER, SADAT SAYS; sometimes just AHA, or OY, or TESTING THE INTERCOM: THREE TWO ONE.

How'd the woman get home from North Carolina? Take your pick. May Jump says C.B S. reports that Shmah told her that Djean told *her* that he'd been monitoring his monitor as usual all that weekend, trying to spring himself and his favorite storyteller out of the pen he'd processed them into, when that picture postcard arrived from K.H.N.C. with the gray granite shaft of the Wright Brothers Memorial on the front and, on the back, Scher's little diagram of her maiden flight, and something went *click*. He hoped it was the muse's key in the lock of his imagination, but in fact it was his new three-thousand-dollar word processor crashing from a local power lapse, and there went his Tale of You-Know-Whom Thus Far, which he had neglected to Save To Disk. Power was anon restored, but not his unfinished story of Scheherazade and her predicament, nor for that matter the word machine: Something had blown.

As he was set to put his fist through the darkened screen, the Pretty Obvious Possibility occurred to him. But no: A pop ending like that wouldn't fetch his old friend to Baltimore-Washington International, much less back to her PTOR. Next day, Shmah came home with the sea-snail shell and the osprey-feather quill Scher had sent him as, oh, mementoes of Kitty Hawk Eleven. She found her husband wishing he'd stayed with his sturdy though erratic fountain pen. Said Shmah Your pal says you might try these, and put the quill and snail shell down on the postcard. When last seen, Shmah went on, she was still to be seen at K.H. Eleven.

This time both of them heard the click, and the box lit up, and as far as they and May can put times together, that was just about exactly when Ms. Scheherazade pffed off from Kitty Hawk and clicked on back home.

Queries C.B S.: THAT'S AN ENDING? Hold on, girls, says May Jump: It

was just then too that friend Djean made some Further Connections—
noted them down with the osprey quill in good old messy black ink on
paper white as a laundered smock or a fresh T-shirt, scribble scribble—
connections between the stuff on that postcard and sea snails and osprey
feathers and the Brothers Wright and Kitty Hawk Eleven and the Keyhole
Big Bird spy in the sky and keys to the treasure and central intelligence
and the omniscopic point of view and Allah knows what else. He embraced
his patient wife and said *Shmah Yisroel*: The story's done; on with the
story.

So they went sailing.

But our collective narrator is obliged to add that when C.B S. and May
Jump get word of all this a few days from now from Djean and Shmah,
whom they happen not to have seen since way back then (that's last "October"), and they pass the news along later yet—next month, say, or next
fall—to us Sherritt-Sagamores in Baltimore, and *we* pass it along later yet
to Andrew Christopher Sherritt, who was present when certain stories got
told on certain sailboats, young Chip is going to go clickety buzz himself
and come up with the most personal question he has ever put to his sister
and his brother-in-law. We'd stayed home from that ASPS get-together
last fall, Kath's told him, 'cause Pete had seminars to preside over and it
was her ovulation time and we were trying as usual to lay the keel for
Chip's niece and nephew, right? Old Yang and Yin there. So excuse him
for asking, but he supposes that a lot of love got made in Baltimore,
Maryland, that Thursday, Friday, Saturday, Sunday, and Monday, no? It
did: also at Nopoint Point and aboard the good ship *Story,* toward that
weekend's end. So, lad? So: Counting back 266 days from our happy
birthday yesterday (but it won't be yesterday by the time Chip gets this
news, fingers his brown bead necklace like an abacus, and goes clickety
buzz), we get . . . KH11! Columbus Day ± a couple—and not only the
eleventh birthday of the ASPS and the tenth anniversary of our first Day
Zero in Dun Cove, but just possibly the very moment when the *Santa
María* of Sagamore sperm Land-Ho'd the Hispaniola of Katherine Sherritt's
ovum; when "Fred" and "Mimi" wound up their sex education and commenced to Something Both and Neither, now snoozing happily in their
twin cribs.

Got it?

Maybe. How does that arithmetic get Scribbler Djean off his plot-hook,
P wants to know, and Scheherazade back to the Islands of India and China?
Chip says he's only crunching the numbers; it's not his story, and we
Sherritt-Sagamores are too busy nursing and diapering these days (and
easing back into our rent-paying labors while working up our coupled
viewpoint for *The Tidewater Tales: A Novel*) to give it much thought.

But we'll give it some, for Scheherazade is in our story as well as in our
stories. Whose bracelet was it got Princess Kate lickety-split through her
labor, *allegro ma non troppo* just as C.B S. foretold, all hands delivered
safely in the Easton Hospital just before and just after midnight by Doctor

Jack Bass, to his happy surprise, and no episiotomy necessary, much less a cesarean? We sense already (P.S. especially, who has piloted such narrative channels before) that you don't get home free just by blowing horns and running up flags and weighing anchor and chugging off for Georgetown. Mister Djean had only one dramaturgical chestnut to fetch from his fire; Professor P and partner have got a peck of them smoking away like Alert-and-Locate signals, or those slash-and-burn Third World farm-fires that show up at night in satellite photography. (Scheherazade declares she can spy them all the way from her PTOR, via her highest-level keyhole.)

Through which now a certain late retired Agency consultant named Douglas Townshend observes to Carla B Silver (in one of those Gypsy receiving-modes of hers) that if the key to the treasure is the treasure, then the keyhole must be the treasury. If the key is missing, Doug declares, there's at least that keyhole to be peeked or whispered through: elementary Tradecraft. His blessings upon the heads of sturdy Pomp and bright-eyed Circumstance, whose godfather he wishes he might have been; upon their mother, to whom he apologizes yet for his contribution to her earlier miscarriage; and upon you, Peter Sagamore, in whom his long-shot investment has paid off: You *are* writing about the Doomsday Factor, are you not?—or *not* writing about it, but in a different way, Q.E.D. and *auf Wiedersehen.*

Whoa-ho-*ho*! will protest Peter. There'll be no spooking off like that, old friend, here in our Ending! Hold that ghost on the line, Carlita, till he answers a few Reallys for us, to help tidy the mess he helped make. Like was that mint tea really spiked, Doug, up there in Carla's Cavern? And what really happened to John Arthur Paisley aboard *Brillig,* and to your late friend The P of D aboard *Reprise,* and to Short Jon Silver, and for that matter to yourself? Loose ends, Douglas, in the argyll sock of our story, which we want knit up—unless the message is too painful for C.B S. to carry.

What say, May? Tell on, Scheherazade.

Match-hand shaking, our friend lights up. That particular mint tea was not laced, though folks Doug knows are perfectly capable of such valentines. The antidote Peter swallowed afterward was a nothing, in this instance, though folks Doug knows are not above either poisoning your tea and faking your antidote, or faking your poison and poisoning your antidote, or poisoning both, or (as in P's case) faking both. The real poison, Doug declares, is the Company we keep, as embodied particularly in F. Mansfield Talbott the Prince of Darkness and his fellows. Do not glorify them, readers and writers. Do not romanticize their exploits. They are an amoral crowd employing immoral means to not especially moral ends: the dirty-tricks department of international grabbiness. A Gypsy curse upon them all.

You want Reallys? Father and son really did die, not together as in C. B Silver's rafted dream, but as in its corrective gloss, with one difference: Having learned from fellow spooks that his son had been tortured to death in Chile by low-level operatives of the government brought into power with the Company's generous assistance, Frederick Mansfield Talbott borrowed his brother's boat for the purpose of reprising J. A. Paisley's suicide, only without the aid of a nine-millimeter bullet in the brain. His DINA counterparts drowned his son in a prison toilet full of diarrhetic shit; he meant to drown himself in full consciousness, cold sober, with enough scuba ballast to keep him truly down for keeps. But climbing the lifelines with eighty pounds of lead off Bennett Point, where Wye meets Miles, he slipped on the dew-wet deck, conked his noggin hard on the metal toe-rail, and never felt the hypothermic night-sea do its job. His anchor held. He has been long since distributed through the food chain, like Kepone. Not an altogether evil man, Frank Talbott's brother; good to his family, in his way—but to hell with him, really.

And Paisley? Q.E.D. And Doug Townshend himself (who now snuffs out his cigarette and signs off)? KGB, very nearly, by another elegant mischance. Operation BONAPARTE having reached a hiatus, in early June Doug was en route to the U.S. embassy in Australia to make contact with a KGB counterpart in the Soviet embassy there whom he had known slightly in other stations over the years. The Russian chap's principal assignment in Australia was to gather intelligence about U.S. intelligence-gathering in Perth and Carnarvon, in particular the Big Bird's song; but he had sent equivocal signals to CIA people in the U.S. embassy that could be read as tentative overtures to defection, and therefore retired senior officer Townshend, an expert in such matters, was dispatched from Bethesda to Canberra to encourage him.

This commission, however, was imperfectly got wind of by another KGB officer back home on the Chesapeake (assigned to monitor and forestall BONAPARTE), who mistakenly believed D. Townshend to have succeeded F. M. Talbott as the Agency's highest-level Doomsday Factor, and who understood Doug's mission to be the liquidation, rather than the encouragement, of Colonel Maydonov in Canberra. To protect his fellow officer, therefore, he set about to nail our friend with a dollop of the Komitět's highest-tech cardiac arrestor in the bustle of the baggage-claim carousel in Sydney's Kingsford Smith airport, where one goes through customs and changes planes for the short hop over the mountains to the capital. But as the Qantas Airways 747 banked over Botany Bay on final approach to Sydney, he was prevented in this design by the rupture of an aneurysm of whose existence Doug himself (lighting his final lifetime cigarette) was unaware. The spook took credit for having completed his assignment, went on to Canberra, reported to Colonel Maydonov that his life had narrowly been saved from a CIA hit, and returned to Washington and Corsica Neck. The colonel, knowing that the CIA had no particular reason to kill him and some reason to keep him alive, took Doug's "assassination" as a warning from his own colleagues, abandoned therefore his tentative plan to defect, and so energetically rededicated himself to his work that under Yuri Andropov's future and brief succession of Leonid Brezhnev, he will become one of the Kremlin's very Commissars of Darkness.

And that (saith the spook of the spook who once warned Peter Sagamore "We lie and lie and lie and lie and lie") is the truth.

Nevertheless, goes on our omniscopic Scheherazade, Operation BONA-PARTE will half succeed. During Ronald Reagan's first presidential year, the Deniston trustees will sell slightly more than fifty percent of the orig-inally proposed wooded campus acreage on Corsica Neck to the Soviet embassy, at the price first offered for the whole parcel. The purchasers, correctly anticipating an end to President Carter's U.S./Soviet détente, lust for privacy more than ever and dare not hold out for a better deal. John James Deniston would be proud of us, Irma Sherritt will declare. To that sum will be added anonymous donations (laundered from the Agency's huge new secret budget) in memorial to the late ex-Congressman Porter Baldwin, Jr., always a friend of The Deniston School, and his campaign treasurer William Sherritt, killed with him (together with the pilot and a third passenger) in the crash of that Easton Air Freight helicopter just off Corsica Neck in the wicked late-afternoon thunderstorm of 29 June '80, as the party was en route from Queenstown up to the Sassafras River on business. In his excitement at Katherine's labor and the running up of *Katydid*'s alphabet flags, Henry Sherritt forgot to VHF his elder son to cancel the Breadbasket granary ceremonies (Willy would have made the flight anyway; Sherbald Enterprises had other bases up that way to touch), and Irma forgot to remind him till the flotilla was halfway to Georgetown. By when, reported Molly then by radio to Irma, her husband had already left home for Queenstown; and thank God he wasn't the pilot, for he was half-tanked on Sherbrook rye. But she promised to leave word with both Easton Air Freight and Sherbald Enterprises that the festivities were can-celled. Her love to Katie! Even over the airwaves, Irm could tell that Moll had been crying again.

Laborwise, our fleet got to where it was going in good time, though Kath's contractions had both accelerated and regularized well beyond the norm for so early in the game. No problems with the Simon Silver drop-off *(Au revoir, Reprise!)* or with Chip's singlehanding *Story* up to rendez-vous with *Katydid IV* at the Georgetown bridge. Two transient slips were reserved through next weekend, when whoever is free and in the mood (it will be Hank, Chip, and Bobby Henry) will return the boats to Nopoint Point. An ambulance stood by at the Sassafras Boat Company for Kath and Peter and Doctor Jack; Bobby Henry was on his way in the Sherritts' saddle-brown Caddy to pick up the other four.

Weatherwise, however, we were just in time. To west-southwest the sky turned soot-black and copper-green. On *Katydid*'s radio and the ambul-ance's, NOAA Baltimore was issuing a tornado watch and severe thun-derstorm alert for that city, the whole upper Bay area, and the Eastern Shore.

P and K smiled: Blooey! But all were concerned for *Reprise,* not to mention *Rocinante IV*. Docklines were rechecked, deck gear doubly se-cured. Doctor and patient conferred, patient and spouse, doctor and ambulance driver. Out over the Bay they heard the first thunder, and word came in now of considerable destruction in the city: large trees uprooted in Druid Hill Park, in Guilford, in Homeland; a great crane toppled by ninety-knot winds at the Dundalk Marine Terminal, and the whole shebang headed our way. Whistled Peter Ninety knots! He'd never *seen* wind that strong. Dangerous even to drive, the party agreed. As birth was not imminent, it made most sense to stay put, ambulance and drivers as well, and keep an eye on the boats—indeed, remain aboard—until the squall blew through: an hour at most. Should the ambulance be summoned to direr work, the Sherritt Coupe DeVille (there it came now) could fetch the drama's principals to Easton Memorial.

What I hear, announced flush-faced Bobby Henry with a wink at Peter Sagamore, she's blowing the daylights out of Tolchester and Rock Hall.

Blooey! Behind Ordinary Point (so the Talbotts will tell us later, who barely reattained in time that familiar shelter), some yachts dragged anchor at the height of the storm—couple of seventy-knot gusts, plenty of fifty-pluses—and made life interesting for those downwind whose anchors held. Simon Silver loved it. Frank and Lee's main concern, and Carla B Silver's, was for Marian, somewhere out there in the thick of it with Captain Donald Quicksoat. By 1900 hours, the violent front had passed; ambulance and Cadillac were negotiating tree-limbed highways on their way to Easton in light rain; *Reprise* weighed anchor and sailed out on the fresh northwesterly, enjoyed a fine clear sunset, and parked for the night in Still Pond Creek, from where the crew ran home today with a stop at Kent Island Narrows to drop off May Jump and Carla and Simon. Through the evening, and all day today, the Talbotts have monitored channel 16 and heard alarums aplenty: reports of two sportfishermen drowned in the storm in small boats off the Patapsco; news of a large cruising ketch blown out of its storage cradle at Rock Hall; word of a helicopter crash off Corsica Neck, names of victims not yet released—Good lord, Frank Talbott says: Do you suppose?—but, thank heaven, no reports of sailboats in real trouble: just the usual chatter of blown-out sails and You-shoulda-seen-its and We'll-be-late-getting-home-hons, better-call-my-office. On the other hand, there's no response when they try to raise *Rocinante IV* or radiotelephone Carla's Cavern and her apartment upstairs.

So they're taking their time, Lee Talbott supposes, hoping she's right: that the salty old pseudo-Spaniard and her kid sister are getting it on at *Rocinante*'s mooring in Bowleys Quarters or Frog Mortar Creek.

She's wrong.

TWO AND A HALF TONS MARIJUANA SEIZED FROM BOAT NEAR OCEAN CITY, Scheherazade hears from C.B S. What's your next chestnut, Mister Sagamore, in need of fetching from the fire? Ah, so: BONAPARTE, she was saying. Breadbasket Inc. The Saint Deniston School for Girls.

Okay: The Russkies get half the extra acreage they wanted, but none of the extra privacy. The Agency people brought in unknowingly by The Deniston School as construction supervisors to relocate a horse barn from the property involved are able to plant (in a few cases literally) additional surveillance devices on or near the grounds, not all of which the KGB debuggers routinely locate and either destroy or make use of to leak disinformation. Not even Scheherazade will tell what, in their dirty, demoralizing, and stupendously expensive business, such snoopers learn and mislearn from one another. When her keyhole omniscope picks up such dreck, she dismisses it from our story.

The blooeying of Easton Air Freight's helicopter virtually into the Soviets' Corsica Neck compound will prove to be everybody's good fortune except its pilot's and his passengers'. The president of Sherbald Enterprises had postponed that scheduled noon rendezvous with his new partners in Breadbasket Incorporated at the old Back Creek granary not because the chopper was down for servicing, as he'd reported to Henry Sherritt, but because his longtime friend and Sherbald cofounder, ex-Congressman Porter "Poonie" Baldwin, Jr., wanted to come along and couldn't get to the Queenstown office until four. It turns out Poonie's heart had been oddly touched by that accidental encounter (on Wye Island, Day 10, outside the gate of Natural Recycling Research) with his childhood sweetheart and first wife, so immensely pregnant now by her handsome and—so Poon understood, though he had not gotten 'round to reading any of Peter Sagamore's fiction—somewhat famous current husband. He bore Katherine Sherritt no grudge for the so implacable grudge she bore him, which he mildly wished could be placated. It occurred to him to follow up that amusing and after all nonhostile encounter with another—festive, unannounced, and short, in the company of her family and family friends at the little granary ceremony—where, by comporting himself with self-effacing dignity, he might lead her to see him in a less unsympathetic light. He would like that, Poonie would, for he remembered warmly, if wincingly, his first and only real heterosexual love, dating back to Heather Foulke-Stoughton's gazebo and beyond.

Katherine aside, he and Willy had other business that Sunday: Sherbald Enterprises had employed a Baltimore acquaintance of Willy's to coordinate the interests of Natural Recycling Research and the New Jersey waste-disposal firms with which NRR expected to do an increasing business as Breadbasket Inc. expanded its feed-grain acreage on the Eastern Shore. The fellow also had connections with an oil-recycling firm in Baltimore that Sherbald Enterprises hoped to acquire: The American Recovery Company, which specialized in dumping benzene, xylene, toluene, chromium, lead, copper, and cadmium wastes into Chesapeake Bay under the camouflage of its oil-recovering facility. He was, finally, a handsome devil, this new chap: a Rumanian-American, whom Poonie thought might be induced to work two sides of the sexual street, as he had worked some others.

The plan, then, was for the four of them—himself, Willy, the pilot, and Lascar Lupescu—to go on from the Sassafras ceremony up to Atlantic City on the Sunday evening to confer with one of their business associates there, and then today to stop at Bridgeport and Price's Pit, both in New

Jersey, to have a look at a particularly successful operation Lupescu had heard of: bribing city garbagemen to spray toxic wastes on ordinary trash before composting it for illegal disposal at the municipal landfill. On then to New York City, to see whether American Recovery could effectively imitate the mob's waste-recycling firms there, which lace nearly half the heating oil sold in that city with toxins that ordinary oil burners spout uncombusted into the sky. A bit of sport Monday night in the Big Apple, *chacun à son goût,* and back home to Maryland tomorrow.

Much bigger stuff, all this, than slipping your Lester Treadways twenty a week to dump a few drums in various Queen Annes County landfills, or tipping your Bobby Henrys extra not to ask what's in the ones they drop overboard after dark from time to time in the deep spot off Bloody Point Light, or mixing a shooter of PCBs with the pesticides sprayed by air on Breadbasket's golden waves of grain, which only dumb animals are going to eat anyhow, right? She cannot swat this chopper out of the sky, Scheherazade declares, before wondering one last time, with Peter Sagamore and Katherine Sherritt, what such fellows as Willy and Poonie really think of themselves and their doings. Compared to the Pentagon and the Kremlin, these Doomsday Factors in our own backyards are no mortal threat, individually, to the world at large. But daily and knowingly, Will Sherritt befouls his own nest and ours, with the same bluff indifference wherewith he passed along his herpes simplex even unto his wife, and Poon his crab lice unto Katherine. *He* fishes in these waters, goddamn it, says Willy, and he eats his catch. He's a dues-paying member of Ducks Unlimited, and sure, the ducks are scarcer than they used to be, and the rockfish have their ups and downs, mostly downs, but he bets there's more Canada geese on the flyway than when the Injuns were around. And there are scores of Willys and Poonies all about us.

Blooey! Baldwin and Lupescu had a couple of scotches in the car en route across the Bay to Queenstown and were late arriving. Willy (we've heard from Molly already) had been coming through the rye before he left home, and prevailed upon the chopper pilot to have one with him in the Queenstown office while they waited. Just as Poonie and Lascar arrived, Molly Sherritt telephoned with the news of Katherine's labor and the cancellation of the granary ceremonies. Disappointed, the three passengers (but not the pilot) nevertheless drank a toast to Willy's sister and Poonie's ex, and decided to fly directly to their business in Atlantic City. How could an experienced pilot be induced to take off, on no urgent mission, in the face of so darkly oncoming a squall? Not even Scheherazade can say, though time and again, from *Story*'s anchorages, we've seen light aircraft overhead in such situations. But lift off they did at 1745, from the pad behind the Sherbald offices, even as Blooey's leading edge swept across Kent Island. They were airborne for less than ten minutes, flying north at a few hundred feet over Queenstown Creek, various Breadbasket corn lots, stands of pine and mixed hardwoods, Reed and Grove Creeks, The Deniston School for Girls. At the height of the storm, they plunged into the Corsica between Red Nun 2 and the Soviet dock at Corsica Neck.

The crash was witnessed by several yachtsfolk anchored in the large bight nearby, which includes part of Deniston's waterfront; but those witnesses had their hands full coping with the squall, and their accounts differ. One says the helicopter was blammed by a massive downdraft and hit the water with its engine running full-throttle; another swears the engine stalled and the craft flipped over; a third (U.S. Navy, retired) swears that a Russian with a walkie-talkie was on the pier at the time and pointed up at the chopper while speaking into his transceiver just before the crash. He does not doubt (this gentleman will write to the editors of the Baltimore *Sun*) that the Soviet vacation compound is equipped with devices to stall the engines of low-overflying aircraft, along with electronic hardware for snooping on our National Security Agency snoopery at Fort Meade and the eighty Pentagon facilities on Chesapeake Bay. A few far-right-wingers will mount a halfhearted effort to beatify their fallen ex-darling, who was perhaps on a highly classified mission of which the Soviets were aware. One of Baldwin's companions will be rumored to have been a present or former CIA agent, perhaps a KGB double agent. . . .

The Soviet embassy will make no comment, though the incident no doubt helped justify their measures to increase security at Corsica Neck. The U.S. Central Intelligence Agency will deny—truthfully, as it happens, in this instance—any present connection with Lascar Lupescu, but only the naive will credit that denial. The KGB, were it given to comment upon such allegations, would make a similar denial, likewise truthful in this instance, and likewise to be ignored, as ought to be all such public statements by all such agencies and the governments they serve, for they lie and lie and lie and lie.

The little fuss soon dies down. Autopsies disclose that Willy Sherritt and the pilot, seated forward in the helicopter, were crushed on impact; that datum suggests a nosedive, though the machine settled finally upright on its skids in ten feet of tidewater. Ex-Congressman Baldwin and ex-CIA/KGB low-level operative Lascar Lupescu, strapped into the rear seats, drowned. Poon's second wife's lawyer (she'd given up Standing By Her Husband) will be obliged to recast her divorce-suit claims into claims upon the estate of the deceased. No great matter.

Guilt-smitten Molly Barnes Sherritt truly grieves. What on earth for? wonders Katherine, who, though shocked, can muster only regret, not deep grief, for her brother's death. Oh, for having briefly trafficked behind Willy's back with Douglas Townshend in Operation BONAPARTE, for her husband's own good, as she'd thought, and maybe the country's. For having not after all been able to conceive a child by Willy, though there toward the end, on the strength of his one-eighty, she'd truly believed she had. The thing in her womb is something else. For a season she'll find some comfort in widowhood, honoring Willy's memory; then she'll be overtaken by the great project of dying stoically of metastasized cervical cancer. In the absence of immediate heirs, she'll bequeath the bulk of her considerable estate to The St. Deniston School for Girls, as the institution will have been named by the time she rejoins her husband in the Sherritt family graveplot.

Scheherazade's position is that what's to be regretted in this matter is that such as Willy Sherritt and Porter Baldwin, Jr., become what they become, in despite of extraordinary privilege and loving parents of good character. It should not be supposed that they were wholly vicious fellows, without any redeeming qualities, incapable of becoming slightly better human beings. But as they turned out to be mainly bad, and not likely much to improve, their surely accidental death need not be greatly mourned nor take up even one additional sentence in this Ending.

Says sleepy Shahryar Hmp. Wrap up that Captain Whatsisname, why don't you: the old fellow with the new young concubine.

With goodly gree, say K & P. Supposedly en route across the Bay from Ordinary Point to *Rocinante*'s Middle River mooring and thence to Baltimore and Carla's Cavern, Captain Donald Quicksoat detoured late yesterday morning down to Still Pond Creek to park for lunch and, you know, a swim; after which just enough of a breeze sprang up to seduce him into trying to sail instead of motoring, despite the threatening forecast and *Rocinante*'s sluggishness in light air. There's a sailor for you. Topless Marian soon grew bored: The heat was woozy-making; there wasn't even a portable radio aboard for her entertainment; and her new lover had proved short on staying power. The afternoon was well advanced before the skipper packed it in and went back to motoring, leaving his main and mizzen sails up in hope of eventual better wind. But the aged diesel turned balky— sounded to Capn Don like fouled fuel injectors—and when the sky ahead went dark, and the first cool breeze came from the northwest, and it was time to shirt up and take precautionary measures, *Rocinante*'s main halyard jammed at the mast truck with the sail not even down to its first reef points. A serious matter, but not yet alarming to a veteran solo passagemaker. He dropped the mizzen and limped into the lee of Pooles Island—exposed from every direction except west and northwest, but the nearest shelter available. There he anchored and bid Marian go below and put on a life vest while he made his way up the mast to either free or cut the fouled halyard before the storm hit. She saw him climb ratlines to the main spreaders, rig the free jib halyard into an improvised bosun's sling, and, with an open clasp knife between his teeth, begin half shinnying, half hauling himself up the rest of the mast, wedging one bare foot at a time between the slack sailsides like a rock-climber on a tricky face. Frightened then by the black sky and water and the rising wind, she went below per orders as Blooey struck.

It cannot have been just another thundersquall, even for C.D.Q. For Mim Silver it was as terrifying an hour as any since the conception of her son. One blast laid *Rocinante* right over on her beam ends; loose gear flew across the cabin, as did the hapless passenger; only the life jacket spared her more than one broken rib and an even more impressive array of contusions than she has. The ketch righted itself, but pitched and yawed violently on its anchor rode. The rigging shrieked; bolts of lightning exploded all about; rain backlashed into the open companionway and soaked everything inside; the whole world seemed to roar. Marian trembled on the cabin sole, covered with loose settee-cushions, vomiting with terror and motion sickness, certain that the boat was going down but too frightened to leave the cabin even if she had believed she could manage to. Atheist on principle, she nevertheless found herself praying from time to time to someone: not that she and the ship and its skipper survive, but that her sister please please please please *please* be pregnant.

At half past six, though thunder could still be heard from the black mass to eastward, the wind and waves quieted; the sky brightened over Pooles Island; *Rocinante* settled down. After calling his name from the cabin many times without response, battered Marian gathered courage enough to climb partway up into the cockpit and look for her companion. The stuck sail was down, she saw, though not furled; it spilled wetly from the boom over one side of the cabin top and deck, billowing now and then in the breeze. She saw a long rope (the unfouled halyard) blowing loose from the masthead. No sign of Captain Donald Quicksoat or, for that matter, his ad-lib bosun's sling. On the whole expanse of the Bay, only one other boat was in sight, too far away to see or hear her: a queer-looking, black-hulled, white-topped thing, sailboat she guessed, but moving as fast through the showery, rainbowed distance as a racing speedboat, and soon gone. Though Marian was neither calm nor knowledgeable enough to notice the fact, *Rocinante*'s dinghy was missing, too. Its yellow polypropylene tether trailed off astern, either chafed or cut through (poly line unravels in either case). The dinghy will turn up tomorrow, blown ashore near Fairlee Creek, clear across the Bay. Its owner will not.

Mim Silver knows little about sailboats except that in warm weather they're neat for nude sunbathing. In a near panic, she retreated below, turned on what she took to be the ship's radio, and went right around its dial, shouting tearfully into the little microphone for help. She heard only static and, on one channel, weather reports. Had she known to push down the Transmit button under her thumb as she hollered, someone might have heard her and asked the boat's name and situation; she could not in any case have said where she was.

Before long, she went hysterical: The crotch of her underpants still moist with Donald Quicksoat's lunchtime semen, she was alone on an anchored sailboat near an uninhabited island in the middle of nowhere. Helpless, sore, too frightened to eat or drink, and eventually spent by her paroxysms, she shuddered and whimpered all through last night in the very settee berth from which, only the night before, while leaking the same *señor*'s infusion, her mother had reached out in the darkness to May Jump.

She's still there tonight, is Mims, still occasionally praying her already-fulfilled prayer; and there we'll leave her, in no danger but frightened almost catatonic. When May and C.B S. reached a Kent Island telephone this morning and heard no answer from Fells Point, and then found no one at Carla's Cavern this afternoon, they notified the Coast Guard, though for all they know, the pair simply crossed wakes with some of Capn Don's cronies, changed course and plans, and are larking up the ICW toward New England waters. Tomorrow morning she'll be found. Her mother and May and her sister and brother-in-law and others will once more pick up the pieces; Allah himself could not restore them.

On with the story, then, Shahryar agrees, but happily nods off before he can exasperate our narrator by asking So where *is* that Captain Whats-isname?

THAT'S IT?

Just about. Not quite. Once over the first great shock of Willy's death, Henry and Irma Sherritt will thrive upon grandparenthood. Given Katherine and Peter's involvement with their professions (rather less on K's part these days, for she takes to mothering like duck to water; lots more on P's, whose muse's gates have swung wide open), they'll have ample opportunity so to thrive. They tell their wide-eyed little heirs the tale of Shorter Point Restored, and other tidewater stories. Peter's brother, Jacob Sagamore, retires early to Fort Myers, Florida, and never revisits Hoopers Island for the rest of his life except once, briefly, for his mother's funeral. Their sister, Sue-Ann Sagamore Hooper, grows ever more estranged from them, not without reason, as her menopause exacerbates the nagging responsibility of their senile mother's care, or vice versa. Nora Sagamore, healthy, cheerful, and oblivious, lives to age ninety-two, much depleting though not quite exhausting the financial resources of her children, none of whom will likely live so long, and whom she is unable even to recognize for the final seven of those ninety-two years. Not poor Nora's fault, to be sure, but boyoboy.

Moving right along, we see no need to reprise Jean Heartstone, whose Magic Language Theory has all but done its job. Ditto Marcie Blitzstein, Yussuf al-Din, Saul Fish, Jaime Aiquina, Ex–Interior Secretary and Mrs. John Trippe, Black Olive Treadway, Florence Halsey, Shirley Ovenshine, Shirl the barmaid of the Madison Bay restaurant off the Little Choptank, the Alice Roosevelt Longworth lady, Buck Travers the intercom installer, Charlene (Charlie) Smart, Judge and Mrs. Somebody Barnes of Chestertown, Frank Talbott's father Judge George and his housekeepers Lew and Cecilia Skinner, Howard the Knapps Narrows bridge-tender, Debbie the moon-faced waitress from St. Johns College in the Treaty of Paris Restaurant in Annapolis on lay day, or Vug, Crump, Fougasse, Dingle, Coomb, Cubby, and Coign. Stavros Petrakis, who drove our Checker taxicab from the 92nd Street Poetry Center down to the Gramercy Park Hotel on the night of 29 June 1964, returned ten years later to his hometown (Heraklion, Crete), where he presently operates a tour-bus service with his brother and two first cousins and suffers from a bladder complaint. Let's see: Dr. and Mrs. Jack Bass's Ericson 39 sloop, *Off Call,* places second overall in this summer's Tred Avon Yacht Club around-the-buoys series, thanks in part to a new suit of Mylar racing sails and in part to the skipper's new high-tech tactician, A. C. Sherritt. Ronald Reagan is reelected to the U.S. presidency in 1984. The world as such does not end before the century, though sundry subworlds do.

Shahryar snoozes. Our tutelary genius, Scheherazade, in her highest-resolution omniscopic mode, serenely orbits the PTOR of these tidewater tales and finds them now all but free of smoldering chestnuts.

All but?

Right. Seems to our projected narrator that this wrap-up inventory, like the one Whatsername delivered to Ma Nontroppo back in Our Story, omits the main thing. What she means is:

ON WITH THE POEM!

Oh, *that,*
          tuts Katherine Sherritt with mild surprise—
Kith at her starboard nipple, Kin at her port,
Doubly draining, twice-delighting her;
Burning our coupled candle at both ends:
At once Exhaustion and Replenishment.
(Drink up, bids Kath: There's more where that came from.)

It's true she spoke in verse in our prologue,
Improbable as such a thing may seem.
And she left that doggerel green-belt poem undone
Like Penelope's web; like Scheherazade's last yarn;
Like *The Tidewater Tales: A Novel,* finished now
But for some wrap-up word, some curtain line. . . .

Or did she? Comrade reader, look again
Through the keyless hole or holeless key of Form.
We thought we lacked a closing rhyme for *cost*
To end our poem with: one less bleak than *lost,*
Remember? But we were in formal fact
Not at the end at all.
          Au contraire.

We'd launched a new stanzaic pair: a Jack
Implying and preceding some new Jill,

As in Ma Goose (though in *our* Genesis,
As C.B S. predicted, it was Eve
Who foreran Adam). Weren't we a brace
Of wiser birds than we supposed? A whole

New ball game! Maybe a whole new tale in verse . . .
or prose: *Our House's Increase,* by P.S. out of Katherine Sherritt Sagamore, its Once Upon a Time the Ever After of:

THE
TIDEWATER
TALES

A NOVEL